THE ROSE

OF

MIDDLEHAM

CHRISTINA SMEE

Published by
Spotted Hen Publications

ISBN 978 0993281 105

British Library Cataloguing in Publication Data.
A catalogue record for this book is available from the British Library.

Printed and bound in the UK by TJ International, Padstow, Cornwall

Typeset in 11pt Georgia by Troubador Publishing Ltd, Leicester, UK

Dedicated to the Memory of
Shirley Anne Thompson-Yates
Who made it all possible

Introduction

The Rose of Middleham is the product of a long journey. It all began back in the 1990s, when quite inexplicably, a slow curiosity about King Richard III developed which led to a compulsion to find out more about this enigmatic medieval king.

I began to read a range of published works, including Josephine Tey's *The Daughter of Time* and thus began the lengthy process of research into Richard's life and the times in which he lived. Like so many others, I could not simply accept the Shakespearean portrayal of a man which, quite remarkably, seems to have been passed down the ages and received as fact. William Shakespeare was a brilliant Tudor playwright but not a reliable historical source, any more than my own novel could be deemed worthy of such an accolade. The result of this early research was a book entitled *Loyalty Binds Me* which was put into print in 2005. Once the limited copies had been sold I thought that to be the end.

My interest in Richard III, however, did not dwindle and I joined Les Routiers de Rouen, the Living History group based at Bosworth Battlefield Centre in Leicestershire. Along with my son, Dominic, we had the privilege of being a small part of the extraordinary events that followed the discovery of the mortal remains of King Richard III under a Leicester car park in 2012. From a personal point of view, even more astonishing was the revelation that Dominic has almost the exact type and degree of scoliosis as Richard III. The following year saw the making of a third Channel 4 documentary, *Richard III: The New Evidence* where Dominic was put through vigorous training similar to that which almost certainly would have been undertaken by Richard himself. The programme proved that it is possible for a man with severe scoliosis to have worn bespoke plate armour, ridden a horse and engaged in competitive foot combat, giving credence to the contemporary sources that we have of Richard's prowess as a military leader.

The discovery of the skeletal remains has not only provided us with unprecedented opportunity for scientific research but has also challenged the traditional view of Richard III as a hunchbacked monster guilty of a series of despicable crimes. The vast amount of research undertaken over many years by dedicated members of the Richard the Third Society and others is at last being given recognition by the wider populace.

The disclosure of these new discoveries about Richard III opened up a challenge to me: to rewrite *Loyalty Binds Me* in the light of that new evidence and, significantly, to draw on my son's own experience of living with scoliosis to enable me to build a more complete picture of the man himself that goes beyond what we know of him as king and military leader.

Why the change of title? Although the novel is undoubtedly aiming to tell in part the story of Richard III, the main character is Christiana, the mother of Richard's illegitimate son, John of Gloucester, hence *The Rose of Middleham*. Historically, as far as I can determine, there is no evidence to confirm who this woman was, although more recently some have speculated upon her identity. Therefore I have taken the liberty afforded all writers of works of fiction and created her myself. To further emphasise, this is a work of fiction although I have used as much historical research as possible to present my Richard as a plausible alternative to the Shakespearean villain we are so familiar with.

This book also seeks to give a taste of what life might have been like in late fifteenth-century England expressed through contemporary religious beliefs, customs, food, clothing and such. Of particular interest was my research into medieval herbal medicine, a fascination that continues to this present day.

Finally, to my readers I say thank you for taking the time to travel life's journey with Christiana and I hope that it gives you as much pleasure to read as I have had in writing it.

A note on context and historical principal characters

Edward, the Black Prince; Lionel, 1st Duke of Clarence; John of Gaunt, 1st Duke of Lancaster; Edmund, 1st Duke of York; and Thomas Woodstock, 1st Duke of Gloucester were sons of King Edward III. Their descendants were engaged in a bitter power struggle for the English crown that set father against son and tore apart family allegiances. This rivalry continued through sporadic warfare between 1455 and 1487.

We refer to this period in our history as the Wars of the Roses, although at the time it was known as the Cousins' War. It was not a geographical feud as some have supposed but rather a conflict between the House of York, represented by a white rose and the House of Lancaster, represented by a red rose.

The family connections are complicated not least because of similar names and titles. It is not within the scope of this book to provide genealogical charts showing the various family connections as these can be viewed in many history books of the period and also on relevant websites.

It was into this unsettled time of divided loyalty, plot and treason that Richard Plantagenet, Duke of Gloucester and later King of England was born, lived and ultimately lost his life.

Edward IV

Born in April 1442 at Rouen, France. He was the son of Cecily Neville and Richard Plantagenet, 3rd Duke of York. He was King of England from 4 March 1461 until 3 October 1470, and again from 11 April 1471 until his death in 1483. He was the first Yorkist King of England. He married Elizabeth Woodville in 1464 and their children include Elizabeth of York, Edward V and Richard, Duke of York. These two boys are referred to as the Princes in the Tower.

George Plantagenet, Duke of Clarence

Born in 1449 at Dublin Castle. He was the son of Cecily Neville and Richard Plantagenet, 3rd Duke of York. He married Isabel Neville, daughter of Richard Neville, 16th Earl of Warwick, in 1469. Their children were Margaret Pole, Countess of Salisbury and Edward Plantagenet, 17th Earl of Warwick. He was executed for treason in 1478.

Richard III

Born in 1452 at Fotheringhay Castle, Northamptonshire. He was the youngest child of Cecily Neville and Richard Plantagenet, 3rd Duke of York. He was King of England from 1483 until his death in 1485 in the Battle of Bosworth Field. He was the last king of the House of York and the last of the Plantagenet dynasty. He married Anne Neville, youngest daughter of Richard Neville, 16th Earl of Warwick. Their only son was Edward of Middleham, Prince of Wales.

Elizabeth Woodville

Born in 1437 at Grafton Regis. She was the daughter of Jacquetta of Luxembourg and Richard Woodville, 1st Earl Rivers. Her family was considered mid ranking amongst English aristocracy at the time of her birth. She had two sons by her first marriage to Sir John Grey; Thomas Grey, Marquess of Dorset and Richard Grey. She married Edward IV in 1464 and was Queen Consort until 1483. Her daughter, Elizabeth of York, married Henry VII. She died in 1492 at Bermondsey London.

Richard Neville, 16th Earl of Warwick

Born in 1428 at Norwich. He was the son of Alice Montacute and Richard Neville, 5th Earl of Salisbury. He was known as the Kingmaker due to the significant part he played during the Wars of the Roses. He was killed at the Battle of Barnet in 1471.

Margaret Beaufort

Born in 1443 at Bletsoe Castle. She was the daughter of Margaret Beauchamp and John Beaufort 1st Duke of Somerset. She had one son, Henry Tudor, by her husband Edmund Tudor. She later married Sir Henry Stafford and then Thomas Lord Stanley. She died in 1509.

Henry Stafford, 2nd Duke of Buckingham

Born in 1455 in Wales. His parents were Humphrey Stafford, Earl of Stafford and Margaret Beaufort, daughter of Edmund Beaufort, 2nd Duke of Somerset. He was significant in King Richard III's rise and fall. He is also one of the primary suspects in the disappearance of the Princes in the Tower. He was executed for treason in November 1483.

Part One

Prologue

There was a chill inside the chapel and a damp mustiness that clung to the air. Light, like arrow shafts, shot from windows set high in the stone walls, fell in golden pools on the patterned floor.

She approached cautiously, holding her breath; afraid to look – yet needing to know. With pounding heart she moved forward to where a hand cart had been left in the middle of the floor; out of place, violating the purity of the holy chapel. Whatever lay upon the cart had been concealed with a piece of course hessian cloth.

The stillness unnerved her; the grey-cloaked figure watching silently from the shadows, the soles of her boots echoing loudly in her ears.

With trembling fingers she slowly pulled back the covering, her breath catching painfully in her throat at the sight of what lay beneath. Thrown like a common thief, naked and irreverently into a cart, was the despoiled corpse of her beloved.

She had only moments; even now she could hear the clinking of their spades as the monks were digging hastily at the floor tiles in the choir; this was to be his resting place, with as much honour and dignity as the Grey Friars could afford him.

Scores of deep wounds and lesions punctured and mutilated his body, staining the skin a hideous black and green and emitting a malodorous smell that nauseated her. His slender arms, lacerated and bludgeoned, were tied at the wrists, bitten raw by the harsh, frayed rope still attached. Hair matted with congealed blood from mortal wounds to his head brushed his face, and the once beautiful eyes were now closed in death.

Was this the man whom she had loved with an intense passion for as long as she could remember? Had it only been four days since she had held him in her arms and felt the warmth of his breath and the beating of his heart? How could this cold, lifeless form be hers?

An unbearable pain fired up from deep inside her and a torrent of anguish and rage engulfed her. Tormenting sobs racked her body as her tears poured forth in sorrow. Startled by the sound of the weeping woman, a young monk left his duties and went across to the cart. In wretched helplessness he stood beside her.

"I have heard it said that he was a good man and loved by many," he whispered, and after placing a comforting hand upon the woman's trembling shoulder the monk returned to the shadows.

York
January 1461

The road leading up to the Micklegate had long since become a quagmire with the endless trampling of foot, hoof and wheel. Alfred joined the press of pedlars, merchants, common peasantry and beggars that surged towards the gate into the city. He was jostled on either side by horse-drawn carts and great lumbering oxen. A thread of nervous excitement ran through the crowd as it cajoled and shuffled forward, the whispering, warbling and babbling rising to a voluble drone. Torches blazing high on the city walls caught the shimmer of rain as it spat down out of the murky twilight and here the stench of human habitation clung to the damp air.

Alfred could not get within reach of the gate and several times his horse shied nervously as a stray dog or pig flitted between its legs. At last he gave up his fight against the jostling masses and turning his horse about ploughed his way back through the crowd.

At first he thought that it was another dog coming too close to its hooves that caused his horse to baulk but as the small figure scampered away and slipped in the rain-sodden mud, Alfred could see that it was not a dog but a child. He slid down from the horse and scooped up the tiny form before it could be trampled upon.

Holding the child under his arm as he would a sack and leading the horse, Alfred managed to weave a path through the now thinning crowd. Reaching an area of open ground he set the whimpering figure down onto the grass. It was a boy of no more than eight years. His thin, tear-stained face was smeared with dirt, his tunic was torn and his skinny legs were barely covered by his tattered hose. His unshod feet were blistered and grazed and his whole body trembled violently.

Alfred squatted down beside the boy. "Where is your mother?" he asked. The child gave no reply.

"Where then is your father? Are you alone?" Alfred persisted. Still there was no response and the man sighed impatiently.

Just then a little girl appeared at Alfred's side and laid a tiny hand upon his shoulder and stared down curiously at the shivering figure. Her grey woollen dress hung in a cobweb of holes about her thin ankles and two battered boots, encasing her tiny feet, were blotched with grime.

"Come along, Christiana. The boy must have a home here about. He will fare well enough. We need to find lodgings by nightfall. Come now."

The tall, broad-shouldered man stood and went back to his horse where it was grazing contentedly on the wet grass and waited to lift his daughter back into the saddle. He turned to see that the girl was not following him.

"He is very cold, Father," she called to him. "We cannot leave him here or he will go frozen or else be taken by goblins." She shuddered at the thought. Alfred sighed wearily; maybe it would do no harm to watch over the boy for one night. Removing his heavy woollen cloak he returned to the child and wrapped it about his thin shoulders.

There were now three of them on the horse as it picked its way along the stony road going westward. Alfred was cold as well as hungry since he had parted with his cloak. As they rounded the next bend in the road he was immensely relieved to see the candlelit casements of a wayside inn.

There were many guests at the hostelry that night but room enough for the three weary travellers. Alfred had a fair supply of groats and pennies in his coin purse but he would still have to be careful. A night's lodging was, however, an unavoidable expense.

They sat at the long trestle tables in the hall eating a hot pottage of bacon and beans. The boy was stuffing huge chunks of hard rye bread into his mouth. Piece after piece he shovelled in hungrily until Alfred reached across the table and gently removed the bread from his fingers. "Have a care, lad. If you carry on like that you will bring it all back up again and that will be a waste of my money, will it not?" he said, chuckling.

Later, after the tables had been cleared and the guests were settling down on the straw-covered floor, Alfred stretched his tired legs and watched the children. The boy was still shivering despite the heat from a roaring fire but Christiana had snuggled up to him, wrapping her arms around his shaking body in an effort to warm him. Alfred smiled. This daughter of his was such a sweet-natured child and so like her mother. She had the look of her mother too with her large gentle eyes and abundance of raven curls.

Presently Alfred addressed the boy. "So, lad, what name do you have and why were you out alone in the thick of winter?" The child sat in silence. Alfred sighed resignedly but his daughter took up the challenge.

"My name is Christiana and Father is called Alfred. What name do you have?" Drawing away from him slightly and tilting her head to one side she studied the boy. In the firelight she could see that his hair was brown like the curlew that called out across the dales and his face would be pleasing to the eye if only he could smile. His eyes, when he looked at her, were the colour of hazelnuts. After a moment or two of thought she announced. "You can be my brother if you want. I do not have any brothers or sisters, do I, Father?"

Alfred's face was at once the image of panic and surprise and he was completely lost for words when just then the boy spoke for the first time.

"William," he said. "I am called William." He sniffed as a spate of tears began to trickle down his grimy face as though the utterance of his own name should bring to mind some memory too awful to contemplate.

Alfred, in his rather clumsy manner, shuffled closer to the boy and wrapped a thick-set arm around him, almost hiding him from view.

"Now there, lad. Do not weep. You just sit there and tell us everything when you are ready."

Several sniffs and coughs later and William was ready. "My father is a soldier. He went away at Christmastide and he has not yet come back. I left the village to look for him; I did not know what else to do." He stopped speaking and stared into the flames dancing in the hearth.

"And where is your mother?" Alfred asked gently.

"I have no mother. 'Tis just father and me. He never lets me go to battles with him. I'm always sick when he kills the pig and so he says I'd be no use on the battlefield. I can fight when I'm a man, he says. He always does come home..." His small voice trailed off and he hung his head sadly. After a while he took a deep breath and continued. "I saw the heads on the gate. They were real heads with lots of blood and eyes that stood out like a pig's on a platter. One of them had a paper hat on like a crown." The boy's eyes glistened as he recalled the macabre scene.

They sat in silence listening to the murmurings of the sleeping and the crackle and spit of the fire. Then William's voice whispered into Alfred's ear, "That was not my father's head on the gate, was it?"

The burly man drew the boy closer to him and answered softly, "Nay, lad. I am sure it was not."

So that was what all the commotion had been about, thought Alfred. The severed heads of noble Yorkist prisoners publicly displayed by the victorious Lancastrians as trophies of the battle fought at nearby Wakefield. Like as not the head that wore the crown would have been Richard, Duke of York and Protector of the Realm. He slumped back against the hard wall with a sleeping child cradled in each arm and thought back on the recent events that had brought him to this place.

The acrid smell of burning in the chill morning air, the billow of black smoke rising like dragon breath into the pearly dawn sky; the screams of the villagers, panic-stricken and fearful, running for the surrounding trees in the mayhem of rider-less horses and stampeding cattle.

Power hungry and drunk to the point of insanity on the free-flowing ale, hordes of victorious soldiers terrorised the countryside in the aftermath of battle. They saw it as their right wherever they went to loot, burn and maim, more often than not their actions sanctioned by their liege lord. It was a common enough occurrence in these troubled times. The blacksmith and his daughter had been fortunate enough to escape with their lives let alone the tools of his trade, crammed into a leather bag and slung over the back of his horse.

Alfred's heart burned with resentment as he thought about the home he had been forced to leave behind, burned to the ground. He and his daughter had lived in a one-roomed shack adjoining the smithy, shared with their black Dales pony and, until last autumn, a fat snuffling pig, the salted carcass of which was hanging from a hook in the rafters. It had not been much but Alfred was content and trade had been going well enough for him to consider building a separate dwelling and enlarging the smithy. He would have probably taken on an apprentice too. Now they had nothing but a horse, a bag of tools and a handful of coins; they were homeless in the bleak of winter. All because the nobility of the realm had nothing better to do than engage in bloody battle for England's crown. He sighed bitterly and kicked a horn cup that lay on the floor with his outstretched foot.

In the dim greyness of the winter dawn Alfred sat on a wooden bench in the courtyard supping ale. The children were still asleep inside. Life at the inn was slow to commence; many travellers reluctant to venture out into the bleak world were still huddled around the dying embers of the fire or else taking their ease in the courtyard. Alfred's bench was by a stall where several horses, his own included, were stabled. As he sat trying to clear his head of sleep he became aware of a muted conversation nearby.

"What is to be done now that the Duke of York's head and that of his son sit on Micklegate? Is our cause now lost?" whispered one man.

"The Duke of York has more sons. His eldest, the Earl of March, proves worthy," returned another.

There followed a brief silence when Alfred could hear only the stamping of hooves and the jingling of harnesses. The second man spoke again. "England needs a king, a real king. Not a weak-kneed sop led from the nose by a woman. There will be no stopping the bloodshed else."

"Hush, man. Think on what you are saying."

"I speak only the truth and well you know it. You mark these words for my Lord Neville will…"

Alfred heard no more as the conversation ended upon the arrival of a serving girl calling the inn to break their night-time fast. He shook his head. More trouble brewing, he thought. Well he had troubles enough of his own, one in the shape of a small boy. What was to be done with him? Come to that, what was he to do about his own future?

On his return to the hall Alfred found William sitting on the damp straw huddled inside the girl's cloak. Christiana was feasting heartily on bread and ale.

"William feels unwell, Father. He will not eat his bread," she announced. Alfred knelt down beside the boy and stared into his ashen face.

"Well, little man, did I not tell you not to eat so much last night?" he chided gently.

William shook his head and whispered, "My arms and legs ache and I have a great pain in my head."

"Too long out in the cold, boy, 'tis all. You will be well soon enough." Alfred ruffled William's tousled locks of brown hair.

Sometime later, having supped and paid their due, Alfred and the children were back on the road.

"Where is it that we are going, Father?" Christiana asked as they swayed gently atop the horse. Alfred wished he knew. He was not sure that York would be the best place to go just now. It would not be easy to find work in rural Yorkshire either as most villages would already have an established farrier. But he would have to try – or starve.

He gave his daughter what he hoped was a reassuring embrace and urged the horse forward. They headed in a north-westerly direction, following the River Ouse. Their sturdy mare picked her way over fallen branches and roots along the rutted tracks meandering over the wild Yorkshire land. Hour upon hour they travelled without sight or sound of another soul, the damp drizzle clinging to vale and hill seeping into their clothing and wetting their skin.

Alfred became increasingly concerned for the boy. His cheeks were flushed scarlet and he was hardly able to keep himself upright in the saddle. It was only Christiana's arms fastened around him that prevented him from tumbling to the ground. Alfred was diligently searching the area for signs of a shelter when William began to groan. Alfred looked down anxiously at the boy and saw that, despite the pinpricked flush of his cheeks, the colour had drained from his face. Alfred barely had time to hoist William from the saddle before he vomited violently, drenching his own scant rags and Alfred's already work-blackened tunic.

The blacksmith sat in despair on the roadside cursing the soldiers who had caused him to be out in this bleak wilderness without shelter, regretting already his weakness at burdening them with a sick child who meant nothing to them. Christiana held the boy's hand as he sat and retched pitifully between sobs, his head hanging between his bent knees.

Would the boy ever stop throwing up, Alfred thought ungraciously. He stood up and moved away a little, rubbing his tired eyes. He thought at first that he had imagined it, but no, his eyes had not deceived him. A small group of white-robed friars was walking two abreast along a narrow track that crossed their path a few yards ahead. They had, it seemed, caught the attention of one of the brothers.

"Good day to you, friend," he called, walking towards them with hands hidden within the voluminous sleeves of his robe. "'Tis not a good day to be out on the road," he remarked, looking down at the two children. "Allow me to be of assistance." Without waiting for a reply he hailed one of the monks standing quietly on the path.

"Brother Clement, have you any peppermint about you?"

A young monk stepped out of the rank and shuffled over, blushing painfully.

"Come, come, boy. The child has more need of it than you." The older monk snapped his fingers and held out his hand, whereupon the younger man drew out a phial from the folds of his robe and handed it to his superior. As Brother Clement returned to his companions the monk offered an explanation. "The good brother has a sensitive stomach, shall we say, but our Lord Abbot insisted that he make this journey today. We have to take provisions to the leper house of Saint Giles whatever the weather. The spirit must conquer the flesh." A mischievous smile spread across his face and he lowered his voice. "He did not think that I knew about the peppermint."

Crouching down and supporting William's head the monk coaxed the mixture into his mouth. "There, that should help ease your vomiting, young man."

"Many thanks, brother," Alfred said gratefully.

"Where are you bound in such foul weather?" the monk asked, returning the empty phial to the scrip at his belt.

Alfred chortled wearily. "God only knows. I'm a blacksmith by trade and homeless, looking for work."

"We are returning to Jervaulx Abbey and our doors are open to you, at least for a while. This boy is too sick to be without shelter."

Alfred's heart lifted. He had heard of the Cistercian abbey nestled in Wensleydale along the River Ure. It was renowned throughout the dales for its large stables of well-bred horses. Alfred accepted the offer of hospitality with a grateful heart. This might be just the chance he was looking for.

Well into the afternoon the small family of travellers with their holy escort progressed deeper into the dales. Alfred kept the boy under his cloak, snuggled against his broad chest. The fever had a firm grip on William now, his forehead afire and his cheeks crimson.

Jervaulx Abbey
Yorkshire
January 1461

It was dusk when they drew up at the great stone archway that formed the entrance to the abbey. A young novice was summoned to tend the horse and Alfred and the children were led to the guest hall where several other travellers had taken refuge. A fire roared in the hearth and the straw on the flagstones was clean and dry.

Leaving his daughter curled up on the straw, Alfred, carrying William in his arms, followed a monk through a side door and out into the cloisters. They crossed an inner courtyard and entered the infirmary. Several fat wax candles flooded the room with light and the air was thick with the smell of herbs. Brother Infirmarir, red-cheeked and stocky, sat dozing by the fireside. Apart from a few aged monks no one else occupied the raised pallets.

Alfred placed William down on the nearest empty mattress as his escort nudged the infirmir awake.

"Your son has a high fever," remarked the monk sleepily, placing a wrinkled hand upon William's brow. "And his feet need attention," he remarked, tut-tutting his disapproval at the boy's badly blistered feet. Alfred saw no gain in attempting to correct the monk's natural assumption that he was the boy's father and stood awkwardly aside as William's sodden tunic and hose were removed. After a while Alfred left William in the hands of the monk and returned to the hall to eat.

After sharing a meal of boiled turnips from a rough wooden bowl and a chunk of course rye bread the trestles and boards were moved to the side of the hall and folk began to settle down for the night. Alfred lay back on a straw pallet with his hands behind his head staring up at the fireside shadows dancing provocatively on the beams overhead. The warmth of the fire and the peaceful murmurings of his companions lulled him into a restful sleep.

Sometime later Alfred woke to the unfamiliar sound of chanting in the distance. As he lay there trying to remember where he was, he realised that it must be about the hour of midnight and the monks were making their way to the chapel for matins. The fire had died to a faint red glow and all around him were the sounds of snoring and mumbling from sleeping bodies. He sat up and looked across to his daughter. By the dim light he could see that she was awake and staring up at him from her straw pallet.

"Father, where is William?" she whispered.

"He is in the infirmary, child. The monks are looking after him."

"I want to see him," she urged.

Alfred remained silent. He knew that they should not leave the guest hall but to his surprise he found that he too wanted to see the boy again – especially if the worst should happen. Maybe if they were quiet they could creep across while the monks were at their prayers.

"You must promise to be very, very quiet then," Alfred whispered at last. Christiana nodded and stood up. She stooped again quickly to pick up something that lay in the straw beside her.

Alfred made for the side door that led to the cloisters, the same one he had taken earlier. Cautiously he lifted the latch – it was open. The cold night air took their breath as they stepped outside. The moon was high in a star-filled sky and flooded the courtyard with its silver light. Silently Alfred led Christiana by the hand across frost-coated cobbles. The singing from across the courtyard continued to reach their ears.

Loud snoring from the warmth of the fireside indicated the presence of the portly old infirmarir keeping soporific watch over his wards. Moonlight pouring in from a high window bathed the small prostrate figure on the bed in silver. Christiana let go of her father's hand and walked over to William.

"He looks like an angel," she breathed softly.

Alfred's heart almost missed a beat, fearing that the boy had already lost his fight for life. He knelt down beside the bed and felt William's forehead; it was hot and damp. "The fever still has him, child," he said.

As he looked down at the small stricken face, Alfred's mind was drawn back six months earlier to when Mary lay on a mattress in the smithy gripped by a raging fever. At first he had failed to notice his wife's condition for all his grief was being poured out on the tiny, perfectly formed body of his stillborn son cradled in his arms. The small room echoed with prayers and incantations of the village womenfolk as they tried to revive his wife with their herbal remedies and superstitious ritual. Finally the priest was called in to perform the last rites and within hours Alfred had lost his beloved wife and a much longed for son. A tiny wooden cross in the village churchyard was all that marked their passing and the blacksmith was left to raise his seven-year-old daughter alone, with no female kin to call upon.

He drew his hands together over the bedcover and still on his knees began to pray in quiet murmurings that God would spare the boy. As he knelt there a notion stirred within him, a desire to adopt the boy and raise him as his own. From the corner of his eye he noticed Christiana bring something out from beneath her cloak and place it under William's hand as it lay limp on the bed. By the time his prayer had ended Alfred's mind was made up: given that the boy endured the night he would take him as his own.

As they tiptoed back across the courtyard towards the warmth of the hall Alfred looked down at the little girl holding his hand. It would be good for his daughter to have a companion of her own age, he thought, smiling.

Alfred went alone to the infirmary early the following morning, leaving Christiana still asleep in the hall. His footsteps were slow and heavy as he walked the short distance across the cobbles. His heart trembled as he opened the door to the infirmary.

He hardly dared to believe what he had prayed for – but there was William propped up on cushions looking a little flushed but with his eyes open. All trace of the fever had gone. Alfred could not contain his relief. He bounded over to the boy and clapping a huge hand on William's shoulder, exclaimed, "Well, son, you are looking better I see."

"Better, yes, but not yet recovered." Brother Infirmarir

lingered behind Alfred. "I do not know where it is you are bound," he continued, "but this child is not well enough to travel in this weather. The abbot has graciously allowed you to stay a little longer until he has recovered strength enough to continue your journey."

Alfred nodded gratefully. A few days as guests at the monastery would do them no harm and maybe give him chance to weigh the situation in the stables. Things might just be going his way at last. Christiana was given permission to visit her brother later that day.

"Look what I found this morning," William said as she came rushing in. He drew out a little carved wooden horse from underneath the blanket. "An angel must have left it in the night."

Christiana looked quickly at her father and giggled. "Well it was mine but now it is yours, *brother*." She emphasised the last word before leaning across the mattress and planting a small kiss on the top of William's brown thatch of hair. Alfred smiled sadly. He had carved that little horse for his daughter in an attempt to ease the grief of her mother's death. It was her most treasured possession.

As William convalesced Alfred busied himself in the abbey stables, lending a hand with the shoeing of their magnificent horses. He also learned a thing or two about equine herbal remedies, something the monks were most knowledgeable about, but not too keen to share.

They did, however, show him their breeding stallions; fine, sleek creatures, pampered like spoilt princes. Alfred would have given much to remain here amongst the brethren as a lay worker but alas, the entire place ran as efficiently as a skep full of bees; from the initiated white robed monks to the skinny young lads who pumped the bellows, all seemed to have his place and no room for any other. Even with his skills as a blacksmith Alfred was hard pressed to find enough to do at the stable yard each day and found himself lending a hand to the elderly cellarer, unable to move some of his heavy barrels and sacks unaided.

After High Mass was sung in the chapel Christiana helped Brother Hosteller to sweep the guest hall and scatter clean rushes on the floor. The grasses here in the monastery had a much sweeter fragrance than the threshings used on the floor of the inn, she noticed.

After dinner, when the monks took rest from their labours, some of the novices were allowed into the outer courtyard where the lay people could congregate. Christiana would join them and sitting on a bench against the wall for shelter from the wind she would watch their comings and goings.

One afternoon, when the sun had dispersed the dismal grey of winter, a young man came to her bench and sat down wearily next to her, slamming a clay board and wooden writing stick down beside him. Christiana peered up at him, a little wary of his temper. He was slightly built with bony arms protruding through his coarse tunic. He had a mass of very dark unruly curls that sprang like coils from his head with no hint of a tonsure as worn by most of the other monks.

"Why have you got so much hair?" Christiana suddenly blurted out in her childlike manner. The young man turned his head to look down at the girl beside him, surprise lighting up his blue eyes, his ill humour forgotten.

"'Tis because I am not yet a proper monk. I am still learning and it is hard work."

"Well I like your hair, it looks like mine. You should keep it. What is it that you are doing?"

The young man sighed. "Latin, French! I am behind in my studies and have to do extra work."

"I can help you if you like," the child offered innocently.

The man laughed, a little unkindly. "You are a child and a girl. What help could you possibly give to me?"

Christiana was not to be put off. "My mother could read a little and she was showing me before she died. Father always said it was a waste of time."

So it came to be that as Alfred worked to repay the monks' hospitality, his daughter spent the short afternoons in the public courtyard with Dominic, learning the skill of reading and writing. William left the infirmary after a few days, his still blistered feet smothered in balm and wrapped in cloth boots. He would sit in the courtyard with Christiana but he had little interest in the strange sounding words she mumbled with the young novice as they bent their heads over their clay boards.

One afternoon a cold sheet of rain blew in from the dales, drenching any poor soul who happened to be outdoors. Dominic took his clay board and sat at a carrel in the cloisters. Christiana and William wandered into the large stone dairy where the monks made the crumbly white cheese from ewes' milk. It was hardly warmer inside but at least it was drier. The children sat on wooden stools and watched the monks turning and sniffing the maturing cheeses; there was little supply of milk in the winter so not much fresh cheese could be made.

A lay servant scurried in through the open doorway, rain dripping from the end of his pointed nose.

"Oswald has arrived, Brother Philip, from the castle, for the cheeses," he announced with a watery sniff. "He's in the hall drying off. How many shall he take?"

Brother Philip looked up from the wooden table, where he was coaxing a semi-sodden lump into a roundel, a spatula poised in each hand. "Eight. No, make that ten. If we have snow it could be a while before he comes again. I will note the ledger." Laying aside his spatulas he disappeared into a storeroom, the dripping servant following behind.

Later that day, when the rain had eased off a little, William and Christiana helped to load up the mule with the large cheeses wrapped in butter cloth together with several pots of abbey honey and watched as Oswald and an armed escort rode away.

"Finest cheese is that, made right here in Wensleydale," remarked the servant proudly to the two children as the retreating mule squelched across the courtyard with its tail swishing furiously.

The day soon came, too soon for Alfred, when Brother Infirmarir declared William recovered enough to travel. The problem of their future could be shirked no longer. The abbot had been unable to provide Alfred with any regular work, a bitter disappointment to the blacksmith. This night was to be their last in the monastery and tomorrow at dawn they would be back on the road.

The work at the stables was finished for the day and so Alfred ambled across the darkened inner courtyard to the storeroom below ground, to see if Brother Cellarer had need of his help before taking to his bed. The aged monk spent a good deal of time here amongst the sacks and barrels where it was dry and sheltered and there were plenty of soft resting places for old bones.

A concoction of odours assailed the nose on entering the underground lair of the cellarer; wheat, corn, hessian sacking, salted fish and mulled wine. A few tiny candles burned in their holders here and there, casting an eerie light in the gloom. Alfred could discern at once that the old monk had sipped a goblet or two of the abbot's best wine.

"Alfred, my boy. Sit you down and keep company with a wizened old monk." He indicated a thick pile of sackcloth beside him on the bench. Alfred stepped over the earthenware jars that dotted the floor and took a seat beside the old man.

"Ye be off on ye travels soon, I 'spect," the old man stated, with slurred speech.

"Aye, on the morrow," replied Alfred with a sigh.

"The boy recovered now then?"

"Indeed he has and I thank God," Alfred replied and meant it.

"Where you off to then?"

"I wish I knew." Alfred could not hide the note of anxiety in his voice. "I need to find a place where there is plenty of work for a blacksmith. Trouble is there are just too many of us about."

"Middleham, my boy," hissed the monk.

"Middleham?"

"Aye, castle a little way farther up the dales. You've heard of the Neville family, surely?" The monk looked suspiciously round at the barrels and pots watching them from the corners of the room.

Alfred nodded. Richard Neville, Earl of Warwick; a great magnate of the north, due in part, it was said, to his fortuitous marriage to a Beauchamp heiress.

The monk leaned over to Alfred and whispered in his ear, "Things be brewing up there so I've heard tell. Anyway, lad, blacksmiths don't just shoe horses do they? They forge weapons for battle and mend tools for masons. They are doing some fine building work up at the castle right now."

This wrinkly old monk quite took Alfred aback. He was rather worldly wise for one who had probably lived secluded in a monastery for most of his life. Still, Alfred considered, he might just have something there. Why should he not make use of the business of war for a change? If he could make a living supplying weapons for men foolish enough to addle each other's wits then why not? If it had not been for a drunken troop of soldiers, he reminded himself, he would not be in this situation in the first place.

"Where is this Middleham Castle then?" he asked after a while.

"North-west, lad. Follow the lie of the River Ure. 'Tis less than half a day's journey."

The bell rang then for compline, signalling also that supper was ready in the hall for the guests. Alfred bid the old man farewell and left him to sleep off his excesses. Perhaps his absence would be overlooked in chapel this evening – he was an old man after all.

It was with a much lighter spirit that Alfred rode away from the abbey at daybreak the following morning. At last he knew where he was bound. He had great cause to rejoice in William's recovery too and the abbey treasury was a little more swollen upon their departure.

Middleham Castle
Yorkshire
Early 1461

Alfred looked out across the undulating plains of Wensleydale, bare and forlorn in winter repose. Way on yonder slopes a few sheep grazed, their gaunt bodies just visible in the sombre light, their mournful bleats echoing through the dales.

Below, cradled in the bosom of Wensleydale, a stone fortress of immense proportion squatted squarely on the landscape. The vast rectangular keep and regimented towers that linked the curtain wall shimmered gold and rose in the last light of the dying day. Stretching out to the east was the bailey, enclosed and protected by its own strong stone wall. Circling the castle was a deep and wide moat lapping gently at the base of steep grassy embankments giving the impression that the whole fortress was afloat upon a green island.

The thought of living and working within those impregnable walls gave Alfred a sense of exhilaration. That castle represented power and wealth on such a scale the humble blacksmith could only dream of. Under the protection of the Earl of Warwick he and his children would eat well, sleep soundly and want for nothing in exchange for hard work and loyalty.

Alfred could see the long white road coming from the gatehouse in the east and running like a ribbon down the hillside. After a while he urged the horse on across the heath in its direction.

"Are we going in there?" William asked, at once alert. "Soldiers live in castles, don't they? Will my father be there?"

"I cannot say, lad," Alfred replied, patting the boy's head.

The closer they came to the castle the higher the walls seemed and Alfred became increasingly apprehensive. How would he go about asking for work? What if the monk had been wrong and there was in truth little enough work? He was strong and healthy, which should go in his favour – having two small children in tow would probably not.

A steady stream of people was moving in and out of the gate under the watchful eye of the armed guard. Carts loaded with wood or animal fodder rumbled up the road and every now and again their contents would be poked or prodded by a soldier with a spear before being allowed to pass through.

The blacksmith's sturdy horse had almost reached its turn at the gate and Alfred was about to try his luck when the sound of cantering hooves could be heard from the foot of the hill. A small troop of soldiers was riding towards the gate, scattering the crowd as it approached. Alfred reined his horse onto the grassy verge to watch with interest. As he waited for the group to pass he noticed that the rider at the fore was having some difficulty with his mount. The big brown courser was rearing and prancing, obviously in some pain. Before reaching the gate the rider was obliged to dismount, releasing a volley of curses at the unfortunate animal, who was now limping miserably.

Alfred could not let such an opportune moment pass and in an instant he was off his horse and grabbing his tool bag to walk over. "My name is Alfred Smith," he called. "I am a blacksmith by trade. If you allow me I can help."

The man eyed him suspiciously for a moment and then nodded his assent. For all Alfred knew this was the earl himself for he wore a tabard bearing the Warwick coat of arms and his cloak was of the finest woven wool. He would have to keep all his nerve if he was to make use of the opportunity fate had placed into his hands. He also had to play to an audience of onlookers who had gathered around them and haste was prudent as the light was disappearing fast.

He caught the reins of the animal and beckoned one of the bystanders to steady the horse's head; putting his own hand onto the quivering flank he ran his fingers gently down to the hoof, held gingerly in the air, talking soothingly to the horse all the while. Grasping the leg gently but firmly in his steady hand he took his pliers and carefully caught the end of a nail and slowly drew it out from where it had been embedded in the frog of the hoof. "This is a badly fitted shoe," he said, looking up at the man. "See, the nail has been run through at the wrong angle."

The other man's face turned scarlet with rage as he bellowed, "That incompetent ass, Jankin. That drunken bungler." He snatched the reins of the horse and stormed off through the gatehouse, calling out behind him, "You, Alfred Smith, follow me."

The blacksmith looked around him in bewilderment at the amused faces. One of the guards smiled and spoke in an aside to him. "Looks like you've made an impression on the steward, Smith, and old Jankin is about to get the boot at last."

Alfred led his horse under the great arch and into the bailey. He followed the steward as he marched in a rage, along a wide road, stopping only when they reached the stables and smithies veiled in shadow at the far end.

"Where's Jankin?" demanded the steward sternly. The stable lads looked around nervously in the direction of one of the stalls. The steward strode up and pulled open the door. An inebriated form toppled out in a heap onto the cobbles. He looked up with bleary eyes at the man towering above him.

"You shod my horse this morning and damn nearly crippled him," he raged. "Last week one of the earl's best horses was burned by a red hot shoe. You have had your last chance, now get out!"

The poor blacksmith was far too much under the influence of ale to protest at his fate and was hardly aware of the hands that lifted him roughly and dragged him down the road towards the gatehouse. The steward called out a parting retort, "'Tis well for you, old man that the earl is away or else you would have been flogged within an inch of your life."

Alfred stood silently by as the steward brought his temper under control. He looked shrewdly at Alfred, noting his muscular physique. He looked across at the two children, too afraid of the man to even move, clinging to the saddle of their horse.

"These two yours?" the steward asked with a nod in their direction.

"Aye, they are," Alfred replied firmly. "But they are good

children. The boy is ready to learn the blacksmith's trade." He waited expectantly.

The steward nodded. "The Earl of Warwick keeps a large stable here at Middleham and an army of masons on site for he has a mind to make the castle grander. There is plenty of work here for a good blacksmith. If you think you are up to the task then Jankin's work is yours. Unless, of course, you are here on another matter?"

Alfred was almost speechless and not a little embarrassed. He stared up the darkening road at the retreating soldiers and the pathetic bundle of humanity slung between them. Well, he thought, one man's loss is another's gain. "I am most grateful for the work and am pleased to offer my allegiance to the Earl of Warwick," Alfred said, after a while. "And to you, my lord?" he added bowing low.

"Sir John Conyers, Steward of Middleham," replied the man.

Christiana had spent the morning making the room adjoining the smithy into a home for her father, her brother and herself. This dwelling was bigger than the one they used to live in; the walls were thicker and sturdily built with a roof of stone.

She moved about arranging and rearranging the few scant objects left by the previous occupant and kneaded the stained mattress to spread out the straw. After her labours of domesticity her father said she could wander around the bailey as long as she kept out of trouble and did not cross the wooden bridge to the castle. That was where the grand folk lived and it was no place for her. William's feet were still sore and he had no mind to wander about, content to sit and watch Alfred's activities at the forge.

The bailey was a vast place, easily the extent of her village, with buildings of every description: from dairy to brew house, to storehouses and barns. Christiana drew her cloak about her and walked around with the natural curiosity of a child. She stopped to look at the ducks paddling in the muddy puddles and the skinny hens that pecked and scratched in the soil. A bony grey and white kitten twined itself around her legs, meowing hungrily and she stooped to pat its matted fur.

Everywhere she looked there were people at work just as in any village. There were carpenters, fletchers, candle makers and washerwomen. Carts piled high with wood, sacks and barrels clattered to and fro across the bridge to the forbidden castle.

Most of the buildings were clustered along the northern side of the bailey and way across to the southern end was a large grassed area. Here the men-at-arms were going through their drill, despite the chill of the day, the captain's voice booming out his orders across the open space. She stood and watched them for a while, admiring their brightly coloured livery and the bear and ragged staff that marked the retainers of the Earl of Warwick.

Facing the castle and to her right side Christiana could see timber scaffolding growing, it seemed, out of the curtain wall. The keep also had a dressing of scaffolding and she could see men walking along planks of wood. They were dragging huge blocks of stone along and lifting them on pulleys up to the very top of the roof. The builders looked very small and she hoped that they would not fall off.

There was just one more part of the bailey left to see. It looked to be a garden way over in the far corner beyond the drill field. She took a path that skirted the grass and entered through a small wicker gate. She could sense at once that this place was unlike any other she had seen thus far. The rest of the bailey's function was purely practical, existing to supply the needs of the earl and his household. This place was tranquil and pleasing to the eye, a quiet sanctuary. She hesitated at the gate, unsure of whether she should proceed. Gravelled pathways meandered around box hedges, flower beds and shrubs, at present bare and colourless but holding the promise of colour and warmth under a summer sun. Benches had been placed around an elaborately carved dovecote where the residents bobbed and cooed in the cool air.

Tucked away against the outer wall was a cottage with small windows and the typical stone roof where a plume of smoke curled upwards to the grey sky. There appeared to be outhouses attached to the main dwelling, including a covered midden and large water barrels standing to attention on one side. Spreading around the front and sides of the building was a very neat and regimented herb garden.

Curiosity was a natural part of the little girl's being and so, stifling her feeling of apprehension, she began to walk along the path towards the cottage, regarding the form and style of the garden as she went.

As she came closer she could see that the wooden door was ajar. At once and without warning a woman appeared in the doorway and caught sight of her. Christiana would have scampered like a cat caught with an eel pie but the woman called out to her. "And who, pray, do we have here then?"

The child stood looking up at the woman. She was round like a barrel with a leather cord around her middle from which hung an assortment of little pouches. Wisps of fuzzy greying hair had escaped her linen coif and framed her plump rosy-cheeked face. She stood with hands resting upon her ample hips, giving her an air of authority.

Finally the girl found voice to speak. "Christiana, my lord," she answered, bowing as she had seen her father do to John Conyers.

At once the woman let out a bellow of laughter, her pink cheeks glowing crimson.

"Come here, girl," she commanded, still chuckling. Christiana did as she was told.

"Now first off I'm no lord, and no lady either come to that. Although my husband, William, God rest his soul, did hold the post of steward a few years back." She looked down at Christiana, who was staring at her aghast.

"I am called Martha," the woman continued. "You had best come inside and we will get better acquainted."

The inside of the cottage was nothing like Christiana had ever seen before; no dwelling in her village looked like this. Wooden trestles with boards bowing under the weight of earthenware bottles, jars, bowls, pans, flagons and vessels of many shapes and sizes ran round the walls. Under the tables were sacks and barrels, one near the door was filled with water, and the floor had a sprinkling of clean, dry strewing herbs. Bunches of dried herbs hung like overloaded grapevines from the low beams and a pungent, aromatic odour filled the air. Near the centre of the floor stood a small charcoal burner with a pan on top and something inside it was gurgling gently, sending a vapour upwards through a hole in the roof.

It looked very much like the infirmary at the monastery; it had the same smell. Christiana looked around to see if there were any sick people. There was a small door set in the far wall but it was closed. Perhaps they were in another room, she thought.

"Do you live in this place?" she asked curiously.

"Of course I do, child," Martha replied. "Now sit yourself down and take some ale." She produced a costrel and two horn cups into which she poured a dark, sweet, fruity smelling liquid. "Go on, girl. 'Tis not poison. I brew it myself." The old woman smiled at Christiana's reluctance to drink.

The girl took a sip and found the drink to be very pleasant and so took a little more. "What do you do in here?" she asked, sitting herself down upon a nearby stool.

"I keep the herb garden to supply the kitchen and to make medicines for the earl and his household. So, are you going to tell me what you are doing here? I do not recall seeing you before."

"No, I have just arrived with my father. My name is Christiana and we live in the smithy. Father is a blacksmith. Do you live here alone?"

Martha drained her cup and smiled. "I did have a husband until a few years back. Like I say, William was the steward and looked after the running of the castle. We lived up at the keep in those days."

"You did!" Christiana was awestruck. "You lived in the castle? Why do you not live there now?"

"I was given this work when my William died. I learned the skill from my mother. It suits me just fine to live here. John Conyers is steward now."

"My brother is called William," Christiana said cheerfully, suddenly recalling the fact that she had recently acquired a brother.

"Indeed," Martha said, taking the empty cup from the girl.

"How would you like to work for me here in the herbarium? I could do with a little help – my bones are not getting any younger and someone will need to take over when I am gone."

Christiana thought about that for a while. "But Father will need me to help in the smithy," she replied.

Martha looked surprised. "But 'tis man's work is that. Your brother will be helping his father, will he not?"

Christiana nodded slowly. Yes, she supposed he would. She had not thought of that until now. William would be Father's apprentice. "I should like very much to come and work here if my father agrees," she replied politely.

"That's settled then, if your father agrees and the steward of course. But you can nowise work with me until you are cleaned up. Look at your rags, girl. Do you not have another dress?"

Christiana blushed and looked down at her tatty mud-splattered dress and shook her head.

"No matter, lass. I will see what can be done." Martha smiled and ruffled the child's dark curls tenderly.

It was not long before Alfred and his young family began to settle down to their new life. It pleased him immensely that his daughter had found a woman willing to take her in hand and to teach her skills more suited to a girl than work in a smithy. He was pleasantly surprised when Christiana came home one day bearing two home-spun dresses of brown wool, neatly made, and not only boots for herself but a pair for William also.

They ate well too, for the first time since the death of his wife. The earl's table lacked for nothing and even the most modest meals were as good as a feast to the blacksmith. The soldiers and the servants who lived and worked in the bailey ate the leftovers from the high table served in their own hall adjacent to the brew house. Mostly the food was cold by the time it reached them but no one seemed to mind. The castle also had its own bakery in the bailey so all in all they wanted for nothing.

The Earl of Warwick had been out campaigning for the Yorkist cause long before Alfred arrived at Middleham, along with the greater part of his retinue and his best horses. Lack of horses to shoe and take care of was no problem to Alfred as there was always a steady supply of tools to mend and weapons to sharpen.

Middleham underwent vast alteration work in the year of Alfred's arrival; there were extensions to the northern range of towers in the curtain wall, including a new northern entrance that would allow access to the castle from the village. The earl's greatest architectural achievement, however, was the erection of an upper chamber over the great hall of the keep. With its rows of tall round-topped windows offering spectacular views over Wensleydale, the upper chamber would be a symbol of the earl's status and power here in the north.

William grew stronger as the weeks passed. His thin limbs began to pad out with flesh and his skin took on a healthier glow. He worked hard and enthusiastically under Alfred's guidance. He was eager to learn the smith's trade and had a natural liking for horses and an instinctive understanding of their needs that made his training a joy.

As well as William, Alfred had a bellows boy to attend the fire and stoke it with charcoal and a portehache, the boy who did the fetching and carrying. Alfred had cause to thank God daily for his good fortune and prayed that England would soon settle her warring feuds and that peace could reign at last over the land.

There was only one thing that troubled Alfred, that being the occasions when he would catch William sitting alone on the stacks of straw in the stables. The boy would have a faraway look of melancholia in his eyes, quite lost in his own little world. Alfred guessed it was at these times the boy would be thinking of his natural father who had died in a battle he was too young to even understand. Alfred would ruffle William's brown hair and leave him alone with his thoughts. He knew from experience that time alone could soothe the pain.

One morning Christiana sauntered into Martha's cottage to find her mixing yet another herbal concoction.

"What is that smell?" the girl asked, wrinkling her nose and watching her mentor stir and pound the recipe with a wooden pestle.

"Oil of bay leaves, sweet almond oil, stavesacre, tansy juice, centaury and salt of sulphur and not forgetting fat of an old hog," Martha replied without looking up.

"For what?"

"A young page up at the castle has got head lice and we have to go and treat it."

"We have?" Christiana's eyes lit up. "You mean *me* as well? I can go inside the castle?"

Martha laughed. "Of course you, child. I have no other apprentice."

Christiana had trouble bridling her excitement as she trotted beside Martha along the road towards the castle. She had been given a sealed jar containing vinegar and held on to it tightly as they went up the green, passing the dairy and the fletchers' hut and the bakery, where the smell of fresh baked bread floated deliciously on the morning air. As they neared the stables and smithies Christiana peered warily across the grass, expecting her father to come out and forbid her to cross the bridge.

"There'll be snow later," Martha prophesied, looking upwards. Christiana followed her gaze to where grey-brown clouds hung ominously over the castle. They reached the wooden bridge that spanned the moat. Christiana took hold of Martha's hand as they clattered across, pausing to look over the stone wall at a pair of swans gliding on the murky water below. Two armed sentries guarded the gatehouse but they let Martha through with a nod of recognition.

Once over the bridge and through the gatehouse Martha made her way across the inner courtyard towards the entrance into the great keep. An enclosed stone staircase ran along the side of the keep, another pair of sentries guarding the foot. Martha stated her business and was allowed to ascend. Christiana's heart was pounding as she walked slowly up the stone steps through a gated archway. She was overawed by the magnitude of the building, even bigger now that she was this close.

They passed under a second gated archway, also guarded,

and reached the top of the staircase. A final archway led into an antechamber, a small room with one high window and a desk at which sat an elderly usher. He looked up from his ledger with a smile as Martha entered with the girl hiding behind her skirts.

"You are expected. My Lady Anne and the children are in the great chamber," he announced. "Godwin here will escort you." He spoke to the young groom who was standing idly by the round-headed doorway leading into the great hall.

The room into which Christiana walked was spacious and very grand. Set into the wall by which they had entered were three large round-topped windows through which the feeble winter light trickled. Rows of trestles and boards were set hard against two walls and a long oak table raised on a platform ran the length of the wall furthest away and facing them. Above this grand table and either side of a single round-headed window hung a banner bearing the Neville coat of arms and a pair of crossed swords. The walls were limewashed and decorated with richly coloured tapestries and murals. In the centre of the tiled floor near to the high table a fire smouldered in its deep rectangular recess, puffing curls of smoke up into the rafters. To their left a carved wooden partition supporting a minstrel's gallery screened the stairwell that led from the kitchen and cellar below. The hall was empty except for a pair of rough-haired wolfhounds snoring and twitching beside the fire.

Godwin led the way across the hall to an arched doorway in the opposite wall where a heavily embroidered curtain concealed another chamber beyond. The groom announced their arrival and then retreated to his post.

This second room was a privy chamber, warmed comfortably by burning logs in the fireplace. Seated before them on a large fur-covered bed was the graceful figure of a woman illuminated by light from three large rounded windows behind her.

The little girl stared wide-eyed at the lady. She had never before seen such a beautiful being. Her gown of pale crimson silk fell in soft folds to the floor. A wide fur-trimmed V-shaped neckline ended at a dark blue velvet girdle that circled her narrow waist. The lady's delicate wrists were hidden beneath matching fur-trimmed cuffs. It was not, however, the gown, beautiful as it was, that caused Christiana to stare in astonishment. The woman wore a dark blue velvet band across her high forehead which curved down to her shoulder at either side. Attached to the band was a long gold cone-shaped hennin with a white transparent veil hanging from its point. Women in Christiana's village never wore such elaborate headwear. Martha stepped forward and bowed reverently. Christiana did likewise.

"My lady, I have the remedy for head lice," the herbalist announced. The lady nodded her head gracefully and stood to her feet. She beckoned to a figure standing within the shadows of the wall. A small boy, looking to be of much the same age as Christiana, reluctantly stepped forward. His clothes were as rich and elaborate as the lady's; grey tight-fitted woven hose and a short red fur-trimmed velvet tunic. He wore shoes of soft black leather with fashionable long pointed toes and his dark hair was cut shoulder length. His eyes flitted shyly from Martha to the lady at his side.

"Francis, Martha is going to wash your hair. You will do as you are bid," the lady commanded. "The grooms will fetch anything you require," she added, addressing Martha.

Jugs of warm water were sent for and poured into a large bowl. The boy was ordered to stand with his head over the bowl while Martha rinsed his long hair with vinegar and water. After that he had to sit still as the herbalist rubbed the liniment into his scalp, a disgruntled frown upon his face.

After a while it became apparent that there were other persons present in the chamber for Christiana could hear stifled giggling from behind her. Turning around she saw two girls sitting on a wooden chest against the wall. Their laughter grew louder until finally they emerged from their seat to stand over the boy, tittering like a pair of doves. The girls looked to be sisters and by their colouring were most certainly daughters to the lady. As they wore no hats Christiana could see their long golden tresses hanging down their backs. The older girl looked to be about ten years of age but the little one was of no more than four or five years. Christiana thought she was very pretty with eyes as blue as a summer sky.

Martha, sensing the boy's embarrassment, addressed the lady. "My lady, may I be so bold as to advise that the Lady Isabel and the Lady Anne be treated also with this remedy for it has been known for lice to jump from head to head."

The giggling ceased forthwith and the girls retreated to their chest. It was Christiana's turn to smile. She cupped a hand over her mouth to suppress the laughter that bubbled up inside her.

"Who were they?" asked Christiana later as they stepped outside into a flurry of falling snow.

"That was the Countess of Warwick and her daughters, the Lady Isabel and the Lady Anne. The boy is Francis Lovell, the earl's ward. He has been sent here while his mother recovers from her illness, God help her," Martha answered, walking briskly back across the bridge towards the warmth of her cottage.

Wind howled across the dales, bringing blizzards of icy snow, shrouding hill and dale in white and making travel almost impossible. The horse troughs were frozen over each morning and William and Jude, the bellows boy, had to go out with hammers to crack their surfaces. Christiana's fingers were so cold she could hardly rub the herbs and mix the potions for Martha. Alfred was probably one of the few people to keep warm, sweating over the heat of the brazier as he melted iron to forge the shoes. Work on the third storey of the keep had halted due to the freezing cold and high winds making work dangerous. Materials could no longer be transported in severe weather so many of the masons had little or no work. All this meant that Alfred's workload was also less and the winter days were long and cold.

When the daylight began to fade Christiana and William would huddle together on the straw mattress in the glow of a few tallow candles and listen to Alfred telling his stories. There were stories of chivalry and bravery, of love and romance. William liked to hear the one telling of how Saint George slew the fierce dragon and sat still as a rock with eyes wide as Alfred described the fire-breathing green-scaled monster and the courage of the knight. Christiana wanted to hear stories of the gallant knight's love for his lady. Whatever the tale Alfred had a skill for embroidering his narrative with a few well-chosen sounds and facial expressions that could evoke tears of laughter or sorrow in the children.

One of the tales the children never tired of hearing was the one about Saint Dunstan, the patron saint of metal workers and smiths. This pious monk lived in a little cell in Glastonbury Cathedral where he had built himself a small forge to make church bells and other metal objects. One day the devil appeared to him in the form of a beautiful young girl to tempt the holy man. However, the monk was cunning and knew it to be a trick. So he took a pair of red- hot tongs and grasped hold of the girl's nose and he knew by her inhuman screams that she was none other than the devil himself. At this point in the story Alfred would stand up and taking hold of his own nose would run around the smithy screaming like a wild boar. William and Christiana would roll about hysterically on the mattress at his performance.

It was now almost April and the weather was still bitterly cold. Despite the almost impassable roads news was still reaching the castle of the earl's exploits on behalf of the Yorkist cause. Nothing could be certain, however, and gossip and rumour spread like wild fire with the arrival of every travel-weary soldier.

No one could refute the victory won for the Yorkists by Edward, Earl of March, against Jasper Tudor at Mortimer's Cross in early February; a triumph it seemed with divine blessing, for had not Edward seen a vision of not one but three suns in the sky on the day of the battle? It was being hailed as the York sun in splendour, each sun representing one of the three remaining sons of the now demised Duke of York.

The matter was far from settled though, because as much of an unwilling soldier King Henry was proving to be, the same could not be said for his queen, Margaret of Anjou. Barely two weeks after Edward's victory at Mortimer's Cross news was in that the Lancastrians had triumphed at St. Alban's, where it was rumoured the Earl of Warwick had been killed; a rumour only to be refuted when it was confirmed that the great magnate had indeed made safe his escape to the Cotswolds.

It seemed that every rider entering the castle had a different tale to tell and Alfred, along with many, wondered how long it would be before the feuding would end and England could be at peace.

One evening a returning troop of soldiers had carried with them news that would appear to settle matters once and for all. Edward, Earl of March, supported by the Earl of Warwick, had entered London on the twenty-sixth day of February and such was the popularity of this dashing young warrior that he met with no resistance when, on the fourth day of March, he proclaimed himself king. No one seemed to be concerned that Henry the Sixth, anointed King of England, still lived.

Middleham Castle
Yorkshire
Spring 1461

John Conyers, the steward of Middleham Castle, was in excitable humour as he came down to the bailey one cold morning in early April to announce the news that the earl was even now on the road heading home. His ardour soon infected the rest of the servants who began a frenzy of activity to prepare for the return of their liege lord.

A raw wind blew across the bailey and an early dusk was rapidly obscuring the outline of the buildings when a loud trumpet blast could be heard down at the eastern gatehouse. Christiana and William, along with Jude, had stood out for hours waiting to catch their first glimpse of the earl and now came hurrying along the road shouting excitedly, "He's here, he's here!"

Alfred, who had remained in the warmth of the smithy keeping his brazier hot and his tools at the ready, came out slowly and peered into the gloom along the road up which Warwick would come.

Within minutes a magnificent black war horse, flanks frothy with sweat and mud from the roads, trotted up to the stables, tossing its noble head in the wind. The earl, a broad-shouldered man with a harsh despotic countenance etched deeply with battle-worn lines, sat well on his horse despite the hardship of travelling in such bitter weather.

Behind the earl came several of his men-at-arms and companions, weary with hunger and fatigued with fighting. Warwick did not pull up his horse at the stables but urged it on over the bridge to where Conyers was waiting to greet him. A couple of stable lads ran on behind the earl to see to the needs of his horse.

The soldiers dismounted in the stable yard where they had to attend their own mounts before taking sustenance themselves. Grooms and stable lads were all on hand to assist. William's face was aglow with excitement at the sight of so many soldiers. Alfred watched as the boy looked expectantly from one face to another in the hope of recognising his father. Some of the men looked to have had a skinful of ale judging by their red faces and the lewd remarks made to the few women present. Alfred sought out the captain and asked for news, more so to appease William than from a desire to know himself.

"Edward, Earl of March, now King Edward," the captain corrected himself, "has led us to victory over the Lancastrians at Towton. By God, it was a bloody battle," he emphasised, bending over to meet William's eye. The boy smiled gleefully.

"Looks like the Yorkists have the upper hand now, lad; Queen Margaret has fled in fear for her life," the captain continued and ruffled William's hair before adding a final parting remark: "The greatest Yorkist victory was the death in battle of that esteemed northern magnate, Henry Percy, Earl of Northumberland, although it pains me to see how great men must fall."

Most of the soldiers having seen to their horses had now ambled away to their victuals and much needed rest. Christiana had stood in the shadows of the smithy overawed and not a little fearful of the men shouting and stomping about.

One man, a mere youth of no more than sixteen years with long strands of greasy hair hanging limply over his face, had arrived at the entrance to the smithy as the captain had been speaking. He had several pieces of plate armour in his hand that he now dropped to the floor with a loud clang.

"Here, smith," he shouted rudely. "The earl's cuisses and greaves for you to hammer back into shape." He looked at William, who was sweeping the earthen floor with a birch besom, and a curious half smile, revealing pockets of hardened gum where once had hung a tooth, spread across his thin lips.

"So, you like to hear tales of battle do you, boy?" he teased.

William nodded eagerly and stepped a little closer to the soldier but there was something in the man's tone that alerted

Alfred. He looked up from his brazier where he had been placing turf to dampen down the fire for the night. He could see that the lad was drunk and he began to feel a little uneasy. He beckoned his daughter to his side and waited, alert, for the man to continue.

Even from her place beside her father Christiana could see the odd way in which the young man's eyes stared from their sockets; it was as though their hinges were askew, for each looked in a different place to its twin.

"There were hundreds of Lancastrians running away, cowards the lot," the man began eagerly. "We chased 'em all across the field, hacking and cutting their limbs and ran 'em out into the freezing River Cock. There was so much blood the river ran red." He threw back his head and laughed. The smile had faded from William's face and he backed away from the soldier. Alfred, disturbed by the sadistic glint in the young man's eyes, had stepped forward to stand beside his son but the soldier was already outside, obscured by the darkness of the yard.

"Their armour weighed 'em down, boy, and they drowned in their own blood," the youth called over his shoulder as he ran away laughing.

Alfred put a comforting hand on William's shoulder but the boy wriggled free and walked dejectedly through to their dwelling.

Warwick did not stay long at Middleham. Rested and refreshed, the earl, the countess and their two daughters, along with a suitable retinue of soldiers and servants, left the castle for London and the court of King Edward the Fourth.

As spring gave way to summer Christiana learned much from the herbalist as together they tended the herb garden. Martha pointed out the usefulness of each plant; the fragrant chamomile for skin complaints, the golden-yellow coltsfoot for coughs, and creamy-white flowers of the yarrow used in the treatment of wounds. Christiana was learning how to identify each plant by its fragrance, its leaves and the proper season for its flowers. There were rows of pennyroyal, wormwood, sage, hyssop, rue, sweet basil, thyme and dill. They would go out to the herb garden together and watch the oily orange petals of the calendula, known also as St Mary's gold, and predict rain if the petals had failed to open by early morning.

One day Martha said to Christiana, "You see that plant over there, the yellow one shaped like a star?" The girl nodded her head. "Celandine is that and swallows pluck off little bits of the leaf and rub it into the eyes of their young."

Christiana spent hours that day sitting beside the celandine waiting for a swallow to fly down, much to the amusement of Martha, who had a wide beaming smile on her face for most of the day.

Christiana took pleasure in watching each new flower open its treasure trove for the first time as the weeks drifted by. There were purple periwinkles, blue irises and peonies. Also they had an abundance of daezes eyes and pink, crimson and white gillyflowers that laced the west wall of the cottage.

The herbalist was sure to make certain that her apprentice knew how to identify the poisonous plants such as wolfsbane, belladonna, hemlock and foxglove. This skill required many journeys to the surrounding woods, heaths and waysides; medicine made from these plants was carefully labelled and stored in a locked chest.

The girl was realising a special friend in the old woman, almost the mother she had never really had chance to know. Martha's vast knowledge of herbal remedies astounded the child but more importantly she was the means by which she could visit the castle and the grand folk who lived there. The herbalist explained that although the countess and her daughters were frequently away with the earl on court affairs they returned as often as possible to their favoured northern residence.

Countess Anne was very fond of Martha's recipes and as such there would always be a constant supply. Christiana made these favourites with great care; white blossom of the deadnettle to dye their long golden hair and wild tansy seeped in buttermilk for a fair complexion.

The castle pleasure garden also flourished under the summer sun and due in no small part to the dedication of the gardener, a quiet man, well past his prime but still agile enough, known simply as Wat.

A circular border girdled the dovecote and in mid-summer a profusion of pale crimson roses flourished amidst their ragged leaves. Martha had informed Christiana this was the Apothecary Rose, used as a symbol of the House of Lancaster. There had been a long tradition of support for the Lancastrians at Middleham until the Earl of Salisbury, the present earl's father, had lost his head supporting the Duke of York at the battle of Wakefield. The Apothecary Rose had adorned the castle garden for a long time; its petals were used to make rosewater and the hips were used in autumn to flavour the honey and to make soothing syrup for coughs.

Christiana's favourite part of the garden was tucked away in the south corner and partly concealed by a box hedge. A sprawling rose bush cascaded elegantly over the high stone wall. Clusters of milky white roses opened out flat in the sunshine looking heavenwards with their shaggy golden faces. At the foot of the wall, beneath the shade of the giant bush, was an old oak-wood bench, shiny and smooth and cracked with age. On hot days, when her work was done, Christiana would sit here and let the intoxicating perfume of the roses enfold her. Martha was not sure when the Rosa Alba had arrived at Middleham but agreed it was a lovely specimen.

Summer ripened into the long golden days of harvest time, a time of plenty, God willing, and a herald to the reds, yellows and browns of autumn. On one such mellow day at the end of the reaping, when swallows circled the sky, Middleham Castle welcomed within its walls someone who seemed to be of little importance, a mere younger brother, but one who was to have such a profound effect upon the life of the blacksmith's daughter that he would leave an impression upon her heart as deep and permanent as any made with a blacksmith's brand.

The new King of England was to be the honoured guest of the Earl of Warwick during his royal tour of the realm. After an elaborate coronation at the end of June, Edward had set off on a journey to establish himself on the throne by showing himself in all his glory to his subjects. The young Edward certainly knew how to behave like a king, a most welcome and indeed necessary change, some said, to the pious Henry who had no stomach for the battlefield. Very few people had speculated upon what had happened to that poor miserable man. Talk, especially amongst the womenfolk around the bailey, was of nothing but the newly crowned king.

"He's the most handsome man who ever lived," one remarked.

"So tall as well, with hair of spun gold, some say," said another.

"Women throw themselves in front of his horse just for one kiss," stated the toothless old hag at the bake house one afternoon.

"Is that for a kiss from the king or his horse then, Bessie?" Alfred laughed as he took his loaves and tucked them under his arm. He, for one, was beginning to think that this king was not human at all with the things folk were saying about him.

Conyers was like a bear with a sore head as he stomped around the bailey checking that the roofs and walls of the stone buildings were all in good repair; making sure there were adequate supplies of all necessities such as beeswax candles, wood for fuel, feathers to make new mattresses and food enough to feed ten thousand men. Rooms on the upper floor of the south range were swept clean, limewashed and kept warm, ready for the royal retainers and servants that would accompany the king.

The Earl of Warwick, astute and cunning as ever, had commissioned a sword be made for the new king, finely balanced with a jewel-encrusted hilt. Richard Neville was taking no chances; now that he had his cousin on the throne he was going to make sure that the young man knew exactly how he should rule his kingdom.

At last the long-awaited day arrived. A pale end of summer sun brushed the turning leaves a fiery bronze and a cool wind swept the dales. The road leading down the hill to the east was lined with villagers. Within the bailey many servants had left their work and congregated on the drill field where a breath of anticipation danced from head to head.

"I cannot see anything," Christiana moaned from her lofty position on top of her father's broad shoulder. William, perched on Alfred's other arm, craned his neck to peer down the road.

"He will be here soon," Alfred reassured his children yet again although they had already been waiting there for almost an hour.

All of a sudden the expectant murmurings changed pitch and a wave of cheering rippled through the crowd on a fanfare of trumpets.

"The king is here, the king is here!" William shrieked, twisting his body round so quickly that Alfred had to shift his weight on alternate feet to keep his balance.

Everybody held their breath and stretched their necks towards the gatehouse. The Earl of Warwick was the first to appear astride his prancing warhorse. Men-at-arms, led by the royal standard bearer followed and then came the king. Carried on the back of an impressive chestnut stallion, King Edward, nineteen years of age, tall and handsome, with breastplate gleaming in the sunlight, made a striking entrance.

Several other representatives from the northern nobility followed, flaunting their banners and Heraldic arms in support of the new king. There was also, riding just to the rear of the king's procession, amongst the earl's family, a youth of about twelve years, grinning broadly at the spectators.

Christiana, sitting patiently on her father's shoulder, watched the colourful procession with awe. One figure, from amongst so many, drew her attention, even from the regal person of the king himself. A small boy with an ermine-trimmed cloak of purple around his slender frame was riding high up behind the king on his horse. He was waving at the people, just like his sovereign. He wore no hat and his hair, gilded with gold, not unlike the king's, swept his shoulders. Christiana thought that he must be someone very important indeed to be allowed to ride with the king.

As the parade passed on out of sight into the inner courtyard the crowd began to break up, muttering words of praise and admiration.

"A fine young buck like that needs to get a wife, and soon," remarked one of the soldiers standing beside Alfred.

"Have you not heard?" replied another. "Conyers has it that Warwick is even now trying to match him with a French noblewoman."

"Well he had better not tarry – half the women in the kingdom will be throwing themselves at his feet, lucky fellow." His companion laughed and together they disappeared into the thinning crowd. Alfred's passing thought was one of bemusement and he wondered if the young king was ready to take a French wife. Like it or not, that was the way with nobility: a marriage was often more of a peace treaty than a love match.

The king and his entourage stayed at Middleham for several days during which time there was much merrymaking and joviality. The whole castle had the atmosphere of a feast day but the steward made certain that the servants did not neglect their duties.

Christiana was very disappointed that she saw nothing of the royal visitor as Edward had brought with him many of his own servants and attendants, including physicians.

Alfred had an added workload making sure that the horses were adequately prepared for the long journey south. When the time came for the king's departure everyone turned out once again to wave and cheer Edward, his entourage and the earl on their way. Christiana looked out for the little fair-haired boy who had arrived with the king and watched sadly as he departed once again astride the great chestnut horse, passing under the arched gatehouse and riding away down the road.

Middleham Castle
Yorkshire
Autumn 1461

"I have something to show you, Christiana," Alfred whispered eagerly. It was early and a chill mist hung in the morning air as his daughter, a little sleepy-eyed, was about to leave the smithy on her way to the herbarium. The blacksmith was standing just within the open smithy where he was cleaning the ash from the brazier before stoking and relighting it.

"'Tis a little late in the season, mind, but these things do happen," he mumbled, laying aside his brush and taking Christiana's small hand in his large calloused one. He led her to the stalls at the rear of the smithy.

"You must be very quiet," he warned, "and no sudden movements."

"Why?" the girl asked, intrigued.

Alfred put a finger to his lips as he entered a large building divided into sections, each housing a horse chomping contentedly on its hay bag. In the very end stall, the largest of all, however, there was no horse; creeping stealthily inside Christiana thought it to be empty and gave her father an inquiring look. Then she heard faint whimpering sounds coming from the corner where piles of clean dry straw had been swept and pressed into a high stack with a wide plateau, reaching almost to the wooden rafters above. Standing tiptoe on a stone trough and pulling herself up Christiana peered closer and gave a startled gasp of joy as she saw, concealed in the straw, a big grey rough-coated hound lying panting on her side. Clasped tightly onto and tugging hard at her nipples were two soft bundles of brown and one of grey.

"Only born last night," Alfred whispered. "Master Perkins, keeper of the earl's dogs, has not seen them yet."

Christiana leaned forward a little closer to see better the

44

tiny blind puppies sucking hungrily in the dim light. A sudden movement in the doorway behind alerted them.

"What are you doing?" William asked, standing there hugging his arms in the cold air.

"William, come here," Christiana called in a low voice behind her shoulder. The boy crept forward and joined his sister on the trough. He put out a hand as if to touch the nearest pup.

"Nay, lad, do not touch; she might not like it," said Alfred. "Best come away now and leave her be."

Later that afternoon Christiana returned to the stable almost skipping along with anticipation at seeing the pups again. She clutched her upturned apron full of scraps of meat purloined from the servants' hall at dinner. She had carefully wiped away the rich sauces so as to make the meat more palatable to the dog.

She came to an abrupt halt at the entrance to the stall for she was not alone. A big thickset man wearing rough dirty hose and Warwick's livery was standing with his back to her reaching over the top of the straw mound. Tentatively Christiana walked forward. She could see that the man held one of the pups in his large hand and was peering closely at the squirming bundle of soft hair. "Well, Lass, you've done well again – with two of 'em anyhow." The man was addressing the large wolfhound bitch lying passively on her side in the straw. "This un's a runt though." He was turning the one grey pup in his hands and pinching the fleshy round feet. The little dog yelped in pain and Christiana gave a startled cry, almost letting the morsels of meat tumble from her apron.

The man turned abruptly around to face the girl. "And who might you be?" he asked gruffly, his eyes narrowing suspiciously. For a moment the girl could find no answer for fear of the man but as she continued to watch the little puppy whimpering in the man's hand she found courage.

"My name is Christiana. My father is Alfred the blacksmith," she said as boldly as she could. "What is wrong with the pup?"

"It has twisted feet. No good to the earl or anybody with twisted feet."

Christiana stared up at the animal. "But it will walk, will it not?" she asked, growing uneasy at the thought of what this man might intend to do with the pup.

"Maybe it'll walk but it won't hunt. Useless lumbering along on twisted feet, seen it afore. 'Twill have to go."

"Go where?" Christiana asked, alarmed.

The man stared at the girl. She could see his square jaw sprouting a coarse growth of beard and gazed up at his grey eyes, impassive and dull.

"You'd best run along to your mother, child, and leave me to do me job." He walked across the floor with long strides, his boots thumping on the hard ground. Christiana dropped the corners of her apron and ran to keep up with the man, leaving the meat unceremoniously scattered on the floor.

Still holding the pup he walked round the building into the stable yard and over to where a large water barrel stood next to the open front of the smithy. Alfred looked up from his brazier to see the Keeper of the Dogs come striding up, his daughter running behind.

"Good day, Master Perkins," Alfred said, laying aside his hammer and tongs and walking out into the fading light of the stable yard.

Ignoring the blacksmith, Perkins walked up to the barrel and dropped the pup into the water where it plummeted like a stone to the bottom. Christiana let out an ear-piercing scream and would have run to the barrel but for the restraining hand on the back of her bodice pulling her away.

"The pup's nowt but a runt, Smith, it needs destroying. Keep the girl away," he ordered before marching off into the gathering shadows. Bewildered, Alfred stood and watched him go.

"Get it out, Father! Get it out!" the girl screamed, tears now streaming down her cheeks.

"I dare not, lass. If the pup's a runt and no good then it's not my place to interfere," Alfred replied, flinching at his daughter's anguish.

"No, no, Father!" Christiana was hanging onto the rim, trying to pull herself up and into the barrel. She could see the little dog pawing weakly at the water in vain, tiny bubbles of air rising to the surface from its mouth. The girl began to kick the wooden sides of the barrel in anger and frustration, yelling at her father.

"Look, look, 'tis coming up," she cried, her hands tightly gripping the sides of the barrel.

"'Tis all but dead already. Come away, lass, we cannot interfere," Alfred said miserably. Christiana would not let go of the sides of the barrel and was sobbing uncontrollably now. Alfred sighed deeply and reaching into the barrel he scooped up the dripping, lifeless form. At once Christiana held her arms out for the pup.

"'Tis dead, child," Alfred muttered, a pained expression on his face. The child snatched the dog and held it close and moving as fast as her legs would allow with the wet heavy body pressed hard against her chest she ran to Martha.

Bursting in through the door, breathless and red-faced Christiana held the pup out to Martha, quite unable to explain its presence for sobbing.

"My, my, what have we here then?" Martha wiped her hands on her coarse apron and eyed Christiana suspiciously. "'Tis not one of the pups from the stables you were telling me about this morning?" The girl nodded, a fresh trickle of tears running down her face.

"Fetch me a cloth and quick about it," Martha ordered, taking the dog from Christiana. The girl did as she was bid, feeling a little calmer now that Martha had matters in hand. The old herbalist wrapped the linen cloth around the cold body and began to rub the chest vigorously. Christiana watched in bewilderment as Martha took the pup's long grey muzzle in her steady hands and forcing open the mouth she began to blow her own breath down deep inside the animal. Again and again she blew and rubbed, blew and rubbed. Still the pup lay limp in her hands. "'Tis no use," she sighed. "'Tis gone."

"Keep trying, Martha," Christiana pleaded. "It was not long in the water barrel. *Please* try again."

Martha shook her head but began again her silent ritual as the child looked on. They both stood by and watched incredulously as the pup suddenly began to cough and splutter and then draw a deep breath of its own. For a moment neither of them spoke, staring in amazement at the gasping animal, and then they both laughed out loud.

"Now, fetch a dry wool blanket and move the pan off the brazier. This little fellow needs to get warm," Martha said.

As the pup lay wrapped in a blanket atop the grill on the brazier warmed by the embers beneath Martha poured herself and Christiana a goblet of spiced wine.

"You had best tell me how you came to have this *dead* pup, child."

Christiana told Martha her sad story while sitting shivering on a stool, her goblet held tightly in her hand. When she had finished Martha nodded her head slowly.

"Now you had best change your dress before you catch a chill, and wrap yourself up in a blanket," she said.

While the girl rummaged through some old garments in Martha's bed chamber the old woman checked on the pup, now sleeping but whimpering pitifully. "This pup needs its mother. 'Tis hungry; you will have to return it and hope the bitch does not reject it." Martha noticed the look of fear spread suddenly across the girl's face and added, "You will have to guard the stable and remove the pup when Master Perkins comes in to check his dogs. If he finds you've duped him there will be trouble. It won't be long afore the pups are weaned and they'll be taken to the kennel with the others. God alone knows what you will do with this one then. You cannot easily hide a full-grown wolfhound dog under a table."

Christiana was determined to do what was necessary and enlisted the help of William, and as he stood guard she returned the pup to its mother. Placing it back in between its brother and sister and drawing its soft muzzle to the teat she left it. She had managed to procure more scraps of meat and as the pups suckled she sat up at Lass's head and fed her the morsels.

"We cannot even tell Father," Christiana whispered to William as he stood on the stone trough peering up at them.

"Where will you hide it?" he asked.

Christiana frowned at her brother. "Anywhere we can for now. And later Martha can keep it."

William laughed. "Look at the size of Lass. That pup's a dog – he will be even bigger than his mother. Will Martha want a donkey in her cottage?"

"You just promise not to tell anyone, William," Christiana said, glaring defiantly at her brother.

"All right, I promise." He sighed and walked away, leaving the girl to her hare-brained schemes.

William kept his promise not to tell anyone about the miraculously resurrected pup but inevitably Alfred discovered their secret. The blacksmith found himself a reluctant participant in the conspiracy to conceal the pup from the Keeper of the Dogs and whenever he or the steward happened to come anywhere near the stable yard there would be a subtle shuffling of feet or uncommonly loud voices to warn one or the other that trouble was afoot.

The pups grew fatter and more boisterous over the weeks and their soft fur-like coats were slowly turning into the coarse hair of their mother. Ulrick, as they had named the third pup, although he could not have been less wolf-like, thrived with care, but the twist of his two front paws had become more noticeable as he took his first lumbering steps, an obvious hindrance to any dog expected to take down a full-grown stag.

Middleham Castle
Yorkshire
Late 1461

The weather was rapidly becoming colder. The sky had turned from pewter to iron grey and once again snow had started to fall in the dales. Inside the stable behind the smithy Christiana sat with legs outstretched on top of the mound of straw, her back leaning against the outer stone wall. A little horn lantern hung from a hook next to her, the light from its candle throwing the stall into quivering shadow.

Beside her the shaggy form of Ulrick slept contentedly, Christiana's face bowed over his grey bearded head resting on her lap. Lass and the other two pups were scuffling playfully in the straw beside them.

Outside, a wailing wind blew a flurry of snowflakes across the unglazed aperture above her head and she snuggled deeper into her woollen cloak. She would have to return to the smithy soon; the early nightfall was almost upon them and Alfred would be expecting her home before then.

She lifted her head and was at once alarmed to see a figure standing just near to the entrance to the stall, staring up at her. The moaning wind had masked his footsteps, silent as a cat, and she had no concept of how long he had been standing there. Her startled cry had awoken the hound, who sat up on his hind legs yelping noisily.

The figure stepped forward and Christiana's fear increased for the boy was none other than he who had ridden up to the castle with the King of England at harvest time; the same boy she was certain had departed with the king and wondered by what sorcery he appeared before her. Surely now that her secret was discovered they would all be punished for their disobedience. She drew her knees up and moved closer to the pup, who foolishly began to lick her face, oblivious of its fate.

Christiana stared down at the boy. Shoulder-length golden hair framed a small round face with a soft chiselled jaw and a long straight nose. He took a few steps closer into the light cast by the lantern and she could see that his cloak was of fine lambswool lined with fur. His calves and feet, visible beneath the cloak, were sheathed in a good pair of sturdy outdoor boots.

"I am sorry I startled you," he said, in a voice that resonated with a strange twang.

Christiana placed a hand protectively on the back of Ulrick's neck and asked, "Did you come here to see the pups?"

The boy glanced up at the lively hound visible on top of the straw as though seeing it for the first time and shook his head. "No, I came in here to get away from George," he replied curtly.

"George?"

"My brother, my older brother." The boy's face darkened.

Just then Ulrick's affectionate advances became over ardent and with his large paws on Christiana's shoulders he pushed her off balance and she tumbled from the stack of straw, landing with a thud at the boy's feet. For a moment she stared up at him in expectant silence before the corners of his mouth curled in amusement.

"Are you hurt?" he laughed, extending a hand to pull her to her feet. Her cheeks were a little flushed but she was not overly hurt and had the good grace to laugh at her own misfortune as she allowed the boy to help her.

Once on her feet the girl found herself staring as though bewitched into a pair of eyes so dark in the candlelight that their colour was lost. She perceived the eyes to be sad or hurt or angered by something or someone and began to sense instinctively that he posed little or no threat to her, lost it would seem in his own thoughts.

The boy stood on tiptoe upon the trough and reached up to pat Ulrick's shaggy head. He peered over to where Lass and her other two pups lay in the straw.

"I heard Conyers say there were two pups and yet here are three," the boy stated, bemused. At once the mirth fell from

51

Christiana's lips and her guard, that had begun to crumble, was back up in an instant. The boy turned his face towards her, waiting for an explanation. She gave none.

"Who are you?" he demanded.

For a moment Christiana considered not giving the boy an answer but then she remembered that he had some connection, possibly a very good connection, with the king and it would be most unwise to ignore him.

"I am Christiana. My father is the blacksmith here." She spoke clearly, holding the gaze of the boy's eyes that stared darkly back at her.

"Gloucester," he announced simply, and the girl was not sure whether he had spoken his own name or not. "My brother and I have recently arrived with my guardian, the Earl of Warwick."

Christiana was only vaguely aware that the earl had returned to his northern residence as her attention had been consumed of late by the demands of the pup.

"So, how comes it that there are three and not two pups?" the boy persisted.

Bracing herself against retribution and defeat, Christiana related Ulrick's sorry tale to the boy who had discovered her secret, adding one final plea. "He can walk well enough and he is a good dog. Please do not tell Conyers. My father will be in trouble." The big steward had a frightful temper and she did not want to be the cause of them being thrown out of the castle like the unfortunate Jankin.

Gloucester was staring at her with those deep dark eyes. After a while he seemed to have come to a decision and said, "I will not let on to Conyers that a runt has been saved. I do not think the dog deserves the penalty of death just for having deformed feet. I have a mind to keep him for myself," he added, ruffling the dog's soft beard.

Christiana sighed with relief that Ulrick was in no immediate danger but then froze at the sound of running feet coming down the length of the stable towards them. It was, however, a more familiar head that poked around the wall, breathing hard and with cheeks of scarlet.

"Richard, there you are," Francis panted, steadying the lantern swinging precariously in his hand. "The countess is most displeased with you. You are to return at once and make peas with George."

Gloucester and the girl exchanged fleeting glances and then burst into laughter at the small boy's misuse of his word. Francis, however, stood before them quite indignant, his little face glowing even redder.

Gloucester ruffled the child's dark uncovered head, saying, "You had best run along back to the countess, and stop following me everywhere like a sheep." Then he thought better of it and added, "No, mayhap you would do better to wait for me, it is dark outside."

Taking hold of the boy's hand he was turning towards the stable door when Christiana called out, "You said your name was Gloucester. Why did he call you Richard?"

It was Christiana's turn to blush with embarrassment as both boys laughed at her. The older inclined his head to her and announced, "I am Richard, Duke of Gloucester."

Francis called over his shoulder as he was being led away, "*And* he's the king's brother."

Christiana could hear Martha's angry tirade before she opened the door to the cottage. For a while she stood outside in the cold and foggy morning air, too afraid even to enter. The object of Martha's frustration seemed to be Ulrick, yet again, and Christiana could well imagine the scene behind the closed door. The dog was barking, Martha was shouting and amidst the confusion there came the unmistakable sound of breaking pottery.

Cautiously, Christiana opened the door and peered into the herbarium. She had to stifle a giggle for the scene before her might well have been any from a play performed in the market place on a feast day. Martha was bending down, her large round posterior elevated, picking up shards of broken pot. Ulrick, imagining it to be a game, was barking and wagging his thick hairy tail, sweeping several other pots of precious remedies onto the floor.

As the girl stepped into the room Martha straightened up, her face red and shiny with sweat.

"Oh, Christiana," she panted. "This dog will have to go. It needs a proper master, some discipline. It will fair ruin me at the rate it knocks things over. Get out of it, cur!" she yelled, giving Ulrick a sharp kick with her boot. The dog was not perturbed, however, and barked all the louder, greeting Christiana with a bounding leap that almost floored her.

After a while the pup flopped exhausted to the floor and Martha began to compose herself. "I have been called up to the castle urgently. You stay here and clear up this mess. Make a note of the broken pots. I will return as soon as I can." Martha took her woollen cloak from a hook on the back of the door, pushed the wisps of stray hair under her coif and bustled outside into the mist.

For several moments after the herbalist's departure Christiana

54

stood and stared woefully at the bits of broken jars scattered across the flagstones. What could they possibly do with Ulrick? She glanced at him; big, grey and hairy, his deformed paws twitching as he dreamt, unaware of the trouble he was causing.

Her eyes returned to the broken jars. She was a child of nearly nine years but she lived in a world where children grew up fast. She was mature enough to understand that it was neither wise nor practical to keep a hunting dog in the herbarium, let alone the impossible task of keeping its existence a secret, feeling sure that Martha would even now be arranging for its disposal. But it was her dog and she was going to keep it.

By the time Martha returned, a little under the hour, the girl had picked up all the pieces of pot, arranged them on a woven reed mat on a bench and identified three separate jars; calendula ointment, oil of St John's wort and comfrey root tincture, all painstakingly grown, dried and prepared.

Martha sat her bulk down heavily on a stool and rubbed her forehead. Timidly, the girl approached. "I am sorry, Martha. There were three jars that Ulrick broke. I have cleaned the mess and—"

"Never mind that just now, child," Martha interrupted. "We need to brew a coltsfoot infusion and chamomile. You fetch the herbs and muslin and I will set the pan to boil."

Martha did not utter one word as she made her infusions but Christiana could see by her furrowed brow that she was thinking deeply about something. Maybe she was plotting a way to rid her cottage of an unwelcome wolfhound.

Just as they were about to leave the warmth of the cottage, wrapped in their hooded cloaks, Martha said, "Bring a flagon of vinegar and two long strips of clean linen."

Christiana stepped carefully over the snoring dog and bent down under the bench where Martha kept a wicker basket full of clean pieces of linen. As she stood with the pieces of linen in her hand Ulrick opened a big brown eye and rolled over with paws in the air exposing his chubby underside. Christiana was about to stop and tickle the pup's belly when Martha's booming voice halted her. "Vinegar, if you please. We do not have all day."

The fog was still swirling damply in the bailey as they walked through the garden and up across the empty drill field towards the castle.

"What will you do with Ulrick?" the girl asked in a small voice, almost lost in the fog. For a while Martha gave no reply, concentrating it seemed upon keeping her infusions steady and hot within their leather costrels wrapped in cloth.

"Well I was a fool to agree to keep the dog in the first place. How we can feed it I do not know. It cannot live off scraps forever." She sighed deeply. "But I have more pressing things to think about just now."

Countess Anne was waiting for Martha in the great hall, her pale face stricken with a worried frown. "Do you have a remedy?" she asked anxiously.

"I do indeed, my lady," Martha replied. "Is the child abed as I advised?" The countess nodded her head and led the way through the heavy curtain into the privy chamber beyond.

"I have had him put in here." The lady led them into a second, much smaller chamber, gloomy with a faint smell of sickness. A fire burned in the hearth and despite the presence of two round-topped windows little daylight had penetrated the winter gloom. A chest near the bed held candlesticks bearing five flickering candles. As they entered the chamber Christiana had noticed the small solitary figure sitting on a coffer in the shadows against the wall, idly pushing counters around a board with one finger.

The countess stood a little distant from the large oaken bed as though afraid of the sickness that lay within. The herbalist waddled boldly over to the bed followed a little timidly by Christiana. In the dim candlelight she could see that their patient was the dark-eyed boy calling himself Gloucester, who had come to the stables just before Advent.

"Richard!" she cried, moving closer and almost sitting on the great bed. Immediately she realised that her behaviour was not acceptable for the look given to her by the countess could have frozen a waterfall.

"It is Duke Richard to you, girl, and you will do well to

remember your place and not overstep it. Martha, see to it that she is disciplined," she retorted.

The herbalist inclined her head and made a show of shooing the girl to one side as she felt the boy's moist, clammy brow. As they stood by the child was seized by a spasm of coughing which shook his slight frame painfully. The countess, pulling out a pewter filigree pomme d'amber from her belt purse, held it to her nose and noticeably took a few steps further away from the bed.

"He coughs like this throughout the night. He keeps nothing down and I fear he will waste away," she whimpered.

Martha unwrapped her coltsfoot infusion and took a pewter spoon from a pouch at her waist. "I will do all I can for the young duke, my lady. Do not over worry," she said calmly and began to spoon the warm liquid into the boy's mouth.

"Should I send word to the king? His Grace is most fond of his brother. Mayhap I should return him to the care of his mother. He has always been a most sickly child. I should be most distressed if..."

"Now, now, my lady," Martha clucked. "You can nowise send this child on a journey anywhere in this weather. Let us see how he fairs with coltsfoot and some of my simples."

Countess Anne dabbed at her brow with her napkin and edged nearer to the door of the chamber. "I will go to the chapel and pray for his recovery. My servants are at hand should you require anything."

As soon as the countess had departed the silent figure keeping watch from the shadows crept forward.

"Why, 'tis little Lord Lovell. I did not see you there; you gave me a fright," Martha scolded gently.

"I beg pardon, mistress, but I... will Richard be well soon?"

Before the herbalist could give an answer Richard began another spate of coughing and Francis watched in distress as he finished by coughing up the coltsfoot infusion, a warm brown stain trickling down his shirt.

"Dear, dear, that will not do at all," Martha tut-tutted.

"He is going to die, is he not?" Francis sniffed tearfully.

"Nonsense, child. He will do no such thing, not if you and I can help it." Martha bent her head down level with the boy and holding out the leather costrel said quietly, "Can you give your friend just two spoonfuls of this coltsfoot every few hours and a little chamomile to drink? Not too much mind, he must keep it down for it to do some good. Can you manage that?" The small boy nodded his head vigorously.

"Now run along and find a servant to change the duke's shirt. And you, come over here," Martha addressed Christiana as Francis left to do her bidding. There was a large shallow bowl and a jug of water on a table near the window and Martha instructed the girl to soak the strips of cloth they had brought in a mixture of vinegar and water heated in the flames of the fire.

A little later when Richard had on a clean shirt Martha wrapped the boy's thighs in vinegar- moistened cloths. "That should sweat the fever out of him," she announced, tucking him warmly up in the thick coverlet. It was not long after that the duke fell asleep.

Martha and the two other children sat on the bed watching the sleeping boy, his hair falling across his face, which had a strange yellow pallor in the candlelight.

"I will take a penny to Saint Mary and Saint Alkelda's on the morrow and ask the priest to light a candle and pray for Richard," Christiana whispered.

Francis smiled at the girl. "He would like your dog better than a prayer. He was going to ask Lady Anne if he could have one of the pups but George has taken both of them."

Christiana looked at the young lord in alarm, her eyes flitting to the door and back.

"Ulrick is a secret. He should have been drowned," she hissed.

"I know what happened," Francis interrupted. "Richard told me."

"But he is my dog," Christiana retorted harshly.

"You are a servant. You cannot have a dog," Francis said indignantly.

"Now, now, you two. You will wake the duke with your bickering." Martha gestured for them to leave the bedside.

"Christiana, my Lord Lovell is correct in this matter. I do not say that it was wrong to save its life but if the duke wants the dog then it will be his."

The girl was still protesting loudly as the two of them walked back to the cottage, the fog of earlier having dispersed, leaving the bailey bathed in pale winter sunshine.

Martha ignored the girl until they had reached the cottage and the door was firmly shut behind them. "Now listen well, child," Martha began brusquely. "If you want to remain here at the castle and not make trouble for your father you will need to know your place. You are a servant, here only to do the bidding of the earl and his family. You own nothing, not even the dress you are wearing, except by Warwick's grace. We cannot keep that dog."

She pointed a finger at the hound curled up in the middle of the floor, its tail wagging tentatively. "Now, stop snivelling and put the pan on the brazier. There is work to be done."

The following morning Christiana walked despondently beside Martha carrying one of the cloth wrapped costrels. Rain was falling steadily, adding a wet misery to the girl's already melancholic mood. The cold mud beneath her feet had begun to seep into her sodden boots by the time they had reached the stone staircase leading to the great hall.

A group of children could be seen sitting around the smouldering fire as Martha and Christiana walked across the tiled floor. The ladies Isabel and Anne, playing with wooden puppet dolls, had their golden heads together in secretive whisperings. Two boys, sitting cross-legged at the far side of the fire, were playing a game of Nine Men's Morris.

Francis looked up as the herbalist approached and made to rise, intent upon following her, but his companion pulled him down with a sharp tug on his tunic sleeve.

"And where might you be going, Lovell?" he demanded.

"To see Richard," Francis replied with shaking voice.

"You have not finished the game yet," the older boy retorted unkindly.

"But you are cheating, George," Francis replied.

"Sit down, Lovell. I have not finished playing yet," George persisted.

Francis, his face glowing with anger and fear, would have obeyed his elder had it not been for the intervention of the herbalist.

"Now then, Duke George, Lord Lovell has agreed to help with your brother's physic and so he will need to come with me." Martha was careful to show all due respect for the duke without losing her own authority over the petulant child.

Reluctantly George let go of Francis's sleeve, muttering inaudible oaths under his breath, and moved across the floor to taunt the girls at play. Christiana stared at his long brown locks, which gave him little likeness to his brother, the king. He looked to be much older than the other children, older even than Isabel, but to Christiana's mind, of royal blood or not, he was a mischievous sort.

The countess was sitting on a heavy oak chair in the chamber with two of her ladies seated either side of her, each embroidering a section of altar cloth.

"Please go through, Martha," she said wearily. "There has been no change in him."

The herbalist pulled aside the tapestry drapes and entered the inner chamber, the two children scurrying behind her. A little light had penetrated the glazed casements although the rain continued to pound down upon them. The drapes had been parted around the bed and Christiana could see the small figure propped up on scarlet bolsters. His eyes were closed in sleep but his face was white as a tallow candle. Martha took the leather costrel from the girl and placed it on the table beside the bed.

"I have to see the countess. You stay here and if the duke awakens you are to give him this." She indicated the costrel containing the coltsfoot infusion. "Pay heed to what I told you yesterday, young lord," she added, passing a pewter spoon to Francis. "We do not want him to cough it up!"

Francis and Christiana sat in silence on the edge of the large bed. Richard's hand was lying out of the coverlet; it looked so cold and so small that Christiana had an urge to hold it. She glanced across at Francis who was staring sadly at his friend. Christiana took the duke's hand in her own warm fingers and held it tight. Presently Richard opened his eyes and looked directly at her. She could see, by the light of day, that his eyes were not so dark; rather a deep blue like the cornflower.

He smiled weakly as he recognised her and asked, "Have you brought the dog?"

Christiana pulled her hand away as she was reminded of Ulrick's impending fate. Francis had got up from the bed and was fumbling with the stopper on the neck of the costrel with his small hands. Christiana walked over to the table to assist him. Together they managed to pour out a spoonful, although much of the liquid splattered onto the floor, and they held it to the duke's lips for him to drink. After a while, when he did not cough, they deemed it fit to administer a second dose.

At that moment Martha returned, waddling over to the bed to where Richard had rested his head back on the pillows and closed his eyes.

"We have given him two spoonfuls of coltsfoot," Christiana reported. "He is very ill isn't he, Martha?" she added solemnly.

Martha sighed. "Yes, child, I fear that he is and we must all do what we can to help him."

"I would like him to have Ulrick," Christiana said decisively. "The duke will be good to him, I know."

Martha looked down at the girl and smiled. "I have spoken to Lady Anne about the dog. She has agreed that the duke can keep it and undergo its training. It will not be allowed on the bed, however, my little Lord Francis." She glared at Francis, who nodded his agreement.

It took several days of coltsfoot and chamomile infusions and vinegar-soaked wraps to draw the fever before the duke finally recovered from his illness. Ulrick proved to be a great aid to his recovery, lifting the boy's spirits and providing the necessary incentive for him to be up and about.

By springtime the duke and his dog were a familiar sight

around the bailey, running and playing in the sunshine. Only Perkins, the Keeper of the Dogs, could be seen with a scowl on his face whenever the huge hound went bounding by.

Spring also saw the return of Francis Lovell to his family home in Oxfordshire upon his mother's recovery from her long illness. Almighty God, it seemed, had been merciful that winter.

"So, young man, you are another George eh?" Martha, in her usual forthright manner addressed the child dangling on his nurse's lap as she attended the wound to his knee. Having wiped away the blood and picked out the pieces of gravel the herbalist applied her agrimony salve and turned to her assistant for the dressing. Christiana, however, was not giving her attention to the matter in hand and Martha had to snatch the bowl, wherein the linen strips were soaking in celery juice, from her grasp.

The young girl, for her part in this little scenario, was gawping at the lady, the boy's mother, standing beside the bench in the herbarium. The folds of the deep blue velvet of her dress cascading gracefully to the floor and spreading like a pool behind her had drawn the young girl's eyes. The shade of blue was the very same as the body feathers of the magnificent bird she has seen strutting around the bailey a few days ago. Wat had told her that it was a peacock destined for the earl's table. If ever she could possess a gown of such splendour it would be of the very same colour.

"Christiana!" The girl felt the sharp prod in the rib from the impatient herbalist and at once felt her face redden. The lady glanced at the servant girl with a hint of humour in her eye and at once Christiana lowered her gaze.

Moments later the lady, the nurse and the child, with a chunk of bread, bearing a dollop of melrosotte, in his little fist, walked away along the path back into the garden and the hot sunshine.

"That, child, was Lady Eleanor Neville, sister to our earl and wed to Thomas, Lord Stanley and their little son." Martha announced in reply to Christiana's question. "And it is not proper to stare at one such as her," she added with a grin.

Later that afternoon Christiana was sent out into the garden to pick a basketful of herbs to Martha's specification; the correct identity of each plant to be a test of the girl's skill. The day was still balmy and hot and a sweet, aromatic scent filled the garden. Before making her way to where the herbs grew in abundance Christiana ambled around the flower beds with her empty basket swinging on her arm. There were many people in the garden; several unknown to the girl and their laughter and joyful chitter chatter irked her somewhat for she had come to think of the gardens as her domain.

There was Isabel and George close to Lady Anne Beauchamp. The peacock lady was also there talking to another finely dressed noblewoman whose spreading black gown was at that moment being trampled on by the small feet of a lively child of around two years; a little younger than the one who had received attention from Martha earlier that day.

"Katherine, you must try to control George for he is set to ruining my gown," the woman chided as the nurse ran in circles around the child's mother in an attempt to catch him. The ensuing giggles from the women and children brought a curt word or two and a stern look from the Earl of Warwick who was conversing with two well-dressed men a little way off near the dovecote.

"Come, Isabel, let us remove ourselves from the company of men and take the children to the white rose garden." The Countess of Warwick took the arm of the woman whose gown was now free of footmarks and led her away followed by all but the men.

Could no-one think of a title other than George for naming a son? Christiana pondered as she watched them disappear around a box hedge; she was now aware of three given this name.

Resigned to her errand and rolling the sleeves of her kirtle the girl walked purposefully towards the herbs. With snips in hand she began to cut her bunches; lavender – easy; rosemary – easy; marjoram, thyme and lemon balm. She moved in deep concentration around the different beds and was not aware of the huge hairy hound until it was upon her.

"Ulrick!" she exclaimed just managing to steady her basket in time. Looking up she saw the dog's master coming towards her; he was not alone. Richard's cousin, Lady Anne Neville came trotting breathlessly behind, her golden curls bobbing on her shoulders.

"Richard, you walk too fast," the child called as she reached the place where her cousin had stopped, at the herbs and the servant girl.

"Why is it then that you are following me everywhere?" asked the young duke, although his voice was good-humoured.

"He remembers you," Richard smiled as Christiana made bold but futile attempts to dispel the dog's advances.

"Richard, you must get him off the herbs before Martha sees what he is doing." The girls watched helplessly as Ulrick's huge paws churned the ground and uprooted the delicate plants.

The duke called his dog in the sternest voice a ten-year-old boy could raise until finally the hound jumped the two or so feet onto the gravel path towards its master, but in so doing unbalanced the little girl beside the duke and sent her sprawling onto the path. At once tears welled up in Anne's eyes and spilled down her rosy cheeks. Christiana noticed the slit in the girl's sleeve and a trickle of blood beginning to soak into the pale-coloured linen.

Richard was at once profusely apologetic as he helped Anne to her feet.

"Take the Lady Anne to Martha, Richard," Christiana advised and watched as the duke put his arm protectively around his cousin's slender shoulder and guided her gently towards the cottage.

Christiana was left to recover what she could of the damaged herbs, replanting the fragile roots into holes she scooped out with her fingers. That task finished she turned her attention back to gathering herbs. There was one left to complete her collection: coriander. There it was, its waxy yellow flowers wafting in the breeze. Christiana plunged her bare arms into the blue-green foliage and broke off the tall stems until she had sufficient and began her walk back to the cottage. While still a short distance she could see Richard and the Lady Anne leave and she hastened her steps.

Remembering her obligatory reverence just in time, Christiana was pleased to see how the boy looked her way and smiled. Lady

Anne looked a little downcast and allowed herself to be led silently away by her cousin as she nursed her sore elbow.

Christiana placed her over-brimming basket on the bench and sat down heavily on a stool. Martha waddled over to the bench and began prodding the herbs with a forefinger.

"Was Anne hurt badly?" Christiana asked.

"Nay, 'twas but a little wound, nothing a goodly rub of calendula will not mend." The herbalist took a flagon of her elderflower ale and two cups from a shelf and as she poured both of them a goodly measure remarked, "Cook has asked for chicory for a syllabub so we can take a walk to the castle when you have taken your drink, child."

Christiana made no reply but sat and rubbed her forearm.

"Syllabubs are a favourite of Thomas, Lord Stanley, so I am told," continued the herbalist. "And while he is a guest of the Earl of Warwick we must do all we can to see that his stay here is comfortable.

"What is wrong with your arm, child?" Martha put down her cup and taking hold of the girl's hand pulled her arm towards her. Christiana flinched as the herbalist peered closely at the angry red rash that had begun to spread along the girl's arm.

"What is it you have been picking?" Martha returned to the basket and upturned the contents onto the bench.

"As you asked: lavender, marjoram, lemon balm, rosemary, coriander, thyme."

"There is no coriander in here!" Martha exclaimed as the girl came over to stand beside her.

"'Tis that with the yellow flowers, surely," Christiana remarked, pointing.

"Nay, fuddle-brained child. Coriander has white flowers. This is rue and you have picked it in hot sunlight and it has burned your skin. Am I to spend all this day tending to the misfortunes of children!"

Christiana began to cry as her arm was becoming very hot and painful and the harshness of Martha's voice was beginning to make her fearful.

"Come, let us put the sap of aloes on this and it will soon cool and heal." Martha turned and moved her pots until she had found a tightly sealed clay vessel. As she gently rubbed the salve into the girl's blistered skin her voice softened. "You have done well this day, child. You are learning speedily the different herbs and I'll wager you will not make this mistake again." She smiled at her protégé and Christiana returned the smile through her tears.

In the cool of the late afternoon the herbalist and her young assistant took a stroll up to the kitchens to deliver the bunch of chicory and other culinary herbs. Christiana was surprised to see the earl and his two male companions still in the garden near to the dovecote as they passed by. Martha's heavy-booted footsteps scraping the gravel alerted the attention of the earl and he turned from his conversation. The herbalist gave a polite nod of her head towards them as she walked past. The girl, however, slowed her steps to an almost standstill and stared at the men; one in particular. He was taller than the other two and slender built. He was immaculately attired in black hose and velvet tunic decorated with large scrolled patterns of gold thread. His face was long and oval shaped with a pointed brown beard. With a pair of shrewd eyes he held the intense gaze of the child until Martha gently nudged her arm, causing her to look to the ground as was proper.

"How often must I tell you not to stare at your betters? This bawdy manner will get you into much trouble one of these days, child." Martha continued to berate the girl as they stomped across the bridge into the inner bailey.

"Have you any notion of who that was? Have you?"

Christiana shook her head, intrigued.

"'Twas Thomas, Lord Stanley, and he's nobody's fool."

"Who was the other man then?" the girl asked. "Was *he* the earl's fool?"

Martha began to laugh, a rumble that started in her belly and bubbled up until it shook and trembled her basket of herbs. "Nay, child, that was John Neville and that one lives in his brother's shadow."

The girl followed the old woman into the kitchens, wondering greatly why it was that she found it necessary to speak in such riddles.

Middleham Castle
Yorkshire
Autumn 1464

During the summer of 1464 Richard Neville moved his family south to spend some time at their castle in Warwick. From here the intrepid earl was in easy reach of London and the court of the young king where he could make himself available to negotiate and manipulate on the young monarch's behalf. George, Duke of Clarence, second brother to the king and now a young man of fifteen, had spent much of his formative years at the royal residence at Greenwich where he had completed his prescribed education and now spent his time in company with the Earl of Warwick.

Duke Richard, a boy of almost twelve years and youngest brother to the king, was left behind at Middleham Castle to complete his training. Most of his hours were spent in learning his lessons: script, mathematics, Latin, music, astronomy and Christian doctrine as befitting one of noble birth. His formal education as page also included social graces, riding, falconry, hunting and the art of warfare. With a small household of retainers the young boy's every need was met except one.

Despite such a rigorous regime there were times when the boy found himself in need of companionship of his own age, now that his cousins were away. It was almost inevitable therefore that as his rheumy-eyed tutor snored in front of the fire on chilly afternoons, the duke sought to amuse himself.

Reticent and taciturn by nature, unlike his garrulous, brash sibling George, the Duke of Gloucester had found perhaps an unfitting but natural friendship with the blacksmith's daughter, younger than him by only one year. The dog, Ulrick, had been a catalyst in the relationship, for it was to be expected that while she had willingly relinquished her pup to the sick boy, the girl would want to see as much of it as possible. As time went on, however, Christiana found that she was seeking the duke for his own company and the dog became merely an excuse.

One dismal autumn afternoon not long after the duke's twelfth birthday he and Christiana were sitting together in the great hall. The boy had been in a nostalgic mood for much of the afternoon as he spoke to her of his family. He talked with great affection of his mother, Cecily Neville, and his sisters Anne, Elizabeth and Margaret, and with much sadness of his father and brother Edmund, both killed in battle. He missed his eldest brother, Edward, the most; his admiration of the king was evident in his words of devotion and praise. The young girl sitting beside him tried to imagine the lives of this great Plantagenet family.

They had their backs against the wooden partition that straddled the south end of the room and Richard was turning the pages of his book, *Vegetius*, paying little attention to the bold declarations of military advice for princely commanders contained therein. The rain, falling heavily outside, was drumming a sombre repetition on the glazed casements overhead. Ulrick lay sprawled across their outstretched legs snoring and twitching in contented slumber.

Christiana glanced sideways at the duke; his blue eyes were dark, shielding impenetrable thoughts. She noticed too how his hair, still brushing his shoulders, was losing its golden hue of childhood. Her eyes traced the outline of the intricately embroidered scrollwork on his pale blue tunic. Her gaze followed the length of his slender legs encased in dark blue hose ending at the trim pointed toes of his soft leather boots. Her eyes then fell upon her own tattered stockings and shabby boots. The plain brown woollen dress that she wore was embellished only with remnants of straw and dried herbs.

Deep within her she had a distinct awareness of something intangible that would always separate them. Her childhood innocence could not explain it fully; she knew only that it existed. The warm feeling she had when she was close to him as now was but a moment stolen from time, not hers by right.

Richard stopped thumbing the pages of his book and let it fall to the floor beside him with a sigh. He turned his face towards hers and smiled mischievously, his mood changing in an instant.

"It is the Feast day of Saint Alkelda on the fifth day of November," he said with a merry sparkle in his eyes. "I should like to go – with you."

Immediately Christiana's desire for adventure was aroused. The prospect of walking clandestine through a crowded fair with a prince was too exciting a challenge to let pass.

"Yes, let us go," she whispered with the air of a conspirator, and heads together in excited whispers they hatched a plan to slip from the castle and join the villagers and travellers on their day of merriment.

The marketplace was crammed to overflowing with merchants, traders, dancers, jugglers and sideshows. Jesters and wandering minstrels spilled over onto the surrounding fields and byways. The feast day atmosphere had begun in the pale grey light of early morning and would continue until the last streaks of daylight had been engulfed by dusk.

Two children, cloaked and hooded with hands tightly clasped, weaved their way through the throng. There followed at a little distance behind these two a shaggy grey dog, large and bony with nose to the ground and tail like a brush held high. Any caring to look would notice the distinct lumbering gait of the dog as it ambled along.

The footways had turned to slime in the dampness of autumn and the thick mud oozed over their boots. In the midst of the marketplace blood from the slaughtered pigs ran red and the air was thick with the smell of roasting hog flesh. Threading their way through the mud, oblivious to the merriment, were the poor, the sick and the disfigured. Dirty and ragged with faces festering with sores, they held out their begging bowls with pathetic, hopeful eyes. Equally oblivious, the crowd passed them by. On all sides colourful booths were erected with traders offering their goods with voluble tenacity; silverware, clay pots, leather costrels, buckles, knives, bone combs, shoes and bolts of dyed cloth. Merchants, on their travels from far-flung corners of the world, brought exotic spices and richly woven silks for those who could afford such luxuries.

A thin gangly juggler in a brightly chequered costume tossed and balanced balls, the jingling bells on his pointed hat an echo of the merriment in his blue eyes. The boy tossed a coin into the upturned basket at his feet and grinned impishly to his companion as they moved on.

At a small booth a toothless old woman with a fine display of facial hair stared long at the young duke and his companion; so intent was her gaze that both began to edge nervously away. She had an assortment of hand-crafted wooden dolls, each brightly garbed, and these fripperies held the girl's attention. Pulling down the hood of his cloak to further obscure his face, Richard produced the penny necessary to secure a purchase from his coin purse and hurried away. Christiana was thrilled with her gift and tucked it away inside the bag on her belt.

Away from the noise and bustle of the traders, on the edge of the marketplace, a troupe of musicians was plucking the strings of the psaltery and harp and breathing sylvan tunes on pipe and flute. The girl stood gazing at their harlequin and chessboard attire, mesmerised by the hypnotic melodies. A young man, looking to be of no more than nineteen or twenty years with dove grey eyes and hair the colour of autumn leaves, sang of faraway lands, dragons, princes and fair maidens. Reluctantly she moved on as she felt a gentle tug on her hand.

Some distance from the smallholdings and cottages straddling the edge of the village there was a patch of common grazing where a few skinny goats nibbled at the sparse grass and a group of boys kicked a stuffed pig bladder one to another. A section of the ground here had been fenced off with rough wooden palings into a horseshoe shape and dug into a shallow pit. Tightly packed around this small arena was an assortment of men and boys, some from the castle garrison, apprentices, servants, villagers and sojourners. The two children moved closer to take a look at the local sport. Two game cocks strutted arrogantly within the enclosure, each trailing his opponent with a beady eye and crimson comb erect. The men around the ring watched their every move as the birds clawed the dirt with scaly yellow talons, metal-capped spurs at the ready.

They were magnificent birds; one white-breasted with a golden mantle down his neck, back and flowing onto his wings, his challenger a black-breasted beauty with a scarlet cape of feathers.

Like a flash of lightning the two came together in a fiery frenzy of scarlet, jet and gold. Amidst squawks and screeches claw struck flesh and tore ferociously, wings flapped furiously and dust flew into the air as a ball of egocentric masculinity cavorted round and round, cheered on by the onlookers who had placed their wagers. For a while it looked as though neither bird was better than the other and the watching gamblers could do nothing but hold their breath and wait.

At first it was nothing more than a quiver of fatigue in the red and black plumed cock but the deep gash inflicted by his opponent was slowly weakening him until finally he succumbed and slumped bleeding to the ground. The victor shook himself ceremoniously to a rapturous applause from those who had backed the champion and a string of oaths from those who had not.

The crowd began to disperse, some pushing forward to claim their winnings, others resignedly walking away empty-handed. A youth of little more than eighteen or nineteen years stepped forward to reclaim his golden game cock and the pouch of silver coins as his reward. As he staggered away, supported on either side by his companions with the victorious bird swinging drunkenly from its wooden crate held in his hand, Christiana felt certain she recognised him. With the strands of greasy dark hair falling limply across his face and the fox-like leer on his lips, it could be none other than the soldier who had returned from Towton full of tales of blood and woe and who she had often glimpsed around the castle garrison.

"The ale's on Ralph!" called out one of his companions before the trio disappeared from view into the throng.

A light drizzle had begun to fall as the young companions with wolfhound on their trail made the return journey to the castle. They passed an old dame in the marketplace selling sugar paste almonds. The boy fumbled under his cloak for his purse and in his haste dropped several coins. With muffled giggles the two friends stooped to retrieve the silver discs from the mud and purchase their confectionery.

By the time the two errant adventurers had made their way hand in hand through the slippery mud clotting on the roadway and across the bailey the light was fading fast. With mouths crammed full of sugared almonds and heads bowed, they were hardly aware of the steadily falling rain that had begun to soak through their cloaks onto their skin and was sending sensible folk scurrying indoors.

They had barely reached the stable block when the sound of hooves, muffled by the mud, could be heard fast approaching from the gatehouse. Glancing behind his shoulder, Duke Richard's quick eye discerned the broad thickset figure of his guardian at the fore of the riders, and by the way he spurred on his mount he was in a hot temper.

Built on to the end of a long low row of stalls was a small square room housing the harness and saddles, the entrance to which was by way of a door set in the side wall. Fearing discovery and to gain shelter from the now torrential rain, Richard led Christiana through the doorway and into the room beyond where the pungent smell of leather filled the air. Ulrick had followed excitedly and the duke had to speak sternly, albeit in a whisper, to calm the dog.

A small iron grill set into the adjoining wall let in light and sound from the stables beyond. A pale flicker from the stable lanterns diffused the grey of dusk, showing up their faces and the regimented saddles along the walls in ghostly relief. It soon became apparent that the earl's arrival at this hour was not expected for all the grooms and stable hands were either about their evening meal or else not yet returned from the fair. Only the high-pitched apologetic squeak of the young lad left behind to keep watch could be heard in reply to Warwick's cursing. The sound of small feet splattering through the mud betrayed the boy's urgent errand to call his fellow servants to duty.

From their concealed position the two children could hear the men removing the wet bridles and cruppers that clung to their horses' sodden rumps. The sudden thud of a heavy boot making contact with a wooden post startled a horse and they heard its nervous whinny.

The constable made a breathless appearance at that moment and was about to receive the full blast of Warwick's temper, the journey from London doing little to disperse his anger.

"By all the saints, FitzHugh, I still cannot believe that Edward could do such a thing," the earl's voice boomed heatedly. Duke Richard shuffled against the harness in an effort to hear better what it was that his brother the king had done to so enrage Warwick.

"My lord?" the constable asked tentatively.

"The king has been married since May."

The constable, knowing well the reputation of the young king, raised an eyebrow.

"Well, my lord, in truth I am surprised he has not taken a wife before this," he chuckled.

"This is no jest," Warwick bellowed. "Why did he not tell me? Damn him. All those wasted journeys to France, sweet-talking Louis for nothing."

"Richard, the king surely has a right to make his own decision regarding a wife."

"The king is little more than a boy and forgets who it was helped him win the crown. He should heed my council," Warwick fumed.

"What of this wife? Is she known to you?" The constable was intrigued.

"The widow of the Lancastrian, John Grey, killed at St Alban's," Warwick replied tartly. "The woman is a leech and an upstart. She brings with her a whole clan of hangers-on all eager for a handsome settlement and the foolish young king will play straight into her hands."

"'Tis not Elizabeth Woodville, daughter of Jacquetta of Luxembourg?" FitzHugh mused thoughtfully.

"Aye, the same, what of it?" Warwick returned abruptly.

"Then witchcraft and sorcery are behind this marriage," the constable sniggered. "Have you not heard the legend that

Jacquetta's ancestor was married to some water goddess? Surely then, there are magical powers in that family."

"What nonsense you speak, FitzHugh. This is a serious political matter, not the stuff of myth and legend," Warwick retorted. "What was that?"

In his effort to press up against the grill Duke Richard had unbalanced a saddle from its post, sending it thundering to the floor. Ulrick, alerted to danger, began to whimper, and the children froze in terror, waiting with bated breath for their discovery.

A pair of sharp hawk-like eyes in a ruddy face presented themselves at the grill and searched the gloom beyond. "Show yourselves. Who dares to eavesdrop on the Earl of Warwick?"

Christiana could feel herself begin to tremble. She looked tearfully at Richard crouched against the wall trying to silence his dog. They were saved it seemed by the fortuitous arrival of the grooms and stable hands muttering apologies and hastily tending to the horses. Warwick's attention was distracted and Richard used the moment to seize the girl's arm and flee. With the dog on their heels they ran through the rain-drenched twilight until breathless and soaked they reached the darkened shadows of the fletchers' hut.

"I must be away to the keep now. Breathe not a word of this news to anyone," Richard whispered. Christiana nodded in agreement. Just as he was about to take his leave Richard looked into her face and grinned. "It was a good day at the fair, was it not?" With his dark cloak sagging heavily around his shoulders and his dog bounding along like his shadow he was gone like a spectre in the rain.

It was during the spring of 1465, the year of her twelfth birthday, that Christiana was first aware of changes taking place in her body. Her hips took on a rounder shape and her breasts formed small hard lumps that blossomed into fullness as the months passed. Martha showed her how to make larger dresses, which she embroidered with small flowers on the bodice and sleeves. She was also allowed to wash her long black curls in the juice of boiled peach kernels over a wooden tub in the cottage where the older woman would watch the young girl with a knowing smile on her face.

In the absence of a mother Martha had also made certain that the girl knew about the curse soon to befall her that would follow the cycle of the moon and a goodly supply of old linen strips and a basketful of blood moss was stored away in readiness. The herbalist showed the young woman how to make the linen pads stuffed with the sphagnum moss and held in place with woollen loops attached to a cord around her slender hips. Christiana was not unduly worried about such things for it happened to all women and Martha, in her wisdom, had said that it was only by enduring the discomfort of these monthly courses that one day, when she was wed to a suitable man, she could conceive and give birth to a child. Even the Lady Isabel could not escape the curse for many times had they taken horsetail compresses up to the great chamber to ease her stomach cramps.

The longer warm days of spring brought with it many distractions for this child on the cusp of womanhood and none it seemed more appealing just now than the activities of the men on the drill field.

A number of soldiers could always be found training here during the summer months; the castle garrison ever had a need to remain fit and alert. The captain encouraged regular training, including archery, to which any able-bodied male servant was encouraged to attend in their leisure time. It must always be necessary for the earl to muster an army of men-at-arms at any time should the king have need.

It was on this field too of course that Duke Richard received his personal training in the skills of riding and swordsmanship, for one day in the not too distant future he would be expected to command his own men and, should the need arise, lead them into battle. At thirteen years of age the young duke was not as sturdily made as many of his peers and Christiana watched with amusement his clumsy ungainly attempts to thrust and parry with his sword. What he lacked in stature he made up for in determination, however, as hours were spent in the heat of the day developing the necessary skills required of a noble warrior.

It was here too that the blacksmith's young daughter realised the first stirrings of womanly passion in her soul. From her safe distance she watched every move the duke made with a fluttering heart, a dry mouth and a head that swam as though seeped in wine. This she knew was more than friendship, more than the fun and games she sometimes shared with the other children in the bailey, more even than the sisterly love she had for William.

At the end of a long afternoon she would return to the cottage to receive a reprimand from the herbalist, who threatened to find her even more work as a means to avoid the temptation of her immortal soul. Christiana knew that Martha's scolding was only half meant by the twinkle in the old woman's eye – and did she not cosset her as if she were a beloved daughter?

One such hot, windless afternoon the pages and squires were going through their paces on the field, each according to position and ability. The young Duke of Gloucester looked tired; his pale cheeks bore a crimson glow and his hair, the colour of cinnamon bark, hung in sweat-laden strands around his face. His instructor was relentlessly reiterating the correct stance and position necessary to attack or defend. Even the hefty built boy he was up against looked as though he had taken enough for one day.

There was at last a little respite and sustenance was called for. Christiana, sitting on the grass twirling the stems of the withering herbs reposing in the pannier at her side, had failed to notice that she had a companion. For several moments now her brother William had been sitting beside her. She was startled at the sound of his voice.

"You spend too much time out here for a girl," he announced firmly.

"Why?" The question was simple yet uttered with no less authority.

"You should be in the garden with your flowers."

"And you should be in the stable with your horses." Christiana turned her back on her brother and bothered a bunch of chamomile, de-heading them in seconds.

William said nothing for a while and watched as the company of men wiped their brows, gathered their weapons and departed.

Brother and sister remained sitting side by side until the field was emptied of all but these two. When he next spoke William's words were dipped in melancholy, uttered to the wind, perhaps never meant for the ears of the child beside him.

"I could do this. I have a great desire to be a soldier and one day I will."

They walked together across the field and round to the stables. Christiana uttered no word to her brother but slipped her arm through his in the hope that this would somehow endorse their friendship.

The stable yard was alive with activity owing to the arrival of one of some import. The Earl of Warwick was waiting to greet his brother, John, as he galloped up to the stables, a small retinue in his wake.

As he drew closer the earl swept his hat from his head and made a low exaggerated bow to his brother. "Welcome, my Lord Earl of Northumberland, to my humble abode."

John Neville threw back his head and laughed. "You have heard then?" He swung his leg across the high pommel of his saddle and jumped to the ground.

"Of course I have heard!" the earl replied with a grin. "Who better to receive the fortune of the great Henry Percy than a brother of mine? Come, Anne and the girls have not long returned from Warwick; they will be pleased to see you. Is your wife Isabel and young George to visit soon?"

The two brothers were walking away now and William and his sister heard but a little more of the conversation: "My family will profit from the making of this king," Richard Neville announced as they disappeared around the corner of the stable wall.

"There, I do believe all is ready." Martha set her last ceramic bowl on the embroidered cloth covering the high table. The pungent perfume of crushed rosemary, basil, marjoram and yarrow filled the air. Servants were already entering the great hall to light the scented candles and replenish the fire with logs. Musicians up on the gallery at the far end of the room could be heard tuning their harps and lutes. Two rough-haired wolfhounds were awakened from slumber by the antics of a jester turning cartwheels across the tiled floor.

Martha turned to the young girl at her side and remarked, "Methinks there will be a fine feast in here this eve."

Christiana smiled wanly; feasting yes and much gaiety and laughter to celebrate the Feast of Saint Valentine. Warwick had invited several distinguished guests from the northern nobility who were even now preparing themselves in lodgings within the castle.

Rumour had it that Warwick's eldest daughter Isabel, now a young lady in her fifteenth year, had formed a romantic attachment to George, Duke of Clarence, and this evening's celebrations no doubt would encourage that liaison, something the earl would see as beneficial indeed; a daughter wed to a brother of the king.

"We should be getting back now, Christiana," Martha whispered. "There will be celebrations for us back in the bailey."

Guests had begun to enter the hall and mingle before taking their allotted places at the long tables. Amongst the first to arrive were Warwick's daughters, looking most attractive in matching crimson silk gowns. Lady Anne, a mere girl of not yet ten years, stood nervously looking about her, a little unsure of herself but not so her sister. The moment the Duke of Clarence sauntered into view Isabel approached the young duke boldly, but lowered her gaze modestly upon reaching him.

Christiana, who stood transfixed at the sight of the rapidly filling hall, felt a sharp prod in her ribs and Martha's voice hissing in her ear urging them to depart forthwith.

"Where is your basket of herbs?" Martha suddenly asked as they approached the foot of the stairs. A flush of colour rushed to Christiana's cheeks as she realised that the large basket containing the dried herbs used to decorate the table must still be in its place where she had set it down earlier.

"Fuddle-brained child," Martha scolded. "You must go fetch it at once before the earl arrives and the feast begins."

Hoisting up the skirts of her shabby brown dress Christiana fairly flew back up the stairs across the antechamber and back into the great hall. Breathing hard she sidled through the richly clad folk towards the high table. The minstrels had struck up a lively tune, drowning the sound of voices. Nearly all the guests had moved to their positions along the tables set down either side of the hall, awaiting the seemingly imminent arrival of the earl and countess.

Christiana could see the offending basket perched on the end of the high table, quite out of keeping with the other adornments. Someone else had also spied the basket with its bunches of herbs cascading over the sides and at that moment, seeing also Christiana in an agitated state, realised the significance of it all. Snatching up the basket Richard walked over to the girl, a faint smile on his lips. Christiana blushed, thanked the young man and felt she ought to bow to the duke although she had never felt the need to do so before.

She watched as he turned and made his way back to the far end of the room from where, as page, he would be expected to serve the earl and his family at the table on the dais. The Lady Anne had also noticed her cousin's presence and smiled sweetly in his direction as he disappeared from sight once again, her gaze lingering.

Seeing how the little lady regarded Richard with warmth and affection Christiana felt a sudden and quite unexpected pang of jealousy. Quickly she spun around and headed once more for the doorway, but she did not get far for she came heavily into contact with Conyers, the steward. The herb basket, taking the force of the impact, shed its load over the tiled floor. Her predicament caused her to hesitate, torn between paying respect to the steward with a bow and stooping to retrieve the herbs. From the immediate rising up of all the guests and a silencing of tongues it seemed that the earl and countess had entered the hall through the door leading from the great chamber.

"Should you not be at the herbarium, girl?" Conyers whispered angrily. Christiana nodded and glancing behind her saw the figures of the earl and lady take their place on the dais.

"Then be gone at once." With that Conyers brushed past her towards the dais, leaving her to gather up as many of the herbs as she dared before making a hasty retreat; any remaining would blend sufficiently with the rushes on the floor.

"You took your time," Martha remonstrated, stamping her feet on the ground at the foot of the stairs as Christiana appeared at its head. With the absence of daylight came an icy chill in the air and Martha's old bones ached with the waiting.

All the way back to the cottage Christiana's heart was in turmoil imagining the love games that would be played in the great hall after the feasting. What love tokens would pass from one guest to another; symbols of affection or mere folly?

At the cottage Martha lit the candles and together with the warm embers of the brazier the place was comfortable. Christiana slumped onto a chair, taking up the grey cat that had curled itself into a ball there.

"Do not be so downcast, girl," said Martha. "We will do our own games for Saint Valentine." So saying she shuffled over to the great table supporting her wealth of herbs and began turning jars and bottles until she found what she wanted. "Here we have it, hemp seed. Now you fill that bowl there half full of water and place it on the floor."

Christiana took the wide shallow vessel indicated, went outside to the water butt and filled it as instructed.

"We used to play this game when I was a lass. Nowt but a bit of fun is this. Now stand there with your back to the bowl like that. That's it."

Martha gave the girl a handful of hemp seed. "Now then, pass the seed over your left shoulder slowly and let it drop into the water. Stop giggling and repeat the ditty."

Christiana did as she was bid, trying to rebuke the smile that tickled her mouth.

"Hemp seed I sow," said Martha.

"Hemp seed I sow," repeated the girl.

"Hemp seed will grow; let him who loves me come after me and mow." And so Christiana repeated.

"Now turn around and look. What do you see?" Martha enthused. The tiny dark round seeds bobbed around and jostled one another on the water until at last they formed a shape.

"It looks like a circle," said Christiana, bending over the bowl to take a closer look.

"No look, it has pointed bits. 'Tis a crown methinks. What does that mean?" she asked excitedly.

Not waiting for a reply – indeed none was forthcoming for at that moment the outer door latch rattled loudly – a smile like a sunbeam lit up the girl's face. Surely, she thought, a crown could only mean one thing – someone with royal connections.

A voice from without was calling. "Martha, Martha, are you there?"

It was Alfred bearing a wooden tray of marchpane dainties. "From the kitchen to celebrate," he said, offering the delicacies to the herbalist. William followed his father into the room, looking rather awkward.

"Father, we are playing Valentine games," Christiana announced gleefully.

"Oh aye, and can anyone play or just the young 'uns?" Alfred laughed.

"We can all play. You go next, Father."

After instruction from his daughter Alfred stood rather clumsily with his back to the bowl and almost upset the water with his large boot. Christiana giggled as her father recited the ditty and dropped the seeds into the bowl behind his shoulder. They gathered around eagerly awaiting the result. When the hemp had dispersed and regrouped into a vague shape Christiana shouted, "It looks like a loaf of bread! Look, Martha."

"So it is. And who might your loved one be then, Alfred?" Martha teased.

"'Tis Bessie in the bake house, Father," Christiana announced to a roar of laughter.

"Come, Will, your turn next," said Alfred.

William, at almost fourteen years of age, was not at all sure that he wanted to play. To his mind such games were female nonsense. He was content enough to munch on the marchpane and sup Martha's ale but as Alfred had partaken of the fun good-humouredly he did not want to lose face. So he took his place, mumbled the required ditty and dropped his handful of hemp into the bowl. They waited expectantly. Christiana thought she could see the shape the seed had formed but said nothing and Martha was just standing there smiling.

"Looks like a horseshoe to me, lad," Alfred blurted out. William had turned a deep shade of red in the candlelight. Martha bustled forward with a handful of seed and declared, "Move aside, I haven't had my turn yet."

Her seeds bobbed and bounced and drew together into another non-descript shape. Once again it was Alfred who deciphered the picture. "A butter churn is that," he shouted.

Martha giggled like a girl. "That would be the old dairyman, Jack. I always knew he had a fancy for me."

Christiana and Alfred joined in the laughter at the image each had in their mind of old Jack, toothless and crook-backed from years of bending to milk cows. Even William could not suppress a smile at the thought.

The bowl and hemp seed cleared away, the four of them sat in the warmth of the cottage drinking ale and eating marchpane. William's sulky countenance and the sidelong glances he threw at his sister did not go unnoticed by Martha and all attempts to engage the boy in conversation were unfruitful. The herbalist had not lived these many a year without becoming womanly wise and thought much on what all this could mean, and was certain she had the measure of it.

It was not long before the sugary delicacies were gone and the ale jug empty, most of its contents inside the blacksmith, and so with lantern in hand Alfred bade Martha a good night and departed with his children for the smithy and home.

The dying embers of the brazier still warmed the smithy and penetrated to the living area beyond. Christiana lit a few tallow candles to disperse the darkness.

"Everything all right, lad?" Alfred asked, as they were making ready for bed. William grunted a reply. Christiana offered up prayers on behalf of her father and brother before climbing into the narrow pallet that was her resting place.

It had been a while since Martha had suggested that she might have a separate bed to her brother and father and glad she was of it too, especially now that William seemed to be growing apart from her; the closeness they once shared as children had all but gone. Her brother's mood seemed to have changed of late and he had become surly and oft-times even petulant. Most strange of all was the way she would catch him staring at her as though seeing her each time for the first time.

For his own part William was confused. He wished fervently that he could talk to his father about all that troubled him but how could he, for was not Alfred Christiana's father too? He thought that he was brother to Christiana, everyone said so and he had no clear memory of his very early childhood, but he knew that there was a time when he was neither Alfred's son nor Christiana's brother. None of this would matter very much if he had not now and for some time had carnal thoughts about the girl he knew as sister. He felt desire that caused him many a restless night and roused him shamefully whenever she so much as looked at him. And this night was no exception, exasperated by those childish Valentine games of folly.

William had heard the priest in his sermons at church warn

men to be on their guard against the sinful, lustful nature of women, being as they were daughters of Eve. Perhaps it was true even of his sister; had he not seen her many a time watching the men in training on the drill field? One in particular.

Long into the cold night William lay awake looking up at the small casement high in the stone wall where he watched the flutter of icy flakes against a sky as black as jet.

It was not many days following the Feast of Saint Valentine that Martha welcomed a visitor to the herbarium. The herbalist was a servant of some standing at Middleham, revered for her skill with herbal remedies as well as her status as widow to the late steward of the castle. It was not altogether surprising then that the old woman should see fit to pay host to her husband's successor with a feast of bread, cheese and a jug of ale.

This particular afternoon Christiana had returned to the cottage after an errand to the kitchen to deliver a supply of herbs for the cooking pot. She carried back with her a large jar of goose fat for use in ointment preparations. She was about to set it down to turn the latch of the big wooden door when to her surprise she found it ajar; the day was still cold with a layer of ice underfoot. Furthermore, there came the sound of voices from within, one of which was Martha's, the other she knew to belong to John Conyers. With jar in hand, Christiana hesitated outside the door listening.

"They are but children, John. I am sure it will come to naught," Martha was heard to say.

"Aye, maybe you are right," Conyers replied. "But the countess is concerned that these two are becoming overfriendly. Her husband has the keeping of the king's brother until he is of age and she sees it her duty to make certain any improper relationships concerning him are avoided."

What followed was something akin to a snigger from Martha. "My Lady Anne or anyone else cannot stop what will be and it would not be the first time *improper relationships* have occurred. You know that well enough, John."

"Aye, but not if we can help it. We need to be seen to discourage any improper relationship between the duke and the blacksmith's daughter."

Behind the door Christiana felt a blaze of colour rush to her cheeks despite the cold air as she realised that it was she and Duke Richard that they were discussing. There followed a lull in the conversation and the sound of drinks being poured and cups clattering on the table.

"You know, John," Martha continued, "the young duke must be lonely, what with his brother George and his cousins spending much of their time at court with their father. He seeks companionship of his own age, nothing more."

"Well that is soon remedied. I have news, not long received, that young Francis, Lord Lovell, is to be made Warwick's ward following the death of his mother. He is to wed Lady Anne FitzHugh, Warwick's niece, and complete his education at Middleham until he is of an age to consummate his marriage and assume his late father's titles."

"There lies the answer for the Duke of Gloucester also, my friend," replied Martha. "He will soon be fourteen years of age and it will not be that long before he can bed a wife."

There came the thud of a cup against the table and Conyers laughed. "That is one task I will not be called upon to do – marriage-making for royalty.

"Jesting apart though, Martha, I could have this girl moved to the kitchen or sent to wash clothes. She would have little opportunity then to pursue the friendship of a duke. She has a privileged position here and it must not be used to her advantage."

Another brief silence followed. "You know, she is also of an age to marry. Maybe you should talk to her father." This absurd suggestion came from the steward.

From her hiding place Christiana bristled with indignation. She would not be forced to wed anyone.

"I look to you then, my friend," Conyers continued. "See to it that the girl gives the countess no further cause for concern."

The scraping of chair legs on the flagstones and the sound of heavy boots moving towards the door indicated that Conyers was about to take his leave. Quick as lightning Christiana disappeared behind the corner of the stone wall of the cottage just as the figure of the big man came into view.

She found the herbalist at work stirring a concoction over her brazier when she entered the cottage a few moments later. Martha made no comment when the girl said the reason for her delayed return was because she had dropped her jar of fat and had to return for another, an act that ordinarily would have brought forth a severe reprimand.

It would appear the old woman had something on her mind, which strangely seemed nothing to do with the verbal exchange Christiana had just witnessed.

"What say you to moving in here with me, Christiana?" Martha began. "There is room enough for two and you would be on hand to work. You are getting older now and soon a woman. 'Tis time you increased your knowledge of herbal remedies, and besides, the smithy is no place for a young woman."

Christiana, much relieved that she was not after all to be instructed on the merits or otherwise of who she should and should not fraternise with, walked over to Martha and took her chubby hands in hers. "You do not need to press the point, Martha. I would be happy to live here. Who would not after the dirty smithy?"

Martha smiled broadly. "That is settled then. I will see your father this very day."

Christiana turned then to put the jar of goose fat away on a shelf and was not certain that her ears had not deceived her, for did not Martha mutter under her breath the words, "I can keep a better eye on you here, my girl."

A few days later, her father having approved his daughter's move, Christiana packed up her meagre belongings and took up residence in the cottage with Martha. Her father had kissed and embraced her as though she was leaving him for good and then laughed at his foolishness. William, leaning against the wall of the smithy, watched in sullen silence.

As to the outcome of Conyers' conversation with his trusted friend, the subject of Christiana's possible courtship and marriage to a hitherto unknown young man was not broached by either her father or the herbalist.

Needless to say then Martha's prophecy came to pass and the friendship between the young duke and the servant girl continued to blossom, although with more discretion than had hitherto been observed.

Middleham Castle
Yorkshire
Autumn 1466

One fine morning towards the end of September the castle bailey droned with excitement. Something was afoot but none would say except that the presence of the young Duke of Gloucester was expressly requested at the stable yard.

Many people were curious it would seem for a sizable throng had gathered on the cobbles outside Alfred's smithy; even the blacksmith had left his brazier and joined William and Jude, waiting with the others. Christiana stood by her father's side and watched as the duke walked into the yard, his dog Ulrick bounding at his heels. With Richard was Conyers the steward, Francis Lovell and the countess with her youngest daughter Anne at her side.

It was not long before a cloud of dust and the thunder of hooves along the road from the eastern gatehouse heralded the arrival of Warwick's men wearing his livery and carrying the standard of the ragged staff and bear. All eyes were turned on the troop as they reached the cobbled yard save Christiana's, which were stealing a fleeting glance at the duke standing in the morning sunlight, a frown upon his dark brow.

The last rider to enter the yard held in his hand an embossed leather halter from which pranced a magnificent white destrier, its nostrils flaring and mane and tail flowing like silk in the breeze. They came to a halt before the duke and the fore rider swept low his pennant and waited. Just then the figure of the Earl of Warwick strode into the yard from behind the stables from where he had concealed himself.

"Richard, Duke of Gloucester," he announced with considerable pomp, "may I present to you this gift, from the stables of Jervaulx, to mark your passing from page to squire."

For several moments the duke, his cheeks flushed with

pleasure, could only stare mutely at the gift. At last a smile lit up the young man's face as he took a step towards the horse, which stood impatiently tossing its head and stamping the cobbles.

Conyers laughed aloud and led the crowd in a rapturous applause. Richard reached out a slender hand to pat the horse's soft grey muzzle, still too overcome it seemed for words.

"The animal has been bred and trained by the monks at Jervaulx, my lord," announced Conyers when the ovation had ceased. "He will make a fine warhorse, but heed well, young man, for he is of high spirits. Your road to knighthood will begin in earnest now and you will be in need of such a steed to take you through your training." Conyers gave the youth a fatherly clap on the shoulder before leaving the yard to return to the keep with the earl and his family.

With the crowd dispersed and about its duties the duke remained in the yard a little longer. He was leaning over the low wooden door of the stall with his chin resting across his arms looking admiringly at his horse as it munched oats from a trough when Christiana came up quietly behind him.

"He is a fine horse, my lord," she said softly.

"Indeed he is and he needs a fine name. What think you of White Surrey?" Richard answered without looking her way.

"White Surrey," the girl mused. "Yes, I like that well. It will suit him."

Richard turned to face her then, a mischievous glint in his dark blue eyes. "I shall ride on the morrow," he announced impulsively. "Nay, I shall do so now."

Christiana frowned. "Is that wise? You heard Conyers. Is he ready to be ridden?"

"He most certainly is. You do not doubt my horsemanship I hope?" the duke replied curtly.

"Never," Christiana answered hastily.

"Good. Then I shall prepare him myself at once."

"Can I come too?" The question came from the boy standing in the shadow of the stable block.

"No you cannot, Francis. I shall ride too fast for you to keep up," Richard replied firmly before turning and walking away. The young lord shot a sullen glance at the girl before shrugging his shoulders and walking away, somewhat sulkily.

Christiana returned to her duties at the herbarium and left the duke to his own schemes. She was busy turning the last of the fresh herbs into potions and storing the dried ones. She and Martha worked in companionable silence well into the morning, pounding, mixing and boiling the sweet-smelling herbs and storing the bottles and jars in neat rows on the wooden shelves.

Just before noon Martha stopped working and wiped her brown wrinkled hands on her apron. Taking up a pannier from the table she began loading it with a various vessels, saying as she did so, "I will be away to the castle, Christiana, to replenish the stores up there." She hesitated before continuing, "I may be a while."

Christiana smiled at her retreating back as she disappeared through the doorway. She knew that Martha would probably be stopping to gossip awhile with her friends up in the kitchen and pantries.

The sun, like a disc of liquid gold, pulsated low in the sky, catching the copper and bronze hues of the dying leaves on the trees in the garden. One or two tired wasps buzzed drunkenly over a clump of grizzled mallow still supporting a few pink flowers. All in the garden was peaceful and quiet.

Christiana sighed and turned away from the door where she had been leaning lazily against the crooked jamb, looking out. She walked back to the table; she was almost finished. She had just put the stopper in the last jar of St John's wort oil when a shadow fell across the open doorway. Turning quickly and expecting to see Martha back early from her errands she was surprised to see Richard standing there.

She stood for a moment staring at him. His white linen shirt was torn at the shoulder and quite filthy; the embroidered red tunic he wore was ruined, gold thread hanging and frayed. His hair was dishevelled and his face blackened with mud. She resisted the urge to laugh at his unbecoming appearance and suddenly concerned that he might be hurt she crossed the room towards him.

"What happened?" she whispered.

He grinned, a little embarrassed. "White Surrey got the better of me. He is a little wild but he goes like the wind. He is a magnificent animal, Christiana."

"I do not doubt it," she laughed, until Richard winced and touched his left shoulder with his fingers.

"I think I may have a few cuts," he said. "Where is Martha? I will need a salve."

"She is on an errand at the castle. I can tend to your wounds... if you permit me," the girl answered timidly, acutely aware at that moment of being alone with the prince.

She could see wet sticky patches on Richard's shirt where cuts on his arm and shoulder had bled and clung to the linen. She indicated a stool for him to sit. The duke, however, did not sit and stood hesitatingly beside her. Christiana's face blushed red as the rose at that moment when she realised that she had broken the rules of etiquette. How could he permit her to tend his wounds? Where was the herbalist?

"What happened, my lord?" Christiana asked in an effort to restore decorum.

"The horse jumped a hedge at a gallop," Richard replied, smiling now. "Trouble was a tree branch got in the way and lifted me from his back. It was fortunate that I held onto the reins otherwise I might have lost him."

"Richard!" she gasped. "You could have been killed. You..."

"I was only dragged a little way," he said, grinning sheepishly.

"Even so, you should be careful."

The girl's eyes were drawn to Richard's shoulder where the cuts were still oozing through the linen of his shirt. It took a great resolve to suppress her natural desire to tend to his wounds. She stepped a little closer to him and their eyes met.

"Have you a salve?" he asked.

She nodded silently, still holding his gaze until at last she moved away to the shelves containing liniments and salves from where she took a large jar of vervain and chamomile.

She needed but a small amount, and taking a smaller clay

vessel she began to spoon the salve into it. As she stirred it to blend the herbs she noticed an ornament pinned somewhat crookedly onto the duke's tunic. It was a curious emblem and she thought to question it but decided that would be too impertinent and intimate a thing to do. However, Richard had noted where her gaze was fixed and offered an explanation.

"'Tis the boar device of the Duke of Gloucester," he stated.

"Why the boar?" Christiana asked gently, sealing the pot with linen wadding.

"The boar is a brave and courageous creature and it was a boar that protected Saint Anthony when he was alone in the wilderness. It kept away other animals and also demons and evil spirits sent to tempt the purity of his heart."

The girl returned his smile and handed over the pot when all of a sudden their peace was interrupted by William bounding into the herbarium, his face flushed and hair darkened with the smoke from the smithy.

He halted sharply at the sight of these two alone and in apparent closeness to one another – any words he may have been about to utter died on his lips.

"I thank you kindly," Richard addressed Christiana. "Francis can assist me with this." With a polite nod towards William Richard left the herbarium.

For a long hard moment William stared at his sister, eyes blazing. She stood like a tree rooted to the ground, matching his gaze but unable to speak. Then abruptly he turned on his heels and strode back out through the door, the purpose of his errand unfulfilled leaving Christiana with so many emotions tangled and knotted like strands of wool caught in a loom.

Middleham Castle
Yorkshire
Spring 1467

"Right glad I am that you are here, Francis," Richard muttered, twisting the tufts of grass around his thin fingers under the warm spring sun.

The boy sitting beside him smiled somewhat shyly and nodded his head. "It is preferable to keeping company with ladies and their fripperies," he muttered.

The duke chuckled. "How do you find your wife?"

Francis's cheeks flushed a little. "Anne is pleasant enough but I regard myself too young to..."

"Give it time, Francis, and all will be as it should. Lady Anne is but a child, but not for long." Richard laughed and leant back against a pile of hessian straw bags on the edge of the drill field, legs sprawled out in front of him and an empty costrel and bread bag by his side.

It had been a most demanding morning for Richard. The weapons he was expected to train with were now heavier and more awkward to wield; gone were the wooden swords from his days as a page. The weighty pieces of plate armour he wore and fought in tired him and his slender body boasted many a bruise from falling off White Surrey in an effort to improve his equestrian skills.

The day's training would not yet end for now that they had partaken of their victuals Richard would be expected to present himself in the great hall to continue his study of Heraldry and battle tactics.

Oft-times of late Richard had been feeling weary but he would say nothing for it was his duty to fulfil the expectation and desire to become a knight; how else could he be loyal and faithful to his beloved brother the king?

Slowly he stood to his feet and walked towards the keep,

Francis at his side. "I shall challenge you to a game of chess after we have supped this eve," Richard informed his friend as they entered the courtyard. Francis scowled a little as he knew that the duke outwitted him at every game.

Richard smiled. "I would challenge my Lord Neville but he is away again at his castle in the south along with my cousins, and besides 'tis good for you to persevere, Francis, for you will become all the better for it." With that they entered the keep and so to their studies.

"Look to your business, girl," Martha chided as she walked beside Christiana along the edge of the drill field. They were making their way to the village where Martha had some errands to undertake. The retreating form of the Duke of Gloucester and his companion exiting the drill field had not gone unnoticed by the young girl. Martha huffed and tut-tutted and quickened her pace.

A gentle breeze swayed the golden heads of the Lenten lilies growing in clusters along the wayside, a poignant reminder that the season of fasting and penance would soon be upon them. It was quiet in the village, many folk about their work with little time for idleness.

Christiana ambled down the hill, past the market cross and along the thoroughfare beside the herbalist, a wicker basket swinging on her arm.

"Here we are then," Martha announced as they approached the faded wooden door of a small cottage. To the side of the door large pieces of the dried dung and animal hair that daubed the walls had fallen away, exposing the birch wattle beneath. As Martha knocked on the wood and waited, Christiana noticed that the rest of the cottage walls fared much the same; only the thatching of the roof seemed to be in good repair. After a moment or two the door opened and on the threshold stood a man. Christiana could see at once that he had been drinking strong ale for his eyes were red and unfocused as they searched the faces of the two women standing outside his door.

"A good day to you, Master Thatcher. How does Eadgyth fair?" Martha inquired.

"You best come inside and see for yerself," Martin Thatcher answered brusquely.

Little light had penetrated the gloom of the cottage despite the numerous holes in the walls and the one unglazed casement. Christiana stood close to the herbalist, wary of the drunken man with the large hands.

A pallet of straw stood in the far corner and atop a pile of stained blankets and old animal skins slept a young woman, not many years older than Christiana. Corn-coloured hair, matted and unruly, obscured her pretty face.

"Eadgyth," Martha exclaimed, crossing the dry earthen floor. She placed her strong hand upon the woman's shoulder to waken her. Slowly Eadgyth's eyes opened, glazed and faraway. Martha glanced down at her blood-stained shift and pressed a hand gently on her stomach. She looked anxiously at Martin sitting heavily on a stool. "She has birthed the babe – what has happened?"

"You are too late," the man spat. "Even your witchcraft has no power here. 'Tis God's punishment on me for keeping a whore under my roof."

Martha had caught the jerk of the man's head towards the hearth and her eyes followed. There in the cold ashes lay a bundle, still and lifeless. At once Martha left Eadgyth's side and snatching up the trappings that swaddled it she uncovered the body of a tiny stillborn female babe. Christiana was close enough to see; the babe's limbs were crooked and shrivelled, fingers and toes mere stumps.

"She lay with another," the man sobbed and pointed a finger at his wife. "'Tis the devil's spawn." He stood and tottered towards the door, Christiana leaping out of the way and almost overturning her basket. Martha returned the babe to the hearth and returned to the bedside.

"What happened, child?" Martha gently brushed Eadgyth's hair from her face. "'Tis true, Martha, I lay with another and this is the punishment I receive for my sin." The woman cried anguished tears.

"Christiana, give me the basket." The herbalist turned to the girl who relinquished her hold of it.

"I did not go willingly but 'tis no matter, I sinned," Eadgyth wept. "Martin suspected somehow... He always wanted us to have children but we were not blessed – and when this happened..."

"Here, drink this." Martha offered a cup of wine with lemon balm. "I will leave some of this here for later." She placed a small stone jar on the floor beside the pallet.

Straightening up Martha muttered resignedly, "'Tis always the fault of the woman. You had something to tempt the man I dare say."

"Ralph needs no tempting, he's like a beast of the wood and under the earl's protection." Eadgyth's words were bitter as she closed her eyes in fatigue, allowing the older woman to wash and cleanse her stained body.

Christiana had little desire to remain in the cottage but as she turned towards the door she hesitated. Where might the man be?

Slowly she opened the door and peered out into the road. A few children were playing jacks on the ground at the wayside; she deemed it safe enough to venture forth.

She walked along the road inclining upwards towards the church of Saint Mary and Saint Alkelda. Christiana had seen the lifeless body of the babe, its deformed feet not unlike those of Ulrick the dog, and it played upon her mind. Did God allow the child to be born disfigured as a punishment? She recalled at that moment her own mother and baby brother. Was his life taken away because of something her mother or father had done? What might it be that had so incurred the wrath of Almighty God?

She sat on the ground outside the walled enclosure of the church lost in her musings. Presently a shadow fell across the place where she, with head bowed, plucked at the spring grass.

"Is all well, child?" It was a male voice that startled the girl for she expected the dark shadow to belong to Martha come looking for her. The figure looming over her wore the black garb of the priest. At once Christiana was on her feet, bowing respectfully before the man of God.

The young priest smiled. "You are not of the village are you?" he asked.

"No, Father, I live at the castle." Christiana pointed to the looming castle wall that dominated the village as though he knew it not.

The man nodded and was about to enter the church precinct when he paused and asked, "What is your business here?" His question was direct but asked kindly enough so the girl thought to settle matters that troubled her mind.

"I am with Martha, we—"

"Ah yes, Martha the herbalist," he interrupted. The world and his wife it seemed knew Martha.

Once again the man turned away but the girl tugged at his robe somewhat irreverently. "I would ask you a question... please," she pleaded.

"Does it concern matters spiritual?" the priest asked, frowning.

"It does. I want to know about God's punishment. Are babies born with twisted arms and legs because their mother has sinned?"

The priest stared at her for a moment before replying. "Well yes, child. 'Tis the sins of the fathers passed to the children. We must always, above all else, guard our immortal souls and through due penance and prayer seek God's grace and mercy."

Christiana nodded, listening intently to the man's words.

"Sometimes these things are a mark of the devil himself," the man continued, thoughtfully.

"Is it all right then if we get people better when they are sick?" the girl persisted.

The priest began to feel a little uncomfortable under the interrogation of one so young, especially as this was reminiscent of conversations he had recently been having with another, one of noble birth. He had not been long under Holy Orders and he knew that many, even within the Church, held opposing views. He recalled the debates he had heard at the great university in Cambridge. There were those who advocated that healing should not be encouraged as sickness was God's way of allowing us to focus upon our sin and so lead to repentance and spiritual cleansing;

something to be prized above physical health. He himself could see no reason why the art of medicine should not be practised as long as due diligence was paid to the salvation of the soul – after all, Our Lord himself healed the sick.

"I think it is well within God's purpose for you to help those who are sick." He smiled and then added, "Remember it can also be a sign of God's special favour and grace upon one who has to endure great physical hardship for it strengthens their faith."

He turned to walk away, feeling certain that he had covered all the theological arguments, and had just reached the gate when there came yet another.

"Do dogs sin?"

The man was saved from having to provide an answer by the appearance of the herbalist waddling up the hill towards them. "Rector Beverley," she called, approaching breathlessly. "Eadgyth, wife of Martin the Thatcher, has need of you. The child she was carrying has been born dead and..."

The priest sighed and nodding his head walked past and back down the road.

"Come along, Christiana, 'tis late. Our other errands can wait for another day; let us go home." Martha handed the pannier once more to the girl and together they began the walk back to the castle, Christiana having much to ponder.

Middleham Castle
Yorkshire
Early summer 1467

As spring warmed into summer the earl and his family returned to Middleham for a few weeks to oversee his affairs in the north. The king, he decided, could manage well enough without him for a short while, the demands of the queen's family more than sufficient to occupy the royal mind at present.

Warwick declared that there would be a petit tourney held in honour of his lady wife, who was always happy to return to this northern stronghold. The earl ever on the move had rarely spent more than a few days here since the coronation of King Edward.

A few young knights from neighbouring families would attend for jousting, the young lords in training would test their skill at the quintain and the castle garrison could have an archery competition. It would be no great spectacle for certain, the entertainment limited to simple feasting and a modest display by the musicians, but it was a distraction looked forward to by all nonetheless.

The pavilion and the tilt for the joust took three days to erect on the drill field complete with a flutter of banners and flags. A long table was set up on a high platform to seat the earl and his family. Trestles and benches were set out on either side of this table for their noble guests and visitors, all under the shade of a colourful canopy. Sideboards and cupboards had also been carried down from the keep and placed nearby from which an abundance of food could be served: cold meats, loaves of bread, sweetmeats and flagons of wine. Warwick had declared the day one of rest and servants not in direct attendance at the tournament were given permission to watch and cheer on their champion. Jugs of ale and platters of bread and cheese were to be supplied for them on open grass on the opposite side of the lists from the pavilion.

On the fourth day all was ready for the entertainment to begin by mid-morning. Warwick, looking resplendent in mulberry hose and jerkin with matching chaperon complete with its hanging liripipe, lorded over the proceedings. Beside him at the long table, Countess Anne, who would award honours to the champions, looked very regal in her dark blue gown cut low to her girdle and wide across her white shoulders. Despite the increasing heat of the day the lady wore a heavy truncated hennin and butterfly veil. The Lady Isabel, now in her sixteenth year, looked very charming in her red damask gown cut in the same style as her mother's. Her younger sister, Anne, looked as pretty as a rose in her saffron-coloured gown and shimmering golden plait.

Christiana's dress of undyed linen had for adornment only a handful of small embroidered herbs on the bodice. She had, however, daringly woven gillyflowers into her raven plait. She accompanied Martha onto the drill field, each carrying a wicker pannier with a supply of lint and ointments should any would-be warrior require treatment. The herbalist had warned her that even these displays, given as forms of entertainment, were not without their wounded.

The drill field was now fairly swarming with people, noble and low-born. William was standing at the end of the lists behind their father, a leather bag of necessary farrier's tools at their feet. Here too were assembled the knights ready to do combat, their squires in attendance bearing their standards and coats of arms. Their horses, tethered close by, were also caparisoned in the heraldic trappings of their riders.

The tourney began with a troupe of musicians blasting their instruments across the field followed by the herald announcing the order of the day's events. A display of archery would be first, open to any. Following that Warwick was keen to show off the skill of his young protégés who would charge the quintain. There would be a break for refreshment and the grand joust would then begin, the day culminating in prize-giving and feasting.

As the challengers for the archery competition made their way onto the field with an assortment of bows and some very crooked-looking arrows Christiana made her way, basket across her arm, to where Warwick's young lords were making ready for the quintain and receiving final instruction from their master. She saw at once the wolfhound, Ulrick, with long coarse beard sweeping the ground as he sniffed around and knew that the Duke of Gloucester would not be far away.

Richard was chatting to his older brother George who, it seemed, had come to Middleham with Warwick. The young man now stood a head and shoulders above Richard and much broader than last she had seen him. Christiana stood a little way off, unsure of whether or not to approach this gathering of young nobles. Periodically the crowd beyond and to her left cheered heartily as a bowman hit his mark. It was Ulrick who sensed his onetime mistress and came bounding over to her, alerting Duke Richard to her presence. It was all smiles when these two met under the disapproving gaze of the Duke of Clarence.

"I came to wish you luck at the quintain," the girl whispered.

Richard's face darkened. "I will need it," he said glumly. "I am none too skilled as yet. These others are older than me and bigger." He jerked his head back towards where George was now engaged in conversation with a group of young men who did indeed all seem much older and certainly stronger made than Richard. Christiana placed her hand over Richard's, where he toyed nervously with the hilt of his dagger secured in its scabbard at his waist.

"You will do well," she said, hoping to sound reassuring, although she had seen the boys at the quintain and it was none too easy a task to perform.

Christiana left the duke then and went to join Martha back at the lists to witness the last of the archers let loose their arrows. A fair few flagons of ale had passed amongst the men judging by the raucous shouts and bawdy banter at this side of the field but at last the judges declared they had a winner. To the surprise of all it was no soldier who won but a young lad apprenticed to the master stonemason still engaged upon the building work of the keep.

There was a short interval as the heavy butts were carried off the field and all the arrows retrieved. Martha, sauntering around the field, spied an old acquaintance and nodded a greeting although she did not make conversation but merely walked on. Christiana noticed his broad shoulders and he was holding a battered leather bag in his large hand.

"Is he a soldier, Martha?" Christiana whispered to the herbalist.

"Nay, lass, although he's as familiar with the battle field as any soldier."

"How so?" asked the girl.

"That is Roger Barber, a surgeon the earl employs to treat the battle-wounded."

Knowing of Martha's distrust of any who would rival her knowledge of healing, Christiana questioned her friend, "Do you not mind that he is here?"

"On the contrary, child, for I welcome his presence; he is better placed than I to perform amputations and arrow extractions.

"Come, do not look so fearful, such injuries are rare at the tourney."

They looked on as the quintain was erected. A sturdy thick post was hammered into the ground and across the top of it was pivoted a wooden beam. On one end of the beam was a large shield painted red and from the other end hung a leather bag filled with stones, all carefully balanced.

A troop of musicians led by a drummer marched around the field as the competitors entered the arena on horseback, six in all. Christiana edged a little closer, arm linked to Martha's.

After the preliminary introduction the riders returned to the end of the ride to await the first charge. A young lord of the Scrope family was handed his lance and a hush fell upon the crowd as he prepared to gallop his horse. With lance held high on his arret he set his mount at the target and charged. Hooves thundered across the hard ground, and with lance couched the rider hit the shield full square, the beam swung on its pivot, the bag came round and floundered in mid-air; a successful manoeuvre. Jubilant applause rose from the crowd.

The following three squires also made successful charges and so the Plantagenet brothers were remaining. Christiana could see George offer the next ride to his sibling. She could almost feel

Richard's nervousness as he hoisted himself into the saddle and took the lance offered to him.

"Do they ride only once?" Christiana asked Martha.

"Nay, lass." It was a garrison soldier standing beside them with a cup of ale in his hand who answered. "They each get three rides to begin with and then the ones with the most successes ride again and so on until they have a winner."

Christiana nodded but turned her head away towards the field at the sound of a horse's hooves drumming past. She held her breath as the lance struck home and the bag shot round. This time, however, it found a target, hitting Richard full in the back and knocking him winded to the ground. Christiana would, at that very moment, have rushed to his aid had not Martha put a restraining hand upon her arm.

"Leave him be," the old woman warned.

For a while Richard lay motionless on the ground amidst the jeering crowd, his horse prancing freely across the field. She could hear Ulrick bark as he too tried to reach his master but was held back by two young lads struggling to keep a grip on his collar.

At last the duke stood shakily to his feet, not so hurt physically, his padded jack absorbing much of the impact, but suffering much humiliation as he walked back to the waiting men, some smiling, others laughing outright. It seemed that brother George laughed the loudest. Back in the crowd Christiana felt her cheeks glowing red, feeling Richard's chagrin almost as much as he did.

George swung himself smugly up into his saddle and galloped off confidently to make his first successful hit and so ended the first round. As the second round began with two more successful hits Christiana peered across to look for Richard.

He was still there, a little apart from the others with head downcast. She sighed and fretted beside Martha but the herbalist warned her to stay put with a stern look.

Christiana was still watching Richard when the jeers of the crowd told her that the third knight had taken a fall. Far from crestfallen, this young man was walking towards his fellow competitors with a broad grin on his face and his helmet held high despite the jeers of the crowd. Duke Richard even managed to return his smile as he walked up to him. By the time the fourth man went up, one of the Scropes of Bolton, the Duke of Gloucester was looking distinctly more confident.

Taking up the helmet offered by a page and mounting his horse for his second ride, Richard held back his sprightly mount to line him up to the target. Taking up the lance he steadied the horse before spurring him on. Nearer and nearer he galloped to the shield until with a loud thud the lance made contact, the bag flew round and touched the rider on the back as he sped past. The spectators held their breath but the impact had failed to unhorse him and he raised his lance in triumph to a tumultuous roar from the crowd.

George gave his brother a curt glance as he took his turn at the end of the ride. It was perhaps not so much lack of skill as an arrogant confidence that caused this young man to fail in his task, and down he came with a heavy crash to the ground at his second attempt.

Under the brightly decorated canopy across the field Christiana had noticed how the Lady Isabel had stood at once to her feet, hand clasped over her mouth, as her cousin took his fall almost it seemed under her very nose.

Stunned, the Duke of Clarence lay prone on his back for several moments before struggling to his feet and marching off the field, not stopping at the gathering of men and horses but stomping away altogether out of sight.

"That is one spoilt young man," Martha hissed in Christiana's ear. It did not escape either of the women's attention that presently the Lady Isabel had excused herself from her pavilion seat and would have walked off in the direction taken by her cousin were it not for her father's hand raised in objection.

Only five competitors took the third round, Duke Richard's last attempt also a success. With the Duke of Clarence disqualified and Lord Dacre spraining an ankle after a fall, it left only four to go on to the next round. Christiana took the opportunity to slip discreetly from Martha's side as her attention was now given to the young man and his swollen ankle.

"You did well," Christiana enthused as she ran up to Richard. The youth's pleasure was evident by the wide smile that seemed to light up his dark eyes. "Where is Ulrick?" Christiana asked.

"I know not," Richard answered, looking around the arena with a frown. "He will be here about."

It was unusual for the wolfhound to be absent for any great length of time, trained as he was to keep close to his master's side, so after a while the duke decided to go in pursuit of his dog. "You will miss the next round if you are not here," Christiana remarked as they moved away. Richard merely shrugged his shoulders.

Away from the lists there were few people about, servants only who had duties to attend and a scattering of men, deep in their cups, idling about. Together the young duke and the servant girl wandered across the bridge that spanned the moat into the inner bailey, which was all but deserted. From here Richard was able to survey the pavilion and the crowd of people in the outer bailey. The scarlet surcoat of the rider galloping towards the quintain was visible from here and they heard the cheering crowd as he dodged the flailing bag.

The duke sighed deeply and was about to turn away when activity at the farthermost end of the drill field away from the lists caught his attention; activity that to his mind was far from sporting. Beside him, Christiana had not seen what had caught her companion's eye and was surprised when, without a word, the duke took off like a bolt from a crossbow along the bridge and down the field. She could do nothing but follow, hampered by her long skirts and the basket that she still carried across her arm and dared not discard.

Lagging behind the duke and breathless, Christiana came upon a chaotic scene. A group of men, garrison soldiers it seemed, were gathered where the half-dozen butts had been placed earlier after their use in the tourney. An empty ale casket lay on its side together with an assortment of upturned cups. Drunk and witless, the men had continued to try their luck with the bow. One, apparently, had decided that a moving target would serve better, for sprawled on the floor, an arrow head piercing his thigh, was Ulrick.

Clarence was amongst those present, and it was towards that youth Duke Richard pounced, fearing his dog dead and holding his brother, in a position to know better, responsible. With fists pounding and a temper that none would have credited the boy with Richard pummelled George's chest. Clarence floored the younger boy at once with a hefty shove.

"Get off me, you stupid boy," he yelled. "It was not me who shot the hound. 'Twas Hodkin. Besides, 'tis only a dog, a deformed one at that." George glanced disparagingly at the panting dog but Richard, back on his feet, was coming at his brother again.

Christiana was on her knees examining the dog's wound just as they were joined by Martha, William and the earl himself. Martha, scarlet-faced and panting hard, could speak no words, William went to stand beside his sister and Warwick, glaring at the two brothers, demanded to know the purpose of this breach of the peace.

George, given opportunity, told his lord of how a few of the soldiers had sought a little sport, nothing more, and the dog happened to wander past. The accused, Ralph Hodkin, not unknown to those present, hardly able to stand without the aid of his companions, sniggered loudly.

Satisfied that there was nothing here of any real consequence, the younger brother not daring to say a word, Warwick gave orders for his soldiers to go dip their heads in the nearest horse trough. The two dukes were ordered to be at his side for the commencement of the grand joust. With that Warwick turned on his heel and marched off.

Richard was now on his knees beside the dog, stoically awaiting the herbalist's judgement. Martha, breath now recovered, lowered herself with some difficulty to the ground. Bending over the hound, it took her only moments to take measure of the situation. Grasping the arrow shaft she gently twisted and pulled, the dog letting forth a painful yelp. "'Tis only a flesh wound and gone in none too deep, and most fortunate that the arrow head is not barbed," she exclaimed. Rummaging in her basket she produced a ceramic pot of honey and walnut paste and handed it to Christiana.

"You apply this to the wound using a clean piece of cloth but first hand me the oil of lavender; you should have it in your basket. One of the ladies has taken badly in the heat."

With trembling fingers Christiana fumbled at the bottom of her basket for the oil and handed it over to Martha who eased herself to her feet and walked off in the direction of the pavilion. With the departure of the soldiers the three youngsters were now alone with the injured dog. Richard took Ulrick's head to soothe him as William held his thigh steady for Christiana to gingerly dab the paste onto the wound, although the boy would not look for fear of turning his stomach.

"What happened, Will?" the girl asked after a while.

Taking a quick glance at the duke William replied, "A lady, one not known to me, took a bad turn, as Martha said. She had no lavender so she sent me to look for you. I came across the soldiers; they were drunk, and not content with the butts had moved to... other targets. Ralph Hodkin was the main one but encouraged I think by Duke George." William paused in his oratory, expecting a comment from Richard, but as none came he continued. "An arrow from Hodkin's bow had just missed a cat by a whisker when Ulrick comes bounding up thinking it all a game. When they started aiming at him I tried to stop them but could not so I ran back to Martha and the earl." He looked across at the duke, who nodded silently.

"I think my Lord Warwick thought someone had been killed by the uproar I raised," William confessed with a grin.

"'Twas just as well for Ulrick that they were all so drunk," Richard exclaimed.

The wound sufficiently covered in paste, the three of them eased the dog to his feet. Ulrick, standing a little shakily, would not put much of his weight on his injured hind leg but otherwise fared well enough.

"This dog has escaped death twice now," Richard laughed as they returned very slowly back to the pavilion.

Duke Richard dutifully took his place at the high table joining his brother, to whom he did not speak, and cousins Isabel and

Anne. William joined Alfred on the field in attendance of the horses and Christiana kept her place beside Martha.

Throughout the remainder of the afternoon each watched the grand joust and the celebratory prize-giving from his or her allotted position according to status. The dog, Ulrick, found himself once again in residence at the herbarium, this time safely out of harm's way, convalescing peacefully.

Middleham Castle
Yorkshire
Late summer 1467

"You should have come down to the herbarium afore now with this young man," Martha reproached Godwin, who sat somewhat agitated on a chair in the anteroom of the great hall cradling his uncovered arm.

"I have been busy," he protested. "The earl is holding council again this morning. You know, complaints, petitions, moans and groans. Like as not he will be back to London and the king soon enough and all his tenants will want their say before he goes."

Christiana held steady a bowl of chamomile tincture as Martha bathed an angry rash that had flared up on the usher's arm. Through the open door she could just see a corner of a long table placed in the centre of the room and a faint murmur of voices came from within.

Godwin began to fret. "Martha, I need to make ready. The petitioners will be here at any moment." The young groom had recently been promoted to usher and took his position seriously.

Martha, concerned that her work should not be interrupted, put a large restraining hand on Godwin's shoulder. Christiana was taking little note of what was going on in front of her for the voices beyond the door were growing ever louder and drew her attention. Voices now raised in anger, although hardly a word could be discerned, reached the ears of those in the anteroom. There was no mistaking the deep resonance of Warwick's voice and surely his adversary was the Duke of Gloucester? Christiana would recognise that voice anywhere. She stood completely still as she strained to pick up any coherent word. The king's name was mentioned several times but nothing much else could be made out.

All of a sudden the great oaken door pushed open and Richard stormed out in a flare of temper. Godwin and Martha, who had been seated, fumbled to their feet and all three turned to face the young lord. Only Christiana looked directly into the face of the duke. Her gaze swept past his flushed cheeks to the pain and anger apparent in the flash of his blue eyes. Then he was gone, his leather boots thumping down the dusty stone staircase.

The three servants looked from one to the other, perplexed. Godwin sighed and pulled down the sleeve of his tunic. "More trouble," he whispered.

But that was not to be the end of the day's troubles, for no sooner had the duke disappeared than a scuffle on the outer staircase drew their attention. Two garrison guards burst into the antechamber dragging between then a scruffy boy of no more than ten years bound at the wrists and wriggling like a convulsive worm. A young woman had followed them up the stairs, flaxen hair flying free of her cap and her pretty face streaked with tears.

Godwin, ready to maintain the proper procedure for the admittance of supplicants, was brushed brusquely aside by one of the soldiers. "Move aside, Godwin," he barked. "This little thief was caught red-handed and Warwick will hear of it."

The distraught woman grabbed the sleeve of the soldier's tunic in protest.

"Please, he's no thief... he's just a boy."

"Keep away, wench," spat the other soldier and shoved her none too gently out of his way. Before the door was closed on the soldiers and their captive another figure had appeared up from the outer staircase. Although a young man in his early twenties his girth was much extended beyond that expected of his age, and his long lank hair falling across his face barely disguised the fox-like leer on his lips. A self-satisfied grin displaying a few toothless gaps was etched on his face as he slinked through the door behind the others.

The woman stood before the closed door, her shoulders sagging in despair, and wept into her hands. Godwin was taken aback by this abuse of his authority but lacking the experience to deal with it he sat down heavily on the chair and cradled his sore arm. Christiana, still holding the bowl of chamomile, stared silently as Martha took the young woman by the arm and led her to a chair.

"Sit you down, lass, and calm yourself," she soothed. "I take it the boy is your son, although I cannot say you look old enough to be his mother. You want to tell us what all that was about?"

The woman sniffed and wiped her face with her grubby sleeve. "Aye,'tis my boy, Clem. He is not yet ten years old but he is no thief, I swear!" Her tears threatened to flow again until Martha placed a comforting hand upon her shoulder.

"Clem was caught with a coin purse, cut from the belt of a soldier as he left the ale house, so *he* says," the woman continued.

"Who says?" Martha asked, although there was little doubt in the minds of those present that Clem's accuser was none other than Ralph Hodkin, the very same who had only moments ago entered the great hall. The young mother spat out his name venomously in confirmation, adding, "He is a soldier here at the castle garrison."

Godwin spoke up at that moment. "Hodkin is known to be a good soldier, well thought of by the earl," he said quietly.

Martha frowned and shook her head. "But why would this Ralph accuse your son of stealing his purse if he did not?"

"'Tis not the first time he has been accused. Last autumn Clem was flogged for poaching pheasant from the earl's land," the woman whispered.

A wry smile crept over the herbalist's wrinkled face. She looked down at the young woman seated before her. "You know, boys of Clem's age have been known to poach and get into all sorts of mischief. How can you be so sure he did not steal Hodkin's purse?"

Clem's mother looked up at Martha, her pale blue eyes brimming with unshed tears. "Well maybe he did poach, we would starve else. But he is no thief of gold coins, that is for certain!"

"Where is the boy's father?" Martha asked gently. The woman looked up quickly at Godwin, who was listening very intently to all of this.

"Well I am just about finished here," Martha announced. "You come down to the herbarium, my dear, and take a goblet of fruit wine to calm your nerves."

The old woman gently took the younger by the arm and led her down the stairs, calling over her shoulder, "Be sure to come down to see me on the morrow, 'tis a nasty rash you have there, Godwin."

Outside a playful summer breeze whipped up the skirts of the three women as they made their way across the bridge and into the bailey.

"We will find out about your son from Godwin a little later," Martha said reassuringly. "Now, what name do you have?"

"Jennie," answered the woman. Martha introduced herself and her young apprentice.

The air inside the herbarium was warmly fragranced with drying herbs and after Christiana had warmed a goblet of fruit wine for Jennie the woman began to relax a little.

"Clem's father, Daniel, is dead," Jennie began, her features looking softly sad in the sunlight from the casement. "My Daniel was a good man, he worked on the earl's estates grading fleeces, but he had one weakness." Jennie paused to rub her fingers together in her lap.

"He gambled – dice, cock-fighting, anything," she said so softly Martha could barely hear her words. "He owed a great deal of money to Ralph Hodkin. I never knew exactly how much, but he could not pay him. When Dan died of a fever last summer Ralph came to see me." Jennie's voice cracked and she swallowed hard to compose herself.

"You know," she continued, "he said I could pay with my body if I had not the money." Tears trickled down her face. She wiped them quickly away. "Clem took a dagger to him when he came back one night. Ralph was only slightly wounded but he made it clear that either I paid Dan's debts or Clem would. Since then he has falsely accused Clem of many things and had him punished."

Martha, who had been sitting on a stool listening, stood up. Christiana could see she was angry by the way she smoothed her apron down over and over. "I always said he was a nasty piece of work that one. Trouble is the earl cannot see it," the herbalist said gruffly. "Now drink up and we will be over to the castle to see what has happened."

Christiana walked a little way across the garden with the

two women as they made their way towards the keep. She was not completely certain that she understood just how Jennie was expected to pay her husband's debts but she had an awareness of such matters that was not far short of the mark. She had not forgotten that it was Ralph Hodkin who had shot an arrow at Ulrick earlier that summer, even though the dog had made a full recovery. Maybe Martha was right; it seemed the soldier could do no wrong in Warwick's eyes.

The two older women had passed through the wicker gate out of the garden but the girl lingered within. The sun overhead was warm, enticing a cauldron of smells from the flowers all around her. The oak-wood bench beneath the cascading rose bush beckoned. It could do no harm to take a little rest before resuming her duties.

She saw him as soon as she stepped out from around the box hedge. He was seated on the bench with legs outstretched and arms folded. She tipped an obligatory bow, a habit she had deemed necessary of late to apply whenever she was in the duke's company, for the sake of any who might be watching.

He turned suddenly to look at her as though her presence had startled him. His dark brows knotted in a frown but softened a little when he recognised who had invaded his privacy. Without waiting for permission she sat down beside the duke. Richard was a youth of few words, keeping his own counsel, but she also knew that he felt comfortable enough with her to share some of his thoughts. After a moment or two of silence, as she had anticipated, the duke spoke.

"Warwick is in a foul temper," he muttered. "I have been in the great hall to witness my cousin's administration of justice but I saw little justice there this day."

"I do not think then that Clem will receive a fair hearing," Christiana muttered under her breath.

"Clem?" Richard enquired.

"The boy, brought in by soldiers just as you were leaving. His mother was with him." She hesitated, not sure how much of this matter she should be discussing with the duke.

"He has been accused of stealing a coin purse belonging to a garrison soldier," the girl continued after a while, and added softly, "What do you suppose will become of him?"

Richard's eyes, clear and wide, searched her face, and once again his brow creased pensively.

"It is not for me to say," he answered after a while. "A flogging? The pillory and an ear-slitting?"

Christiana shivered despite the warmth of the day. She had seen several floggings in the village marketplace and wondered how the frightened youngster would withstand the sharp lashings across his bare back. As for the pillory, where Clem's legs would be tied through two holes in a hinged plank of wood and his ears nailed to a cross beam, the very thought of it repulsed her. After enduring a suitable number of lashings he would be torn from the beam, thus slitting his ears and marking him for life as a criminal.

"'Tis a harsh punishment, the pillory," Christiana murmured, thinking of the boy's mother. "Especially for one who is innocent."

"If the boy is guilty of theft then he must take his punishment," Richard stated solemnly. "But let us hope that he gets a chance to put his case for Warwick's foul humour has been the reason the castle dungeon is even now holding a half-dozen so-called perpetrators of the law. More like those who have dared to upset the great Earl of Warwick." He finished his oratory by kicking up the gravel of the path with his boot.

Christiana was a little taken aback by this uncustomary outburst but nowise afraid, indeed she admired the passion in those deep blue eyes.

"Why is it, do you suppose, Warwick is in such a temper of late?" she asked.

"I cannot be sure but he has been like a bear in the baiting ring ever since his return from France. Whatever the reason, he should see that the king's law is justly served. I would see it so," Richard ended hotly.

"That is a most commendable virtue, my young duke, but not always an easy one to uphold."

The sudden appearance of one richly dressed and well-spoken

from behind the box hedge startled them both. It had been two years since she had last seen the face but Christiana recognised it at once; the oval shape, the piercing gaze of the eyes and the distinctive long pointed beard.

Richard made to rise, for he too had recognised the person of Thomas, Lord Stanley, Earl of Derby.

"Sit down, Richard." Stanley sat beside the duke on the bench, seemingly unaware of the existence of the servant girl, who stood in the presence of her betters and now felt at a loss as to what she should do next.

For certain she could no longer remain here but she thought to make the same use of the box hedge as had the lord. Cunning was not the sole preserve of the nobility after all. Without the provision of such innocent and well-placed objects such as box hedges, overhanging eaves and doors left ajar, the good folk of the land would live their lives in total ignorance of the rest of the world, both near and far. By such means vital information had been obtained that could alter the course of events, be it for the good or ill of others.

And so it was without any pangs of conscience that Christiana, slipping quietly away, stood far enough from the bench for her own breathing to go undetected but close enough to hear every spoken word.

"There may be times, young man, when it is not always possible to do the right thing. Someone such as yourself can be caught up in a political battle where your hand is forced to save your head. You will learn of such matters as you grow older.

"I can tell you what has angered your guardian," Stanley continued. "You know, do you not, that for some time now His Grace the king has been moving towards an alliance with Burgundy? Your sister Margaret has been offered as bride for Duke Philip's eldest son, Charles."

"Indeed, Burgundy is England's most important market overseas for the export of wool. An alliance would be most desirable," she heard Richard answer.

"You are well informed, young lord. However, it would seem

that Warwick was sent on a wild goose chase to France once again to forge a friendship with Louis. Warwick does not favour friendship with Burgundy – something to do with the Woodville connection I believe. The earl did not approve of the king's marriage to Elizabeth Woodville for certain and now the king will not sanction Warwick's plans to marry his daughter Isabel to the Duke of Clarence."

So, thought the girl hiding behind the box hedge, rumour was founded and there was something betwixt these two. She heard no reply from Richard to this snippet of information.

After a while Duke Richard was heard to ask, "Do you have business with Warwick, my lord?"

"I heard he was home so I took opportunity to settle a matter of no great importance. But be assured, young prince, I do not intend to end up in the dungeon or on a pillory." The earl laughed at his own wit.

Another brief silence followed before Lord Stanley added, "I must be away to find my wife and our brood. She is on a brief visit to her brother before lying in for the next."

The sound of crushed gravel underfoot was heard as the older man stood; time for the servant girl to make a hasty retreat.

Middleham Castle
Yorkshire
January 1468

The Earl of Warwick had returned from the king's court to his northern stronghold at Middleham for the Christmastide festivities, having been away once again since early autumn. Not merely for the sake of his daughter, Isabel, but for the furtherance of his own ends, Warwick had the miserable George in tow. The previous autumn Clarence had been summoned to court to answer the king's displeasure. Edward knew well enough that although he had not given royal approval of his brother's intention to marry their cousin Isabel, George was forging ahead with the necessary preparations; he had applied to Rome for papal dispensation on account of the two of them being kin.

Warwick and Clarence had intended to move south after the Feast of Epiphany but the weather had taken a turn for the worse and now they had become imprisoned by the elements, the roads out of the village impassable. This was naturally a welcome turn of events for the countess, who saw little of her peripatetic husband, and also for her eldest daughter, eager to pursue a courtship with the Duke of Clarence.

Situated in the north-east corner of the great hall was the oratory, a small private chapel for the use of the earl and his family, and in addition to this Middleham Castle had a larger, more corporate place of worship. This, being situated on the upper floor of a three-storey building attached to the east wall of the keep, was entered from the antechamber at the top of the stairs to the keep. This larger chapel was for the benefit of both the earl and his household, although many of the servants preferred to make the journey to Saint Mary and Saint Alkelda's in the village to observe the more important feast days and celebrations.

Within this larger chapel there was an elaborately painted wooden rood screen and mounted above was the imposing statue of the Christ crucified looking down on all. There was also a finely carved altar chest containing the silver plate. The earl and his family sat in the upper part of the chapel while the servants stood in the lower area.

One particular Sunday morning not long after Epiphany a bitterly cold wind howling outside blew into the chapel from beneath the windows set into the north walls. Christiana shivered under her woollen cloak as she attempted to listen to the words of the chaplain as he recited the Latin Mass in his pious monotone, to the accompanying drone of the whistling wind.

An ethereal white glow filled the inside of the chapel, a reflection from the deep snow drifts covering the broad sweep of Wensleydale, and illuminated the small congregation.

Seated nearest the altar were the earl and his wife looking comfortably solemn in their heavy fur-lined mantles. Behind their parents sat Isabel and Anne, young ladies of sixteen and eleven years, elegantly wrapped in rich sable.

Occupying the same bench as their cousins were the Dukes of Clarence and Gloucester together with young Francis Lovell, all looking princely in their cloaks lined with miniver and black velvet berets.

Behind the family stood the servants of note; ladies-in-waiting upon the countess and her daughters, Conyers and the constable and various clerics holding office under Warwick to name but a few. The lesser servants huddled at the back included the herbalist and her young assistant; the earl had opened his chapel on this occasion to servants whose journey into the village was hindered by the snowfall.

After a while Christiana gave up trying to follow the words of the chaplain so instead she focused her attention on the family at the front of the chapel. George sat close to his cousin Isabel, so close that the arm he passed surreptitiously beneath her cloak went unnoticed by most of the congregation. A barely concealed titter from the lady brought a sharp look of reproof from her mother.

This act of censorship did nothing to dampen the ardour of the eighteen-year-old duke, however, with much wriggling and shifting along the wood, continuing even during the distribution of the Sacrament, to the obvious embarrassment of the priest. This unseemly and rude behaviour had not escaped the attention of Clarence's younger brother and several times Christiana was made aware of Richard's disgust by the nudges and pokes he gave his elder brother.

Mass concluded and the congregation proceeded to file slowly out of the chapel, emerging in the antechamber and so on down the outer staircase. Martha and Christiana were amongst the last to leave the chapel and upon entering the antechamber they caught the sound of raised voices through the open door to the great hall. George was shouting in a tone of mockery and condescension, "Brother, you are so strait-laced and far too pious. Methinks you should take Holy Orders."

They heard Richard's voice, raised in anger, reply, "It is disrespectful to behave like that in the presence of God. You bring dishonour to the Lady Isabel in front of Warwick's household and servants."

"A pox on the servants," George retaliated. "And as for the fair lady, she was enjoying the attention. Wait 'til you are a man, little brother, then you might enjoy the company of a woman. Should you be up to it, of course," he sniggered.

George's remarks fired anger in Christiana's heart. The lighter-haired and undoubtedly good-looking Duke of Clarence, although not as tall as their brother, the king, certainly towered over the Duke of Gloucester. Living as she did amongst soldiers, who were notoriously vulgar, Christiana at fourteen years of age was beginning to understand the lure of carnal temptation that led to sin. However, the inference of George's words was unprovoked and utterly unjust. Furthermore, Richard was given no chance to defend himself for at that moment they heard Warwick's voice ordering Clarence into the great chamber for private counsel.

Within the antechamber the usher had looked up from his desk with quill poised over his parchment as he listened intently to the heated discussion between the brothers. Martha, seeing how pale and thin the young man looked, demanded that she take a look at his arm.

"You really must see that this arm is treated, Godwin," Martha chided as she examined the rash. Seeing how the herbalist was at once preoccupied, Christiana took the opportunity to sidle unnoticed into the great hall.

She found Richard standing in the shadows, his back against the wall. Softly she approached in the gloomy silence. His dark eyes held the glint of angry tears as she searched his face and despite the thick fur lining of his cloak she could sense that he was cold, shivering even. Christiana stood near to him and enclosed her warm hand around his slender fingers, icy to the touch, and pressed them gently as a tear fell slowly down his cheek. The girl felt no need for words and let the moments pass in companionable silence.

Richard shifted his weight from one foot to the other and drew his shoulders away from the wall with a pained grimace on his face.

"Is all well, Richard?" Christiana asked after a while.

"Aye, 'tis but the cold, nothing more," he replied with a faint smile. "I have pressing matters to attend to; you may be about your duties." Before he left her Richard drew her fingers to his lips and left the faintest impression of a kiss.

Stepping out into the courtyard a whirlwind of snow fell upon her in a frenzy of cold white flakes. Bending her head and drawing her cloak tightly about her she made haste towards the covered arch of the gatehouse spanning the bridge. The courtyard was deserted but for one figure hunched up in the shelter of the thick stone walls. As she passed under the arch she could see the man, a soldier of the garrison, pissing onto the virgin snow banked up under the wall. Nothing unusual in that, she thought and moved on.

The man turned then and Christiana gave a start as she recognised him as Ralph Hodkin. She quickened her pace to reach the far side of the archway but Ralph was quicker. Like lightning he had her arm in a tight grip and pulled her roughly towards him. Her breath came in audible gasps and her heart raced as he pinned her against the jagged stone wall.

"Where are you going in such a hurry, wench?" His face moved close to hers, his cheeks were flushed and his eyes bloodshot. She could smell the odour of ale, sharp and stale, on his hot breath. "I need a wench to keep me warm in this foul weather," he hissed.

She stood in fear and trepidation, trembling like a rabbit before the fox, too numb to move. A wave of terror swept over her as the man held her down by the shoulder with one hand and forced the other under her cloak and into the bodice of her kirtle. His icy fingers enclosed over her small breasts and he squeezed hard. He pushed his face closer to hers in an attempt to match his thick drooling lips to hers, the rough unshaven bristles along his jaw grazing her cheeks.

"Bah, you've naught here of any use to me – you're still a bairn. Another few years and you'll be a comely enough wench though," he sniggered, giving her breast another sharp prod.

It was with immense relief that Christiana could see the portly figure of Martha just visible in the swirling flakes coming from the direction of the kitchen, picking her way precariously through the snow. She had her head down against the wind and did not at first notice the two figures under the gatehouse. Ralph had also picked up movement and like a disturbed rat in a kitchen he scurried back through the arch and across the courtyard to lose himself in the shadow of the stone walls.

"You still here?" Martha was quite startled to see her young assistant standing under the gatehouse as she passed through. "I thought you would be back at the herbarium by now – why do you tarry in the cold?"

Christiana said nothing and pulled the hood of her cloak over her head to hide the hot tears that were stinging her cheeks.

The girl was thankful to link arms with the older woman as they proceeded with caution along the slippery road. She needed the reassurance of Martha's presence after her encounter with

Ralph as much if not more than a steadying hand against the icy path underfoot.

"Who was that you were speaking to just now under the gatehouse?" Martha asked casually. "The guard? 'Tis a thankless task standing guard in this weather," Martha continued to herself.

They had reached the wicker gate and Martha fumbled with the frozen latch. Once inside the warmth and shelter of the herbarium Martha removed her heavy cloak and shook off the cold balls of snow that had clung to it.

"Godwin's arm is healing at last, though slowly. I thank God it seems nothing too serious."

Christiana nodded. She was still thinking about how Ralph had touched her body. He had done the same to Clem's mother – and she remembered poor Eadgyth in the village. Were all men like that, she wondered? She knew little of men in general but she felt certain that her father would not behave in such a way towards a woman. Since her mother's death she was convinced her father had not so much as looked at another woman.

"Here you are, Christiana, something to warm you." Martha was standing over her, holding out a cup of hot fruit wine. "Are you not well? You look flushed." Martha's wise twinkling eyes searched her face.

Christiana forced a smile. "Yes I am well enough, just cold and wet."

"Well this snow is here for a good while yet. Let us hope that our supplies are enough to see us through to the thaw." Martha sat her heavy bulk down on the stool next to the girl.

Christiana sat before the glowing woodstove with fingers tightly wrapped around the warm cup. After a while Martha spoke. "I know how you feel about the Duke of Gloucester," she began, thinking Christiana's sullen mood to be due to her preoccupation with the young prince.

Christiana shifted uncomfortably on her stool and set down her cup of wine untouched. She was aware of the pool of tears that were forming in her eyes and lowered her head. Martha moved her stool a little closer to the girl. "You are a young woman now and bound to have all sorts of passions and emotions, most of which are just a passing phase."

Christiana sat silently regarding her fingers as Martha went on. "Duke Richard will grow to manhood and is certain to wed a fair lady of noble birth." The warm salt tears spilled over Christiana's eyelids and down her cheeks.

"He will like as not leave Middleham one day soon and never return. You cannot have him and to think otherwise will cause you much pain and a wasted life. He will not look upon you as any more than a wench with whom to satisfy his desires. 'Tis the way of noblemen," Martha continued.

More tears cascaded silently down the girl's face until the herbalist could bear it no longer. Reaching out she took Christiana in her arms and held her close, muttering, "My poor child, my poor child," as the young girl wept copiously, her mind a whirlpool of emotion.

Middleham Castle
Yorkshire
Lent 1468

"I fear I shall die of a surfeit of fish," Martha exclaimed, shuddering. They were returning from the servants' hall in the bailey where every remove had fish in one form or another: salted, dried, pickled. "I must be certain to have a plentiful supply of dill sent to the kitchens; maybe that will help a little."

"'Tis but a short time to remember our Lord Jesu's time in the wilderness and His Passion, Martha, and then we can celebrate Eastertide and the glorious resurrection," Christiana announced as they neared the cottage.

"Aye, well, that is as maybe; there is still work to be done. We must tend to the tansy for they will be wanting their pudding up at the keep come Eastertide."

"Is the earl at Middleham for Easter?" Christiana enquired.

"Nothing is certain where the earl is concerned," Martha replied, stooping to gather some fresh dill from the herb garden. "He may well move south to his castle there or is more likely to be tailing the king. The Duke of Gloucester, I believe, will be away after Easter as he is to accompany his sister, Margaret, on her wedding journey."

So it began, Christiana mused; Richard would be spending much of his time away from Middleham as summoned by the earl or the king.

Martha had decided that day to do an inventory of all her herbal remedies. There were jars, flasks and bowls all over the table spilling onto the floor of the cottage. She needed no record for everything she made she kept a note of in her head. Her assistant, however, made use of the knowledge she had gained whilst at the monastery of Jervaulx and had begun to make labels and keep a small ledger, much to Martha's amusement.

"We had more than this, I am certain," Christiana frowned as she turned the bottles on the table. Martha was sweeping the floor with a birch twig besom and paid no attention to the girl.

Christiana turned to her ledger and there it was: three clay bottles of powdered alum and now there were two. Maybe one had broken, she considered. Two jars of dried hyssop had also disappeared, along with a jar of juice of the waybread.

Sometime later Martha laid aside her besom and sat heavily upon a stool.

"Someone had better run up to the kitchen with that dill while there is time enough to flavour our fish on the morrow." Martha indicated the dill beginning to wilt in its basket on the floor. "And take up some of that dried parsley while you are about it," she finished with a wearisome yawn.

Christiana was more than glad to be relieved of her cleaning chores and a chance to encounter the duke up at the keep, however remote, was always a welcome distraction.

The sun was pleasantly warm on her head as she walked along the road towards the inner bailey. The only sound to be heard was the chitter-chatter of birdsong in the air; games and frivolities were forbidden during Lent and only essential work could be done. Christiana smiled at the thought that Martha considered cleaning the cottage to be essential work.

It was quiet in the kitchens. The spit boy was scrubbing the large drip tray in readiness for use once its forty days of idleness had passed. Several boys were chopping the onion, swede and parsnip for a pottage, with hardly a word exchanged. Christiana emptied her basket of dill and jar of parsley onto the end of a large table. As she was about to leave the kitchens her sharp eye caught sight of a well-dressed figure hesitating at the foot of the stairwell. Ever inquisitive Christiana moved forward and recognising the boyish figure of Francis, Lord Lovell, she smiled and curtsied. The boy, however, did not enter the kitchen but instead pulled the girl by the arm closer to the recess and so out of view of those in the kitchen. His face wore an anxious frown.

"Are you not well, Lord Lovell?" Christiana asked at once. "Are you looking for someone, something?"

"Aye, milk, mayhap," Francis answered uncertainly.

"You will not find any milk, Francis, for 'tis Lent," Christiana whispered, somewhat perplexed. "Unless 'tis almond milk you seek?" the girl offered, but she received no reply.

Francis turned to retrace his steps back up the stairs, hesitated, and eyes searching the girl's face seemingly for an answer, he spoke. "Christiana, will you come to Richard? I do not know..." He got no further in his pleading for Christiana was at his side like a limpet as they climbed the stairs.

It took several moments to reach the duke's chamber for Francis employed much stealth to avoid detection. Pulling aside the heavy tapestry separating the chamber from the stone passage they found Richard sitting on a wooden chest with arms hard pressed across his stomach, his face pale and beaded with sweat. Crossing the room to him Christiana noted the large empty bowl at his side. She looked at Francis for explanation. For answer the boy took up the small vial reposing on the bed nearby and handed it to the girl. She could see a small heap of crystal powder on the coverlet where its contents had spilled and there also was a horn spoon sticky with honey from a clay pot.

"It is alum," Francis offered.

It was indeed and now she had the measure of why they were missing a jar from the herbarium. She knew it could be used as an emetic but there her knowledge ended.

"Lent is a time to purge and cleanse the body of its sin," Francis spoke with trembling voice.

"We should send for Martha," Christiana announced, afraid that the duke had done himself some harm.

At once Francis was gone, leaving them alone. The girl knew not how she should proceed; the second time she was left alone to give succour to the prince. She merely sat and watched the troubled expression on the duke's face and waited.

"I have sent a trusted servant to the cottage," Francis informed her on his return to the chamber.

"How much alum has he taken?" Christiana asked.

It was Richard who answered, "One spoon with honey." He

took up the bowl and leaned over it expectantly but produced nothing more than fruitless retching.

It seemed like an age of waiting, the three of them in silence, before the rotund figure of the herbalist appeared from beyond the tapestry. At once Martha had the matter in her control, asking questions, placing a chubby hand upon the duke's stomach and feeling his clammy brow.

"Alum is a fine emetic but slow to act," Martha declared. "Take another spoonful and be done with it as is your intent, but no more, you understand me, young lord?" She took up the vial of alum and mixed a good spoonful of the powder with a little honey and gave it to Richard. "There, now we wait. I will go find the countess and inform her."

"Please do not," Richard pleaded, rubbing his stomach.

"The earl and countess are with their guests and I should be in attendance," Francis stated nervously.

"Then you must be about your duties as I to mine." Martha offered a leather costrel to Christiana. "When the vomiting ceases you are to give him this – 'tis an infusion of dill, peppermint and ginger. Return at once to the herbarium when the duke is well, at *once*." Martha glared at the girl and turned to leave the room but having a few more snippets of wisdom for the young duke she tarried.

"The biting stonecrop taken in wine is more effective, my lord, and maybe next time you have the need you will come to the herbarium." Having given her instruction she left the room, Francis Lovell hard on her heels.

The second dose of alum had the desired effect and it was not long before the duke, with head low over the bowl, was vomiting copiously. With one hand Christiana held the bowl and the other she placed gently upon his shoulder.

When at last Richard lifted his head with breathless gasps she removed the bowl and wiped his face with her apron. She would wait awhile before giving the calming infusion.

"Shall I assist you to the bed?" she asked.

Nodding silently Richard stood and walked to the bed where

a soft pile of embroidered cushions and bolsters were spread. He sat back against the cushions and closed his eyes. What should she do? She wanted to be close to him – she always wanted to be close to him. In the silence she could hear no sound; no one moved about on this side of the castle. She took up the costrel of herbs from the floor where she had placed it, removed the stopper and taking Richard's fingers she wrapped them around the vessel. "Richard, you must take this, it will soothe your stomach." Her words were gentle, encouraging.

As the duke sipped at the infusion Christiana sat alongside him on the bed and waited. Beside the duke and partially covered by the cushions she noticed an open book. The lettering was precise and bold; the illuminations, though faded, were skilfully painted in hues of red and gold and blue. She reached out a hand and pulled it closer. The duke showed no objection. The words were not Latin as she would have expected. Richard, having taken all the infusion, had laid aside the costrel and now sat watching her.

"It is a Bible," he whispered. "Translated from the Latin into English by John Wycliffe." Richard spoke as though it was the Holy Grail they had before them.

"'Tis a most beautiful thing," the girl conceded. She knew this duke, as young as he was, to be known for his piety.

"And rare, and frowned upon by the Church," he continued with a faint smile.

Christiana recalled Francis's words earlier about Lent being the time to purge and cleanse the body of sin.

"What sin do you have, Richard, that would require cleansing?" It was a bold question to ask of a prince.

Richard's eyes darkened and his countenance gave no secrets away. Christiana, remembering Martha's words, bowed her head, about to stand. "I will take my leave of you now, my lord, if it pleases you."

Richard, however, had put out his hand and held her arm to prevent her leaving.

"Sit down," he said gently. The girl obeyed. The young duke then did something that caused the girl to tremble, a little afraid.

He took up the edges of his shirt and lifted it up over his head. He said nothing more but turned slowly away from her to face the wooden carvings of the bed board.

In the weak light of the chamber she could see at once that Richard's backbone was not straight but rather it curved away slightly to the right before straightening again at his neck; somewhat like the curved blade of a sickle but not so pronounced.

Christiana stared in wondrous silence for never had she seen such a thing before. She reached out her finger and very gently traced the pathway of his curve. At once she felt his body tense beneath her touch. He turned then to face her, anguish in his dark eyes. "This is my sin," he muttered painfully.

The girl could bear it no longer and reached out to enfold him in her arms. She felt the warmth of his chest against her bodice and trembled. "None but Francis know of this," he said, his voice a gentle whisper in her ear. "I have Francis look..." His voice quivered like a bow string. "It is getting worse."

Christiana held him closer and let her tears fall gently onto his bare skin. After a while he eased her away and took up his shirt. The girl remembered then a conversation she had had only last year with a man of God and tentatively she voiced her thoughts. "Are you certain this is the mark of sin, Richard?" she began. "I have asked Rector Beverley about this and something like this can also be seen as God's favour, one with Christ's suffering."

The duke paused with his shirt held in his hand and stared into the face of the girl. Their eyes locked and held the gaze, a puzzled frown upon the young man's brow.

"I too have conversed with Rector Beverley," Richard answered after a while. "I cannot say I know for certain... Francis says it is the mark of the Reaper who gathers souls for hell." Richard hung his head sadly.

Christiana pressed her hand on the duke's arm. "Richard, do not speak thus for 'tis false." Christiana's words were earnest, solemn. "You have the mark of God's grace and favour, do not doubt it," she continued.

"Do you truly believe that?" Richard lifted his head and his deep blue eyes sought an answer from the depth of her soul.

"With all my heart," she replied.

"You must return to the herbarium," Richard whispered urgently as they heard footsteps approaching along the stone passageway beyond the drapes.

She stood and walked towards the exit. As she parted the tapestry she heard Richard's voice, barely audible: "Pray to the Holy Mother for me, Christiana."

"Always," was her reply before disappearing stealthily into the shadows, the disembodied footsteps echoing in the distance.

Middleham Castle
Yorkshire
Summer 1468

The two women had laboured all morning under the heat of the brilliant July sunshine, raking weeds from the herb beds and watering the young shoots. It was quiet around the castle this summer as the earl was about his business and had taken all his family with him, Duke Richard included, and there was little relief from the monotony of work.

Martha stood up slowly, pressing her fingers into the small of her back to ease the pain. "My, 'tis warm today!" she exclaimed, looking up into the sky. "Methinks it is high time for bread and ale. Come on."

The old woman's portly hips waddled as she walked along the gravel path towards the herbarium. "There is still a wedge of cheese from Jervaulx in my stone jar. We can have that too," she announced to the girl who walked obediently behind her carrying two small metal hoes.

It was only slightly cooler inside the cottage where they sat and ate their mid-morning meal.

"This afternoon I need to make up some more oil of lavender. Oh aye, and a goodly measure of yellow loosestrife, for some of the masons up at the castle have come down with the flux. 'Tis the unusual heat I should say. Godwin's skin rash has flared up again. Now I know I made up a salve of marshmallow and comfrey last week to try on that."

Martha put down her horn cup and looked enquiringly at her young companion.

"Is all well, Christiana? You have uttered scarcely a word all morning."

The young woman pushed back the dark locks from where they had fallen across her cheek and smiled wanly. "Aye, I am well," she replied softly.

"The steward spoke to me yesterday about you," Martha announced suddenly. Christiana looked up quickly, her lips rapidly becoming dry.

"Do not look so fearful." Martha laughed. "You are of an age to be considered as a properly paid servant. I left Conyers in no doubt about your abilities as a herbalist and wages are to be negotiated for you. He knows I am not getting any younger and soon there will be a need for my replacement."

Christiana smiled with relief and her rosy cheeks dimpled into a smile. It would appear then that her position was secure with no further consideration to be given to finding her more menial work.

Martha was reaching up onto a high shelf to locate the jar of skin salve and had her back to Christiana when she said, "'Tis time now for your father to consider your future, lass, and start to look for a suitable young man for you to wed. 'Twould put an end to all this daydreaming then."

Christiana felt her face flush scarlet. So, she thought irritably, Martha and Conyers were still conspiring to marry her off. Martha, still fingering the jars on the upper shelf, muttered to herself. "Now where is that darned salve?"

The girl, seeing a chance to avoid any further discussion on the matter jumped down from her stool and over to the shelf, locating the pot immediately, concealed as it was behind a leather costrel.

"I have the salve," she called, moving towards the door. "I will take it up to Godwin."

"Aye, and do not return until you have tended that arm. 'Tis through neglect that young man has such a nasty rash."

Christiana was all but through the door and on her way when she heard Martha calling out, "Now there is a comely young man in a good position and not yet wed."

The girl quickened her step in keeping with her mounting annoyance at Martha's interference. Her father had never once mentioned marriage to her although maybe he considered the matter best broached by a woman. She doubted that they were also seeking to marry her brother off to some serving wench at the castle; William would be free to make his own choices.

She was still fuming when she arrived hot and breathless at the bridge that spanned the moat. She paused to watch a pair of white swans glide majestically through the water. Such was the paradox of the young woman's mind that she should at that moment begin to focus her thoughts upon the unmarried men that she knew. Who were they? Skinny and foolish lads who took pleasure in throwing stones at the cats in the bailey. The other unmarried men were the soldiers at the garrison, most considerably older than her. There was Ralph Hodkin, for one – her blood ran cold as she recalled his groping fingers and putrid breath.

She waited until an empty cart had rattled over the bridge heading down the long wide road towards the eastern gatehouse before continuing on her way to the keep. The usher was not, as was his custom, stooped over his desk when Christiana entered the antechamber. Instead he was sitting on a bench against the wall nursing his arm, a pained expression upon his face. He attempted a smile as the girl approached with her remedy. A young page, filling inkpots at the desk, left his task and sat beside Godwin looking concerned.

Expecting a degree of resistance Christiana said abruptly, "Martha insists that this salve is applied to your arm – at once."

Godwin said nothing but rolled back the sleeve of his shirt exposing skin red and swollen with blisters. She was taken aback by how angry and sore the arm looked. Taking a piece of lint from her belt pouch she set about gently covering the arm in a coating of the pungent ointment. She worked silently and meticulously, taking care to cover all the affected parts.

After a while she glanced up from her work. Godwin was leaning back against the wall, his eyes closed. She regarded him for a moment or two; his features were certainly not unpleasant to behold, he was not that many years older than her and he did indeed hold a good position at the castle. She recalled Martha's words, but what of marriage? Surely he would be looking for a woman of better standing than herself? Besides, wedlock was all but impossible for her while her heart belonged to another, however improbable a situation that might be.

She was unaware that her hand holding the piece of lint was poised in mid-air until a gentle nudge at her elbow drew her back to the task in hand and a small voice beside her whispered, "You have missed a bit there."

Christiana smiled apologetically at the page and resumed bathing the usher's arm. Godwin had opened his eyes and was looking at her now and smiling. Christiana blushed deeply, embarrassed that she had been assessing this young man's potential as a future husband.

The door to the great hall opened at that moment, a much welcome distraction for Christiana. Francis, Lord Lovell, his tumbling thatch of dark hair obscuring his eyes, stood before them. Godwin was at once on his feet, likewise the page, and all three of them bowed to the young man.

"My Lord Lovell," Godwin said. "Is all well?"

"Very well, usher. Is there news in yet from London?" the boy asked eagerly.

"Indeed there is," Godwin whispered with a smile. "A messenger arrived with news for Conyers this morning. The earl, the countess and the young ladies are expected home very soon. All went well, it would seem, with the departure of the Lady Margaret from London to her new husband, Charles of Burgundy."

"And what of the Duke of Gloucester?" Francis asked eagerly.

"Well, Warwick's letter does commend the duke's diligence in escorting his sister on part of her journey and although not specifically mentioned as returning to Middleham, I am sure that he will arrive with his cousins," Godwin speculated.

This news was most pleasing to Christiana also, who had the greatest desire to see Richard again – and soon.

Middleham Castle
Yorkshire
All Soul's Day
November 2ⁿᵈ 1468

"Are you certain you will not come, Martha?" Christiana persisted as she placed the lighted candles on the ledges of the casements around the cottage.

"Nay, lass, one Mass in the day is enough for me. Besides I have to make the soul cakes." The old herbalist was cleaning the brazier of its globules of oil and dried herbs in readiness for the round flour cakes she would cook slowly and keep aside should any dear departed soul return this eve.

"You do not go alone?" Martha queried.

"Nay, I am to wait for Father and William at the wicker gate; I should not want to meet any witches or goblins on my way to the village." Christiana laughed as she now balanced unsteadily on a stool to hang a bunch of dried wormwood of considerable size from the hook in the middle of the lintel. "There, I should like to see any goblin get past that," she declared, jumping to the floor just as the stool overbalanced.

"Have a care, my girl, or else 'twill be more than goblins you will need to fear," Martha remonstrated. "Now, have you the amulet?" she asked, draping the girl's heavy wool cloak across her shoulders.

Christiana patted the linen pouch stuffed with dried vervain and dill that hung from a thin hemp cord from her belt and smiled.

"And the alms?" Martha continued.

"Not enough to ensure safe passage for all the souls in Purgatory but sufficient for my purpose. Now I must be gone for Father will be waiting."

A light drizzle was falling on the folk making their way solemnly to the church of Saint Mary and Saint Alkelda in the village.

Christiana walked beside her father in silent reverie, William following behind. The girl's thoughts turned from her own mother for whom she would have the Mass to William, who she doubted not would be thinking of his own father killed in battle. Her brother was not overly observant of the many feast days that beset their seasons but the Feast of All Souls was one he had kept since their arrival at Middleham.

The flickering yellow glow of the many candles in the dwellings made a welcome guide to the pathway of those shuffling up the hill to the church from the marketplace. Rector Beverley was awaiting them to lead a candlelit procession around the graves of the departed. Once inside the church there rose a mustiness from the damp wool cloaks of the congregation huddled into the nave that mingled with the heady perfume of burning incense.

Throughout the Mass Christiana stood beside her father and brother making Confession, receiving the Eucharist and dutifully reciting the necessary prayers. She tried to recall memories of her mother but in truth there were not many and those that remained were fading rapidly. She felt her mother's love and saw in her mind the abundance of black curls that tickled her skin whenever her mother held her close. She hoped that she had done enough to secure her mother's passage from the purgatorial state to the joyous glory of heaven.

At the stone cross in the marketplace she joined the servants and retainers of the Earl of Warwick as they trudged through the mud-laden road upwards towards the castle. At a bend in the road Christiana's boot slipped on a patch of mud that had taken many unawares and would have gone the same way downwards were it not for the hand that caught her arm and steadied her.

With trembling heart she beheld the face of her protector shrouded by the hood of his cloak.

"Richard," she whispered. "I was not aware of your presence in the church. I thought you would take the Mass in the castle chapel."

"Then my disguise has worked," returned the duke with a smile. "I have little desire to join my family at present." He said no more but taking the girl's arm he led her up the hill some way behind the now retreating throng.

The last of the servants were dispersing as they walked towards the cluster of buildings that made up the outer bailey of the castle. The rain too had ceased and a silver moon lit the edges of a few scudding clouds. Neither duke nor servant it seemed had any desire to part company and the quiet of the darkened garden beckoned. They huddled together on the bench beneath the bare branches of the white rose, eerily skeletal in the pale moonlight on this eve when witches and goblins walked the earth.

Christiana put her fingers protectively around the herb pouch hanging from her belt and moved closer to her friend. "Why did you not go to Mass in the chapel in the keep?" the girl asked boldly of the duke.

"My Lord Warwick has much bad humour of late and is once again in contention with the king who will not give consent for Cousin Isabel to marry our brother George. There is much discord within the walls and I would sooner have my own company for the feast of All Souls," Richard answered solemnly.

"What of Lord Lovell and Lady Anne; their company is pleasant enough surely?"

"Indeed, Francis is a noble friend and Cousin Anne is always pleasing company but she is Warwick's daughter and a mere child," returned the duke.

"And you, my lord, are ever the man at sixteen years," Christiana teased with a smile.

"For one such as I, childhood is a fleeting moment blown away by the storms of life." Richard's answer was serious, tinged with sadness.

"Have there been many storms in your life?" Christiana asked gently.

The duke sat pensively for a while, the cold wind blowing his hair across his face where his hood had fallen away.

"I have given much thought to my father this day," he answered quietly. "The Duke of York was killed at the Battle of Wakefield along with Edmund his second son, my brother.

"I know my father was a good man and did what was noble and right. My mother always told me how I reminded her of him. I should like to think that were true."

Christiana recalled how it had been for her and her father after that battle and how they had been forced to leave their village. "What happened after Wakefield?" she asked gently.

"We were saved by Edward who was declared king the following March," Richard answered vaguely.

"I remember a time earlier when we were living at Ludlow and after a skirmish at Ludford Bridge Lancastrian troops rode into the town and entered the castle." Richard shivered in the cold and moved his back painfully against the bench.

Christiana reached across and took the duke's cold hand in hers. "What happened?" she encouraged gently.

Richard inhaled deeply of the cold air and exhaled a cloud of vapour into the night. "I still hear her screams...

"There was none to save us; father and my brothers were gone, fled into exile. There was Margaret and George and me with our mother. I had not many days before seen my seventh birthday. Mother gave me a book although I could not yet read." Richard paused and looked down at the gravel path touched with silver in the light of the moon.

Christiana's mind was trying to weave together the incomplete tapestry. She recalled Clem's mother, Jennie, and her story about Ralph Hodkin last summer and then her own encounter with the man earlier this year. In truth she felt she had the measure of it although Richard had not said so in plain words. Whatever had befallen Duchess Cecily at that time had certainly been a violation of sorts witnessed by her three youngest children.

"After the Battle of Northampton Henry was captured and we moved to London. My father returned from exile and mother went to meet him. Edward visited us every day until mother returned," the duke continued.

Richard shifted on the bench then to look directly into the face of the girl beside him; she could see the glint of light in his eyes. "I do not know as yet how far Warwick will go in his quarrel with the king but my father and brother Edmund gave their lives fighting for this realm and Edward has and always will have my loyalty."

It was several moments before the spell was broken and they drew apart and stood to their feet as Ulrick the hound came bounding towards his master with yelps and barks of joy.

With the Duke of Gloucester and his dog disappearing along the dark road towards the keep Christiana was left to face questions back at the cottage.

The girl played down her absence with a smile as Alfred, William and Martha rose from their seats as she entered. It was the herbalist, however, who voiced their concern. "Where have you been, child? Your father has been beside himself with worry; we thought you had been spirited away by goblins or witches."

"'Twas not witchcraft that kept me, Father, but a friend. We were talking in the garden. I have come to no harm – see?" Christiana spread her hands before them and took a few steps across the room to embrace her father.

Alfred, relieved enough that his daughter had returned safe and well, said no more. He accepted her explanation with a nod of his head and approached the door to take his leave. As William followed his father out of the cottage he paused and whispered an aside to his sister: "Was it the sullen blue-eyed duke that you tarried with in the garden?"

Christiana gave no answer but stood in silence as he passed her and out into the darkness beyond the door, her cheeks burning crimson.

Middleham Castle
Yorkshire
January 1469

Christiana had been sent on an errand to the keep. The Countess of Warwick and her daughters were suffering from the winter ague and had requested remedies from the herbarium.

Armed with a concoction of syrups and infusions made with horehound, sage, rosemary, wild garlic and ginger the young girl battled her way through the whirling snow storm that raged through the bailey and entered the covered archway to the outer staircase.

No sooner had Christiana stepped into the antechamber than she was brushed aside by the burly, irate figure of the earl as he flew from the great hall and ran down the great staircase to the outside. The girl was left in the swirl of his wake, only just saving her basket from a spillage. At once Godwin, the usher, was on his feet to offer his support and escorted Christiana through the doorway into the hall.

Once inside it became apparent that she had entered into the aftermath of a family feud. At the far end of the hall near the dais Anne Beauchamp, with cheeks flushed and dabbing her brow with her handkerchief, was urging the young Duke of Gloucester to calm. "Richard, you must not challenge the earl while you are subject to his authority and within these walls."

"I am subject to the king's authority, madam," Richard retaliated.

"You are sixteen years of age, my lord, placed here by the king for your training and improvement. You will show proper respect to my husband."

Christiana, her basket clutched tightly to her chest, watched earnestly as Richard's eyes darkened and his face took on a veil of anger, suppressed only by respect for his patron. Standing in the shadows at the side of the hall were the countess's two daughters, also listening to the altercation between their mother and their cousin.

Richard gave a curt bow to the ladies before turning on his heel and striding across the tiled floor. He paused briefly to catch the eye of the servant girl standing nervously near the doorway and then he was gone. Christiana may have followed the duke just then but for the stern words of the countess echoing across the hall.

"Do you bring the remedies, girl? Then do not tarry, come hither," she called.

Christiana glanced back towards the doorway to make sure the duke had indeed departed and then walked towards the ladies, the jars and bottles jingling loudly in her basket.

The countess walked through the tapestry hanging into the inner chamber, followed by the Ladies Isabel and Anne. Christiana sidled through on their shadows.

"Well, what has Martha sent?" the countess demanded.

Christiana unpacked her basket, showing the horehound syrup and wrapped infusions, sure to be cold as stone by now. She smiled kindly at the young Anne Neville whose sore red eyes and trickling nose told that she was indeed suffering from the winter ague. As the remedies were administered and the infusions warmed on the fire the subject of their earlier conversation resumed.

"I do not see why Cousin Richard should interfere in this matter of my proposed marriage to George," Isabel announced. "It is not as though it concerns him."

"It concerns him because it has put a wedge between your father and the king," her mother answered. "Richard has an unshakable loyalty to the king."

The seventeen-year-old Isabel tossed her fair head. "'Tis not just this, Mother," she offered. "A wedge was put between Father and the king when Edward decided to marry Elizabeth Woodville. George says that Edward risks the stability of the realm by elevating the Woodville clan."

Christiana had finished preparing the herbs and had no further desire to remain in the chamber. She shuffled from foot to foot impatiently.

"Leave us, girl," the countess said harshly, seeming to notice Christiana's presence for the first time. The servant girl wasted no time and bobbing a curtsy departed forthwith.

The snow was still beating mercilessly down onto the bailey as Christiana fought her way back to the cottage, the icy flakes stinging her eyes and cheeks. Flinging open the door into the welcoming warmth she was not at first aware of their visitor. Placing her basket on the bench and divesting herself of her sodden cloak and hanging it on its hook by the door, she then became aware of John Conyers. He was seated at the table partaking of Martha's best ale and marchpane delicacies left over from Christmastide.

Christiana gave the steward a bow and sat down upon a stool a little distance away from the table.

"Was all well up at the castle, child? You took your time," Martha chided.

"Aye, the remedies needed heating again but all is well." The girl sighed wearily.

"Warm yourself a cup of spiced ale on the brazier, you look chilled," Martha said a little more kindly and smiled.

"As I was saying, Martha," Conyers continued with his conversation, "I was at Hornby for Christmastide visiting my son, John. There is a good deal of unrest here in the north. Folk like it not that the earldom of Northumberland has been snatched from the Percys."

"Was not Henry Percy killed at Towton?" Martha asked, refilling Conyers' cup.

"Aye, but he has a son and heir languishing in the White Tower in London."

The old herbalist nodded her head, remembering now that she had come by this piece of information. "Well I suppose it was too much to expect that young King Edward's reign would remain peaceful for long."

"I think Edward's reign would be, shall we say, less of a challenge if he did not give precedence to the queen's kith and kin over the noble lords of the land."

Christiana, sitting quietly and sipping her hot ale and listening to this conversation, realised that it endorsed the one she had heard earlier at the keep. Surely Edward had been king long enough now to sort out a few minor problems caused by his wife, she thought wearily, and wished just then that she had the table close enough on which to rest her head. All of this family squabbling seemed to the young girl no different from any other, except the nobility were less vulgar in their altercations than the common folk, whose arguments oft-times ended in a good wife beating, many of which she had witnessed in the village. It would not be long, she surmised, before Edward was reconciled to his kin; they were of the same blood when all was said and done.

In this, however, the young woman could not have been more wrong.

Middleham Castle
Yorkshire
May 1469

"Martha?"

The old herbalist looked up, squinting in the sunlight. "Yes, child."

Christiana swallowed nervously. "The comfrey should be in flower about now... up on the marsh... should I take a pannier and go see?"

Martha slowly straightened up her portly figure from over the herb beds where she had been picking out weeds. She regarded her young assistant with a raised eyebrow.

"'Tis but the first week of May; there will barely be leaves out yet, let alone flowers ripe for plucking."

Christiana lowered her head. "There may be enough for us to use – we are in need of poultices. The leaves then at least...?" Her voice trailed off as Martha, her hands resting on her hips, stood looking at her with a wry smile on her wizened face.

"Think you that I did not see the Duke of Gloucester leaving the bailey not an hour since with a fine raptor tethered to his arm?"

The young girl blushed painfully. In an effort to redeem herself from her feeling of guilt she said quickly, "The duke will be flying his bird down along the riverside, Martha, whereas I shall be up on the marshland picking comfrey."

Martha's brow puckered and she sighed deeply. "What am I to do with you, girl?" she lamented.

Seeing how she was on the verge of winning this battle, Christiana grinned and said boldly, "Someone has to go pick the herbs and you cannot, dearest Martha, can you?"

"Get along with you, cheeky lass." Martha laughed, waving her away.

Christiana rummaged under the benches in the cottage for a

flat-bottomed pannier before setting off down the road on her way to the marsh that lay betwixt the wood and the river beyond the confines of the castle walls.

With the blossoming and ripening of maidenhood the young sixteen-year-old girl had become aware of the intense physical attraction she bore for the Duke of Gloucester. Their friendship kindled as children had flamed into something more dangerous, more forbidden, and the poor girl seemed powerless to control it.

If these feelings had been confined within her breast alone maybe she could have tamed them, given no fuel with which to fan the flame. But they were not hers alone; indeed she felt certain they were not.

The memory of the May Day Feast was so vivid it swam in her head like the giddy perfume of the May blossom. They had all gathered on the grass in the bailey around the mulberry tree which had been garlanded with sprigs and wreaths in abundance. Trestle tables groaned under the weight of pastries, pies, frumenty and marchpane Jack in the Greens. Bells and pipes rang out under the warm May sunshine as everyone danced in frivolous abandon amidst a shower of blossom and greenery; all that is, with the exception of the Duke of Gloucester. That young man could barely breathe without the permission of the Countess of Warwick. The lady guarded him closer than his own dog. Any attempt to so much as walk in Christiana's direction would be countered by polite but firm resistance.

It seemed that the Lady Anne, now a young woman of almost thirteen years, was also under orders to trail her cousin for she was hardly more than a foot from his side for most of the afternoon; a task not wholly disagreeable by the radiant smile on her face.

Inevitably the duke did manage to give his guards the slip, albeit briefly; a moment long enough to convey to Christiana all she needed or hoped to know. The opportunity was found during a particularly boisterous dance known as a farandole, one deemed altogether undesirable for ladies of noble birth, the countess forbidding her daughters to participate. Joining hands in a long line the dancers performed a follow my leader act to music, dipping and twirling, twisting and turning to the whim of the leader, in this instant John Conyers after a skinful of wine.

More by design than chance Christiana found herself hard pressed against Richard in the medley. Forsaking his partners on either side he at once wrapped his arms tightly around the girl and held her close. In that fleeting moment one look into his eyes and she knew his mind, the passion of his desire she felt in his loins. It was over as fleetingly as a snowflake melts in the hand but it was enough.

And now on this fine May morning her musings had led her to the riverside. She turned to walk up across the marsh; a treacherous place in the winter, but now a boggy damp stretch of open land clogged and choked with clumps of reed, sedge and yellow iris. In the silence she could hear the little reed buntings twittering from stalk to stalk.

Growing in abundance at her feet were the hairy leaves of the comfrey, and as Martha had foreseen only a few of the plants were as yet just in bud, showing promise of the pink bell-shaped flowers to come. She bent down and very gently began to lift a few of the plants out of the wet soil, taking care not to damage the fragile roots.

She moved around the marsh to make her selection over a wider area and as she did so a flicker of movement in the sky overhead caught her eye. She straightened up and peered into the blue. The arrow-shaped profile of a bird could be seen high above gliding gracefully on silent wings. As it soared nearer she could see that its underside was streaked brown and buff. Suddenly the bird folded its wings and went into a spectacular near vertical dive; seconds later it had an unsuspecting wood pigeon in the grip of its strong claws. The raptor was Richard's peregrine falcon and Christiana watched as it descended into the scrub with its prey.

Some way below her the River Ure sparkled like a silver snake in the sunlight. Along its grassy banks the lone figure of a man walked. Presently he entered the undergrowth where the bird had come down and moments later emerged clutching the plump limp body of the pigeon, the falcon hooded and tethered upon his gloved arm.

The sun warmed her and a gentle breeze wafting the sweet smell of the grasses through the air ruffled her gown. She stood watching the young man, little more than a boy of not yet seventeen years, and a silent battle raged in her breast. He had none of the charm and charisma so evident, it was reputed, in his two older brothers, and to him, she may never be anything other than a childhood companion or a common wench available for his pleasure, but Richard possessed an inexplicable fascination that drew her to him like a moth to a candle.

Presently, another youth could be seen walking beside the river towards the duke. A floppy-eared black and white spaniel, with nose to the ground and tail high in the air, trailed behind him. Christiana had not been aware that Francis Lovell had accompanied Richard on the hunt but she should not have been surprised for these two had bonded like brothers.

High up on the marsh the girl held her breath. What would the duke do? He could continue on his way along the riverbank with his companion and soon be out of sight or he could cross the marsh to where he could surely see she was waiting. He looked up and stared in her direction for a moment or two before handing his falcon and a bag containing the quarry to Francis. Richard waited until the boy, his dog and the peregrine had turned a bend in the riverbank and disappeared from view before climbing the gentle path across the marsh. Within minutes he had reached her.

The wind caught his hair turning it a rich tawny in the sunlight. A faint dark shadow of beard growth ran along his well-defined jawbone, a feature of maturing manhood that did not go unnoticed by the young girl standing before him as she lowered her gaze, blushing prettily.

"You should not be out here alone," he said smiling.

"Oh I am safe enough," she replied confidently. He raised an eyebrow to question the surety of her statement.

"Footpads and lawless men wander the roads, my lord, on the

lookout for lone travellers," she explained. "They have no purpose in walking the marshes."

Richard laughed at her childlike reasoning.

"And you, Christiana, do you have a purpose in walking the marshes?"

The girl blushed and quickly held out her basket with its few wilting plants. "I am about my work, my lord, – see, I am picking comfrey for the herbalist."

"Ah I see," Richard replied, still smiling.

"You are teasing me," she said, a little vexed.

"No, indeed," he laughed. "Let me take your basket, it looks heavy. We will walk up here." He snatched the pannier and indicated the line of trees fringing the wood on the higher ground.

"I saw your bird take its prey," Christiana panted as she struggled to keep up with the duke, who despite his lean frame was by no means feeble and was climbing the hillside way ahead of the girl.

"Yes, she is a fine bird," Richard called behind his shoulder. "I hope Francis returns her safely to the mews.

"And you will have to move faster than that if you want your comfrey back," he provoked her, holding the basket high above his head.

She came up breathing hard, her dark hair blowing recklessly in the breeze, her coif having been snatched from her head by a bramble as she climbed. Heedless of her attire she had almost reached striking distance when Richard turned and ran towards the trees that edged the open grassland. When she finally reached him he was sitting with his back against the trunk of an old willow, laughing at her.

"Sir, you lead me a merry dance. The comfrey is mine for I have picked it, if you please," Christiana said, trying to sound indignant but laughing despite herself. She flung herself down on the grass beside him and made to snatch her basket which he held at arm's length above his head. Her hand missed its mark but caught instead the duke's arm which in turn upturned the pannier, showering him with the comfrey.

They laughed as she leant close, picking the sprigs from his hair and tunic. She was so close to him that she could see her own reflection in the sparkle of his eyes; like sunlight on a meadow of cornflowers. She felt his warm breath, fragranced with honey and cinnamon, on her face. Her whole body quivered with desire for him and she found that she could not, nay, would not move away. The laughter died on his lips and he made no attempt to remove himself from her side either, as should have been only right and proper for she was a common maiden of fifteen years and he a duke of the blood royal.

It was as if by mutual consent that they each drew closer still to the other and when Christiana felt the first touch of his lips on hers, as warm as honeyed mead, a ripple of tingles shuddered down her spine. His second kiss was firmer as he pressed himself against her and she could feel the rapid thumping of his heart next to her breast.

What followed was foreseen; they had been thus close before but now the time was ripe for surrender. When his fingers sought the hem of her gown and raised it she did nothing to prevent him. With the unsure, trembling hands of youth he touched her secret places, lovingly, tenderly. There on the soft cool grass she gave her maidenhead to him willingly, with a sharp tremor of pain that fired within her a deeper desire for him. His hair gently brushed her cheek as he moved inside her. She closed her eyes and let her own body be roused and intoxicated by his until with an eruption of ecstasy she knew his seed had flowed within her.

They lay coupled beneath the dappled leaves of the wispy willow until their breathing had slowed to a gentle rhythm. When they had drawn apart he held her still in his arms and caressed her cheek with a sprig of comfrey blossom. Looking up at him she thought that she had never seen any man more beautiful and knew that she could never, ever love or desire a man more than she did Richard at that moment even though a chasm as wide as the sea separated them and she could only confess her love to the fleecy white clouds drifting aimlessly in the blue sky overhead.

Christiana had much difficulty setting her mind to her work over the following few days. She would pause frequently in her tending, drying or pounding of herbs to relive the moments she had spent with Richard up on the marsh. She cherished the memory of the warmth of his body against hers, which would leave her skin tingling with goose bumps. She would often catch Martha staring silently at her from a distance, a questioning frown creasing her brow, but the girl was giving nothing away.

It was a week or two later, one sunny afternoon, and the young girl was still mooning around in a daydream. She was returning from the dairy at the far side of the bailey where she had taken a skin balm to the cowman. A few days ago a skittish cow had kicked the old man, tearing the skin on his shinbone. He had continued stoically with his work but Martha had made sure he had his wound tended to daily.

With her eyes downcast, following her booted feet peeking periodically from under the hem of her kirtle as she walked, her thoughts were once again with the gallant young squire who had won her heart.

She had not set eyes upon the duke since that fateful day and Christiana began to grow concerned as the days drifted by. Could it be that he was angry with her? Would their sexual intimacy change the hitherto nature of their friendship? Was it enhanced, or maybe spoiled forever?

Without realizing it her footsteps had led her not back to the herbarium but to the smithy. Looking up she was startled out of her daydream by an awareness of her surroundings. Her feet had come to rest a short distance from the open front of the smithy and here she stood watching the scene before her.

Alfred had his head bent low over the forge as he fashioned a bar of iron, flattening and shaping it skilfully against the anvil. Christiana could feel the intense heat from where she stood in the brilliant sunshine. Her father's face glowed red as beads of sweat poured down his cheeks and soaked into his smoke-blackened shirt. Away to the side, some distance from the fire, stood Jude holding the halter of a grey destrier. How the boy had grown since first she came to Middleham some eight years past; no longer a bandy-legged sapling of a lad, Jude was tall and broad with strength enough for two.

Christiana gazed at the horse, standing docile and calm, a few flies buzzing around its half-closed eyelids, and she wondered at the courage of these steeds who carried their masters into the conflict and mayhem that was the battlefield. She smiled wryly; for certain they were not all this placid, they had known a few wild and dangerous beasts.

Her brother, William, stood alongside the horse's rear flank and with head bowed he grasped the fetlock, picking up the hoof and holding it steady in his strong hands. When Alfred was ready he carried over the shoe tightly held in tongs and placed it down on the upturned hoof where it fizzed and sizzled, sending a puff of smoke skywards. Once measured, Alfred returned the shoe to the anvil for its final shaping before it cooled. Christiana continued to watch her father as he clasped the horse's strong leg skilfully between his knees and tapped six nails into the cooled shoe, now aligned neatly on the hoof, three on either side, and hammered a caulkin to each point. William took over then, and gripping the horse's leg between his knees he began to file and smooth the cracks on the horny hoof.

Christiana had watched the craft of shoeing horses for most of her childhood and there were still times since she had been living with Martha and her herbs when she missed the raw masculinity of the blacksmith and his work. As Jude led the big grey away to check the shoe Alfred straightened his back and turning, saw his daughter for the first time. A beaming smile lit up his scarlet face. Christiana seemed to notice what had not been apparent to her before and the smile she returned to her father was tinged with sadness. The thick black curls that had once adorned his head were thinning and sprinkled with silver and his face etched with lines. How could it be that she had failed to notice that her beloved father was growing old? She had given little thought to the passing of time that had brought into being her blossoming to womanhood and would even now be beckoning Alfred ever closer to his maker;

'twas the wheel of life that carried on its spokes all living things. She felt somewhat disconcerted as to why she should be thinking about such matters, her humour of a sudden very fragile.

William caught sight of her then and came out into the yard. His cheeks were flushed and his shirt clung in damp patches to his body.

"Anna!" he called.

He was growing fast too. At sixteen years he stood almost as tall as Alfred. Christiana watched him as he scooped cold water from the rain butt over his hot face.

"Are you well, Anna?" he asked, concerned. "You look pale."

She stared into his face and held the gaze of his brown eyes for a moment as the water dripped from his chin onto his shirt.

"Yes, William, I am well," she replied with a half-curved smile. "'Tis only the heat."

Without lingering further she turned slowly and walked away, drying the stray tear that had trickled down her cheek with a finger.

Middleham Castle
Yorkshire
Late spring 1469

The longer, warmer days drifted along and by the end of May the bailey had begun to bake hard and dusty under the warm sun. The heat was beginning to make Christiana unusually tired and lethargic; so much so that one particular morning she found herself at a loss within the garden.

She had spent the first few hours since daybreak picking the flowers and leaves of the herbs growing in their beds outside the cottage. That task completed she had strolled aimlessly along the pathways looking at the flowers; clusters of purple loosestrife, woodbine and meadowsweet. She paused for several moments to watch the antics of a honeybee over the sweetly fragrant lavender.

She still had not set eyes upon Richard since that day in early May but thoughts of him drove her to distraction. It troubled her much that the young duke had found no way to slip from the castle to meet her. She herself had had no recent cause to make any visits up there; it would appear that all the residents were presently in good health.

She knew Martha was watching her from the doorway to the cottage. Dearest Martha, what a blessing the old woman had been to her, but at times her almost bewitching way of seeming to know all the thoughts inside her head unnerved her. Christiana moved away from the garden and Martha's scrutiny and let her footsteps lead her to the white rose on the south wall.

She felt the warmth of the bench as she sat down. The fragile rosebuds quivered in the light breeze. She closed her eyes and drew in the fragrance of the garden. The only sound was distant birdsong; all was at peace.

After a while she sensed a shadow falling across the ground before her and she opened her half-drowsy eyelids. Richard stood in riding attire, leather hose and tunic and sturdy boots. He spoke not a word. With trembling heart she stood to face him, fearful of the seriousness of his countenance.

"Are you troubled, my lord?" she asked tentatively.

For reply he took a step towards her and enfolded her in his arms. The joy and relief she felt to have him hold her thus caused tears to spill down her cheeks. Easing herself away Christiana looked earnestly into Richard's eyes.

"Are you unwell? Can you not tell me? Is it...?"

"Sit down, Christiana," Richard said gently, shaking his head. They sat together on the bench, knees touching and hands tightly clasped.

"I am leaving Middleham," the duke began.

"Leaving? You mean for a while. You will return soon," the girl said, her fear growing. "You always return... after a while."

"Not so soon I think – if at all." Richard lowered his head.

"But why? It is your home. The earl is your kin, surely..."

"No, Christiana!" Richard returned sharply. "This is no longer my home. Not if Warwick has no allegiance to the king, and he does not I swear it. He has poisoned our own brother's heart against Edward. That which I feared has come to pass and I am needed at my brother's side. I must go... it is impossible for me to stay."

"When?" Christiana asked abruptly.

"Soon... this very day. I ride to join the king's men at Nottingham."

The girl gasped. "Am I to see you again?" she asked tearfully.

"I cannot say. I will remain with Edward until God delivers us from this treachery. Loyaulte Me Lie," he whispered softly.

Christiana looked down into her lap trying to stifle her falling tears. Richard was and always would be fiercely loyal to the king; not for him the selfish vacillating allegiances of the Duke of Clarence. Loyalty Binds Me was no idle motto of the Duke of Gloucester.

Beside her the duke had stood and was holding out a hand to her. With pounding heart she allowed herself to be eased gently to her feet to face him. Once more he took her in his arms and kissed her long and hard and deep, a kiss that left her breathless and longing for more.

"Christiana, you do know that nothing can become of our..." He hesitated. "Friendship," he whispered at last. She nodded silently.

He did not have to state the obvious, she thought, a fearful anger rising in her breast. "Do you regret our union, my lord?" she asked coldly.

Richard shook his head. "Never," he answered, pulling her closer to him. "There is but a chasm between us that can never be bridged. We are destined to take opposing paths, you and I. You must know that it has to be so," he finished, sighing deeply.

Christiana could do no more than incline her head, such was the weight of sorrow on her heart.

Richard took something from the pouch hanging from his belt and handed it to her. She held in her fingers a collar chain of woven gold. In the centre hung a golden roundel engraved in leaf enamel. Petal-shaped claws held a large stone of jet within a ring of garnets. It was a fine jewel and certainly the most exquisite piece the blacksmith's daughter had set eyes upon.

"Richard, 'tis beautiful." Her lips trembled as she breathed the words.

His fingers gently clasped hers. "See the jet. It was mined at Whitby, here in Yorkshire, and 'tis marked on the reverse with my crest." He took the jewel and fastened it around her neck. "Keep it, Christiana, to remember me when I am gone," he said, smiling.

"I need no jewel to remind me of you," she answered as fresh tears filled her eyes.

"Now I must go. Farewell, my dearest friend." His final embrace was short, his parting kiss a mere caress. In a few strides he had rounded the box hedge and was gone.

Christiana sank down heavily upon the bench and wept. It was here sometime later that a very anxious old woman found her and offered a shoulder upon which the young girl could vent her tide of painful loss.

"Here, drink this, slowly." Martha handed Christiana a cup of warm infusion of ginger. "How long have you had this nausea?" she asked.

Christiana shrugged. "A few weeks. I thought it was something I ate but..."

"Did you bleed with the last moon cycle?" Martha interrupted briskly.

"Well, no."

"And the month before?"

Christiana shook her head. The herbalist threw up her hands. "I knew as much. You are with child," she exclaimed.

The young girl sat motionless, the cup of ginger in her hand, her face glowing yellow in the stream of morning sunbeams pouring in through the open door, her pale lips parted.

"Drink that," Martha ordered. "And do not look so shocked. I take it you do know how this condition came about?"

Christiana lowered her eyes, shaking her head slowly.

"What! You mean to say—"

"Yes, yes. Of course I do, Martha," Christiana spluttered. "I just cannot believe that it has happened." She rubbed a hand across her abdomen as yet still flat, her lips curling into a smile.

"Well it has and now we must think on it. I do not know how William will take this," Martha mumbled.

Christiana looked up suddenly. "Martha! Surely you do not think that...? Will is my brother."

"Brother!" Martha exclaimed, chuckling. "Now you know he is no more your brother than I am."

There was little to be gained in refuting the fact, the old woman was too astute, but in all truth William had been her brother for so long it seemed to her that all was how it appeared.

Seeing the look of bewilderment on the girl's face Martha said, "How do I know? Any fool can see the way the lad looks at you. Not with the eyes of a brother for certain. Besides which there is no likeness. You are your father's daughter, no mistake, with those black curls – now William, he's much fairer."

"But, Martha," protested Christiana, "there is no likeness betwixt the king and the Duke of Glouc..."

"Ah, the Duke of Gloucester, now we have it. I always knew you would not be strong enough to keep away from him. The curse of Eve, that's what it is," she sighed. "And does our princely knight know he is about to be a father?"

"How can he? He has left to join the king's court and with all this talk of rebellion who knows when he will return," Christiana replied mournfully.

"Well there's many a by-blow with royal blood in its veins. Yours will not be the first, or the last," Martha replied pragmatically.

"'Tis well I think for me that the earl and his family are away for I should not like to face them just now," Christiana mumbled to her cup of ginger, now rapidly cooling.

After a while the old woman's brow wrinkled. "You do not have to. I have laurel berries," she whispered gently.

Christiana stood quickly to her feet, spilling the now cold cup of ginger, and put a hand protectively on her belly. "Never, Martha!" she retorted indignantly.

"You are far too earnest, my dear. You will make a good mother to be sure. But do not become over fond for much can happen."

Christiana thought at once of her own mother and the now fading memory of her travail and subsequent death and she shuddered. "I will not think of such things, Martha," she said determined. "I will set to making a birth girdle and saying my prayers to the holy mother this very night." She sat down again, her thoughts turning to the days and weeks ahead.

After a while the young woman asked a question of her friend.

"Have you ever been with child, Martha?" She realised that her friend had never spoken about her own bygone days.

The herbalist sat down wearily on a stool next to Christiana, her face suddenly dark with sorrow. "Aye, I did have children," she recalled sadly. "I birthed five babes, all boys, but not one survived beyond ten years. Young Will, named for his father, lived the longest. 'Twas the scarlet fever that took him." Her pale blue eyes shone with a liquid haze, looking deep into the past.

Christiana placed a hand on her friend's knee. "I am sorry if I have caused you pain through remembering. I did not mean to."

Martha wiped her eyes on her apron and smiled. "It was many a long year passed before we came to Middleham. We served the Beauchamps in those days. My William was usher to the great hall. I have delivered and nursed countless babes since then and soon there will be another," she added warmly.

"Did you deliver the Ladies Isabel and Anne?" Christiana asked.

"Nay, lass. They were born at the earl's castle at Warwick. But I have brought most of the scallywags running around the bailey into this world and a few more in the village besides. So you will be in good hands."

Christiana smiled, reassured that she would indeed be in no better hands when her time came.

In the meantime there were other matters to worry about. "I saw Conyers in here yesterday, Martha," Christiana remarked quietly. "Does he have any news? Is talk of rebellion mere rumour?"

The old herbalist shuffled her ample derriere on the stool and leaned over the table, closer to the girl. "Nay, lass. If Conyers has the measure of it something is afoot," she whispered. "Many here in the north are rallying under the banner of one Robin of Redesdale."

Christiana's brows puckered.

"You may well crease your brow, my girl." Martha's voice was almost inaudible now and she looked around the room at her sacks, bottles and jars, all waiting silently for the answer.

"'Tis Sir John Conyers of Hornby, son of our own steward."

"In rebellion against the king?" Christiana asked in disbelief.

"You will breathe not a word, *not a word*. Do you understand?"

Christiana nodded her head in solemn agreement. "But what of our steward; does he...?"

"I should think not but his allegiance is with Richard Neville, Earl of Warwick, as is all within this castle."

"But, Martha, surely our first allegiance is to the king. If Warwick rebels where does that leave us?"

"Let us have no more talk of treason within these walls, Christiana," Martha stated vehemently. Our earl and his family are on their way to Calais; as captain of its great fortress he has business to attend to there and I am sure a rebellion against his king has not even crossed his mind."

If Christiana knew the earl as well as she thought she did then rebellion was like as not foremost in his mind; even though he sailed for Calais.

Martha took the cup still grasped in Christiana's hand. "I will heat this up again and be sure to drink it this time." She bustled over to the brazier and prodded the embers with an iron rod.

"Should I tell father and William about this child?" Christiana asked tentatively.

Martha drew a sharp breath. "Nay, lass," she announced. "As I said, anything can happen, there is time enough yet."

Christiana inclined her head and smiled. Martha's answer pleased her for in truth and for reason she could not quite fathom she did not want her brother to know that she carried the duke's child in her belly.

Dust billowed into the air in the wake of the galloping horses as they moved at speed up the winding road to the castle. Watched curiously by the small band of soldiers from the eastern gatehouse, the banner of the bear and ragged staff flew into view – the earl had returned.

At once the castle garrison was thrown into panic; no one, it seemed, not even Richard FitzHugh, the constable or John Conyers, the steward, had been alerted of Warwick's impending arrival. It was now mid-August and little had been heard of the intrepid earl for some time.

Hot, dusty and travel-weary, the riders reined in at the stable yard to be greeted by a bewildered Conyers. It came as no surprise that Warwick, in characteristic bombastic manner, should berate his servant for neglecting his duties. It did, however, come as a great surprise, indeed shock to all those present in the yard that August morning, to see the person of King Edward himself amongst the horsemen under Warwick's command.

Under heavy guard and looking bone-weary Edward nonetheless cut a striking figure sitting upon his grey charger.

Conyers, unsure of his position, recognised at once his sovereign lord and hesitating momentarily, stepped forward in obeisance. A flash of anger glowed in Warwick's eyes but he made no attempt to question the man's loyalties, merely ordering him to see that chambers were made ready for their guest.

Over the following days a strange air seemed to prevail over the castle; folk were worried, unsettled. Not altogether a prisoner, Edward was allowed to come and go as he pleased within the castle walls, although never without an armed escort. Many stared sadly at his pale face as he walked in the garden or around the inner courtyard, a conspiracy of whispers following his every move, not knowing quite how they should behave when the king's path crossed theirs.

Christiana was now well into the fourth month of her pregnancy and beginning to feel much stronger. Her heart had leapt with joy at the first fluttering movements of the child growing inside her. The generous cut of her gown was concealing her steadily thickening waistline – just. Maybe the time had come for her to tell her father and William her close-kept secret.

When she had become aware that Warwick held the king captive, she had feared greatly for Richard's safety. Martha's oft-repeated words of wisdom, "No news is good news," failed to comfort her.

One fine afternoon Christiana visited the smithy to deliver a concoction of equine herbal remedies made by herself and Martha at Alfred's request. A pile of plate armour and broken weapons littered a corner of the yard and Christiana stared at it forlornly. It was unusually quiet, the only sound the clanging of metal as the blacksmith hammered out dents and blows from pieces of battered armour. Alfred looked up from his work as she approached and acknowledged her presence with a nod of his head.

"I have the horse medicine, Father," she said, offering the basket.

"Thank you, child," answered Alfred, bending his head to his work once again. Christiana wondered, somewhat irritably, how old she would be before her father and Martha stopped referring to her as a child – especially as she was soon to have one of her own.

William came out into the sunshine just then to relieve her of the basket of bottles and jars. After placing them on a bench inside the smithy he took up several long-shafted billhooks and bound them together with two pieces of rope.

"These are ready, Alfred. I'll take them to the armoury," William announced. The blacksmith nodded his assent.

"Walk with me, Anna?" William offered.

She hesitated for a moment and then decided that perhaps this would be an opportune moment to ask for news of Richard. William, working at the stables, was well placed to receive any gossip that entered the castle. Also, if courage did not fail her, she could tell of her own news while she had her brother's ear. Prudence dictated that she would not want knowledge of her condition to reach his ears through servants' prattle as surely it would in a few more weeks.

"Is there any news of Rich... the Duke of Gloucester, William?" She broached the subject cautiously after they had walked along in silence for a while.

Her brother's tone was not as she had expected or hoped for. He exhaled tetchily. "How should I know?" he replied. "Maybe you should ask his brother, the usurper."

"I cannot get an audience with Edward," replied the girl, taken aback by William's use of the word usurper to describe the king.

"Nor should I care to speak with the Earl of Warwick for his part in this treacherous rebellion has proved true," she continued hotly.

William stopped in his tracks, the poles of the billhooks he was carrying scraping loudly on the dusty ground. He turned a grim face to her and hissed urgently, "Have a care to what you say here, Anna. With Warwick within the walls you are best holding your tongue."

They continued in silence along the road, over the bridge spanning the moat and into the inner courtyard. The armoury was housed in the north-east tower and it was towards that building that they directed their steps.

Several soldiers were idling about in the heat of the afternoon, drinking ale and throwing dice. Christiana's sharp eye caught the figure of a young woman seated on the bench in their midst. She was unknown to Christiana but with so many servants, retainers and workers coming and going it was impossible to know of everyone. The woman looked to be older than her, possibly of around twenty or so years. Her abundant hair hung about her shoulders in a mass of red curls and her gown was cut low, revealing ample creamy breasts. Christiana frowned at her bawdy manner and familiarity with the soldiers.

William delivered the weapons to the Master of Arms and they began to retrace their steps across the courtyard. They had gone no more than a few paces when a slurred voice called out from a bench where the drink flowed and the tongues wagged freely, "Will, come and take a jug of ale with us!"

William glanced across at Christiana. "Not now, Ralph," he called back. "There is more work to be done. You never know when you will have further need of the bills."

"Aye, lad," Ralph returned. "And soon will be the day when you join us eh? Young Will here is showing great promise with pole arms and he has some skill with the bow."

A colour rose to William's cheeks as the men at the tables raised their cups in agreement. The young redhead unwound her curvy body from the soldiers at the bench and slinked a few steps closer to where William stood with Christiana at his elbow. A pair of vibrant green eyes took in the tall muscular blacksmith and her full red lips curled seductively.

"I am sure you are very well skilled with your arrow," she purred.

William's face reddened deeper as a bellow of laughter erupted from the group of men. Christiana's cheeks flared up in angry embarrassment at this outburst. Unconsciously she slipped a hand through William's arm, desperately wanting to get as far away from Ralph Hodkin as possible but aware of the cool sparkling eyes of the woman burning into her. They moved slowly over her face and down the length of her kirtle to her boots and up again, coming to rest on the thin leather cord that circled her waist. The woman threw back her fiery head. "I knew as much," she laughed.

With the heat still stinging her cheeks Christiana marched quickly away towards the gatehouse.

"Who was that dreadful woman?" she demanded when they were out of earshot.

"How should I know?" William snapped.

"And what did Ralph mean, you are skilled with the bow? Have you been training?"

"You should know that very well, Anna. 'Tis law that all men have skill at arms. Warwick himself ordered an increase in training a few months back."

"Warwick ordered it so that his men can fight against the king," Christiana retorted sharply.

"And who do you suppose is the king, Christiana?" William hissed.

"William, 'tis Edward of course," she replied, notably shocked.

"Is he? Not all would agree with you there, sister. Henry still lives and so does his son, Edward, Prince of Wales."

Christiana fell silent. Her mind had been so fettered by thoughts of Richard of late that much it seemed had passed her attention. She glanced across at William as he walked a step or two in front of her. The years spent at the blacksmith's forge had strengthened his arms; he was tall, almost a man. His natural father had been a soldier, she recalled, so maybe battle fever was in his blood.

"You will not take up arms against the king will you, William?" she whispered anxiously.

William rounded on her then and grasping her shoulders he spat out, "Pay heed, Christiana. Warwick is my liege lord and yours. You will do well to mark that." So saying he released his hold of her and strode off down the road towards the smithy, leaving Christiana bewildered and tearful.

The following morning, after a restless night, Christiana rose fully determined to speak at once to her father and William. When he knew that she carried the Duke of Gloucester's child in her belly then her brother may think again where his loyalties lay. She also felt certain that the wench they had encountered yesterday at the armoury had guessed at her condition and she was most anxious that her father should hear the news from her own lips and no other.

However, a certain incident at the herbarium prevented her from fulfilling her desired course of action at that particular time, although it afforded an opportunity to use to her benefit.

They were barely up from their bed when a loud banging shook the cottage door. It was John Conyers looking as though he had spent a sleepless night and in need of a tonic.

"I have news, Martha." He began once settled onto a cushioned seat. "Warwick was privy to the uprisings here in the north and used them to his advantage, returning post-haste from Calais. There was a clash of arms at Edgecote Field and although the rebels were victorious my son John was slain."

Martha placed a comforting hand on the man's shoulder. "I am sorry for it, John," she said gently.

"I fear I have taken the news badly," he rubbed a hand across his unshaven chin, "especially as it has been long in coming. There was confusion on account of him masquerading as Robin of Redesdale. I am to leave soon to take the news to his mother and wife."

"Let me make you one of my simples before you go, to give you strength." Martha rummaged amongst her herbs on the bench and as she did so Conyers offered more information. Christiana sat unnoticed in the corner of the room.

"Our lord Warwick had more than a military interest in travelling to Calais," Conyers continued. "His daughter Isabel was married to George, Duke of Clarence, on July eleventh by Warwick's brother, the Archbishop of York."

"Well, not exactly unexpected but certainly in defiance of the king," Martha commented as she stirred a mixture over the wood stove.

"Warwick has sent orders for the execution of Earl Rivers, the queen's father and her brother, Sir John Woodville," Conyers continued.

"And that should please some who say that the queen's kin have more influence over the king than the blood royal of the land. You might think Edward himself were of common stock the way he favours the Woodvilles," Martha chuckled.

From her stool, out of view, Christiana felt a rising sense of panic that something dreadful had become of the Duke of Gloucester and would have boldly asked the question of the steward were it not for what followed: the metal pan Martha had been holding slipped from her grasp, splashing its hot contents over her bare foot. Christiana acted at once, drenching the foot with scoops of cold water from the rain butt to ease the pain and applying a goodly coating of honey. It was not a bad burn but enough to keep the old woman off her feet for a day or two. Cursing under her breath at her unusual clumsiness, Martha perched herself on a high stool in the doorway of the herbarium, resigned to giving orders.

The mixture of valerian and melissa was made up and dispensed to the steward who went on his way, full of concern for his friend. When a groom arrived at the cottage later that day with a request for a remedy to ease indigestion, it was Christiana who carried the costrel containing a hot infusion of meadowsweet up to the castle.

"It must be sipped slowly while still hot, remember!" Martha called from her perch as the younger woman strolled off through the garden.

Like as not it was the earl himself who was in need of the remedy, Christiana thought as she clattered over the bridge and into the fortress. His bad temper had very likely given him bellyache. She noticed that the guard had been doubled as she walked up the broad staircase and into the antechamber where Godwin nodded her silently through into the great hall.

Warwick, face like thunder, paced the tiles at the far end of the room. Christiana trembled somewhat as she approached the great magnate, costrel clutched tightly in her hand.

"My lord." She bowed demurely and offered the meadowsweet to the earl.

"Not me, wench," he roared. "In there!" He stabbed a finger at the curtained doorway into the great chamber beyond. In bewilderment she walked through to be greeted by a well-dressed servant who jumped up nervously from his seat to receive her.

"Do you bring the remedy for indigestion?" he asked, pointing to the costrel. The girl nodded.

"Move aside and let the girl in." The man spoke sternly to a guard standing outside the door leading to the smaller chamber on the right.

The room into which Christiana entered was a small vaulted chamber, richly decorated with tapestries. Sunlight trickled warm and hazy through two casements bathing the interior and lighting up the livery of yet another guard standing rigid and stony-faced against the wall. She remembered that this was the chamber where Martha had tended to the king's young brother; many years ago now it seemed.

A tall regal figure reposed on the bed, his long legs resting on a wooden chest at its foot. His fine tunic was cut short in the Burgundian court fashion and his neck and fingers were garlanded with jewels. Christiana hesitated in bemusement, staring at the man before her.

"Why do you stand there, girl, when your king has need of some relief?" he shouted, rubbing a hand vigorously over his stomach. Christiana bowed very low and took a few cautious steps forward as he eased himself up to sit facing the girl.

"Your Grace," she whispered, holding out the costrel. "The herbalist has made an infusion of meadowsweet to ease your discomfort – it should be sipped slowly."

She peered up into his face, which was tired and pale looking, but still with a sparkle in his pale blue eyes. With his great stature and blond curls she remarked to herself how little resemblance he bore to his younger brother Richard, although undoubtedly there was a likeness.

"How do I know that this vessel does not contain poison? Mayhap my cousin sends a servant to do his evil work," Edward mocked, standing to his feet.

Christiana looked helplessly across at the guard who continued to stare impassively ahead. She had nothing to rely upon but her own wit. Taking a deep breath she stepped forward and addressed the king. "I am sure that there is none here who would wish to harm your person, but if it pleases Your Grace, I will take the drink first to put your fears to rest."

Edward smiled broadly. "Spoken like a true subject! What say you?" he called to the guard, who taking one step forward bowed his head and replied, "The girl is well known here, my lord king. She is assistant to the herbalist; they are to be trusted."

"Indeed!" cried the king. "As if I should trust any in Warwick's household. And why the man does not keep a physician within his walls is a mystery to me."

Christiana removed the stopper from the costrel and taking a horn drinking vessel from a table she poured out a little of the meadowsweet and drank it. The liquid was still hot but would not remain so for long.

"Your Grace, you need to drink while the mixture is still hot to feel the benefit," she said boldly.

Edward regarded her for a moment or two before taking the costrel and sipping its contents. As he drank she regarded him closely. Dare she ask the one question that had burned on her lips and had so troubled her heart these past months? A question the man before her would almost certainly have the answer to. She glanced sideways at the guard who had retired to his post assuming an attitude of near slumber. If she did not take her chance now the moment would be lost.

With all her courage she stepped a little nearer to the king and in an almost inaudible voice she asked, "Your Grace, have you any news of the Duke of Gloucester? Do you know, is he well?" She swallowed hard and waited.

Edward stared at her curiously. Then he threw back his golden head and laughed heartily, causing the guard to look warily at them. Still chuckling, the king put out an arm and drew her closer to him. She began to feel a little uneasy for she was not unaware of his reputation with women, but she stood still and waited for his answer.

The king whispered softly in her ear, "How comes it that a servant girl, a very pretty servant girl at that, takes such an interest in the well-being of my younger brother?"

Christiana could feel the flush beginning at her neck and spreading right up her cheeks to the very roots of her raven hair. She averted her eyes to the floor and at the same time touched a hand to her abdomen, a gesture not unnoticed by Edward.

"Well, well," laughed the king. "It would seem that our Dickon is not as strait-laced as he would have us believe."

After a while his face hardened and he lowered his tone. "My dear, do not concern yourself for the young duke, he is safe enough. Things did not go well for us at Edgecote Field and he lies low for now until this present trouble blows over. Warwick does not dare do me any harm and will release me soon from this pretence of captivity." He smiled knowingly and a look of relief dimpled Christiana's red cheeks.

The king stepped away from her then and belching loudly declared that her remedy was the best he had known yet.

It was with a much lighter spirit that Christiana returned to the herb garden. It pleased her immensely to have word at last that Richard was safe. It cheered her to see the king in fine fettle too despite his potential danger. She hoped that Edward's assumption was correct and that Warwick would release him soon.

As she turned in through the wicker gate into the garden she was surprised to see Alfred down by the herbarium. It was most unusual for him to visit Martha during the day unless he was unwell. She quickened her step. Alfred had noticed her approaching and walked out to meet her. She could see at once that his face was grave.

"What is it, Father? Are you sick?" she asked.

"Is it true that you are with child?" Alfred demanded, ignoring her question.

Christiana felt the pain of guilt sear her heart. Alfred took hold of her hand and held it tightly in his large rough one. "Why did you not tell us sooner? The knowledge of it has come by tittle-tattle in the bailey. William..."

"What of William?" she asked, feeling her face redden for the second time that day. In silence she crossed the short distance to the herbarium. Through the open doorway she could see Martha, standing somewhat awkwardly on her bandaged foot and dabbing at William's eye with a piece of comfrey-soaked linen as he sat on a stool before her.

She paused as Christiana's shadow darkened the doorway. As William turned his head towards her she could see the stain of bruising around his left eye and cheekbone. Pain and anger flared up in his hazel eyes as he stared at her.

"I am so sorry, William, I did not tell you," Christiana said regretfully. "What happened?"

There was no reply from the young man who continued to stare at her, his gaze coming to rest on her girdled waist. It was Martha who answered for him. "William was defending your honour, it would seem. There was a brawl at the stables. It may have been wiser to have spoken out sooner," she concluded sadly, not forgetting that it was she who had advised against it.

It was of little use telling William that she would have told him that morning had it not been for Martha's accident. She had tarried too long; the blame was hers. She went closer to William and offered him her hand. He waved it away brusquely and stood up, brushing aside Martha's hand, still holding the linen pad.

"What did he do? Take you at the back of the stables? I suppose he thinks it's his right to have a servant girl, or maybe you just threw yourself at him like a whore." William spat out the words angrily.

"Now then, lad, there is no need for that," Alfred protested hotly but William was already storming off through the garden and back to the smithy. Indignant at his daughter's humiliation, Alfred would have been hotfoot on his heels had not Martha stayed him with a hand on his shoulder.

"Leave the boy be for now," she said quietly. "Do not be too hard on him. Return to your work, Christiana will fare well enough here."

The blacksmith sighed deeply and looked into his daughter's tear-stained face. With no further word he turned and walked away.

"It was not like that," Christiana sobbed.

"I know, child, I know," Martha said soothingly. "William will come round soon enough. Like as not he feels the fool before the other men."

Martha knew the young man's outburst was due to more than wounded pride but she was wise enough to hold her tongue.

As the summer months drifted by into the warm laziness of autumn Christiana's waistline slowly disappeared as the womb nurturing her unborn child grew. Her small breasts began to swell and her cheeks bloomed like spring flowers kissed by the sun. Martha fussed around her like a broody hen, asking after her health and lovingly preparing copious infusions of lady's mantle for her to sip.

Sitting on a stool in the herbarium to ease her aching legs and back Christiana would pound the herbs and mix and stir the remedies but her eyes would see far beyond the root or aromatic leaves of her medicines. Her thoughts as always were never far from the father of her unborn child.

The intrepid earl left Middleham at the beginning of September with King Edward in tow. By the end of October it was known that, as foreseen, Edward had found himself no longer Warwick's prisoner. The earl had released the king having first obtained pardons for himself and the Duke of Clarence. Edward had ridden triumphantly into London reaffirming his right to kingship with Gloucester, his loyal brother, at his side.

Christiana received well the news that the Duke of Gloucester had been made Constable of all England just a few days after his seventeenth birthday, a position formerly held by Earl Rivers, the queen's father, executed at Warwick's command.

Fortunes did indeed have a way of swinging back and forth. Christiana was no longer naïve enough, however, to imagine that now Edward seemed to be firmly back on the throne all would be at peace. Many felt that Warwick would stop at nothing in pursuit of his own ruthless ambition.

From time to time Alfred would linger self-consciously in the doorway of the cottage to see how his daughter fared. On one such occasion he arrived bearing a carved wooden cradle that Martha made him return to the stable at once.

"You cannot bring that in here afore the babe is born. Do you want to tempt fate?" she rebuked severely. Christiana called out her gratitude to her father as he mumbled his apologies and hastily retreated, banging the cradle against the doorway as he did so. There was never any sign of William at the herbarium and she was much grieved by his indifference towards her.

As the weather turned colder Martha was kept busy preparing the rosehip cough syrups and lozenges that would soon be needed in abundance. She had requisitioned the services of a young girl from the dairy to run errands to and from the castle, and each morning Tilly would arrive at the door, red-cheeked with the cold, awaiting her instructions. Christiana was well aware of how fortunate she was to have Martha; most other women of her social standing would be working from dawn till dusk almost to the day they were delivered of their child.

Martha had forbidden Christiana to leave the herbarium, warning her of the treachery of the ice-covered road and pathways underfoot. She was more than thankful to be indoors now, warming herself by the burning brazier. As she sat there she could feel, and at times even see, the tiny limbs of her child pushing outwards as it moved within its womb.

Her afternoons were spent bringing to completion the birth girdle with its embroidered images of the saints and her evenings were spent in prayer. She would pray for her father and brother and Martha. She would call upon Saint George, that brave and gallant knight in stories from her childhood, to keep Richard safe, wherever he might be.

Christiana dearly hoped that her baby might live and she would earnestly petition the Virgin Mother and Saint Margaret to let it be so. The joy that she longed to feel when she held Richard's child in her arms was tempered by the fear of her travail, unknown and fraught with danger. She could not forget that her own mother had died in childbirth and that her fate and that of her unborn child lay in the hands of Almighty God.

Part Two

During the last days of January Christiana began to feel a tightening in her belly and as time went on the pains grew more intense. When she mentioned this to Martha, the herbalist confirmed that her time was drawing nearer and called in the chaplain to hear the young woman's confession and to serve the Blessed Sacrament.

The following day Christiana woke early to discover a layer of ice on the inside of the glazed windows and peering out she noticed a light covering of powdery snow on the sleeping herb garden. Martha appeared in the doorway moments later, her arms laden with bundles of lady's bedstraw, the golden yellow blossom now dulled and wilted but still exuding its heady perfume. "This has been drying out nicely in the corner of a barn," she announced before scattering her load onto the bed.

Throughout the morning Martha would eye Christiana suspiciously, looking up from her lucet to stare at her for a moment or two.

"You unnerve me, Martha, with your constant watching," the young woman laughed. She was sitting on a stool at the bench moving jars and pots about in an aimless manner and every now and then she would touch her belly and grimace.

"Just making certain all is well," Martha returned unperturbed.

Then towards the end of the afternoon as the day was losing its light and Martha was searching for candles to put in her lanterns Christiana suddenly shrieked in terror. She had felt a gush of warm liquid trickling between her thighs, wetting her kirtle and the stool beneath. "Martha! What is happening? My baby!" she cried.

Without any ado the herbalist took hold of Christiana's arm and easing her to her feet she guided her to the bed of straw in the adjoining room.

Christiana was eased down gently and the ties of her bodice loosened and her skirts raised. She could feel Martha's firm but gentle hands removing her boots and stockings and placing the birth girdle across her swollen belly. Another wave of pain gripped her and she knew the mattress to be soaked. She grasped Martha's hand and demanded to know whether she was to bleed to death.

"Nay, lass, that was water not blood. I have seen that happen afore, do not fret. Now lie still while I untie this coif. Your hair must be loose otherwise the cord will tie itself round the babe's neck."

Christiana lay on the bed moaning as her pains were coming faster and deeper. The old woman, having lit the candles on the shelves and in the lanterns on the hooks, returned to the bed and took the girl's hand. She advised her to breathe deeply with each contraction; advice wasted upon the girl, who considered a hearty scream would be of more benefit.

Christiana's labour continued for several hours during which time Martha cooled her sweating brow with rosemary water and watched anxiously for signs of life between her raised legs. Although pain had dulled her wits, Christiana was aware that Martha had left her side, returning moments later with something that she tied around the girl's thigh. She lifted her head to look; it was a length of dried agrimony, its yellow blooms still bright and pungent with its spicy aroma.

"There, that should move things along," Martha proclaimed confidently. Indeed every constricting pain served to push the babe closer to the outside world. Then, as though from a distance, Christiana could hear Martha's voice, declaring with great fervour, that the head was visible. Christiana had a compulsive urge to bear down and push... and push... and push. Breathless and panting and moaning with the effort she made one final strain, expelling the tiny form into Martha's waiting hands.

"The Lord be praised! You have a son, and one of the easiest travails I have ever known," she announced as the child drew its first breath and cried heartily. The young mother slowly took the weight of her exhausted body onto her elbows and saw her babe for the first time. Slippery and wet from the birth fluids, a small, perfectly formed male child with eyes tightly shut and little face wrinkled and red. A mass of black hair sprang from his head and clung to the back of his neck.

Martha took a sharp knife and severed the cord attaching the child to his mother. She gently rubbed a little salt into his delicate skin to clean it and swaddled him in a linen cloth.

"My, oh my I do believe I can see teeth in that tiny mouth." She laughed as she placed the babe into his mother's arms, a touch reluctantly.

Christiana felt the sharp tingle in her breasts as she guided the tiny mouth to her nipple. The soft lips sought a hold and sucked steadily. Tears of pure joy fell in rivulets down Christiana's cheeks as she cradled her son to her breast.

Following the delivery of the afterbirth, Martha busied herself washing and cleaning Christiana and fetching fresh linen and straw for the bed. Much later, the child fed and swaddled and lying asleep in her arms, Christiana looked up at Martha sitting wearily beside her on the bed and asked, "What day is this, Martha?"

The herbalist smiled broadly. "The second day of February in the year of our Lord fourteen seventy," she replied, a stray tear meandering down her wrinkled cheek.

"'Tis Candlemas," the girl remarked. The day of Purification of the Blessed Virgin and the day the infant Jesus was presented in the Temple. How blessed Christiana felt that the Holy Mother had indeed been watching over her.

"Rector Beverley will be blessing the beeswax candles in the church this eve," she continued. "Shall you go, Martha? I would like a candle for our casement."

The herbalist pondered for a while and then nodded, smiling briefly. "Aye, there is ever a need for candles and the tallow burns too quickly. A beeswax candle would mark well the birth of the babe."

Tilly, Martha's erstwhile dairymaid, had run through the snow to shout the news to Alfred at the smithy. She had returned with the message that the blacksmith could be expected at the cottage at the end of his day's work.

"He will not wait that long if I know Alfred," Martha guessed as she sat on the edge of the bed with the tiny child squirming across her ample lap. "Fetch the pot of capon grease, Tilly. Then you can be away to the dairy for now," Martha ordered. The girl pulled a face at this latter command, knowing full well that she would be called upon to do other more menial tasks as there was little to be done in the dairy this time of the year, and disappeared into the herbarium for the grease.

"In forty days we will make the journey for your purification but first this little one will have to be baptised. Do you have a name for him?" Martha asked as she rubbed capon grease into the creases of his skin.

Christiana had not given any thought to the naming of her son. Should she wait and consult Richard first? She realised foolishly that the Duke of Gloucester would have no knowledge of this child and indeed may not ever have if he should not return to Middleham. She shook her head sadly.

"Martha, do not wrap him so tightly. I like to feel his arms and legs," Christiana snapped suddenly as the herbalist began to wind the strips of swaddling tightly around the babe's limbs. She paused in mid-flow to raise a questioning brow to the young inexperienced mother who had dared to question her wisdom.

"Surely you do not want him to grow crooked arms and legs do you, as he will if they are not straightened out now."

Christiana thought about it for a while and then announced, "The cat does not bind the limbs of her kits and see how well they grow."

Martha gaped open-mouthed at that remark – no answer could she find.

"Besides," Christiana persisted, "I have heard it said that the Scots do not bind their children and they do not have crooked limbs."

"Proves nothing," scoffed Martha. "They are naught but bloodthirsty barbarians."

The sound of banging wood on wood followed by an eruption of expletives from the herbarium beyond brought a welcome end to the debate for both women. A tall shadow darkened the doorway and there stood Alfred, awkward and hesitant.

At once Christiana cried out, "Father, father, come in, come in. See your grandson."

As he entered the room, dragging the cradle behind him, Alfred was ordered at once, by Martha, to warm his hands. This he did by thrusting them under his armpits without once taking his eyes off the child now cautiously being wrapped in linen cloth. Alfred's joy had rendered him speechless when at last Martha handed over the small bundle. He opened out the sheet and let his eyes roam over the perfectly formed body with its abundance of black hair. Slowly he shook his head as a tear flowed over his eyelid and down his cheek.

"If only Mary were here to see this," he whispered at last. Christiana watched silently with a tight knot in her throat. After a while she asked, "Did you have a name for the son you lost – my brother?"

Alfred blinked back his tears. "Aye, we named him John."

"Then John shall be the name for my babe. You and William and Martha are to be his godparents," Christiana announced to her father. Alfred turned his brimming eyes to his daughter. Once again words failed the big blacksmith but he did manage a very broad grin.

The following day Christiana lay propped up against the pillows on her bed, John sucking at her breast, his tiny hand clutching her finger tightly. She turned her head to the window and gazed thoughtfully at the fat beeswax candle reposing there in its clay holder since Martha had returned with it. A pale sun, low in the sky, was slowly melting the icicles hanging in rows from the eaves. The only sound within the herbarium was the faint rustling and stirring of the herbs hanging from the wooden beam as the warm air from the brazier caught and jostled them. Martha was out and about her work and all was tranquil and at peace.

Christiana's thoughts as ever were never far from Richard. She wondered where he was, what he was doing. There was constant talk of unrest and nothing seemed certain save for the steadfast loyalty of the Duke of Gloucester to his brother, the king. Edward and Richard on one side, Warwick and Clarence on the other; a family divided. Where did that leave the folk at Middleham? William had reminded her last summer that their allegiance was to the lord of the castle, the Earl of Warwick. Well who knew what changes of fortune there may be in the wind, she thought, sighing deeply and closing her eyes as the babe continued to suckle.

A sudden movement beyond the open door into the herbarium startled her. Martha had returned, or so she thought, but these were masculine footsteps stamping across the floor. Christiana waited with bated breath, drawing the child closer to her.

She sighed with relief as William's tall muscular frame filled the doorway. Like their father he stood awkwardly, hesitant to enter. She smiled at his ruffled brown hair and warm hazel eyes. "Come inside, William. You are welcome," she called.

He stepped closer, staring down at her naked breast; the child's head had fallen away in sleep. Hastily she fumbled at her kirtle and pulled the folds of cloth together. Wrapping the child in the linen cover she held him out for her brother to see. "This is John," she said softly.

William sat down cautiously on the edge of the bed and stuck out a nervous finger to touch the raven crown, withdrawing it at once as though the head were hot.

Christiana laughed. "You can hold him if you wish," she said.

William shook his head and attempted a smile, somewhat embarrassed. "I have a gift for him," he said quickly, drawing open his cloak and pulling out a small object from the pouch at his belt. It was a set of pegs fashioned from smooth coral and tied about with a red ribbon. "I bought it from a pedlar at the fair last autumn. He said that it would keep away evil spirits and help the teeth to grow." William grinned and added, "By the look of him he needs no help in growing teeth."

The babe's mouth had dropped open exposing two little milk-white teeth protruding from pink gums. Christiana took the teething ring and smiled. She reached out a hand and pressing William's fingers she whispered, "Thank you for coming."

They sat in silence for a while as the child slept. There was between them an uneasiness that Christiana sorely regretted; the closeness they once shared had all but faded with their childhood.

The sound of Martha returning and clanging about amongst her bottles in the adjoining room broke the awkward silence. William said his farewells and departed.

The frost lessened its iron grip on the earth over the following few days and although still wet and cold, travel was a little safer.

The time came for the Sacrament of Baptism and so Alfred and William together with the castle chaplain braved the icy chill wind to make the journey to the cottage. The chaplain had with him the holy water and chrisom cloth to be used in the baptism of the newborn infant. He also produced a small vial of oil of frankincense with which he anointed the child. Christiana wondered greatly at this for it was of no trivial worth and she suspected that Martha may have divulged the paternity of the babe.

After the solemn ceremony had been performed they were joined by Tilly and Jude to mark the occasion by partaking of the caudle, made from wine, oatmeal and almond. Martha produced a flagon of last year's fruit wine and everyone drank to the health of the child after which the chaplain departed to the keep.

As she suckled her infant Christiana lay back on the pillows and listened to the celebration in the herbarium. She felt a great sadness as she lay there on the bed. The one person who should have been at this feast was notably absent, and looking down at the tiny bundle of manhood snuggled to her she felt an overwhelming desire for Richard's presence. Her tears began to fall in abundance, wetting the tiny dark head cradled in her arm, and for several long moments she could find no comfort to ease the longing of her heart.

On the fourteenth day of March, being the forty-first after her confinement, Christiana left the warmth and comfort of the cottage to attend church for her purification. Martha carried the child in a woven basket lined with lambskin, a gift from the steward, John Conyers. The fourth member of the party was Tilly, the little dairymaid, trotting eagerly alongside the sleeping babe.

A timid sun, low in the sky, greeted Christiana on this, her first day out of doors and she looked with wonder upon the clusters of Candlemas bells that still lingered around the bailey, their tiny white heads quivering bravely in the cold breeze.

As they made their way under the arch of the eastern gate at the far end of the bailey the duty guard, a broad thickset soldier with many years of loyal service to his credit, and a well-known figure to Martha, hailed them. "Where are you bound?" he called.

"To the village, Thomas, to church. 'Tis time for Christiana here to give thanks for the child," Martha answered.

The guard peered briefly into the basket over the old woman's arm. "You will do best taking an escort, Martha. These are troubled times. You cannot be sure who is friend and who foe. Wait there and I will summon a couple of men." He turned on his heel and disappeared into the guardroom housed in the gatehouse, returning moments later with two soldiers. One was tall, well-built and mature in years but despite the violence of the battlefield, a man still able to show a courteous manner and a friendly face.

Christiana recoiled abruptly at the sight of the second man. With the unmistakable waft of his putrid breath came the vivid memory of his groping ice-cold hands and drooling lips. She shuddered beneath her cloak and moved closer to Martha and the basket containing her precious bundle. Whoever the enemy might be he could be no worse a foe than Ralph Hodkin.

"You all right, Christiana?" Martha asked, regarding her suddenly pale face with concern. "You are not faint I hope. Too long abed I expect."

Christiana grabbed hold of Tilly's hand, somewhat too forcefully to the surprise of the girl, and moved on down the road. "Do not be troubled for me, Martha. I am well," she called irritably to the herbalist.

They walked on in silence for much of the way but Christiana was ever aware of the pair of bloodshot eyes boring into her, searching for a seed of recollection. She prayed that he would find none. However, they were nearing the gentle slope to the church when Hodkin suddenly stabbed an accusing finger towards Martha's gently swinging basket.

"This must be Duke Richard's little love child." His lips curved into a sneer, delivering the honeyed words with a sting. "Who'd have thought it of him eh? Thin as a green stick sapling. And who are you that you'll only be bedded by a duke?" He sneered at Christiana, who turned blood red and felt a trembling in her limbs. The company had come to a halt and Martha turned a face livid with rage on Ralph but before she could say a word the other soldier placed a warning hand on her arm.

Stepping up to Hodkin he gripped the man tightly by the shoulders and spoke in a calm voice that rang deep and clear in the chill air. "You hold your tongue, soldier, if you know what's good for you, otherwise you'll answer to Thomas Tempest – after you've answered to me."

Browbeaten into silence Ralph hung back from the others, sulkily muttering oaths under his breath. Christiana was more than relieved when entering into the pale sunshine once more from the dark interior of the church only the broad figure of the older soldier could be seen waiting patiently outside the walled churchyard.

Returning through the village, Martha, a little ahead, was talking avidly to Tilly about the ways of babes and Christiana found herself in step with their guard. Ever eager for information she thought to question the soldier; he seemed genial enough as he swaggered along beside her.

"Is there news of my Lord Warwick?" she asked.

The man did not reply immediately, weighing up it seemed the measure of the situation.

"In truth there is nothing to tell. King Edward has the upper hand in this power struggle – for now," he replied at last, and glancing up at the basket bobbing gently on the old woman's arm he asked, "Does Hodkin speak the truth?" He broke off and nodded enquiringly at the basket.

Christiana's cheeks blushed a little but she answered in the affirmative. The soldier sighed deeply.

"Power can change hands with such speed on the battlefield; fortunes, and lives, lost or gained on the swing of a sword. You just take care of yourself and your child. None of us can change the workings of Almighty God, only pray for his favour." He smiled at her, a small pitying smile, and they continued their journey home in silence.

Middleham Castle
Yorkshire
March 1470

"Martha, let me go – please."

The old woman paused as she fumbled amongst her jars and bottles searching for the tincture of valerian. "Well, if you feel up to it," she said unsurely.

"I am well enough and ready for work, Martha. I feel like a hen in a coop here every day. It has been nigh past a month since John's birth and one journey out for my purification in all that time," Christiana pleaded.

A page had just departed after delivering his message. The Lady Anne, it seemed, had taken ill with poor nerves and awaited their attendance.

"You know that Lady Isabel has returned and is soon to give birth to her first child? It may prove awkward up there for you just now." Martha nodded towards the wooden cradle where John lay warm and snugly sleeping.

Christiana sighed a little impatiently. "I cannot hide away forever. It will be good to see the countess and see how she has received knowledge of John's birth." She had now joined Martha and began to turn a few earthenware jars until she had found the dried lavender and rosemary. "See, I shall advise a hot soak in these. It always calms the nerves."

Martha relented. "Aye, but not for the Lady Isabel, mind. You can take her an infusion of lady's mantle. I will prepare it now."

A little later Christiana had a basketful of herbal concoctions swinging from her arm as she made her way across the drill field. The garrison soldiers were going through their paces in the morning mist, a poignant reminder that Warwick was as always at the fore of political tension.

Thankfully there was no sign of Ralph Hodkin as she crossed

over the bridge to the inner courtyard. The recent encounter with him had rekindled long-suppressed feelings of fear and she hurried to reach the covered staircase leading to the great hall.

Godwin received her at the antechamber and waved her through. The Countess of Warwick was awaiting her arrival. The skirts of her gown rustled as she stepped forward. Her face was waxen and she wrung her hands repeatedly.

"Has Martha not come?" she asked rather coldly, looking behind Christiana towards the great oak door.

"No, my lady," Christiana replied simply. "She has sent these herbs."

The Lady Anne glanced at Christiana's basket briefly and announced, "Very well. It is my daughter Anne who has need of them."

As Christiana followed the countess through to the great chamber beyond, the lady turned to whisper over her shoulder, "You will conduct your business quietly. The Duchess of Clarence is resting. She arrived home only yesterday eve and now it seems is to partake of yet another long journey."

The room into which they had entered was warm but poorly lit. The grey of the early spring day failed to dispel the gloom despite an array of beeswax candles flickering brightly. The Lady Anne, little more than a child of not yet fourteen years, sat on the edge of a cushioned chest. She wore no head covering and her hair fell in a golden cascade about her shoulders. Her eyes like two blue moons shone round and large in her colourless face. Her breathing came in quick spasms. Christiana approached apprehensively and took the girl's cold thin hand in hers.

"How long has she been unwell?" Christiana turned to enquire of the mother who hung back a little, her fingers constantly weaving and rubbing together. "My lady-in-waiting came to me just after daybreak to say that my daughter had taken ill. We have..." She broke off and rubbed a hand wearily across her forehead.

Christiana put her basket down onto a carved wooden table nearby and took out the tincture of valerian and a horn spoon. She showed it to the countess who peered at the label and nodded.

Christiana measured the required amount using a quill dropper onto the spoon and bade the girl drink. She did so and shuddered as the liquid slid down her throat.

Christiana removed the jars of lavender and rosemary from her basket and placed these on the table also. "Martha has advised a hot herbal soak, my lady," Christiana once again addressed the countess.

This announcement seemed to shake the lady from her melancholy for she said at once, "Indeed, how wise. I will send for hot water. I myself will bathe also." Feeling of some use the countess turned and walked to the door.

"My lady," Christiana whispered after the countess had left, "is there some reason for your anxiety? Does something trouble you?"

Anne sat still as stone, her lips trembling slightly. Christiana took her hand and sat beside her on the chest. After a few minutes had elapsed Christiana could see the faintest hint of crimson in the girl's cheeks.

"Are you troubled because of your sister, my lady? Is she not well?" Christiana asked, glancing across at the half-drawn hangings on the tester bed.

Anne followed her gaze and replied softly, "Her child is due in May. She was unwise to travel from her home to visit us as it was and now she must make the journey to Warwick on the morrow. She is so tired."

"Can she not stay here with you and the countess until her child is born?" Christiana asked, quite alarmed that a woman of Isabel's standing should contemplate such a journey in her condition.

"It is not possible," Anne lamented. "We have all been summoned to Warwick by the earl. We are to be prepared should the need arise."

Christiana desired greatly to know what the earl's plans might be but she dared not ask for surely it would be taking advantage of her position with the Lady Anne, so obviously distressed.

However, the young lady herself seemed more than willing to divulge her family secrets. She glanced a second time at the hangings on the bed, leant her head a little closer to the servant and whispered, "Isabel believes that Father will take us all to France to the Lancastrian court, in exile there, should events not go his way in England. The earl is… well there is much unrest."

Christiana sat in silence, her heart pounding in her throat. What events could Anne possibly be talking of, she wondered? She shot a nervous glance towards the bed and listened for signs of stirring from within; all seemed quiet. Anne continued.

"Isabel speaks to me of King Henry's son, Edward, Prince of Wales, who is a most handsome man, reputed to be bold and courageous, quite unlike his father," she tittered. "I was very young when I saw him in London and I can scarce remember." The girl lowered her voice still further. "She also has it that the earl is losing interest in her husband Clarence and would use me instead to further his ambition."

Christiana raised an eyebrow questioningly.

"Marriage!" Anne emphasised under her breath. "I cannot see Father forging an alliance with Margaret of Anjou, however – there is much bitterness between them. I believe that Isabel imagines too much."

"Is the prince much older than you, my lady?" Christiana asked, thinking of all the highborn girls reputed to be wed to much older men in order to forge family alliances.

"Not much, I think. He is the same age as Cousin Richard, I believe."

At mention of the duke's name Christiana at once became ill at ease and hoped that his recent paternity would not now become the subject of their discussion.

"Isabel says Richard has a most sour countenance and swears that Prince Edward is the more handsome," Anne continued with a snigger, her cheeks by now displaying a healthy glow.

"And indeed he is," a voice called from behind, causing both young women to turn startled faces towards the bed, where Isabel was moving aside the drapes and slowly placing her bare feet onto the rush mat on the floor. "Sister, you forget yourself," Isabel remonstrated as she walked heavily over to the chest, whereupon Christiana was on her feet at once.

"It is most unwise to gossip with the servants, Anne. Do you not know that this girl has born the Duke of Gloucester's bastard? She could be a Yorkist spy for all we know." Isabel's blue eyes sparkled with malice.

Anne, however, was clearly of the opinion that her sister's fears were misplaced for she at once began to giggle. "Isabel, Christiana is a herbalist, nothing more. And Mother says that Richard was just sowing his wild oats before the shackles of marriage."

The sound of voices and footsteps across the tiled floor beyond the door heralded the long-awaited return of the Countess of Warwick. She entered the chamber followed by her ladies-in-waiting and a troop of serving girls bearing pitchers of hot water, a pile of towels and a wooden lead-lined tub.

Spared further humiliation, Christiana turned to the countess and bowed low.

"The Lady Anne is feeling much better now and here also is an infusion of lady's mantle for the Lady Isabel. It will be of benefit to her. If you please I shall take my leave, my lady." She forced out the words, willing the tears stinging the back of her eyes to stay put.

The countess dismissed her with a wave of her hand and snatching up her empty basket Christiana fled from the room. Hurrying down the outer staircase into the cold early spring air she let her tears fall. Was that really all she had meant to Richard, the means by which he could satisfy his desires? Of course she herself had thought it often enough but to hear it spoken aloud somehow forced home the truth. Was she just as much a pawn in the world of men as the Ladies Isabel and Anne? She put a hand to her throat where hung the jewelled pendant, the duke's parting gift. Was this a token of his love or just a payment for her services, she thought bitterly.

By the time she had reached the cottage her anger had given way to a feeling of despair. Her little son was still sleeping peacefully in his cradle; his father was far, far away on a campaign for the king and for all she knew could already lie dead on a field of blood. Such was the fragile nature of her world.

Spring gave way to summer in the endless cycle of the seasons and Christiana's son grew bigger and stronger every day, taking on more and more the likeness of his father; although his hair even at this tender age was darker, his eyes were as blue as cornflowers.

Martha had relinquished her authority over the swaddling bands and as his mother whiled away the hours tending the herb garden John would lie in his cradle gurgling and kicking his little arms and legs freely. The old herbalist would stare down into the cradle shaking her head and tut-tutting loudly whenever she happened across the babe, but nary a word would she utter.

Alfred was a frequent visitor to the herbarium, bringing with him the various roughly carved toys he had made for his grandson from pieces of scrap wood he had scrounged from the carpenters. Another surprising visitor to the cottage was the old man, Wat, who tended the flowers in the garden. Tottering along on his shaky thin legs he would hover over the child in his cradle and peer down through watery blue eyes, a toothless grin on his wrinkled face. It quite amused Christiana to watch the old man look at the babe thus and then simply walk away back to his flowers.

One night, after a hard day's labour picking the herbs ready for drying in their wooden trays or tying in bunches to suspend from the beams, Christiana and Martha received very little rest. The infant had developed a bout of bellyache, crying relentlessly and vomiting any milk he took from his mother. By daybreak Christiana was in a state of nervous exhaustion as she paced the floor of their chamber, cradling the child in her arms.

Martha could be heard lighting the wood stove and clanging the bottles and jars in the adjoining herbarium. A little later she bustled into the bedchamber holding a horn cup and spoon.

"Here, I have anise for the child. You lie abed," she ordered, "and let me tend to him." Fatigued and tearful Christiana handed over her child and fell wearily onto the bed, where within moments of touching the pillow she was sleeping soundly.

Around midday Christiana awoke to the sound of hammering outside the cottage. She lay on the bed in the hot stickiness of the day; the sun was pouring in through the window, baking the room like an oven. She could feel her head aching as the constant hammering pounded her senses.

Leaving the bed she walked into the herbarium where a pleasantly cool breeze wafted in from the open door. John lay asleep in the cradle wedged between barrels and sacks in a cool corner. Shading her eyes against the brilliance of the sunlight Christiana stepped outside and was surprised to see William hard at work constructing what appeared to be a small pen from planks of wood. He looked up as she approached and smiled wanly.

Martha, who had been standing beside the blacksmith, turned to her assistant and asked, "You feeling better?" Christiana nodded before turning to the rain butt and scooping up a handful of cold water to splash over her face.

"Will's making a pen for John," Martha announced, pointing to the square-framed structure. "'Twill keep him out of harm's way now he's crawling about a bit. Of course it needs lining with sacking on the inside," Martha declared with emphasis as she directed her gaze at William. "Or else the child will have a fistful of splinters."

Christiana expressed her thanks to her brother and turned to go back indoors, the bright sunlight hurting her head.

"Anna!" William called, straightening up and laying aside his hammer. "Do you care to take a walk with me?" he asked. "This is all but finished and I have no work at the smithy. What say you?"

Christiana looked in surprise at Martha as if to say, how could she go off and take a walk just when she had a mind to?

Martha, however, was already waving them away. "John is well and fast asleep. A walk will do you good, blow away the cobwebs," she replied brightly.

Christiana glanced across at William, who was watching her expectantly. If he was offering an olive branch to heal their bruised relationship how could she refuse, for did she not love her brother?

The river glistened in the sunlight and bubbled peacefully as it trickled by. The sense of tranquillity it evoked found a way into Christiana's heart and immediately she felt a lifting of her spirits. They turned onto the broad sweep of marshland high up and it was here they sat side by side looking down on the river below. The last time she had been up here it had been with Richard. She brushed aside the thought; even if he had only used her nothing could quench the burning desire she still had for him.

Looking down she absent-mindedly began to twirl the pink-white star-shaped flowers of the bogbean that grew in abundance around her.

"Is there any news, Will?" Christiana asked tentatively. "I know little but that Conyers has halted the work on the upper chamber of the great hall on account of the uncertainty over Warwick's fortune."

William began tugging at the tufts of grass pensively. "It is now known that John Neville, brother to the Earl of Warwick, surrendered his lands back to the Percys in March. The Northumberland heir was released from the Tower after swearing his allegiance to King Edward," William replied after a while. This piece of information seemed to be as good as any with which to begin but in truth the news he had been privy to that morning was not going to be received well by his sister.

"I am sure that will please many here in the north for the Duchy of Northumberland has long been in the Percy family," Christiana replied.

"Aye, that it will, but John Neville remained loyal to the king even though Warwick did not and for that he has been given the title of Marquis of Montague."

"I am sure that will make amends," Christiana replied wryly. "But, Will, is there not any news that might concern us here at Middleham?"

"You know of the Yorkist victory at Hornfield in Rutland?" William asked.

Christiana nodded. "Conyers informed us that the Earl of Warwick, his wife and daughters had fled to France in April after the earl and his son-in-law, Clarence, had been declared traitors to the crown by King Edward. There my knowledge ends."

"It has been reported that their ships were fired upon off the coast of Calais," William continued softly. "Lord Wenlock, he is now Captain of Calais, refused them anchorage in port. The Lady Isabel, heavily pregnant, gave birth to her babe and it lived but one day. The little body was tossed into the sea for want of a better resting place."

William was certain that this news would have caused his sister grief and watched in silence as the tears began to well up in her eyes.

"Poor Isabel," she sobbed. "Poor, poor Isabel." Christiana's tears fell steadily as she imagined a mother's grief at the loss of a child and the irreverent disposal of its little body.

After a while she asked, "Is there news of Anne?"

"Well it comes as no surprise that Warwick has managed to betroth his youngest daughter to the Lancastrian Prince Edward at Tours Cathedral, not that long since," William chuckled. "No wonder Warwick is being called The Kingmaker. I should say there is no longer any doubt where Warwick's loyalties lie and I would wager that he is even now gathering an army of exiled Lancastrians in readiness to overthrow Edward Plantagenet," William continued.

Christiana's sorrow at Isabel's loss was matched by her loathing of the duchess's father, whose selfish ambition had almost certainly caused his daughter to lose her child. She buried her face in her hands to hide her tears. At once she felt William's arms around her, drawing her close. Her whole body ached with fatigue and sorrow; there was comforting warmth in William's chest as he pressed her head to him, gently smoothing her hair as she wept.

"You should forget Gloucester," he whispered as he held her. "I doubt he will return to Middleham. If Warwick does see Henry back on the throne then Richard, along with his brother Edward, could well find himself in exile – or worse. If Edward does keep his throne then Gloucester will have no cause to show his face in these parts – it will be a courtly life for him. A servant girl and her bastard son will not bring him back."

Any solace Christiana thought she could gain from William's arms was vanquished in an instant to be replaced by anger, nay fury. Like a scalded cat she sprang apart from William, throwing off his arms.

"Do not ever speak to me again of the Duke of Gloucester, William. I see we are divided in this war, brother." She glared at him with eyes ablaze. "If your loyalties lie so far with the Earl of Warwick maybe you should join his army of Lancastrian rebels and keep well away from Richard's son, my son – and me!"

With legs trembling so violently they threatened to give way and tears blinding her eyes Christiana picked up her skirts and hurtled through the boggy grasses and along the riverbank, hardly pausing for breath until she had reached the castle gatehouse.

The horse shifted its weight nervously on its hind leg as William tried to grasp a handful of black fetlock. After several attempts the blacksmith dug his elbow sharply into the ribs of the beast, causing it to whinny loudly in protest.

"Lad, what's troubling you this morning? If you're not calm how can you expect the horse to be?" Alfred looked up sharply from his anvil after biting his tongue for some time now and being unable to do so any longer. "Take a walk, Will, have a drop of ale – Jude here can take over."

William was on the point of shouting down his father but as his eyes met Alfred's he saw nothing but concern blazing in their brown depths and thought better of it. He released the horse's leg and stomped outside, the brilliant sunlight momentarily stinging his eyes.

He could do with something to settle his stomach; he felt all knotted up inside. He ought to go to the herbarium and ask for a remedy but he could not face Christiana at present.

William knew he had always loved the girl he called sister ever since the day he had laid in the cold mud outside the gates of York and peered up into her lovely face. As they had matured into adulthood William's feelings had grown deeper, often fired with anger, frustration and even jealousy. Until two days ago when she had let loose upon him her emotional tirade he had failed to realise the true extent of Christiana's feelings for Richard, that slightly built, solemn duke with an unfathomable countenance. Now William had been left in no doubt and any hope that she might have returned his affection, however slight, now that the duke was out of the way, had died a death up on the marsh for certain.

He kicked at the stones beneath his boot as he walked and tried to dispel any thoughts of Christiana from his mind. He might as well take some ale, he thought miserably, and have good company to share it. He strode briskly across the bridge and turned towards the north-east corner and the armoury; there would always be one or two soldiers idly drinking away the hours.

The moment he stepped into sight a couple of men hailed him from a bench where they were seated, making a great show of cleaning their weapons and supping steadily at their jugs of ale as they worked. William slumped down on a bench nearby.

One of the soldiers threw back his head and called towards the open doorway of a store. "Hey, Rowena, bring another jug for our friend!"

William could see a few dusty wooden barrels standing on the straw amongst a pile of rusty, bent pole arms.

A buxom wench appeared in the doorway carrying a jug full to overflowing, slopping much of the ale onto the hot, dry ground. William raised his eyes to her face as he took the drink and recognised at once the fiery curls and green eyes of the very same girl who had embarrassed him here last summer. He felt a red heat scorching his cheeks as he took a long drink of the cool ale. His first mouthfuls left him feeling nauseous, he was so tense, but as he drained the jug he began to feel more relaxed.

Rowena nestled her curves beside him on the bench and draped a smooth bare arm around his neck. The soldiers were sharing tales about their accomplishments in warfare. The fact that the king had defeated Warwick in the battle of Hornfield in Rutland was no deterrent for they were obviously looking forward with excited fervour to taking an active part in any further fighting that might take place between the followers of the earl and those of King Edward.

There was much laughter as the men discussed the rout at Hornfield during which many of the rebels had discarded their livery coats so as not to be recognised by the king's men. The battle was rapidly becoming known as Losecoat Field.

William listened with mounting envy. The lot of the blacksmith was not a bad one as far as it went but he knew that it would never be enough for him. Deep down he had a desire to be a soldier just as his own father had been.

As he sat in the hot sunshine listening to stories of courage and chivalry the spark of desire was being fanned into a flame. Rowena very obligingly kept his jug full and it was with increasingly blurred vision that William watched his companions sand, oil and rub down the metal halberd blades and axe heads until they had a considerable pile on the floor beside them.

"Well, we'll be off for our meal now, Will," one of the soldiers announced, yawning and stretching his arms wide. The others stood, dusted down their tunics, and, with sniggering glances at William over their shoulders, they walked away.

William peered up into the sky. It must be way past midday. He had not eaten a thing since dawn that morning. He ought to be getting back to the smithy. He banged the jug down on the bench and stood to his feet. Immediately he felt overwhelmingly giddy and sat down heavily back onto the bench. Still beside him, Rowena laughed outright at William's plight and pouted, "Well now, handsome blacksmith, methinks you need a bit of help finding your horses." She coiled her arm tightly around his waist and slowly lifted him upright. He wobbled momentarily before staggering forward. He had the strange sensation of floating but he maintained a vague sense of contact with the hard ground.

Without any notable recollection of how he had arrived, William found himself on a bed of thick straw at the back of a barn, he thought to be somewhere in the bailey. Lying on his back he looked up at the swaying wooden rafters overhead. Locks of flaming hair were tickling his nose and cheeks and he could feel Rowena's warm, ample breasts pressing hard against his chest as she lowered herself over him. He began to respond to her as she reached down and ran her fingers along the insides of his thighs and up between his legs. It was not long, however, before William realised that he would not be able to fulfil her obvious expectations. The copious amount of ale he had consumed sloshed about inside him like milk in a butter churn. With her weight pressing heavily on his stomach he knew that he was going to be sick. Groaning pathetically and shoving Rowena aside, he had the presence of mind to roll himself over onto his front before casting the contents of his stomach into the straw and then passing into oblivion.

The barn was shrouded in twilight from the half-open doors when William came to his senses. His head throbbed like a beaten horseshoe and his stomach felt queasy. Someone was cradling his head in their lap and gently wiping his face. He thought it must be Rowena but her touch could never be so gentle and that wench was nowhere to be seen. He focused his eyes in the dim light and could see the hazy silhouette of Christiana peering down at him, an anxious frown on her brow.

"William, we have been so worried about you. Father was concerned when you did not return for your meal."

Every soft caress of her fingers on his face and hair pained his lovesick heart and he pushed aside the girl's hand ungraciously.

"Well, you do not need to worry yourself on my behalf," he spluttered, "I am not a child." He staggered shakily to his feet and made for the door.

Christiana stood hastily and held out a hand to assist him. "William, I am so sorry for what I said the other day. Can we not be friends, you and I?" she implored.

For a moment William's watery hazel eyes flickered across his sister's face. "Like you said, Christiana, you have made your choice in this war and now I must make mine." With his head fit to explode and a throat as dry and coarse as a pig hide, William shuffled out of the barn and back to the smithy.

She knew it was not much of an excuse but Christiana was anxious to know how her brother fared. Alfred would most certainly not be in further need of any equine herbal remedies and Martha would not be pleased if she knew they had been taken from the store but she hoped they would both understand her need of them.

Thoughts of William had plagued her mind for the past week, ever since she had found him in a drunken stupor in the straw of a barn after searching for him for what seemed like hours and receiving a rebuff for her trouble. She feared that her words, spoken in hot temper on the marsh, had served only to push him further apart from her and their father.

Her bottles jingled conspiratorially in the bottom of her basket as she approached the open smithy. Alfred was sitting on an upturned barrel taking a drink of ale, his work seemingly done for the day although it was a few hours yet till sunset. He looked up as his daughter approached. "Good afternoon, lass. Is all well?" he asked, smiling.

"I am well, Father," Christiana replied, stepping forward and holding out the basket. "I thought you might be in need of more horse remedies," she added feebly.

Alfred looked at the basket with an odd frown on his face and wiped the sweat from his brow. "Aye, well I suppose so. There's always a need. Have you time to sit awhile?" He took the bottles from the basket and placed them under the bench against the wall.

"How is my little grandson?" Alfred called as he went inside the smithy to fetch Christiana a cup of ale and himself a second.

Christiana smiled broadly. "Oh he is fine. He crawls around now getting into all sorts of mischief. We've had to clear the floor of all our things. The herbarium looks twice the size it was before," she laughed.

They sat together on the bench drinking the cool ale. Christiana looked around the quiet yard; Alfred seemed to be alone. "Where is William?" she asked.

Her father shrugged and took a long drink from his cup. "As if I should know. He is rarely here these days and when he is he hardly speaks a word," he replied bitterly.

"We had an argument the other day. I told him to keep away from me and John," Christiana said, her lips quivering slightly. "I was angry, upset. You do not suppose he has a mind to leave us, Father?"

Alfred turned to face his daughter. "I cannot say, lass. I have loved that boy like a son and hoped that one day he would follow me in the trade," he sighed deeply. "He's maybe just restless, finding his own path in life now he's a man. You know."

Christiana nodded silently, not altogether sure that she did know. They spent nigh on an hour together talking of naught but trivia, enjoying each other's company and in all that time she saw nothing of her brother William.

The early evening air was warm and still as she returned to the bailey. She ambled slowly along the path towards the cottage swinging her now empty basket back and forth in her hand. Still some distance away she looked up and noticed Martha sitting on the bench outside the door bouncing John on her ample lap. She could hear her singing and making the strange noises folk often inflicted upon infants. The old gardener, Wat, was standing nearby, enjoying the entertainment as much as the child by the sound of his laughter. Christiana smiled and decided to leave them awhile to their game.

She turned away and began to traverse the pathways amongst the flower garden and hedges. She rarely sat under the white rose these days; the memory of Richard's departure was too painful to recall.

With the ladies away and what servants remaining at the castle about their work there was no one to take a stroll amongst the lovely flowers. Christiana sat on a bench near to a tangled display of late summer blooms abuzz with drowsy insects and thought about her life and how much it had changed in the course of her seventeen years. She had lost a mother and gained a mother in Martha; she had lost an infant brother and then found another. She had met her true love and now he had gone and left behind a baby son. It brought a sad smile to her lips to think of it all.

She looked up from her reverie, certain that she had heard music. She turned her head, listening. Floating on the still air were the unmistakable notes of a flute. It was a sweet, mournful tune and coming nearer.

It was not many moments before the musician rounded the corner of the path, lost in the joy of his playing and came to an abrupt halt, startled by the presence of the girl on the bench. His face flushed crimson as he muttered an apology.

Christiana rose from the bench. "Nay, Godwin, 'tis I who should apologise. I ought to be back at the herbarium."

The young man stepped hastily forward. "Please, do not go. Sit awhile if you would, unless your babe...?" he hesitated, somewhat embarrassed.

Christiana smiled and sat back down on the bench. "My babe is faring very well I think with his adopted grandmother."

Godwin nodded, sitting down beside the girl. "Ah yes, Martha."

"I did not know you played the flute. You play very well," Christiana said, drawing the conversation away from John.

Godwin smiled broadly and Christiana was reminded once again that his features were not unpleasant to behold. She lowered her eyes as she felt her cheeks begin to redden.

"How is your arm?" she asked, forcing herself to dwell upon more practical matters.

For answer Godwin turned up the sleeve of his shirt and held out his arm. The skin was almost a healthy-looking pink with little sign of blistering. "See, you are a good physician," he chuckled.

"Oh no, Master Godwin, I am no physician," Christiana replied with chagrin. "Such are not to be trusted. One came to the castle on the occasion Countess Anne took bad with a fever and you should have seen what he had with him. Jars, a length of tubing and instruments more fit for torture than healing. He spent more time consulting his astrological charts than he did in attendance upon my lady."

Godwin laughed. "But, Christiana, they are most learned men. They are taught in the great universities, both here and abroad."

Christiana sniffed and shrugged. "It matters not. Herbal remedies will always be the best."

Godwin was still chuckling at her and she eyed him suspiciously. "Well, Master Godwin, I will bid you a good day. Some of us have work to do." She made to rise from the bench but Godwin, his face once more serious, put out a hand to touch her arm.

"I am sorry, Christiana. I did not mean to offend you. I know that the earl and countess hold both Martha and yourself in high regard. Please sit and allow me to explain."

The touch of Godwin's hand had been warm and comforting and for the second time in this man's company Christiana found herself blushing but she did as he bade her and sat.

"I had a mind to study the ways of the physician myself at one time," Godwin began quietly. "Alas, it was not to be. My father would not hear of it. He would not waste the family fortune on flights of fancy, as he called it."

Christiana sat very still, waiting to hear more of this young man's mysterious past.

"Who is your family?" she asked after a while.

"The Scropes," Godwin replied.

"The Scropes of Bolton?" Christiana asked, still further intrigued for the Scropes were a family of some note here in the north.

Godwin grinned. "Well, they are a branch. I am a distant kin. You know, youngest son of the youngest son?" he said almost apologetically.

"But you are in a good position here at Middleham, are you not? Usher to the earl," Christiana enthused.

"Yes I am and happy for it in the most part." Godwin's voice was tinged with sadness and Christiana wondered why it should be so.

As the balmy twilight fell and a bouquet of perfume rose from the flowers in the garden, Godwin played his mournful tunes on his flute and Christiana listened, enthralled. Returning later to the cottage she smiled to herself, pleased to have made a deeper acquaintance of Godwin, whom she had thought little of until this day.

Middleham Castle
Yorkshire
Autumn 1470

"You shouldn't be here, William, when there's work to be done. Get along back to the smithy, lad, and look sharp." Alfred stood facing his son square on and waited for William's response. The small group of soldiers gathered around the tables at the armoury downing their midday ale sat expectantly, eager for a possible confrontation to break the monotony of their day.

William sat slouched on a bench with his back against the stone wall and his feet up on the wooden table in front of him. The jug by his side was half empty. Rowena, pink-cheeked and giggly, had one arm draped over his shoulder. Alfred was disgusted by William's attitude of late; if the constable, Lord Richard FitzHugh, had been within the walls instead of away looking after the earl's interests elsewhere, this relaxed, undisciplined attitude would not be tolerated. Alfred felt his anger rising.

"William, you are a blacksmith not a soldier. You belong at the smithy, not here drinking ale in the company of loose women," he shouted.

A murmur of sniggers went up from the men, while Rowena, unscathed by the inference of Alfred's words, giggled and leant her flaming curls against William's neck.

Alfred's patience was all but lost. He took a step towards William and bellowed.

"God's truth, son, pull yourself together and get back to work!"

William, fired with courage courtesy of the ale he had consumed, stood up and brushed the girl aside.

"Son! That's just it, is it not, Alfred? I am not *your* son am I? You might be a bloody blacksmith but my father was a soldier. He died at Wakefield didn't he eh? And you know something, Alfred? I am going to be a soldier just like my father!"

Alfred's silence spoke the full extent of his pain and shock. His hurt was expressed so vividly upon his face that every man around the tables sat speechless. After a few long agonising moments the big blacksmith turned and slowly walked away. As the dejected figure disappeared from view William took up his tankard and threw it hard against the stone wall.

By that evening a cold autumnal wind had brewed up and began to whip around the castle walls in a furious frenzy. Huddled inside the guardroom soldiers snored in heaps on the floor lulled into sleep by watered down wine from a recently tapped barrel. William drew his cloak around his shoulders and listened to the first pattering of raindrops on the stone walls outside. The wind whistled through the arrow slits and around the door teasing the flames of the huge torches into submission.

He had felt too miserable to return to the smithy that afternoon. He had not drunk any more ale nor had he any wine and now he was cold sober and unable to sleep. He should not have spoken as he had to Alfred. He owed much to that man who had been more than a father to him. He did not understand himself sometimes. He felt so restless and frustrated and angry. It was true, he had been spending more time in the company of the garrison soldiers, drinking and taking his pleasure with Rowena. He had been anxious to prove his manhood having failed miserably at his first attempt. He always felt physically satisfied after his lying with Rowena but he was always left with a sense of guilt and shame afterwards. He knew it was because of Christiana. He was enamoured by her beautiful brown eyes and cascade of ebony curls, her gentle nature and selflessness. If he caught a glimpse of her suckling her child, rocking him gently and singing to him, William would feel pangs of passion dart through his whole body until it hurt. His anger was directed at the Duke of Gloucester who, in his mind, had snared Christiana's heart in a trap disguised by such virtues as piety, loyalty and noble birth. Richard's attributes served only to enhance his own sense of unworthiness.

William's thoughts were jolted back to the present by the sound of the great wooden door creaking as someone pushed it open and edged inside in a shower of icy raindrops. The soldier stumbled over the inert bodies and sat down heavily beside William.

"'Tis unseasonably cold out there tonight." He shivered, rubbing his fingers together.

William could see that the man had been drinking and he could smell the ale on his breath. Ralph Hodkin, however, had learned to hold his drink – he had consumed enough over the years to function well enough with or without it.

The two men sat in silence for a while, the only sound being the pounding rain flung against the stone walls by a hot-tempered wind. To pass the time and because his rival for Christiana's affections was foremost on his mind, William opened up a conversation with the soldier.

"How goes it with our king and his loyal brother? What news do you have to cheer me on such a foul night?"

Ralph sneered. "News to cheer? Well, I have got news that might be of interest to some. For all we know, boy, our good King Edward could well be drowned in the Wash, along with his puny brother to boot. 'Tis said the Wash is a cruel sea and shows no mercy. How does that take you for news?"

William sat upright, at once alert. Ralph lowered his voice to a whisper. "But of course, as a supporter of the Yorkist king you will be devastated by such news." His tone was loaded with sarcasm but failed to hit the mark with William who was thinking, much to his shame, about Richard and how, if it were indeed true, the demise of that young prince would certainly advance his chances with Christiana.

After a few moments when his companion did not answer Ralph waded in a little deeper.

"You know Warwick is back?" he asked with a gentle nudge in William's side. William inclined his head; that much he did know.

"Warwick's brother, Montague, turned against the king at Doncaster, miffed at having his earldom of Northumberland restored to Henry Percy. Well, King Ned doesn't even bother trying to fight against the combined forces of Warwick, Clarence and Montague so he turns tail and makes for the east coast. Gone to his brother-in-law Charles, Duke of Burgundy, no doubt."

William turned to Ralph, a wry smile across his face. "How comes it you are so well informed?" he asked.

The soldier gave a sly chuckle. "Because I make it my business to be so. And I am well paid for my knowledge," he answered.

There followed a few more minutes of silence broken only by the howling wind and the sonorous snores of their comrades.

"I have watched you, William," Ralph began quietly. "You are skilled with the halberd with your strong arms and you are nimble on your feet. A soldier needs to know he is on the right side, if you follow me." He spat into the straw. "There will be a restoration of old Henry to the throne now, lad, and when or if Edward cares to come home we will be waiting."

Ralph gathered his cloak tightly around him. "You think on my words, lad," he said before slumping down to the floor and making himself comfortable for the night.

William thought about nothing else for the rest of the cold miserable night. He did not want to stay at Middleham all his life. Maybe, when the time came for the next battle, he would be ready.

Middleham Castle
Yorkshire
Winter 1470

"Now who can that be?" Martha looked up at the sound of a loud knocking on the door. She laid aside her sewing, more shifts for the child who was putting his knees through them at a fair rate, and waddled to the door.

A flurry of snowflakes swept into the herbarium as she opened the door, the cloaked figure outside not waiting for leave to enter. Pushing the oak door closed against the icy onslaught the visitor removed his hood and stood red-cheeked with the cold but smiling.

"Why, Godwin, this is a surprise. Is it your arm? Have you...?" Martha spluttered, looking from the usher to Christiana, whose face had turned an identical shade of red to the man's.

Martha raised her eyebrows before nodding her head. "Enter, enter. You are welcome," she said. "Let me take your cloak. Christiana, a cup of hot spiced wine for the usher."

Christiana stood and placed John, who she had been bouncing on her lap, back in his pen where he began to wail in protest until she threw in a few little carved wooden horses and the coral teething pegs.

With the wine warmed and spiced and handed round Christiana took a seat between Martha and Godwin and waited for the usher to announce the purpose of his visit. He did so without preamble. "Lord Richard FitzHugh," he always gave the constable his full title, "has returned this very day from the Earl of Warwick. He is in London giving his full support to Henry who it seems has been restored to the throne. There is more reason for Warwick to rejoice as his youngest daughter Anne is to be wed to Prince Edward of Lancaster; the 13th day of December I do believe at Amboise Cathedral."

Christiana shifted uncomfortably on her stool. Godwin

continued. "The earl is anxious to see that his affairs are looked to in his absence, naturally. Sir John Conyers has been most diligent on the earl's behalf and most of the revenues from his estates have been collected."

"Yes, yes," Martha interrupted, impatient at the man's rhetoric. "This is no more than would be expected of a man in his position. What of it?"

Godwin shot a patient look at Christiana who smiled in return. "Well, Martha," continued the usher, "we, that is to say all the servants at the castle, have been invited to a feast for the celebration of Christmastide. Conyers has been given leave to provide food and entertainment, as long as expenditure remains modest, you understand."

Now Martha and Christiana exchanged glances. "What sort of entertainment will there be?" Martha asked.

"The usual, dancing, minstrels, just a few mind. Oh, and a mystery play."

"A mystery play," Christiana repeated, suitably impressed.

"There is a troupe of players at Wakefield even now, Christiana. As long as the roads are passable they should be with us during Advent," Godwin said, smiling.

By the Feast Day of Saint Nicholas at the beginning of Advent the snow covering the dales and woodlands had thawed a little, making it possible for folk to go out and about collecting mistletoe, holly and any green foliage they could find with which to make the kissing boughs and decorate the great hall.

By the time the tables, cupboards and walls were festooned in seasonal verdure, and a little to spare to decorate their own modest dwellings, the residents at the castle were beginning to believe that Christmastide would indeed be a joyous occasion.

Late one afternoon the troupe of mystery players and minstrels, together with trunk loads of paraphernalia, arrived cold and wet to a hearty welcome. Lord FitzHugh had even organized a party of nobles to join him on a hunt to bring back the Yule boar, a necessary part of the festivities.

The celebration of Christ's birth began with the Angel Mass at midnight and Christiana, Martha and Alfred joined many folk on the journey to Saint Mary's and Saint Alkelda's under a cold, starry night, lanterns held aloft lighting the way.

The second Mass, the Shepherd's Mass, celebrated at sunrise, saw fewer folk out on the road; the pious, heavily cloaked and bleary-eyed, shuffling once again into the cold church. Christiana had gone to the Shepherd's Mass with her father, Martha offering to stay indoors with the babe. They returned in the brilliance of a sunlit winter's day to a cup of hot spiced wine and an ambience of excitement and wonder.

By late noon the sun had disappeared and a frosty chill once again settled on the castle. Conyers, in consultation with the chaplain, had agreed to open the chapel to any who preferred not to make a third journey to the village to hear the final Mass of the day, the Mass of The Divine Word.

Feeling that all due respect and reverence had been paid to the Divine Christ child, folk turned their attention to the forthcoming feast with increased fervour. It was as they were preparing themselves for the festivities that Martha made an announcement. "I know 'tis not yet the time for gifts, Christiana, but this should not wait for Epiphany." So saying, the old woman opened the heavy lid of a chest and pulled out a plain but newly made gown the colour of sunlit chestnuts and soft as fur.

Christiana gasped. "Martha, this looks like fine-woven lambswool," she said, feeling the cloth.

"'Tis lambswool, aye, but not so expensive. I have money enough to pay for it," Martha mumbled, holding up the garment to Christiana to check its size and fit. "Now make haste, girl, we do not want to miss the disguisings."

Sometime later and Christiana was ready. The gown was a perfect fit and her hair had been combed and tied neatly beneath a linen coif. There remained but one addition to her attire: Richard's garnet and jet jewel. Martha frowned slightly as she tied the clasp at the nape of Christiana's neck, but she said nothing.

With John tucked warmly beneath the woollen folds of

his mother's cloak and Martha in a gown the colour of a ripe Wensleydale cheese, the three set off against a biting wind towards the great stone keep.

Godwin was not at his usual post in the antechamber when they arrived and Christiana looked around the empty room expectantly in the hope of seeing him. There was no one but a surly guard on duty. The great hall was a cauldron of light and colour all awash with sounds of laughter and gaiety. Minstrels were strolling around plucking and blowing their instruments into tune. Ulrick, stiff with age, sniffed nonchalantly around the company before flopping heavily beside the blazing fire where he slept peacefully.

Alfred and Jude approached the herbalists shortly after they entered the room. The blacksmith, looking uncomfortable in such grand company, peered around the hall nervously. Christiana noticed that her father had made an effort to wash the charcoal smears from his hands and face and to clean most of the smuts from his tunic.

It was not long before Conyers announced the commencement of the mystery play. As it was to be performed indoors the traditional moving stage was done away with and everyone was urged to sit as close to the edge of the room as the trestles and boards would permit in order to create a space for the players.

A hush fell upon the hall as a trumpet blast heralded the arrival of the main characters, suitably robed and masked. Kneeling, sitting or craning their necks, the audience watched in wonder as the mystery of the Nativity was acted out before their very eyes from the Annunciation to the visit of the Magi bearing gifts.

It was during the visit of the shepherds, when there ensued a period of mayhem as the two scrawny sheep ran amok in the crowd, that Christiana noticed that Godwin had appeared at her side. In a freshly brushed tunic of scarlet cloth and his dark hair neatly coiffured he looked most appealing and Christiana found herself smiling sweetly at him. He remained at her side until the last of the wise men had deposited his gift, courtesy of a local goldsmith, and the crowd gave up tumultuous applause.

There followed a further lengthy delay as Conyers and several ushers organised the seating arrangements; correct etiquette, of necessity, was almost abandoned. Lord FitzHugh, the constable, and Sir John Conyers, the steward, presided over the feast at the top table on the dais. Christiana found herself and Martha near the upper end of their table just below the clerics and other highborn servants. Alfred and Jude were happily seated at the far end of the table with the soldiers of the garrison.

John was taken away from the main feast to join the few young children who lived in the bailey and their attendants leaving Christiana free to enjoy Godwin's company and with whom she shared a drinking cup.

Before the food was served Conyers stood and called for a toast to their absent lord, the Earl of Warwick. They raised their cups to drink to his health and prosperity and to affirm their own allegiance to him. There was also a tentative toast to Good King Henry before the Yule boar was presented and carved. Removes consisting of pottage, birds, fish, bread and sweetmeats followed together with a moderate flow of wine.

"'Tis most unusual to see so many different folk together to feast," Christiana remarked. "I cannot but wonder what the earl would make of it if he were here."

"Indeed it breaks all bounds of etiquette," Godwin replied, helping himself to a scrawny colly bird from a silver platter. "Warwick's position is by no means secure and he plays a risky game. I believe he allows such a generous feast in order to keep the loyalty of all his servants. Middleham Castle is of great importance here in the north and cannot be seen to fall into ruin."

It was just as well that Godwin remained most attentive and polite as they ate, for Martha was unusually quiet. Once or twice Christiana glanced Alfred's way and wondered, not for the first time, where William could be.

It was getting late into the evening of what had already been a very long day for many when the boards were set aside in readiness for the dancing. Alfred, looking a little more relaxed with a bellyful of wine, approached his daughter as she was bidding Martha and John a good night.

"We will be away now," he said. "Jude and a few of the men are going back for a game of dice."

"You will not stay for the dancing?" Christiana asked, feeling at once as though she was being abandoned.

"Nay, lass," Alfred laughed. "My old pins are too shaky for such cavorting." He bent down to kiss the crown of John's dark head and was just turning to walk away when Christiana caught his sleeve.

"Where is William? I have not seen him all day," she asked. The blacksmith sighed.

"He is down at the gatehouse doing a turn at the watch. Do not fret over him. Stay and enjoy the dancing."

Christiana did not want for a dancing partner as Godwin was ever hers as they joined in the carol dancing and a farandole so that by the end of the evening she was quite fatigued. Retrieving her cloak from the antechamber Christiana walked wearily down the outer staircase, not refusing Godwin's insistence that he accompany her back to the cottage.

The stars sparkled like diamonds in a cloudless velvet black sky as Godwin, one hand holding a lantern, the other looped through Christiana's arm, led the way along the frozen tracks into the bailey. His usual banter had, it seemed, dried up, for the usher uttered not a single word all the way to the cottage; Christiana was grateful that the journey was not a long one for both their sakes.

On the approach to the cottage Christiana was certain there had been just the flicker of a shadow in the candlelight, moving quickly away from the casement, and she smiled.

"Does something amuse you?" Godwin asked seriously.

Christiana chuckled and shook her head. "Nay, Godwin. It has been a most enjoyable feast. Conyers should be commended for his effort," she said sleepily.

"Indeed," Godwin replied. He stood there in awkward silence for a few moments before snatching up Christiana's hand and kissing it gently, and then turning quickly on his heel he marched away, his little light bobbing ever fainter.

It was of no surprise to the girl that Martha was not abed even at this late hour. Christiana would say nothing beyond once again applauding Conyers for the feast and thanking Martha for her gift with a kiss before taking gratefully to her bed.

Outside the town of Barnet
North of London
The eve of 13th April 1471

William eased himself down deeper into the thick grass trying to find a comfortable position to rest, although there would be little chance of sleep that night. He fidgeted with his heavy padded jack and laid a hand reassuringly on the halberd and sallet lying at his side.

The long march south had been tiring. His feet were swollen and sore with blisters and many soldiers, William included, were suffering with the flux; the food they had foraged had come from a most dubious source. The large quantity of cheap wine carried in large wooden casks and consumed freely on the journey was the mainstay of their morale.

It was only last month that King Edward had arrived back in England heading an army financed, albeit reluctantly, by his brother-in-law, Duke Charles of Burgundy. The Earl of Warwick had been prepared and his forces had mustered at Coventry. There, Richard Neville had waited for the Duke of Clarence to join him with his army on their way up from the Cotswolds. The king had gathered his forces outside the city gates and offered the earl a pardon. Warwick had laughed in the face of the king's messenger and refused Edward's challenge to come forth and do battle. With no one to fight the king had led his army away.

Sometime later Warwick's trust in his son-in-law, Clarence, was dealt a severe blow with the news that the brothers had been reconciled near Banbury, due in the main to persuasions by the Duke of Gloucester. George's troops were now added to those of the king. That so many had turned their support to Edward in so short a time was indication of the popularity and strength of the Yorkist king, something William tried hard not to think about on this, the eve of his very first taste of battle.

And so, as he sat here camped just north of the town of Barnet, feeling the cold of early April, his nerves as taut as a bowstring and his stomach as tight as a hemp rope knot, William began to question the sense of it all. He would not easily forget the pain and anger in Christiana's eyes the day he joined Warwick's retinue and marched from the castle. Nothing, it seemed, would shake his sister's loyalty to the Yorkist cause.

His desire to be a soldier at last fulfilled, William sat and waited throughout the long night listening to the taunts of intermittent gun fire and dozing as a dense fog crept in and smothered them all in a damp blanket.

It was barely dawn the following day when Edward advanced to attack. The fog was still thick and heavy with the sulphuric whiff of gunpowder. William was deployed in the small reserve of foot soldiers commanded by Warwick and placed behind the centre division under the command of John Neville, Lord Montague. The Earl of Oxford had command of Warwick's right division and the Duke of Exeter the left.

At the first cry of advance and trumpet call William was on his feet, halberd in hand. Archers on the front line let loose their volley of arrows blindly into the mist. William in the midst of the reserves waited with bated breath as the two armies advanced, ready to lock in hand to hand combat, their pole arms at the ready.

A shout had gone up that the three divisions of the opposing armies had misaligned in the dense fog. To his right William sensed that Oxford, realising the situation, had taken advantage of the sloping ground and charged down to meet Hastings' advancing attack. William could not see very much in the gloom, fuelling his already heightened sense of fear, but he could hear the rattle of armour, the clash of weapons and the soul-piercing screams of butchered men. Flashes of yellow flame from the handguns split the grey here and there like the fiery breath of demons from hell.

Warwick gave the order for his reserve to advance and William followed the banner of the ragged staff and bear, barely visible. He was terrified. His stomach was churning and he felt certain that he was going to cast up his breakfast at any moment.

He gripped his halberd by the shaft, hands spaced wide apart, and strode out to meet the enemy. On seeing the figure of a soldier materialise out of the vapour, weapon poised to strike, William hesitated. As the edge of the blade glinted momentarily before coming down at an angle towards his face, William felt the fighting spirit surge through his veins and instinct told him that it was either kill or be killed. He threw up his pole and angled it deftly to block the force of his opponent's thrust and in the next instance had twisted and plunged the length of the long blade full into the belly of the Yorkist soldier with a dull, slicing thud. The pointed and shaped blade had embedded itself into the thick padding of the soldier's gambeson and William had to twist and turn his weapon to remove it; as it withdrew a gush of hot red blood flowed in its wake followed by a dribble of soft writhing bowel. The pain and terror in the man's eyes lasted only seconds before he crumpled lifeless to the ground. The sight and the sound and the gut-wrenching stench of fresh blood caused William's stomach to heave, but it was of little consequence. With the strength of his arms and the power in his shoulders he fought and hacked his way into the advancing line, hardly aware of his own actions.

By now the Duke of Gloucester had swung his men round into position on the right and a hand-to-hand massacre followed. The Yorkist onslaught proved too much for the Lancastrians and their front line dissolved. Many fled as William battled on. The falling bodies on either side hindered his progress; he could no longer wield the long shaft of his weapon for the crush of the dead and the dying.

The fog had by now all but dispersed and as the line thinned William caught a fleeting glimpse of the Earl of Warwick in blazoned surcoat retreating desperately on foot towards a thicket of trees and a waiting horse. William's loss of concentration, albeit for a second, cost him a severe blow to the head, dislodging his helmet and sending him sprawling on to a heap of sticky, wet and bloodied bodies.

A muffled medley of sounds assailed his ears as a piercing pain exploded inside William's head. A brilliant light burned through his eyelids and he could smell the grass crushed beneath his cheek. A sharp blow to his side caused him to cry out.

"This one's still alive!" A deep voice sounded somewhere above his head; then another.

"Stay your hand! I know this one. William? William?" Someone was shaking his shoulder.

William slowly opened his eyes and blinked painfully in the morning sunlight. He made a feeble attempt to lift himself up onto his knees. An unknown hand was assisting him. He felt groggy and the pain in his head was unbearable. Someone was squatting beside him offering him a flagon of wine. He drank a few mouthfuls before retching as the smell of fresh blood that still hung in the air filled his nostrils.

"All is well, William, take ease and rest awhile." William looked up then at the one who offered him solace to find it was none other than the Duke of Gloucester. Even in his weakened state William had a mind to fear the Yorkist prince. He tried to scramble to his feet but Richard had a hand firmly on his shoulder. "William, the king is willing to grant a pardon to any who will swear allegiance to him," he said firmly.

The blacksmith looked steadily at the young duke, face smeared with blood, armour dulled with gore and filth. A dark patch was forming just visible at the edge of the pauldron that covered his right shoulder. "You might as well, William. Warwick is dead," Richard continued in a whisper.

The duke turned his head and stood to bow as a tall figure strode up to them. Clad in surcoat bearing the royal arms over an impressive harness of armour and fair hair ruffled in the breeze, the person of the king was instantly recognisable by William.

"Come, Dickon. Have that wound tended to, we march on London shortly. Make haste, brother," Edward called before moving away.

Richard extended a hand to William and waited for him to move. William stared into the eyes of the man, a youth of his own age, his rival for the affections of the girl he loved, and reluctantly he took the hand offered in truce.

A little later William sat with his back against the bole of a tree eating stale bread and drinking warm ale. He had been given a herb for his head and the pain was beginning to ease somewhat and apart from one or two slashes across the back of his hands he seemed to have survived his first battle fairly unscathed.

Behind him the villagers and several monks from Saint Mary's church of the Abbey of Saint Albans were helping with the task of burying the dead and offering whatever treatment and comfort they could to the wounded and dying. Horses fit enough to stand had been rounded up and were now in their midst being prepared for the march to London.

Ralph Hodkin had also survived the battle and now sat beside William, heartily stuffing himself with bread and ale. The ale, as ever, had loosened the man's tongue and he began to give his own version of the battle, although it soon became apparent that he was not present for much of it. He had been assigned to fight under the banner of the Earl of Oxford. At the commencement of battle Hastings' troops had fled towards Barnet under attack and hotly pursued by Oxford's men. Ralph, along with many, had given chase all the way into the town. Seeing how more was to be gained by looting the townsfolk, the urgency of the battlefield was soon forgotten.

Ralph put his hand under his gambeson and pulled out a handful of silver trinkets. He winked knowingly at William. "I paid well for my booty, mind," he whispered on ale-scented breath. "Warwick opened fire on us as we returned to the field. The bloody fools thought that Oxford's livery of the star was Edward's sun in splendour. Still, I live to fight another battle." He patted his thigh where a coarse bandage, blotted red, covered a superficial wound, and downed another mouthful of ale.

William looked with growing disgust at the man beside him. The battlefield was just a place of opportunity for him, while for many others it would become their grave.

A few yards in front of them a young squire was helping the Duke of Gloucester to remove his armour. Richard had his back to them and they watched as a monk soaked a piece of lint in a foul-smelling solution and removing the right sleeve of the duke's doublet began to wipe away the blood from the wound in his shoulder.

From where he sat in the shade of the tree it appeared to William that the young duke was reluctant to remove his shirt completely, somewhat hampering the monk's ability to tend the wound. This seemingly insignificant observation was soon forgotten moments later, however, when William's attention was caught by the sound of wailing moans a short distance across the field.

"Who is that over there? I have only just noticed him," William asked. Following the direction of William's gaze Ralph saw the thin scantily dressed man sitting in the shade of a thick oak. His long hair hung in bedraggled strands about his shoulders and several days of beard growth had spawned on his face. With his wild staring eyes and bony fingers tugging at the grass whereupon he sat he looked for the entire world a madman.

Ralph guffawed sarcastically. "Why that, dear William, is good old King Henry, God bless him. He's come along as guest of his cousin Edward. It was to restore him to the throne that Warwick gave his life and that of his brother Montague. Still, we are on the right side now, eh, Will?" He laughed, digging his elbow sharply into William's side.

William's dislike of the man sitting beside him was growing ever stronger. His allegiances were as fickle as the wind, with no regard or loyalty for any but himself. Maybe he still had a lot to learn about warfare, and he was not just thinking about the use of weapons, but for his own part William felt justified in being on the wrong side. He had been loyal to Warwick, his liege lord, and that, he reasoned, was how it should be.

He looked across at the pathetic figure of Henry as he muttered incoherently to himself and then over to where King Edward stood giving orders to his men, and William's mind, it seemed, was made up. He drained his cup and stood to his feet. He walked over to where the Duke of Gloucester was redressing in arming doublet. He stood a little distance from him and bowed.

"My lord," he croaked a touch nervously. After clearing his throat he proceeded. "I am ready to swear allegiance to King Edward and to you, my lord, as his loyal brother. I am willing to serve. I have skill as a blacksmith as well as a soldier."

Richard looked up and for a moment or two said nothing as William continued to stare into his dark eyes and blood-splattered face. After a while the duke answered.

"A pardon will be granted in exchange for loyalty. Now, tell me how is your sister? She is well I hope?"

William felt his face redden. It was not for him to divulge the fact that the duke had a bastard son, every inch his likeness, waiting for his return at Middleham Castle. Instead he replied simply, "Christiana was well enough the last time I saw her, my lord. I thank you."

Not long afterwards William was taken to Edward and there before him went down upon his knee swearing lifelong allegiance to his sovereign lord. As he gave a hand to preparing the horses prior to their march to London, William caught sight of Ralph Hodkin grovelling before King Edward and kissing the proffered ring on his finger. His acute awareness of the dishonour and self-abasement of Ralph's false allegiances sickened William to his stomach.

It was with the triumph of victory still ringing in their ears that the king and his troops were to hear the news that Queen Margaret of Anjou, her son Prince Edward of Lancaster and his new bride had landed safely at Portland in the south of England on the very day the Yorkists had won the battle at Barnet.

Edward's return to London after Barnet was to a victor's welcome made more joyous with the news that his queen had given birth to a son during his time in exile. This was no time for family reunions, however, as matters of great urgency pressed upon the king. Edward knew his enemy and there were few more ruthless than Queen Margaret, fighting for the rights of her son in the absence of a husband capable of defending his kingdom.

Edmund Beaufort, fourth Duke of Somerset would need little persuasion to lead an army in support of the queen for was it not rumoured that his own father, Edmund Beaufort, second Duke of Somerset, was indeed the true father of this Prince of Lancaster?

King Edward knew well enough that this second Duke of Somerset had been the great antagonist of Richard, Duke of York, declared Protector of the Realm when King Henry lost his sanity. There was much at stake when these two rivals met for with both their fathers dead these two sons continued the battle between the York and Lancastrian cause.

Word had reached King Edward that the Lancastrians, once back on English soil, were intent upon crossing the River Severn into Wales to join forces with the Welsh, in particular Jasper Tudor. The city of Bristol had declared allegiance to Queen Margaret and her son and supplied their army with artillery, greatly strengthening their force. Edward had anticipated the Lancastrians' next move and sent word to the citizens of Gloucester to hold fast against

Queen Margaret. This they duly did and the Lancastrian army had little choice but to press onwards towards the next river crossing.

It had been a long, hard and exhausting fox and goose chase to reach the Lancastrians in time to prevent them entering Wales and Edward's men fared little better than their enemy, who reached no further than Tewkesbury before being intercepted by the king's troops.

William could no longer feel the pain in his sore, blistered feet and the pangs of hunger in his stomach had long ceased when the enemy at last came into view. The king wasted no time in ordering his army into three divisions. Edward himself took command of the centre, with Clarence under his watchful eye, for he still had little faith in that brother's loyalty. William Hastings took his right division and the Duke of Gloucester the left, facing troops under the command of the Duke of Somerset.

There was a great wooded area to the left of Gloucester's division and to counter any surprise attack by the Lancastrians, Edward, ever an effective and shrewd commander, dispatched a troop of some 200 spearmen to guard his flank. It was into this detachment that William was deployed.

Battle commenced with each side teasing the other with cannon shots, which could be heard but not seen from the thick of the trees where William waited with pounding heart and churning stomach.

It was not long before it became apparent that Somerset, a cunning commander with the advantage of having previously reconnoitred the land, was leading his men, hidden within hedged lanes, around to the west with the intention of attacking Gloucester's division from behind.

The spearmen waited, arms at the ready, listening for the rustling of leaves and crunching of stick and twig underfoot, waiting for the emergence of the enemy.

It appeared, however, that Somerset was not wily enough for he had undershot his mark, breaking cover just to the left of the king, leaving himself wide open for attack and unable to be aided by Wenlock and Devon who had the centre and left command.

With Gloucester leading the charge from his division and the king joining his brother from the centre it only left the 200 spears to join the foray and Somerset was surrounded on three sides.

After that the Yorkists pressed home with such force that the entire Lancastrian army broke apart and fled. There was some talk later of dissention in the ranks but whatever the truth the outcome was the same: a sound victory for Edward Plantagenet. It was with much elation that William joined his fellow soldiers in pursuit of the defeated Lancastrians, running them across the Swilgate towards the muddy waters of a millpond in a nearby meadow. Many others reaching the safety of the town sought refuge in the church and abbey.

It was as William was returning to the field that he heard the news that the young Lancastrian Prince Edward had been amongst the slain as he fled towards the town.

The following morning saw the execution in the marketplace of Edmund Beaufort, fourth Duke of Somerset, and a handful of other nobles taken captive at the battle. William, having no stomach for public executions, returned to the field to finish the necessary task of treating any injured horses, repairing their shoes and with his dagger ending the suffering of those beyond saving.

It was here at early noon that the Duke of Gloucester approached him. William was just tapping in the last nail of a horseshoe when he looked up to see a rider approaching. Looking tired and bone-weary despite his youth, Richard sat astride his mount, equally soiled with battle mire, and called to the blacksmith, "We need horses, William, ready to march this day, a dozen or so."

William released the horse's fetlock, letting the hoof drop to the ground. "Aye, my lord, there are enough fit to be ridden." He nodded towards the enclosure where several horses were grazing under guard.

"Are you well, William?" Richard asked unexpectedly, but not waiting for a reply continued, "I would have you ride with my men. We are to pursue the Queen Margaret. The king is most anxious for her capture and must leave that task to me for there is news of a skirmish in the north to which Edward himself goes to quell."

William looked up at the prince and met his eye. Five months short of his nineteenth birthday and yet Richard had showed remarkable courage and skill on the battlefield and a fierce loyalty to his brother that was quite astonishing in a world where treachery and self-gain were commonplace. William felt a newfound surge of admiration for the young duke despite still nurturing a wave of jealousy against him that would not quite be quenched.

"I am both willing and able, my lord, to take orders from you. Horses can be made ready to ride forthwith."

"Good man." Richard inclined his head, turned his horse and rode away.

"My lord, Pilkington sends news. The queen and her ladies have taken refuge in the priory at Little Malvern." The soldier had come running into the camp and now stood flushed and panting, steadying the long sheath of his sword at his side and bowing quickly.

The duke stood to his feet to meet the messenger. "Is the queen under guard?" he asked.

"Yes, my lord. Pilkington has them locked in a cell at the priory awaiting your orders."

Richard's face was darkly earnest. He rubbed a hand across the stubble on his chin and glanced upwards. Grey clouds scudded across the sky threatening to blot out the remainder of the day's feeble rays. "How far is it to Malvern?"

"Not far, my lord. We could be there by nightfall," replied the soldier.

Darkness was almost upon them and a few cold drops of rain had begun to splash onto the faces of the riders as the stone walls of the priory loomed darkly before them. Huge torches illuminated their way, sending menacing shadows dancing on the pathway to the great arched doorway. William for one would be thankful enough to spend the night under a roof. It had taken three days before Margaret of Anjou had finally been run to ground; the damp and cold of battle camps was beginning to seep into his bones.

A small postern opened in the great wooden door in response to the ringing of the bell and a hooded monk solemnly greeted the duke. After leaving their horses with the grooms the men were led into the hall where a welcoming fire roared in the hearth. The soldiers, divested of boots and cloaks, set to eating the supper provided by the monks. The duke, along with William and one other, were taken to the prior.

It was a rather tall, gauntly featured man with strands of silver hair circling his tonsure who greeted the young duke. The elderly cleric made a show of protest at giving up his royal guest, who after all, had sought sanctuary in the house of God. It was but a feeble protest, however. He did not want to risk incurring the king's displeasure and thus mar the peace and stability of his final years as prior of this poor lowly place. Therefore he gave up his guest almost willingly.

Richard asked to see the prisoners and the three soldiers were taken along dimly lit stone passageways that led to a large low-beamed chamber. A huge iron grill partitioned off part of the room; within its bars was a padlocked door. It was a prison befitting its occupants; candlelit and furnished with raised pallets and stuffed mattresses. A small table held platters of bread and cheese and a flagon of wine.

The burly figure of Robert Pilkington, a trusted soldier of Yorkshire blood, stood up straight against the stone wall and despite his obvious fatigue bowed his head as his master approached.

"Good work, Robert," the duke commended. "Return to the hall and take food and rest. Set a watch for the night, we leave at first light."

Pilkington shuffled gratefully from the room under the watchful eyes of the same hooded figure that had escorted the duke and his companions to the cell. William turned his attention then to the two female prisoners held behind bars. One, looking pale and fearful, sat upon the bed; the other paced the floor, eyes blazing angrily like a she-wolf. "So, you Yorkist pig," she spat as the duke approached her cage. "What do you propose to do with me?"

"That, madam, will be a matter for the king to decide," Richard replied tersely.

"The king!" screeched Margaret of Anjou. "Henry, my husband, is the king of England." Her words were deeply accented in her native French tongue as her anger rose. "This is treason—"

"Madam," Richard interrupted. "I fear your hopes for the future of the Lancastrian cause are all in vain. They died on the battlefield at Tewkesbury." His voice was strangely cold and the impact of his words cooled the woman's fury. She caught the bars with her jewelled fingers, her hands trembling. "Your filthy servant said that you had killed my beloved Edward – so it is true!" she cried.

William heard a strangled moan from the figure on the bed. Slowly she arose, a young girl, sallow-faced in the candlelight, the hem of her green silk gown thick with mud. Her eyes were red with crying and even now fresh tears glistened on her cheeks. "Is this true, cousin, does my husband indeed lie dead?"

Richard nodded slowly. "The prince was mortally wounded on the battlefield and lies in the abbey at Tewkesbury. He will be interred with all due respect, my lady. You have my word."

There followed a snort of mistrust from the queen which was ignored by the duke; he was looking with earnest into the eyes of the young girl. The widowed Princess of Wales closed her eyes and swallowed the painful lump in her throat. "And what of my father?" she asked quietly. "Is he also dead?"

"Killed at Barnet, my lady," Richard replied softly.

Anne Neville turned slowly away and walked over to the bed where she was joined by the dejected and sorrow-torn queen.

A clatter of boots along the stone passageway heralded the arrival of the first watch and the duke and his two soldiers returned to the hall for victuals. William was intrigued by the pained expression on the face of the young duke as he walked in silence beside him.

Early the following day, after a simple meal of bread, meat and wine, the company left the priory in a blaze of sunshine after the night's downpour, with a very disgruntled Margaret of Anjou a closely guarded prisoner in their midst.

A messenger intercepted the Duke of Gloucester within hours

of the commencement of their journey with further unwelcome news: the Earl of Warwick's nephew, Thomas Neville, known as the Bastard of Fauconberg, was fast approaching London bent upon laying siege to the city. Richard pressed on hastily, anxious now to meet up with the king, who was himself making his way south to London.

Battle-weary and tired, William rode just behind the duke. Not naturally over talkative, the young man seemed sullen and deep in thought. William noticed how he would keep glancing across at his young cousin, sitting hunched and red-eyed upon her chestnut palfrey, hardly caring where she was or where she was bound; his dark eyes full of concern.

William thought much about these young cousins as they rode mile upon mile across meadow and marsh, through hamlet and wood. He looked yet again to where Richard had drawn his horse alongside the Lady Anne, trying to engage her in conversation. It amused William to see how futile the duke's attempts were for the young lady had nothing but a frosty glare and tight lips for her cousin.

The Duke of Gloucester delivered his prisoners to the king at Coventry where a covered carriage was procured to convey the ladies on the remainder of their journey. They all turned southwards, the king having a great many men now under his command, heading for London to see what chaos awaited them in the capital.

Middleham Castle
Yorkshire
June 1471

"Should you not be about your work, Master Godwin?" Christiana admonished the usher with a smile. Godwin was kneeling beside John, who was strapped to his walking gin, teasing the child with a wooden puppet, holding it just out of reach as the boy waddled forward to reach it.

"There is little work at present. The countess has not yet returned; it is believed that she has taken sanctuary down south fearing the king's displeasure after the treachery of her husband." The usher laughed as he urged the child closer to the puppet held limply in his hand.

Christiana was bending over the cottage garden plucking at the ever-rampant weeds that would entwine themselves around the precious herbs given half a chance.

"You are too cruel to my son. Let him have the puppet," she said, sounding cross but smiling still.

"Nonsense, you must encourage him to walk. Is that not right, Johnny?" Godwin shook the puppet in front of the child and retreated a few steps to allow the boy, tethered to the post of his gin, to follow. However, Godwin had failed to notice the wooden basket full of plucked weeds placed on the floor nearby and tripped over it, landing with a thud on his rear end. John, being far more entertained by this performance than the prospect of having a puppet, let forth bubbles of laughter.

Christiana stood up and unable to suppress her own mirth held out a hand to assist the usher to his feet. Godwin, his face a mask of pain and shock, rubbed the affected part vigorously and began to laugh, despite himself.

"Does no one here about have any work to do?" Martha's stern voice cut through the laughter as she appeared in the doorway of the cottage, wooden spoon in hand and her apron streaked with a green-brown liquid. She took one look at the upturned basket with its spillage of weeds and soil and the wooden puppet splayed on the ground and tut-tutted gravely. "You gave me such a start with your frivolities I upset the pan on the brazier – look at my apron. Now I shall have to make some more," she chided.

"I am sorry, Martha, there was an accident," Christiana said, picking up the basket and smiling at Godwin. The usher, however, was no longer amused. Turning a little crimson in the face, he cleared his throat.

"I must return to my duties. Good day, Martha, Christiana," he said earnestly and with a slight incline of his head he walked away down the path. Christiana unstrapped John from the gin and followed Martha inside the cottage, where she placed the baby in his pen and gave him the puppet.

"I am sorry if I spoiled your fun, Christiana," Martha began as she wiped away the spilled liquid that was trickling down an iron leg of the brazier. "I am out of good humour this day. I fear that the death of the earl has upset me more than I cared to imagine." She sat down heavily on a stool and let the cloth fall to her lap.

Christiana was quite surprised by this remark. Although saddened by the news of Warwick's death she could not say that she was overly distressed. He had after all been a treacherous man whose ruthless ambitions had kept the country's nobility in the throes of war. His death would surely mean a more peaceful reign for the king.

"He did take up arms against Edward, Martha," she emphasised softly.

"Aye, I know that, girl. But he also put the king on the throne remember. And I have served the earl and his household here for many a long year," she sighed. "Still, I expect Clarence will be our new lord now through his wife Isabel. I cannot say I care much for him but along with most other folk I serve where my best interests lie. So, if George has a mind to keep an old herbalist in his household then that is just as well for me."

At least George now knew at last where his allegiance should lie, Christiana thought, knowing from recent news that the duke had been reconciled to the king prior to the battle at Barnet. Nevertheless the prospect of George as Lord of Middleham did not over please her. Then another thought struck her.

"Do not most of Richard Neville's estates belong in right to the dowager Countess of Warwick now that she is widowed?" she asked.

"That may indeed be true, lass. But can you ever see a woman keeping her inheritance when a man stands in her way?" Martha replied with a wry smile. "Then there is the matter of attainder – Warwick was guilty of treason against the king. We shall all just have to wait and see how the king decides our fate. In the meantime life goes on."

Christiana walked over to the pen and removed the puppet; the child had fallen asleep on the straw mattress with it clasped in his chubby arms. She lifted the figure into the air where its wooden limbs jangled together and it stared at her with a lopsided grin on its oddly painted round face.

"Godwin is most generous with his gifts," Martha remarked as her gaze fell upon the puppet. Christiana placed the figure down on top of a hessian sack and sat on a bench.

"Aye, he is," she sighed.

"Maybe the man is serious, Christiana. You know? You and him?"

The girl stared at the puppet for a while before replying. "I think he is too serious, Martha. He is a good friend but I think he takes life and himself a little too seriously. He needs to laugh a little."

"I think he hopes to gain more than friendship from you." Martha hesitated and then asked cautiously, "Has he spoken to you of a betrothal?"

"Good Lord, no," Christiana replied firmly and feeling at once that she had been too dismissive of her friend, she added, "As I have said before, Martha, Godwin is a very dear man and good company but beyond that—"

"You should not accept his favours if you have no intention of letting your relationship develop," Martha interrupted rather brusquely.

Christiana looked across at the stool in the corner where an assortment of silver hair decorations and combs lay in a heap; all gifts from Godwin.

"You should consider yourself honoured if a man such as he were to make you an offer of marriage. 'Tis about time you put an end to all this nonsense over the boy's father. But heed my words, Christiana, do not lead this Godwin a merry dance. He deserves your honesty," Martha warned, standing slowly to her feet to finish her cleaning task.

Christiana lowered her gaze to her fingers clasped tightly in her lap. How could she answer? Martha was of course right in all she said but how did she feel about Godwin? Could she see herself as his wife and he as John's father? What of John's natural father? Was there not still the deepest desire for him in her heart? What if Clarence, in spite for his younger brother, should turn her and her son out of the castle? How would William feel if she wed Godwin? Surely he would be pleased for his sister? Her brother had not yet returned from battle but there had been no ill news concerning him so they could only wait. There were so many questions and too few answers and it did little good to dwell on matters that were in the hands of God.

She had, however, grown very fond of Godwin, serious as he was, and she would not like to be the cause of his grief. However, he had not so much as hinted about betrothal or marriage and until he did so she would have no decision to make.

A sudden loud and urgent banging on the door startled both women who jumped up together, exchanging anxious glances before Martha flung aside the door. Jude, blackened from the soot of the smith's forge, face red as a beetroot and hair ruffled and windswept, stood on the threshold clutching his side and panting breathlessly. Martha, taking his arm, tried to pull him inside the cottage but he resisted. "Nay, Martha," he spluttered, fending her off. He turned a grave and frightened face towards Christiana and gasped, "You must come at once to the smithy. *At once!*"

Wensleydale
Yorkshire
July 1471

The air was thick with the scent of early morning, the fragrance of summer foliage rising upwards as the sun warmed it. Shafts of golden sunlight filtered through the canopy of leaves as their horses plodded on wearily through the trees.

William had been away from home some four months and as he sat upon his horse he pondered upon all that had passed in that time: Warwick, his liege lord, was dead and so was the old king, Henry (dying of melancholia from a broken heart, so it was said). King Edward was firmly back on England's throne and he, William, was returning from battles in which he had begun by fighting on the opposing side.

Edward's arrival in London after the battle of Tewkesbury had in fact been a triumphant one; riding at the head of his thirty-thousand-strong force, a king surely now reinstated as rightful sovereign.

It had been a close-run thing from all accounts given to the king on his return: the Bastard of Fauconberg and his five-thousand-strong army of men had launched a heavy attack on London Bridge, Aldergate and Bishopsgate. It was only the timely intervention of second Lord Rivers, leading an attack from the Tower with five hundred men, which forced the Bastard into retreat.

William recalled the scene in the yard at Westminster Palace as the king was greeted by the City Mayor, Aldermen and members of the Merchant Companies, whose loss would have been great indeed had Warwick's nephew succeeded with his raid on the city. A family of some note waiting to greet the king had drawn no little attention to themselves, William remembered, not least because the younger woman had turned a few heads, notably one being the king's own. John Lambert, wealthy merchant, his wife Amy, and their daughter Elizabeth with her husband William Shore, appeared almost on equal footing with the king as they stood clad in all their finery and sumptuous clothing. Edward had stared long and hard into the beguiling, almond-shaped eyes of Mistress Shore for much longer than decorum allowed. The lady, for her part, showed no more virtue by holding the king's gaze and smiling bewitchingly at him. William chuckled to himself as he thought about the reputation of this extravagantly flamboyant monarch.

It was not long after that when the Duke of Gloucester had led a sizeable force of the king's men out of London into Kent in pursuit of Thomas Neville the Bastard. William had been there to witness Thomas's surrender of the fleet and after that was given leave to return north.

That the king had finally appeared to have put an end to the uprisings was of no little consequence but the drama which followed his two younger brothers was no less significant; William had much to tell on his return home.

The company of horsemen, foot soldiers and wagons passed through the trees and into the open. Ahead in the distance they could see the castle; strong, solid and majestic as it glinted in the morning light. The sight gladdened William's heart. His mind went back to his very first glimpse of Middleham some ten years ago. It must have been almost from this very spot where as a small boy of around eight years he sat snug in the arms of the big blacksmith astride the old Dales pony.

Sitting astride his steed, hot and dusty from the long journey, every bone aching and in need of a hearty meal, William longed to reach home. His thoughts turned to Christiana; her honest, open face with gentle brown eyes and black curls tumbling down her back would ever haunt his dreams. He had allowed his bitter jealousy to corrode their relationship and for that he was sorry.

During the months he had been away from home William had matured beyond his eighteen or so years; facing death on the battlefield had a way of catapulting a boy into manhood. He had come to realise that man's allotted time on earth was a very precious thing, too fragile to waste on foolish emotions. He had a good deal of wrongs to right and if what he surmised to be true came to pass then Christiana would have no further need to look longingly at the Duke of Gloucester.

Then there was Alfred, whom he had treated worst of all. Had that man not been as a father to him and how had he repaid that love? By turning his back on his trade and running away to war. He did still have a mind to making soldiering his life's work; it was certainly more lucrative than blacksmithing, he thought, patting the swollen coin purse under his tunic. He would make amends with Alfred before he went away again; give him his earnings at least, as a token of his repentance.

Horses' hooves clattered on the cobblestones as they stumbled wearily into the stable yard. Sore from many a day in the saddle William slid gratefully from his horse, giving it a pat on its arched neck. Grooms and stable hands came forward to relieve the soldiers of their mounts and the footsore marchers of their armour and weapons.

William looked around for Alfred and thought it strange that the blacksmith was not here to look to the needs of the horses. He would find him later; there was someone else he wanted to see just as badly if not more so. He did not wait to take bread and ale to refresh him but instead made his way towards the herbarium. He was in need of a balm to relieve his blistered feet but the more pressing reason for his visit was to see Christiana.

The sun shone brilliantly overhead, showing up the rows of herbs and flowers in all their glory, enticing from them a welcoming aroma. Despite his stiffness William felt a lightness in his step as his boots crunched over the gravel path leading to the cottage. Outside on a patch of grass the child, John, now almost eighteen months, tottered happily around on his gin trying to catch the ginger kitten that pranced and leaped before him. Each time the animal moved beyond the extent of his tether the boy would squeal and extend a pair of chubby arms.

"How you have grown, little one," laughed William as he bent over to ruffle the child's thatch of dark curls. "Where is your mother then, eh?"

At that moment Martha appeared at the doorway to the cottage – if indeed it was Martha for her appearance had changed almost beyond recognition. Her cheeks were pale and hollow and her once merry eyes were devoid of all sparkle, sunk into her dough-like countenance. Her gown hung limply across her hips, no longer as rounded as they had once been.

On seeing William bending down to the child she threw herself at once upon his arms, moaning.

"Oh, William, thank the Lord you have come before it is too late!"

Greatly afeared, William shook the old woman from him.

"God's Truth, Martha, what is wrong?" he demanded. The herbalist continued to weep. William led her inside the cottage looking around him wildly for signs of Martha's distress. All the jars and bottles seemed in order, the brazier was in its usual place, herbs were drying in bunches from the roof beams. Everything, in fact, was where it should be except...

"Where is Christiana?" he shouted, his brown eyes searching Martha's tearful face. She gave no answer but shook her head. William looked towards the closed door leading to the inner chamber.

Martha, following the line of his gaze, put out a hand and grasped William's arm firmly, saying, "Sit down, lad. William, hear me out and then you can go through."

William was just pulling a stool out from under the bench when the inner door opened very gently. Looking up and expecting to see Christiana, William was bewildered to find the usher, Godwin, standing there, his ashen face grave. He shook his head slightly in Martha's direction and William looked from one to the other before striding across the room. He had one hand on the door latch before Martha halted him with the words, "Christiana is well enough. 'Tis Alfred. Now sit down please, lad."

William sat reluctantly on the stool, feeling a rising panic in his stomach. He waited as Martha and Godwin exchanged a few whispered words and the usher had left. Martha came and sat on a stool close by.

"There has been an accident at the smithy. I cannot say exactly how it happened but it seems that a horse went mad; a wild beast Conyers took a fancy to at Richmond Fair. Anyway it took fright as Alfred tried to lift its hoof and reared up and... and..." She began to weep again. William took her firmly by the shoulders.

"What happened, Martha?" he demanded.

The herbalist looked at the young man with great teardrops dulling her vision and took a deep breath. "The horse kicked him in the head and he was thrown against the brazier. His leg was badly burned. Jude... Jude took a knife to its throat to bring the animal down and then Conyers had a fit of rage for the horse had cost him a good many bags of silver."

William sat stunned for several moments taking in Martha's words. "But you have treated his wounds?" he asked after a while.

Martha shook her head. "I did what I could for his leg but it does not heal and festers with poison. I have no knowledge of the damage done to his head. He lies most times in a raging fever and scarcely makes any sense at all."

"Is there nothing you can do?" William asked desperately.

"No, William, nothing. We can only wait for the end and pray that God will be merciful."

"What of a physician?"

"William!" Martha laughed, almost bordering on hysteria. "There is none here with the authority to bring in a physician for a mere blacksmith now that the earl is gone." She sighed wearily and placed a hand on William's shoulder. "Go in to him," she said gently. "Christiana is with him, poor child. She has hardly left his side since we carried him here a month since. I am so very sorry, lad."

The room was dimly lit, the shutters half drawn across the window to keep out the light. It was stiflingly warm inside. The multitude of herbs hanging from the beams could do nothing to mask the stench of rotting flesh that clogged the air. For William it was as if he had returned to the battlefield but without the rush of fighting spirit that suppressed his natural feelings of disgust and repulsion. He had to fight down the waves of nausea that swept over him as he walked across the room.

He was aware of Christiana sitting silently beside the bed but his eyes were compelled to look upon the figure of his father lying in the grip of death beside her. His face was grey save for the brand of a horseshoe that burned red into the skin at his right temple. His eyes were closed and strangely at that moment he appeared almost at peace. For one dreadful moment William thought that perhaps he was too late. He stared dumbstruck at Alfred's face and swallowed hard. Beside the bed Christiana turned her face to her brother and spoke gently. "I do not think he feels much pain. For most of the time he lies oblivious to all, full of Martha's poppy juice. There are times when the fever takes him and it is then that he cries out for you. He has been waiting for your return. God be praised that you have come home."

William could not take his eyes off Alfred and stood like a stone statue as the tears began to form under his eyelids. Christiana rose from her chair and kissed her father's forehead. She placed a hand on William's shoulder and guided him out of the room. Martha had a goblet of strong wine ready for him but William, his face white as alabaster, waved it aside, saying, "I do not feel well, Martha."

Martha opened wide the outer door and placed a stool on the threshold. "Come, William, and sit down here." She eased him down onto the stool and gently pushed his head between his knees. "There, lad, the feeling will pass in a little while."

William sat with his head bent as waves of blackness ebbed and flowed before his eyes and became aware, as though in a dream, of a child crying. He sensed a woman brush past him and go outside. He could feel the sweat rising on his forehead and soaking through the palms of his hands. He felt dreadfully ill and utterly exhausted. He could feel Martha's firm hand on his shoulder bringing him comfort as she would to a child. He was also aware of another person, a man, speaking in hushed whispers outside the door.

After several moments his head cleared a little and the nausea passed. Martha made him drink the cup of wine before he walked slowly back to the garrison to join his fellow soldiers. He desperately needed sleep. As he staggered through the sun-drenched bailey William began to realise the extent of the shock and grief he felt at the accident that was to bring about Alfred's untimely death.

On the third day following William's return to Middleham there was a change in Alfred's condition. Martha had to continue with her duties and Christiana had the needs of the child to attend to so William had taken his turn at the dying man's bedside.

The weather was hot and humid. Gathering black clouds foretold a coming storm. William sat on the chair staring with unseeing eyes through the wide-open casement. Prickly rivulets of sweat trickled down his back and his shirt clung damply to his chest. A murmur from the bed broke into his thoughts and he turned his attention at once to Alfred. His eyes were open, large and delirious with pain. He was trying to raise his hand off the coverlet and William grasped it firmly in his own.

"Father," he whispered. "'Tis I, William. I am come home."

"My son." Alfred forced out the words on a painful whisper. "Thank God, thank God."

"Hush now, Father. Do not try to speak, just rest."

"I have loved you, William, like a son," Alfred spluttered.

William, choking back tears, shook his head. "I do not deserve to be called your son. I am sorry..."

"Nay, lad." Alfred shook his head, breathing hard for several moments. "Nothing to be sorry for," he gasped.

Alfred closed his eyes and William, fearful, squeezed his father's hand. "Shall I fetch Christiana? She is just outside with John."

William went to stand but Alfred's eyes flickered open and he mumbled. "Not yet, not yet. William, promise, promise me, take care of your sister; see that she marries well... you... you... could." Alfred's fingers gripped William's hand feebly but he was unable to say any more. William felt ill at ease. What was it that Alfred asked of him? Was he asking that he marry his daughter? How could he promise Alfred such a thing? He could not be certain even now of her feelings for him. Even after he had made attempts to heal their rift would she want him enough to marry him? He would certainly never force himself upon her. What of this usher, Godwin, who seemed a little too familiar with his sister?

Alfred was growing agitated. He tried to speak but nothing came out but a spasm of coughing. His choking and spluttering brought Martha hurrying in through the door to his bedside. She calmed the sick man with soothing words and wiped his brow. His coughing ceased at last although his eyes still pleaded with William for an answer.

William sighed heavily. "Father," he said finally, "I promise that I will always be a brother to Christiana till the end of my days." What else could he say, in truth? It seemed good enough for Alfred, however, for upon hearing these words his body slumped as though from it a great tension had been released. He closed his eyes and slept.

Martha, cloth in her hand, paused in wiping Alfred's brow and looked up quickly at William with an expression of sadness in her grey eyes.

Two days later Alfred breathed his last. On either side of the bed sat his daughter and his son, each holding one of Alfred's work-roughened hands as torrents of rain hammered relentlessly on the closed shutters outside. United in grief, there was no need for words between these two and together in silent witness they beheld their father's passing from this earthly life into the next, the only sound the melodious tones of the chaplain muttering his prayers at the foot of the bed.

"What is it betwixt those two?" William's face darkened at the sound of laughter coming from outside the open cottage door. Martha looked up from her mixing to watch Godwin and Christiana walking side by side along the pathway towards the herbarium.

"Well?" William demanded when Martha did not answer.

Martha put down her spatula, wiped her hands on her apron and pushed the door to before sitting down on the stool beside the young man. "I do not think there is anything between them, in truth, William. Although I dare say Godwin would have it otherwise."

"Indeed!" William replied, scowling.

"Do not fret, William," Martha soothed. "You are over anxious on your sister's behalf." The utterance of the word sister brought about a distinct, though subtle, change in William's countenance, reaffirming Martha's long-held belief that William saw more than a sibling whenever he looked at Christiana.

"Godwin has taken a fancy to Christiana, true enough, and plies her and John with gifts, but he takes it no further. As for Christiana, methinks she looks at him as no more than a companion," Martha continued softly.

"Aye well, as Christiana's nearest male kin I am responsible for her now and she will marry where I say," William said defiantly.

Martha smiled at the young man. "You forget, my boy, we all belong to the lord of the castle and no one will be wed until the matter of ownership has been settled. I dare say it will be our George."

William sighed. "Well that may take longer than we imagine for *our* George and his brother Richard are in dispute over Warwick's land and nothing was settled when I left London."

At that moment the door flew open and in waddled John, closely followed by his mother. "I can no longer keep him in that gin, Martha, for he can undo the strap," Christiana said, taking hold of her son around his chubby waist and tickling him until he collapsed in fits of giggles.

"Will. I did not know you were here," she said, seeing William seated at the stool.

"He has come for some balm for his feet," Martha answered for him and stood to fetch the salve from the bench while William and Christiana stared at one another in awkward silence.

"Christiana!" Godwin's voice called from the herb garden. "Christiana, bring the boy here for there is a fledgling sparrow flown the nest. Hurry!"

Christiana swept the child up into her arms and with an apologetic smile hurried outside.

"You keep those birds off my seedlings!" Martha called after her.

That William was hurt by Christiana's friendship with Godwin, however non-committal it may be, was plain to see in his brown eyes as he stared up at the old woman standing over him with the wooden bowl in her hand. Poor boy, she thought, and with a bid to lighten his mood she laughed and said, "Come on then, lad, take off them boots. You are not so much of a man that you can do without a motherly touch. Let me see how those blisters fare."

As Martha's gentle hands rubbed soothing balm into William's sore, road-weary feet she looked up into his face and met the eyes of the young man. She had great affection for this rough but gentle youth and wished she could find a way to bring his heart some peace. She thought on the potions her mother used to make with St Mary's gold and heartsease for the love-struck young lads and maidens in her day and smiled to herself. She had no faith in such fripperies and would sooner Nature take its course.

Middleham Castle
Yorkshire
Autumn 1471

One fine afternoon in autumn, Christiana, returning from an errand to the kitchens, passed through the wicker gate into the garden. The flowerbeds were sleepy with dying foliage and seed heads hanging forlornly in the glowing pale yellow of the insipid sunlight. As she walked along the gravel paths her eye was drawn to the mound of earth at the corner of the garden with its ring of brown and withered Michaelmas daisies at its summit.

Hesitating only briefly, Christiana made her way towards the grave, plucking a handful of the purple daises, symbolic of farewell, as she went. After removing the decayed flowers and replacing them with the freshly picked flowers Christiana stood in silent reflection. At the first sign of the autumn mists Ulrick had died. The old dog had simply stretched himself out beside the blazing fire in the great hall and fallen into a deep sleep from which he never awoke. Conyers had presided over the burial of the hound in an undisturbed corner of the garden.

Christiana smiled as she recalled Martha's face when she discovered what the arrangements had been for the disposal of the dog's body. The old woman looked near apoplectic, declaring fervently that she hoped for such an honourable resting place when her time came. Martha had always maintained that the dog's unnatural longevity was due to the choicest cuts of venison passed to it under the duke's table; fare that would swell many a peasant's belly. Christiana would never forget that Ulrick had been the main catalyst in her growing relationship with the boy duke and for that alone the hound deserved a marble sepulchre.

As she turned away from the grave still deep in thought, the figure of a man, just passing through the gate out of the garden, caught her attention. She could not be certain for it was just a fleeting glimpse but if her suspicion was confirmed then the return of that man was anything but welcome.

She hurried along to the herbarium to find Martha deep in her ritual of stirring and blending. "Is all well?" the herbalist asked without turning her head from the mortar.

"Aye," Christiana replied, reaching down to her son who had his arms spread wide ready for his mother's embrace. "Martha," Christiana continued warily, "did someone come to the herbarium just now?"

The herbalist, concentrating on her work, muttered, "Bah, 'tis not enough grease in this. Now where did I put it?" Martha looked up as Christiana handed her the pot of goose fat and muttered her thanks.

"Has anyone been here?" Christiana pressed Martha again.

"Aye, just now," Martha replied absent-mindedly, her spatula, balancing a glob of fat, poised in mid-air. "The captain of the guard; it seems he has developed a nasty skin rash, although if you ask me—"

"Captain of the guard?" Christiana interrupted.

"Aye, Ralph Hodkin, lately appointed captain of the castle garrison. Though if you ask me not a wise choice."

"Then why has he been given such a responsible task?" Christiana asked in bewilderment.

"Now, lass, do not take on so. 'Tis not our business who is favoured and who is not but as it happens Conyers recommended him."

"Conyers recommended him?"

"Are you going to repeat everything I say?" Martha asked, becoming quite bewildered as to the reason for Christiana's persistence.

"It would seem that Warwick had Hodkin set for the task and Conyers is honouring a promise made by the old earl," Martha continued. "Even during the absence of a lord this castle needs to be defended and alert although he will not be long in the post if he keeps up his drinking and gambling."

Martha laid aside her spatula with a sigh of satisfaction. "There, the salve is ready to be taken to the captain." The old woman caught the momentary flame of fear light up Christiana's dark eyes and asked, "Have you had a run-in with Hodkin? Because if you have—"

"No, Martha," Christiana interrupted quickly. "I like not the look of the man, nothing more."

Martha stared at her young friend with a not altogether convinced look on her round face. "Well, I have an errand to the kitchens so I shall take the salve," she said and let the matter rest there.

"I could use your whole supply of this, Martha," William grinned wistfully, "and still not have enough."

"Aye, well, you use it sparingly and bind your feet before putting your boots on – and take care not to get your feet wet." Martha handed William the pot of marigold ointment.

"Martha, I am a soldier not a court fop," he laughed. "I dare say I shall be wet more than I am dry and not just my feet."

"Where is it you are bound?" Martha asked.

"I am summoned back to London and the duke. This visit was but a little respite after the battles. I dare say I will not be gone long unless there is any further unrest.

"Where is Christiana?" he added, looking around the herbarium as though expecting her to emerge from behind the sacks and bowls lining the room.

"She went up to the kitchens with a basketful of dill and thyme but that must have been an hour since..." Martha's voice trailed off.

William sat on the stool looking somewhat dejected. Martha had not said that Christiana was with Godwin but he knew it all the same. She pushed a cup of her best wine into William's hand. "Stay awhile, she may return soon."

He took the wine and drank half the cupful. "You know, Martha," he said after a while, "'twould be better if Christiana did marry Godwin. At least then she would have the chance of a respectable life."

William drained his cup and stood to his feet. "I had best be going. There is much to be done before we leave."

"You could marry Christiana yourself, Will," Martha said boldly before he had reached the door. William turned with a wry smile on his lips. "I?" he smirked. "I am Christiana's brother. Everyone here knows me to be. I have no document to prove otherwise. Besides, it is of little consequence for Christiana does not love me. She sees only a brother when she looks at me. I am no prince. What could I offer her? If Godwin, for all his education and position, is not good enough for her, then I shall never be," he said sadly, his hand upon the door latch.

Middleham Castle
Yorkshire
December 1471

"Wat!" Christiana walked up to the old gardener as he swept leaves from the pathway with a birch twig broom. He did not look up but carried on with his task; a thankless one as the wind would disturb his pile just as it formed in substance.

"Wat!" Christiana spoke a little louder. The old man jumped, startled at the sound of his name. "I am sorry to disturb you but could you watch John for me?" Christiana asked. "I am needed up at the castle with Martha."

The old man looked down at the little boy holding his mother's hand and a toothless grin creased his reddened cheeks. He dabbed at his watery eyes with a grubby sleeve. "Certainly I will, Mistress Christiana," he replied gleefully.

"You can go inside the cottage," she announced. "'Tis warmer in there and you can watch the herbarium for me. I shall not have to lock up then."

Christiana watched her son toddle off happily with the old man and turned to Godwin. They walked along leaf-strewn pathways where the once glorious apparel of summer now hung as tattered rags on bare-boned twigs and branches. A sharp gust of wind sent a shiver through her and Christiana drew her cloak closer to her. Despite the chill of the day Godwin paused along the pathway before opening the wicker gate into the bailey.

"Christiana," he began, his eyes searching her face earnestly. He looked awkward, trying to find words to convey his thoughts.

They were friends; he should feel he could speak his mind to her, Christiana thought. She smiled encouragingly.

"I wanted to," he hesitated. "I have a gift for you," he said finally and drew back his cloak to unfasten a leather pouch from his belt.

Before he had even undone the drawstring Christiana said,

"Do not think I am unappreciative of your gifts, Godwin, but you do not need to seal our friendship with any token. We are... well, friends."

He looked up then, the gift now in his hand. His cheeks were flushed and a light glinted in his dark eyes. Christiana grew uneasy; instinct told her that this would be no ordinary gift and its purpose more than a token of friendship; even more than a bauble to mark Twelfth Night. Indeed, the gift when it was presented was a beautiful trinket. Unfortunately for Godwin he had chosen to express his love through a necklace and memories of Richard's parting gift rushed giddily into Christiana's head. This jewel, lovely as it was, had nowhere near the value of the other. But that was of little consequence to Christiana. She glanced down at the string of silver filigree laced with beads of coral held in his hand and then up into Godwin's face. The wind blew his dark hair over his eyes and he brushed it aside with a finger before saying, "I had hoped, Christiana, that we could be more than friends. I have long admired you and wish for nothing more than for you to be my wife. I have grown fond of your boy, John, and would see him as my own. I feel confident that the matter can be arranged once the lordship of Middleham is settled." He paused; waiting it seemed, for her reply.

She stared into his face; handsome and intelligent, yet with a boyish innocence. She realised that Martha had been so right. Godwin was everything and more than any woman of low birth could ever expect. With his occupation as usher they would want for nothing and he would love her well. She would have to be nothing short of insane to refuse him.

She hesitated, placing a hand over his, still holding the necklace, contemplating the decision in her mind. She always knew that Richard would marry some day and there was no guarantee that the duke would acknowledge John as his son; it was common knowledge that his brother the king had a handful of bastards, sired since his marriage to Elizabeth Woodville and none openly acknowledged. There was no news as yet on the settlement of Warwick's estates or for certain of what had become of the countess; her own future and that of her son seemed as unclear as that of the nobles who ruled the land. What choice had she? For the sake of her son surely she must accept Godwin's offer?

"Dearest Godwin, I am deeply fond of you and your proposal is very generous, for one in my position would be a fool to turn you down." She smiled, not altogether with joy, but answered as earnestly as she could. "If my brother gives his consent and our liege lord, whoever he may be, allows it then I shall be your wife."

The poor man was almost beside himself upon receiving the news that he had so desired to hear. He confessed that there was no urgent errand to fulfil at the keep and it had all been a ruse to be alone with her.

"Let us find Martha and tell her at once," Godwin gushed.

Christiana tempered his enthusiasm with a gentle hand on his arm. "Godwin, there is time enough. Allow me to ponder on this; we do not need to be hasty, for nothing can be done until things are settled."

"For certain, for certain," he replied. "You have made me a most happy man, Christiana." Godwin smiled exuberantly.

She took her leave of him then, declining his offer to put the necklace around her neck, for to do so would displace the one already put there by Richard. She returned alone to the cottage, feeling the enormity of the decision to accept a proposal of marriage lying heavily upon her heart.

Middleham Castle
Yorkshire
Spring 1472

"What's up with you, lad? You've said naught all morning." Ralph kicked William's foot with the toe of his boot. They were outside the armoury sorting through the weapons, cleaning, oiling or laying them aside for repair.

William was sitting on the bench rubbing goat marrow onto the blade of his halberd, the shaft steadied between his knees. Ralph, as was his wont, had done very little, shifting pieces around, kicking at bits of wood, drinking ale. William had not seen the man actually pick up a weapon since they had been there, which was just after breakfast.

"If 'tis a woman that troubles you, lad, take it from me they're not worth it," Hodkin continued, standing to his feet and helping himself to another cup of ale from the barrel on the table.

William was beginning to feel irritated by the man but continued to ignore him. He had not long returned to Middleham to the unwelcome and disheartening news that his sister had accepted a proposal of marriage from Godwin the usher. Maybe he should have listened to the advice of the old herbalist and asked Christiana to marry him; it was too late now, although betrothal vows had not yet been pledged as ownership of the castle had not yet been established.

He was shaken from his reverie by the slurred ramblings of the Captain of the Garrison, who chose at that moment to put voice to the thoughts that circled round in William's own head. "That wench in the cottage with the old witch, now she has done well for 'erself. First she gets bedded by the duke and then gets a proposal of marriage from an usher – not bad for the daughter of a blacksmith."

William dropped the greased rag he held in his hand and put the halberd carefully down on the ground before standing to his feet. "I will thank you not to talk about Christiana in that manner as though she were a common camp whore."

"'Struth, Will, she is no more than that, cut from the same cloth as us, only she goes about as though she was above the salt. She would never give the likes of us a second glance." Hodkin tottered unsteadily on his feet inches away from William.

"Be careful, Hodkin. That is my sister you are talking about."

"Bah, sister be damned," the captain retorted.

William reached out his hand and grabbed the front of the man's jerkin and would have struck out at him but then thought better of it; he wasn't worth bruising his knuckles for. The man did not have the respect of his subordinates and William would wager he was not going to keep his post for long. He settled for delivering a hard shove which sent the captain sprawling to the ground, before walking away.

"Are you well, Martha?" Christiana had entered the cottage, a wriggling infant balanced on her hip, to find the herbalist seated at a stool and looking flushed.

"I am a little breathless and out of humour but I am well enough," Martha replied, stirring a mixture in a wooden bowl set on the table in front of her. "Now I have the cowslip and betony in here but it does need some waybread... now have we any?" The herbalist muttered to herself, "And 'tis a few sprigs of sage or was it thyme needed at the kitchens? I could well do without a visit to the village this day." Martha stood to her feet to search amongst her jars and pots for dried plantain leaf.

Christiana put the child into his wooden pen with a few of his carved playthings and turned to the old woman. "I can run the errand to the village to save your legs. What is the remedy and who is it that ails?"

Martha sighed in relief. "Conyers has asked that I look in on the weaver's daughter; it seems she has the falling sickness. It would be of much help if you could finish this infusion and take it to her and I will take the herbs to the kitchen – but what of the boy?"

"Wat is in the garden, I will ask him to keep an eye on John – he never minds doing so."

It was not much later when Christiana pushed open the wicker gate to leave the garden on her way to the village, a basket containing infusions and oil of lavender across her arm. Looking up she noticed William walking from the direction of the keep, bound for the smithy no doubt. She waved her arm and called a greeting to her brother. At first the man did not respond, with head down he seemed lost in thought. He had just spent a second morning at the armoury finishing the task of sorting the weapons, this time without the company of the captain. William heard his sister's call the second time and walked towards her.

"Are you well, sister?" he replied. "But of course you must be for you are soon to wed. I gave no objection to the usher when he sought my permission for your hand, for what man would not be happy to see his sister make so fine a marriage?"

Christiana noticed the touch of sarcasm in William's voice. "Walk with me, William. I have an errand in the village and would sooner have your company than go alone." The thought that she might encounter Ralph Hodkin niggled in the back of her mind.

William's eyes met those of his sister's and fleetingly their gaze locked. He sighed resignedly; he would sooner keep her friendship than lose it, even when she became another man's wife.

The wayside to the village was awash with the colour and scents of spring, caressed by the warm breeze. They walked for a while in silence as Christiana perused the abundance of God's providence: bluebells, celandine, wild garlic and dog violets.

"Tell me the news from London, Will, for I have a desire to know – everything." Christiana's pace had slowed to a standstill under the shade of a birch tree. William too stopped walking but said nothing.

"Conyers has announced to us that the king has given lordship of Middleham to the Duke of Gloucester until a quarrel between his brothers George and Richard can be settled." Christiana's voice was quiet. "What has become of Countess Anne? For these lands belong by right to her," she continued.

He sighed and removing his jacket spread it on the ground beneath the tree. When they had sat, the basket of herbs between them, he told of what he knew.

"After the death of her husband, Countess Anne of Warwick took sanctuary in Beaulieu Abbey where she remains," William began.

"And Will, is it true that Richard is to marry Lady Anne Neville?" Christiana's voice was small, almost faraway. William looked deeply into the warm brown eyes of his sister and pondered: surely it could not pain Christiana to know of Richard's marriage? She knew this day would come and besides she would be wed herself soon. He knew that she would be content with nothing less than all the knowledge in his possession.

"Lady Anne Neville, widowed and fatherless at fifteen years of age, fell under the guardianship of her brother-in-law, George, Duke of Clarence," he began. "It was, and still is, George's intention to secure all of Warwick's land for himself, including that belonging to the countess, through his wife Isabel." William paused and plucked at the bluebells on the ground beside him.

"Go on," Christiana prompted with a hand on his arm. "You are going to tell me that Richard proposed marriage to Anne in order to wrench some of the land off George for himself."

"There are those who would say so," William replied. "But I have seen for myself and I believe that Richard's affections for Anne are genuine."

Christiana continued to sit in silence.

"Lady Anne Neville will be a good and fitting wife for Richard," William continued pragmatically before pulling up a clump of bluebells and chuckling. "You would not believe the lengths to which George has gone to keep his brother away from Lady Anne. He even had her disguised as a kitchen maid and hidden in some wealthy household but Richard found her." William smiled as he recalled the incident, himself a witness, and remembered the look of surprise on the young girl's face when she discovered that the cunning George had been outwitted by his younger brother.

"This business has caused much dissention between the

brothers," William pressed on. "So much so that the king himself is likely to intervene. Some of Warwick's northern lands have been granted to Richard, and George, under duress, has agreed to the marriage upon condition that his brother makes no further demands on what he sees as his by right of marriage to the elder daughter.

"It is by no means over for I do believe that Richard will press for a greater share in the fortune. The Papal Dispensation had just arrived from the Vatican when I left London and Richard and Anne were making preparations for their marriage."

There was still no response from the woman and William had an urge to put his hand over hers – and he did so, pressing gently.

When she finally looked up into his face it was with an expression of stoic acceptance, giving little away. "This is to be expected, Will. The duke must make a favourable marriage and as you say, Anne will be a fitting wife." Her voice was steady, controlled.

William nodded his head – it was done; she had her answers, though what good they would do her he knew not. They would all have to wait and see how life unfurled. It seemed certain that married to Anne Neville and given his position as Lord of the North Richard's home would continue to be here at Middleham – for better or worse for all concerned.

He stood and offered a hand to his sister. "Come, Christiana, you have an errand pending in the village – do not neglect your duties."

As they made their way along the road Christiana's eyes were drawn to the hovel where once had lived the thatcher and his wife. It sat now in woeful disrepair; even the roof had shed its reed coverings. Someone had made use of it as a shelter for their cow, whose head was even now protruding through the door. Walking past Christiana frowned sadly as she recalled to mind the happenings within that dwelling some five years ago now.

The weaver's cottage was at the far end of the village set within a neat plot of land. In contrast to many of its neighbours this dwelling seemed to be in a good state of repair; the weaver was obviously doing well for himself.

An anxious-looking woman answered their knock at the door and beckoned them inside. The first thing Christiana noticed upon entering the spacious interior were the two looms filling most of the room. They were quiet today; the weaver did not seem to be at home. The woman led them to a second room beyond a closed wooden door. In here stood a large spinning wheel; a basket of carded wool of various hues lay beside it on the floor. A young woman sat at the spinning stool, her attention on the fibres as she teased them through the spindle. She looked up as the strangers entered and her eye did not overlook the handsome young blacksmith.

The weaver's wife drew back a tapestry in the corner of the room and lying on a pallet within was Christiana's patient; a thin, pale girl of no more than fourteen years. She stared with vacant, glazed eyes. For the first time since they had arrived, the mother spoke. "Annette has the falling sickness. Her convulsions leave her weak; it takes a good deal of time for her to come back to us," she explained.

Christiana followed the woman into the partitioned area. William remained in the main chamber.

"You are not surely the herbalist from the castle?" the woman continued. "You are little more than a child."

"Nay," Christiana answered. "I am assistant to the herbalist. 'Twas Martha who prepared the physic." She opened her basket and took out the sealed bottle. "Here is a drink made with herbs reputed to help keep away the falling sickness. Martha advises taking two sips three times daily." Christiana handed the bottle to the girl's mother. "You should pray to Saint Anne for healing," she added, although Martha had said no such thing. She also left the woman with a small vial of lavender oil before opening the tapestry and stepping back into the room.

William had occupied his time with the attentions of the spinster, Annette's elder sister, Joan, it seemed, for these two were now engaged in pleasant talk and smiles. Christiana frowned at her brother before walking briskly through the cottage and outside into the road.

Middleham Castle
Yorkshire
End of July 1472

The afternoon shadows were lengthening. Way out on the dales the distant call of the curlew could be just heard above the plaintive bleats of the grazing sheep. Caressed by the warmth of the sun the herbs and flowers had opened in fullness with sweet-scented breath that still lingered in the peace and tranquillity of the garden. High on the stone curtain wall a blackbird sang his requiem to the dying day. The melodious warble, melancholic in its beauty, washed a feeling of sadness over Christiana.

She had to fight back tears as her thoughts turned to her father. A full twelve months had passed since Alfred had departed this life and she still grieved for his loss. Her sorrow was especially heightened at present as all her emotions seemed to be on the edge of spilling over.

She knew of course that Richard was back. Who at the castle did not? His arrival had caused quite a stir, she recalled, everyone wanting to welcome the new lord of Middleham and his young bride. Christiana, herself, however, had seen nothing of the duke or his wife in the two weeks since their return. She longed for nothing more than to see Richard again but the prospect filled her with dread and fear.

Would she still love him? Or would she discover that in his three-year absence her feelings had grown cold and died? It would be better if they had, she thought bitterly.

What of his wife? How would she take to having her husband's bastard and his mother in her household? Would the duke find employment for Godwin at another of his northern households once they were wed? That was another matter which troubled her – how much longer could she put off the pre-nuptial betrothal that would seal her fate? They did not have to wait for Papal

Dispensation before they could wed, unlike the Duke of Gloucester and his intended bride. Godwin had informed her that the duke had consented to their union, William voiced no objection – only she tarried.

How would Richard take the knowledge that he had sired a strong healthy son? Would he admit paternity? He must surely know of John's presence by now and yet he had not been to see them once.

"Mama, more!" A little voice beside her reclaimed her thoughts and she looked down to find that she was holding the flat-bottomed pannier at waist level, far too high for John to put his rose petals in.

"Oh I beg pardon, my love," she murmured, bending down so that her son could release his handful of soggy crimson petals into the basket.

"Be careful of the thorns," Christiana warned as they continued to walk carefully amongst the bushes, gleaning the fallen petals and where occasionally Christiana would pluck an entire bloom from its stalk and add it to her collection.

A little while later Christiana sighed, straightened her aching back and said, "Well, John, I think we have enough. 'Tis getting late and time to go back."

"More!" John said defiantly.

"No!" Christiana said firmly. "We have enough."

The boy's bottom lip began to quiver and he pulled back on her hand as she tried to lead him away. Christiana looked down at her son's head of long dark tresses and thought that this wilfulness must be a sign of his royal blood, for whom but nobility could do as they pleased?

To placate the child she bent down and whispered, "We will go to the white rose and gather a few more petals and then you will be a good boy and come home without a fuss."

This chance to stay in the garden and further delay his bedtime seemed to please John for his little face lit up at once with a smile. In that very instant Christiana saw in her son the face of his father and her heart began to race wildly.

They were almost at the box hedge screening the white rose rambling over the south wall. It had taken a while to reach it for John's little legs were growing tired despite his determination to keep going.

As soon as they turned the corner and she saw the sprinkling of pale petals spread like a gown on the ground she regretted her decision to come here. To her fragile heart it seemed only yesterday when she had stood beneath its fragrant boughs to be held closely in Richard's arms.

Grasping John's hand tighter she urged him on. "Just a few more and remember these roses have thorns too."

She had just bent down to pick up a handful of petals when something startled her. They were not alone; someone was sitting on the far end of the oak-wood bench beneath the rose tree. His face was almost obscured in shadow but she would know those features anywhere. He too had been alerted by their presence and he stood and walked into the golden glow of twilight.

His hair was longer and surely darker; all trace of his boyish pale tawny curls had disappeared and its brown shade like the bark of the mighty oak glimmered in the fading light. The passing of time had also matured and finely honed his features. He stood silent as a shadow as those unmistakeable deep blue eyes penetrated her very soul.

She began to tremble and could do nothing to prevent the tears that had welled up in her eyes from falling down her cheeks. She knew then beyond any possible doubt that she still loved this man and so longed for his embrace, to feel once again the closeness of his body against her own. But it would never be. Not now or ever again. Never had the chasm between them seemed so wide and not least because he was married and she too was about to embark upon that blessed sacrament that excluded all others.

The certainty and power of her emotions filled her with a great fear. She could not move; her legs, like trees, seemed rooted to the spot. She knew she should have bowed before her liege lord but even this she could not do.

It was only the repeated sharp tugs on her hand that broke the spell and she became aware of her son still at her side, his own face showing signs of anxiety at the strange behaviour of his mother. Bending down she gathered John into her arms and together they stared at the man before them.

The duke seemed to be struggling with feelings of his own for he had uttered no word as yet and Christiana failed to fathom what lay beyond that dark, mysterious façade. Richard stared long and hard at the boy until he finally found voice. "My son?" was all he said.

Christiana nodded silently and then watched in bewilderment as the duke inclined his head towards her and walked away.

It was not many days later that Christiana was summoned to the keep by the Duchess of Gloucester. Christiana was expecting such a command and it came under the guise of a need for white nettle blossom and tansy juice. The messenger arriving at the door of the herbarium also took pains to ensure that the younger herbalist should be the one to deliver the concoctions in person. Christiana nervously fumbled with the folds of her grey wool gown, brushing away the wisps of dried herbs that habitually clung there. Her hands were shaking as Martha handed her the costrels. "Do not worry," Martha assured her. "She will nowise turn you out. What cause has she? Do not forget that the duke has given consent for you to marry the usher."

There was an unusual chill in the air for early August and Christiana shivered slightly as she ascended the outer staircase to the great hall. Surprisingly too, Godwin was not at his usual desk in the antechamber to give her an encouraging smile; only a young clerk who lifted his head from his work as she entered.

"If you have come to wait upon the duchess," he said, looking at the costrels in her hand, "then you must go to the south side for that is where the lady has her chambers. The duke has the rooms here in the keep as his own," he added in a knowing whisper.

Christiana smiled and inclined her head politely, ignoring the obvious inference of the young man's words. Let him think what he would, she thought, as she retraced her steps back to the inner courtyard. She turned to her right and passed under the small archway beneath the chapel and so on towards the chambers within the south range. She had to stop a servant and enquire of the way to the duchess's chambers for the castle was vast and largely unfamiliar to her save for the keep itself.

The arched doorway leading to the Lady Chamber was half concealed by heavy tapestry drapes, which were surreptitiously pulled aside before she had reached the entrance. There she was confronted by a rather sour-faced woman whom she did not recognise.

The lady, for her fine gown told her that she was such, approached from the other side of the curtain and stood looking down at her in a somewhat haughty manner. Although considerably senior in years to Christiana she was by no means an old woman and her face would have been pleasing to behold if she did not appear to be wearing a permanent scowl. "My lady," she called behind her shoulder. "It would appear the serving girl has arrived with the herbs."

Christiana was beckoned inside. The chamber was dappled with light as scurrying clouds in the sky beyond the casement played hide and seek with the sun. A pretty young girl with eyes wide as a frightened lamb and coils of brown curls escaping from under her ill-fitting coif was standing beside the bed, nervously folding gowns that lay there.

The Duchess of Gloucester was standing at the window with her back to the door. The lady did not move as she spoke. "I do so love this castle. It is good to be home."

She turned slowly to face Christiana and smiled. No longer a child, she looked radiant in her blue velvet gown trimmed with ermine and finely embroidered with crimson thread. Her fair hair was drawn back under a cone-shaped hennin of the sort favoured by her mother, the dowager Countess of Warwick.

However, her youthfulness was evident in the almost childlike way in which she held out her hands as she crossed the room, her pink cheeks glowing. "You have brought the nettle blossom," she said gleefully. "Mother always had our hair washed in this when Isabel and I were girls. There is nothing in London or France to compare with Martha's recipes," she whispered with a smile.

Anne took the jars from Christiana and beckoned her to sit on a wooden chest. Christiana hesitated. The formidable lady-in-waiting who had remained silent until now had moved a little closer and now cleared her throat audibly, disapproving no doubt of the young lady's familiarity with the servants. At once Lady Anne's colour rose painfully and she inclined her head a little in deference to the older woman.

"Now, my lady," the other began, taking the jars from the duchess's hands. "If I may be so bold, before the day grows colder you should bathe at once and I shall wash your hair." Turning then to the little maid by the bed who stood gawping at them all, her duties forgotten, the lady snapped, "Sybil, go to the kitchens at once and fetch hot water and a tub, and you, girl," she addressed Christiana, "you may return to the herbarium."

Christiana bowed to the duchess and retreated thankfully from the room. There would be little to fear from the young duchess while that dragon was around, she thought. The poor lady would have no authority in her own household.

She had reached the inner courtyard when the sound of running feet coming from behind halted her. Turning, Christiana found the maid, Sybil, hurrying after her.

"She's an old witch that one," the girl panted as she fell into step alongside Christiana.

Smiling in agreement, Christiana asked, "Who is she?"

"Lady Anne Tempest, a relative of John Conyers. She will keep the duchess under her thumb, that's for sure." The girl looked quickly around her. "But she won't master the duke. Have you seen him? He is quite handsome, though very stern looking. I should not like to cross him."

Christiana stared at this very young girl who had more than enough to say about matters that did not concern her. "And who might you be?" she asked.

"Sybil Tomkins," the girl announced with a smile that lit up her pretty face. "I have been sent from Sheriff Hutton. The new duchess requires a bigger household now, especially when she starts having her babies."

Christiana, feeling her cheeks redden, stared open-mouthed at the girl. "Should you not be about your duties, Sybil?" she said irritably.

"Indeed, that is where I am going now, we can walk together. So who are you then?" Sybil continued as they paused at the entrance to the ground floor of the keep.

Christiana bristled, feeling slightly under interrogation, although she was amused by the girl's amiable personality. "I am Christiana, assistant to the herbalist. We share a cottage in the bailey," she announced, bracing herself for the inevitable, for surely nothing was going to escape the attention of this little vixen.

"Oh, so you are..."

"The woman who has borne the duke's bastard son – yes I am," Christiana finished defiantly.

"They were talking about you the other night," Sybil continued unabashed.

Christiana had been about to walk away under the arch back to the bailey but her curiosity roused she asked, "Who was talking about me?"

"Why, the duke and duchess," Sybil replied, smiling sweetly. She bent her head nearer to Christiana's, close enough for her to catch a hint of rosewater on her breath, and whispered, "You have nothing to fear. Your position is safe enough here now that you are to marry the usher."

Christiana felt her heart beating painfully. How dare this mere child speak to her thus? "You should heed well this advice, Sybil," she began hotly. "If you do not learn to curb your tongue and guard the secrets of the bedchamber you serve you will not keep employment here for long." Christiana breathed heavily, staring into the wide innocent eyes of the girl before her. Sybil at last had the grace to blush. She even bowed to Christiana before scurrying through the doorway towards the kitchen.

Returning to the cottage Christiana was not sure whether to be amused by the foolish girl or angry at her impertinence. She was clearly only a child who would end up in hot water if she did not mature soon and judging by those wide lamb-like eyes no malice was intended.

Christiana's mind was once again a cauldron of emotion, relieved to hear that she was to be allowed to remain at Middleham but the reminder of her forthcoming betrothal unsettled her.

Middleham Castle
Yorkshire
Autumn 1472

"Christiana, a word, before you are about your duties." Godwin was standing at the foot of the staircase leading to the great hall; he was obviously waiting for her.

She was about to enter the south range where her arrival was expected imminently, but she paused and turned her head towards the usher. Godwin's smile was warm. "I have news, my love."

Christiana approached and returned Godwin's embrace.

"I have made arrangements for our betrothal with Rector Beverley," he said eagerly. "It is all set for the day following the Feast of Epiphany; we shall make the betrothal promise and then forty days hence we can be married. I can tarry no longer, Christiana. I have secured a house in the village with a garden enough to grow your herbs and for John to play. I believe the duke will settle an annuity upon John... you know, as his father." The usher's eyes sparkled merrily.

"You will not have to work – unless the duchess wishes you to," he called as he took the steps two by two back to the antechamber, leaving Christiana bemused and speechless.

Lady Tempest was waiting for Christiana as she entered the lady's chamber. "You took your time, girl," was her surly greeting.

Christiana bowed courteously and glanced across at the great tester bed where Martha sat and beckoned to her. Christiana's attention at last turned to the purpose of her visit: the Duchess of Gloucester lying pale and sickly atop the sumptuous coverlets of the bed.

"Where have you been?" Martha hissed as she approached. "Do you have the ginger?"

Christiana took a small leather costrel from the linen script slung across her shoulder and handed it to Martha. "Is all well with the duchess?" she asked nervously as Martha plumped up the duck down pillows and gave the young lady the costrel from which to drink the infusion.

"Aye, Christiana," Martha replied with a smile. "The duchess is with child and feels a little unwell. She will be fine with plenty of rest and care."

"That is good news indeed, my lady," Christiana replied with a faint smile. Anne drained the costrel and sat back on the pillows, a weak smile curving her red lips. "I pray that all goes well and I can provide my husband with a healthy son as is my duty," she murmured softly.

"I am sure all will go well, my lady," Martha said reassuringly, tucking up the covers around the duchess as though she were still a child. "You lie there and rest. I shall send more ginger if you need it and prepare a tonic now that the cold weather approaches," she continued warmly.

Christiana walked over to the casement and looked out upon the surrounding dales. It was a glorious view; the leaves in all their red, gold and bronze flying in a windswept frenzy over the scattered dwellings and settling within the castle walls. She could hear Martha talking briskly and with authority to Lady Tempest, as was her way, commanding respect from high and low born alike, although Christiana did not decipher a single word. Her thoughts once again turned to Godwin and their forthcoming betrothal. She felt certain that a woman of her low birth should feel great joy at such a momentous event in her life, and yet she did not – and this lack of happy anticipation pained and troubled her.

She seemed unable to reason with herself. The duke was married, his wife expecting their first child. She had hardly set eyes upon the man who had fathered her child and barely acknowledged his existence; the man who had robbed her of all reason. What sickness ailed her? She must marry Godwin soon and be done with it.

A sharp poke in the ribs caused her to turn abruptly, barely able to stifle the cry of pain that was on her lips. Sybil was standing beside her and whispered, "You are daydreaming, mistress. The herbalist awaits you."

Horrified, Christiana looked up to meet with Martha's impatient glare and the perceptible look of disgust manifest upon the lady-in-waiting's proud face.

"What is wrong with you, girl?" Martha demanded as they hurried through the chapel archway. "You cannot expect to have the respect and trust of Lady Tempest and her kind if you do not even keep your mind on your work. You still have a great deal to do to prove your worth in this household. You must keep your position because you are a good herbalist and not by virtue of the fact that you are mother to the duke's bastard, at least until you are wed to Godwin and then maybe you will be given a new position elsewhere."

They had passed through the wicker gate before Christiana spoke. "I do not think that will happen, Martha" she said quietly.

"You do not think what will what happen?" Martha asked irritably.

"That we will be sent away from here once we are wed. I have seen Godwin this day and he has bought a house in the village and set the date of our betrothal – after Epiphany."

"It will be a relief to the duke, I am sure, to see you properly taken care of and life can go on as it ought."

They had reached the cottage door and Martha turned the latch.

"I should not want to leave here, to leave you," Christiana said sorrowfully. At the sight of tears in the eyes of the young woman Martha's temper cooled and she held out her arms.

"Come hither, child, I am sorry. I would nowise see you leave either but it is how things must be."

"I still love Richard, Martha. What am I to do?" Christiana wept.

"Our duke is married to Lady Anne and you must accept it and that legitimate sons will follow, God willing. You should be happy for him for she will make a good and proper wife. He has no further need or desire for you. Your path lies with Godwin, a good man, and you must embrace it."

For several moments Martha held Christiana in her arms and prayed that this young woman whom she loved as a daughter would be able to accept the right pathway for all their sakes.

"I have no desire to go to the fair, Godwin," Christiana said impatiently as she moved jars and bottles hither and thither to no real purpose along the shelves.

"But there will be merchants from all over York selling their wares," Godwin persisted. "We can buy all we need for our house."

Christiana sighed and finally ceased her pointless task, turning to face the man she was to wed. "Very well, we will go," she smiled.

Godwin held up the fat purse hanging from his belt and shook it. "See, I have coin aplenty, we shall want for nothing."

Christiana reached for her cloak hanging on its hook beside the door. "Martha, are you to come with us?"

"Nay, you go without me. I trust you will purchase anything we have need of. I will stay here and amuse the child."

Christiana's face belied a touch of disappointment but the old woman was not about to give in. "'Tis too cold for my old bones walking around and around. Be off with you and leave me be."

Contrary to Martha's view the weather was mild; the autumn sun was glowing yellow and there was not even the hint of a cold wind, making the walk from booth to booth a pleasant one. It amused Christiana to see that Godwin had brought with him a large wicker basket slung on rope handles across his back; evidently he was going to be true to his word.

The fair weather had enticed many folk out of doors and they had to jostle quite a crowd, Godwin's basket becoming somewhat of a hindrance. In his precise, organised manner the usher had quilled a list of items required to make up a cheerful home and soon his carrier was brimming with bolts of cloth, spoons, trenchers, pots, candles and holders. For things that could not be carried Godwin placed orders with the craftsmen.

On their travels they happened upon a scene where there appeared to be an altercation between the village weaver and a finely attired wool merchant. As it was Godwin's intent to buy more cloth and the price asked by the local weaver was more favourable than that of visiting tradesmen they lingered.

"Come now, Master Weaver, you would not have me give away my wool."

"Nay, but neither would I see you rob me of my living by charging such extravagant prices."

"'Tis no more than the going rate," replied the wool merchant.

There appeared then an interruption in their discourse as a young woman approached the weaver and smiling sweetly linked her arm through his. "My daughter, Joan," he announced, returning the girl's smile.

"Father, have you coin?" she asked, still smiling. "I wish to purchase a comb."

It appeared that the weaver had affection for his daughter – or was it weakness? – for at once he reached into his purse and took out a handful of coin and handed it to her. She took it gratefully and with a sweep of her long chestnut hair she floated into the crowd once more.

Christiana stood by, intrigued. The wool merchant, not an altogether unhandsome man, regarded the retreating back of the girl and turning to the weaver said, "I am certain we can do business, Master Weaver, and reach an amicable agreement for a contract. I have a house in York. John Stapleton is the name." With that he bowed his head and left the weaver to his customers.

Godwin was a little annoyed at being kept waiting for his basket was heavy but he greatly desired to purchase finely woven lambswool cloth, enough to make a bridal gown for Christiana. His eye had caught a bolt of deepest cornflower blue. There now followed an argument between the usher and the herbalist for his intended bride was adamant that the price was far too high and she would make do with the dress that Martha had given her last Christmastide.

They were still arguing, though good humouredly, when, having bought chewitts of hog roast, they were seated together on stuffed hessian sacks; Godwin had his hand protectively on his bolt of blue cloth.

The crowds had dispersed somewhat as it was getting late and darkness was creeping in. Torches were being lit here and there to provide light enough for the traders to pack away their goods. The hostelries in the village and the wayside inns in the surrounding dales would be full this night; the annual fair was always a prosperous time for Middleham. They sat in silence now eating the last of their meat and watching the movement of people. Across the way a few folk lingered where the brewsters had their barrels of ale; amongst them was William and he was not alone. The tall graceful figure of Joan, the weaver's daughter, stood close and they whispered and smiled together. After a while they walked off into the gloom, William's arm around the girl's slender waist.

"'Tis late, Godwin," Christiana announced suddenly. "I need to get back to John." She stood to her feet and brushed the crumbs from her skirt.

"John will be well, he is with Martha. Do not fret." Godwin stood hastily to his feet, his meat not yet finished.

"I want to go home," Christiana declared, walking briskly away from the fair and towards the road that led to the castle, Godwin hard pressed to keep up with the great load on his back.

Middleham Castle
Yorkshire
Advent 1472

A fierce wind pummelled the cottage door sliding icy tendrils beneath its frame, rattling bottles and jars and rustling the dried herbs hanging from the rafters.

It was far too cold to sleep so Christiana lay awake huddled beneath the blankets pressed close to John who lay sleeping peacefully between her and Martha. She watched the shadows flicker wildly across the chamber walls as the trees and bushes outside the cottage were tossed and whipped frantically in the moonlight.

At first it sounded nothing more than the wind at the door but after several moments of listening Christiana was certain that someone was knocking urgently. Careful not to disturb the child she sidled out of bed and reaching for her cloak on top of the chest she wrapped it over her shift. Shivering in the cold air she crossed the herbarium to the door.

"Who is it?" she demanded in a harsh whisper.

"'Tis Sybil, open up," came the reply.

Christiana drew back the bolt and the door, aided by the wind, flew open. The young girl stood on the threshold, hair and cloak blowing wildly about her as she fought to hold on to the horn lantern that was being tugged from her grasp.

"The Lady Anne has taken badly and you are to come at once," the girl announced as soon as she had stepped inside and the door was firmly shut.

"How do you mean, taken badly? What are her symptoms?" Christiana demanded urgently.

"Well – she is in pain," Sybil offered.

"Does she bleed?"

"A little – yes."

"God have mercy!" Christiana gasped and turned at once to the rows of bottles shining silver in the moonlight. "Light some candles, Sybil, so I can see," she commanded.

Before long Martha had joined them and mixtures of shepherd's purse and horsetail had been hastily prepared and placed in a strong wicker basket. Leaving the child sleeping soundly and careful to extinguish the candles they left the cottage with nothing more than their shifts beneath their cloaks and a pair of boots on their feet.

The three women, their lanterns casting eerie shadows along the stone walls, made their way slowly across the inner courtyard and on to the south range. The duchess's bedchamber was roomy and warmed well enough although the beeswax candles flickered alarmingly in their holders. Heavy velvet curtains, a deep maroon in the dim light, shielded the tiny figure on the bed. As soon as she saw Martha approaching Anne struggled to sit and reaching out to her she cried, "Martha, I am so very afraid. I do not want to lose my babe."

"There now, child," the old woman soothed, wrapping her large fingers around the duchess's small hand. "Just you lie back now and let me take a look at you."

Pulling aside the coverlets Martha looked for tell-tale signs that would indicate all was not well. She found only a few spots of blood on the lady's shift and upon the bed linen. She turned to Lady Tempest who was standing at the bedside, an anxious frown on her pale face.

"Have you changed these sheets?" Martha demanded. Lady Tempest shook her head. "Then all may still be well," Martha said encouragingly. "Lady Anne, you must drink these. They will help prevent the babe coming away. You must rest and not leave your bed until you have delivered this child," the herbalist added firmly.

A harsh prescription indeed, thought Christiana, as she removed the costrels containing the medicine from their basket. The duchess's child was not due for another six months at least. But confinement to bed so early was worth the inconvenience if it meant a healthy child at the end, she reasoned.

"Should a physician be sent for?" Lady Tempest asked as she gently eased the covers over Anne, now lying peacefully on her pillows.

"That will depend upon the duke," Martha replied, a little chagrined at the suggestion that her own expertise could be bettered by a physician. "I dare say it would do no harm," she conceded after a little thought. "I take it the duke does know of his wife's condition?"

"He does indeed," Lady Tempest replied. "It was he who ordered Sybil out on such a night as this to fetch you. The duke awaits your counsel in the great hall."

"I shall return at first light with more of this," Martha announced as she replaced the empty costrels in her basket. "Remember, rest, plenty of rest," the herbalist warned before nodding to Christiana to follow her out of the bedchamber.

The wind had abated a little as they crossed the inner courtyard towards the keep. Christiana caught Martha's arm. "Someone should go back to John at the cottage." She paused. "You are tired. I can find the duke and tell him about Anne."

Martha stared at her assistant as the wind whipped her gown and sent tears streaming down her face. "It is my responsibility to talk to the duke, Christiana," she replied curtly.

"But, Martha, I can tell him as much of this matter as can you," Christiana pleaded.

After several moments of standing in the bitter wind the old woman capitulated. "I am always the fool when it comes to you, my girl," she said resignedly. "Remember your position." With her final warning Martha walked slowly away into the night, her lantern bobbing like a beacon on a stormy sea.

Christiana hurried up the outer staircase, her footsteps echoing loudly in the silence. She tiptoed past the sleeping guards slouched against the wall at the entrance to the great hall. Inside was deathly quiet and cast in shadow. The flames of the fire still burned scarlet and gold within the iron grill lighting up the dais and its bare wooden table. The warmth beckoned her for she was now very cold with only a thin shift beneath her cloak.

The duke was sitting alone on a carved chair pulled up close to the fireside. Beside him on a small table stood a large jug of wine, half empty. He was slumped in the chair, his legs stretched towards the grill and a silver goblet held precariously in his left hand. With the other he rubbed at his forehead as though to ease a pain.

"My lord," Christiana said clearly as she approached for she did not wish to startle the duke. He, however, made no response.

"My lord!" she repeated a little louder, and moving closer still she knelt down and placed a hand on the arm of his chair. He turned his face towards her, a little flushed, and not, she thought, from the heat of the fire. He had been drinking – a good deal. This shocked her somewhat for drunkenness was the very last vice she would hang upon this man. He stared at her as though seeing her for the first time.

"Richard," she breathed softly and the sound of his name from her own lips caused her to tremble. She took a deep breath and said gently, "The duchess is sleeping now. Martha has given her potions to help stay the babe. If she rests and does not become over anxious then maybe all will be well. Martha recommends you send for your physician as a precaution."

There, her duty was performed. He drank another couple of mouthfuls of wine. She wanted to tell him it was of no use drinking himself sick, whatever his reason for doing so – but she dared not. He put out his hand and touched her cheek in the briefest of caresses but it was enough to warm her aching heart.

"How I have missed you," he whispered, staring deeply into her eyes. Then suddenly, as though he had touched hot embers he pulled his hand away.

She should not be here, she thought. Her task was complete and now she must leave. She began to ease herself to her feet.

"Where do you go?" the duke demanded brusquely.

"Well, I... I thought to take my leave. I have told what I came to say, my lord."

"You will not leave me, Christiana," he commanded. "Sit down, here." He tossed her an embroidered cushion from the back of his chair. Obediently she sank down on the cushion beside him knowing she should flee and yet longing to stay.

He drained the cup and replenished it from the jug on the table. Christiana grimaced as he spilled some of the red liquid down his tunic. "He is a fine boy," Richard said, and added, "my son," as though she would not know to whom he referred.

"He is indeed, my lord," she agreed.

"It would appear that I have sired yet another bastard." He laughed, seeming to find humour in words that shocked Christiana. She said nothing.

"Aye, a girl," Richard continued as though she had begged the information. "I have heard word this very day. The mother has died and named me the father of her child, although in truth she is no babe but an infant of over one year."

"You do not need to tell me this, Richard, 'tis none of my concern," Christiana said quickly.

"No?" he said, glaring at her bleary-eyed. "Do I not tell you everything, all the secrets of my heart? Are you not mine own, black-haired witch, for you hold me in your spell." He clutched her chin in his hand and pressed his face close to hers. She could smell his wine-scented breath but her lips were left bereft of any kiss.

Once again he drew his hand away but this time she caught it and held it tight and said defiantly, "I am no witch, Richard, but I am, I think, your truest friend.

"Tell me of this babe, this girl. There is no dispute that you are her father?" she asked gently.

He shook his head in confirmation and took yet another sup of wine before replying, "She is named Katherine and of her mother there is little to tell. It was a chance meeting en route to Burgundy... I was in exile with the king. I..."

Christiana shook her head in bewilderment but this, it seemed, was one secret he was not able to share with her for he turned his head and took another gulp of wine. There fell a silence between them for a while as the duke stared into the dancing flames.

"So I become a father yet again even as my wife lies in danger of losing my only legitimate heir," Richard muttered at last.

"Does Anne know of this child?" Christiana asked, afraid that knowledge of the child may have brought about the duchess's present unhappy state.

"No indeed," Richard emphasised. "And neither must she, for now."

"I will say nothing of this, you have my word. What is to become of the child?"

"She will be well provided for, a suitable household. It will be arranged."

They sat in silence once again, neither seeming aware that their fingers were still entwined. The firelight lit up their faces and shone in the goblet as the duke continued to sip the rich red wine. At last he banged the goblet down on the table beside the jug and shifted uneasily in the chair. "I do hope she will prove herself a good wife," he said, addressing the flickering flames.

"I am sure she will, my lord, and all will be well with the babe," Christiana replied, silently praying that she would be right on both accounts.

Further moments passed and Christiana could feel the warmth of his breath upon her cheek, so close were they. Her fragile heart was in turmoil. How should she read the measure of it? Had Martha been wrong? Did this man think more of her than a mere servant at his disposal? She did not doubt that he had true and proper affection for his wife and as social graces demanded there could be no better match for this prince than Anne Neville. It was perhaps that lady's present unhappy state that caused her husband to soak his sorrows in a cup or two of wine. For her own part, blacksmith's daughter though she may be, she did not doubt her love for this man; strong and true as ever it could be and with his son to love and nurture she knew that as long as she had breath and it was within her power she would be here for him.

After a while Richard gently caressed her cheek with his finger before turning away. "You may go," he whispered. "I will send for the physician but see to it that Anne is given all due care."

Christiana stood without a word, nodded her head in reverence and departed.

Middleham Castle
Yorkshire
Christmastide 1472

"For one who makes betrothal vows come Epiphany you have a face that would curdle milk," Martha remarked.

Christiana had been unsettled throughout the festive season; she had no humour for the dancing and merriment in the servants' hall. She had made excuses to Godwin whenever he urged her dance or watch the jugglers and minstrels sent by the duke to entertain.

She now sat sullen and quiet on one of Martha's simple folding chairs with its faded wool cushion; resting her back on the wall of the cottage she cradled her sleeping child in her arms. She smiled down at his round rosy-cheeked face, cherub-like in slumber, where locks of dark hair coiled untidily across his eyes. With gentle fingers Christiana brushed them back under his linen cap. It was strange, she thought, how the boy did not have the golden hair of childhood endowed upon his father, but rather her own raven colouring.

The herbalist paused in the working of her needle and stared sadly at the young mother but said no more. She felt she had the measure of the thoughts that occupied the girl's mind and she was afraid.

It would not be long before Godwin would arrive to escort his belle to the great hall where the promise of a feast and dancing enthused all participants. By virtue of his status Godwin had been invited to share in these celebrations with other highborn servants. Rising to her feet Christiana carried her son to the bed where she laid him down and covered him with a lambskin, silently watched by Martha.

Christiana had taken the silver filigree necklace from the little wooden box where it had stayed since Godwin had given it to her twelve months ago. It was time to put an end to this charade. It grieved her to think of the hurt she would cause Godwin for he did not deserve this but neither did he deserve a wife whose heart belonged to another.

She had just put her cloak about her shoulders covering her now faded chestnut-coloured gown when the knock came upon the door. Godwin stood outside, shivering in the cold winter wind, but his face held a warm smile. It was with a heavy heart that Christiana left the cottage to walk the long road up to the keep.

The dim light was fading fast and shadows engulfed the garden as they walked. Voices could be heard and lanterns bobbed in the darkness as others made their way to the great hall.

The wicker gate swung closed behind them and Godwin reached into Christiana's cloak to take her hand; she could bear it no longer. They had reached a dark place where shadows deepened, where the pathway to the stables met the bridge that spanned the moat. Christiana stopped and moved to where the moss-laden wall curved onto the bridge. She waited for cloaked figures to pass by and burst forth in an urgent whisper, "Dearest Godwin, I am deeply fond of you. You are indeed a good man and worthy of any woman but I cannot marry you. It would not be fair to marry you or any man unless my heart was wholly theirs. When you marry, Godwin, you deserve to have a woman who loves you utterly." She caught her breath and stood silent before him.

He stared at her for a moment and then gave her a crooked little smile. "But life is not like that, Christiana. Do you not know how many marriages are nothing more than contracts to secure wealth and power? Even a weaver would not sell his daughter unless his trade could benefit from it. I dare say our good duke has married the Lady Anne for gain. Love seldom, if ever, comes into play."

He took her hand and pressed her cold fingers. "If we have a fondness for one another, and I can truly say on my part there is more, then that is more than most and certainly enough to build a life upon."

Dear, dear Godwin, she thought. Could she ever love him as

much as he deserved? Could she lie with him night after night longing to be in the arms of another man? In all truth she could not.

She took the trinket from her belt purse and with trembling fingers held it out to the usher. Godwin did not move but stared at the woman before him, utterly unable to fathom her reasoning. Was she a fool? Did she imagine herself to be a character in a tale of hapless love? If he had been honest with himself he should have foretold this, for had she not been showing him the signs? Now it was to no purpose to try reasoning with her any longer. Suddenly this rejection turned to pain and anger.

"What will you do, Christiana? How will you live, a woman without a man? Do you not know what you are turning down?"

The cold wind blew about them and Christiana shivered but there was no comforting arm to warm her.

"I suppose you could always marry that blacksmith come soldier," Godwin continued. "You will not have much of a life and then he will go off to battle and like as not leave you a widow. What of your bastard son then?" Godwin caught his breath. He had said enough – too much.

Silent tears began to course down the woman's face. "If it is William of whom you speak you are mocking me," Christiana retorted. "He is my brother and nothing more. I will take my chances in this world without a man. I am sorry for it but I will not marry you, Godwin."

The man all but snatched the necklace from the woman's hand. Turning away with head bowed and the wind stinging the hot tears on her face she made her way back to the cottage and into Martha's waiting arms.

It appeared that the final celebration of the season, the Feast of the Three Kings, or Epiphany, was to pass with no less fervour than those preceding it, for the duke had commissioned a mummers' Nativity play to be performed for his guests in the great hall and after for the servants in their hall in the bailey.

The end of the long season of merrymaking was nigh and the

servants were glad of it for there was more work for them on such occasions keeping the lord of the castle and his guests fed and entertained. They did, however, look forward to the mummers' play and there was much eager anticipation within the bailey.

This mood was not shared by the women in the herbalist's cottage, however. Melancholy hung like a rain-sodden cloud over the benches with their array of bottles and pots, dripping even onto the small dark-haired boy who sat silently in the pen tossing his little wooden horse from hand to hand.

"We should go for the sake of the boy," Martha declared, laying aside her mending and rising slowly to her feet. "This mood will linger else and cripple us like a poison."

Christiana sighed. Martha was right, and besides, Godwin would not be in the servants' hall, having watched the play in the great hall earlier.

Conyers was overseeing proceedings when they arrived. Food was being brought in from the kitchens and the boards were covered with cloth ready to receive the platters, plates and bowls, all without the ceremony and fuss required in the great hall of the keep.

When the company of servants was assembled and their places taken at the boards Conyers thanked God for His provision and the duke for his benevolence and the feast began.

The time was spent in pleasant conversation, although sometimes a bawdy remark was to be heard along the table where the garrison soldiers sat. Many folk engaged Martha and Christiana in discussion about their ills and ailments and soon their mood lightened.

It was as the tables were being set aside to make way for the mummers that Christiana first noticed William. He was standing with a young woman, slim and graceful with chestnut hair falling loosely down her back. Christiana recognised her as Joan, the weaver's daughter. Indeed the weaver and his wife were close by in parley with Conyers, the steward. The young herbalist felt a jolt in her breast and a return of the melancholy that had all but vaporised.

A rapturous applause went up from the gathering just then as the company of players entered the hall with their elaborate costume, decorated masks, drums, pipes and tinkling bells and an assortment of snorting, barking and bleating animals.

"My, that did my humour much good," Martha chuckled as they walked back to the cottage some hours later. "Did you see King Herod? What a fearsome man; he made you afeard did he not, little man?" She reached out and pinched John's chubby leg as he dangled on his mother's hip beside her. The boy waved his stick with its coloured rags in the air and chuckled.

"Have you spoken to William since my betrothal to Godwin was broken?" Christiana asked, dressing down the smile upon the older woman's face.

"Nay, lass. I have said nothing but be assured he knows for there are no secrets within these castle walls," Martha replied.

"He seems to have taken a liking to the weaver's daughter," Christiana commented, setting her son down to waddle the last few yards to the wicker gate.

"Aye, well, who can blame him?" Martha sighed pragmatically. "'Tis time he sought a wife and settled down, though to my mind a soldier makes not a good husband."

Christiana opened the gate and scooped John up into her arms again as Martha gave her a sideways glance and shook her head sadly.

Middleham Castle
Yorkshire
Spring 1473

Winter reluctantly lessened its iron grip and melted into spring with a pale sun that glistened in the dripping icicles and turned the frozen cart ruts to puddles of icy slush.

John saw his third birthday with neither father nor uncle there to mark the occasion. Once again the Duke of Gloucester was summoned to court by the king where the Duke of Clarence continued to make demands for the right of all of his late father-in-law's estate.

The Duchess of Gloucester made a favourable recovery from the fear of miscarriage and with adequate rest the remaining weeks of her pregnancy were progressing well. For her extended lying in Anne had requested that she and her ladies be allowed to occupy the suite of rooms in the round tower at the southwest corner of the castle.

These chambers had their own fireplaces and so were easy to keep warm. Embroidered drapes were placed across the windows to keep out the light and the walls, freshly lime washed, were hung with heavy tapestries. Anne's relics and prayer book were brought into the darkened room and all was made comfortable and secluded for the duchess and her unborn child.

Almost daily Martha or Christiana would come and go bearing infusions of lady's mantle and basketsful of herbs to gladden the heart and perfume the rooms. The herbarium seemed to have a constant cauldron of boiling orrisroot to produce the violet-smelling perfume with which the laundry servants could soak the duchess's bed linen.

The pleasant days of summer were upon them when a messenger arrived at the door of the herbarium with the news that the duchess's labour had begun and Martha's attendance was required forthwith.

Armed with bundles of lady's bedstraw they prepared to leave the cottage at once. "What of John?" Christiana asked suddenly. "I cannot leave him alone. Wat lies ill with a fever and Tilly..."

"Then you must bring him with us," Martha stated impatiently. "You must learn the art of midwifery, Christiana – your attendance is required. I doubt that fop of a physician the duke has up there knows anything of birthing and her ladies are either too old to remember their travails or else too young to know of any."

Snatching up the little wooden puppet in one hand and taking hold of her son by the other Christiana reluctantly did as she was bid.

At the duchess's bedchamber an anxious Lady Tempest met them. "Her pains have begun. The physician has examined her and all is well and the chaplain has heard her confession," she said a little breathlessly. Upon seeing John standing forlornly beside his mother clutching his puppet to his breast, she shrieked. "Why have you brought that child in here? Are you bereft of your senses?"

"The child cannot be left alone and I require my assistant," Martha replied briskly.

Sybil was standing close to the bedpost looking pale as milk and for the world as though it was she and not the duchess about to give birth. Firmly of the belief that the birthing chamber was her domain Martha began giving her orders.

"Sybil!" she called to the trembling girl. "Take John to the kitchens and see that he stays out of harm's way. Make sure that plenty of hot water is brought up and linen cloths, cold water, lavender and rosemary. And be quick about it!" she called to Sybil's retreating back.

The physician, who had been standing silently outside the birthing chamber, was forbidden entrance. Martha was horrified that the man had gained any access at all into this place of feminine intimacy and banished him at once to the furthermost reaches of the castle.

Authority and proper order established, Martha turned her attention to Anne. Like a frightened lamb she lay on the great bed, her face glistening with perspiration and a look of terror ablaze in her blue eyes. As Christiana arranged the bedstraw in loose bundles around the mattress Martha eased up the duchess's shift to check the baby's progress, muttering soothing words to calm the fearful girl.

"It will be a while yet," Martha announced, placing her chubby hand on Anne's swollen abdomen. "You ladies can go back to your sewing." The little knot of ladies standing wide-eyed around the bed quivered indignantly at the suggestion that they should leave their lady in her time of travail.

Pails full of hot water and armfuls of linen duly arrived although nothing was seen of Sybil, and Christiana hoped that her absence meant that she was taking care of her son. It was several hours before Anne showed any signs of delivering the babe and all her attendants could offer were words of solace, a wiping of her brow and a hand to crush when the pain became unbearable.

The sliver of light sneaking through the parted window drapes slowly withdrew, the only indication that dusk had arrived, and the ladies of the bedchamber lit a few more candles. Martha examined Anne and declared that all seemed to be progressing well, although fatigue and exhaustion threatened to overcome the poor lady, who was not of a strong constitution.

Sounds of the night drifted in through one small aperture in a casement; the distant hoot of an owl, the shout of the watch. By now Martha and Christiana were the only ones keeping vigil at the bedside; the others were pacing the floor or else kneeling in prayer for Anne's safe delivery of a healthy male child. A violent outburst of pain from the duchess brought them all rushing at once to the bedside, however, to witness the first appearance of a little head with its crown of black hair. With shouts of encouragement amid a good deal of screaming, the head was followed by the tiny torso with its frail arms and legs.

"The Lord be praised!" Martha exclaimed. "The duke has a son."

Anne lay back on her pillows, her golden tresses hanging damply about her face and shoulders. Martha presented her with the precious babe and she smiled in relief before closing her eyes.

Once the necessary birthing ritual had been performed and the duchess was made comfortable announcement of the birth was made to the steward and the wet nurse sent for. It was as Martha and Christiana were leaving that Sybil finally returned to her lady's chamber. The girl looked a little flushed and her hair in fuzzy brown curls escaped her linen coif. "I have heard the duchess has delivered a boy. Is all well?" she gasped breathlessly.

"Indeed it is," replied Martha. "And you had best not neglect your duties any further for there is much still to be done," she added, nodding over to where the ladies of the bedchamber were clearing away soiled bed linen and bowls of lavender-scented water.

"Where is John?" Christiana asked, catching Sybil's sleeve as she brushed passed them.

"Oh, he is well enough. He has been sleeping soundly in the kitchen for hours."

A few days later Christiana took a turn to call upon the duchess with freshly prepared herbal tonics.

Clattering over the bridge to the inner bailey Christiana gave a cautionary glance across to her right where stood the guardhouse. It was never far from her mind that Ralph Hodkin was still within the castle walls and in a position of authority now as captain of the guard, making him a dangerous man. Like a starving wolf that bayed at the full moon he was to be avoided at all costs. Hurrying along under the arch of the chapel she arrived at the lady's bedchamber a little breathless.

Christiana found the duchess in good spirits. Propped up on her pillows there was a rosy glow in her cheeks and a distinct sparkle in her eyes.

"I am pleased to find you looking so well, my lady," Christiana remarked, setting down her basket. "There must be good news indeed to cheer you," she added, noticing that Anne held a rolled-up piece of vellum in her hand.

"Indeed there is," Anne replied, waving the scroll in the air. "This is from my husband."

Christiana lowered her gaze to hide the blush that had crept furtively to her cheeks. Talk of Richard with Anne was never going to be easy although his wife did not seem to object to his being the subject of their parley. She opened up the vellum and her eyes began to dart back and forth over the neat script. "He says that he deeply regrets that he will not be home for the birth of our child but has obtained permission from the king for my mother to be brought here where she is at liberty to remain." The duchess looked up with a broad smile on her face.

"That is indeed good news, my lady," Christiana returned pleasantly.

"The countess is presently seeking sanctuary in Beaulieu Abbey. She feared reprisals after my father's death and I thought never to see her again but now dear Richard has invited her home."

Anne continued reading: "She is to be escorted by the duke's trusted servant James Tyrell and we are to expect their arrival before summer is over."

"Lady Beauchamp will welcome the birth of her grandson for certain," Christiana said with a smile.

Anne put down the vellum and lay her head back on the pillows with a sigh. She drew a hand across the bodice of her shift and rubbed her swollen breasts.

Christiana noticed the wet patches where milk had soaked through. "You should bind your breasts, my lady, to stop the flow of milk," she whispered gently.

"I know," Anne replied sadly as a single tear appeared in the corner of her eye and trickled down her cheek. "I watched yesterday as Jane suckled my son and I wondered how it must feel. You will have suckled your son, Christiana. What is it like?"

Christiana felt the rush of heat once more in her cheeks. This was the first reference Anne had made to John since her return and what answer should she give to such a question? Should she tell the truth? That watching her baby son gently pulling on her nipple as he fed, his tiny fingers tightly clasped around her own, had given her such a feeling of maternal joy that was beyond words?

She stared into the wide innocent eyes of the girl before her. "'Tis not so much about feelings, my lady, but a necessity of life for those of us born to it; of no more significance than our own eating or drinking." She ended with a smile so contrived and false that she quickly added, "Could you not try for yourself, my lady, for a day or two perhaps?"

Anne looked horrified at the very suggestion. "No, it would not be proper. I could not," she stammered. "Lady Tempest would forbid it and whatever would my husband say if he knew the thought had even entered my head?"

"Then you will do well to let your servant bind your breasts and think no more of such matters. Think instead upon the return of your mother."

"You give wise counsel, Christiana," the duchess replied, beaming at her herbalist. Aye, thought Christiana, wise maybe but false indeed.

"Now, you will take a message to the usher of the great hall for me," Anne announced brightly, her mood changing. "I should like him to script a letter to the duke in all haste, for our news cannot wait."

Christiana arranged the costrels of herbal tonics on the table beside the bed and prepared to take her leave of the duchess.

"You might have an eye open for Sybil, my chamber maid. I have not seen her all morning," Anne called as Christiana left.

Christiana gave no thought to the errant maid as she climbed the outer staircase to the keep for her heart was pounding at the prospect of coming face to face with Godwin again. She had seen nothing of the man since she had rejected his proposal of marriage at Christmastide. There had been no chance encounters or otherwise since that day and Godwin's absence at the cottage had passed without comment.

The figure of a young girl scurrying down the stairs almost knocked Christiana off her feet, such was the speed and excitement of her progress.

"Sybil!" Christiana remonstrated. "Have a care. Where do you go in such a hurry? The duchess is awaiting you in her chamber." The maid had halted abruptly, her cheeks scarlet and her coif askew. "Sorry, mistress. I am on my way." The girl then bowed to the herbalist, a gesture that both annoyed and amused Christiana, for the maid clearly had no understanding of etiquette.

With much trepidation Christiana entered the antechamber of the great hall. It was not Godwin, however, seated at the desk but another. This man was well attired in a finely woven garment of a deep red hue. Bolts of cloth of varying colours lay strewn across the desk obscuring any parchment that lay beneath. The weaver, for that was who Christiana recognised the man to be, gave the young woman a curt nod of his head as she entered.

The usher entered almost immediately then through the doorway from the great hall. He stopped abruptly upon seeing Christiana.

"Well," demanded the weaver, "have you found the steward?"

"I, well, no," Godwin stammered.

"I cannot hang around here all day, I have work to do. You mark my words, usher, and be sure to tell Conyers I shall be back. I am about to do a most profitable deal with a wool merchant in York and I need to know my market." The weaver snatched up his samples and turned to leave.

"Maybe next time, Master Weaver, you can send warning of your arrival," Godwin offered, finding his composure at last.

As he brushed past Christiana the weaver dropped two of his bolts of cloth. He bent to retrieve them, his face as florid as his tunic, and muttered something about the place being full of serving wenches before making a hasty retreat.

Godwin and Christiana smiled, their gaze meeting warmly, and any anxiety Christiana felt dispersed at once. "Are you well, Godwin?" she asked. "Does your arm trouble you?"

"I am well enough and the rash sleeps for now," Godwin replied. "And you?"

In truth Christiana had been much troubled in her mind since Christmastide. Her rejection of Godwin had left her saddened that maybe she had lost a friend. The possibility that her brother may have plans to pursue the affection of the weaver's daughter also somehow troubled her; she always missed him when he was on campaign with the duke. For now, however, it appeared that Godwin at least might remain a friend of sorts.

"I am well, Godwin, I thank you. Lady Anne has asked that you send at once to inform the duke of the safe arrival of his son," she replied.

"'Tis done already, at Conyers' request." The usher smiled and began to tidy his desk. Christiana thought it pertinent to take her leave and content she left Godwin to his business.

The ladies of the castle were out in the pleasure garden taking in the delights of the summer air. The Duchess of Gloucester was venturing forth for the first time following the birth of her son, accompanied by Lady Tempest and Lady Skelton. Lady Scrope and Lady Thomas Lumley joined them; the duchess's household grew ever larger.

Anne looked radiant, not only because the sun warmed her pale skin and the scent of the roses lifted her spirits, but mostly due to her mother's presence, now seated beside her on the bench. The other ladies were strolling along the gravel paths followed by a troupe of minstrels singing ballads to the tune of lute and harpsichord.

"It is so good to have you home, Mother," Anne said, taking the countess's hand.

"And this is my home?" Lady Beauchamp asked bitterly.

"For certain, Mother," Anne laughed.

"None would think I had home or title of any sort the way your husband and his brother fight between themselves like a dog with a bone," the countess retorted.

The younger woman blushed. "I am sure the dukes have your interests at heart, ensuring that the Beauchamp and Neville lands are, well, safeguarded for the future," she finished lamely.

"Talking of Gloucester, does he have his wife's interests at heart? I take it from the early production of an heir that there is one area of your marriage at least that is not lacking."

"Mother!" exclaimed the duchess, her blush deepening. "Must you talk of such matters openly? Someone may be listening." She looked around the garden quickly.

"You are such an innocent, my sweeting," the countess laughed. "I merely meant, well..."

"What did you mean, Mother?"

"Well, simply this; you come with the goods, my love. No Anne Neville, no castle, no lands." The countess sighed and clasped her daughter's hand. "Does he treat you well? Is he a good husband?"

"Oh yes indeed. He has treated me with all respect and care. He is a good man."

"Then he is fond of you at least and that bodes well for an amicable marriage. And what of you, daughter, where lies your heart?"

The duchess did not answer for a while, pondering. "I was truly grieved when my Edward of Lancaster was killed," she said sadly. "I loved him well and did not think to find another I could care for as much. Richard is kind and gentle, if a little sullen at times. Now we have a son, the first of many I pray, I hope to find contentment in this marriage."

"Then I am happy for you, dearest Anne." The countess smiled. "Your father would have been pleased too, I am sure, that you have found a good match in this prince. If Gloucester keeps favour with the king then all cannot fail to go well with you, daughter. And now that the queen has produced a second son for Edward and all seems at peace in the realm, for once we can be at ease."

"You are well informed, Mother, for one in sanctuary these past two years," Anne observed.

"Gloucester's servant James Tyrell had much to say on our journey to the north," the older woman confessed. "He has divulged much and his service to Gloucester is admirable. Your husband inspires loyalty as well as gives it. I do believe there is nothing Tyrell would not do for his lord.

"I was saddened to hear of the death of your father's sister, Eleanor. I have it that her widower Lord Stanley has made a most profitable marriage to Lady Margaret Beaufort; her fourth husband I believe." The dowager added this remark with a wry smile.

"I would wager 'tis she who has made the profitable marriage for Richard believes she will make much use of Lord Stanley's wealth and position," Anne replied.

The afternoon sun was gloriously warm on their faces, a welcome change from the cold interior of the stone castle. For several moments both ladies sat in companionable silence.

"Have you any news of my sister, Isabel?" Anne asked after a while.

"The last I heard she was in the south – Somerset, and has a fine, healthy daughter this year past, praise God." The dowager hung her head sadly then, remembering the tragic circumstances of the birth and death of her first grandchild. "If only George were as loyal to the king as his brother," she muttered. "I should fear less for Isabel then."

The Duchess of Gloucester took her mother's hand and pressed it gently as both ladies closed their eyes and continued to enjoy the warmth of the summer sun.

The patter of light footsteps and a shadow falling across the bench disturbed their peace. The countess opened her eyes quickly, for she had begun to doze, to find a small dark-haired boy standing before her. His little round face wore a serious expression and in his tiny hand he held a sprig of rosemary, which he duly offered to the lady. The countess took the offered herb. The child's face lit up with joy before he turned and scampered away down the path.

"Who was that boy?" the countess asked as the child disappeared from view. "He seems familiar somehow."

"That was John, Richard's bastard," Anne replied without any malice in her voice.

The countess raised an eyebrow. "Ah yes, now I recall. What became of his mother?"

"Christiana, she is still here. They live in the cottage in the garden. You must remember Martha the herbalist, you have not been away that long, Mother," Anne chuckled.

"For certain, I do. Is the old woman still alive then? Your father used to call her an old witch but he esteemed her knowledge of herbal remedies above all others." Her face dropped its smile then and she became serious once more. Turning to her daughter she said, "You must not mind too much about your husband's mistresses. It is the way of all men."

Anne smiled knowingly. Did she not have a bastard sister herself duly acknowledged and accepted by her own father?

"As long as you remember that you are his wife and always will be and do not let any woman rob you of that status then—" the dowager continued.

"Mother, please," Anne interrupted. "Richard is not like that; he is not, I am certain. This child, John, is... well... Christiana means nothing to Richard. She is a servant and a good herbalist. I am very fond of her. Richard allows her to stay because, well, he is kind-hearted."

Just at that moment providence dictated that the subject of their conversation should walk into view. Observed from a distance, Christiana could be seen ambling slowly along a pathway with a pannier slung across her arm. She paused intermittently to pick at the herbs growing at her feet. Her movements were firm yet graceful as her raven locks fell about her shoulders like a silk veil.

"Well she has certainly become a very pretty wench," Countess Anne conceded, "but how drab." She compared Christiana's faded green kirtle, looking tatty even at this distance, with her daughter's luscious gown of crimson satin. "No, my sweeting, I do not think you have much to fear from that one. Although I like it not that she is hidden away from view down here.

"Come let us join the others. You must not neglect your duties. Lady Scrope will need rescuing from that formidable Tempest woman."

The countess rose from the bench and smoothed her gown. "As I do not have many ladies of my own as yet I shall instruct you, daughter, in the art of handling your own."

Middleham Castle
Yorkshire
Autumn 1473

The long hot days of summer gave way to the warm balmy days of autumn. This was a busy time in the herbarium when the last of the herbs were picked and dried and stored for making salves, tisanes, infusions and decoctions.

"I hear our William is home," Martha remarked as she sorted her bunches of dried herbs on one such busy day.

Christiana looked up briefly from her grinding, a shadow darkening her face.

"You do know that he is courting Joan, the weaver's daughter?" Martha pursued without looking at the younger woman.

Christiana felt the heat sting her cheeks and her hand ceased its labour, pestle poised over the wooden mortar. "What is that to me?" she replied softly. "I should be glad to know that my brother has found happiness and a future with this woman."

"Humph!" Martha responded. "And what of you, my girl? You have rejected your one chance of a marriage proposal. Godwin—"

"I do not wish to talk of this Martha," Christiana interrupted sternly. "I have made my choice and let that be an end to it."

And that was an end to the matter until a few days later.

A slight breath of wind caught the yellowing leaves of the plants and lifted some, whose time was ready, and gently spun them to their final resting place upon the ground. It always seemed to Christiana that a tinge of melancholia hung around the last remnants of the ebbing summer and somehow seeped gently into her soul.

The garden was tranquil and warm. Mother and son sat together on the bench near the dovecote. Christiana was attempting to teach John to play jackstones but the boy's little fingers were as yet too clumsy to catch the smooth pebbles as they fell. He had, however, a determination to succeed which occupied him – for now.

Martha had consented to finishing the work in the herbarium alone, allowing Christiana to take her son into the garden to distract him; there was a limit to the length of time the child would remain content in his pen with just a few toys for his amusement.

The sound of bubbling laughter reached their ears, that of a young woman, followed by William's voice in mock reprimand. The sounds grew louder, signifying that the couple were approaching nearer. Presently the soldier stepped from the cover of the box hedge into view, his arm provocatively draped around the weaver's eldest daughter. Christiana returned her focus upon the pebbles in her hand but the child's eyes lit up in recognition of his uncle. "Unca Will," he cried, shuffling to the end of the bench and flopping to the ground.

William received his nephew graciously with a quick glance in the direction of the woman still seated on the bench.

"Joan has come for more of Martha's physic," William announced by way of explanation. "Her sister, Annette, has further need," he continued, re-establishing his grip on the girl's waist, to which her response was another bubble of laughter.

"Can you prepare it, sister?" William continued without taking his eyes off Joan, who smiled sweetly at the attention.

"'Tis the herbalist you should consult, brother, not I," Christiana replied somewhat sourly.

For less than a moment's passing William's eyes caught those of his sister and held a wordless gaze before the man inclined his head to the woman and turned towards the cottage, Joan at his heels.

Christiana sighed deeply and ruffled the black curls of the small boy who had returned to sit beside her on the bench. The melancholia of the season had begun to seep into her bones.

The seasons changed; autumn through to winter through to spring. Christiana continued to work alongside Martha, increasing her knowledge and understanding of the herbs they grew and used.

The child, John, likewise grew in stature and likeness to his father, the Duke of Gloucester.

Duchess Anne's baby son, Edward, thrived despite his sickly nature and it was much comfort to Anne that she had her mother close by as she felt the absence of her husband keenly.

The news that the long dispute between the king's brothers was now at an end preceded the return of the duke by a matter of weeks. The king himself had finally intervened and carved up the late Earl of Warwick's fortune between his brothers to his liking. Parliament had sealed the decision and no more was to be said. Richard, Duke of Gloucester, endowed with the title Lord of the North, was at last on his way back to claim legal ownership of his castle at Middleham, amongst others.

When Richard did return in early summer, tired and dusty from the journey, Christiana witnessed the joyful reunion of husband and wife in the great hall for she happened to be there on an errand for the steward. Her heart was heavy with longing as she watched the warm embrace and kisses plentiful Richard had for Anne.

Christiana saw very little of her brother and knew him to be spending his free time in the village at the weaver's cottage. For her it was a lonely existence at times and the busyness of her work pushed from her mind the thoughts of what might have been and thoughts of what could never be.

All through the summer and into the gold and reds of autumn Christiana continued in her duties to serve the lord of the castle and his household. Her son was her joy and the core of her existence.

Middleham Castle
Yorkshire
Autumn 1474

One sun-filled day in autumn Martha and her assistant were bending over their garden, picking and raking, when shadows darkened the ground. The old herbalist looked up and squinting into the sunlight saw the figure of Conyers, the steward, standing over them. She noted that he was looking somewhat portly these days. Beside him stood an unknown figure dressed in black with the strap of a large leather bag slung across his shoulder. Christiana was already on her feet thinking that their visitor might be William Beverley, the rector.

"This is Lempster of London, physician to the duke." Conyers introduced the stern-looking man whose nose resembled the hooked beak of a bird. "He wishes to look around the herbarium at your physic and herbs," Conyers continued.

Martha too was on her feet, wiping her hands on her apron. "Does he indeed," she retorted. "And why may I..."

"Now, now, Martha," Conyers said gently. "The physician has authority from the duke and you will give him your assistance." He put his arm around the old woman's shoulders and cajoled her towards the cottage door.

Christiana followed, entering the pungent gloominess of the cottage wherein the physician immediately began to turn and peruse the many bottles and jars on display, Martha following him around her domain like a sheep. Conyers took Christiana aside and whispered, "Lempster will need your assistance and you must be discreet."

Christiana nodded and waited for the purpose of Conyers' visit to unfold.

"Where do you keep myrrh and saffron, poppy seed pods and cinnamon?" the physician demanded.

"They are spices of great worth," Martha replied indignantly.

"I do not need an old herbalist to tell me their worth – produce them immediately."

Martha, muttering expletives under her breath, dragged a heavy wooden chest from under the bench, took a key from her belt and opened it; having done so she stood aside, sighing heavily.

Conyers led her to a stool and bade her sit. "A message has been received from the village. The weaver's wife has asked that you be sent with remedies for her daughter. The falling sickness has returned." He placed a hand upon her shoulder and smiled. "You should go where you are needed. It will be of no use fretting here. Lempster will not stay long."

Martha gave the steward a long cold stare, relented and stood to her feet. She made a great deal of fuss grinding, mixing and banging bottles but at last her basket was full of remedies and she left the cottage with a loud thud of the door in her wake.

Conyers left soon after, taking John with him. Alone with the formidable physician Christiana watched as he produced from his leather bag a pair of brass weighing scales and an assortment of weights from a wooden box lined with blue velvet. Using the smallest of pewter spoons he carefully measured a powdered drachm of this and a scruple of that, taking his remedy from a thin sheet of parchment produced from the pouch at his belt. In silence he slowly mixed, heated and prepared a warming poultice of exotic spices and several of Martha's most potent herbs, and having wrapped it in linen placed it in a wooden box which he enclosed within a leather bag.

"Have you knowledge of measurements and weights – can you discern such matters?" Lempster asked as he walked briskly towards the keep with long purposeful strides, the young woman all but running to keep pace.

"I have some understanding, yes," she answered breathlessly, thinking that Martha rarely relied on such matters, having the measure of all things secreted away in her head.

"Then I shall have the receipt written down and sent to you so that you can make it again when needed. You have a set of weighing scales, I presume?"

"I believe so..." Christiana hesitated.

"I shall see to it that you have a proper pair precisely calibrated for your use," Lempster announced.

They had reached the keep where the physician continued his journey without a by your leave from any until he arrived at the duke's bedchamber. There he grovelled with many a bow and a bob.

"My lord, I have the relief you require, made to a specific receipt from the East."

Richard was lying beneath the bed covers clearly in some pain by the look on his face. He noted Christiana's presence by the briefest of glances her way.

"Now, my lord, remove your shirt and sit astride this chair, if you please." The physician snapped his fingers and a youth nervously stepped forward from where he had been standing amongst the shadows along the wall. He drew Richard's shirt over his head and laid it aside. As the duke sat in the required position Lempster turned to Christiana and hissed a warning. "Of what you are about to see you will breathe not a word to a living soul. The duke trusts your discretion," he added with a sniff as though the sentiment were foolish.

The woman nodded silently and watched as the physician applied the warming poultice to Richard's back and covered it with strips of linen which he first dipped in a bowl of water warming in a pot on the fire. Christiana was not afraid of what she witnessed for had she not seen this before? Richard, a mere youth, had showed her this and foretold that it would worsen; and indeed it had. The curve of his spine was deeper, more pronounced. She marvelled at how it could be that he lived and fought and commanded armies when surely he must be in some measure of pain.

"This must remain thus for half an hour," Lempster announced, drawing from his bag an hourglass and placing it on the table beside the bed. "The linen strips can then be removed and the back washed with warm water." He addressed the groom of the bedchamber. "By your leave, my lord, I shall look upon your lady wife and your son to see that they are in good health." The physician made his way to the tapestry hangings at the arched doorway.

Richard addressed the groom, "Alan, see to it that the good physician finds his way to the duchess's chambers, Lady Tempest is expecting his arrival."

Lempster paused momentarily, realising that the duke's command would leave the servant girl alone in the bedchamber with her lord. He said nothing, however, and inclined his head respectfully. After all, he had witnessed similar or worse behaviour amongst the king's courtiers in London.

Alone with Richard, Christiana at once went to his side, kneeling down upon the hard floor, tears welling up in her eyes.

The duke smiled. "Do not be anxious for me, Christiana, this brings me much relief. I trust you can prepare it when I need more?"

She returned his smile and nodded although her tears had escaped and trickled down her cheeks.

"Lempster has tried to persuade me to be racked," Richard laughed.

Christiana stared in horror. "You mean tortured on the rack?" she whispered in disbelief.

Richard laughed again. "Aye, I do believe so although I am yet to be persuaded that it would be for my benefit and well-being."

Christiana smiled and stared at Richard's arms as they rested upon the high back of the oak chair.

"You must not be worried on my account," Richard continued, turning his head to meet her troubled countenance. "I do not intend to be racked; I was tortured enough when I had two teeth pulled by the barber surgeon in London."

Now Christiana laughed with the duke. Richard rested his head against his arms. "I am content to remain as God has made me," he whispered and closed his eyes.

When the groom of the bedchamber returned several moments later he found the duke alone sitting on the chair just as he had left him, giving him no reason to ignite malicious gossip or rumour.

By the time Christiana returned to the cottage Martha's errand was also complete and the herbalist was at her bench pounding and grinding her herbs. John too had been brought home, asleep in Conyers' arms, and now lay content in his pen.

"How did you find Annette, the weaver's daughter?" Christiana asked as she poured them both a cup of elderflower ale from a flagon.

"The poor girl is sick but she may find some relief from my herbs and prayer."

They sat and drank as Christiana divulged the purpose of Lempster's intrusive visit to the herbarium, saying only that the duke had a common back pain. Martha did not question or evoke any further information for she seemed occupied with thoughts of her own.

Given Martha's reaction to having her authority usurped by a physician prior to her leaving, Christiana was puzzled by her complacency and asked, "Is there no other news from the village, Martha? Is all well?"

"No, no other news. Now we must be getting along for we have been taken from our work for long enough this day." She put her cup on the table with a clink and stood to her feet.

There was indeed news from the village but she would say nothing. Life was as tangled and complex as the back of a tapestry hanging. There was much to be said for getting daughters betrothed at an early age, the earlier the better, as had happened with Anne FitzHugh, wife of Francis, Lord Lovell, a child-bride of five years.

Had her eyes and ears deceived her or had they conveyed true in their witness? Had she seen and heard the beautiful Joan, sister to the ailing Annette, in deep and whimsical talk with John Stapleton, wealthy wool merchant of York? Had she seen their fingertips touching and his lips caress her rose-red cheek as her father looked on unabashed? Martha shook such thoughts from her head. Maybe it would not be long before some matter of great importance took the duke away and William with him.

Middleham Castle
Yorkshire
Winter 1474

"'Tis a wet and miserable day," Martha complained as she blew into the cottage on a swirl of wind and rain. "Let us hope we have enough remedies to see us through this winter." The old woman shivered and removed her cloak to let it drip dry on the peg behind the door.

"Here, drink this." Christiana offered a cup of hot spiced wine. "We can ill afford you to be sick, dear friend." She smiled.

"Aye, God help us all if that should happen," Martha laughed. "The duke will have to bring in one of his physicians and it will be God help us then!"

The old woman eased herself down onto a stool and sipped the warming drink. "There is a bout of winter vomiting up at the keep," Martha continued more seriously now. "I pray that little Edward is spared for I cannot see him surviving if that gets a hold of him, poor child."

"How is Richard?" Christiana asked with concern in her voice.

"The duke is well. Do not fret for him, Christiana," Martha warned. "Now, we shall busy ourselves preparing syrup of rosehips the rest of this day and be certain that you and the boy take plentiful measures."

The light of the day was fast disappearing by the time they had bottled the last of the syrup. Christiana lit the candle stubs as Martha covered the child with the lambskin as he slept in his pen. The rain continued to lash down upon the rooftop and pour down the glazed casements.

"Did you hear that?" Christiana asked.

"Hear what?" Martha replied. "Nowt but the wind and the rain."

"Martha, there is someone outside." Christiana was at once at the latch to open the door. The wood swung inwards with a spray of cold rain, revealing a wet and pale-faced man barely able to stand upright on the threshold.

"William!" Christiana cried. "Heaven help us. Martha!" she called just as the herbalist reached her side, and not a second too soon for the soldier crumbled to his knees before them. Both women thrust out an arm to steady the man who would surely have fallen prone at their feet were it not for the timely arrival of another at the door.

"Jude, thank goodness you are here," Martha exclaimed as she stood aside to allow the young man to assist Christiana in pulling William to his feet.

Sometime later they had between them stripped William of his sodden attire and had him on the bed beneath wool blankets and animal skins.

"He has been unwell for some time," Jude explained as he sat on a stool sipping a cup of hot spiced wine. "But being the man that he is has carried on regardless until today when he is no longer able. 'Tis well for him I followed him here from the stables."

"Aye, 'tis the way with men; either they are stoical when ill or else act like babes," Martha commented sagely.

"What do you suppose to be wrong with him, Martha?" Christiana asked quietly.

"I cannot be sure, lass. He has a fever for sure but there is no rash on his body or black lumps," Martha replied thoughtfully. "Like as not 'tis but a winter ague common to all and with proper care will soon be back on his feet. He is a strong lad."

Martha waddled across to her bench to chop the garlic and onion and look for the jar of dried feverfew leaves. Jude, warmed within and dried sufficiently to attempt the return journey to the stables, bade them farewell.

Christiana prepared a bowl of vinegar and taking a piece of butter cloth began to gently wipe the sweat from her brother's brow.

"Martha?" Christiana called softly without ceasing her bedside task.

"Aye, lass," Martha returned to the bedchamber.

"Do you not think it would be well for me to go into the village to see how folk are faring? If we have the winter ague here at the castle maybe others in the village are also ill." She hesitated momentarily. "I was thinking of the weaver's family, you know Joan, she may have this fever also and be in need of our help. And then there is Annette, the girl."

Martha said nothing but her face wore a ponderous frown.

"I think William would like to think that we have looked in upon Joan... if he does indeed have a heart for her," Christiana continued softly.

Martha's sigh was deep and touched with sadness. "Aye, lass, maybe you are right," she replied. "But nowise shall you go anywhere this day. Wait a while until this deluge has ceased."

William lay abed for several more days and received all the care and physic the two women could offer. Martha slept on the truckle at the foot of the bed while Christiana took for her repose a straw stuffed mattress which she shared with her child. As with Alfred the women were prepared to give up their bed when the sick had need of it.

The rain abated to a drizzle after a day or two, allowing Christiana to make her visit to the village, with the duke's consent. She squelched along the rutted roads with a basket of herbal preparations swinging on her arm. She made her way to the weaver's cottage; maybe the man's wife would know of any who ailed in the village.

Christiana waited patiently outside the door for her knock to be answered. She glanced upwards into the grey bleak clouds scurrying by and knocked a second time. She was about to turn away when the door opened and facing her was the weaver's wife.

"Good morrow," Christiana said politely. "I thought maybe you were not at home."

"Ah yes," returned the woman, holding a skein of wool about her arms. "'Twould be the noise of the loom, muffles the sound of the door knocks. Come in." She pulled the door wide to allow Christiana to enter.

The weaver's youngest daughter Annette was sitting on a stool at the loom. She looked up at Christiana as she entered and smiled wanly.

"I am come from Martha to see how you fare," Christiana began, walking over to the girl. "There are many at the castle suffering from the winter ague and William, my brother, is taken badly. I am..." The young woman stopped speaking then as she noticed for the first time the person of John Stapleton, the wool merchant, also present in the room. He was standing beside Joan in the shadows of a darkened corner and Christiana began to sense that she had somehow entered upon a scene that she should not have witnessed. There seemed nothing untoward, however; it was certainly not out of the ordinary for a wool merchant to pay a visit to a weaver.

Christiana glanced at Joan. Her soft chestnut curls framed a pretty round face with cheeks tinged red as the rose, a complexion not indicative of ill health. Indeed looking around at the faces of the weaver and his family none seemed to be troubled in the slightest by the malady that inflicted the castle dwellers and Christiana felt a surge of awkward silence.

It was the weaver's wife who spoke. "I thank you kindly for your concern and making the journey, Christiana, but as you can see we are all well. Even Annette here has not been taken with the falling sickness these few weeks past."

"I shall bid you all a good day then and be on my way." Christiana inclined her head towards the weaver and let her eyes rest upon his eldest daughter's face for a brief moment before turning towards the door.

Outside the door Christiana hesitated to pull up her hood for the rain had begun again as the clouds overhead darkened. Before she had adjusted the handle of her basket on her arm the door opened and Joan sidled out.

"Is William very sick?" she asked in almost a whisper.

Christiana regarded her for a moment or two, her mind still unclear. "Aye, he is," she replied after a while. "He lies abed in Martha's cottage with a fever. Maybe you should pay him a visit, if you have a care for him."

Joan turned her head back to the half-opened door and stepped a little nearer to the other woman. "When I have a chance I will," she answered quickly.

Christiana gave no reply and pulling her hood closer over her head she walked away.

William remained at the cottage for a few more days before he had recovered sufficiently to return to his duties. Christiana made no mention of the niggling thoughts in her head to Martha, for they were just that: thoughts without substance. In all the time William remained in their care they saw nothing of Joan, the weaver's daughter.

Summer 1475

During the summer of 1475 the duke was once again at the king's side on campaign in France, putting a large retinue of men-at-arms at Edward's disposal.

One notable absence on this cause was William, who had been assigned to lead an armed escort for the dowager Countess of Warwick and her daughter, the Duchess of Gloucester on their journey south to Warwick.

The Lady Anne had the greatest desire to see her sister Isabel again. They had not met for nigh on five years and now Isabel had a son, Edward, born towards the end of February of that year at Warwick Castle.

The duke reluctantly agreed for Edward, his son and heir, to travel with his mother, before leaving for France.

William oversaw the journey with no great haste, allowing plentiful rests on the way, the mild weather greatly aiding their comfort.

Upon their arrival at Warwick Castle beside the Avon River they found Isabel pale-faced though well enough and very pleased to see her mother and sister.

"Martha sends you some of her potions." Anne smiled as she kissed her sister's cheek.

"I swear that old woman is a witch." Her mother laughed good-humouredly as she helped Anne to unpack the jars and costrels.

Isabel's countenance darkened. "Do not jest about such matters, Mother," she said sadly. "I hear nothing but talk of witchcraft from George. He is convinced that sorcery was afoot when Elizabeth Woodville married Edward. I swear my poor husband is losing his mind and rambles on about secrets that only he knows and how he is the rightful heir to the throne," Isabel ended tearfully and a little breathless.

"Come, come, Isabel, let us not talk of such matters for this is a joyous occasion for you have given your husband a son and heir."

"Heir to what? There is little to inherit – Anne's husband has seen to that." The Duchess of Clarence wiped at a stray tear on her cheek.

"Do not be bitter, sister," Anne admonished gently. "Do not forget George's treason. The king has been more than generous; George's lands match those of Richard's and more."

"Ah here are the children," Anne Beauchamp announced, somewhat relieved, as a nurse entered the chamber carrying a sleeping child of four or five months and holding the hand of a pretty girl child of almost two years. Little Edward of Middleham, now also two years of age, was brought in by his nurse after a period of rest following his long journey.

At once the mood lightened as the children were fussed over and petted. Little Margaret, Isabel's daughter, was a special joy to her grandmother and aunt and they passed a pleasant afternoon together, forgetting for a while the tension of the political world into which these little ones had been born.

The visit to Warwick was over all too soon and it was with a heavy heart that Anne bade farewell to her sister and made the long journey north once more as the golden glow of summer began to fade.

Middleham Castle
Yorkshire
Summer 1475

"'Tis quiet up at the castle with the duke in France and the duchess at Warwick and half the servants away with them," Martha sighed, setting her empty basket down on the table.

Christiana looked up from her work, pounding fresh herbs in a wooden mortar.

"This coltsfoot is almost ready," she commented. "Where is John? He will need to take this soon; his cough is most persistent."

"Cough or no cough that little scallywag needs a firm hand, Christiana. I have just found him trampling on my herbs and had to shoo him away." Martha sighed again and sat heavily down upon a chair.

"Can you make ready this coltsfoot and I will go find him," Christiana said, and taking up her straw hat she went out of the cottage, leaving the door wide on its hinges to coax in the breeze.

Martha had the coltsfoot infusion warming on the brazier and she had started the muslin bags of bitter herbs as required up at the keep by the time a hot and dishevelled mother made an appearance at the cottage with a wriggling child on her hip, coughing violently.

"He had managed to open the latch on the gate and was halfway across the drill field by the time I caught him," Christiana said wearily. "You have been forbidden to leave the confines of the garden. You are a wilful child," she continued sternly.

Martha took John from his mother and sat him on a stool. She waited until his cough had abated before giving him two spoonfuls of the prepared infusion.

"Catch your breath and take a little ale, Christiana, and then you can leave the boy with me and run an errand to the keep."

Christiana sat down heavily on a stool, grateful that Martha was here to support her in her struggle to nurture and discipline her son, although it was with the latter that she needed the most help.

It was not long before John was sleeping soundly in his pen. Martha was heaping two large flat-bottomed panniers with bunches of lavender, lemon balm and fennel for strewing on the floor and muslin bags aplenty stuffed with tansy, rue, wormwood and yellow loosestrife for hanging in the garderobes and filling the clothes chests.

As she handed the baskets to Christiana Martha said gently, "The child lacks a father. No good ever came of a boy who lacked a father."

Martha's words were still stinging her ears as she entered the inner bailey and made her way towards the kitchens. She would not allow herself to regret her decision to reject Godwin, the only father her son was likely to have. John would do well enough once his uncle Will returned home; the boy should spend time at the smithy watching the work of the blacksmith for one day that would be his trade.

There was an air of excitement within the kitchens as she entered but the merry banter and babble ceased no sooner had she crossed the threshold. That scatty chamber maid, Sybil, seemed to be the centre of attention and the reason quickly became apparent, sending a flush of colour to the cheeks of the herbalist. Christiana had caught the glint of silver from a trinket hanging around Sybil's neck and the unmistakable deep pink glow of coral beads as she flaunted her gift to butlers, kitchen maids and spit boys.

Evidently unaware that the bauble she possessed had once belonged to another, Sybil came forward to declare that Godwin, the usher, had proposed marriage and once the necessary formalities had been seen to then betrothal vows would be made; the necklace was a sign of his commitment.

Christiana's head was reeling with the surprise of seeing what had once belonged to her around the neck of another, and more than that was the absurdity that Godwin should choose one such as Sybil to take as wife. Had the man lost all reason? She forced a smile upon her face and all but shoved the baskets into Sybil's arms, commanding her to be certain to make good preparation for the return of the duchess, whose arrival was expected any day.

She should have returned then to the cottage but she felt compelled to see Godwin so she ascended the outer staircase and entered the anteroom of the keep.

The usher was at his desk and rose to his feet as Christiana entered. He knew by the look on her face that she was privy to the news of his intended betrothal. He took her hand and led her to a chair, sitting himself beside her. Still holding her hand he spoke without preamble, "You know?"

She nodded and he continued. "I have a fondness for Sybil and she for me, I believe. For certain she does not have your degree of common sense and stability but I truly believe that we can be happy. You would not deny your friend the chance of happiness?"

Christiana smiled. "Never that," she said. "I am very fond of you and would be pleased to see you make a good marriage. Sybil is a sweet-natured girl, though I fear a little reckless."

Godwin pressed her hand. "I would want no less for you, Christiana, one day..."

She smiled but she knew that her fate had been sealed the day she rejected this good man.

"So, Sir Usher, is this indeed a love match or maybe the lady comes with a vast fortune to ease the pain of married life?" Christiana teased.

Godwin took her jest in good humour. "Sybil is from a worthy family here in the north," he replied. "Although her father's fortunes changed for the worse when Edward took the crown, there should be a modest dowry but nothing more. There, does that please you?"

"Immensely," she replied, and on an impulse she opened her arms to catch his embrace, feeling again the warmth and fondness of what might have been.

The Duchess of Gloucester found a rather vexed husband upon her return to Middleham. It would appear that the military intent in France had not quite gone to plan and her husband's arrival at the castle had preceded hers by only a matter of days. Edward's intentions were not so much military as diplomatic and commercial. A peace treaty, which involved a substantial payoff to Edward for withdrawing his army, had been negotiated and trade agreements between the two countries were secured.

The signing of the treaty on the bridge at Picquigny in late August, by King Louis of France and the King of England, had one notable absence amongst the witnesses; namely the Duke of Gloucester, who it was said regarded the treaty as a dishonourable surrender and a betrayal of public funds put forward for the campaign.

For once it was not his brother, George, accredited with any blame but John Morton, Bishop of Ely, and one-time supporter of Henry VI, who forged the terms of negotiation.

Unlike his liege lord, William's return home was viewed with eager anticipation for he had made up his mind to go at once to the weaver and ask for the hand of his eldest daughter in marriage. He could fool himself no longer. He would never be anything other than a brother to Christiana; he could not hold her to blame for they had been raised as such. Her unfathomable obsession with the duke had cost her a favourable marriage, the like of which would never come again; she might as well try to dance on sunbeams.

As for Joan, William considered her to be a most worthy woman. Her father seemed to be making a reasonable living from his cloth in the village and at local fairs. He could not object to giving his daughter to one in the employ of one of the most powerful men in the kingdom. He had sorely missed Joan during winter last when he was taken badly with the ague and could not understand why his sister had not sent word to her in the village that he was indisposed. Then after that Joan had travelled to York with her father to aid him in his business. She would not be away long, so said the weaver's good wife on his last visit to the village, before he departed for Warwick earlier that summer.

It was still early in the afternoon when the duke and his retinue had arrived back at the castle. Not wishing to waste any time

William lingered only to stable his horse and take a deep drink from a costrel of ale.

The walk to the village would give him time enough to make coherent sense of the jumble of words that tossed around in his head. Straight to the point and without beating about the bush would be how the weaver would like it.

The early autumn sun was still hot on his uncovered head and his shirt was soaked with sweat by the time he arrived at the weaver's cottage. The door was open; William halted on the threshold. He could see the weaver at his loom, his wife and younger daughter sitting on stools carding wool. It was fortunate perhaps that Joan was not at home; asking for a woman's hand in marriage was something a man had to do alone. He knocked on the door and entered, bowing respectfully to the weaver and his family.

"Will, I bid you a good day, lad." The weaver looked up from his work and offered a greeting. "Are you come on an errand? Those herbs concocted by that old witch up at the castle have weaved their magic on Annette here; she has been well these past few months." The weaver chuckled at his own wit.

The weaver's wife left her carding and went through a door leading to the kitchen outside to fetch a jug of her home-brewed ale. William suddenly felt nervous. It was going to be difficult getting to the point if he could not even get a word in.

"So, Will, sit you down on a stool and state your business," the weaver ambled relentlessly. "Talking of business, I have recently forged a very lucrative contract with a wool merchant in York. You tell Conyers that he will not find a better bolt of woven cloth than mine. I shall be up there—"

"I beg your pardon, Master Weaver," William interrupted brusquely, his nerves beginning to get the better of him now. "I have come here this day to ask for the hand of your daughter, Joan, in marriage. I have a modest income as a soldier, I am certain promotion up the ranks will not be long in coming and..."

He stopped abruptly for the weaver had begun to laugh, a hearty belly laugh that shook his body and rattled his loom.

"You are jesting with me, lad," he chuckled breathlessly. "Now don't take this to heart, I've seen you around my Joanie and I dare say you're fond of the girl, but she's part of the contract." The weaver continued to laugh as William felt his face glow redder. "I've given her to John Stapleton, the wool merchant. He has some of the finest fleeces in the north. Don't you worry on her account, lad – he has fine clothes, a fine house and fine coin aplenty. You can take Annette here with my blessing. She'll suit you better, Will, and I dare say I'll be hard pressed to find anyone else for her."

William was angry but greater than his anger was his deep humiliation. He could do nothing but turn on his heel and stride out of the cottage, the sound of the weaver's laughter drumming in his ears.

Middleham Castle
Yorkshire
Winter 1475

William received well the news that the Duke of Gloucester was to spend some time away from Middleham at his other northern strongholds of Sheriff Hutton and Barnstable. As chief steward of the north, Richard's duties took him across much of Yorkshire and Cumbria.

William had been more than ready to leave his work at the smithies and join the duke's retinue once again. For a while he had been able to immerse himself in the life of a soldier, riding out in protection of his lord, and thoughts of Joan and her beau were left far behind. Winter was slow coming that year and the duke took advantage of the milder weather to settle affairs on his estates before returning to his wife and son.

It was quiet about the castle, the Christmastide festivities long over, and William soon settled to his mundane duties on his return home.

One grey, overcast day, William, his work complete, had a mind to visit his sister and the old herbalist at the cottage. There was always excuse enough to have more balm for his feet and he surprised himself by how fond he had grown of the boy, John.

On his arrival at the cottage William found Martha taking her ease in a wooden chair on a faded cushion. The child was at her feet, his dark head of curls bent over an assortment of wooden toys. He appeared to be acting out a childish scene with horses, knights and a castle he had constructed using some of Martha's bottles, jars and baskets. William smiled and squatted down beside the boy to join in his game.

Christiana seemed intent on concocting a strange pungent mixture for which she was carefully measuring each part using a pair of brass scales. Periodically she would add to the pan slowly bubbling on the brazier. William glanced up at the old woman who merely shrugged her shoulders.

Sometime later Christiana had her remedy suitably heated and wrapped in linen strips. "I am away to the keep, Martha," she announced, taking her cloak from its peg on the door.

"I will walk with you." William sprung to his feet.

"As you wish," Christiana replied with a smile. Although she had not encountered Ralph Hodkin in a long time the thought that he still abided within the castle enclave still niggled her mind, especially in the dark, melancholic days of winter. She would be glad of her brother's company on the walk to the keep.

"I was sorry that Joan did not accept your offer of marriage, Will," Christiana offered tentatively as they strode out side by side. She had not had opportunity to speak to her brother since the unfortunate incident last autumn, which had become known to all at the castle within days.

"She did not get chance to turn me down, Anna, for she had already been promised to the wool merchant by her father." William sighed. "We seem to be destined never to wed, you and I," he continued.

They had reached the keep and the outer staircase before William enquired, "Who is the physic for, Anna? You have not said."

"'Tis for the duke," Christiana replied as she began to stride up the steps to the antechamber. Once there she was allowed through to the great hall by the usher, William following.

"Surely you do not enter the duke's privy chamber, Anna?" William whispered as they crossed the patterned tiles.

"Richard has need of this remedy for which I alone have the receipt. Do not interfere in my work, brother," Christiana returned sharply before stating her business at the arched entrance to the chambers beyond. "Thank you for your company and good day." With that she disappeared beyond the drapes.

The light was fading and the great iron sconces were being lit in the hall as Christiana emerged sometime later. Her heart was still trembling and her fingers shaking as she gripped the empty wooden casket. It had been difficult to apply the hot poultice to Richard's twisted back as though he were merely another of the many folk she attended daily in the course of her work. She rubbed and pressed the aromatic herbs and spices onto his bare skin in the manner shown to her by Lempster, the physician, all the while under the watchful eye of the groom of the bedchamber. Surely her hand did not linger over long as she wound the strips of linen around his torso to contain the heat?

It was with these unhappy musings within her head that she descended the outer staircase and entered the inner courtyard. It was cold and grey, a flicker of pale light from the torches casting monstrous shadows on the stone walls.

She turned towards the bridge spanning the moat and quickened her pace. Ahead a figure sat on the low wall this side of the archway. She froze in panic, turned about and in fear would have fled back up the staircase to Godwin but the man called out her name.

"Anna!"

She sighed with relief and walked towards William. Instinctively she took his arm as they moved under the arch. William, it seemed, was not yet ready to move on.

"You have been over long for one who has but to deliver a remedy," he announced curtly.

"I have had to administer the remedy also, William." Christiana's reply was equally tart.

"Indeed! How convenient," he retorted.

"What is your meaning, William?" Christiana felt her anger rising and turned to face her brother's inquisition.

"And what, pray, could possibly ail the duke to the extent that he needs a woman to administer the remedy that could not be done by the hand of a man servant?"

Christiana could find no immediate reply to this question for what she was privy to was not common knowledge.

"There, I knew I had the measure of it. You are playing with fire, Anna. You risk everything you have here, including your son.

You are worth more than a common whore that slinks around in the shadows." William had caught Christiana's hand and held it tight as his words came hard and fast and his brown eyes flashed in the torchlight.

He should have expected what came next but the blow left a hot sting as her tiny hand came down upon his cheek with all the force it could muster.

"You know nothing, you know nothing," she cried as the angry tears fell. She tried to shake her hand free of his grasp but he held it still tighter.

"Anna," he pleaded. "You must rid yourself of this madness. You have turned your back on the only proposal of marriage you are ever likely to have and for what? Richard is wed, he has a son and heir and more to follow, God willing. It pains me to know that you will end your days as a lonely old woman..." He finished on a sigh, letting go of her hand and looking down at the ground.

Christiana did not move away, her anger giving way to fortitude. "Brother," she whispered. "You cannot know how much I love Richard. I would have wed Godwin if I could have but he deserved better than I could give. I am content with what I have: John, Martha... you." She hesitated and looked into the eyes that now stared painfully into hers.

"I swear to you that I have crossed no boundaries and Richard's marriage bed has not been violated. As long as I am able I shall continue to be a loyal servant to the duke and his household... nothing more and nothing less."

She wiped at the tears that wet her cheeks and attempted a smile.

"I am sorry, Anna," William said gently.

"We will say no more on this matter," Christiana answered, and taking her brother's arm once again they walked across the bridge into the bailey and on towards the cottage as the shadows deepened and the night air grew cooler.

William thought that he knew a great deal more of the extent of his sister's love for the duke than she imagined, for did he not himself know and experience daily the pain of unrequited love?

The year 1476 saw the Duke of Gloucester heading a solemn procession from Yorkshire to his birthplace at Fotheringhay in Northamptonshire for the re-internment of his father, the Duke of York, and brother, Edmund, Earl of Rutland, killed at the battle of Wakefield sixteen years earlier.

It was not long after the duke's return from Fotheringhay when an incident occurred which was to set the course for change in Christiana's life.

Returning to the garden after a visit to the kitchen to deliver a replenishment of herbs, Christiana paused, with basket over her arm, to check the trays of herbs drying in the afternoon sun. She prodded and turned them thoughtfully.

Francis, Lord Lovell, it seemed was spending a few days at the castle with his close friend the Duke of Gloucester. Gossip amongst the kitchen maids had him a most handsome man. Christiana smiled as she recalled the small shy boy who followed Richard like a lap dog wherever he went. She tried to calculate his age; he was a little younger than the duke, in his early twenties she thought, an age when most young men were setting afire the hearts of young maidens. Christiana did not forget that Lord Lovell had a wife.

The turning and rearranging of the herbs now to her satisfaction, Christiana straightened up and walked across to the herbarium. The door was open and inside she could see Martha's ample figure sitting on a stool as she crushed dried flower heads in a mortar with a heavy marble pestle. Christiana looked about the garden; it seemed unusually quiet.

"Martha, have you seen John?" she called.

The old woman stopped work and shrugged her shoulders.

"Nay, lass. Not for a while. He's like as not out in the flower beds with Wat."

Casting off the empty basket Christiana turned and walked quickly across the herb garden to where the ornamental flowers grew. She looked out upon the dovecote and empty benches, the circular beds of red roses – nothing. At six years of age and somewhat headstrong it was becoming increasingly difficult to keep an eye on her son's movements. She tried to stem the flow of rising panic as she headed towards the far wall and the box hedge; a veritable maze for one so small.

Before she had reached her destination she saw the figure of an old man come hobbling into view. "Mistress Christiana, have you seen John? I have missed him these past hours and thought him to be with you," the gardener cried with an aged voice cracked with emotion.

"He cannot be far, Wat. He will be out in the bailey, I am sure," Christiana replied with an effort to calm herself. With heart pounding she dashed through the wicker gate and out toward the drill field. She had a great fear that the boy may have wandered into a training session and be caught in the cross thrust of poleaxe and halberd. Fortunately the field was devoid of any soldier; at their meal at this hour.

Her next hope was the smithy and the boy's Uncle Will. He loved to be taken to watch the blacksmith labouring over his hammer and anvil; but there was no little boy watching gleefully as she rushed into the yard, only William bent over his work.

"Will!" Christiana cried. "Have you seen John? He has gone missing." By now she was close to tears.

Dropping his tools William came out to her. "No, I have not seen the boy in days."

Her feeling of dread was exacerbated by the appearance of Martha, panting and red-faced, waddling into the yard. She shook her head in confirmation that there had been no sighting of the child.

There was a dreadful thought that had squirmed its way into her head: that somehow Ralph Hodkin had a hand in John's disappearance.

As Christiana began to tremble she felt William's arm go around her shoulder. "We must inform the duke," he said gently.

"Nay, William," Martha protested. "The boy is like as not to turn up within the hour full of mischief and we will have raised an outcry for nothing."

"And what if the boy is hurt? The duke will not thank us for keeping this from him – he is the child's father," William said, looking to Christiana.

The old woman sighed. "What say you?" she asked, also looking at Christiana, who was wiping at the tears that had begun to surface from beneath her eyelids.

"Well, why do we tarry?" Martha cried resignedly, not waiting for any further comment, and led the way across the bailey towards the keep.

The young groom could see by the anxious expressions on the faces of these unexpected visitors demanding an audience with the lord of the castle that something was amiss.

"I will inform the duke of your request," he said and slipped beyond the door to the great hall. He returned moments later with permission for them to enter. With William at her side, Martha resting her legs in the antechamber, Christiana pushed open the great door and entered.

Two men were seated at a table near the fireside, a merrills board and a jug of wine between them. One of the men was Richard, the other she did not at first recognise.

The men stood to their feet as Christiana approached, Richard smiling jovially, unaware of the grave nature of their visit. Leaving her brother standing, Christiana, making no pretence of reverence, started forward and began at once to plead her case.

"Richard, John is missing. Nothing has been seen of him for hours and I fear for his safety."

At once the glory of their afternoon's hunt and the merriment in the company of a long-standing friend were forgotten. The duke's eyes now dark and troubled looked hard into the face of the woman before him. Her word, it seemed, was not to be doubted for

320

he at once declared that the castle would be searched, including the cellars.

He turned to address his companion who Christiana could now see to be Lord Lovell.

"Francis, you take soldiers and make a search of the village. Question all you see. William," Richard called to the blacksmith. "You and I will ride along the riverside and the marshes." As the three men turned to leave the hall Richard approached Christiana and took her hand. "Fear not," he whispered, "I will find him."

Before he could leave Christiana put out a hand and touched the sleeve of his garment and whispered, "Richard, there is one amongst the garrison who I would not trust, one of whom I am afraid."

The duke looked earnestly into her eyes and a frown creased his brow. "Who is this whom you fear?" he asked gently.

She hesitated. Should she say? There was no evidence against him. To be afraid of a man was no proof of his guilt.

"Who is this man?" Richard asked again.

"Ralph Hodkin," she replied.

"The captain of the guard?"

Christiana inclined her head in confirmation.

"Nothing is known against him. The constable has not reported any problems," Richard replied. "Has he done something that gives you cause to fear him?"

Once again Christiana hesitated. Had he? In truth nothing more than a molestation of her person and that many years ago now. She cast her eyes to the floor and shook her head.

She felt Richard's fingers gently lift her chin and his eyes met hers. "You are distressed with worry," he began. "But I will have this Hodkin sent to me for questioning." He smiled reassuringly and turned then to join the others.

She followed them through into the antechamber from where the duke began ordering the guard to inaugurate a search of the castle building for the lost boy. Martha returned to the cottage where it was hoped the child would return unharmed of his own free will. Christiana remained in the antechamber waiting for any news. Godwin, who had been working with much concentration on ledgers at a small desk, left his task and sat with Christiana in companionable silence.

The shadows were beginning to lengthen as the duke, William and a company of a half-dozen men rode out along the riverside and towards the marsh. The only sounds of the late afternoon came from the river fowl and the gentle tapping of their horses' hooves on the stony bank. William peered into the deep waters of the Ure, dark in the shadow of overhanging trees. Richard rode alongside him following his gaze for any movement or sign of a child. The other men moved out in different directions to scour the marsh.

They had been about their search for what seemed like hours without seeing hide nor hair of any other living soul; even the water birds were disappearing into the growing blackness of the river, and William was beginning to despair of finding the boy either alive or dead, when the duke was hailed by one of his men.

They turned to see the soldier advancing towards them down the slope leading from higher ground. Sure enough he carried astride his horse, and dwarfed by his own sturdy figure, a small boy, but as they approached William could see that the child was fair-haired, not dark like John.

"My lord, I found this little scallywag up yonder and I swear he knows something of John's whereabouts," the man declared as he rode up. The child was thin and dirty with a pale tear-stained face and large brown eyes turned in terror towards the duke sitting astride his fine horse.

The three men dismounted, with his captor holding steadfast to the back of the boy's frayed tunic as he squirmed and wriggled like an eel on a hook. The soldier gave the boy a sharp poke in the back. "Tell the duke what you know of John," he demanded. The boy shook his head in silence until a second dig in his ribs coming sharper and harder than the first caused him to yelp in pain. This time Richard held up his hand in protest.

"What makes you so sure this boy knows anything?" he asked of the soldier.

"Because, my lord, I found this clutched in his grubby hands."

He handed Richard a small pewter boar: the emblem of the Duke of Gloucester. Richard took the badge and turned it around in his fingers. The word John had been engraved into the back; evidence indeed that this was the very same given to his bastard son on one of his rare visits to the cottage.

Richard knelt down on the grass and gently took hold of the boy's shoulders. "Do you know who I am?" he asked. The boy, trembling violently, kept his eyes on the man's face and slowly nodded his head. "If you know anything of John, anything at all, you must tell me. Do you understand?" Again the boy nodded but remained firmly tight-lipped.

William, who had been standing nearby holding the reins of the horses, noticed the boy's feet for the first time; poorly shod with stockings soaked through up to his scrawny knees. The child had obviously been in the river and William tried to think back at what he himself might have been doing at his age. Then he was struck by a thought and beckoning the duke over he whispered, "I think perhaps the boy is afraid of you, my lord. If he were to be caught poaching in the duke's rivers he would fear punishment."

Richard nodded his head, seeing the child's sodden attire and catching the inference of William's words. He approached the boy and went down on his knees once again on eye level with the fear-stricken face. "John lives up at the castle with me and sometimes I let him go fishing in my rivers. If you are a friend of John's then it is all right for you to fish in my rivers too. Do you understand?"

William caught the obvious guffaw of the soldier standing alongside the boy but Richard ignored it. Still regarding the child intently he continued. "Now, were you fishing in the river with John?"

William looked upwards at the darkening clouds with their rings of crimson and gold and prayed that this diplomatic approach to obtaining information would not take too much longer. There was, however, a slight change to be seen in the boy's countenance. Richard caught it too and pressed on. "Do you know where John is?" The boy nodded.

"Will you take me to him?" The response was given by way of a vigorous nod of the head, still without any words.

"Good lad." The duke smiled and gently squeezed the boy's shoulder. He stood to his feet with a sigh of relief.

In the antechamber of the great hall Christiana stared forlornly at the servants as they lit the candles on the desk and those in the iron brackets over the door. Godwin took his cloak from its peg on the wall and placed it around her shoulders. She smiled gratefully at him.

Thoughts had been tossing around in her head like a pair of dice; one showing optimism, another, despair. He was sure to be found, the village was not so big. But what if he had fallen prey to a cut-throat or met with an accident? What if Hodkin were somehow involved?

A movement on the outer staircase sent her heart racing with expectation and fear. It was the duchess and two of her ladies, all wearing fur-trimmed cloaks over their gowns and carrying horn lanterns.

"Christiana," Anne said solemnly. "I heard word that your son is missing." The young duchess lowered her gaze, unsure of what she should say. Christiana was touched by her concern and attempted to smile but all she could manage was tears.

Anne stepped forward and put a hand on her servant's shoulder and guided her through into the hall. "Come in from the cold and take some wine," she said, handing her lantern to Godwin. Candles had been lit within the hall and the fire burned brightly in its pit. A servant came forward to pour them wine as the ladies sat on cushioned chairs alongside the fire. The malmsey wine did indeed warm Christiana inside but her heart remained cold.

Anne sipped from her cup. "My husband will find your son, I am sure of it," she said encouragingly after a while.

"I pray it will be so, my lady," was all Christiana could utter in reply.

The world beyond the casements of the great hall gradually turned black as night fell. Christiana felt sick with worry and hampered by an impulsive urge to stand and pace the tiled floor. She glanced across at Anne who sat companionably silent, taking tiny sips of her wine periodically, so Christiana had to content herself with turning and weaving her fingers beneath the folds of Godwin's cloak.

The sound of footsteps and voices from beyond the door reached their ears and Christiana was on her feet at once. Francis Lovell was the first to enter followed by the duke. In his arms he held his son; flaccid and lifeless as a wooden puppet.

Christiana could only stare at the dangling limbs and ashen face, feeling as though she herself would collapse in a faint at any moment. Richard strode purposefully across the hall carrying his child towards the great chamber with Christiana at his side. Francis remained behind in the hall with the duchess.

The boy was soaked to the skin, his tunic torn across the chest and he was missing a boot. There was also a nasty wound, dark with congealed blood, across his forehead. His mother tried to take John out of Richard's arms but the duke would not relinquish his hold of the child until he had reached the great tester bed whereupon he laid him down.

"In God's name, Richard, what happened?" Christiana cried.

The duke sat down heavily on the bed catching his breath. Christiana was frantically feeling her son's body for signs of life; his skin was warm and she felt the whisper of a breath on the back of her hand as she held it close to his lips. She removed his sodden clothes and wrapped him in the linen bed sheet.

"He has been fishing along the Ure with a lad from the village," Richard explained. "Nothing much can be got from the boy other than John seems to have slipped on a mossy boulder and struck his head. Luckily the water was shallow and the boy managed to haul him out on the bank and there left him, not knowing what else to do. It was only by chance that one of my men came across the boy, otherwise we may not have reached John before nightfall."

Christiana was looking at the wound on the child's head as Martha arrived with her basket of concoctions. With bustling efficiency she nudged the boy's mother from the bedside and proceeded with her own examination. "How long has he been like this?" she asked anxiously, lifting up the boy's drooping eyelids.

"I cannot say," replied the duke. "He was unconscious when we found him and his companion had no comprehension of the passing of time." He stood and began to pace the floor, gnawing on his lower lip nervously. Christiana stared at Martha, looking for reassurance. All knew that injuries to the head were the worst possible kind and the longer it took to regain the senses the darker the prospect. Both women had a vivid recollection of Alfred's head injury and the grievous outcome of that.

"Has he taken in much river water?" Martha asked suddenly and began to knead the child's chest and stomach with her podgy fingers.

"It is not likely. The boy pulled him clear of the water before he swallowed over much," Richard replied wearily. "Can you restore the boy, Martha, or should I send for the physician?"

The old woman dabbed at the wound on John's forehead with a piece of cloth soaked in water to clean it and then applied ointment of comfrey before answering the duke. "I have done all I can, my lord. He is in God's hands now." She hesitated for a moment before adding, "If he does not regain consciousness soon then you should call your physician."

Martha gathered up her basket and left the chamber, shaking her grey head sadly. Richard sat beside Christiana on the bed. His brow was furrowed and his dark eyes were pained with grief. She could sense too that the cold and damp was causing pain in his back as he shivered slightly. She looked down at the small metal object he held in his hand; it was the boar badge he had given to John. The boy had cherished that gift from his father and wore it pinned to his tunic every day.

Silence sat heavy in the air and drew together father and mother in mutual sorrow and fear. The minutes ebbed away until quite suddenly the boy moved his head. His eyes flickered open and his lips parted in a moan. "My head hurts," he gasped, bringing a hand up to his forehead.

Christiana smiled. "Yes, my love, it will for a while." She looked on as he at once began to cough and splutter. She pushed him forward as a surge of murky brown river water spewed from his mouth and laughed with relief; now she knew that he would be well.

Richard gave his son a smile, one that spoke of his own relief and affection.

"You will be wanting this back now," he laughed, holding the badge up to the boy who had sunk back down on the pillows. John smiled in recognition of his treasure and let his eyelids close once more.

"My son will sleep here this night," Richard announced. "I can keep a watch over him beside me in the bed." Seeing the look of doubt appearing on his mother's face, he added, "Do not worry, all his needs will be seen to."

"Then I shall return on the morrow, my lord," Christiana replied softly. As she turned to leave the duke's bedchamber, Richard said, "God be praised that the boy is safe and well."

She walked across the empty hall where the embers of the fire had burned low and out into the deserted antechamber. Her footsteps were heavy with fatigue as she made her way down the great stone staircase, passing only the sentries on watch. She was grateful for Godwin's cloak as she stepped into the chill of the night air; black with a sprinkling of stars overhead.

Crossing the bridge that spanned the moat she halted abruptly at the sight of a lone figure sitting on the stone wall. For one panic-stricken moment she thought it might be Ralph Hodkin, but was relieved when the man stood and walked towards her.

"Will, you gave me such a fright," she sighed.

"How is John? Martha passed by an hour or so since and said that he remained unconscious from the blow to his head."

As she began to relate to William that all looked to be well with her son, the blessed relief washed over her anew and she began to weep. She felt William's arms enfold around her, pulling her into a warm embrace. As she stood before him, her face buried in the coarse linen of his shirt, and breathed in the odour of his manliness, she realised that all she had wanted up in the keep was for Richard to reach out and hold her in his arms; but he had not.

"Come," William said gently. "Let me take you home."

Early the following morning, after a night of restless tossing and turning, Christiana rose and made up infusions of vervain and valerian and a fresh supply of comfrey ointment. In the golden mist of a summer sunrise she set out across the bailey towards the keep.

A groom escorted her to the duke's private chambers where she was conducted to the inner room. A table alongside the wall held the remains of a meal: chunks of bread, slices of meat, some cheese and cups of ale. She eyed it hungrily for she had not yet broken her fast.

Her son was sitting up in the bed wearing an overlarge shirt with the pewter badge, hanging lopsided by a bent clasp, pinned to its front. He smiled broadly as she entered. Richard, fully clothed in murrey hose and doublet, was standing by the window.

She poured a measure of the vervain onto a horn spoon and offered it to her son. She took a piece of lint and began to apply more comfrey salve to his wound. "You are well now, my son. You can come home this day. Martha waits to see you and Wat..."

She felt Richard's presence beside her and his hand upon her shoulder. "I would speak with you, Christiana," he said. "In the hall." She bent forward to kiss John and then followed the duke out into the deserted hall.

"It is my intention for John to remain here at the keep," Richard began without preamble. "I will not have him running loose and undisciplined."

Christiana reddened with indignation at his inference to her failure to control the boy. "I know he should not have been by the river unattended but I am sure that he does not make habit of leaving the bailey. I will ensure that it does not happen again," she rambled.

"You do not seem to understand, Christiana," Richard replied firmly. "John is my son and as such he must be brought up in the proper manner befitting his birth. Tutors will be appointed for his education and he will be taught skill at arms..."

"He can be taught the skill of a blacksmith by his uncle, to serve you well. And what of a mother's love?" she cried, horrified by the duke's proposal.

"A son of mine will nowise be a blacksmith," Richard retorted, equally perplexed. "And as for a mother; he is six years of age and soon he will no longer require a mother if he is to become a man. Besides, he will have the duchess to impart the necessary social graces."

"No, Richard, you cannot take him from me; he is my only child," she pleaded, hot tears stinging her eyes as she took a step closer to the duke.

"Do not presume to tell me what I cannot do, Christiana," Richard replied angrily. "The boy will be trained for knighthood and there is an end to it. Would you sooner I sent him away to Sheriff Hutton or to the Percys at Warkworth to carry out the task?"

Christiana shook her head wildly as her tears fell. She trembled at the touch of his hand on her sleeve. "We must do what is right for the boy. It is his future," Richard said, his tone less harsh.

She stared long and hard into his eyes; dark and deep blue portals to a soul that held the very essence of her being. Inclining her head she whispered, "My lord, I beg your forgiveness for my outburst. You must of course take charge of your son." With that she made a low reverence to the duke and with his leave, departed.

What turmoil filled her head as she crossed the bridge into the bailey. In truth the duke was right. It was a wonder that he had not claimed his son before now; maybe it was out of concern for her feelings that he had not.

All she had longed for was to have Richard's arms around her once more but that could never be and now he had taken her son, his son, from her, and she was left here a servant in the bailey where she belonged. Wretched tears spilled down her cheeks as she ran through the garden into the herbarium.

In the days following Richard's claim to his son the duke, true to his word, had questioned the constable of the castle and the captain of the garrison. Notwithstanding the fact that soldiers were not expected to live the life of monks, there was nothing in Hodkin's behaviour that could condemn him. FitzHugh, the constable, was aware that on occasions the captain let overconsumption of ale cloud his judgement and for this the soldier was reprimanded.

The duke had summoned Christiana to inform her that unless she or anyone else had anything more substantial against the man then Hodkin would be at liberty to remain in his post as captain of the garrison. Christiana understood and accepted Richard's judgement; his sense of justice compelled him to do no more without evidence, but she continued to be wary of the man nevertheless.

Middleham Castle
Yorkshire
Early 1477

Christiana slowly turned the wooden spoon inside the iron pot on the brazier, lost in thought; the cold, dark, inactive days of winter stirred a melancholy within the young woman. She tried to picture in her mind how life played out for those abiding in the castle; her son John, his half-brother Edward and his mother, the Duchess of Gloucester, and not least among them the duke himself. What trivial pursuits occupied their time? Games of chess, merrills, stories and song from the minstrels? However John spent his time it would be all to the purpose of making him a son his father could be proud of.

The fat in the pot bubbled and thickened. Christiana sighed and removed the pot from the heat.

"'Tis ready, Martha," she called to the older woman who had her head bent over the table along the wall where she was pounding dried roots to a fine powder. "I have a mind to take a walk, there is little to be done in here," she added and took a cloak from the hook near the door.

Martha watched her assistant leave the cottage without a word; she knew how difficult it must be for the young mother to be without her child.

Richard and Anne were home having spent the Christmastide festivities in London. They had taken young Edward and her son John with them. The castle had been an empty, cold place that Christmastide.

A chilled wind blew grey clouds across a grey sky and wrapped her grey gown tightly around her legs. The garden was dull with dried remnants of its former glory and few birds had braved the squall to sit in the branches of the trees and shrubs. There was, however, one other who had ventured forth in the gale and that was a small child, blown like a ship down the path that led to the wicker gate.

"John!" the woman exclaimed, recognising at once her beloved son. "What are you doing out in this foul weather?" She scooped him up in her arms and embraced his slender body.

"I am come on an errand to procure your services for the Lady Anne," he gasped after his feet had been put down again upon the ground.

Christiana smiled at the formality of his speech – he was quick to learn, this boy of hers.

"Is my lady unwell?" she asked, concerned.

"I cannot say for certain, Mama. It was Lady Tempest who sent for you," the child replied.

Hand in hand they crossed the bailey and over the bridge into the inner courtyard. Here the wind had lost some of its aggression and Christiana sought to converse with her son before they entered the south range and the duchess's quarters.

"Are you well, my son? Do you see much of your father?" Two questions – time was valuable.

John turned his small, round, rosy-cheeked face up to his mother and nodded his head. "Yes, Mama. I have been in my father's chambers this morning, I have been reading his Bible," he announced proudly. Christiana remembered that Richard had in his possession a Bible written in English and smiled.

Just then another figure entered the courtyard from the direction of the keep, gown flapping like sails and a hand pressed to his head to prevent the theft of his hat by the mischievous wind.

"That is Rector Beverley," John informed his mother, who of course was already familiar with the village priest. "He spends much of his time here, talking with father. They talk about God all the time."

Christiana laughed and allowed the boy to lead her chivalrously through the arched entrance and along the passageways to the duchess's chambers. Once there John disappeared silently and Christiana was left to face Anne's lady of the bedchamber alone.

Lady Tempest smiled, albeit somewhat forced, at the herbalist.

It would appear that Christiana's presence in the household was beginning to be accepted.

Richard's wife was sitting on the edge of a coffer at the foot of her great bed, her pretty face pale and wet with tears. Across the coffer and atop the bed were an assortment of furs and silks. Christiana approached and bent her head in reverence.

"I have received news this very day that has left me feeling quite unwell." Anne removed the fur and silk, handing them to Lady Tempest, and indicated the seat beside her on the coffer. Christiana sat obediently.

"My sister, Isabel, has died of child bed fever," the lady continued. "It would seem that she gave birth to a son, Richard, October last." Anne smiled even as her tears continued. "Named I think for our duke, who shares the babe's birth month."

Christiana put a comforting hand upon the cold delicate hand of the duchess, watched hawk-like from a distance by the Lady Tempest.

"Isabel never recovered from his birth and the babe also died this January gone."

"My lady, I shall send physic to your chamber to calm and lift your spirits," Christiana spoke gently. "And what of your mother, is she well?"

Anne shot a furtive glance at her lady of the bedchamber before drawing closer to her servant. "Mama has received a letter from George in which he rants about poison and sorcery being the cause of his wife's death. I fear the poor man has lost his mind."

Christiana stood and was about to take her leave when into the chamber walked the duke. He was hatless, his hair blown untidily in the wind and his cheeks ruddy. For the briefest of time their eyes met before Richard crossed the room to his wife. Anne was on her feet to receive his embrace as she spent her grief upon his shoulder.

Christiana stood transfixed nearby, feeling the sharp stab in her heart before Lady Tempest with bejewelled hands waved her out of the bedchamber.

The young woman's humours were truly out of balance by the

time she reached the herbarium but out of respect for the duke and his wife she dutifully prepared the herbs as promised. She was, however, spared a return journey to the castle to deliver her concoctions as Martha took them herself, wishing to convey her condolences to the dowager Countess of Warwick on the demise of her eldest daughter.

"I still miss Father," Christiana said forlornly, placing her little posy of rosemary, periwinkle and St John's wort at the foot of the rough stone that marked Alfred's grave. Straightening up she felt the warm touch of William's hand on hers as they walked in silence through the churchyard.

They came across a stone bench in the shade of the church wall and here they sat in the peace of a summer's afternoon, Christiana's thoughts buzzing like a bee from flower to flower. It had been six years since the accident at the smithy had claimed the life of their father and brother and sister had come together to mark the occasion. True enough the passage of time had dulled the anguish but there were still days when the sense of loss filled her with fresh pain.

Although nigh on twelve months had passed since his father, the duke, had claimed her son, she still felt his loss keenly. There had been but few occasions when she had had any contact with John, seeing him mostly from a distance as a servant would view the highborn not in their direct care. She consoled herself with the knowledge that his education would be to his benefit and he was at least nearby.

A young couple ambled along the pathway a little distance from where they sat. Christiana could hear the joy in the girl's laughter as she linked one hand through her husband's arm and the other rested protectively upon her gently swollen belly. Christiana smiled a little sadly as she watched them pass. At least Sybil would keep any child born of their union, she mused.

The duke had recommended Godwin to assist Thomas Barowe, his senior clerk, overseeing the documents and ledgers that necessitated the administration of his fortress at Middleham. With an increase in salary Godwin had married Sybil in late spring of last year and taken a house in the village, a larger one it seemed than the one originally intended for her and John, for with Sybil there came a modest dowry enabling them to set up adequately for their future. The Duchess of Gloucester agreed to release her chamber maid at the time of her marriage, her present cortège of ladies well able to attend to the needs of the bedchamber.

William shifted his weight on the bench, thoughts of his own filling his head; thoughts of frustration that he had reached the age of four and twenty years and had thus far failed to secure himself a wife. Satisfying his desires with the wenches in the alehouses whenever he was on campaign with the duke left him overflowing with emptiness, for it was no satisfaction at all.

The memory of his humiliating attempt to procure the weaver's daughter as wife still pained him but now after two years had passed it sometimes brought a smile to his lips. At least he had not set eyes upon Joan since that day; she was now mistress of a grand merchant's house in York, unlike the woman sitting beside him on the bench, her tiny hand in his, who was a constant reminder of something he could never have.

William stood to his feet a little abruptly and sighed. They should be returning to the castle; good use must be made of the weather before the onset of autumn. The building work begun many years before by Richard Neville was all set for completion in the next few months and one of the blacksmith's tasks was to keep the masons and carpenters supplied with well-sharpened tools.

"Is all well, William?" Christiana asked as she walked beside him, her arm linked into his.

"Aye," he replied with a forced smile. "Just thinking on my tasks this afternoon; you know, the treadmill of life."

They reached the newly built northern gatehouse and the guards, recognising them, allowed them access through the piles of stone and wood that lay scattered thereabouts. As they walked across the wooden bridge into the bailey Christiana turned to William. "Father would have been so proud of you, Will. He would not have asked for a better son," she said.

He stared at her for a moment before allowing her the briefest of smiles, touched by her sentiment but reminded painfully of their ill-fated kinship.

Middleham Castle
Yorkshire
Autumn 1477

Martha and Christiana were returning from their meal in the servants' hall. The October afternoon was grey and miserable and an icy squall pounded their faces as they walked through the bare garden.

Once inside the cottage Martha rubbed her chubby hands over the warm brazier.

"Winter has come early methinks, and the summer was naught to speak of," she mused. "Let us hope that the snow keeps away for the fair." She looked across at Christiana who was sitting on a stool staring pensively at the floor.

Ignoring Martha's remarks on the inclemency of the weather she asked, "Did you hear talk just now in the hall of..." she hesitated. "Ralph Hodkin, losing his position as Captain of the Garrison?"

"Aye, I heard it," confirmed Martha, eying the younger woman a little suspiciously. "I foretold as much and not before time. Duke Richard will not tolerate such incompetence in his men. The man should consider himself fortunate that he still has any position here at all."

"He was drunk, so I heard," Christiana muttered.

"Aye. William reckons Hodkin was the instigator of yet another brawl amongst the men of the garrison. There is no respect for the man and hence no discipline. Thomas Tempest has the position now."

Christiana nodded thoughtfully. It now seemed likely that an incident occurring just last week, in which Ralph had given her further cause to fear and loathe him, had followed the garrison brawl which had led to the man's demotion: Hodkin had sauntered into the herbarium late one afternoon, during Martha's absence, demanding attention. The side of his face was badly bruised and his left eye puffed and swollen. As much as she despised the man she could not but treat him; refusal to do so could be construed as insolence and give him more cause to vent his spleen.

She handed him a pot of salve of comfrey with instruction to apply it to his face.

"How can I do so, wench," he roared. "Can I see my own face? Here, you do it." He thrust the pot back at Christiana. Taking up a cloth she began to dab at the bruised face, all the while standing in dread of the man. She concentrated her gaze on the purple blotches of skin so that she would not have to watch his roving eye hungrily seeking the stays of her bodice. She felt certain that his fingers would have followed the line of his eye had it not been for the timely and most welcome return of Martha.

"So, are you in agreement?" The sound of Martha's voice shattered her reverie.

"You have not been listening to a word I've been saying, have you, girl?" Martha reprimanded.

"I am sorry, Martha. I am tired," Christiana replied somewhat untruthfully. "Please tell me again. I am listening, truly."

Martha sighed. "Well, 'tis like I said, I think it is best for you to take charge of the preparations of the medicines from now on. Some of our more potent remedies require an exact measurement of ingredients and a little too much of one or a little too much of another can have fatal results. My eye is not as sharp or my hand as steady as once they were."

Christiana smiled at her long-time friend and mentor. "I will of course do this, Martha, and I shall help with the ledgers and accounts for I have seen you struggle over them by candlelight." This observation was less to do with failing eyesight than a dislike for such formality. "But there will be no more talk of old age; there are years of life ahead of you yet," Christiana said cheerfully.

The cold northerly wind did nothing to dampen the spirits of the good folk of Middleham and on the fifth day of November the fair went ahead. Indeed it was such a success that it went on for three days, attracting traders and visitors from far and wide. Martha,

337

William and Christiana wandered around the booths, marvelled at the jugglers and fire-eaters, bartered for wares and partook of great chunks of roast hog and jugs of ale.

The unrelenting northern wind had blown in a flurry of cold December sleet, shrouding the dales in a mist of melancholic gloom. Christiana had not long opened the door to a sodden bundle of cat fur meowing pitifully from without and was even now rubbing its scrawny body with a hemp sack when a heavy pounding began on the wooden door.

"Have a care! You'll flatten that door!" Martha shouted, rising to her feet. She opened the door to a boy, face red raw from the wind and limbs dripping wet. "Heaven help us," Martha exclaimed. "Are we to take in every waif and stray this night?"

Coming up behind Christiana peered over Martha's shoulder at the boy, trembling so violently with cold that he was unable to speak, and recognised him at once. Pulling him inside she said, "'Tis Jack, Godwin's servant boy." Jack could only nod his head in confirmation.

"Is it Sybil?" Christiana demanded, to which the reply was another nod of his head. Martha had been to the village little more than one month since to check progress on the young woman's pregnancy.

"God have mercy!" she cried and crossed herself.

"This poor boy won't make the journey back on foot," Martha stated, turning to Christiana. "You run up to the smithy and fetch a cart while I find what I need here."

By the time Christiana had returned to say that William had a cart and horse ready to take them into the village, Jack was recovered a little, wearing dry clothes that had once belonged to John and so were a tight fit, and supping mulled wine. Martha, with a concoction of herbal brews in a covered basket, was waiting impatiently beside the door.

The journey to the clerk's house was not a pleasant one. Seated on the floor of the open cart, huddled beneath hessian sacks as the wind whipped icy sleet across their faces, they bumped and bounded along the rough stone-pitted road.

At the sight of Godwin standing in the doorway holding up a lantern to light their way, all Christiana's sore, aching limbs were forgotten. Gone was the fastidiously attired clerk, clean shaven and hair neatly combed. In his stead was a vulnerable young man beside himself with worry. His dark eyes were wide with fear, the bristled stubble he had allowed to grow across his jowls a stark contrast to his pale face. His shirt, sleeves rolled to his elbows, was creased and smeared with what looked to be vomit.

Christiana's heart began to race; all did not bode well. As she entered the room, dimly lit with candlelight, her worst fears were confirmed. Martha had no sooner walked in than she marched straight back out to the street to send William to the church and summon the rector, William Beverley.

Sybil lay prostrate on the bed that took up a corner of the room, curtained off from the rest of the living area. Her hair was loose in a wild mane of brown curls about her shoulders and her pretty round cheeks burned red as she panted with pain and fatigue. Her shift had been drawn up to her waist exposing bare legs bent at the knees and trembling violently. A vast pool of blood spread out beneath her buttocks.

"'Tis past my time, Martha," she moaned as the old woman approached the bed. "Save my baby, my baby!"

"Hush now, child," Martha soothed as she stared despairingly at the young woman. Christiana held Sybil's hand as Martha carried out her examination. After a while she straightened up and approached the ashen-faced husband. Taking him by the arm she guided him away from the bed and in whispered tones she commanded him be seated on a chair. "I fear the child to be dead and may soon claim the life of your wife. I am very sorry, Godwin. Sit you here and we will do all we can."

Martha returned to the bed where Sybil continued to writhe in agony. Christiana cooled her brow with lavender-scented water and watched in alarm as her pallor turned grey. She glanced down the bed at the spread of blood that grew rapidly. Her fingers trembled as she fumbled with the phials and costrels in Martha's basket. Nettle, yarrow; what use were herbs when it was a miracle

339

needed? But try she must and seizing the yarrow she held up Sybil's head and thrust the open costrel between the girl's blue lips. She duly swallowed the mixture but moments later it was vomited back. As Christiana wiped Sybil's mouth she could see the fear of death in the large brown eyes that stared up at her.

Christiana looked up at Martha across the bed where she was shaking her head slowly. With an overwhelming sense of helplessness they could do nothing but wait for the inevitable. All the painful memories of a similar incident in the village several years ago came flooding back to Christiana's fraught mind. Martha called Godwin over to the bed where he sat holding his wife's hand as her life ebbed away before him. Sybil's anguished moaning had ceased and all that could be heard now was her slow rasping breath. Godwin sat silent and still as alabaster, his eyes looking far beyond the wretched creature on the bed.

It was as Martha tried to soak away some of the blood from between Sybil's legs that she noticed for the first time two red circles on the inside of her thighs. Peering closely she saw the raw swollen welts with angry sores where the skin had become infected. Frowning, Martha turned to Godwin for explanation.

"She was cupped," he muttered.

"I can see she was cupped, lad, but who in God's name did it?" Martha demanded. Godwin stared in horror at the herbalist and swallowed the great lump in his throat.

"Well?" Martha insisted.

"A barber-surgeon. He was at the fair. Sybil had... a bladder problem I think it was, and the man recommended wet cupping to draw blood and relieve inflammation." Godwin's voice was cracked and pained with emotion.

"Aye well, it looks as if—"

"Martha!" Christiana interjected sharply. "'Tis of no good use to dwell on such things now. Let him be."

The three of them turned as the door latch rattled and the boy, Jack, entered on a gust of icy wind followed by William Beverley the rector. The blacksmith's voice could be heard calling from outside, urging the boy to remain with him, under the pretext that the horse needed rubbing down now that it had stopped raining.

Martha and Christiana left the bedside to make way for Rector Beverley. By the time the priest had reached Sybil, her suffering had all but ceased and as he anointed her with the oil of extreme unction peace came to her at last.

Godwin allowed himself to be led from the bedside like a child. Christiana eased him into a chair and kept her hand upon his trembling shoulder. "I am so very, very sorry, Godwin," she whispered.

The rector, his task completed for now, called Martha back to the bed to lay out the body in readiness for burial. Christiana sank down on her knees before her friend and took his hand lying limp and cold in his lap. "Will you not return with us to the castle?" she offered. There was no response from the distraught man.

"Christiana, here if you please, I require your assistance," Martha called out. Reluctantly she went to Martha's aid, stripping the bed linen and washing down Sybil's still warm corpse. As they worked in grim silence fetching clean linen and such herbs as Sybil kept in her modest kitchen, William Beverley tried to bring some comfort to Godwin. The poor man, however, did not move or respond to any words of human kindness.

"I am fearful for Godwin," Christiana whispered to Martha. "He should come home with us."

"He will not want to leave his wife. He must stay here and work out his grief in his own way. He knows where we are if he has need of us." Martha gathered up her potions and headed for the door. "Come, we are done here."

It was such a heart-rending act to leave her friend thus but there was no more she could do for the present and so Christiana walked across to Godwin and kissed him gently on the forehead before departing.

Outside, the cold of the night air hit her hard and Christiana shuddered. The boy was standing shivering by the horse's head and she heard Martha's voice. "Look to your master, young Jack, he has much need of you now." The child stared dumbly at the old woman and shuffled back into the house.

Christiana felt tears falling down her cold cheeks and of a

sudden the world seemed to spin around her. She attempted to walk towards the cart but her legs had become like ingots of lead and she began to falter and would have stumbled into the wet mud underfoot had it not been for William's strong arms sweeping her up onto the floor of the cart. There she lay against Martha's shoulder and wept all the journey home and long, long into the night.

A day or two after Sybil's internment in the churchyard of Saint Mary and Saint Alkelda Christiana called upon Godwin only to find the house locked up and empty. Rumour had it in the village that the clerk had gone to York to take Holy Orders. Whatever the truth, Christiana was never to see her friend again.

Middleham Castle
Yorkshire
Early 1478

The year had not long begun when the Duke of Gloucester was summoned to London by his brother, the king. It seemed that George was causing Edward more trouble. This time he had instigated the king's displeasure by seeking a suitable marriage with Mary of Burgundy, heiress of Charles the Bold.

Anne was a little concerned that her husband had to leave, although she would nowise voice this opinion to him, for their little son of not yet five years had developed a troublesome winter cough and she fretted much for him.

Midway through February, however, Christiana was pleased to note much improvement in the boy as she visited Edward's private chambers late one afternoon.

"Here is syrup of honey and lemon, my lady, for young Edward," Christiana said, placing the costrel on a carved wooden table. "He is much improved I think."

The duchess smiled warmly as she watched her son rolling on the floor with a grey wolfhound puppy. Edward's curls, blond like his mother's, were fanned out on the wooden boards as the boisterous dog attempted to lick his face.

"Eddy," his mother laughed. "You must not let Beowulf behave so. Show him that you are master." It was all to no avail for the dog had the advantage of size over the boy and all poor Edward could do was giggle helplessly.

As Christiana stood watching this spectacle the door from an inner chamber opened and in walked a boy of around eight years. He approached the duchess and made a polite reverence, turning then to the servant present; the sight of the woman momentarily threw him off guard and he stood staring. Christiana likewise stared at the child, small and thin with dark hair falling about his shoulders, and held the gaze of his deep sapphire eyes. He looked most regal in his doublet of blue velvet and perfectly fitted hose of a lighter hue. It always took her by surprise whenever she saw him how quickly he was changing under his father's guidance. She had to fight down an urge to rush to the boy and take him in her maternal embrace.

"Have you finished your studies, John?" the duchess asked keenly. John did not take his eyes from his mother's face but answered the lady in the affirmative.

"Then you may spend a little time with Edward; you can play merrills," Anne announced kindly. "Thank you, Christiana, you may return to the herbarium," she added to her servant.

Christiana walked slowly over the wooden bridge in deep contemplation. A sharp wind blew around her legs and sent icy fingers groping across the bodice of her gown but she made no attempt to draw her cloak closer. She passed the stone huts of the fletchers, the candle makers and the dairy, seeing none of the buildings and eying not a soul within the cold bailey. She could not return to the cottage just yet for seeing her son had brought about a fit of melancholia and her mind was too full of sorrow to take to her work. She needed a time of reflection to ponder on those who had been taken from her: her father, Godwin and his Sybil, Richard and her son.

She paused at the smithies, all lying empty and their forges long cold. Since completion of the northern gatehouse and the upper storey of the keep all work had been centred upon the stable yard smithies. Perhaps she could find a little solace in this quiet place. Maybe the soul of her father would see her and bring her comfort as he had so often done in life.

She sat down wearily on a bench and stared around her. Here and there lay broken tools lying in redundant repose, bits of bent metal and splintered wood. She gazed down at her grey woollen gown where pieces of dried herbs had attached themselves and began to pick at them, immersed in thoughts of sadness. She knew that Martha would not approve of such musings for they led to idleness and incurable melancholia; and the devil made work for idle hands. Hard work and nothing less was her adage.

She did not hear any noise but caught only the fleeting movement of shadow, by which time it was too late to make her escape. Swift as a hawk a foul-smelling hand was clamped over her mouth as she was jerked violently to her feet. She had no time to recover her shocked senses before she felt herself being shoved roughly into the darkened interior of a smithy.

She had been thrown to the floor and the man was straddling her prostrate body before she had seen her assailant for the first time. Ralph Hodkin had pressed her firmly to the ground and worse, she had caught the edge of a sharp implement as she went down and a terrible pain now burned in her thigh, bringing a rush of tears to her eyes.

"So, wench," he hissed. "We are alone again and this time no fat old crone to come between us." He turned his head and spat into the straw, a slither of spittle catching her sleeve. She tried to cry out and wriggle her body from underneath him but his weight upon her constricted her breathing and pain in her leg had sapped her strength.

Ralph's rough fingers grazed her cheek in a caress as his breath, reeking of ale, came hot and clammy on her face. "You are nothing but a common wench. You are wasting your time strutting your cunt at the duke; he's not interested in you – puritan as a parson's arse is Richard now that he has a pretty wife and son." His fingers moved down to her neck and grabbed the laces of her kirtle, pulling on them violently. His hand, cold and vicious, was inside her bodice, squeezing her nipples painfully.

"I like you well, you are a comely wench, but you think yourself above me. Only dukes are good enough to bed you eh?" he drooled.

"Please, no!" she begged, as the pain in her leg seemed to surge through her whole body. She felt his weight lessen across her stomach as he groped lower, reaching for the hem of her gown.

"I'll show you my cock's as good as any duke's," Ralph leered as his hands wrenched her gown upwards, exposing her nakedness. She tried to slide out from under his legs as his fingers picked at the laces on his hose. She could not move her leg, but free of his full weight she began to scream and at once felt the full force of his hand across her face.

She was almost oblivious to the hurt he caused her as he thrust himself brutally inside her. All she could see was the blurred outline of his vile face and the greasy strands of his hair flopping into her eyes and feel the burning pain in her leg.

After what seemed an eternal passing of time, his seed spent and his lust satisfied Ralph lifted himself off her. She lay there moaning softly and desperately trying to pull down her gown with fingers that did not seem to be hers. It was some time before she realised that the man had gone and that she was alone. She lay there unable to move; the pain in her thigh, a cold heat, rendered her helpless and nausea swept over her like a tide.

It was dark and bitterly cold in the old smithy before anyone found her. She could hear the calling of her name, way in the distance across the dales.

"Anna, Anna, wake up."

A flickering light, bright and painful, lanced her eyes; she stirred and moaned and then felt strong arms underneath her, lifting her, carrying her. She saw nothing but dark shapes in deep shadow and the faint glow of the swinging lantern held by the hand that supported her as she was carried, the icy wind stinging her near naked breasts and shoulders.

Martha was beside herself with worry for the missing woman, greatly increased when she saw the torn and blood-soaked garments.

"Lay her here on the bed, Will." Martha's voice was cracked with emotion. "You can go now, lad. I will see to her."

"I am not leaving her until I know what happened." William's voice was no less distraught.

Martha began to tear at the young woman's kirtle in a bid to remove it. Her chubby fingers trembled but at last the kirtle lay in tatters on the floor; Christiana's shift remained intact to preserve her dignity for try as she may William was going nowhere.

"Sweet child, who did this to you?" Martha asked gently as she wiped blood from the wound in Christiana's leg. William stood close by holding the bowl of rosemary water used for the purpose. There was a silent rage deep within him, held in check – for now.

It was not until a poultice of agrimony and yarrow held in place with strips of linen soaked in celery juice had been applied to her wound did Christiana show any response. It came in the form of bitter tears falling down her face. William could do nothing but take her in his arms and hold her firm. "Tell me who did this, Anna, for I must know," he whispered close to her ear. She said nothing.

There was only one man known to him within the castle walls with the baseness of character enough to violate a woman thus; but he must be certain. Without releasing her from his embrace he spoke the name: "Ralph Hodkin?" He felt her body stiffen. He held her closer. "And did he force himself on you?"

At once her imprisoned pain and humiliation broke free and she sobbed uncontrollably on William's shoulder. When the well of tears had run dry he eased her gently down onto the pillow and stood to his feet. A dark look like gathering storm clouds marred his handsome face and eyes black as flint put a great fear into Martha's heart as the man pushed past her and strode across the herbarium to the door. The noise of its slamming shut echoed in the silence behind him.

The old herbalist warmed a cup of spiced wine for her daughter, for surely this woman, though no blood kin, was as much her daughter as any could be, and bade her drink. She climbed into the bed beside the younger woman and pulled the thick wool blanket over them both and prayed. There was nothing else to be done, but wait.

A loud, persistent banging on the cottage door at first light woke the women. Martha had not yet reached the latch before the wood was flung open and the figure of FitzHugh, the constable, strode across the threshold.

"There has been an incident up in the guard room. The one-time Captain of the Garrison has been beaten to within an inch of his life and requires your urgent attention. The perpetrator is held under lock and key awaiting a trial upon the duke's return."

Martha's wit was not so dulled by sleep that she failed to take in the measure of the situation, but she squared up to the constable with barely concealed rage. "You will have to find another to tend the wounds of a man who forces himself upon a woman and gets what he deserves." She folded her arms and stood immovable before the man whose authority was sacrosanct in the absence of the duke.

"You will do as I command or find yourself similarly incarcerated," FitzHugh answered hotly.

Martha felt her face redden but knew she had little choice; for Christiana's sake she must go.

"Then you must go with me for I fear I shall kill the man myself and gladly hang for it," Martha retorted angrily before throwing a few pots of her less potent remedies into a basket and following the man out.

From her bed in the adjoining room Christiana had heard every word and her heart raced with fear for her brother.

Martha returned sometime later carrying a basket of vegetables and grain from the kitchens with which to make a pottage for Christiana.

"Did you see Will? How is he?" Christiana asked anxiously as soon as the herbalist entered the bedchamber.

"Nay, lass, I was denied a visit." Martha sighed sadly. "I must look to your needs now, Christiana," Martha said with her usual aptitude for practicality. "I will say no more on the matter of Hodkin other than the hellhound fares well with more attention than he deserves."

Christiana grasped well enough the inference of her words and nodded silently.

That night Christiana lay restless on the bed, drifting in and out of sleep. Martha's potions dulled the pain a little but her mind was in turmoil. Her fingers went to the dressing Martha had bound to her leg. There was something amiss but she knew not what. She felt sullied and shameful and for the first time in her life she knew what it was to really hate another human being. There was something else; something of little significance that should not have mattered, but it did, immensely.

In the dead of night she woke in a cold sweat and knew – her pendant was gone. The jewel that Richard had given to her was no longer around her neck. She touched the place; it had gone. It must have fallen in her struggle with Ralph. Either that or he had taken it and if so she had seen the last of it for sure. After that there was no more sleep to be had that night.

The days passed and the days turned to weeks. Martha's daily applications of comfrey and agrimony tightly bound with clean cloths gradually brought about the healing of the wound on her thigh. It still pained her to walk and she still carried the bruising, now mottled green and yellow, from Hodkin's blow across her face.

There was no news concerning the return of the duke and William remained a prisoner in the keep. There were few visitors to the cottage and save for Martha's occasional calls to the guard tower to tend to the captain's wounds they lived very much in isolation.

"You have not conversed with me much this day, Christiana," Martha remarked gently one grey miserable afternoon. "Does your leg pain you? I can make you a potion if needed." The two women had been sitting side by side at Martha's table all morning, grinding and pounding, mixing and pouring.

Christiana put her pestle down, sighed deeply and hung her head, her raven locks falling across her face like the veil of rain that fell beyond the cottage door.

Martha turned on her stool and took the other woman's hand. "Tell me what ails you so that I may help." She could see the teardrops falling and soaking into Christiana's lap.

"My courses have ceased." The woman's voice was filled with fear.

The older woman did not reply immediately, trying to calculate the passing of time.

"I have the measure of it, Martha. My courses are always timed with the moon cycle and... I have the same nausea I had with John."

349

"God have mercy," Martha exclaimed. "I have pennyroyal. 'Tis best to take it now before your belly swells." She got down from her stool and began to search the jars on the upper shelves for the required herb.

After a while Christiana spoke. "I do not think I can, Martha. It would be no less a murder than if I gave you monkshood in your wine."

Martha turned from her searching, a look upon her face akin to disbelief and exasperation. "Christiana, you must. What are you going to do, pass this one off as another one of the duke's bastards?"

"I do not know what I will do," Christiana moaned, horrified that Martha would say such a thing.

Nothing further could be said of the matter as just then a gentle rapping could be heard on the wooden door. Irritated by this untimely visitor Martha opened the door just enough to see who it was disturbed their peace. Standing there cold and wet was William Beverley, the rector of Saint Mary and Saint Alkelda's. Martha stood aside to allow the man to cross the threshold.

Rumour that the herbalist's assistant had provoked the attention of a soldier and then instigated a beating of the man by her brother had reached the ears of the village priest who felt duty-bound to hear her confession and offer absolution for her sins. He felt it prudent to make the call himself and not involve the castle chaplain who held pastoral responsibility for the duke and his family.

Christiana made a full confession of her sins, including the sad fact that she was with child. It was an impulsive move for the man's sudden appearance had given her little time to consider her plight. Besides, she knew that she would not be blameless in the eyes of this man – or any man. She could not hide her shame and without confession she could not be absolved of her sin.

Hospitality compelled Martha to offer the rector a cup of spiced wine after the necessary penance was declared and before making his journey back to the village.

"I do not think it will be long before the duke returns," he offered as he sat and sipped his wine. "Although it will be to the unwelcome news that peace within the walls of his castle has been disturbed in his absence."

Martha, ignoring this last comment, drew up her stool, eager to hear any news of the duke's return. Christiana held her cup tightly with head bowed. How could she face Richard after this?

"A licence has been granted at the request of the duke to make St Alkelda's a collegiate church. This will mean great status for our church and the village," the rector continued. "There will be a ceremony with much pomp and reverence and of course the duke will want to be here for that."

"That is welcome news indeed," Martha replied.

"The good duke will want to see that this matter is settled and your brother will have his petition heard, I am certain." Beverley took another sip of his wine before turning a solemn face to Christiana.

"My child," he began softly. "This will be no small a matter for our duke to contend with. His needs and reputation must be upmost in our minds." He paused before continuing, "I commend the duke for accepting his bastard son and providing for him a fitting education."

Another pause. "This unfortunate incident, however, is another matter," he continued slowly. He reached out and took her small hand in his. "Maybe, for your sake and that of others, you should consider taking Holy Orders. With your knowledge of herbs you would serve our Lord best in the care of the sick."

Christiana sat in stunned silence. She gave the rector a tearful smile. He patted her hand before releasing it. "I will make enquiries for somewhere suitable." His wine finished and his duty done William Beverley bade them farewell and departed.

"It pains me to say so, Christiana," Martha said, returning to her stool. "But I do believe he is right. You have rejected a chance of marriage and you will be a constant thorn in the side of our good duke. You may find if the holy sisters are merciful they will take your child also. Think on it, my dearest love." Martha turned away and wiped her tears with her apron.

It was one quiet afternoon, when Martha's work was well in hand and a gentle breeze carried the aroma of early spring through the open doorway, the two women were sat on a bench against the wall in the herbarium, working silently.

Christiana's full attention was given to the sewing of a new kirtle; her small bone needle slipped in and out of the linen as her fingers worked deftly.

She did not see the shadow fall across the open doorway and her reverie was broken only by Martha rising quickly to her feet with a gasp. Christiana looked up and as she stared she began to tremble and then she wept. Pulling herself to her feet with the support of the bench, the kirtle and needle in a heap on the floor, she walked to where her brother waited. He was thin, unshaven, dirty and the smell of incarceration hung all about him.

"William," she cried and held out her arms to embrace him. Martha said nothing but busied herself preparing a tonic and vegetables for a pottage.

Christiana was full of questions but Martha reprimanded her. "Wait awhile, child. He needs sustenance – and a wash."

Christiana fetched water from the trough outside and heated it on the brazier while Martha used the last of her onions and beets and a goodly handful of barley to make a meal. There was also a little of the loaf of bread left over from that morning.

Sometime later Christiana watched on as her brother, smelling sweeter, wearing an old under shirt procured from their basket of rags, ate and drank eagerly like a half-starved wolf. Christiana remembered the last time she had seen him eat so ravenously; many years ago in a hostelry outside York, a small boy lost and abandoned. Her lips quivered with a smile.

"So, what has happened then, Will?" Martha asked as the last of the food disappeared.

"Richard is home," William announced, giving his sister a furtive glance. "He brings ill tidings. Clarence is dead."

The women made no reply but waited for him to continue. "He was executed for treason on the eighteenth day of February.

Richard is most distraught and it appears that he tried all ways to form a truce between his brothers – but to no avail.

"There has been talk that George's death was by drowning in a vat of malmsey wine."

Martha sighed. "Well I cannot say I am surprised at his execution although the method seems strange. He was always double-minded and fickle that one. I daresay the king had little choice although for certain 'tis sad news."

Christiana reached out a hand and touched her brother's sleeve. "What happened to you, Will?"

"I gave Hodkin his due, only stopping short of killing him. FitzHugh has had me under lock and key like a common felon. Fortunately for me the duke understood when I told him everything." He paused and looked into Christiana's tear-stained eyes. She felt her cheeks redden with shame; even William did not have the full measure of it.

"I was released with no further enquiry," William continued.

"And what of Hodkin?" Martha asked.

"Escaped the duke's retribution."

"How so?" Martha asked.

"The duke was not a mile from Middleham when Hodkin availed himself of a swift horse from the stable and a sackful of silver, riding off into the moors or who knows where," William finished wearily.

"A good riddance," Martha retorted. "Let us hope that is the last any of us see of him."

William turned to Christiana then and asked gently, "How do you fare, Anna?"

An answer to this question was about to fly from the lips of the old herbalist when Christiana shot her a look that killed it before it took flight. Checking herself then Martha busied herself removing the bowls and spoons from the table and taking them outside to soak in the trough.

"I am mending well. Martha's healing hands have closed the wound in my leg and see, the bruising is fading," Christiana said gently, turning her discoloured cheek towards him.

"Then all is well and life can be as before now that Hodkin has gone." William smiled reassuringly.

"Aye, all is well once more," Christiana replied, touching her belly and sighing sadly.

A few more weeks passed, the weather grew warmer and the green shoots and buds bloomed and so did Christiana. Although hardly visible as yet she made for herself an apron with many folds to conceal her swelling belly.

Then came the day Christiana had been dreading; it dawned a warm balmy morning mid-April. The cottage door was open and the herbarium was filled with the sweet aromatic scent of herbs.

It was not, however, the shadow of William Beverley that darkened the threshold but that of the Duke of Gloucester; received with no less dread. The women turned from the bench and bowed in reverence as the man entered.

Christiana's eyes were averted to the floor as was proper and she felt her heart pounding and her cheeks redden. Richard sat down on a nearby stool and the women rose from their obeisance.

"Leave us, Martha," the duke commanded softly. "I would speak with Christiana alone."

"As you wish, my lord," the old woman replied. "I will see that none disturb you." With a slight bow Martha went outside to her herbs, closing the door behind her.

"I know of this heinous deed that has been done to you and I am sorely sorry for it," Richard said quietly, crossing the room to where Christiana stood. "Word is out for Hodkin's arrest and if he tries to sell my silver then we will hear of it."

Christiana could not help the tears that coursed down her cheeks and closed her eyes as she felt Richard's warm fingers gently wiping them away. With one swift impulsive movement he drew her into an embrace and as she leant her head against his shoulder, breathing in the smell of his hair, the warmth of his skin, it was as though these nine years past had never happened and her longings filled her afresh with torment.

After a while Richard gently drew apart from her and indicating the two stools they sat side by side. For a few moments Richard said nothing and she could see the working of his jaw in anxious apprehension. She waited.

"What I am about to say is not easy and I wish it could be otherwise," he began. "It is time that you were gone from here. I had hoped that you would have accepted Godwin's proposal of marriage, for you would have been well taken care of.

"William Beverley has informed me that he is seeking a place at a suitable nunnery for you. Unless you have a preference to take holy vows I have another offer for you."

Richard paused and looked down at his fingers rubbing nervously together. "I can readily find you a position at one of my other castles: Pomfrey, Sheriff Hutton, Barnards. Your skill as a herbalist would be welcome in any household. You must decide, Christiana, only know that you can no longer remain here."

What could she say? Hodkin's words as he debased her came back to torment her. Did she regard herself as better than others of her status? Who was she that she should demand life always went her way? She was a blacksmith's daughter – nothing more. It was time she remembered her place.

Richard was still speaking: "Our son possesses a liveliness of mind, an activity of body and is inclined to all good custom. You can be pleased at this and fear not for his future."

She still could find no words with which to respond but Richard seemed to understand. "Think on it, Christiana," he said and after the briefest of kisses on her cheek he departed.

No sooner had the duke passed through the wicker gate into the outer bailey than Martha appeared demanding to know all.

"Christiana, you can nowise be sent to another castle any more than you can stay here with Hodkin's sprog growing in your belly," Martha exclaimed with exasperation after she had heard the purpose of Richard's visit. "What are you thinking of? Does he know you are with child?"

"I know not, I know not," Christiana cried helplessly. "My confession to the priest is surely secret, even from the duke."

"Enough of this," Martha retorted angrily and bustled over

to the shelves where she reached for the pennyroyal. She took a goodly measure of the dried herb and stirred it into the hot water in a pan on the brazier. Having strained it through butter cloth into a cup she handed the brew to Christiana. "Here, drink this now and be done with it." Her words were harsh.

Christiana's temper flared and she swept the cup from Martha's hand whereupon the clay vessel shattered into a myriad of pieces on the stone floor. "For the love of God, I will not," Christiana cried and covered her face with her hands, weeping sorrowfully.

Martha too was crying as she took the besom and brushed the shards of pot under the bench.

A little later and tempers suppressed by Martha's strong wine, the old herbalist felt she could enter once more into the fray for this matter must be settled one way or another.

"You know there is another path to take, Christiana," she said softly.

Christiana turned her reddened tear-stained face towards her and listened.

"I feel certain that William would marry you and accept your babe as his own. Work could be found anywhere for him as a good blacksmith. You could go away, start a new life together. I am sure that the duke would see to it."

The wine seemed to have recalled her good sense and Christiana was ready to voice her resolve. "Nay, Martha, I would not have William bear the burden of my foolishness and sin; he does not deserve that. I will pray that Mister Beverley will find a merciful priory that will have compassion on a poor woman and her unborn child. This is the right thing to do for the sake of all. 'Tis time I considered others and not myself." She bowed her head and this time there were no tears.

It was not many days later that William Beverley paid them another visit. He bore the news that the Benedictine Nunnery at Marrick near Richmond might be willing to accept Christiana. The rector had pressed upon the Prioress Christiana's skill in herbal remedies and her penitent nature and she seemed willing to consider his request.

After this Martha wasted no time in securing a replacement assistant, choosing Tilly, the dairy maid, confident that the girl could be trusted with the simplest of tasks at least. The next few weeks were spent teaching the girl the rudimentary skills of herbal remedies; she proved willing if a little slow-witted.

Christiana dutifully assisted Martha in the task of preparing her successor but with each new morning her sadness grew. The day was fast approaching when she would leave her home and all those she loved most dearly: Martha, William, her beloved son John and Richard, to whom she had vowed her life until such time as he had no further need for her. It seemed that such a time was now upon them and it crushed her heart like a leaden weight.

She spent her days in silent acceptance and her nights in sorrowful repentance and regret. She ate little and slept little, becoming paler and thinner daily; although the child within her grew, seeming to drain her very being of life.

The month of April had hardly ended and the weather was becoming much warmer. This was always a season of joy for Christiana when new life bloomed and blossomed all around them. The scents and hues of spring always swelled the heart with gladness; but not this year. The woman was constantly watching and listening for the swing of the wicker gate that would herald the arrival of William Beverley bringing news that all was ready for her departure.

One hot and humid afternoon the three women were tending to the herbs in their beds, plucking at the weeds that constantly threatened to strangle. As Christiana straightened up from her work she felt a sudden sharp pain burn across her belly causing her to bend double again. There followed a second pain and then a third. By this time Martha and Tilly were at her side guiding her into the cottage. It took some time for Christiana to reach the bed for the agony crippled her.

Martha had the yarrow and horsetail prepared in next to no time. She even took a handful of shepherd's purse growing in an untended corner of the garden and boiled that; all to no avail. Several hours later and Christiana was purged of the child within her, a tiny scrap of flesh that hardly looked human in form.

Tilly cried for it was her first witness to such a thing, although she had seen many an aborted calf in her young years. Martha was relieved for this event may change Christiana's fortune but she voiced no opinion for she could see the woman felt her loss keenly.

Christiana kept to her bed for many days following the loss of her babe, falling into a deep, dark melancholy. Martha bade Tilly bring in as many pots of melissa as grew in the garden in the hope that its lemon scent would disperse the woman's bad humour. It was one thing only that caused Christiana to leave her bed, bathe in the wooden tub and put on her kirtle and that was a message sent from the duke himself by the hand of his groom of the bedchamber, requesting a jar of exotic spices for his back.

Christiana would allow neither Martha nor Tilly access to this receipt for it was hers and hers alone to brew. No one was going to deprive her of this last intimate moment with Richard, one last farewell; whether her fate now lay in service at another castle or in the nunnery at Richmond. The poultice would not be hurried and Alan was waiting patiently for her on a bench in the herb garden when she had finished.

They walked in silence to the keep, Christiana clutching the precious jar wrapped in linen strips to keep warm. At the inner courtyard Alan paused at the foot of the stairs leading to the great hall and Richard's chambers.

"I will take this to the duke, Christiana," he announced and held out his hand to her.

She drew the jar closer to her bosom. "But surely I must administer this," her voice cracked. "Lempster did instruct me to..."

Alan gently prised the jar from her possession. "Christiana, you forget that I too was present in the chamber when Lempster applied the poultice. I am capable of doing this and it is seemly that I do so. The duchess has requested your presence in her chamber." He turned from her and disappeared up the stairs and so to his duties.

Christiana did not hurry along the passageway to Anne's chamber, dreading the fate that awaited her. The duchess was alone when Christiana entered the room; not even the formidable Tempest woman was to be seen. Anne welcomed her with a smile and after Christiana's bow of reverence bade her servant be seated on a coffer.

Christiana looked into the eyes of this beautiful, delicate creature who was Richard's wife and tears began to fall. Anne sat beside her and spoke gently to her servant. "Christiana, I am privy to all that has befallen you; all has reached my ears and I am sorry for it." She blushed a little and bowed her head.

"I have heard the conversations between my husband and William Beverley," she continued. "I also know that a place has been found for you in the kitchens of Pomfrey Castle. By the duke's grace you are to choose: a nunnery or a kitchen servant."

Anne fell silent for a moment pondering her next words. She pursed her lips in resolve and continued. "I have been given to understand that you also possess some skill in the art of reading, a rarity indeed in a servant."

"Yes, madam," Christiana replied. "This is so."

"Then I should like it if you would move from the cottage and live here in the keep. My mother, the dowager countess, has failing sight and requires a companion to read to her. She has taken a fancy to Richard's copies of *Tristan and Isolde* and Chaucer's *The Knight's Tale*." She chuckled at the idea that her mother should enjoy such romantic writings. "You will see more of your son living here and you can of course spend some time at the herbarium when required."

"But, my lady, surely the dowager countess already has ladies who could perform this duty well enough?"

"For certain she does," the duchess replied and reaching out took her servant's hand and held it. Christiana felt the smooth cool skin of her fingers around hers and waited for the duchess to continue.

"Christiana, my mother does not trust you and I fear she would always doubt your integrity were you to be sent to Pomfrey, where my husband spends much of his time when he is away." Anne's voice was quiet and solemn.

"I have talked with my mother about this, Christiana, and in truth it would be better for you to come under the protection of the duke's household here in the castle. My mother feels that you would cause less embarrassment to the duke to be under her authority than left to your own devices at liberty in the castle enclave – any castle."

Christiana at once felt as though she were being scolded for wanton behaviour but what could she say in her defence? "Maybe it would be better for all concerned if I went to the nunnery, my lady," was all she could say.

"That is of course your choice. It is not a decision to be taken without due consideration but it would solve the problem," Anne replied gravely.

Christiana could not prevent the tears that rolled down her cheeks as she realised how much of her future would be decided by those who ranked above her in social standing.

"Richard does not want to send you away for certain although he knows that he should." Anne's gaze fell then to her embroidered gown and she pondered on the swirls and patterns of the silver thread.

"Men see these... incidents... as the fault of women's inherent sin," she whispered, a pale rose hue colouring her cheeks. "But Richard has reason to think differently."

Christiana too had lowered her gaze in the presence of the duchess and waited.

"Richard was just a young boy when he witnessed the defilement of his mother at Ludlow after a Lancastrian victory... he understands your plight."

Anne's words had recalled a memory from her early days at the castle; Richard had spoken to her of this very thing and little did she grasp the full meaning of his words then. Now she had the full measure of them and more.

The woman before her understood her husband well. It must be a great sacrifice for her to open her home to the servant who had borne his bastard son and a deeper sense of respect and loyalty towards her blossomed in Christiana's heart.

"I value your skill as a herbalist and your loyalty as a servant has been proven," Anne continued, smiling directly into the other woman's eyes. "I know Richard and I trust him. I hope I know enough of you to trust you also."

Christiana felt a compulsion to fall to her knees before the duchess and pledge an oath. "My Lady Anne, I swear to you that I shall be a true and honourable servant to you and your lady mother and your entire household. I will be worthy of the trust you have placed in me, so help me God."

As she walked back to the cottage, tears still flowing in abundance, Christiana understood that as much as this decision to move to the keep was costing the duchess, it was costing her as much – if not more.

Christiana had spent her last night in the comfortable old bed with Martha and this was to be her last day at the cottage that had been her home for seventeen years. The wound in her leg was fully mended save for the scar that would ache every now and again, when she would rub a little calendula salve into the skin. Her face showed no sign of bruising now and all that remained of her tribulation were the inner wounds that she feared would never truly heal.

From her position atop her well-worn stool she could see beyond the open door to where Tilly even now was bent in earnest over the herbs. Christiana's eyes came to rest on the sea of rosemary bobbing gently in the breeze, each sprig bearing delicate blue flowers; symbolic of remembrance, a poignant sign of her final day.

She drew her gaze to the familiar rows of bottles and jars sitting on the bench, the pestles and mortars, phials and dishes all in order. She hoped Tilly would remember to keep the wolfsbane, arsenic, digitalis and such like locked securely in the chest to prevent any accident of error.

Bunches of dried herbs hanging from the rafters above her head wafted their perfume down onto her. It was going to be so hard leaving all this and the old woman who had been as a mother to her these past seventeen years. She swallowed the lump, hard as a walnut, in her throat and looked across at Martha. The herbalist was sitting on a stool at the far side of the room concentrating her efforts upon cleaning the spills from the neck of a clay flagon, her soiled rag moving up and down, up and down until it seemed a hole would soon appear in the vessel. Sensing the younger woman's eyes upon her she looked up and smiled wanly.

It was Christiana who found voice to speak. "Do not forget it is I who will be doing the ledgers as promised. Tilly is not ready by far to take on such a task."

Martha gave the flagon a little respite, waddled across the room to Christiana and placed a chubby hand on her arm. "You belong up there with your son. It will be well for him if his mother is a lady's companion and wears fine clothes." There, she had spoken aloud what they had both been avoiding all morning.

"When I first came to Middleham as a girl I imagined it would be so wonderful to live up in the keep and wear fine gowns and attend the feasts with the ladies. Now that the chance has come I find that I do not want it. I shall be stifled up there with nothing to do all day but read and sew fripperies," Christiana said mournfully.

"You are too valuable a herbalist to be put out to pasture. I will hold you to your promise of keeping my ledgers, so do not fail me. Do not forget your humble friends either when you are parading around in all your finery," Martha laughed, dabbing at the corners of her eyes with her sleeve.

The old woman sat on the stool beside Christiana and a moment later her expression became serious. "Be warned, Christiana. Take care to give none the opportunity for gossip and slander. I have lived amongst the nobility and believe me I know how cruel they can be to one who is not their own. All up there will know you to be the mother of the duke's bastard and will be looking to catch you out."

"There will be nothing for anyone to find with which to discredit me, Martha," Christiana stated firmly. "The duke has a wife and son to whom he is devoted." She drew a deep breath and sighed. "I am nothing to Richard save a common wench and

John was conceived in the passion of his youth. That the duke has acknowledged his son and provided for him I am grateful and I should hope never to behave in such a way as to bring shame upon the duke, his wife or his household."

"Aye, I pray that it will be so for fortune favours you, my girl, when your path could have been so very different." Martha embraced the younger woman with tears in her eyes and kissed her friend as though an expanse of sea were to separate them instead of a herb garden and a few satin gowns.

Christiana was given a room on the upper floor in the west range. It was of modest proportions with an arched window and a fireplace. A heavy tapestry curtain hanging from a pole across a stone archway separated this chamber from that of the countess. She was to share this room with two companions, ladies of noble birth in waiting upon Anne Beauchamp.

The young woman had not been long in their company before realising that they regarded her with much suspicion. Knowing her to be the mother of the duke's bastard they hinted greatly at the favours she must be doing in exchange for such an honoured position.

Such a notion was reinforced by the countess herself one day, not long after her arrival, and occurred as they were together as Christiana was being measured for her new gowns. Knowing that the duchess favoured the colour of saffron, Christiana chose cloth of forest green and another of peacock blue; one of silk and the other of velvet. She had refused a fashionable hennin and chose instead a plain linen coif as a headdress. A pair of embroidered cloth shoes, a luxury indeed, new leather boots and a heavy woollen cloak completed her wardrobe.

"You have a very comely figure and a fine display of raven hair, Christiana," the countess remarked as a servant twisted and coiled her tresses under the coif. Christiana made no reply but bowed her head in acknowledgement of the compliment paid to her.

After the tailors and servants had been dismissed and they were alone and Christiana was tying the laces of her old brown dress, the countess stepped forward very close to her companion and looked intently at her. "My daughter is very fond of you," the lady whispered. "She has accepted well enough, as all wives must, that husbands will have their pleasures before wedlock certainly, as also some will violate the marriage bed itself."

Christiana felt the heat of indignation sear her cheeks but she dared not make any reply.

"Do not look so injured, my dear. I know Richard and so do many others, although that will not stop tongues wagging. Taking a servant wench in the hot blood of youth is one thing but to break marriage vows, as far as the duke is concerned, is indeed quite another matter. So I sincerely hope that you will give me no cause to doubt his good reputation. The duke merely has a desire to act honourably towards his bastard son and his mother in agreeing to our request."

The countess sniffed and shrugged her slender shoulders as though dismissing the subject from her mind. "Come to me this evening after the meal and read to me," she concluded with a cool smile and glided gracefully from the chamber.

Christiana took Anne Beauchamp's words as a warning and wondered greatly that she should find herself in such a fearful predicament.

Middleham Castle
Yorkshire
Summer 1478

In early summer of the same year the Duke of Gloucester announced to his household that His Grace, King Edward was to be the honoured guest within their walls.

The queen, Elizabeth, and their eldest child, also Elizabeth, a young lady of twelve years, were to accompany the king, together with several other persons of the English nobility.

The newly decorated and furnished chambers on the upper floor of the keep with their high arched windows offering splendid views across Wensleydale were to house the king and his grand entourage. Fine carved wooden chests from Flanders and large comfortable beds with canopies of brocade curtains furnished the rooms and plush woven tapestries and heraldic banners were hung where the sunlight could show them off to their best advantage.

Christiana had worked tirelessly under the direction of the duchess to arrange the bowls of dried herbs and scented candles that were to enhance and perfume the royal apartments. She carried armful upon armful of lavender, rose petals, thyme and rosemary leaves round and round the spiral staircase. Despite the tedium of her labour Christiana was very much looking forward to meeting Edward again, all the more so because her present position in the castle would allow her to see more of him. She smiled to herself as she recalled how the king had discovered her secret the last time he had been at the castle. She rejoiced that on this occasion he would be a more welcome guest.

The duke, at six and twenty years of age and more than capable of commanding large retinues of men-at-arms, was showing some sign of anxiety as preparations to receive his royal guests were underway. Christiana noticed the habitual working of his lower jaw, present whenever he felt uneasy. Could it be perhaps that

Richard was a little apprehensive at the thought of entertaining the queen under his roof? Christiana had heard it said that following the death of the Duke of Clarence there was little affection between the queen and her brother-in-law.

At last all was ready and the long-awaited day finally arrived. The weather was warm but somewhat overcast, a gentle mist settling along the dales and around the stone walls. Christiana, wearing her newly made gown of green silk, was feeling nervous, as she would be more conspicuous a servant now that she was required to attend the countess and she hoped her limited knowledge of etiquette would not let her down.

She sat with Anne Beauchamp in her chamber. That noble lady displayed no sign of eager anticipation of the arrival of her king and sat nonchalantly in her great chair. The window was slightly ajar and Christiana had her ears stretched for the sound of Edward's coming. The noble travellers were to arrive through the newly finished north gate thus allowing the common folk a glimpse of their sovereign lord as he rode through the village.

A sudden fanfare of trumpets blasted the silence causing Christiana to jump nervously. "My lady, should we not move to the hall to greet the king when he arrives," she said.

The countess turned a pair of ice-blue eyes on her attendant. "I do what I have to for the sake of my daughter, but I do not forget that Edward was responsible for the death of my husband," she said coldly. With that she rose to her feet and walked slowly along the passageway and wooden bridge crossing over to the keep.

Several persons of note, having arrived at the castle several days before, were already gathered in the great hall, most of whom were unfamiliar to Christiana. Two ladies-in-waiting joined the countess and together the small group waited silently to one side.

Christiana looked for Richard amongst those gathered. She saw him standing at the far end of the hall by the great wooden door waiting to greet his brother. How splendid he looked clothed in tunic and hose of darkest burgundy with a velvet cape about his shoulders. Anne was by his side wearing a saffron fur-trimmed Burgundian gown and gold embroidered hennin. Jane Collins stood behind the duke and duchess holding little Edward's hand, trying desperately to calm the excitable five-year-old. There was no sign of her son John at present but she knew that he would likely be in attendance on one of his father's guests.

A great hush descended upon the hall as the outer door was opened and the steward announced the arrival of His Grace, King Edward and his queen, Elizabeth. As he entered every head bowed in silent reverence and for several moments Christiana could not see the king, only the newly laid patterned tiles of the floor. When she finally looked up she allowed her eyes to appraise the tall Plantagenet king. The long journey had hardly diminished the brilliance of Edward's attire, richly embroidered and of the deepest peacock blue. She did notice, however, that the king was somewhat more portly than she remembered from his previous visit. Not in excess but certainly well padded around the middle and on the jowls.

"Dickon, dearest brother!" Edward exclaimed at the sight of the duke on bended knee before the king. With outstretched arms Edward took Richard in a warm embrace. Christiana smiled. For all his kingly pomp Edward was still the devoted elder brother.

Christiana's attention moved to the queen, standing gracefully at the side of her husband. She was tall and slender with finely shaped features. Just a touch of red hair could be seen under the band of an elaborate hennin, framing a smooth heart-shaped face with its pair of almond-like violet eyes. Her gown, the colour of ripe cherries and trimmed with ermine, trailed behind her and a string of white pearls circled a swanlike neck.

She held out a slender hand but offered only the tips of two fingers to the Duke of Gloucester, who bowed to kiss the hand of the queen. Her gaze was cloaked in majestic aloofness but Christiana could see the look of contempt with which she regarded the duke who stood somewhat shorter than she. Christiana felt a pain of humiliation on Richard's behalf. How dared Elizabeth Woodville, whose father was of common stock, condescend to be kissed by a descendant of the Plantagenet dynasty and a son of the House of York? Richard, however, behaved with the utmost courtesy before the queen, smiling benevolently at her.

The young Elizabeth waited shyly behind her parents clasping her fingers nervously in front of her. She had inherited all of her mother's beauty but with features softened by youth and looked a very becoming maiden in her velvet gown of pale green. The duchess stepped forward to greet her niece and immediately the girl's face melted into a smile.

On the third day following the arrival of his royal guests the Duke of Gloucester gave a lavish feast in honour of the king and to mark the occasion when the church of Saint Mary and Saint Alkelda received collegiate status and the village elevated to the standing of a town.

Although the licence was applied for in February the statutes bestowing the honour upon the church were drawn up early in July and at the duke's request inscribed in English, not Latin as was usual.

Mister Beverley, who had resigned his position as rector, was made its first dean. It was a grand affair when the dignitaries from York named the stalls for posterity and in honour of the saints: Saint George, Saints Ninian and Cuthbert, Saints Barbara and Katherine and Saint Anthony. Christiana had smiled to herself when she heard that Saint Anthony, the patron saint of swineherds, was a named saint and remembered how Richard had told her why he had taken the boar as his device.

Much preparation was needed before a feast fit for a king could be presented; beasts were slaughtered and prepared for the spit, and a wealth of spices had been procured from overseas merchants to flavour the food: ginger, cinnamon, nutmeg and mace, galingale and cubebs. The finest grown vegetables were selected and the biggest carp from the fishponds to be prepared for table. A supply of pure white sugar loaves, carefully stored to prevent damage, had been carved into elaborate shapes worthy of any Italian sculptor. The venison was provided courtesy of the king for Edward had shot the arrow that had felled the noble beast on a hunt the day before.

Every servant in the castle and a few besides, beyond its walls in the fields and orchards, worked long and hard to prepare for the feast. The great hall and the huge kitchens beneath bustled with activity. The enormous ovens, pulsating with heat, baked the bread, pastries, pies and trencher loaves. The kitchen boys turned the handles of the great roasting spits until their arms ached. Pail upon pail of water was drawn from the wells at either end of the kitchen and carried back and forth.

Christiana was given leave to assist Martha in preparing the potherbs and sweet violets for culinary use. Great bowls of sweet-smelling flowers and aromatic herbs were placed in the hall and coloured ribbons and banners festooned the canopy that had been erected over the upper table. It gave Christiana much pleasure to work once more alongside her old friend and a sense of pride that she was in some small way able to serve her sovereign king.

On the day of the feast Christiana was summoned to assist the countess with her dress. That great lady had elected to wear a crimson gown with elaborate patterned embroidery in silver thread. She sat on the edge of the bed in her chamber and fussed with her headdress. Not her usual choice, she sported a butterfly hennin adorned with silver beads and a flowing transparent veil. For some reason known only to Anne Beauchamp the band of the hennin would not sit well upon her greying head. She pulled and twisted the band until Christiana and the ladies in attendance feared the whole thing would fall apart.

"Methinks the lady wishes to usurp Her Grace – for a butterfly is her favoured headdress," said a fraught attendant in a whispered aside to Christiana.

Christiana was becoming agitated for she wished to attend to her own modest dress and time was moving ever forward. At last the countess gave up the fight and allowed her ladies to fit the headdress. In a temper all but one of her attendants were dismissed. Greatly relieved Christiana made haste to her own chamber and there donned her gown of peacock-blue velvet. She had brushed and powdered it and hung sprigs of lavender about the seams for days in readiness for this occasion. She drew her dark curls under her coif, smoothed the folds of her gown and went to find her mistress to make ready for the feast.

There was such a humdrum behind the wooden screen at the south end of the hall where guests and servants mingled. Minstrels were warming up their instruments and filing up the staircase to the gallery above. Two huge hairy hunting dogs were bounding around, picking up the scent of excitement that hung in the air.

A single trumpet call announced the proceedings underway and the Surveyor of Ceremonies formerly welcomed the guests into the hall.

Earls and countesses, lords and ladies and clerics, the steward, the marshal, the sewer, the pantler and ewer all assembled. Before the guests could be seated the laverer was summoned with his large decorative silver bowls. Into these he poured herb-scented water from a silver lion-headed aquamaline. Each guest was required to file past the bowls where they stood on side tables and dip their hands into the fragrant water. The king and his royal family would wash their fingers in a hand-basin presented at their table by the marshal.

Long tables had been positioned at either side of the upper table, running the length of the sidewalls and all covered with lavishly embroidered cloth. On the table to the right hand sat the highest ranking guests and to the left the lesser, falling away in order of importance until the least sat furthest from the elaborately decorated salt dish and therefore the king.

The duke's guests had been drawn from the nobility and gentry of the northern counties, many of whom were tied by blood and marriage and quite unknown to Christiana. Henry Percy, Duke of Northumberland, now in possession of his father's lands after swearing his allegiance to King Edward, was present. Sir Thomas Burgh of Gainsborough and servant to the king, John, Lord Scrope of Bolton, John, Lord Zouche and Ralph, Lord Greystoke were amongst many. The guest list would not have been complete without two of the duke's closest and most devoted friends, Sir Richard Ratcliffe and Francis, Lord Lovell.

Christiana's place was at the lower end of a table to the left. Above her sat the Countess of Warwick and her attendant, a woman of noble birth. At the far end of the opposite table, that on the king's right hand, were seated the clerics and dignitaries from York, at Middleham for the church's collegiate ceremony. With them also sat the almoner and Thomas Barowe, secretary to the duke, William Beverley, the newly appointed dean and his ministers and the duke's accountant.

A trumpet fanfare heralded Edward's entrance as all turned in deep reverence to their king. He took centre position on the upper table, which was raised on a high dais looking magnificent in his elegant robes and exquisite jewels.

The canopy under which was placed his chair ran the length of the table and the queen, beautifully attired, her cool pale eyes surveying the room in thoughtful silence, took her place on the left hand of the king.

With eyes averted Christiana waited until the duke and duchess had taken their seats and Edward had given permission for his subjects to rise from their obeisance.

Once her duty to her king was done, Christiana's eyes drifted past them all and came to rest upon the person of the Duke of Gloucester. Sitting to the right of the king Richard looked almost vulnerable and her heart ached for this young prince. His clothes were of emerald green woven with regular patterns of gold thread; his tunic was of a more modest length than the one worn by his brother who always flaunted the latest fashion from Burgundy, presently irreverently short. Richard's fingers and neck were adorned with jewels and upon his head sat a beret of black velvet.

To the right of her husband the Duchess of Gloucester waited calmly for the feast to commence. On her left hand the queen's twelve-year-old daughter sat in wide-eyed wonder at the assembly.

After the ceremonial unveiling of the salt, the pantler, with his long fringed portpayne across his shoulder, carried in the loaves with all due reverence. Taking his gleaming silver knife he deftly cut the upper crust of one large and elaborately coloured loaf and presented it to the king, bowing low as the offering was accepted. The remaining loaves were then expertly cut into deep trenchers for use by the other guests. The cupbearer came forth to the upper table whereupon he tasted the wine poured by the butler into a magnificently carved silver cup.

A toast was drunk to the health of the king and queen and a second to the Duke and Duchess of Gloucester. This was the signal for the musicians to strike up and amidst a fanfare of trumpets the feast began. As the dishes were presented the steward and the chief cook would have to taste them before the king and his family could eat.

Christiana watched in bemusement as a troop of brightly attired servitors, each bearing symbols of their rank, marched to and fro with their dishes. The upper table was served first and food from these dishes was then offered to the guests on the king's right-hand table. Presented before His Grace were fish dishes, meat and poultry dishes, vegetables and salads, jellies and cream dishes, all highly decorative and coloured. The game and venison were expertly carved, paying due regard to ceremony and etiquette. A gasp of approval went up as the stuffed peacock, resplendent in all his glorious feathers of green and blue, was paraded before the king on a silver platter.

Christiana shared a plate and cup with a female servant of equal rank sitting to her left. Between the removes there was much entertainment; jugglers, dancers, magic and mime. There was an abundance of food of which she tasted only a portion. She was far too excited to eat a great deal and spent much time watching her fellow feasters.

Christiana studied her son's face as he went about his duties as a young page enthralled by all he heard and saw. At eight years of age, and having lived for a while in the splendour of his father's household, to experience a feast fit for a king seemed beyond his imagination. Richard had also recently begun to refer to his bastard son as John of Gloucester, a seal of his accepted paternity; an accolade that pleased Christiana immensely.

Further up the table Christiana could just make out the tiny figure of five-year-old Edward sat atop a pile of thick velvet cushions; his father, the duke, had broken tradition and allowed the children of his household a brief time at table. A jester had walked in front of him and waved a wooden stick from which hung an array of coloured ribbons. He shook his head, jingling the bells on his three-pointed hat. Little Edward laughed helplessly at the sight and would have toppled from his high perch were it not for the Lady Jane grasping hold of the back of his tunic.

Christiana looked across at the table on the dais. The king had just accepted the sotiltee an elaborately carved sugar sculpture of a crown in honour of his royal person. Edward's face was flushed with pleasure and wine. He was conversing animatedly with the duke. His words were lost in the hubbub of the occasion but the two laughed heartily together. Christiana smiled – there was no mistaking the deep affection and mutual respect each of these brothers had for the other. The queen apparently did not share their humour for she sat stony-faced dipping a slither of venison into a bowl with her long graceful fingers before turning to engage her daughter in private conversation.

As widow to the one-time steward of the castle Martha ranked as a servant of some worth. Her knowledge of herbs commanded much respect within the noble household. Thus she had been invited to the feast and now sat a little to Christiana's left looking quite resplendent in her pale gown and white starched cap. As she caught the eye of the herbalist and smiled, Christiana thought, not for the first time, how strange it seemed to be sitting here as part of a nobleman's household, sharing the splendour of the king's feast and yet still very much a servant.

The hours slipped by until well into the afternoon the feasting finally came to an end. A further toast was drunk to the king and Edward staggered to his feet, bloated and stuffed and not a little merry on the surfeit. The queen, in a swirl of purple silk, bowed to her husband as he retired to his chambers on the upper floor, no doubt to be purged of his excesses before rejoining his guests a little later. The children too were carried away by their nurses and attendants. Christiana bade a goodnight to John and watched him leave with the others, his young earnest features glowing with pleasure. The clerics too withdrew from the company after the feasting to assist the almoner in distributing the alms and the trenchers to the poor at the castle gate.

The countess had recovered her humour and showed no sign

of following her weary daughter to her rooms. However, her lady attendant had been dismissed on account of her discomfort from an excess of food and wine. Christiana had been ordered to remain with the countess in her place.

The trestle tables were cleared and moved to the sidewalls of the hall and the great rush lamps were lit high up in their iron sconces. There was to be dancing for any willing and able. The York Waits, a band of musicians of high repute from the city of York, had been commissioned to entertain the king and even now the sound of sackbut, flute and bagpipe floated through the air.

Many of the lords and ladies and their attendants remained behind. A great feast given in honour of an eminent guest was one of the few occasions where many members of the household could participate.

Martha excused herself and retired to the cottage, patting her even more rotund figure as she departed. Christiana sat quietly to one side waiting for the first dance to begin. The knights and their ladies faced one another in their sets across the stone floor. The minstrels struck up with gusto and the dance commenced. Weaving, dipping and twirling, a multitude of coloured gowns swished amongst brilliant tunics and tabards.

Throughout the dance Christiana's eyes never left the figure of the Duke of Gloucester. He was nimble and graceful upon his feet and danced expertly. His face was flushed and he smiled warmly at his partner. The dance ended and the dowager Countess of Warwick was escorted to her seat, panting and hot-cheeked. Christiana smiled at her, pleased that the wine and rich food had cooled the heat of her earlier temper.

As the next dance was called, a tall dark-haired figure approached from across the room. A young man of maybe four and twenty years with emblazoned surcoat over a tunic of deepest murrey stood before them. With dark eyes flashing warmly he bowed low and addressed Anne Beauchamp. "My lady, would you do me the honour of accompanying me for this dance?"

The countess offered her hand in greeting to the young lord. "Why, Francis, it has been a while since our last meeting. It is good to see you again. I fear, alas, I am unable to accept your kind offer. I am fatigued and must rest awhile." She smiled, still flushed and breathless.

"But, my lady, 'tis a gentle dance and one that progresses," persisted Francis. "You will not have to dance with me all night." He smiled mischievously.

"Later, young sir, later. In the meantime take my attendant Christiana here. Her legs are younger than mine. She will make a more worthy partner."

Francis, Lord Lovell, turned his gaze then to the young woman seated beside the countess and his eyes shone in recognition. "Christiana, the herbalist, I remember. So you are still in service here then?" He held out his hand and with a quick glance at the countess Christiana acquiesced. "I am no longer herbalist, my lord. I am in waiting to the countess as you can see." There was no time to converse further as they took their places and the music began. It was a slower dance, the steps of which Christiana was familiar. All ranks of society knew how to dance for it was a common pastime on feast days and celebrations.

Francis danced well. He held her hand and turned her about without once treading on her feet. She smiled at him as they parted company for their next partner. The same could not be said of him, however. A rather clumsy earl, stumbling all over the place, he completely missed several of the steps altogether. She passed him on with relief. On they came, some old, some young, some portly and some thin as reeds. There were knights, lords and noblemen, soldiers and servants. She weaved and pirouetted, dipped and twirled with man after man and indeed, once with an elderly gentlewoman who was utterly befuddled.

She held out her hand to receive her next partner. He caught it steadily. Her eyes looked across at the gold pattern embellishing his green tunic. His fingers were warm as he pulled her towards him and circled her waist with a firm arm. They were close, close enough for their breath to mingle. She caught the smell of him, the warmth of him as she locked on to the deep blue eyes that were penetrating her own. With pounding heart she savoured every second until he was torn from her grasp by the noble woman to her right. It was with trembling legs and fluttering heart that she returned to her seat at the end of the dance.

Elizabeth Woodville, Lady Scrope and one or two others had joined the countess's circle as the more energetic took to the floor for a farandole. Christiana watched in amusement as the Duke of Gloucester led his young niece a merry dance, dipping and diving until the poor child was quite flushed and breathless but obviously enjoying the experience immensely.

"You have a delightful young daughter, madam," remarked Lady Scrope, listening to Elizabeth's laughter as she was escorted by her uncle back to her nurse on the far side of the hall.

"Indeed I do," agreed the queen with an affectionate smile.

"Mayhap there is to be a betrothal to a worthy noble prince, my lady?" the dowager Countess of Warwick boldly enquired of the queen.

Christiana, sitting silently beside the countess, her eyes turned as they were towards the revellers, had nonetheless caught the sudden blush of colour rise on the queen's cheeks.

The countess, it seemed, was also aware of the impertinence of her remark for she hastily added, "I merely inquire now that George Neville, my late husband's nephew, once betrothed to the young lady is no longer... er... in favour."

Christiana began to feel distinctly uncomfortable in such noble company and moved surreptitiously away from the circle of ladies but close enough not to appear negligent of her duty, hoping that the countess would soon find the merriment too much of a strain and excuse herself.

The minutes slipped by, the dancing continued and likewise the whispers and gossip amongst the ladies. Christiana sat silently watching the dancers. There was a young man, perhaps two or three years younger than Richard, however, who had caught the attention of the herbalist. It was not his fine stature or handsome features that held her gaze but his arrogance of manner that put her in mind of the late Duke of Clarence. He was partnering the young Elizabeth of York in a pavan but his remarks appeared curt and rude for the blush upon the cheeks of the girl was one of painful embarrassment, not maidenly modesty.

"I see you too have noticed Henry Stafford." This remark, coming of a sudden from a woman sitting herself abruptly down beside her, startled Christiana, who only just managed to suppress a cry of surprise.

"Forgive me, I did not mean to take you unawares, Christiana," the woman, said smoothing the folds of her red velvet gown.

"I beg pardon, my lady, but I am not familiar with many of the duke's guests for I have not been long in the service of Lady Anne Beauchamp."

The woman smiled and Christiana caught in her face a glimpse of familiarity but could not place it. Christiana's remark seemed to amuse her for she continued: "I would wager that you would have to be in the service of Lady Beauchamp for many a year to become familiar with the intricacies of this family.

"Take our Henry over there," she inclined her head towards the young man still dancing with the king's daughter. "He is the second Duke of Buckingham married to Catherine Woodville, sister to our queen and by any account not overly pleased with the match. His Uncle Henry was married to Lady Margaret Beaufort until his death a few years ago. That lady has now taken for husband Thomas, Lord Stanley, whose first wife was Eleanor Neville, sister of the great Earl of Warwick."

The women's eyes followed the object of their scrutiny as he walked across the hall to where a very elegant and finely dressed couple were conversing with the Duke and Duchess of Gloucester.

"I do not see Thomas, Lord Stanley, for I am familiar with his face," Christiana commented.

"Nay, I dare say Lord and Lady Stanley will have better things to do than attend a feast given by the Duke of Gloucester.

"Come, Christiana, let us take a walk in the garden before the light fades," the older woman announced with a chuckle, seeing the look of bewilderment on her companion's face. "I have not yet introduced myself and your Lady Beauchamp, it appears, has taken her leave and left you behind."

Indeed there were several vacant chairs and so it seemed that Christiana's services were no longer required. She stood to her feet and followed her companion who was walking across the room towards the door.

The early evening air was balmy and heavy with the scent of herbs and flowers as the two women strolled along the pathways, pausing at the benches near to the dovecote where they sat side by side.

"You and I share a common existence," the older woman began, breaking the silence that had accompanied their walk. "Forgive me for keeping you in ignorance for so long. I am Margaret Neville, bastard child of the onetime Earl of Warwick and half-sister to the Duchess of Gloucester, married these fourteen years past to Sir Richard Huddleston."

This announcement did little to relieve Christiana of her sense of confusion and she sat there silently on the bench beside this most intriguing woman.

"Your son will be provided for with all the necessities of one who is a true heir. Richard is an honourable man, as was my own father, for all his many faults. Alas, my own mother, though nowise neglected and cast out, did not fare as well as you, Christiana," Lady Margaret continued with a smile.

"Richard must hold you in high regard to allow you to have such a position in his household, and what is more, Richard's marriage to Anne is strong enough to risk the reputation and standing of his wife."

Christiana hung her head and intertwined her fingers in her lap, waiting for the warnings, the hostility, the casting of aspersions. Instead, she felt a warm hand gently cover hers and a softly spoken voice. "I should like you to consider me a friend," Margaret whispered. "My mother was in love with my father and I grew up with her pain. My father took as wife the Lady Anne Beauchamp as befitting his rank and status; my mother understood and accepted that but it still hurt."

Foolishly Christiana felt tears roll down her cheek and the hand pressed her fingers gently. "You will be the one to lose if you ever break the bonds of trust. Be wise and you will remain near to your son until he makes squire at fourteen – then he is lost to you forever."

Christiana had heard these warnings from the lips of others; the countess, Martha, within her own mind, but here was a woman who she felt truly understood her part and was prepared to stand as friend.

"My husband's lands, endowed to me by my father, lie in Coverdale not far from here should you wish to seek me out," Margaret continued. "I am certain that I shall be seeing more of my sister too in the future."

Christiana lifted a tear-stained face to her companion, dried her eyes on her sleeve and together they walked back to the great hall.

The weather remained favourable for the next few days and many guests taking advantage of the warm and balmy hours swarmed the garden in the bailey. Knights and ladies and children, closely managed, would idle away the afternoons on the benches around the dovecote or roam the pathways to admire the flowers. The king and his brother together with their noble guests spent the mornings hunting, returning hot and dusty and occasionally bearing the carcass of a stag or a boar across the back of a horse. After bathing and a change of clothing they would walk with the ladies in the garden until it was time to retire to the hall to eat.

It was late one afternoon and Christiana was on her way across the bailey to visit Martha, holding the hand of her eight-year-old son. Earlier that day she had read to the countess who, soon tiring, had asked to be put to bed. So Christiana had delivered her mistress into the hands of her ladies-in-waiting and went in search of John. She had discovered that the child had accompanied his father and the king on a hunting trip. On his return she had asked leave to walk with her son in the garden.

The day was still warm after a sprinkling of rain and the mellow sun lingered as the shadows began to lengthen. John trotting now at her side was very eager to relate the events of the afternoon. He seemed more at ease away from the formalities of the castle. He was telling his mother of how he had been taken on horseback with Lord Lovell, who told him that he used to live here himself when he was a boy. "Did you know him then, Mother?" asked the child.

"Yes, John, I did. It was when the duke was a boy and the Lady Anne and her sister Isabel were young girls," Christiana replied, holding open the wicker gate to allow her son to pass through. He stopped as he entered the garden and looked up into her face, dark eyes searching hers. "You must be old, Mother, if you have lived here all this time," he announced with childlike innocence.

Christiana ruffled his hair and chuckled. "No, my son, not that old, I was a mere child myself when I came to the castle."

Turning about, John's sharp eye caught sight of Martha in the distance bending over her herbs and without further ado ran on slender legs towards her. Christiana smiled. She decided to let Martha have a few quiet moments with her adopted grandson for the old woman saw so little of him these days. Christiana walked along the gravel paths around the garden enjoying the hue and perfume of the flowers now at the height of their summer glory. Few people were in the garden for it was approaching the hour for evening meal and Christiana wondered perhaps if the bench by the white rose would be occupied. She would repose there awhile until John was ready to return.

As she approached the place from the screen of the clipped box hedge she slowed her steps for her keen hearing had discerned voices, one of which was that of the king.

"Come, dearest wife, your jealousy is ill-founded I tell you..."

"Nay, husband. You lay too much honour on your youngest brother: wealth, position," replied the queen.

"Well, my love, your own family, the Woodvilles, have not done so badly since you were espoused to me now have they?"

Elizabeth Woodville exhaled impatiently. "I would not trust those shrouded features and quiet disposition. One wonders at the workings of his mind..."

"Now hold your tongue, madam." Edward's voice was raised in anger. "There is no other man in my entire kingdom I would honour and trust more than Dickon. He rules the north well and keeps the peace with Scotland better than any before him. Of his loyalty there is no doubt. No one will speak ill of my brother in my presence – not even you, my dearest queen."

"Brother be hanged!" she sneered. "The man is dangerous, like his brother before him."

"You forget yourself, wife," Edward hissed. "You forced my hand over George and I will not—"

"Come, come, Edward," she interjected with a low chuckle. "We all know that Clarence was executed for treason against his king and country."

"Well, know this and mark it well. Should I die with our Edward still a minor, then Richard, Duke of Gloucester, is to be Lord Protector of England, and no other."

"Then you are a greater fool than I took you for, husband," came the queen's retort.

From her hiding place, Christiana sensed that the conversation, nay altercation, she had inadvertently overheard and liked not the sound of, had come to an end. Either His Grace or the queen could round the hedge at any moment and she would be discovered an eavesdropper. So, quick-witted as ever, she took a deep breath, taking in the musky scent of the still wet leaves of the box hedge and boldly sauntered around the end of the hedge looking to any as though she were merely continuing her walk, unaware of the royal presence. She had taken only a few steps when the ruffled person of the queen, pink-cheeked and perspiring in the sun, almost collided with her as she endeavoured to escape her incorrigible royal husband. Undeterred, Elizabeth Woodville quickly vanished towards the castle and Christiana walked on.

She did not, however, continue her journey unnoticed. Edward hailed her and bid her come to him. She halted, turned and made a low reverence to the king. Sitting on the wooden bench his long legs were sprawled out in front of him. He was still wearing riding habit of leather tunic and leggings. There was a jewelled hip belt at his side holding a silver gilded dagger. His blond hair shone like gold in the sunlight.

"I know you. You were at the king's feast the other day," he called.

"Yes, my lord king," she replied, inclining her head.

Edward continued to look at her for several moments as though trying to recall the answer to a mystery that escaped his memory. "What is your position here?" he asked.

"I am attendant to the Lady Beauchamp, Your Grace."

"Ah, I see. But you have not always been so?"

"No, Your Grace, I was assistant to the herbalist for many years."

"That is it!" He slapped his thigh as recognition dawned upon him. Christiana began to blush under his interrogation. "I remember you. You are the one who has borne the duke's bastard son." Christiana's countenance reddened further in confirmation of the king's suspicions.

"Well," he said, "I cannot say I blame my brother, you are a comely woman. Have you regard for him?" he teased.

Christiana hesitated, unsure of how she should answer such a question put by the king; surely he took advantage of her position?

"Come, come. You can be open with me. There is no other in this place. Tell me your secret," he laughed. "I swear I shall keep it safe."

She took a deep breath and replied, "My affections for the Duke of Gloucester are as strong and true as ever they could be but they are locked away deep in my heart, my lord king, where none but those who have authority to look would ever find them."

Edward raised an eyebrow. "Bold words indeed! You would do best to guard your heart well, young woman, for naught can come of your affections. Richard has the wife of his choosing fitting to his own birth and a son and heir to his estates; not for him the frivolities of courtly life."

He turned his gaze from her with a sigh and muttered, almost to himself, "I miss Dickon. He comes so rarely to the palace these days." His face darkened as he sat in silence for a moment or two. Christiana was just wondering whether or not she should take her leave when she felt a small hand thrust into hers. Standing beside her, John, suddenly recognising his sovereign lord, gave a long, low, somewhat exaggerated bow. Edward turned to look at the child and laughed heartily. "So this is my brother's son? A fine-looking child, he resembles his sire well."

The king stood and looked hard at Christiana and then down at John and smiled, a twinkle in his eye, before turning and walking away.

As Christiana returned to the castle, she pondered upon the person of the king. It was said that he had many mistresses, and one, Jane Shore, he openly flaunted at court. How unlike his brother he was. But for all his reserve and piety and impenetrable dark features, it was the younger prince, and he alone, who still held captive her heart.

The king did not stay at Middleham Castle for many more days after that. Affairs of state called him back to London. Christiana was among many who turned out along the road in the bailey to watch the departure of the royal party. The king had chosen to leave the castle via the east gatehouse in preference to the newly built north gate to allow his brother's household to pay final homage to his royal person.

As Edward passed under the arch, splendidly attired, astride his black steed, it was to be the last many there would see of that handsome and flamboyant Yorkist king.

Christiana's life in the keep was rapidly becoming one of tedium. As one used to work and activity, as foretold, she found the leisurely activities of reading and needlework pertinent to ladies of noble birth somewhat boring.

If opportunity availed itself Christiana would take an unhurried walk to the herbarium to visit her dearest friend, Martha. She had noticed of late that the old herbalist was looking tired and her usual briskness of gait was tempered by stiffness.

"There, a hot infusion of meadowsweet to ease the pain in your bones." Christiana offered the cup to Martha who accepted it gratefully. It was early afternoon one warm day in late spring and the countess was taking her ease on her bed and had no need of Christiana's services.

"You should have Tilly make up this infusion daily for you," Christiana advised.

"Ah, if only the girl had half your wit and understanding, but alas..." Martha replied, sipping her drink.

"Does she not prove worthy?"

"She is willing but not so able. It will take time but I dare say she will make a herbalist one day." Martha smiled.

Christiana was perusing the ledgers when Tilly walked in through the door, her arms full of sprigs and sprays of early blooms, stopping abruptly when she saw her predecessor at the table.

"Come in, girl," Martha commanded. "Do not dally in the doorway, you can start to bunch for drying and chop for fresh and bundle for the kitchen as I showed you last week."

Christiana smiled to herself as she bent her head over the ledger; the same old Martha. Conversation turned to chit-chat about the weather and the garden for there seemed little in the way of gossip at present.

A second shadow darkened the doorway and Christiana turned her head to meet the eyes of her brother, William, standing on the threshold. Christiana felt herself unaccountably blushing. She had seen little of William since her defilement by Ralph Hodkin a year earlier, their respective positions at the castle keeping them apart. She noticed, however, that he wore the murrey and blue livery of the duke for he was now a trusted retainer and did little work as a blacksmith.

Martha beckoned him inside whereupon he stated the purpose of his visit.

"The duchess has a visitor in her chambers who has been taken ill. I bring the message as I was coming here anyway," William announced without taking his eyes off Christiana, noting her sumptuous velvet gown beneath the rough hessian apron she had donned.

Martha stood to her feet and hobbled over to the shelves and taking down a jar of calendula, chickweed and comfrey ointment she handed it to the soldier with a smile.

"This salve is more potent than the last. How you can be retainer to the duke with feet like yours I know not," she laughed.

Christiana had also stood. "What is the nature of the lady's illness?" she asked.

"'Tis Lady Margaret Huddleston who is overcome by nausea, so her servant informs me," William replied.

Tilly had abandoned her work and was staring open-mouthed at the handsome young soldier in the cottage and Christiana had to push her aside to reach the jars of ground ginger.

A little while later and Christiana was walking towards the keep, her brother at her side and a warm infusion of ginger in a covered costrel in her hand.

"It is good to see you, Will, how are you faring?" Christiana asked.

"I am well, and you?" William replied politely.

"I lead a life of leisurely boredom for the most part but I am well," Christiana said with a smile.

A silence fell between them after this exchange of pleasantries. Christiana felt it foolishness that such etiquette should exist between brother and sister. As they approached the keep and about to go their separate ways she asked, "How is it that Lady Huddleston visits the countess?"

"I know not other than she has recently arrived with her husband who is in deep counsel with the duke and a James Harrington concerning matters of a long-standing feud."

William said no more and turned to go when impulsively his sister reached up on tiptoe and kissed him on the cheek. "God bless you, brother," she whispered and walked away.

There was a babble of excitement in the duchess's chambers as Christiana entered with her remedy. The two sisters were engaged in pleasant conversation and their ladies were all smiles, their needlework forgotten.

"Christiana, my sister has good news." Anne greeted her servant with a smile.

Margaret stood to her feet, her cheeks a little flushed. "'Tis long in coming but I am with child," she announced. "But it is causing a sickness in my belly that I like not."

Christiana bowed respectfully and walked across the room holding out the costrel of ginger. "'Tis common to all women, my lady," she said, "but fear not, it will pass."

After she had taken of the ginger and declared she was feeling much improved Margaret Huddleston let it be known that she wished to take a stroll in the garden to take in the air. Her only companion would be Christiana who would give her good advice on the herbs she should grow in her own gardens.

"'Tis a most pleasant garden indeed," Margaret remarked as she sat on the bench near to the dovecote, breathing deeply the warm scents of spring.

Christiana wanted the confidence of this woman and felt she could be bold without giving offence to one, though bastard born, was regarded as noble. "Forgive me for being so forthright, my lady, but is there perhaps some ongoing dispute between your husband and the Duke of Gloucester?" she asked, picking up a thread sewn earlier by William.

Margaret's brow creased. "No indeed, what causes you to imagine such a thing?"

"Well, he may be mistaken of course, but my brother, William, retainer of the Duke of Gloucester, seems to think that there is a long-standing feud between the duke and Sir Richard and one James Harrington," Christiana ventured.

"Ah no, Christiana, Harrington's feud is not with the duke. Richard is a staunch ally of the Harringtons." She sighed and drew closer to her companion.

"It is a most dreadful thing the way men wrestle for power," Margaret whispered. "The Harringtons of Hornby have always been loyal supporters of the House of York but Thomas Harrington and his son John were killed at the battle of Wakefield along with the Duke of York."

Christiana nodded silently. This she knew for her brother had been orphaned as a result of this war and the duke had lost his father and a brother.

"Harrington's heirs were two young girls and the power-hungry magnate Thomas, Lord Stanley, given wardship of the children by the king, thought to marry one to his son and the other to a nephew thus securing Hornby Castle for himself.

"Thomas Harrington had a second son, however, James, the same who even now sits with our Duke of Gloucester in his chambers. This James took matters into his own hands and declared wardship of the girls himself and fortified his castle at Hornby.

"Although the Harringtons continued to give loyal support to Edward, after his re-establishment on the English throne in fourteen seventy-one the king favoured Stanley's power and influence over the Harringtons and forced Harrington to surrender Hornby to Stanley.

"When King Edward appointed his brother, Duke of Gloucester, Lord of the North, things did not look good for Stanley. Richard, with his sense of justice, is taking steps to take Hornby out of Stanley's hands and place it into the hands of its rightful heirs, the Harringtons."

"And what of your husband, Sir Richard?" Christiana asked tentatively.

Margaret laughed and took the younger woman's hand. "We are here to visit my sister with our news," she declared, placing her other hand across her belly. "My husband, not unaware of the situation, has merely offered his counsel.

"I suspect that decision by the king greatly upset his brother's sense of justice but I will say one thing," she continued, "Gloucester's faithful service to his brother has brought stability to the north and given him strong and loyal supporters."

"I imagine that Thomas, Lord Stanley, does not take it well that the duke favours Harrington's part in this feud," Christiana whispered.

"No indeed," Lady Huddleston agreed.

Christiana was not surprised to hear this anecdote concerning Richard's rule in the north but what did surprise her greatly was Margaret's knowledge of matters that were usually the reserve of men. She smiled at her friend who must have gleaned her thoughts for Margaret laughed aloud.

"Men regard women as having very little wit and see us merely as chattels to own and produce heirs to their estates. For the most part we are left to our sewing and weaving and feminine fripperies. They forget that we have ears and eyes and wit enough to use them. A foolish man ignores a woman at his peril." She laughed again.

"Please do not misunderstand me, Christiana, I am more than content in my marriage to Sir Huddleston and even more so now that I can provide him with an heir." She patted her belly once again and stood to her feet.

Taking the younger woman's arm Margaret Huddleston directed her footsteps back towards the keep. "Come, let us return to our needlework, for who knows what gossip we may then be privy to."

"You have done well, son." Richard put an arm around John's shoulder and gave the boy a gentle hug. "Lord Clifford makes a worthy opponent and you matched him well."

John, still breathless from his dual using wooden sticks to represent the broadsword, looked up into his father's face and smiled.

Christiana, watching this pair from a little distance across the drill field swelled with maternal pride. At eleven years of age, John of Gloucester had all the promise of becoming a worthy soldier like his father whom he resembled in both appearance and nature.

She followed discreetly behind as they made their way back to the keep. The late morning sun burning down upon her covered head told her that it would soon be time to eat.

"'Tis the distance you hold your hands apart on the shaft that determines the thrust of the pole arms, John." The duke was still discussing the tactics of hand-to-hand combat with his son as all three entered the great hall.

Trestle tables had been laid out to the side of the room and even now many members of the duke's household were taking up their positions as servers brought out the trenchers, platters of meat and jugs of ale.

Christiana was about to join them – John would take his meal with his father in their private chambers – when the countess entered the hall from those very rooms and was heading their way. Judging by the blackness of her countenance she was not in good humour.

"Well, this makes for a very pleasant scene," she hissed sarcastically upon reaching them. "Mayhap you should pay more attention to your wife, my lord, and matters concerning your own kin." The countess stood before the duke with ice-blue eyes that froze the smile on her son-in-law's face.

"Is Anne unwell?" Richard asked anxiously, striding towards his chambers, the most direct access to his lady's chambers from the hall being that way.

Christiana thought to take her place at the trestle table, concerned that all eyes had turned on the duke and countess, but Lady Beauchamp thought otherwise.

"You will not sup while my daughter has need of you," she said sharply and followed the duke out of the hall, a bewildered servant at her heels.

Leaving John in the duke's chamber they crossed the wooden bridge that led from the inner chamber to the south wing and so on to the duchess's privy chamber. Christiana wondered greatly at this sudden illness for Anne seemed well enough last evening as she sat and talked to her mother after supper.

As they entered the duchess's room Christiana was surprised to see Tilly and not Martha at the bedside. The girl was clearly out of her depth concerning such matters for her face crumpled into tears at the sight of the herbalist rushing towards the bed.

"Calm yourself!" Christiana commanded in a harsh undertone as she brushed the girl aside.

Duchess Anne, white-faced and fearful, lay on the great bed. Richard, sitting beside his wife and taking her tiny hand in his, asked gently, "My love, what ails you?"

Anne turned a tear-stained face away from her husband and muttered words that were barely audible. "I live only to please you, my lord, and yet it seems I have failed you – yet again."

"What in God's name are you talking about, Anne?" Richard asked in bewilderment, looking around for his mother-in-law to provide an answer. The countess, however, was standing ashen-faced by the door.

Even before Lady Tempest, her arms full of blood-soaked sheets, appeared from behind the curtained-off latrine, Christiana had guessed at the truth. She caught Lady Tempest's eye and the lady-in-waiting inclined her head sadly.

"Tilly, pour the countess a cup of wine and bid her sit awhile before she faints," Christiana whispered urgently to the young girl at her side. She then turned to the duke. "My lord," she said softly, beckoning him away from the bed.

"It would seem the duchess has lost the child she was carrying. 'Tis merciful it had not been long growing."

"She was pregnant?" Richard muttered, paling visibly.

"It appears so, my lord. Now, with your leave, I must be away to the herbarium to fetch herbs to stem the bleeding." The duke nodded his head silently and with a short reverence Christiana hurried from the room.

Once outside the cold stone walls of the castle the brilliance of the sun blinded her momentarily and caused her to sweat as she made haste towards the cottage. This was the second child Lady Anne had lost, she thought grimly; the other had been almost ripe for birth when it had fallen away, a tiny male child. Like her sister, Isabel, the Duchess of Gloucester seemed too delicate a creature to produce a brood of strong healthy heirs. Christiana pondered on how this second miscarriage would affect the duke for she knew how he must long for more sons. He would, she felt certain, hide his own feelings of disappointment for the sake of his wife, who was after all still a young woman and may yet give him the sons he desired.

Pushing open the door of the herbarium she called out for Martha. The old woman was nowhere to be seen. Greatly perplexed Christiana walked towards the door to the inner room. It was not like Martha to shirk her responsibilities without good reason.

Good reason there was for the old woman was lying on her bed looking weary and much discomforted.

"Martha!" Christiana exclaimed rushing over to the bedside. "What has happened?"

The herbalist attempted a smile, which resulted in nothing more than a painful grimace.

"'Tis just my legs, child," she said a little breathlessly. "They are swollen and I cannot walk for the pain. How is the duchess?"

"She has miscarried a child none knew her to be carrying, not even the duke," Christiana whispered, noting with much concern how bloated Martha's knees and ankles were.

"Ah!" Martha sighed. "She is not strong that one."

"I must return to her with the shepherd's purse; Tilly has no experience of such matters, poor girl. I will send her back here with instruction on how to tend to you, dear friend."

As she went about preparing her infusions Christiana felt her anger rising. She should be here helping Martha and not following the countess around like a little lap dog.

Her remedies prepared at last, Christiana returned to the castle. The duke had left his lady's bedchamber and the duchess was in the care of her mother and her ladies. An examination of the duchess revealed that she was losing very little blood – a good omen – but it was not Anne's physical nature that concerned Christiana.

The lady lay placidly on the bed as her ladies tended to her needs, her blue eyes turned away from them all, staring at some unseen image far away. She took her physic and ate a little of the food sent up from the kitchen but her face remained sad and forlorn.

Long after Christiana judged her to be well enough to resume her normal duties, the duchess remained in her bedchamber with none but her mother for company, shunning even the presence of her own husband.

Middleham Castle
Yorkshire
Autumn 1481

The last rays of sunlight barely penetrated the inside of the fletchers' hut where Dan sat with legs outstretched astride an upturned barrel. With knife in hand he carefully tapered one end of the ash-wood arrow, letting the curls of wood fall into the straw at his feet.

"Come, man, there's barely enough light left to see by. Stop work and take some ale." Ned, his apprentice, sat with his back slumped against the rough wooden wall of the hut steadily supping more than his share of ale from the barrel, the toe of his boot resting heavily on top of a sack of goose feathers.

"Nay," replied Dan, "I'll just finish this'n afore dark." Squinting in the fading light he took one of the barbed arrowheads from the wooden box at his feet and fitted it for size over the arrow shaft – perfect. He bent over to the small black cauldron of glue and stirred it with a spatula. The thick bluebell paste had dried to a hard lump.

Uttering an oath he kicked over the cauldron and turned around on his barrel to face the younger man. "Get ya great 'eavy boots off the feathers, Ned. They be no use as fletchings if they be flat. And keep off the ale, lad. There'll be trouble if the duke catches you in this state."

"Humph, duke's got to catch me first." Ned slurred his words as he reached over to refill his cup at the barrel and to sling the sack of feathers over into the corner of the hut. "Come the morrow and I'll be as sober as any monk in a monastery."

"Be that as it may, lad, but the duke has a face fit to curdle milk of late."

"Aye well, we all know what's wrong with him don't we?" Ned winked at the older man who threw him a bemused frown.

"Come on now, Dan. Don't take on like you 'aven't heard," Ned chuckled. "The Lady Anne keeps her lord from her bed, denying him his marital rights, 'tis said on account of the wench he keeps up at the castle more than willing to oblige him."

Dan let drop the knife from his hand. "God's Truth, man! From whose lips do you get such nonsense?"

The youth let his gaze rest on the horn cup in his grasp. "Rowena says..."

"Rowena! Not that harlot that frequents the garrison? Since when could a man trust anything she says?"

Ned glared bleary-eyed at Dan before continuing. "Rowena don't frequent the garrison no more. Duke had 'er thrown out of castle. Serving wench at The Old Bull in town now. Anyway," Ned paused to belch, "why else would the fair Anne shun her husband? And the wench has borne his bastard – what more proof d'ya need?"

Dan stood to his feet and brushed the wood shavings from his tunic. "Well I can't say as I know much about the woman except she was herbalist here in the bailey; seemed a respectable enough sort when I went to her for a salve for an old battle wound. What I do know is that Duke Richard has a reputation for being pious and strait-laced down at the king's court."

"Well down at the king's court is not 'ere is it?" Ned retorted, slumping further down the wall, satisfied that his argument was won.

"I need to stretch my legs afore bed," Dan said, moving towards the half-opened door. "The duke's private life is no concern of mine nor of yours either, Ned. If you put as much effort in your work as you do gossiping you might yet make a fletcher. Gossip is best left to the womenfolk who have nowt better to do."

Richard hurried along, his cloak drawn tightly about his shoulders against the biting wind. There was a churning sickness in the pit of his stomach and a throbbing pain in his head. Damn these servants and their malicious prattle, he thought bitterly.

He had been returning from his evening walk around the

bailey and the northern gatehouse to check that all was well with the twilight watch. There had been recent reports of a gang of lawless men and footpads over Witton way and he had had his mind on the safety of the surrounding villages when he had passed the fletchers' hut. The words he had caught from within its walls had set his temper rising, all the more so because they were a little too close to the truth for comfort and yet as far from the truth as it was possible to get.

He ambled up the broad staircase to the keep, passing beneath the flickering flames of the rush lights high on the stone walls.

"Beowulf!" he called to his dog, which had paused at the foot of the stairs to sniff at the stones; he waited as the huge hound galloped past him and disappeared through the door into the anteroom.

Inside the great hall a few still lingered before nightfall and bed. The days were becoming shorter now and the servants had lit the torches and thrown a few more logs on to the blazing fire. Two clerks were sat in its warmth, immersed in a game of merrills. The ladies had all retired, save one: Christiana, who sat in conversation with the young boy in the chair at her side.

"How is your head now?" she asked.

"'Tis much better, Mother," the boy answered with a smile.

"If the pain returns send to the herbarium for more willow bark but remember not too much or it will make you sick."

John humoured his mother with a smile as if she did not know that soon he would be a man and then nothing would be beyond his wisdom. "How is Martha?" he asked after a while.

"She is back on her feet at last but I do fear for her well-being. We forget at times how old poor Martha is."

"How old do you suppose her to be?"

Before his mother could answer John had noticed the dog bounding across the tiles from the far side of the hall, making a straight pathway to the fireside.

"Beowulf!" the boy called, ruffling the dog's hairy coat as it skidded to a halt. "'Tis Eddy's dog," John added by way of explanation.

The duke had followed the animal into the hall and even in the firelight Christiana could see that his eyes had a flinty glare and his lips were tight shut. "John, fetch me some wine," he growled at his son who, without a word, stood to his feet to serve the duke.

"Is all well, my lord?" Christiana asked, also standing, much concerned by the man's temper. The clerks too had interrupted their game, stood to their feet and turned inquisitive eyes to their lord.

"You should be abed at this hour, child," Richard snapped, snatching the wine from the boy. Bowing low to his father and with a quick glance of bewilderment at his mother John left for his chamber. Without a word the clerks, catching the sign from the duke, had gathered their board and counters and were making rapidly towards the door, their long gowns flapping wildly in their wake. There was no other in the hall but Christiana and the duke and the disinterested hound at the fireside.

Richard took a gulp of wine and slammed the goblet down onto a table. "Do you know that she refuses me into her bed?" he said, his voice low with anger.

Christiana sensed the pain beneath his outburst and took courage. "Richard," she said gently, moving a little nearer and touching his sleeve. "Anne has lost two babes. She feels greatly the shame of failing you as a wife. Do not be angry with her for all will be as it should in time."

He stared at her, the light from the fire flickering in his dark eyes. She was close enough to feel his breath in her face as his chest rose and fell with the effort to calm himself. His lips parted as his face drew nearer. Her heart began to beat fast in the silence but it was no kiss that left his lips but words that cut her deeply.

"You should never have come here. You should have remained in the bailey, nay, gone from this place altogether." He turned from her and marched across the tiled floor, disappearing into his chamber.

Later that night Christiana lay uneasily on her bed listening to the gentle snores of her companions. She stared at the tapestry hanging on the wall beside her; the hunters and their hounds, the fleeing hart just beyond the reach of the flying arrows, all bathed in silver moonlight.

Her eyes were swollen and sore with crying. Now more than any other time since her departure did she long to return to the cottage. She knew that living so intimately with the duke and his family she would be caught in the crossfire of their troubles. There raged within her breast a battle of desire and loyalty; her constant longing to know the love and intimacy of the man who held her heart and soul and the sworn oath of trust and devotion she had made to that man's wife.

She closed her eyes and drifted into sleep; bunches of fragrant herbs floated before her eyes and she heard the comforting crackle of the little brazier set on the flagstones. And then the little brazier became the red-hot heat of the blacksmith's forge and there in the smoke and heat stood her father. As she watched his ruddy face and the might of his arm swinging down on the anvil there appeared, as though from the sky, a multitude of white rose petals floating down and burning to a cinder on the forge. She awoke as the cinders faded before her eye; after that there was very little sleep to be had that night.

The following morning, thick-headed and sleepy-eyed Christiana joined her fellow servants in the great hall to break their fast. There she learned that the duke had risen before daybreak and left Middleham for matters pressing at Pontefract. He had left behind him a coolness in the air that had little to do with the chill of autumn.

"Did you not get this looked at when you were on campaign?" Martha asked brusquely as she bathed a wound still red from conflict in William's shoulder.

"Aye, there was a surgeon in the camp," William replied, wincing as the old woman rubbed at his flesh as though she were scouring a pan.

"Did he use honey? Rosewater? I think not for this is not healing as it should."

"Martha, I was given the best care. Do not fuss for 'tis but a flesh wound and the blade was wiped clean as it sliced through my padded jack." William chuckled before pulling his shoulder away from Martha's grasp. "I would sooner have Christiana's touch for she is gentler than you."

Martha flicked the linen cloth she held in her hand around the soldier's ear.

"There, 'tis done. You will need a little salve on this though so do not put on your shirt," she remonstrated.

The salve applied and shirt replaced Martha held a cup of hot spiced wine to the man and taking one herself she sat beside him at the table and sighed heavily.

"Is all well, Martha?" William asked.

"Aye, there is nothing untoward, Will, 'tis just that I feel my age these days and I miss Christiana more than I would have imagined."

William nodded sympathetically and asked, "How goes it with my sister at the keep?"

"Your *sister* fares well enough I do not doubt although I am certain she must find a life of waiting upon the whims and fancies of the nobility to be tedious and constraining for one such as her."

"You may well be right, dear Martha, but at least she is nearer to John at the keep – and his father."

"You do not bear malice against our duke on account of Christiana's obsession with him do you, Will?" Martha asked tentatively.

William pondered the question for a minute or two as he sipped his wine. "There was a time when I did, but no longer. Christiana is a besotted fool and the duke is... well he's a man... you know."

"Aye, a man who is true and loyal to his wife. Christiana may be a fool to lay her heart at Richard's feet but she has more than she deserves given her status. She knows she is fortunate and she is not so much of a fool to throw it all away for the work of a kitchen maid in some far flung castle," Martha returned.

William too had been thinking much about Christiana since his return from the Scottish borders and how different their lives might have been had Alfred not brought them here to the castle and secured himself a position as blacksmith all those years ago.

"I hear that all went well for the duke on this latest skirmish." Martha's voice broke into his thoughts.

"More than that, Martha," William replied with a sense of triumph. "'Twas a resounding victory over the Scots. We have had these border clashes before but this time..." William held his cup out for Martha to replenish it. "The duke marched us right into Edinburgh and even the garrison at Calais fired their guns in salute. What say you to that, Martha?"

The old woman made no comment, indeed none was required for the soldier would waste no time in the telling of the campaign that had resulted in his visit to the herbarium, now that opportunity had opened up.

"Berwick-upon-Tweed is back in the hands of the English, and for good now I should say. Our noble duke Richard has once again proven to be a skilled military leader, working well alongside the Duke of Northumberland to bring about this victory. He also forbade his soldiers to despoil the town after its capture and I for one say that marks him as an honourable man."

"Well I dare say there would be none to disagree with you

there, lad," Martha commented. "Although not many share our duke's virtues, I hope the king recognises the worth of his younger brother."

"Always, Martha, and for this victory reports have it that the king is elated."

"Ah well, rejoice while you may," Martha continued pragmatically. "For who knows what may lie around the corner."

William stood and flexed his shoulder. "Martha, do not think so gloomily for there is peace with the Scots thanks to Richard and Edward has had a trouble-free reign these many years past. What could there be to worry about?"

Part Three

Middleham Castle
Yorkshire
Early April 1483

"The day has turned chilly; I wish to return to my chamber," the countess announced wearily. Obediently Christiana took the lady by the arm and gently eased her up from the bench where they had been sitting.

A few early flower heads shivered in the wind as the ladies left the garden. At the wicker gate Christiana turned to look over her shoulder towards the herbarium to see if she could catch a glimpse of Martha at work. There was no sign of the old woman, only the slim figure of a young girl bent over the herb beds. Christiana sighed sadly; she was worried about her friend and had been for some time.

The countess's progress was slow through the bailey and along the bridged moat towards the inner courtyard. The wind blew coldly here, rippling the green water and whipping the skirts of the two women as they crossed over. Christiana regretted leaving the castle without her cloak as the first drops of squally rain spotted her blue gown.

Just as they passed under the eastern gatehouse a clatter of hooves could be heard as three riders, wearing royal livery, entered from the northern gatehouse and reined in their horses on the cobbled courtyard. The women halted as servants approached to relieve the soldiers of their mounts.

"I bring an urgent message for the Duke of Gloucester." Christiana's sharp ears picked up the words of one of the men as she guided the countess across the courtyard towards their chambers in the west wing and thought little of it; more trouble at court, she surmised.

Once inside Christiana helped the lady off with her cloak and poured her a goblet of wine. A crackling fire in the hearth soon warmed and relaxed the countess. Presently she spoke. "I should like to see my daughter and grandson. Enquire if the duchess is well enough to spend a little time with her mother."

Christiana found the duchess in her own chamber sitting beside a warm fire with Lady Tempest and two others, their tongues working as fast as their needles. Lady Anne seemed in good spirits as Christiana delivered her message. It was now over eighteen months since the duchess's miscarriage with no indication of any pregnancy since although rumour had it amongst the ladies of the bedchamber that relationships were fully restored between the lady and her husband.

Anne looked up from her work and smiled. "For certain, I will visit my mother. I have sat long enough beside the fire this day. Lady Tempest, ask Jane Collins to fetch Edward, if you please. Lady Catherine you can come with me, I would hear more of your brother's adventures in the Holy Lands. Tell me again, how did he..." Anne's voice trailed off as she left her chamber arm in arm with her companion, Lady Tempest bringing up the rear like a gaudily dressed galleon.

As ever when she had a little time to spare Christiana would look for John and if neither had duties to perform then a little leisure could be taken in one another's company. At thirteen years of age her son was progressing very well in his training towards knighthood. Despite her earlier misgivings she had to admit that John's future under the guidance of his father far exceeded anything she could ever have given him. It would be only a matter of a year or so before he would begin his training as a squire and that would inevitably mean leaving Middleham for another of his father's northern seats.

It was usual at this hour for the soldiers to be out on the drill field but a glance through the casement of Anne's chamber revealed a spring storm in the making. Iron-grey clouds were blowing across the sky releasing a steady downpour of rain and in the distance a rumble of thunder could be heard echoing across the dales.

Leaving the south wing – she would never cross the high wooden bridge to the keep unless given leave to do so – she stepped out into the cold wet courtyard. She wrapped her arms around her for warmth as she ran up the outer staircase of the keep. The usher at the desk in the antechamber did not so much as look up as she hurried through the great wooden door.

In the corner of the hall near the wooden partition and raised on a platform was a long oaken table where a jumble of parchments, quills and inkpots together with a locked silver-bound chest covered its gnarled surface. It was here that the duke carried out the business of his estates, receiving petitioners from all over his vast land.

None it seemed had petitions this day worthy enough to brave the elements for the hall was empty. The duke, however, was at his desk, slumped forwards with his head resting against his folded arms. Cautiously she approached the table, treading softly on the tiles. "My lord," she whispered. "Are you unwell?"

There was no reply so she moved a little closer. "Richard, 'tis I, Christiana." She spoke louder, more urgently. "Are you unwell?"

Slowly he lifted his head from his arms; his blue eyes, deeply pained, stared at her from an ashen face. "You are sick, my lord," she said and touched his arm.

"Aye," he whispered hoarsely, shrugging off her hand, "sick to my heart."

Christiana knew not what she should do but for certain she could not leave the duke in his present state. "Shall I fetch my Lady Anne?" she suggested. Richard shook his head and leaned back in the great chair. His eyes searched her face for a moment before he spoke. "My brother is dead."

"Brother, my lord?" she asked foolishly.

"Aye, my brother, Edward the king, is dead. Is there another?"

"Merciful Jesus," cried the woman and made the sign of the cross.

"I have just received word from Lord Hastings," continued the duke. "Edward died suddenly on the ninth day of this month. I can scarcely believe the truth of Hastings' words, but see, here is the letter bearing his seal." He waved a hand at the curled parchment before him on the desk and looked up at her, his lips trembling.

405

Christiana felt her own eyes fill with tears. She swallowed the hard lump that had risen in her throat. Her sorrow was not merely for Richard's loss but her own as well. Indeed, the whole of England must surely mourn the premature passing of King Edward.

After a while the duke composed himself. "There is much to be done," he muttered. "Where is Thomas Barowe?" He stood and walked towards the door leading to the antechamber, calling orders to the page to summon his secretary. Christiana turned slowly away, leaving the duke to do what had to be done.

Richard, Duke of Gloucester, and an armed company of men were set to leave Middleham by the afternoon of the next day. With the death of the king, still in his prime, and his son and heir a mere boy of twelve years, the duke could waste little time in reaching London where he would assume his appointed role as Protector of the Realm, a position his father had been forced to take during the unstable years of Henry the Sixth's rule. This matter of pressing urgency would not, however, stand in the way of Richard's duty as a devoted brother and his first desire was to call for a Requiem Mass at York Minster where prayers would be offered for Edward's departed soul.

On the cobbles of the inner bailey, under a warm April sun, soldiers had gathered, their horses restlessly tossing their heads. Others had come up from the bailey and now stood in a jostling line along the bridge ready to move at the duke's signal out through the gatehouse.

William, seeing a small gathering of women just visible within the confines of the inner courtyard, spurred his mount on around the waiting horses and crossed the bridge. The Duchess of Gloucester, holding the hand of her young son, was exchanging farewells with her husband. Christiana, a little apart from the other ladies, was staring forlornly at them and William, who had his own farewells to make, could nowise reach his sister without causing a disturbance amongst his fellow soldiers.

At length the duke mounted his steed and with nothing more than a brief glance Christiana's way led his men out of the castle under the stone arch. By the time William was in hailing distance of her his sister had turned slowly away to follow the ladies back across the yard towards their chambers. He spurred his horse into an angry prance on the cobblestones before passing under the gatehouse.

The weather remained fair and they made steady progress to reach the approach into Northampton early in the morning of the twenty-ninth day of April. Lodgings were procured on the outskirts of the town and the company rested to await the arrival of the young king according to plan.

The twelve-year-old boy was travelling east from his home in Ludlow on the Welsh Marches where he had been living under the guardianship of his maternal uncle, Anthony Woodville, Earl Rivers. Along with the Duke of Gloucester, travelling from the north, Henry Stafford, Duke of Buckingham, was riding from Brecon in the west. Northampton had been suggested by Earl Rivers as the most suitable rendezvous for them all to gather forces to escort the young king to London in preparation for his coronation.

Beyond the casements the morning light gathered strength and its rays penetrated the dim greyness within. William sat at a table in a corner of the hall throwing dice with three companions.

"I wish he would sit down. He unnerves me with his constant pacing," said one, letting the wooden dice fall with a sharp clatter onto the table's hard surface.

"Aye well, Tom," sighed another, "the duke has much to trouble him of late. You look to the game, lad, for that's another groat you owe me."

William eased back a little in his chair and watched as Richard walked up and down the flagstones, his brows dark and sombre, and his left hand clasping the hilt of the sword at his belt. Rob's words were true enough, he thought. Ever since the duke had received further word from Hastings in London his mind had been ill at ease. The Woodville clan were clearly taking advantage of the situation with blatant disregard for Duke Richard's position as Protector of the Realm. The queen was signing writs to force an early coronation of the king and she had seized a considerable portion of the royal treasury and concealed it within the walls of Westminster Palace.

A platter of bread, cheese, meat and ale was laid out on tables and the duke had finally sat to partake of these victuals when the door flung wide to admit a breathless soldier. At once Richard was on his feet to receive news from his scout. William watched as the soldier caught his breath sufficiently to give his report in a hushed whisper into the duke's ear.

When Richard turned back towards his men a dark shadow covered his face and his eyes were ablaze with resolve. He called his men-at-arms to him: William, Robert Harrington, Charles Pilkington and Tom Danyell, amongst others.

"Scouts report that Rivers and the king were still a way ahead of us ten miles north of Weedon where they should have turned off for Northampton. They have not yet arrived, so where are they and to what purpose did Rivers fail to keep our rendezvous?" The duke's voice, cold and hard, addressed each one of his loyal supporters with earnest.

"Furthermore," he continued, "every inn and lodging house in this town and beyond is full of Rivers' men. Where is he and where is the king?" Richard rubbed a hand across his brow, etched and lined with anxiety.

"The road south of here leads to Grafton Regis, and the Woodville manor. Keep off the road and see what you can find. Make haste for I suspect treachery is afoot. Buckingham should be here ere long and I need the full measure of the situation."

Thus briefed the small band of armed scouts left the town and took the road south. It was not long before the road skirted a densely wooded area and the sunlight dimmed. They rode through the trees, their horses' hooves snapping the twigs and fallen leaves along the way. As they neared the Woodville manor Harrington signalled for them to dismount and merge with the shadow of the trees. Two of their number were elected to remain behind with the horses while the remainder, William amongst them, continued on foot to search the area.

Before long they came upon what they were looking for: concealed under leaves and branches and close by to the roadside were four carts loaded with arms and armour all bearing Woodville devices.

"For certain someone expected the duke to pass this way unawares on the morrow," said Pilkington, covering up their find again.

"Aye," returned Harrington, "someone who takes Gloucester for a fool – leaving this lot unguarded."

Reining in on the cobbled yard of the inn sometime later the company of scouts witnessed the arrival of the Duke of Buckingham. The Duke of Gloucester was there to meet him.

"Cousin!" hailed the younger man upon seeing the Duke of Gloucester's worried countenance. "Is all well? I am not late am I?" he jested. "Is our king within?"

"That he is not, Henry," Richard declared, moving forward to take hold of his horse's rein. "Send your men into the town to find lodgings and you join me here."

Once inside the hall, Harrington's report of the consignment of hidden arms did not appear to take Richard by surprise.

"Anthony Woodville, Earl Rivers, preceded your arrival by minutes, Henry. Apparently he was forced to move the king on to Stony Stratford, south of here, where he waits for us," Richard announced with quiet sarcasm.

Buckingham smirked. "Why so?"

"'Tis through lack of suitable accommodation for the king here at Northampton."

Buckingham laughed outright. "Does he take you for a fool? His intentions are plain as day. Where is the man now?"

"Back at his lodgings, dressing in his finery no doubt, for I have invited him to sup with us tonight."

Forewarned of treachery it was no hardship for the duke to take evasive measures. At sunrise the following day, after a very congenial supper with the Dukes of Gloucester and Buckingham, the unsuspecting Earl Rivers found himself under arrest and at the mercy of the Lord Protector, whose authority he had failed to do away with.

The Duke of Gloucester and a company of men set out to circle Grafton Regis by way of Towcester intent upon riding straight for the Rose and Crown Inn at Stony Stratford. Meanwhile the Duke of Buckingham and his men rode through the unsuspecting ambush and relieved their would-be attackers of their contingency of weapons, joining Gloucester's forces at Stony Stratford by mid-afternoon.

It was plain by the look of astonishment on the faces of the richly attired men before him that the Duke of Gloucester was the last person they expected to see. Rounded up like errant sheep they faced Richard in the hall of the Rose and Crown: Earl Rivers' half-brother Richard Grey, the king's chamberlain Sir Thomas Vaughan and Sir Richard Haute together with a handful of the king's personal attendants.

Standing close by the door to guard its way William watched with interest as Duke Richard paced the flagstones, his hand steadying the hilt of his sword and a look of anger in his dark eyes.

"Your coup has failed, Grey!" he snapped as he ceased his pacing and stood before Earl Rivers' brother. "Did you take me for such a fool that I would not discover your true intention?"

Richard Grey's face paled and exchanging a quick glance with Thomas Vaughan he stammered, "My Lord Gloucester, we are pleased indeed to see that you have arrived in safety. My brother took the road north at first light to meet you."

"I do not doubt it," the duke retorted.

"My lord." The elderly Thomas Vaughan, his thin fingers clasped in front of his finely woven tunic, stepped forward. "At my recommendation the Earl Rivers secured these lodgings for the king." He gestured around him with a bony hand.

"The boy was weary of travelling and in need of a comfortable bed as befitting his birth. The earl was on his way to inform you of the change of plan." Vaughan bowed his head politely and waited to see how Gloucester would receive this explanation.

The duke was not to be deceived and merely sneered at the

old man. "It was Anthony Woodville himself who put forward Northampton as a rendezvous. Easy then to have the king and his entourage hold up here while an ambush was set for me at Grafton Regis. You never intended for the Lord Protector to ever reach London did you?" Richard glared coldly from one man to the next, his eyes coming to rest upon the person of Richard Grey, whose lips had parted ready to utter a protest. "Save your words for your trial, Grey, for I have the evidence against you – four cartloads of weapons concealed under trees along the roadside at Elizabeth Woodville's manor."

Gloucester snapped his fingers and William steadied the long shaft of the bill in his hand, holding it across the doorway as several armed retainers rushed forward to take by force Richard Grey and every member of the king's household there present.

The young King Edward, fifth to bear that name after his father, was summoned before his Uncle Richard in the now almost deserted hall. Dressed in black and gold tunic with matching leggings, a head of rumpled golden curls and with the thin gangly legs of youth, the boy held himself with much dignity before the scrutiny of the deep blue eyes of his uncle. All of his young life had been spent under the protection and guidance of his mother's kin. He knew little of his father's younger brother with his dark brows and solemn features.

The boy king demanded at once to know the cause of his uncle's outrageous behaviour towards his protectors. It was William's belief that Edward knew nothing of Rivers' failed coup as he watched the boy's pale bewildered face as the discovery of the plot was laid before him.

"Your father was most unwise to place you in the hands of your mother's kin for they are a treacherous and scheming lot," Richard was saying quietly.

"I will not believe such accusations against my Uncle Anthony," the boy returned in a small high-pitched voice.

"Believe it or not as you wish," Gloucester continued, "but the evidence is there; proof of a plot against the life of the Lord Protector." The boy looked down at his feet and shook his head sadly.

"As king you will have much to learn of the treachery of men," Richard said, staring down at his nephew's blond head.

Edward took a deep breath and lifting his head he stared into the eyes of his uncle with tearful defiance. "There is nothing treacherous about Earl Rivers and if my father the king saw fit to trust his loyalty then so do I."

Despite his brave words the child's legs began to shake and Richard called for wine and bade him be seated. As he drank the rich red liquid the young king pondered his fate. He had a suspicion that his mother the queen had never been popular with England's more aristocratic nobility, but he doubted she would stoop to conspiracy. He knew also of his father's desire that his brother, Gloucester, be made sole Protector in the event of his minority rule. He was sorely vexed to find himself in such a dilemma. He rubbed a hand across his jaw; it was paining him much as it often did when he felt troubled. He wished for the advice of his dearest friend and tutor, Thomas Vaughan, but he was allowed no such counsel.

Eventually, feeling as though he had been left with no choice, Edward surrendered himself to the protection of his Uncle Richard and watched sadly as his maternal uncle Rivers, Richard Grey, Thomas Vaughan and Richard Haute were led off, bound for incarceration in Gloucester's northern strongholds.

"Sir Richard, I am most pleased to see you for we have had no news since my husband left for London in April." Anne extended her slender hand to the noble man standing before her.

"The little news I bear, my lady, I fear is not good," Sir Richard Ratcliffe replied solemnly.

The Duchess of Gloucester seated herself on a plush cushioned chair positioned discreetly in a far corner of the great hall and indicated a second for her guest after she had summoned a page to serve wine.

"I have under armed escort Sir Richard Grey, son of Queen Elizabeth. He is to remain here under guard awaiting instruction from the duke," Ratcliffe whispered now that they were far enough removed from wagging ears.

Anne's pale complexion paled further but she sat in silence waiting for the knight to continue with his report. "Sir Anthony Woodville and others are also incarcerated here in the north following discovery of a plot against the person of the Protector of the Realm."

The duchess knew her husband had been appointed this role by the late king and it seemed that Richard's worse fears of a Woodville bid for power were being realised.

"Lady, I would not wish to panic you," Ratcliffe continued. "When I left the duke he was preparing to escort the young king to London. Once there I am sure he will have matters under his control with all speed."

Anne nodded her fair head and smiled weakly.

"I am to remain here, my lady, and when you have prepared I am to take you to London in time for the coronation of the king set for the twenty-second day of June. I have here a letter from your husband in which he hopes to reassure you and earnestly seeks the pleasure of your company."

He took a rolled parchment bound with the seal of the Duke of Gloucester from inside his cloak and handed it to her.

Anne moved to the wall of the great hall where a beam of sunlight from the huge windows struck the coloured mosaic tiles on the floor and afforded more light by which to read. After a few moments the duchess looked up and her eyes met those of the knight's in mutual understanding; a power struggle of great magnitude had begun which could have far-reaching consequences for them all.

"And now, good sir, I forget myself," Anne said, summoning a level of cheeriness. "Pray rest here awhile and I will go see a chamber is prepared and food is brought for you and your men."

Ratcliffe stood and bowed as the duchess gathered her gown and swept gracefully from the hall. He sat and stretched his legs, closing his eyes wearily.

A few moments later and the quick patter of a child's footsteps across the floor drew the attention of the knight. A small fair-haired boy of nine years, cheeks flushed from running, was bounding across the hall to stop abruptly before the figure reposing in the chair.

"Oh!" spluttered Edward. "I thought you were my father come home." The child stood uncertainly, his face turning a deeper scarlet. "I... I saw his horse in the stable yard."

Sir Richard leaned forward in his chair to face the boy. "Ha ha, young sir," he chuckled. "That would be Grey Lady, my old mare. She does resemble White Surrey now you come to mention it but I will wager she is faster."

"Never!" declared the boy with fervour.

Ratcliffe stood to his feet laughing gently as the duchess entered the room followed by a young page. "Sir Richard, a room has been prepared for you and your men in the west range. The kitchen servants will send food to you and if you require anything further see Colin here." The young page inclined his head respectfully. Sir

Richard took Anne's hand and planted a kiss upon it. "You are most kind, my lady," he said and followed the page out of the hall.

The duchess knelt down before her son and taking both his little hands in hers she smiled into his small round face. "We are to make ready for a long journey. There is much to do and prepare."

"Where are we going, Mother?" the boy asked excitedly.

"To London, Edward; to your father," Anne smiled broadly. "Now run along and find Lady Jane and send her to me in my chamber."

Anne waited until her son had disappeared from sight before turning to the small group of ladies sitting silently, working their needles, embroidering a new altar cloth for the chapel.

"A word, Christiana," Anne commanded, walking a few steps to the side of the hall, a discreet distance from the others and to where her servant followed.

"You are to prepare a chest of the most commonly needed herbal remedies to take with us on our journey to London for the crowning of our young King Edward. You will need to make yourself ready for I shall require you in attendance." The duchess spoke softly before leaving the hall and entering her husband's privy chamber.

Christiana walked slowly down the outer staircase and into the sunshine caressing the bailey with its warmth, her head whirling with thoughts. It seemed such a long and dangerous journey to be going to London, although William had been there many times. Indeed, her brother would be there now in attendance upon the duke. As she began to imagine all the great places William spoke of – the royal palace, the magnificent Abbey of Saint Peter and the wide flowing River Thames with its multitude of trading ships – she began to feel a surge of excitement; it would be a momentous occasion – London at the coronation of a king.

When all was ready for departure a few days later young Edward suddenly took ill and his physician advised against his making such a long journey. John of Gloucester was also to remain behind with his half-brother; the duchess saw no reason why he should go to London as the duke had not made any mention of his bastard son in his correspondence to her.

It was with a feeling of excitement and not a touch of sadness to be leaving her son behind that Christiana sat astride her chestnut palfrey and knew the castle to be shrinking ever smaller behind her as she rode away across land unknown and a future uncertain.

Baynard's Castle
London
9ᵗʰ June 1483

The Lady Anne stood by the glazed window in the solar of Baynard's Castle, the riverfront home of her mother-in-law, Cecily Neville. Low evening sunlight burning through the panes of glass picked up its green hue and cast it over the lady's face and soft lambswool gown. The sweet smell of lavender and rosewater clung to her skin and her golden hair, still damp from bathing, hung loosely down her back. Lady Alice Skelton and Dame Anne Tempest sat quietly in the shadows, working the coloured thread of a tapestry, the gentle clonk-clonk of the wooden loom breaking the silence.

Christiana made a perfunctory bow at the door before walking over to a small table in the corner of the room. Taking up a pewter goblet she poured a goodly dose of thyme and rosemary infusion from the flagon she carried with her.

"My Lady, here is a tonic. It will calm you," she announced, offering it to Anne. "The journey has wearied you but this will give you strength."

The Duchess of Gloucester sipped her drink and attempted a smile. Sitting on a cushioned chair she allowed her herbalist to rub oil of heartsease and lavender into her forehead and temples. She relaxed visibly as the soothing aroma took effect.

"'Twas a great pity our little Edward could not make the journey to be with his father. Do you think he will soon be well?" she asked, her eyes closed.

"His physician said it was just a summer chill and would soon pass," Christiana replied as reassuringly as she could.

"Mayhap you are right. But I do worry sometimes about the boy, he seems so weak and sickly somehow."

Anne sighed and opened her eyes as Christiana replaced the

stopper in the jar of oil. "I fear he would find London overpowering at this time, the noise and great crowds of people," the duchess continued.

"Indeed, my lady. The streets are bursting with all manner of folk eager to see the young king crowned. It will be a joyous occasion."

Anne sighed deeply and began to fret with the great opal ring on her finger. "I have been out onto the streets of London," she remarked pensively. "And I heed no rejoicing, only fear and anxiety. The people do not want a boy king, Christiana, and even less do they want to be ruled by the queen mother and her kin, as indeed they would if my husband's power as Protector were to be snatched from him."

An impatient tut-tutting came from a figure near the wall and the swishing of pearly tartarin preceded the ample figure of Dame Anne as she left her loom and approached the duchess. "It serves no purpose to worry about such matters, my lady," she admonished. "Our good duke has matters well under control I am sure. You are tired and must rest now. I shall send Master Joseph to summon Agnes."

With that Christiana was wafted towards the door by the lady's flowing skirts as she beckoned the usher, who was loitering beyond the doorway, to summon the duchess's chambermaid.

Making her way along a narrow passageway leading to the herbarium in the cellars of the palace where she shared a bed with the other servants, Christiana felt ill at ease. Once again Dame Tempest made certain that she knew her status. A woman of low birth, she had, however, been given a position of some importance as attendant to the ageing Countess of Warwick. That had been at Middleham and now in London it seemed that her status was once again to plummet.

Duchess Anne's words had also kindled her own feelings of apprehension. No one wanted to see days of violence and unrest that many knew from bitter experience could precede the coronation of a boy king.

It was still oppressively warm inside the solar despite the retreating rays of the sun. The Lady Anne sat perfectly still as her maid, Agnes, drew a bone-handled comb through her hair and with nimble fingers worked a braid which grew in length down the lady's back.

"Shall I prepare your bed, my lady?" the older woman asked, stepping back to admire her handiwork.

"Thank you, Agnes, yes, but I have a mind to await my husband's return before I retire."

"But, my lady, the duke may not return for several hours yet, and you do look so weary; maybe you should rest awhile," Agnes suggested hesitantly for she was not long in the duchess's service and knew not her humours well enough to be as yet too bold.

"I am well enough, Agnes," Anne replied patiently. "See to my bed and bring me some wine and then you may leave." Agnes curtsied without further words and withdrew to her lady's bedchamber.

Alone, Anne acknowledged to herself that she did indeed feel weary. The journey from Yorkshire had tired her more than she imagined for she had been in London now for four days and not yet recovered her strength.

She found herself thinking of her herbalist Christiana and with some little annoyance began to marvel at her good health and vigour. How was it that her hair was still as black as the raven and her cheeks always held a rosy bloom? There was always a sweet-smelling perfume about her too, the inescapable aroma of her labour.

She crossed the room to the casement and tried the metal handle, and giving it a forceful push it flung open. At once, a rush of cool air from below hit her full in the face, its sharpness almost intoxicating, carrying upon it the damp, dank smell of the river.

Leaning her elbows on the stonework she looked out below. A pale moon had risen, showering the water with dancing moon drops. After the hustle and bustle of the day all was now strangely quiet and still. A lone oarsman rowed his way upriver towards a small jetty, his lantern swinging precariously on its pole.

Anne's mood suddenly turned melancholic and she sighed pensively. She felt annoyance at the way Dame Tempest seemed to go out of her way to keep any news from her. She resented being treated as a child, or worse, a woman too fragile to know the truth.

Her thoughts turned to her husband. After eleven years of marriage to Richard she still knew him not. She was unable to penetrate that outer shell, those dark eyes always guarding his deepest thoughts and feelings. There was one person, however, she knew to be privy to those thoughts, one woman to whom he went when he had need to share the troubles of his heart. Even though she did not truly believe that Christiana shared his bed she knew the herbalist had captured his heart and it was that knowledge that hurt her most. For that very reason she also felt so wretched that she had failed to give her husband the one thing he longed for: more sons.

Her placid nature tempered her jealousy, however, for she felt she had much to thank God for. Richard was a good, caring husband, despite everything. She also had to concede, though be it grudgingly, that she held certain affections for Christiana. There was strength in the woman that she admired, notwithstanding her skill as a herbalist. Anne shared her father's mistrust of physicians with their lethal and often fatal attempts to cure the sick.

A smile spread across her pale lips as she recalled to mind an incident that had occurred on their journey south. The duchess, in common with all ladies of noble birth, rode side-saddle, or was borne along by litter. She had, however, noticed that Christiana rode her chestnut mare astride, like a man, despite her cumbersome skirts. Anne marvelled that any woman could ride thus such a great distance without undergarments, the female hose designed to be gartered at the knee. Unable to contain her curiosity any longer, the duchess had found an opportunity to speak to Christiana one day as they stopped near a stream to water their horses. Christiana had explained that she had been riding horses since she could walk and riding astride like a man was how her father had taught her. Then she did something that caused the duchess to gasp in amazement and turn her cheeks a deep shade of red; Christiana lifted her skirts to reveal legs encased in a pair of loosely fitted frayed hose, complete with braies. "I borrowed them from William," she had said quite matter-of-factly.

The sudden banging shut of the solar door jolted the duchess from her daydreaming. Turning from the window, she was startled to see her husband, still wearing his outdoor boots and a cape, storm into the room followed closely by their cousin Henry of Buckingham.

"My lord, is there something amiss?" she asked.

For a brief moment Richard's dark eyes met hers and their gaze locked. His face was pale and tired and he forced a smile. "Nay, my love, 'tis matters of state, nothing to concern yourself with," he replied wearily.

"But, Richard," she began fervently, suppressing a quiver of anger, "I am your wife. Surely you can share your burdens with me?" She reached out a thin hand to touch his cape.

"A beautiful wife who should not concern herself with the affairs of men." Henry Stafford stood beside her, smiling, his pale blue eyes at once both patronising and flirtatious.

Anne stood silently before the men, glancing from one to the other. After a while she said quietly, "Then I will bid you a goodnight, my lord husband." With the briefest nod of her head towards Buckingham she withdrew to her chamber beyond the heavy tapestry drapes.

Richard flung his cape on a coffer, not waiting for his servant to assist him, and kicked off his boots. "I will not believe this of Hastings, Henry. Are you certain your sources are true?"

"Completely trustworthy, cousin," replied Buckingham, removing his own cape and walking over to the table where he poured out two goblets of wine. "It is but a fragment found concealed within the pages of a merchant's book but evidence enough to implicate Hastings in a conspiracy to do away with the Duke of Gloucester. And then there is the matter of the unearthing of a plot not two days ago implicating Hastings, Morton, Stanley and Thomas Rotherham, Archbishop of York, of all people. A plot to take matters into their own hands and effectively strip you of the Protectorship."

"Yes, yes, you have said enough already." Richard took the goblet of wine offered to him by his kinsman and drained it before slumping down on the nearest coffer. "My Lord Hastings has been a loyal and steadfast supporter of this family for..."

"Come, come, Richard. Loyalties are fickle – you know that. Men adhere to any while there is much to gain." Buckingham sipped his wine slowly.

Richard ran his fingers through his uncovered hair. "Hastings gave me his support against the queen—"

"And what of the queen?" Buckingham interrupted. "Fleeing into sanctuary with her children once the coup to overturn your authority had failed. And then there is the matter of the royal fleet taken to sea under the command of Edward Woodville with half the treasury on board. I think there is more than witchcraft afoot here, cousin."

"Witchcraft?" Richard queried, rubbing his temples.

"Aye. Surely you know of the stories concerning Elizabeth Woodville and her mother Jacquetta of Luxembourg?" Henry Stafford replied incredulously. "Your brother's court was awash with such nonsense. You have been away too long in the north, my friend."

Beyond the tapestry drapes to the privy chamber the Duchess of Gloucester listened. She had heard of such things for had not her sister Isabel been convinced that Elizabeth Woodville had used black magic to bring about the downfall and death of her husband George?

She sighed wearily and approached the high wooden bed. And so it begins again, she thought as she covered herself with the cool linen sheet, Agnes having withdrawn from the chamber through an archway that led to the servants' quarters. With her head on the soft down pillow Anne drifted into an exhausted sleep.

"Consider this too, cousin," Henry continued. "Even if your Protectorship keeps the peace for now, and that I doubt, it will all come to an end when Edward is of an age to rule freely. What do you suppose will become of you and I then and all others of the true blood royal?

"You saw the way the boy balked at your authority at Stony Stratford. He mistrusts you and who can blame him seeing how he has been cosseted by his mother's kin all his life. Can you honestly expect that woman to keep her distance and allow her son to reign unfettered by Woodville influence? It would be most prudent, my lord, if you were to write to your supporters in the north to send armed forces south post-haste," Buckingham continued solemnly.

Richard sat on the coffer holding the empty wine goblet in his hand. A sudden wave of nausea swept over him and his arm felt weak. The goblet fell from his hand and he would have fallen from the coffer had Buckingham not steadied him. Seeing his pale cheeks and the beads of sweat forming on Richard's brow Henry was at the door at once calling for a physician.

It was not, however, a black-garbed man who answered the summons but a young woman holding in her hands a leather costrel. She bowed to the duke.

"Where is the physician?" Buckingham demanded.

"There is none, my lord. It will take time to fetch one for it is nightfall. I am in attendance upon the Duchess of Gloucester as herbalist to the duke's household. I have here a tonic and lavender water."

Buckingham regarded her through slanted eyes for a moment or two before giving his consent. "Yes, yes, be about your business and make haste."

Christiana approached Richard who by now was made more comfortable on a chair with velvet cushions. He lifted his head as she approached. Removing the stopper from the costrel she held it to Richard's lips. After he had drunk, she knelt down on the floor before him. Taking a portion of butter cloth soaked in lavender water from her bag she began to wipe his brow and cheeks, all the while uttering not a word.

She was almost finished and noting that Buckingham had moved to the table to pour himself another goblet of wine Christiana took from her belt a linen pouch containing vervain and leaves of angelica. She quickly pressed it into Richard's hand. "For protection," she whispered and smiled as his eyes met hers.

"How did you come about this wound, William?" Christiana asked the question of her brother as she dabbed the raw edges of a knife wound in his right arm with rosewater and honey.

"I have told you," he replied, wincing. "Out on the streets; a scuffle involving a mob of peasants, nothing more."

Satisfied that the wound was clean, Christiana searched the unfamiliar rows of herbal preparations for a jar of walnut ointment, saying, "You were escorting the Duke of Gloucester through London this day. Did the scuffle involve him?"

Opening and closing several drawers to no avail she finally found some strips of linen bandage up on a high shelf. When she turned back to face William there was a patient smile of indulgence on his face. "You never stop worrying about him do you? And there was I thinking you were concerned for me." He laughed good-humouredly but Christiana ignored his teasing.

"Well?" she demanded.

William shifted uncomfortably on the stool as the cold walnut paste stung his open wound. "Actually, yes; it was all to do with the duke. I think he had a mind to go out amongst the folk of London and sound them out for support. This day for some reason he chose to throw off his mourning cloth and went abroad wearing purple of all colours. Now if that is not certain to upset folk nothing will," he added wryly.

"There is rumour that Richard intends to take the crown for himself. What say you to that?" Christiana asked, winding the strips of cloth around William's arm.

"I say that you are making that too tight," William rebuked with a smile. "I will need to move my arm you know." Christiana grinned apologetically.

"It looks that way for certain," William continued. "I too have heard the rumours. I would wager the young Duke of Buckingham is as much behind Richard's bid for the throne as any. He has stuck to Gloucester like a leech since they met at Northampton and there are more meetings behind closed doors than you can imagine."

Christiana paused in her winding. "It has not been easy for Richard. The queen only released the young Duke of York yesterday from Saint Peter's to join his brother in the White Tower. Elizabeth Woodville has not exactly given her support to the Protector in all this. 'Tis little wonder that Richard has not been himself of late."

"How so?" William asked but his question went unanswered as a maidservant entered the herbarium and spent several moments clinking amongst the earthenware jars on a wide shelf until she finally found what she was looking for.

"What have you there?" Christiana called, as the girl was about to leave.

"'Tis oil of lavender, Mistress," she replied holding out the jar. "Lady Manleverer has a headache."

"Be sure to return the jar," Christiana advised as the servant departed.

"It seems most remiss that a servant can just walk in here and help herself to the potions," Christiana grumbled as she secured the ends of William's bandage before sitting down on the stool beside her brother and sighing deeply.

"Richard has hardly eaten or drunk anything these past days and sleeps very little according to his servants. I am afeared for him, Will. Do you think his life to be in danger?"

William looked intently at his sister for several moments before he replied. "A conspiracy against the duke was unearthed. It involved William, Lord Hastings, Thomas, Lord Stanley and some bishop by the name of John Morton."

"'Tis the beheading of Lord Hastings without trial that has angered many. He was much respected, not least for his loyalty to King Edward. This much I do know," Christiana replied.

"The duke had good reason to suspect all those involved.

Buckingham presented the evidence; it was indisputable. Hastings had a fair trial and his guilt was determined much to the regret of the Duke of Gloucester."

"And yet Lord Stanley is still at liberty is he not?"

"Aye, let us hope that Richard does not live to regret that decision."

"Richard must have been fearful of treachery for I have heard that he has sent Sir Ratcliffe back north, less than a week after his arrival in London, to summon his supporters south," Christiana muttered.

"Aye and then you will not be able to move in London without clashing with soldiers wearing the livery of the white boar. Our duke is certainly effective and efficient in all he does. No one else would be able to quell a Woodville uprising."

William touched his sister's sleeve and smiled as her dark eyes regarded him sadly. "Do not over worry for Richard, Christiana," he said gently.

He stood to his feet and walked towards the door but paused and turned to face his sister once again. "I was down at Saint Paul's two days ago and witnessed the public penance of Jane Shore, one-time mistress of King Edward and Lord Hastings among others. She was made to parade barefoot along sharp flint stones before a cross and carrying a lighted taper. She cut a sorry figure wearing nothing but her under kirtle before being thrown into prison."

William hesitated before continuing, "It is rumoured that Mistress Shore had some part in this conspiracy and Richard always takes the moral high ground in these matters." He sighed and took a step towards his sister. "Have a care with your conduct, Christiana. You are here in attendance upon the duchess but everyone will know you to be the duke's mistress. The royal court is a hotbed of gossip." William did not wait for a response to his words of advice but walked from the room, leaving his sister to her work.

A day or so later the Duke of Gloucester was seated on a high-backed chair in the great hall of his mother's home. He still could not shake off this lethargy and his head ached from lack of sleep.

He fingered the linen amulet tied to his belt and thought about Christiana. Did she also suspect witchcraft to be responsible for his present indisposition as he himself certainly did?

He looked up as an usher entered the hall. It would appear that Robert Stillington, Bishop of Bath and Wells, was in the antechamber and sought an audience with the Lord Protector.

When the elderly sallow-cheeked man entered with his billowing gown and black hat Henry Stafford, Duke of Buckingham, was behind him.

The bishop bowed low and walked stiffly over to where the duke had risen from his seat to greet him.

"My lord," the bishop began, declining an offer of wine from Henry Stafford.

"These are indeed troubled times. There is much rumour and hearsay on the streets of London. You have heard, no doubt, talk of your brother Edward's marriage to Elizabeth Woodville and the validity of it?" The man hesitated, waiting it seemed for a response from the Duke of Gloucester.

Richard, however, made no such comment but sat on his chair with legs outstretched before him and waited for the bishop to continue.

"My conscience compels me to speak of what I know," Stillington continued.

"There existed a pre-marital contract between Edward and Lady Eleanor Talbot, daughter of the Earl of Shrewsbury."

Richard's attention was now fully on the man before him. He had heard the rumours but surely that was all it was: rumour.

"How can you be certain of this contract?" Richard asked gravely.

"Because, my lord, I was witness to it."

Richard raised a brow. "Indeed, and where is this contract now?"

"It is no longer in my possession, my lord." The bishop looked awkward and fingered the rosary on his belt. "I served your brother well. I was Lord Chancellor twice and... I did what I thought best at the time. I cannot produce the contract and neither can I the lady for she is dead. My lord, you only have my solemn word."

Stillington hung his head and waited. Moments passed; it seemed the Lord Protector was weighing this information in his mind.

It was Buckingham who stepped forward, thanked the man for his confession and escorted him to the door.

"By God, Richard, you know what this means!" Buckingham exclaimed, pouring two goodly measures of wine and handing one to Gloucester. "With an invalid marriage to Elizabeth Woodville, all of Edward's children are bastards. Young Edward is barred from taking the throne."

Henry Stafford's eyes glinted. "Now we put an end to this scheming and upstarting. We have nothing less than a vacant throne and only one deemed worthy to take it."

Richard looked up quickly into the face of the man before him. None could say that Buckingham lacked ambition. Could he be certain of the meaning of his words?

"Can we trust the word of this bishop? My brother was married to Elizabeth Woodville for nigh on twenty years; she bore him nine children," Richard asked cautiously.

"This is no time for sentiment, cousin. If the church recognises a previous troth-plight who are we to argue? Besides, why should the man lie? Was this bishop not arrested once and imprisoned for some trivial misdemeanour? Mayhap his conscience got the better of him that day too and Edward had to silence him."

Richard sipped his wine. He had much to think and ponder upon.

The following day the Duchess of Gloucester joined her husband in the privy chamber of the solar to break their fast. Richard sat darkly morose and uttered no word. Anne, not a little concerned for her husband's troubles, remained silent also, stabbing at the meat on her plate with her knife but eating little.

Presently a young groom entered the chamber and bowed nervously to the duke.

"I have an urgent message, my lord, from Duchess Cecily. She requests that you meet with her at once, and alone, in her privy chamber."

Richard exchanged a baffled frown with his wife after the boy had left them. Dame Cecily had had the briefest of encounters with her son and daughter-in-law since their arrival at her castle. In mourning for her eldest son, the king, she had withdrawn to the solitude of her chambers and there remained.

The duke was greeted warmly by his mother. The elderly lady took him in her arms and with all her frail strength she embraced him. Her dark eyes were brimming with tears as she released her hold of him; her only remaining son and of them all, her dearest child, always loyal, always loving, ever pious and faithful.

"Richard," she said, dabbing at her eyes with palsied fingers. "How like your dear father you are." She sat down on a high-backed cushioned chair and beckoned her son to the one beside her. For several moments the lady seemed preoccupied with the folds of her black velvet gown, smoothing and tugging intently. The duke waited patiently, wondering greatly to what purpose he had been summoned.

"I leave for Berkhamsted on the morrow and before I go there is a matter of the gravest importance of which I must speak," Cecily said at last. "I do not say much, my son, but I hear a great deal. I should have spoken out on this matter when George..." Her voice faltered.

Richard's forehead creased in a frown at the mention of his brother's name. His mother took the long sleeves of her gown and began dabbing at her eyes once again. She reached out for Richard's hand and encased it tightly between her own, with fingers grey and thin and devoid of any jewel.

"You are in the gravest danger, Richard," she whispered urgently. "You do not need me to tell you how much of a threat the Woodvilles will be to you once they have young Edward in their grasp."

Richard looked up at his mother's troubled face. It would be as well for her to return to the convent and far away from all this political upheaval. "Do not worry for me, Mother," he began reassuringly. "I know the situation."

"You do not know, my son," she interrupted harshly. "Edward

must never be crowned King of England nor must any of his siblings."

Richard bit on his lower lip. So, his mother was also aware of Bishop Stillington's confession of a pre-marital contract and her own sense of piety had led her to acknowledge her son's wrongdoing.

"I have a grave confession to make, dearest son," Cecily continued, squeezing Richard's hand a little harder. "I have made this confession to my priest and have received due penance and now I must speak of it to you. Edward, my son, was not your father's son. Any rumour you may have heard is truth. His father and yours are not one.

"To my utter shame he was sired by an archer of the garrison at Rouen. I shall spare you the details. Edward should never have been king – his son should never become king. George knew of this shameful secret and so Elizabeth Woodville persuaded Edward to put him to death."

The lady's tears flowed unchecked. "Richard, you must take the throne. You are the only one with enough authority to break the power of the Woodvilles. The realm cannot have a boy king, therefore George's son can be ruled out. For the sake of the Plantagenet dynasty, it must be you. If you do not then you will go the way of our George and there will be another bastard on England's throne."

The Duke of Gloucester sat in stunned silence. His heart was pounding; sweat was breaking out in sharp tingles on his forehead and the palms of his hands. He had no reason whatever to doubt his mother's words.

Cecily continued, "I have been through this once before with your father. He felt compelled to seize the throne from poor, insane Henry who had no kingly qualities and stood to rule all England through his wife Margaret of Anjou. You stand now where your father stood many years ago as Protector of the Realm and the same path lies before you, Richard... you must embrace it. If you do not then your father and brother Edmund gave their lives for nothing."

This knowledge certainly gave him a greater reason to consider the throne for himself. He was a soldier not a king; but surely a king should also be a warrior? Stillington's accusation was now of little consequence although that would be the one he would stand by for the sake of his mother's reputation.

He stood to his feet to face his mother who was on her feet and fully composed now that the burden of her confession had been lifted. "I have said what my conscience compelled me to, Richard. Now you must do what is in your heart to do. I will leave the world and England to the mercy of God."

As the duke bowed before his mother she caught the sleeve of his tunic and whispered, "Be very careful whom you trust, my son. Those closest to you may yet prove the most treacherous. Your brother made a most unwise choice in marrying a Woodville and that will have far-reaching consequences for you, Richard. God be with you, my beloved child."

With a heart as heavy as lead Richard turned and walked from his mother's chamber.

Baynard's Castle
London
26ᵗʰ June 1483

Many people, including the Duchess of Gloucester and her attendants, had poured into the great hall at Baynard's Castle to witness the purpose of the sudden arrival of so many notable dignitaries.

Christiana, having heard of their coming, had slipped surreptitiously from the herbarium and now stood amongst those gathered, watching and waiting. She recognised at once the person of Sir Edmund Shaa, Lord Mayor of London, seen on several occasions at the castle, at the head of many of the city's leading figures. It was quite a gathering of lords and nobles including bishops and clerics, all regally attired in their cloth of office.

The Duke of Gloucester had been summoned to the great hall and now sat patiently before them in a high-backed chair of polished oak. A stream of expectation flowed in muted whispers from head to head as many of those present sensed this to be a seal upon the events of the past few days.

On the twenty-second day of June an eminent doctor of theology from Cambridge by the name of Ralph Shaw had given a public sermon from Saint Paul's Cross wherein he put forth Richard, Duke of Gloucester's rightful claim to the English throne. Two days later Henry Stafford, Duke of Buckingham, in a speech to the Mayor and Aldermen of London, reiterated Richard's claim and further endorsed it the following day to an assembly of noble lords. Buckingham pressed upon them the corrupt nature of the Woodville influence, the immoral lives of Edward's courtiers, the pre-marital contract that invalidated his marriage, all of which he seasoned with a good measure of the common knowledge of Woodville witchcraft and sorcery. In contrast to this was Richard, Duke of Gloucester, whose character was impeccable, loyalty unshakeable, birth and lineage unquestionable.

A great hush now fell upon the gathering; all eyes were upon the Duke of Buckingham as he stepped forward and held out to Richard of Gloucester a rolled parchment of much length and breadth. In eloquent tones that rang around the hall Henry Stafford read out the Bill of Petition, with its many signatures, confirming Richard's entitlement to the throne of England and formally requesting him to accept the title of King.

Christiana held her breath and felt her heart tremble in the brief moment of absolute silence that followed Buckingham's oration. She could scarcely believe her ears when Richard, Duke of Gloucester, powerful northern magnate, Protector of the Realm and her childhood friend, accepted the grace bestowed upon him.

The king, as he now was, left the great hall amidst a tumult of rejoicing and was ceremoniously escorted to Westminster Palace for the presentation of royal robes and sceptre and there to take possession of the marble chair reserved solely for a king.

Meanwhile at Baynard's Castle Christiana was about to return to her work, wondering once again where all this would lead, when Dame Tempest appeared like a spectre at her side.

"The Duchess of Gloucester requires a remedy for a lady attendant; she has, it would seem, a summer chill. See to it at once," she ordered before hurrying off. There were some things that were bound never to change, Christiana thought tetchily as she made her way slowly to the herbarium.

She was surprised to see William seated on a stool when she arrived, until she remembered that his wound still required attention. He was, however, being adequately attended to by one of Cecily Neville's maidservants. Ignoring Christiana's presence as she clattered and banged amongst the jars and bottles on the table, William commented upon the girl's gentle touch and warm fingers.

Finally Christiana stood before William, throwing him a disapproving stare, and slightly flushed she snapped at the young woman, "When you have finished with that arm – you do not need to use the whole roll of bandage – I need a heartsease and lemon balm tisane, laced with honey." Blushing, curtsying and almost tripping over William's boot the girl disappeared into the room beyond the stone archway.

"You are bad-tempered this morning, Christiana," William teased. "Could it be that you do not approve of our new king?"

Christiana did not think that Richard's usurpation of the throne, for that was how some would view it, to be a matter for jest. "I hope he knows what he is doing," she whispered earnestly.

"Of course he knows," William chuckled. "He will make a right good king and judging by the cheering crowd on the way to Westminster just now so do a great many other folk."

Christiana was not altogether convinced and stood wiping some brown powder from the table with the side of her hand.

"Just think of it, Christiana," William continued undeterred. "We shall be here in London for the coronation of a king; the celebrations, the dancing, the feasting."

"I should not think there will be a place for a herbalist at the coronation table," Christiana lamented. However, a few days later and her fortunes took a turn for the better.

Christiana was summoned before the woman who would soon be crowned Queen of England. Anne received her reverence and greeted her with a smile, beckoning her over to a window seat.

"There is someone arrived from the north that I think you will be pleased to see," Anne whispered. "She has come here under the protection of the northern men-at-arms summoned by the duke, or I should now say king."

Anne stood to her feet and gestured to a woman sitting amongst the knot of ladies at the far end of the chamber.

"Margaret!"

At the sight of Anne's sister leaving her companions and stepping forward, her smile natural and agreeable and her eyes sparkling blue as periwinkles, Christiana could not conceal her joy, releasing a wide sunlit smile across her face.

"My sister has need of a lady-in-waiting for hers is indisposed," Anne continued with a smile. "She has requested you, Christiana. Now that I am queen there will be no shortage of attendants and there are sufficient herbalists, apothecaries and physicians in the royal palace so I am certain that you can be spared."

Christiana's joy deepened as she made a low reverence to the queen.

"We are to make preparation to leave here for Westminster Palace in a day or two. Our coronation is set for Sunday the sixth day of July." Anne paused, her cheeks blooming red like the rose and she breathed a heavy sigh. Christiana reached out a hand and dared to touch the fingers of a queen with a gentle caress of reassurance. Anne smiled.

Within days the Great Wardrobe had moved with military precision from Baynard's Castle to Westminster Palace.

The royal residence, despite its sumptuous wall hangings, tiled floors and lavishly carved furniture, had all the air of a custodial dwelling with corridors long and cold where footsteps echoed and whispers flew like night owls.

Christiana's apprehension, growing daily at the prospect of working within unfamiliar surroundings presided over by pompous court officials, was tempered somewhat by the knowledge that she would be under the direct eye of Lady Margaret Huddleston.

They had not been long at the palace when Anne's tailor, Henry Ive, arrived with a lively troupe of apprentices and servants to take measurements for the royal robes. The queen's chambers bustled with titters and exclamations as servants scuttled to and fro displaying samples of cloth of blue velvet, crimson satin and white damask, ready to make up into splendid gowns for Anne's attendants. Lady Huddleston and Christiana were measured in turn for their own gowns to be made ready for the imminent coronation of the King of England and his queen.

"Hark how well the crowd cheers," Anne said somewhat nervously. "I can hardly believe that this has come to pass. I feel at times as though I am in a dream."

Christiana handed the duchess a goblet of malmsey wine and stood beside her at the open window to where they could see a crowd had begun to gather along the riverfront. "It seems as though the whole of London has worked hard to bring about this coronation, my lady, and I feel it will be the grandest the city has ever known," she remarked pleasantly.

"We have been quite overwhelmed by the gifts we have received." Anne swept a hand around the chamber indicating the abundance of cloth of gold, perfumes, exotic spices, tapestries and vessels adorned with jewels.

"You must see my gift for the king, it has just arrived," Anne said suddenly with childlike glee. She opened the lid of a wooden coffer and pulled from it a sumptuous gown of purple cloth of gold embellished with garters and roses and lined its full length with white damask. Christiana gazed at the gown but dared not place even one finger upon it. Instead she smiled her approval.

An usher entered the chamber at that moment to inform the duchess that the barge was ready and waiting at its moorings. Through an arched doorway leading from an adjoining room there appeared, as one shimmer of silk, Anne's ladies-in-waiting, Dame Anne Tempest regal and efficient at the fore.

Anne began to smooth down the folds of her gown with small fingers. "How do I look?" she asked.

"Like a queen," Christiana replied, fastening the gold clasp of Anne's mantle. Careful not to be seen by any roving eye, Christiana reached under the folds of fur and placed a small velvet pouch into

Anne's hand. "This is a small phial containing valerian, my lady, should you require a sleeping draught this night," she whispered.

Anne smiled weakly and then quite unexpectedly she leaned towards Christiana and kissed her lightly on the cheek before departing at once with her ladies.

Christiana went to the window and waited for the royal party to emerge below. A grand barge bobbed gently on the water with its green and white paint gleaming in the sunlight and its canopy covered in a multitude of wispy, fluttering ostrich feathers. Just visible from the window, Christiana could make out the gold crown and white lion bearing the royal arms hanging high over its prow.

Further out on the river a small procession of barges of the City Companies flying their insignia waited to escort the king and queen to the White Tower. The closest barge was that of the Lord Mayor of London, Sir Edmund Shaa, who was seated beneath a billowing red canopy.

As the king came into view on the quayside to a thunderous applause and a fanfare of trumpets, Christiana's heart almost missed a beat. Majestic and noble, it took only minutes for Richard to cross the flagstones and onto the awaiting barge to disappear at once beneath its voluminous canopy of feathers.

With the noise of the crowd and the salutes from the barges still in her ears, Christiana turned from the window and in the silence of the empty chamber began to feel a strange sense of unreality. Since the shocking news of King Edward's death in April, till this day, scarcely three months later, events had moved with such haste; she had left her home and her son in the Yorkshire dales for the first time in almost twenty-three years and entered a scene of pageantry and ceremony for the coronation of a king. Could it really be that the youth who had captured her heart and sired her son and once shared her world at Middleham was now King of all England?

She sat down heavily upon a coffer, her knees trembling somewhat, but the arrival at that moment of several ushers shouting orders left her no time for further reminiscence.

An animated Burgundian woman introducing herself as Lady Francine entered the queen's private chambers and the smile on her pleasant face gave Christiana some comfort for she was beginning to feel all at sea in this sumptuous palace.

Everywhere, it seemed, red-faced servants were dashing to and fro and tempers flared. There was a great deal left to be done. The king was to remain at the Tower for the great ceremony of the creation of the Knights of the Bath, which would last until well into the afternoon of the following day, the fifth of July. The king and queen would then travel in a glorious procession back to Westminster.

The Lady Margaret had naturally accompanied her sister to the White Tower; Christiana was left behind at the palace to assist the ladies minor with the honoured task of preparing the queen's robes and chambers for the coronation itself.

The queen's coronation robes had been made up and delivered by a servant of the Great Wardrobe and had to be hung and made ready for the morrow. Christiana had fairly scrubbed her hands raw with soap to ensure that they were clean before taking the crimson velvet mantle and gently brushing out its folds.

"It appears that all items of the queen's wardrobe have now arrived," Francine informed her as she carefully laid out the laces of the white damask kirtle to prevent knotting. "Considering the speed with which preparations have been made it is a wonder."

Moving closer to the younger woman she whispered, "Lady Skelton and Lady Poleyn will be here shortly to check that all is in order. I do not think we are to be trusted and I certainly would not want to cross Lady Skelton." She laughed merrily before adding, "I would not steal these garments for they do not suit my complexion and are far too small."

Christiana found herself smiling at Francine's good humour and began to relax a little. "Lady Anne, the queen, has more attendants than I can imagine," Christiana began. Some I am familiar with and others... well, have you knowledge of them all?"

Francine smiled as she finished arranging the kirtle and began sorting the furs that had been draped across the bed. "Of course, some of the ladies were in waiting upon Elizabeth Woodville and there are those more recently given the honour of attending our Queen Consort.

"Lady Grace Poleyn has not long been in service to the queen," Francine continued. "She is sister to Sir Thomas Manleverer who is married to Lady Elizabeth, another of Queen Anne's ladies. Lady Grace's husband John Poleyn is esquire of the royal cellar. So you see, Christiana," she finished breathlessly, "I am far too knowing for one in service, am I not?"

The two women were still laughing when two ladies of noble birth entered the chamber. At once Lady Francine's face assumed a serious attitude and she inclined her head politely to the queen's ladies.

"Have all the queen's gowns arrived, Lady Francine?" enquired Lady Skelton, the older of the two.

"Yes, my lady. All are safely here."

Lady Skelton inclined her graceful head and sighed. "So many preparations and so little time," she remarked. "Of course this coronation was not intended to include a queen," she added coolly.

A little later when Francine, Christiana and two others were alone, folding the bed linen, sweeping the floor and busying themselves with the comfort and preparation of the queen's chambers, the woman from Burgundy sought to make better acquaintance of her companion.

"You are from the north are you not?" the woman asked as she assisted Christiana in the task of brushing the folds of the great velvet bed hangings.

Christiana paused with the feather duster in her hand.

"Come, *chérie*, do not be timid," Francine replied pleasantly. "Everyone knows who you are and you are better to have a friend than a foe at court. Now tell me, you knew the queen from Middleham did you not?"

"I did, yes," Christiana sighed resignedly, knowing at once how it was this woman came about her knowledge. "Anne and her sister Isabel and Rich— the king. We were all children there. Francis,

Lord Lovell, was there too for a while. They were happy times." Christiana smiled, taking her feathers to the velvet once more.

"So, you had a childhood friendship with Richard... how intriguing." Francine giggled mischievously.

Christiana felt herself redden and thought to steer the conversation into less blustery waters and so asked directly, "And you, Francine, have you been at the palace long?"

"*Oui*. I came to England just after the marriage of Margaret of York to the Duke of Burgundy." Francine did not seem offended by this intrusion of her private life. "I am a distant relative of the duke's but alas for me an embarrassment to him."

"How so, my lady?" Christiana asked with sudden interest, realising that this woman was or had been more than a common chamberer.

"Well, *chérie*, long ago I was in love with a man at Duke Charles's court. Pierre was so dark and handsome and very quick with the sword." She sighed nostalgically. "He was an ambassador from France, but Duke Charles never trusted him; said he was a spy. You know alliances have never been good between Burgundy and France. The English king, Edward, favoured friendship with Burgundy over France and this I think will cause problems for King Richard.

"But I made a great show of my love for Pierre. Duke Charles had the perfect excuse to send him back to France and me over to England to forget Pierre. I hated it at the palace at first. I was a foreigner struggling with the language and of course I missed Pierre so very, very much. So you see, we have much in common; we can be companions, you and I."

Palace of Westminster
London
5ᵗʰ July 1483

Christiana was amongst the throng of servants gathered in Westminster yard to salute the arrival of their king and queen and knew nothing of the grand procession that had accompanied them on their journey from the Tower. Loud blasts of the trumpet could be heard long before the first men arrived, lords and knights of the realm, aldermen of the city, a troupe of minstrels and members of the clergy.

Following on came two noblemen wearing crimson velvet doublets and mantles trimmed with ermine draped across their shoulders. Large beaked hats of crimson cloth of gold and ermine trim topped their heads. These two nobles were Sir Edmund Shaa, Mayor of London, and lawyer and close friend to the king, Sir William Catesby. Immediately preceding the king rode the Earl of Surrey brandishing the sword of state in its bejewelled scabbard, flanked to his right by the Duke of Norfolk, now Earl Marshal of England, and to his left the Duke of Buckingham, now Lord Great Chamberlain.

Then came the king, resplendent in blue cloth doublet and stomacher from which hung an array of nets and pineapples wrought from strands of gold thread. About his shoulders hung a long gown of purple velvet lavishly furred with ermine. Watching, awestruck, from a distance, Christiana took in every detail from his jewelled collar to the embroidered garter of the Order down to the gilt spurs on his heels. She noticed too that the king had chosen White Surrey to carry him on this prestigious journey.

Above the king's bare head a canopy of red and green embroidered silk with silver bells at each corner fluttered gently on four gilt staves supported by four knights of the realm.

Following the king were his henchmen, the Master of the King's

Horse and still more lords and noblemen and finally officers and other members of the royal household. Amongst this last group were the men-at-arms and Christiana spied William dressed in new livery of red cloth bearing a large cloth emblem depicting the white boar of Richard the Third.

Whatever would her father make of all this? Did he ever imagine that bringing two little children through the gates of Middleham Castle in Yorkshire would lead them onto this road? Christiana's thoughts returned to the present, as the queen's entourage was about to enter the yard.

Anne's attendants were richly and magnificently robed in accordance with their status. The queen herself rode in an open litter carried on poles between strong palfreys draped in white damask. The litter was cushioned and adorned with white damask and white cloth of gold garlanded with ribbons and bells.

The queen's robe was of white cloth of gold, her mantle and train trimmed with ermine and woven with gold thread. Anne's hair, hanging loosely about her shoulders like spun gold, was capped with a gold circlet encrusted with pearls and jewels. Bells tinkled on the magnificent canopy held over the queen's head as the procession made its way into the palace yard. Several onlookers close by murmured at the splendour of it all and Christiana could not help wondering what spectacular pageantry awaited their eyes on the morrow, the day of the coronation.

Twelve of the queen's ladies-in-waiting, all attired in blue velvet gowns bordered with crimson satin, were in the rear of the great procession mounted upon palfreys bearing crimson saddles; Lady Lovell, Lady Katherine Neville, Lady Margaret Howard and of course the familiar face of Lady Margaret Huddleston amongst others.

It seemed to take an age for them all to enter the yard and several moments longer as everyone dismounted in preparation for the ceremonial offering of spiced wine. At this point Christiana, along with several other palace servants, returned to their many duties; Christiana to the queen's chambers where she would assist in making Lady Margaret ready for supper in the great hall.

Within the passageways and up and down the stairs fraught officers of the household continued to shout orders to their underlings well into the night. During supper Christiana made certain that Lady Margaret's bedchamber was made ready; linen was clean and perfumed, candles were lit, floor swept. She was then dismissed for Anne and her ladies would have much to discuss, matters not fit for the ears of the lowborn.

It was getting late but Christiana, wrapping a cloak about her shoulders, slipped quietly down a staircase that led out into the yard. A pale moon was up and shone its waxy face from a clear black sky. There were very few about now and hidden in the shadow of the stairwell she looked out upon the quiet yard. The cool air calmed and relaxed her. Across the way she could see a group of grooms and stablemen talking softly under the light of a lantern and wondered if William was amongst them.

A sudden movement from the Jewel House drew her attention and alerted the grooms. Black-garbed figures had emerged from the great doorway. Each bearing a candle, they walked two by two in solemn procession across the yard, flanked by two guards and led by clerics bearing a great velvet cushion upon which rested an ampulla containing the anointing oil.

From her hiding place Christiana watched this last ceremony of the day with a sense of peace. The strange band of men left the yard bound for the abbey and as the final little flicker of candlelight disappeared from view beyond the gates Christiana felt of a sudden very tired. It had been a long day and an even longer day lay ahead of them on the morrow; a day the likes of which she would not expect to see again in her lifetime.

The queen's household rose early on the morning of the sixth of July to a pearly gold dawn heralding a glorious day and to the guttural jibber jabber of the palace doves perched on the casement sills. Their incessant chatter was soon drowned by the babble and murmur of many voices within.

Christiana had slept surprisingly well but doubted that many others had been so fortunate. Sailing around the queen's great chamber, snapping orders to their own handmaidens, the royal ladies looked distinctly bleary-eyed.

The Duchess of Norfolk along with Lady Scrope, Lady Skelton and Lady Tempest had the great privilege of bathing the queen and making her ready for her coronation. Once bathed, they dressed the queen in her smock, kirtle and royal surcoat. With seventy annulets through which the silk laces were thread it took several moments of patient standing before Anne's kirtle was secure around her slender waist. Nimble fingers soon laced the sleeves of her kirtle. Emerging from an inner chamber wearing a crimson velvet mantle trimmed with miniver the queen caused many a gasp at the great length of its train.

As for yesterday's procession, Anne's fair hair was to hang loosely down her back and be held in place with the gold circlet, its many jewels sparkling in the morning sunlight. With all attention on the queen and her noble ladies little attention was paid to Christiana but Lady Francine offered her assistance. Theirs were matching gowns of tawny damask bordered with black satin. Daring not to look at her reflection in the polished brass Christiana was content to receive words of admiration from Francine as she coiled her raven hair high at the back of her head and capped it with a matching headdress.

Waiting for the signal to move down to the great hall Christiana watched as Lady Margaret Beaufort began to lift and gather the ample train of the queen's mantle. An unexpected wave of nervousness overcame Christiana as the full realisation that she would be part of this momentous occasion finally hit her. If it were not for the sudden indisposition of Lady Huddleston's own servant she herself would not be here.

An usher appeared at the doorway announcing all was ready. With dry mouth and trembling hands Christiana took her place beside Francine and waited to follow the queen and her ladies.

The king and his nobles had preceded the queen into the great hall and the royal couple now took their places upon their canopied chairs to await the arrival of the ecclesiastical procession from the abbey.

Standing beside Francine within a sea of crimson gowns Christiana could sense she was not alone in her nerves. All around within the sound of silence she could hear coughs, shuffling of feet, a tiny high-pitched giggle here and there. Everywhere there was such decadence and wealth; the magnitude of such would have been beyond even the imagination of her poor neighbours in the village where she grew up as the daughter of a blacksmith. Peering amongst the line of men-at-arms in their scarlet livery she saw William looking far more at ease than she. Maybe a jug of ale had calmed his nerves, she thought with envy.

All eyes turned as the Abbot of Westminster, his archbishops, bishops and clergy entered bearing with them the royal coronation regalia. A greater hush fell upon the already quiet room.

The procession to the abbey was underway and Christiana followed in a haze of colour, pageantry and splendour. Within the cold stone walls of the Abbey of Saint Peter much of the ceremony went unheeded by Christiana. Positioned where she was at the very end of the great train of guests, the figures way down the aisle performing an age-old ritual of prayer, anointing and crowning with solemn oaths seemed so very far away. She stretched her neck to catch a glimpse of the man seated upon Saint Edward's great chair beside the altar as the Archbishop of Canterbury lowered the crown to his head.

She shivered in the chillness of the abbey and felt the warmth of Francine's hand as it closed momentarily over hers. A few stray tears trickled slowly down her cheeks and she hastily wiped them away with the sleeve of her gown.

In due course the queen was crowned with solemn splendour and then the Mass was sung. Following this the Archbishop of Canterbury, the king and queen and their attendants retired to the shrine of Saint Edward behind the high altar. It was a while before they re-emerged and during that time a subdued whisper had wound a thread amongst the guests at the farthest end of the abbey.

Finally the king and queen stepped back into view wearing their royal gowns of purple velvet trimmed with ermine. All was now ready for the return to the palace and once again Christiana took her place at the rear of the queen's procession.

Brilliant sunshine dazzled her eyes as they stepped into its summer heat. Swept along in a blaze of sound and colour by the cheering crowds they soon reached the cool of the palace yard. Returning to her chamber the queen rested as the hall was made ready for the coronation feast. Divested of her heavy robe Anne sank gratefully down onto her bed. She looked pale and visibly tired. Her ladies fussed over her, bringing her wine and wiping her brow. Christiana withdrew to her own small chamber to await the forthcoming festivities, grateful herself for a little respite.

At four of the clock the king and queen left their chambers and entered the hall to take their places at the marble table. Christiana took her place at the rear of the table placed to the left of the king's table amongst the queen's ladies and noble women. She had attended a feast similar to this at Middleham in Yorkshire when Edward, King of England was entertained. This ceremony, however, was to be conducted with more attention to pomp and ritual than many seated here this day had seen before.

A fanfare of trumpets heralded the start of each elaborate course led in by liveried sergeants at arms. Dishes such as roe deer coloured purple, peacock redressed in all his fine feathers, decorated open pies and tarts, soups, sauces, sumptuous fish dishes and sweetmeats passed before Christiana's bemused eyes.

During the afternoon, unhindered by such attention as was being lavished upon the king and queen, Christiana was able to relax and enjoy the rich food and tête-à-tête with the queen's sister who sat beside her.

They watched with intrigue as the lords and ladies of the English gentry and others of foreign blood in London for the occasion ate, drank and conversed.

"That must be Lady Stanley, seated beside Lord Thomas?" Christiana observed. "She bore Queen Anne's coronation train. She has a most distinguished face, does she not?" The younger woman was watching how the lady's features remained aloof and set, giving nothing away, as she conversed with her neighbour.

"Aye, a face as distinguished as her line of husbands," Lady Margaret tittered softly.

Christiana raised a questioning eyebrow and paid a little more attention to the lady with the long noble face, framed by a gabled hood of gold brocade.

"Thomas, Lord Stanley, great magnate of the north, is Lady Margaret Beaufort's fourth husband, although her first marriage to John de la Pole was annulled as the lady was a mere child."

Christiana waited as Lady Margaret took a mouthful of fish in cream sauce and then, curious, she asked, "The lady must have many sons, having three husbands?"

Margaret laid her silver spoon beside her plate and turned in her chair closer to her companion. "The Lady Margaret Beaufort has but one son, Henry Tudor, by her second husband Edmund Tudor, a man many have said was her one true love," Margaret whispered. "This son has become the focus of her life and there are rumours that she will stop at nothing to further his cause; that being the English crown."

"Does this Henry attend King Richard's coronation?" Christiana asked, looking around at the sea of unfamiliar faces.

"Nay, he is in exile in France and has been for many a year since the Yorkists gained the upper hand in this cousins' war."

Christiana was much relieved to hear it although she felt a great confusion concerning the kith and kin of the great Plantagenet dynasty. Her eye fell upon the person of Henry Stafford, Duke of Buckingham, as he stood near to the great door of the hall conversing with two court officials. Now there was one of the blood royal with whom she was more familiar; had he not been Richard's most ardent supporter, forwarding all Gloucester's legitimate claims to the throne?

"There is one at least in whom we can put our trust," Christiana said, giving voice to her thoughts and looking in Buckingham's direction.

She heard the older woman breathe a sigh of uncertainty beside her.

"He brings to mind my father, the late Earl of Warwick, called by some the kingmaker," Margaret said softly. "Buckingham has the same ruthless, ambitious spirit within him."

There was no time for Christiana to respond for at that moment the great door to the hall was pushed open and the entrance of a great black charger adorned in red and white silk commanded all attention and a hush fell upon the whole place.

"'Tis Sir Robert Dymock, the King's Champion," whispered Margaret.

The rider, equally matched in splendour to his horse, urged his mount towards the king's table and bowed low in the saddle to his sovereign. In a deep voice that echoed around the hall he sent forth a challenge: "Is any person here present who, declaring that King Richard is not true heir and rightful inheritor of the crown, would now offer to defend that view with his body?"

An expectant silence descended upon the hall followed almost at once by the cry, "King Richard!" which multiplied and reverberated as one voice. Whereupon the King's Champion turned to his sovereign lord and cast before him a polished gauntlet. Having retrieved it from his squire, Sir Robert once again threw down the gauntlet in the middle of the hall before the guests and a third time at the door.

Returning to the king he made a second obeisance before Francis, Lord Lovell, stepped forward offering Sir Robert a large gold cup of wine. He drank from it and cast out the remainder onto the floor, the crimson liquid bubbling on the tiled stones. Holding his cup high in his right hand for all to see, he spurred his horse on and out of the hall.

After this the Garter King of Arms proclaimed Richard King of England, France and Lord of Ireland to deafening cheers and foot stamping. The final ceremony of the day, for it was now too late for the third course to be served, was the offering of hippocras and wafers to the king and queen by Sir Edmund Shaa, Mayor of London. It was now getting so late that even the long summer daylight had faded to be replaced by great torches and candles flickering and smouldering in their holders.

As Christiana rose with the others to make their final reverences to the king and queen she realised just how tired and light-headed she was. From many accounts there were still more ceremonies to come; processions, dancing and jousting. No doubt there would be bonfires and merrymaking amongst every one of the king's subjects both within the town and much farther afield for some time yet to come. For now though, Christiana would be more than happy to find her bed and sleep.

Before the final coronation ritual on Sunday 13th July, when the anointing coif would be removed from the king's head to be replaced by a gold circlet, there were many feasts and pageants to be endured.

It was at the end of a week of feasting and the great hall of Westminster Palace was full of revellers all making the most of the king's generous supply of food and wine. The great tables had been cleared and set aside, the king and queen having departed an hour or so ago. Many people were enjoying the entertainment provided by the court jester; others were standing around or sitting in small groups talking animatedly or else in close intimacy.

Christiana was seated to the side of the hall observing the comings and goings of those assembled. She was hoping that her brother would join the merrymakers for she had not seen him since before the coronation and desired to question him on events happening beyond the palace walls.

Lady Huddleston had taken her leave, with no further need of her servant, soon after the king. Christiana thought to do likewise when her attention was drawn to a couple who had thought to make secret of their conversation for they had settled on chairs along the side wall of the hall and not too distant from Christiana.

Feeling as though there may be much to gain by being privy to their parley Christiana tried to pick up snippets of their conversation whilst ostensibly concentrating her gaze upon the ludicrous antics of the jester and his dancing monkey in the middle of the hall. Besides, who would notice the presence of a lowborn servant, one-time herbalist and mother to the king's bastard?

"He does not have a strong hold on the crown, dear nephew.

For all your gallant attempts to put him on the throne can you keep him there?" Lady Margaret Beaufort's tone was deeply unctuous.

"Parliament and Church accepted well enough his claim," Henry Stafford replied.

"Ah, but what say others? It lies not easy with some that Richard can usurp the throne with no evidence other than a tale spun by an old bishop."

"I think there was more to it than that, my lady."

A roar of laughter from the audience drowned the rest of his words as the jester began to make swipes at his monkey with his colourful batons. The monkey, for his part, dodged the blows skilfully, running circles around his master.

"And then there is the problem of two little princes still in the White Tower," Lady Beaufort was saying smoothly. "'Tis a wonder our king can sleep easily in his bed with those two boys a constant reminder of how he has sullied the name of their dear father. They could well become the focus of a rebellion."

"Then of course there is your own dear son," Buckingham began, changing the focus of their conversation.

"Let us talk of him in a more private place, Henry." Lady Beaufort's regal head with its long narrow nose and close-set grey eyes pivoted on her swanlike neck to survey those seated close by.

Although still watching and seemingly enjoying the entertainment, any attempts to glean further knowledge were thwarted for at that moment Christiana's attention was commanded by her brother William, who had just entered the hall.

Rising from her seat she went over to greet him and suggested at once that they might take a stroll in the palace gardens.

The air was cooler now as shadows lengthened. There were a few courtiers taking in the dank riverside air of the privy garden and William guided his sister to a wooden bench in a secluded corner.

"So much seems to have happened with such speed," Christiana began as soon as they were seated. "I can scarce take it all in."

William pressed his sister's hand gently. "Aye, we have come a long way since our days at Middleham. 'Tis a very different path we tread now, the way of political danger and intrigue."

Talk of their home enticed a memory from her mind and she sought an answer from her brother.

"There was a man brought in as a prisoner at Middleham just before we left. He seemed young, of good standing. What is to become of him?" she asked.

Will sighed. "Richard Grey, son of Elizabeth Woodville by her first husband. Orders were given for his execution on the twenty-fifth day of June at Pontefract, along with his uncle Anthony Woodville, Earl Rivers, and two others of the young Prince Edward's household."

Christiana shook her head sadly. "The king and queen will leave London soon for their Progress through the realm. Let us hope that there will be an end to further rebellion and bloodshed."

William hoped so too but would nowise put a wager on it. "Buckingham is likely to remain in London for a short time before joining the king on his travels seeing as Elizabeth Woodville remains in the abbey of Saint Peter and there may be further unrest," he said guardedly.

A quartet of courtiers passed by under the star-studded cerulean sky and no words were exchanged between these two on the bench for a moment or two until the sound of laughter faded.

"We must stay loyal to him though, Will," Christiana whispered. "No matter where it may lead us."

What else could he do but agree? Loyalty bound them all.

On this Sunday morning, the thirteenth day of July, the final Mass of the coronation week having taken place, the vast wagon trains were being loaded up in the palace yard ready to move out to begin the king's Royal Progress throughout the realm.

Christiana stood in the herbarium checking the supplies of salves, potions and herbs, marking them off on a parchment ledger with a goose quill before arranging them neatly into a deep wooden chest. The herbarium was at this hour deserted save for the monk whose domain it was and who could now be heard moving about amongst his bottles and jars in the adjoining chamber.

Lady Huddleston and her lady-in-waiting, now fully restored to her duties, had departed to her northern lands. Indeed, now that most of England's nobility had returned to their own estates and affairs and the presence on the streets of Richard's men from the north had diminished somewhat, a cautious air of tranquillity fell upon the streets of London.

Christiana's mood lightened as she stepped out into the palace yard later that afternoon. All was bathed in glorious colour and golden sunlight. White Surrey, resplendent in scarlet drapes, was waiting impatiently tossing his head for the arrival of the king.

Queen Anne was being assisted into the saddle of a pale grey mare suitably adorned in scarlet and gold trappings. Although Anne would travel some of the way on horseback Christiana knew that she would be too frail to ride throughout the whole journey. Besides which it would be unseemly for so gracious a lady to do so. An elaborately decorated horse litter and roofed chariot had been prepared for the tour and Thomas Hopton, the queen's Gentleman of the Chare, was to accompany Anne and see to her travelling arrangements. Christiana did have a freshly made pot of calendula ointment, invaluable in soothing chaffed thighs, should the queen require it.

Swinging herself deftly into the saddle of her own palfrey and arranging the folds of her green linen gown, Christiana caught the eye of the queen and exchanged a knowing smile.

The king led the great procession from the palace yard alongside his nephew, John de la Pole, Earl of Lincoln. Henry Stafford, Duke of Buckingham, as foretold, did not accompany the royal party.

Although at times arduous and tiring, the king's Royal Progress during the summer of 1483 was one Christiana would not forget. She remained with the king and queen as part of the household of personal servants who saw to their daily needs. The vast wagon train carrying their belongings went on ahead to prepare for the king's arrival.

455

They arrived first at Greenwich and from there to the great castle at Windsor, a favourite of King Edward's and his final resting place in Saint George's Chapel. It was then on to Oxford, the seat of learning, where the king paused at Magdalen college to hear the academics debating moral philosophy.

It was whilst lodging under the roof of Minster Lovell, home of his friend Francis, and taking advantage of less formal a setting in which to relax, that the king received news of a most disturbing nature.

Messengers under an armed escort rode in all haste from London to report the discovery of a plot to release the two sons of King Edward from their protective custody in the Tower, with the intention presumably of putting the elder boy, Edward, back on the throne. The conspirators included all three of Queen Elizabeth's remaining brothers.

The king wasted no time in having his royal secretary, John Kendall, pen an urgent response to his Chancellor, John Russell, to increase security around Westminster Abbey where Queen Elizabeth still sought sanctuary.

By the end of July the king had moved his entourage on to Gloucester, where at his lodgings the Duke of Buckingham arrived late in the afternoon and his entrance into the great hall turned the jovial gathering sour. Seeing that his friend's humour did not suit the company of minstrels and ladies playing merrills the king took the young duke aside to an inner chamber.

"Was your journey not smooth, Henry?" Richard asked as he poured a generous measure of wine into a goblet and offered it to the duke. Taking the vessel Stafford drank from it – too quickly for he coughed and spluttered.

"Sit down, Henry," the king commanded, "and tell me what troubles you. Mayhap you can tell me how it goes with our Lady Elizabeth Woodville," he added invitingly.

Richard did not fail to notice the almost indiscernible flicker in Buckingham's eyes as he brought the goblet up to his own lips to drink. Richard replenished Buckingham's wine goblet. "So, Henry, what news do you bring from London?"

Stafford placed his goblet down on the table that stood between them. "Something mayhap Your Grace does not wish to hear," he replied.

The king raised an eyebrow questioningly.

"Rumour, Your Grace, it spreads like the plague."

"Rumour?" Richard's tone was almost casual.

"That you have done away with the late king's sons and because of it people are ripe for rebellion."

"People, what people?" Richard demanded frostily.

"Those loyal to the late King Edward and who see his son and heir as the rightful king," Buckingham replied without taking his eyes off Richard's face.

The king's eyes glinted like flint. "And if I have done away with Edward's heir then who else do these rebels propose to put on my throne?"

Buckingham hesitated in his reply, so the king continued. "Do you forget my brother George's son, Edward of Warwick? Should I not have him done away with too? And what of Elizabeth, my niece – does she contest my throne also?" The king's anger was rising and he slammed his goblet down on the table spilling the ruby red liquid over its surface.

Henry Stafford sighed heavily. "I merely point out, Your Grace, how fragile a hold on the crown you have. You have many enemies."

"I have enemies, Henry, as you rightly say because of rumour and where does this rumour start? London, Henry, where I left you to check any unrest which you have seemingly failed to do."

Now Buckingham felt his rage grow. "I hope you do not count me as your enemy, Richard." The statement came in the guise of a threat and Buckingham's use of familiar terms was not lost upon the king, but Henry would not let the moment pass and pressed on. "Do not forget that it was through my support and loyalty you were even able to seize the throne."

"Your loyalty and support has been well rewarded with offices and titles," the king returned pointedly. "And before you cast up your old grievance I have done all I can to settle the Bohun land on you; the political situation, as you well know, is complicated."

For several moments the two men glared at one another like a pair of stags at the rut before Richard spoke, his voice now calm. "Do not overstep your position, Henry," he warned.

"Your Grace," the duke relented and bowed low. "You have my uttermost allegiance. It is only through concern for your status as king that I venture to suggest that the two young sons of Edward will continue to pose a great threat to the crown and you should give careful thought to what should be done with them."

Richard's dark eyes grew black. "Those boys have been declared illegitimate and barred by the Great Council from taking the crown," he whispered. "They pose no threat to me. I would dare to say that my greatest threat comes from those closest to me. You are my friend and ally, Henry, do not give me cause to doubt your loyalty." The king paused, allowing his words to take effect, before continuing, "Mark you well these words, friend; do not try to manipulate me for I remember another who tried to use King Edward to further his own greedy ambition and it did him no good."

There was nothing else to be said and after a perfunctory bow Henry Stafford left the king's presence. He was hungry and in bad humour. The meeting with the king had not progressed amicably, the reason being to his mind that news of Elizabeth Woodville's plot from her sanctuary at Westminster had reached Richard before he had.

The following morning Henry Stafford, having spent a miserable sleepless night, entered the great hall intent upon sounding out the king's humour. The hall was empty except for the presence of three soldiers wearing royal livery standing guard and an unassuming drab-clothed man sitting at the clerk's table. Stafford sauntered over to the desk and standing over the shoulder of the man seated there regarded his documentation. There seemed to be nothing of any particular significance: receipts for household expenses, nothing more. Indeed the man was rolling a warrant commissioning oats, hay, beans, horsebread and peas for the king's horses.

The duke's snigger alerted the man who had been deep in concentration and now fumbled hastily to his feet with a bow. "John Green, my lord," he stammered.

Stafford waved a jewelled hand in arrogant dismissal of the work of one who was of no importance to him. "Be about your work, John Green, for I would not wish to delay you."

"Very well, my lord," replied the servant. "I leave within the hour bound for London and there is much still to do."

The duke gave a curt nod of his head and moved away to seek out the king.

William was contemplating leaving his post on the door of the great hall, where he had stood for the last two hours, in order to urinate at the fireplace, when the high and mighty Duke of Buckingham strolled back into the room and straight to the table where John Green was gathering papers into a leather bag. There was a brief exchange of words, none of which William could hear, a fumbling with a seal and the passing of a scroll from one man to the other. And if he was not mistaken, a much stuffed bag of coin also exchanged hands.

Within minutes the duke had left the hall and William was relieved to see a change of guard enter. Out in the stable yard William made a play of checking the shoes of Green's horse before he departed for London. The man stood impatiently by, eager to leave.

"There, I do believe your steed is now fit to travel. You cannot be too sure; the roads are rough and a cast shoe could cost you valuable time," William commented as he straightened up to face John Green. As he held the stirrup leather ready for the man to hoist himself into the saddle, William whispered, "What have you in that bag that is the business of the Duke of Buckingham?"

The man's face turned a deep shade of red. "I have but warrants for horsebread and the like, nothing more, if it is of any concern of yours."

"Anything that might be of concern to the king concerns me," William replied sternly. "I was privy to an exchange of words and the passing of a scroll between the duke and yourself. You can tell me what you have or else the king will know of it."

John Green did not open his leather pouch but placed a hand across it protectively. "It is but a letter to the Constable of the White Tower, Robert Brackenbury, asking after the health of the two princes still residing there," he muttered. "I see no harm in that and have agreed to deliver the letter on behalf of the king."

William could speculate no further for at that moment the Duke of Buckingham entered the yard from the far side and stood looking across at the two men standing beside the roan mare. Seeing his chance to escape further interrogation Green snatched the stirrup leather from the soldier, mounted his horse and turned it towards his travelling companions waiting at the gate.

William crossed the yard, bowed his head to the duke and entered the hall; the knowledge he had come by seemed of too little worth to dwell upon.

On the second day of August the Royal Progress left Gloucester heading towards Tewkesbury, with one notable absence; The Duke of Buckingham was bound for his stronghold at Brecon and to one he had incarcerated there at his pleasure; John Morton, Bishop of Ely, arrested and held ever since his part in the Hastings' plot to overthrow the Duke of Gloucester had been discovered.

Time spent at Tewkesbury was seasoned with sadness for both the king and his queen for here at the abbey were the final resting places of Richard's brother, George, Duke of Clarence, and Anne's sister Isabel, Duchess of Clarence.

As Christiana watched silently as the king and queen went down on bended knee to receive a blessing from the abbot she wondered at the secret thoughts of each.

Surely Richard was remembering the battle fought here in 1471; a resounding victory for the Yorkists and one of personal achievement for the young duke, in command of his own men and not yet nineteen years of age.

Did the queen remember that it was this very battle that took the life of her first husband, Edward of Lancaster, a youth of seventeen years? The queen had been comforted by the news that their nephew, little Edward of Warwick, was on his way to join the royal party at Warwick Castle where he was to be brought under her protection. The king had issued orders that Edward was to become his ward after his guardian, Thomas Grey, had fled sanctuary and escaped to France.

The king's parting gift to the Abbot of Tewkesbury was three hundred and ten pounds; rent from the late Duke of Clarence's estates.

The sun was shining on the royal procession as it entered the gates of the great fortress at Warwick mid-afternoon of the eighth day of August.

Queen Anne and her ladies took to her chambers forthwith for the journey had greatly fatigued the lady. Christiana too was grateful for a period of rest; they were to remain at Warwick for the coming week.

She was concerned for the health of the king who would always remain active and attentive throughout his travels. However, she knew that within the privacy of his chambers he would surrender to the pain that he bore stoically in the presence of his subjects. With this in mind, having seen to her first duty, the queen's needs, she went in search of the herbarium sited in the bailey. It seemed an ordered and well-run place and she was satisfied that it could supply the necessary ingredients for the king's prescribed poultice, although some of the more exotic spices she had brought with her.

As she returned to the keep through the pleasant grounds which overlooked the River Avon she realised the folly of her quest. She could not relinquish her desire, her need to care for Richard. As king of all England he would have an army of servants, physicians, grooms, clerics and personal retainers at his disposal to attend his every need. She would be overlooked and rightly so. As deep as her longing to be close to Richard was, she had made a promise to the queen never to give anyone any cause to doubt the king's loyalty and faithfulness to his wife.

Two days later and the queen and her ladies were taking a pleasant stroll in the gardens when they were alerted to the arrival of young Edward of Warwick.

After taking food and drink and a little rest the boy and his nurse joined the ladies in the garden. Anne was overjoyed to see her nephew safe and well. She was grateful to the king for making arrangements for the boy to be placed in one of his northern strongholds. She pondered upon the fate of her two other nephews, Prince Edward and Prince Richard, and prayed that they too were secured and well in the White Tower in London; the focus of a recent Woodville plot.

Christiana, a little distant from the noble ladies, regarded the boy with an air of curiosity. He was fair-haired like his Neville kin and she remembered with sadness his poor mother, Isabel. He did, however, have a strange look about him, dull and melancholic, as though he lacked in part his sanity, but he seemed amicable enough as he allowed his aunt to kiss his cheek fondly.

Towards the end of their stay at Warwick William sought the company of his sister and suggested a rendezvous in the garden. It was to be mid-afternoon when the queen and her ladies took their ease in their chambers.

Christiana was seated upon a bench admiring the fragrance and hue of the summer flowers – betony, lady's bedstraw, bellflower and violet – when William came strolling towards her. He appeared agitated, a little tense.

"Is all well, brother?" she asked after their greeting.

"Aye, well enough," William's reply was hesitant.

"You have news? Is the king well?"

"The king is notably more at ease, although ever vigilant. Your son is to receive a knighthood in York when little Eddie is invested as Prince of Wales," William added cheerfully.

Christiana's smile was as bright as the Saint Mary's gold growing at her feet.

"This I do know, Will. The queen herself informed me this very morn." She laughed. "I do not think this is the news you have bade me come to the garden to hear, brother."

William's face darkened and his voice lowered. "The king is sending me on a mission to root out any hint of rebellion. He does not trust the Duke of Buckingham."

"Surely Henry is steadfast; arrogant maybe, but loyal," Christiana whispered.

"Who knows? It is for this reason I am sent."

"How are you to find out such a thing?" Christiana asked, not having any notion of the workings of espionage.

"I am useful to the king as a commoner and not easily recognised. I can masque as a blacksmith and frequent alehouses and hostelries. You would be surprised at what a man will let slip when he is deep in his cups."

William paused and took his sister's hand in his. "I may be gone for some time. There is little to gain in returning to the king if I have no news to bring."

They sat in silence for several moments; William, it seemed, was reluctant to take his leave.

It was Christiana who broke their peace. "It is good to see young Edward here. The queen was glad to see this nephew safe."

"Aye, he is to be sent to Sheriff Hutton to reside there with the king's nephew, John de la Pole," William replied.

"There has been much talk about the king's other nephews. Some have even said that Richard has done away with them to secure the throne for himself. I cannot believe he would do such a thing even in his desperation to prevent a Woodville conspiracy." The woman's voice was cracked with emotion.

"Do not even let such thoughts into your head, Christiana. But be assured the king will do what is best. I have heard him talk of the possibility of removing the princes from the Tower to safer lodgings; Middleham, maybe."

He stood and offered his hand to Christiana. "I leave at first light on the morrow. There will be three of us to travel although we work alone."

Christiana stood and embraced her brother warmly. "Take care, Will, and Godspeed."

The Royal Progress moved from Warwick to Coventry and then to Leicester and so on to Nottingham, moving ever northwards.

At the end of August the Royal Progress reached the city of

York and there at the Archbishop's Palace the king and queen welcomed their only son and heir, Edward of Middleham. It was a joyful reunion but marred with sadness. None could fail to notice how frail and sickly the young prince looked. Christiana dared to wonder whether it was in truth something more than a summer fever that ailed the boy as she observed his pale face and sunken eyes.

In stark contrast the king's bastard son, John, was in vigorous health. He had accompanied his brother on the journey from Middleham but whereas John had ridden upon a noble steed, Edward was carried along in a litter.

Christiana brewed a strengthening tonic of honey, lemon, ginger, dandelion and burdock. Her heart trembled as she witnessed the tears pool in the queen's eyes as she gave the cup to her child.

The citizens of York had received their king with such pageantry and pomp that it put Christiana in mind of the coronation itself. There could be no misplacing the loyalty of these northern subjects; their love for Richard was steadfast and true, even if it was not always so for his brother, Edward.

Many had gathered to witness the investiture of young Edward as Prince of Wales set for the Feast of the Nativity of the Blessed Virgin Mary, the eighth day of September. During their stay at the palace the king and queen received ambassadors from King Ferdinand of Aragon and Queen Isabella of Castile who proposed a marriage between the king's son, Edward and a Spanish princess. This visit offered a few days of pleasant distraction as the king awaited the arrival of the robes and wall hangings by the hand of his trusted servant James Tyrell, necessary for the prince's investiture.

In the evening of the appointed day, there to witness the ceremony was a great gathering of church officials and nobility in the splendour of the Archbishop's Palace. In royal robes of cloth of gold the boy looked so small and frail as he presented himself before the king to receive a sword, cap of estate placed upon his head, the gold ring on his finger and the staff of gold in his hand.

This was perhaps a poignant moment for the little prince's mother as now more than ever she would feel the need to provide more sons for the king.

It was at this time too that the king's bastard son, John, received his knighthood, along with the king's nephew, Edward of Warwick. It was a proud moment for Christiana sitting amongst the onlookers as the king with his sword daubed his son a knight of the realm and praised the boy's virtuous character, which showed great promise of loyalty and courage to come. John's princely robes of scarlet and gold blurred before her as Christiana wiped away the tears in her eyes. It was indeed a momentous occasion, marked with yet another lavish feast.

On the twelfth day of September, under a heavily armed escort, the Prince of Wales and his mother, the queen, departed once more for Middleham. Christiana was to return with them to resume her duties as companion to the dowager Countess of Warwick.

Edward of Warwick also left York in the company of the king's nephew John de la Pole, Earl of Lincoln, bound for Sheriff Hutton, recently declared a royal household and fit to meet the needs of the young prince or any the king had a desire to send there.

Saddened though she was to leave him, Christiana felt the time had now come for her own son, John, to spend his time with his father and wished him a fond farewell as he rode off at the king's side as the Royal Progress took them south once again.

There was an emotional reunion awaiting Christiana at Middleham Castle, for Martha, whom she had not seen for over five months, was overjoyed to see her. It pained Christiana to see that her friend seemed to have aged significantly in her absence. There was a distinct stiffness in her gait as she tottered across the herb garden and took Christiana in a warm embrace, unable to conceal the tears that fell down her soft wrinkled cheeks. The wisps of frizzled hair that escaped her cap were white as virgin snow and the once capable fingers quivered with palsy.

"My, my, lass, look at you, such fancy clothes and look at your hair – 'tis different," Martha croaked.

Christiana laughed as she picked up the skirts of her green silk gown to walk down the path to the herbarium. "'Tis the fashion in London, Martha. Ladies of noble birth wear their hair drawn right back and look, I even have a hennin." She tapped the velvet band of her headdress and added, "Although I doubt that this will be long worn now that I am home. As for the gown, 'tis a cast off from one of the queen's ladies. And see this, the badge of the king's household, hundreds were given out at his coronation." She tapped the pewter boar pinned to her velvet cloak.

As she walked into the herbarium the girl, Tilly, jumped down from a stool and bowed hastily, then checked herself as she recognised the well-dressed stranger and then stood bobbing up and down in a most comical fashion, her cheeks glowing ever more pink.

Christiana, concealing her mirth in a cough, turned away but Martha, with her usual brusqueness, barked, "Do not stand there like a deranged puppet, girl, fetch a jug of mead and a wedge of Wensleydale."

As the girl bobbed and tripped her way to the pantry at the back of the cottage Martha and Christiana chuckled loudly.

"'Tis good to have you back," Martha smiled. "How is it that you return in such finery? Have you been well met by the countess? You know how she—"

"All in good time, Martha, here comes the mead," Christiana interrupted and walked forward to relieve Tilly of her burden before she could further embarrass herself.

"I'll wager they have none of this in London, eh, lass?" Martha said as she handed a wedge of cheese to Christiana.

"Nothing to touch it," replied the other woman, watching Tilly through the open doorway, now bent over the beds picking the last of the fragranced herbs.

Martha was as eager to hear the account of the king's coronation and Royal Progress as Christiana was to tell it.

The late summer sun had barred the garden with shadow as her story came to an end. Tilly had discreetly disappeared from earshot and only the late lament of a distant blackbird could be heard.

Martha shook her head slowly. "Who would have thought it, that little fair-haired boy, and the youngest son, would have become the king of all England."

"There was a great deal of trouble and mystery surrounding Richard's coronation but maybe all will be well now and he can begin his reign in peace."

Martha rubbed her chin thoughtfully but said nothing; news concerning some of these troubles had reached their ears here in the far north.

"And how goes it now with our Will and young John?" Martha asked, sipping her mead.

"William is away on the king's business," Christiana replied vaguely, "and John is travelling with his father about the realm and back to London." She smiled proudly to which Martha chuckled.

"I dare say our William will have plenty to tell us when he returns," Martha announced, shifting her weight on the stool to gain relief from the pain in her joints.

Whatever news William did bring with him would not be for their ears, Christiana thought soberly. "Prince Edward is home," she offered.

Martha sighed sadly. "Poor boy; he has not fared well since springtide. His father was a sickly sort as a child but he made it through by God's grace so who knows?"

Just then Tilly came into the cottage bearing an armful of herbs and shivering slightly in the evening chill.

"I must be about my duties, Martha," Christiana said, rising from her stool. "The countess is expecting my company this eve." After kissing her friend on the cheek she left the cottage feeling a tinge of sorrow for what she was leaving behind.

William had not been long in London when he sensed the general mood of its inhabitants. Something had changed since the coronation; this was not a city rejoicing in the aftermath of the crowning of a new monarch.

He found lodgings near to the Fleet Bridge and crept around in shadows, saying little to anyone. He had a wool coat lined with linen that concealed a pouch of coins, another pouch hidden inside his hose and a third hanging on his belt at his side. Here too he kept a bollock dagger and a second short-bladed weapon was secured to the inside of his coat. His horse was a common rouncy; sturdy and reliable but lacking any form likely to draw attention to its rider.

He frequented many alehouses, taking care not to consume over much and covered as wide an area of the city of London as he could, also venturing into Westminster.

At first all William could discern was a common feeling of unrest; whispers in corners, individuals gathering on street corners. Then one evening he was sitting in the darkened corner of The Old Bear when he caught sight of a man he had thought never to cross his path again. The unmistakable strands of black oily hair hanging limply across his face as he conversed with his companions roused a feeling of anger and disgust in William. He wanted nothing more at that moment than to let the man feel the sting of his steel blade at his scrawny neck.

William checked his emotions, moved deeper into the shadows and listened. Fortunately Ralph Hodkin's loud voice put him within earshot of the blacksmith. It soon became apparent that Ralph was feeding any who would listen a vile rumour concerning the king.

Interspersed with cups of the tavern's strongest ale a tale unravelled: King Richard, usurper of the throne, had ordered the murder of his nephews, mere children, imprisoned against the will of the people in the White Tower. The truth was out for Sir Robert Brackenbury, the Constable of the Tower, had received orders from the king himself; orders that commanded him to perform the vile deed himself. Being a man of honour and integrity, Brackenbury naturally had disobeyed.

Hodkin appealed to any sense of godly justice that might be lying latent in the hearts of his listeners but William had heard enough to sicken him to his stomach, and for fear of discovery, he quietly left the tavern. There was something about Brackenbury receiving orders from the king that niggled in his mind.

Over the next two or three nights William's ears detected the thread of this rumour picked up and carried along like the filth and stench in the city drains. He also discovered, by prowling around the more prosperous areas of the city, that Lady Margaret Beaufort was instigating covert raising of funds within the city from her former residence, Woking Palace in Surrey. A finely dressed youth, whose office gave him little standing and whose loyalties were negotiable, had offered this piece of information in exchange for a hefty bribe from William.

A few days later William came closer to knowing the peculiar reason for Lady Beaufort's sudden need for capital, married as she was to one of the wealthiest men in the realm.

Living in the crowded city where foulness and malodour abounded and the food came from a most dubious source did not suit William. It was not long before he began to suffer from acute stomach cramps and flux. He had no choice but to seek a remedy or else abandon his mission. He found a tall narrow wooden building in Westminster, home to an apothecary.

He entered the dark interior and was greeted with the smells of herbal concoctions so familiar to his nose. The drably dressed cleric behind his tall desk asked William his symptoms, although by the way the man rubbed his hand across his middle it should have been obvious.

"Hawthorn is what you require," the apothecary announced simply. "It will take a while to prepare. You may be seated and wait." William sat on the cushioned chair indicated, grateful that he could now rest his legs and clutch his stomach with ease.

A few moments passed and William became aware that a second person had entered the apothecary's house. He saw the hem of the black robe of the cleric swish past him as he wrestled with a painful spasm in his gut.

"A good day to you, Caerleon, eminent physician."

William could hear the oily voice of the apothecary. "How fares our good lady, the queen?" His voice was lowered.

Caerleon uttered a guttural cough and William guessed by the way his robe twisted that the man had turned in his direction.

"A stranger from out of town; his stomach has not yet hardened to the delicate London fare." The apothecary chuckled good-humouredly. "Your physic will be ready shortly," he called to William. "But if you have a need to use my privy chamber 'tis beyond the drape," he laughed.

Even through his discomfort William could fathom that he had been offered a brief, if unintentional, opportunity. Still pressing his stomach William arose slowly from his chair and pulling back the heavy curtain he entered the room beyond. He did not, however, proceed any further but took up a position against the limewashed wall where he could see through the parted drape into the apothecary's shop. He prayed that any intelligence would be forthcoming for it would not be long before he would have to avail himself of the facility graciously offered.

"The lady fares better this day than of late," Caerleon continued now that they were alone. "And do not refer to her as queen. The Lady Beaufort has written to assure our Lady Elizabeth that her efforts to raise money to support her son Henry Tudor are proceeding well."

"And of what concern is that to... Lady Elizabeth?" the apothecary asked as he stirred a foul-smelling brew in a metal bowl.

"Elizabeth Woodville has given her support for Tudor's desire to take the crown from the usurper providing that he marries her daughter, Elizabeth of York. So you see, Simon, matters are moving at great speed and money is required to finance an invasion. Are you with us or not?"

"Aye, well I cannot say I care much for the northern upstart. We have prospered well under the Woodvilles. I am certain we could all benefit from a little Welsh influence eh?" The apothecary delved into the pouch at his belt, produced a bag of coin and passed it surreptitiously to the physician.

What followed was or may have been of great advantage to William had his circumstances been different. As Caerleon fumbled with his leather bag, into which he deposited the donation and the physic handed over by the apothecary, a scroll fell unnoticed from

470

the folds of his voluminous cloak and fluttered to the floor, coming to rest out of sight beneath the chair vacated moments earlier by the soldier.

It was perhaps unfortunate that William at that moment had the greatest need to bolt from his hiding place and outside to the covered midden. When he returned much later the shop was empty and his two bottles of hawthorn were ready and waiting.

A quick glance to the floor beneath the chair indicated that the scroll had not yet been missed. William thanked the saints for his good fortune and as the apothecary turned his back to place payment into the wooden box on the table behind him, the cunning soldier had stooped and retrieved the parchment, stuffing it unceremoniously into his coat.

Three days later William had recovered sufficiently to bring his report to John Howard, Duke of Norfolk, residing in London on the king's business. From William's findings and those of his fellow informants and others Norfolk was beginning to build up a very grim portrayal of events. He still needed the detail but the net was closing in.

"Now to focus on the part Henry Stafford has to play in this and his wily houseguest John Morton, Bishop of Ely," Norfolk mused, tapping his fingers on the polished oak of his board as William waited. At the mention of Henry Stafford's name William recalled the suspicious nature of a letter John Green was to deliver into the hands of Robert Brackenbury, Constable of the White Tower of London. He spoke of what he had witnessed at Gloucester to the Duke of Norfolk.

"That would explain much," Howard mused, rubbing his creased brow with jewelled fingers.

"How does work as a blacksmith at Brecon Castle take your fancy?" the duke asked after a while. "Pay particular attention to one Reginald Bray who may very well be staying under its roof."

William was about to take his leave when he remembered the scroll he had in his possession. It was somewhat crumpled and warm from its hiding place next to his chest but he produced it and tossed it on the table before Norfolk.

"Now this is interesting," the duke said, unravelling the parchment. William inclined his head to see what mysteries it contained. It meant nothing to him; just a series of odd drawings and lines with words he could not fathom scribed here and there.

"Do you know what this is?" Norfolk asked, turning the parchment round in his hand.

William shook his head.

"This is an astrological chart mapping the stars and reading fortunes and predictions. How came you by it?"

William relayed his story. The duke leaned forward in his chair.

"Lewis Caerleon, you say? The Welsh physician and astronomer, in attendance on Elizabeth Woodville," he mused. "I will have this chart interpreted and if it turns out to have any connection with King Richard Caerleon will find himself in serious trouble."

William, unfamiliar with such matters, puckered his brow.

"Casting the future of a king of England using the stars without his permission is a treasonable offence," Norfolk replied.

By the beginning of October John Howard, Duke of Norfolk, had gathered sufficient knowledge of a proposed rebellion to write to his king with almost every detail. Uprisings were planned in the southern counties: Kent, Berkshire, West Country and Wiltshire. Henry Tudor was expected to land in Devon with a large force and meet up with Buckingham at the crossing of the River Severn; their destiny London.

In the meantime the king had tested the loyalty of his kinsman Buckingham by summoning him to court; a summons he declined. Richard warned his loyal subjects in the north to prepare for battle.

Middleham Castle
Yorkshire
December 1483

The only sound to be heard was the crackle and spit of the logs burning on the fire; the one cheerful thing in the room. A grey dismal pallor pressed against the outside of the glazed casement; the sun had not strength enough to find its way through.

The countess sat on her great chair supported by plump duck down pillows. Two ladies-in-waiting, their gowns spread over the chest at the foot of the tester bed, sat in silence, their bronze needles pulling thread.

Christiana stared at the flames' hypnotic dance and felt her eyelids droop. The book she had been holding, the story of Sir Gawain and the Green Knight, began to slip slowly down her lap. The countess's sudden snort jolted her and she caught the book just in time to prevent its fall.

Bleary-eyed and only half awake Anne Beauchamp demanded to be put to bed; the short winter day was already over as far as she was concerned and Christiana was dismissed. She hurried from the chamber in the west range and out into the inner courtyard. It was not so late for there were still one or two people going about their duties in the damp swirls of mist.

She shivered beneath her cloak as she walked through the herb garden; even this place seemed to have been robbed of all its joy by the weather. Gently pushing open the wooden door of the cottage Christiana entered into its gloom. There was no wind to coax the hanging herbs to release their aroma and only a faint perfume filled the air.

A young woman was sitting at the table resting her head across outstretched arms; a discarded pestle and mortar lay beside her, a task unfinished.

"Tilly?" Christiana called, coming closer.

The woman looked up, blinking as she focused her eyes on the visitor.

"Oh, I am sorry, Christiana, I must have fallen asleep," she muttered.

"How is Martha?" the other woman asked, moving towards the inner door.

"I cannot say there is any change – no worse, no better."

Indeed that was how Christiana found the old woman, lying motionless on the bed, eyes closed, shutting out a world too weary to regard. Her breathing was gentle and easy. She did not appear to be in much, if any, pain. Christiana sat on the bed beside her friend and stroked the snow-white hair that tumbled in a grizzled heap across the pillow; her chin in slumber spread like dough across her neck. Martha had lain here for weeks now, her life slowly ebbing away. Christiana came every day and sat with her although she doubted the old herbalist even knew of her presence.

The shadows had lengthened and the room was engulfed in darkness before Christiana stirred from her vigil. She had heard voices in the adjoining herbarium: Tilly and a boy, a groom from the keep, asking about a remedy for the steward. Slowly she eased herself to her feet and gently kissed her friend's forehead.

As she entered the herbarium she found Martha's young apprentice close to tears. Tilly was fumbling around looking for some herb or another, feebly lifting the bottles and jars on the table.

"You are tired, Tilly, let me help you," Christiana offered. "What is it you require?"

Tilly lifted her head and stared at Christiana, tears welling slowly in her eyes. She sniffed and took a deep breath. "I should have made ready a mixture to ease John Conyers' cough but it slipped my mind and now I fear the steward will be angry. 'Tis not your place—"

"I should say it is precisely my place," Christiana interrupted sharply and picking up a hessian apron she tied it over her finely woven lambswool gown.

Within the half hour an infusion of coltsfoot was prepared and a semblance of order had been restored to the herbarium.

"You must let me take on some of your work, Tilly," Christiana said, pausing at the open door about to leave. "The ledgers I can continue to do until you are confident enough to take over but I can also lend a hand here when my duty to the countess does not keep me at the castle." She smiled at the younger woman before drawing her hood over her bare head.

She stepped out into the garden holding aloft a lantern for a curtain of cloud had veiled the starlight, although at last the fog had lifted. She hurried along the darkened pathways towards the keep. It pained her much to leave Martha at this time and she had no great desire to sit with the countess listening to the pointless twittering of her ladies. She felt that if such a thing were possible she would die of boredom.

As the days merged into endless night the castle that she loved began to take on more and more the feel of a prison. Seldom did Martha open her eyes and as she sat in silent vigil at her bedside Christiana's thoughts dwelt oft time on those now in London. After a suitable period of rest Anne had returned to court to join Richard: her first call of duty to her king and husband. She wondered greatly about life at court with the king and had a great longing to be there also with Richard. She found herself thinking much of her brother William and at these times a great feeling of loneliness would come upon her. She would have given much to have him here beside her at this time with Martha dying and Christmastide almost upon them.

Christiana's heart was not in the Christmastide festivities taking place in the great hall although for the sake of the young prince the occasion had been joyful to distract him from feeling the absence of his parents.

Slipping away at the first opportune moment Christiana had spent much of the day at the cottage. Martha seemed to sense the day was blessed for she had opened her eyes and allowed Christiana to feed her a little warmed pottage from a horn spoon. That had been a source of cheer to her melancholic heart.

It was now the afternoon of the Feast of Saint Stephen and

Christiana stood silently before the casement of the chamber. She looked up at the flakes of snow spinning and twirling in a downward spiral as they tumbled from a leaden sky. They seemed possessed of a magical light that transformed the courtyard without and brightened the room within.

Behind her the countess was in good spirits seated beside the flickering fire playing a game of fox and geese with her ladies. Every now and again a squeal of delight could be heard. Christiana did not turn at the sound of footsteps on the wooden floor and the voice of a young page. "My lady, there is a... person in the hall."

"A visitor on such a day as this? Can Conyers not attend to him?" The countess pushed aside her wooden board and began to rise from her chair.

"I beg your pardon, my lady, but he requests to see... Christiana."

The countess's companion turned from the window to catch the awkward look on the boy's young face as he stepped to one side.

"I trust that FitzHugh is aware of strangers within the castle?" Anne Beauchamp declared, somewhat startled.

"Oh he is no stranger, my lady," replied the page, glancing quickly at Christiana before backing furtively towards the door, awaiting leave to depart.

"You had best see who it is that awaits you then for I have a game to finish." The countess waved her servants along with a jewelled hand.

Climbing the outer staircase of the keep beneath a flurry of snowflakes Christiana's heart was pounding faster with every step. Who could possibly be awaiting her? It was someone who should have paid their respects to the countess in the first instance.

Across the hall, near the dais, stood a slightly built, well-dressed young man with a short sword hanging at his side and a goblet of wine in his hand.

Christiana laughed as she ran across the wooden floor to embrace her son. "John! *Sir* John," she exclaimed, almost knocking the goblet from his hand. "Why all the secrecy? You had me worried."

Now it was John who laughed. "I could hardly just walk into the countess's chamber now could I? And it appears that the steward is indisposed. The place is as quiet as a graveyard."

"It is so good to see you. Have you come all this way alone?"

"As if he would." She heard the voice of a man as he stepped from the shadow of the cupboard where he had stood hidden from view.

"William!" she cried, tears of joy and surprise filling her eyes. "How glad I am to see you." And then the delight went from her voice as she added, "Our dearest Martha is dying."

The smile faded from William's face. "I am sorry to hear it. We would have been here sooner if the weather had not delayed us. I will go to her now," he added softly and kissed his sister gently on the cheek before leaving the hall.

John and his mother took chairs beside the fire where a boy of no more than twelve years appeared at their side and poured Christiana a cup of wine and replenished John's goblet. As the boy withdrew to the far side of the fire John inclined his head and leaning towards his mother he whispered, "That is Robert Belle, my groom. His father, John, is cofferer to the king."

Christiana sipped her wine and smiled. "He is not much younger than you, my son," she observed.

"The king sends his greetings, Mother," said John.

"How is Richard?" Christiana asked with affection.

"He conducts himself well enough in public but in private I know that he is full of fear. I do not think that rebellion last autumn was the last we shall be hearing of his enemies."

"I have heard of this rebellion, John, but talk of it can keep for another time for you must rest awhile." Christiana reached across and brushed aside her son's dark hair where it had fallen across his eyes. "You take on more the likeness of your father by the day," she whispered. "Take care to stay out of trouble when you are in London."

They finished their wine in silence before the glowing fire. Presently John spoke. "I should like to see my brother before he takes to his bed. Please excuse me, Mother."

He left her alone by the fireside with her thoughts. Right glad she was to have her son and her brother back with her, however short their visit might prove to be.

"I thought to find you here," Christiana said, walking along the stone floor of the long stable block carrying her small light. William was lying on a blanket atop a stack of hay at the far end, a horn lantern hung on a hook above his head. The only sounds to be heard were the snorts and stomping of the horses at rest in their stalls.

"There is a bed for you at the castle, Will. You do not have to sleep in here," said Christiana.

"No, I do not have to but here I can keep a watch on the horses," he called down to her.

"There are stable lads to do that," she smiled. "Come down here so I can talk to you."

"I like it better here, sister. I am close to my work and I can come and go as I please," William said as he slid down the stack, scattering a spray of yellow straw and dried meadow flowers.

"This is no longer your work, Will," his sister replied softly.

"Well I like to return from time to time... you know, to where it all began," he replied nostalgically.

"You would do better up there," Christiana indicated the hay loft overhead. "'Twould be warmer."

"Aye well, if I have a mind to I can take a more elevated position." William upturned two buckets for them to sit on. Ever astute, Christiana was aware of a possible double meaning in William's words and asked, "Has Richard offered you more than this for your services and loyalty? Many men have been greatly rewarded by the king, so I have heard."

"Be that as it may," William replied. "I am content enough with what I have – for the most part. I am fed and clothed well; I have a purse or two of silver and a good sturdy horse to my name. What else should I desire?" He stared at her, the light from the lantern lighting up his brown eyes and brushing his fair hair with gold. It seemed to the woman in those few moments that his face looked so very sad and yet strangely it was not with a feeling of pity that she held his gaze.

"There are some things money cannot buy, Christiana," he said mournfully before lowering his gaze.

"John has spoken of an autumn rebellion," Christiana announced tentatively. "Little news has reached my ears although the guard was strengthened here at the garrison. Is Richard in great danger, Will?"

William stared into his sister's dark eyes. She always had a need for knowledge and he would do well to speak the truth to her as he knew it to be.

"Buckingham proved false, just as Richard suspected. He was lured by John Morton, who he had under house arrest, to join the rebels. Margaret Beaufort, Lady Stanley, has been in correspondence with Elizabeth Woodville, still claiming sanctuary in Westminster Abbey and together they have schemed to put Henry Tudor, Margaret's son, on the English throne."

Christiana's brow creased. "How is this possible, Will, for I have heard that this Henry, Welsh born, has no royal blood. Why should Englishmen give him their support?"

William sighed. "Tudor has a slight claim to the throne by virtue of his mother's royal connection but 'tis very feeble. King Edward, God bless him, left a power struggle in his wake and his dubious marriage to Elizabeth Woodville had the beginnings of a heavy and troublesome burden to put upon the shoulder of his youngest brother.

"Richard has built up loyal and powerful support here in the north which has angered many southerners and fuelled by malicious rumour that Richard has done away with his nephews in order to gain the throne for himself they rebelled in support of Tudor. The uprising was put down ere it took flight, Tudor's fleet failed to make dry land and Buckingham was executed."

"There is one then surely that Richard has overlooked," Christiana spat out angrily, her mind reeling with rumour and not rebellion. "Edward of Warwick, not declared a bastard, who is under a bill of attainder which can be reversed, is even now living under the protection of his uncle – why kill Edward's sons and spare George's?"

William caught his sister's hand as the glint of fury burned in her eyes. "We know the truth, Anna. But people are fickle and will believe anything they want to," William declared gently. "The Lancastrian faction is poised and ready once again but if all they have is the watered-down blood of a Welshman to spearhead their cause then we should have little to fear."

"Has all opposition to Richard's rule been dealt with, Will, as it should be?" Christiana asked softly.

William sighed and shuffled on his seat. "'Tis a strange thing, Anna, for some would say our king is too lenient. He has declined to punish Margaret Beaufort, Lady Stanley, for her part in this rebellion. Instead he has ordered her husband to keep her under house arrest and a close watch on her. I pray that this move will prove to be enough. As for Stanley himself, there lies a mystery for I cannot imagine the man to be unaware of his wife's traitorous activities and yet the king rewards him with Buckingham's forfeited estates and elevates him to Lord High Constable of England, a position formerly held by Buckingham."

"Maybe he is just being diplomatic," Christiana offered.

William said nothing for a while and picked at the pieces of hay that had clung to his clothes.

"Conyers intends to replace Martha with a herbalist from Rievaulx," Christiana said, directing their conversation to matters closer to home. "Of course that will not be until the spring thaw; I cannot say when the Lord will take our dear Martha."

"How does that decision rest with you? Are you not expected to take her place for you have the skill?" William asked.

"For certain I should like to step into Martha's shoes although it pains me to think of being without her. As to skill I have plenty but not enough; travelling the length and breadth of the realm with the king I have seen that there is still much to learn. It seems also to me that learned physicians are taking the place of herbalists, especially women, and I like not that concept. Whatever is to become of me I shall have little say in the matter, I fear. If I am to remain here in service to the countess then so be it but I must confess, Will, that I have no liking for such work."

Christiana finished on a note of such self-pity that was so unlike her that William felt compelled to strengthen his grip on her hand. A sudden rush of cold wind blowing under the outer door wafted the hay and rocked the lantern in its cradle. Christiana shivered in the cold and gripped tightly William's hand as though she sought comfort and assurance from his touch.

"Are you to stay long, Will?" she asked softly.

"Nay, we are to return as soon after Twelfth Night as the weather permits. The king wants us back at Westminster for the opening of his first Parliament mid-January. As you say, my work is that of a soldier now."

"'Tis what you always wanted," Christiana smiled sadly.

"It is getting late, Christiana, you should be getting back to the countess," William whispered.

"She will not miss me I think. At this hour she will be snoring enough to shake the castle walls and so will her ladies." A single tear had crept unbidden to her eye and trickled slowly down her cheek.

"Stay here this night," William offered softly, his heart pounding. In fear that his suggestion might be misconstrued he added the word 'sister' to his proposal. "The hay loft will make a warm and dry bed as you say and I have more than one blanket," he went on. "Up there daybreak will wake you well before it reaches into the castle walls and you can be away before ever your mistress stirs."

William's invitation seemed very welcome of a sudden and with only a moment's hesitation Christiana found herself giving consent and laying down a musty woollen blanket across a bed of hay. She hung her little lantern on a hook from the beam above her head.

For a long while she lay on her back listening to the sounds of the horses below and breathing in their warm smell. Memories of her early childhood floated dreamily in her head bringing such a sense of comfort she had not felt in many a year.

Beside her, William lay on his side with his back to her. She could not tell whether he slept or not. It was as though time had run backwards and they were two small children once again in their father's smithy except that now they were grown and this was no brother that lay beside her. She turned onto her side and snuggled closer to William's back and very, very gently she placed a hand on his shoulder. There she slept peacefully until a grey winter dawn roused her.

Middleham Castle
Yorkshire
Early January 1484

It had been quiet in the stable yard all morning, nothing going out or coming in. The horses were all stabled under cover munching on their oats. With the unexpected presence of one of the king's personal retainers the stable boys and grooms had made themselves scarce, along with the blacksmith, who saw no purpose in hanging around an empty smithy.

William was in sullen mood as he sat on an upturned barrel within the shelter of the smithy to eat his midday meal. The small loaf of bread was stale and the cheese had a leathery texture but he had little appetite. He discarded the food and drank instead from his jug of ale.

For certain Martha was not long for this world and as regrettable as it was the old woman had had a long and fruitful life and was no doubt ready to meet her maker. It was Christiana who gave him cause for concern. How would she fare after Martha's passing? With him and John away soon back to London she would feel the loss of her friend all the keener.

He looked up sharply as his eye caught the sight of movement. A bony mule, heavy laden with hessian sacks and leather pouches, ambled into the yard, a portly white-garbed monk at its side. Despite the chill wind and a covering of frost still on the cobblestones the man was panting hard.

"A good day to you, Brother," called William. "'Tis not the weather to be out in. Step inside and warm yourself at the brazier."

"I thank you, young man," came the reply. William smiled at the monk's form of address. At two and thirty years of age he would hardly have described himself as young.

"I have a supply of cheese and wine from the monastery at Jervaulx," the monk said, waving a fat hand towards his mule before walking inside to the smithy. "Oh and there are some earthenware pots of new made ink. I must take care with those," he mumbled. "'Tis all recorded here on the ledger." He patted the scrip hanging at his side and turned to rub his hands over the glowing embers.

"The weather is bad for sure." The monk's face shone red in the firelight and little beads of sweat formed like dew drops on his forehead.

"I wonder that you are out on such a day. A man can be buried alive in a sudden snow drift on the moors," William remarked.

"Aye that he can," mused the monk, nodding his head nonchalantly. "I bring supplies and a message for Conyers," he mused absent-mindedly.

Suitably warmed the monk stepped out again into the cold. A few light flakes of snow had begun to flutter from the grey sky and he peered upwards as he shuffled over to his mule.

"I had best be getting this lot up to the keep," sighed the monk and began to lead the mule towards the road.

He had only gone a few yards when the blacksmith hailed him. "A moment, Brother; your mule has a loose shoe, let me tap it back on!"

The monk hesitated. "No need to bother yourself. It will suffice until I return to the monastery."

"The mule could well slip in this ice. The shoe is neither on nor off." William strode across the cobbles and now had the animal's leather rein in his hands. "Come, it will not take long."

"He only lets Brother Simon touch his feet," the monk mumbled awkwardly as he followed William back to the smithy. "A right temper he has," he added nervously.

"Nonsense, 'tis only a beast of burden. Now hold his head steady," William insisted.

With the hind leg grasped firmly between his thighs William managed to secure the shoe but not before, with a steady blast of braying and much bucking, the mule had dislodged several pouches and bags from its back. Red-faced and breathing hard William reached down into the straw to retrieve the fallen bags cursing the mule under his breath, much to the amusement of the monk.

"I warned you to leave him to Brother Simon," he chuckled. "You should have taken the bags off first. Oh my, oh my!" He gasped in horror as he remembered the clay inkpots and it was William's turn to laugh as the monk bent down and fumbled amongst the fallen pouches lying in the straw. It took several moments for the good Brother to realise that the precious vessels were still tightly secured to the back of the volatile mule.

William was still chuckling to himself several moments later as he leant on the wall of the smithy, the monk and his mule had certainly brightened his mood, when out of the icy swirls shot a figure, breathing hard from running.

"Uncle Will!" John gasped, halting before him, the snow jewelling his dark hair. "Mother says you are to come now. 'Tis Martha's time."

William felt strangely unreal trudging through the falling snow towards the cottage, his mood once again plummeting. Tilly met them at the door and ushered them into the room beyond the herbarium wherein lay Martha. Christiana sat on the bed holding the old woman's hand. She turned her head as William approached, a pained, tear-washed expression on her face. He was too late, for it seemed that even within the last moment Martha had gone, passing away silently like cloud shadow across water.

William walked up to the bed and looked into his sister's face. The almost imperceptible nod of her head confirmed his thoughts. He gently took the still warm hand, soft and wrinkled, in his own and kissed it.

Christiana stood to face him. As with Alfred's death many years before their mutual grief united them. William wrapped his arms around his sister and drew her to him. His embrace went beyond the need to comfort; he became aware of her body pressed against his and his sorrow turned to longing. Their bodies parted and William found himself touching her cheeks with his roughened fingers and then he kissed her full on the lips. Suddenly afraid of himself he turned from her and left the cottage.

From his place by the window John looked down at the figure on the bed. He felt a little numb, saddened at the loss of the old woman who had meant so much to him as a boy. As he too departed, leaving his mother and Tilly to do the things that women did at times like this, he took with him one lasting memory. The embrace he had witnessed between his mother and his Uncle Will had seemed natural enough given the circumstances and yet the kiss did not seem the sort a brother would give a sister. It was too tender, somehow too intimate.

Standing watching them together he had been struck by their unfamiliar likeness. His mother was so dark and petite; William was tall, broad and fairer. He knew well enough that not all siblings were alike. He would not be easily recognised as brother to the Prince of Wales, who had his mother's golden hair and pale eyes.

Then there was Katherine. His father had taken him to meet his half-sister, a little younger than he, and now soon to be given in marriage to one William Herbert. She had hair the colour of oak bark and eyes to match. For some reason he could not quite fathom he had never mentioned their meeting to his mother.

He pondered much over this feeling that told him that all was not proper between his mother and her brother and resolved to one day seek an answer – and soon.

Yorkshire
Early January 1484

They reined in their horses and from their lofty position looked down on that magnificent fortress. A golden hue from the winter sun bathed its walls in glory and the peaks of snow on the parapets glistened like sugar cones.

Across the dales in dell and ravine only hardened drifts still had a hold while on the higher ground the browned grass stood wet with melted snow. Some way in the distance they could hear the Ure, its waters swollen and dark, tumbling and roaring in its bed.

After a while they rode on going southwards; William, John and his groom Robert together with four armed men. William regarded his nephew as he rode beside him and pondered at the boy's unusual silence. It was perhaps that he was missing his mother now that their leave of absence was at an end and it was time to join his father once again in London.

Although the snow was melting William knew that they would have to make good speed before nightfall when another freeze could well grip the land. There was barely a word exchanged between them as they rode across hill and dale, carefully skirting the fallen trees and debris brought down by the gales and flood water which now festooned the road.

The journey south was familiar to William and he knew that it would not be long before they reached their first resting place. Daylight had almost faded and there was a raw chill in the air as they caught sight of the small hostelry nestled deep in the shelter of a hillside and guarded by a circle of bare-boned oaks.

After a welcome supper of warm pottage and bread the four soldiers joined the only other two guests at the inn for a game of dice. John sat in the shadows of the wall, his arms resting on his bent knees, staring pensively ahead. His groom, Robert, was curled up on his cloak asleep beside the fire.

William watched the young man, the boy he had always thought of as nephew, from the other side of the room where he sat cross-legged sharpening the blade of his dagger along a whetstone. He could almost be watching the king himself the way the boy puckered his dark brows, shielding hidden thoughts.

Presently William stood to his feet and went across to John. Sitting himself down beside the young man he asked, "Is there aught wrong, lad? You have uttered nary a word since leaving the castle."

John turned his dark eyes to William and held his gaze, weighing his thoughts carefully. The reply he gave was in the form of a question, asked boldly and one that William had not expected to hear. "You are not my mother's brother are you, Uncle Will?"

The blacksmith said nothing for a moment but seeing no reason to lie to the boy now that he had guessed at the truth or found it out, he replied simply, "No, John, I am not."

The boy inclined his head slowly and then threw William such a look of austere suspicion that it startled the soldier. He put down his dagger and whetstone and placed his rough hand on the boy's arm. "You can be certain beyond doubt that Richard the king is your father," he said gravely. "Alfred, your mother's father, found me as a boy of seven years, orphaned by the battle of Wakefield, and took me as his own son. I knew no one but the womenfolk in the village where I lived. My father was always away at one battle or another. It was after Wakefield and I found myself joining the throngs of people going up to York that Alfred and Christiana found me. She begged her father to look after me. While much of my life before that day remains a haze I shall never forget your mother's kindly face. Alfred was the only father I really knew and I have been a brother to Christiana ever since."

"But you do not love her as a brother," John stated, looking earnestly at his uncle.

William smiled. "You imagine much for one so young."

"I do not imagine, Uncle, I see," John replied.

"Do you indeed?" William picked up the stone and began running the blade of his dagger along it once more.

"I have loved your mother like a man loves a woman, if you take my meaning." William's face darkened as he stared down at his hands. "For all the good it ever did me. I might as well have been conceived of Alfred's seed for I will never be more than brother to her." The blade of the dagger moved faster along the stone.

A raucous bellow of laughter came from the dice players holding out their cups to be replenished by a serving wench.

"Go easy on the ale, men," William called sharply. "We have a long journey ahead on the morrow."

"She loves my father I know and yet she cannot have him either." John sighed, his words almost a lament on the tribulation of love.

"Let us hope that your father the king finds you a suitable bride and that you do not have the burden of being in love with another." William smiled, a little more light-hearted, and looked up at the unglazed casement where a few feathery snowflakes fluttered against a dark sky. "We must get some sleep for there will be an early start and let us pray that this snow will not settle."

It took them several more days to traverse the frozen roads but as they moved south so the winter seemed to lessen its iron grip. Finally, cold and weary, the seven travellers reached their journey's end. Entering through the city gates around midday into a throng of bustle and filth they pushed their way along narrow streets of bare-footed children and squealing pigs to the Palace of Westminster.

Middleham Castle
Yorkshire
Early February 1484

"I am most pleased to see you again, Lady Margaret." Christiana smiled at the older woman as they walked together through the castle garden. All around them the tiny frost-laden Candlemas bells had bravely pushed their heads through the cold ground to greet them as they passed. They had all lost their charm on Christiana, however; nothing would be the same without her beloved Martha.

Lady Huddleston spread her modest lambswool gown of yellow weld across the bench, wrapped her cloak closer and beckoned the other woman to be seated beside her.

"I too am glad to be here," Margaret answered kindly. "Now, what news is there from court?"

Christiana blushed, a little embarrassed, for with the departure of her brother and her son little news had reached her ears. "With the putting down of Buckingham's rebellion last autumn nothing else is known," she offered. "Maybe the threat to Richard has passed."

Lady Margaret Huddleston took a rather sharp intake of breath. "Do not believe it, my dear," she replied somewhat sternly. "The threat grows ever stronger."

Christiana felt the cold shadow of foreboding pass over her spirit; she shivered despite the tepid warmth of the afternoon. Margaret, not unaware of the other woman's concern, wrapped her warm fingers around the slim cold hand of her friend.

"Richard is doing all he can to prepare for this invasion, for it will surely come."

Christiana felt the sting of unshed tears well up under her eyelids. "This Henry Tudor has no claim to the throne; no one will give him their support."

"Great damage has been done to our king's reputation. He is not popular in London where rumour spreads like a plague; not surprising considering he has spent most of his life building a kingdom here in the north."

"But, Margaret, Richard was fiercely loyal to his brother King Edward. He brought together the northern barons and kept the peace with Scotland." Christiana felt the tears trickle down her cheek and wiped them with the sleeve of her gown.

"Loyalty means very little in this cousins' war," Margaret answered grimly. She paused only for a moment, unsure whether or not to give voice to the knowledge she had only just that morning received from her husband. "Richard, my husband, informs me that Henry Tudor has made a solemn vow in the cathedral at Rheims on Christmas Day last to marry Elizabeth of York, Edward's eldest child. That will strengthen his claim to the English throne if nothing else will," she announced solemnly.

"I wonder greatly that Elizabeth Woodville can support such a union. Would she not want to fight for her son Edward's right to the throne? For if one is considered a bastard then surely all? This of course if Edward lives..." Christiana's voice trailed off mournfully.

Lady Margaret sat in rigid silence; what answer could she give for who knew the truth?

"I want to go to Richard," Christiana whispered tearfully.

"I am summoned to my sister, the queen," Margaret replied softly. "It may be that she would welcome you also at court for she too is in need of loyal friends.

"Now come, we must go to the countess. She is most concerned about her grandson, little Edward. How do you find his health?"

The two women left the bench in the garden and walked back towards the keep. Christiana too was troubled by the frail health of the little prince and conveyed her worries to her companion as they walked.

They found the countess on the approach to the prince's chambers in the south-west tower of the castle. Her ladies flittered around her like caged birds; her concern for her grandson was evident in her pale, drawn face. She greeted Lady Huddleston with a less than cheerful smile.

The little prince looked up from his board game, his golden curls framing a milk-white countenance wherein his pallid blue eyes stared dully as the visitors entered.

Jane Collins, Edward's nurse, moved her counter across the board and left her chair at the table to approach Countess Anne. "The prince seems a little better this morn, my lady," she offered with a curtsy. "I thought to take him for a stroll in the garden once his physician has visited." The woman looked expectantly to the countess who inclined her head briefly.

Later that afternoon Christiana was once again taking in the sights and smells of the garden, this time as part of the countess's small entourage of ladies. They ambled slowly along the gravelled pathways, sweeping the stones with their trailing hems. Edward walked alongside patting the hairy back of his dog, making an effort to keep up with its long-legged gait.

Christiana and her companion, Lady Huddleston, withdrew to the rear of the group, slightly apart from the others.

"The boy looks so much younger than his ten years," Margaret whispered sadly. "'Tis a great pity that the queen has not produced any more children for all her thoughts and effort will be directed to him. Let us pray that this one will thrive."

Christiana smiled at the sound of Edward's laughter as he ran with his dog and remembered his father at this same age, but her heart was heavy. "Will you stay?" she pleaded, suddenly afraid. "I feel so alone in this place, neither fowl nor fish."

Margaret chuckled at the woman's choice of words but she understood. "I will stay as long as I am able," she said, linking her arm affectionately through Christiana's.

"Will, what say you to coming into town with Dick and me? Look out for a decent tavern."

William was just banking down the brazier with a few pieces of turf, sending a billow of peaty smoke into the air. "Aye, why not," he coughed. "Give me a few minutes to clean up and I'll be with you."

Before joining his companions William walked around to the stable block where the king kept his large and impressive collection of horses. He passed John Frisley, clerk of the king's horse, and hailed him. He put a hand to his stomach; there was that irritable pain he had felt earlier.

He found John brushing out the coat of his horse, a grey stallion of unusual dappled markings and a snow-white mane. "How goes it, John?" William called jovially. The boy looked up at his uncle and smiled.

"My work is done here for the day. What say you to coming to town for a while?" William asked.

"You can drink ale here at the garrison, Will," John replied, moving the hard-bristled brush over his horse's flank.

"Aye, but 'tis good to get away from the palace, lad. You look as though you could do with a change," William pleaded.

"I do not know, Will. I am still under the guardianship of my tutor and he might not approve of my going out alone, especially with the king sitting at his first parliament," John replied morosely.

"Well your tutor is not your gaoler is he? Besides you will not be alone. My companions and I are well armed, not to mention that sword by your side. What harm can there be in a few hours of pleasure for yourself?" William persisted, rubbing his stomach. Finally John acquiesced, throwing his brush to one of the stable lads.

"I am sure you would have rather been with the king and his parliament as he makes decisions for the good of his subjects eh?" William enquired of John as they walked to the belfry in the yard where the others were waiting for them.

"My father thinks me too young to become embroiled in politics. He sees me developing a military vocation and has promised me a position to that end," John remarked without enthusiasm. "Should you not be with the king, Uncle?" John asked as they vacated the palace enclave.

"The king has sufficient guard for his needs; I am content to give a hand at the stables. It serves the king well that I can turn my hand to many tasks," William replied, thinking of his days as a royal emissary.

Leaving the dank fish-smelling banks of the Thames the four men headed for the narrow crowded alleys of the town. William glanced up at the lavender sky where a sweep of stars had begun to twinkle. "I hope one of you lads has a lantern," he remarked jovially. "I for one do not want to tread in this foul mess on the way back to the palace."

"You do not suppose a man in my position would walk these streets not well armed with a sturdy lantern do you?" Bill Watson laughed as he pulled out the aforementioned object from beneath his cloak. Richard Dull, known to his friends as Dull Dick, and William Watson were footmen to the king and both acquaintances of William.

The first tavern they happened upon, a ramshackle, timber-framed building in the heart of Cheapside and displaying a crooked painting of a black bull, was crowded.

"Must be something worth coming here for," remarked Bill as they fought their way through sweating bodies concealed in eye-stinging smoke from the fire. Dick called to a serving wench for a flagon of ale and four cups. There was a table in the corner, near the fire, occupied by one body slumped senseless across its ale-soaked surface. Bill gave it a nudge with his elbow and the inebriated soul fell to the floor with a bump.

"Well, lads, the ale's not bad for London; naught like Yorkshire

494

ale though." William raised his cup to his companions and downed half of its contents, grimacing slightly as he placed his cup on the table.

They drank, talked of home, played dice and after their third flagon of ale John began to feel comfortably merry. The smoke was making him drowsy and he leaned back against the rough limewashed wall and watched the others battle out the last game of dice; he had not the luck to stay the course.

After a while he grew bored and his eyes wandered around the room. There were a few less people now but the room was still full. He chuckled at the fellow on the other side of the fire whose large mangy dog drank ale from his flagon while his attention was turned to the buxom young girl sat on his knee. At another table a heated discussion was in full swing between a thin, wiry, balding man and a formidable-looking red-faced woman – his wife, no doubt.

A lone figure sitting in the far corner of the tavern caught his roving eye. He looked to be a well-built man of around mid-forty years although his outer garments cloaked much of his body. A pair of dark eyes stared from beneath an abundance of long black hair, liberally sprinkled with grey. That their gaze was directed straight at John there was no mistake and the boy began to feel most uncomfortable.

Beside him on the bench William too was now out of the game and John turned his attention to his uncle. "Are you unwell?" he asked as William, his face creased with pain, pressed against his stomach with folded arms.

"I know what's wrong with him," offered Bill, turning from the game. "I warned him against eating that shellfish earlier. You cannot trust anything those old men bring up the river in those filthy boats."

"Aye well, remind me to listen to your advice next time," William gasped and in the next instant was on his feet and rushing towards the back door of the tavern.

"Now he'll pay the price," laughed Bill heartily.

"Should I not go to him?" John asked anxiously.

"Nay, lad," Bill replied, still chuckling. "It will not be a comely sight. You stay here and I'll go nurse him." He turned to Dick before he left. "Call the game a draw. Go find a wench for some more ale. I dare say Will should need a good top up when he's finished puking," he said gleefully.

Alone now on the bench John felt a touch uneasy. He hoped that his uncle was not suffering too much and made a pledge to himself never to eat shellfish. He began to think that he should have gone to him after all when without warning a man sat down on the bench beside him. It was the dark stranger from across the room. Slightly alarmed, John edged away looking around the room; there was no sign of Dick and the door leading to the midden was still shut.

"Well, well," said the stranger, "if it isn't the young John of Gloucester." The man spoke with a thick Yorkshire accent and John turned a curious face towards him.

"Should I know you?" he asked politely.

"You may or may not know me," replied the stranger evasively. "But I know you and your mother. Tell me, how is the lovely Christiana?"

John did not at all like the way he uttered his mother's name. "Who are you that I might send her your regards?" he asked, trying to keep his composure.

"Let us say that I am an old friend of hers and of your father," the stranger smirked.

"I hope you do not speak ill of the king," John said angrily, forgetting that he had always been warned against drawing attention to his identity in a public place.

"Indeed, I do not. God Bless his Grace King Richard is what I say – though some would not agree," he added under his breath.

He put out a large roughened hand and touched the green woven fabric of John's sleeve and bringing his ale-reeking mouth closer to the boy he whispered in his ear, "A word of advice, my young prince. Men are not always what they seem and loyalty comes at a high price, too high for some. Tell that to your father if you've a mind."

The back door of the inn opened just then and John turned his head to see Bill enter, leading a pale-faced William by the arm. John jumped to his feet to assist his uncle to a chair. When next he looked the stranger was gone. Dick appeared suddenly at the table, a smile on his face but no sign of any ale.

"Can we go back to the palace, Will?" John asked quietly.

William forced a smile. "I am sorry, lad, I spoiled your night out."

"'Twas not you who have spoiled the night, Will," he said, helping his uncle to his feet.

The cool evening air hit John full in the face as he stepped out into the street. As Bill's lantern bobbed before them they navigated the narrow alleyways back to the palace with taunts from his companions each time William had to stop to vomit again.

John walked in silence beside them brooding over the face of the stranger he had met in the inn and whether or not he should know him or be afraid of him.

Middleham Castle
Yorkshire
Late April 1484

The night was unusually chill; the heavy wool coverlet could not keep the warmth in Christiana's bones. She tossed and turned, disturbing the slumber of her bedfellow. At that very moment, before any words of protest could leave the woman's lips, the curtain to Lady Beauchamp's bedchamber parted and a servant entered unannounced.

"My lady, you must come at once." His voice, like an omen of doom, echoed around the chamber, rousing all the ladies from their sleep.

Christiana was the first to her feet, reaching for her cloak. Someone covered the countess's slender shoulders with a velvet cape; Lady Huddleston was lighting candles from the lantern carried by the servant; soon they were ready to depart. The countess would allow none but the bastard daughter of her late husband and the herbalist to accompany her.

Candles flickered and shadows danced in the gloom of the prince's chamber. Poor Jane Collins was beside herself, kneeling tearfully at the bedside of her charge. It would appear from the mutterings of the physician and others that the boy had taken ill with a malady of such speed, leaving him in the grip of a raging fever and a severe pain in his head.

The physician ordered the boy to be bled and purged; to no avail. Then concoctions of foul-smelling liquid were poured down his throat, which did nothing but make the prince sick. All the while they had to endure the child's pitiful cries for his mother; a helpless plea as the poor woman was miles away at Nottingham.

Christiana was allowed to examine the boy but like the physician was at a loss as to the cause of his illness. The only unusual symptom she noted was how the boy recoiled fiercely whenever a candle light was brought near to his face. They had to tend to his needs in near darkness. The castle chaplain was awoken from his bed and offered prayers and anointing for the child's soul.

"Margaret," Christiana whispered to her companion. "I fear there is nothing more to be done. How can this be? The king's son and heir..." she lamented sorrowfully.

Lady Huddleston wiped away a falling tear and patted the arm of the younger woman. "The child is in the care of God now," she returned with stoic acceptance.

Finally as the day broke with its pearly hue the life of the little prince ebbed away and death brought him peace. For a long, eternal moment of time there was absolute silence around the bed; it was the darkest day ever to dawn upon Middleham Castle. Then the loud, anguished wailing of the countess pierced the silence.

The little body was prepared and laid to rest in the private chapel and the castle was draped in cloth of mourning. The dean of the church in Middleham, William Beverley, arrived to offer what comfort he could to the mourners.

Christiana helped where she could and watched as a small procession left the castle, their destination Nottingham and the king. Amongst them was Lady Margaret, ready to give succour to her sister, the queen. There was nothing else to be done now but wait in hopeless resignation for the return of the king.

Christiana sat on a bench near the dovecote with a basket of herbs on her lap. In pensive mood she had a hand inside twirling the fragrant leaves. Conyers was still negotiating the services of an experienced herbalist from Rievaulx; it would appear the matter was more complicated than he had envisaged. Fortunately for Christiana it had meant that her knowledge and assistance was still required at the cottage.

There was an eerie silence all around her; even the doves had ceased their cooing and sat with puffed up feathers and melancholic eyes. Christiana looked up at the great walls of the keep with a heavy heart and tried not to let her thoughts dwell upon the king within. She had kept away from Richard, leaving him to grieve with his family, taking refuge in the herbarium where she had helped Tilly prepare elixirs to bring comfort to anguished hearts. She had also gathered the ingredients for the king's poultice should he have a need.

The sound of footsteps advancing along the gravel path drew her attention and she raised her head as the lone figure of a woman halted before her. The lady sat down on the bench beside her and spoke in a small cracked voice. "I beg of you to go to the king. He is beside himself with grief and will not be comforted. Not even his closest..." her voice trailed off.

Christiana turned to the woman in surprise; of all the people she could imagine making such a request, Anne Beauchamp would be the last. The countess's face was pale and it was clear from its puffiness that she had shed recent tears. "My daughter has been unable to finish her journey home. She has collapsed with a broken heart," Anne said tearfully. "I thank God her sister is with her."

Christiana closed her eyes and sighed. "I cannot do anything for the king, my lady. He will not want to see me for surely his anger will be turned against me for I could do nothing to save..." Her throat had swollen painfully and her words seemed caught there as if barbed.

She felt the countess's hand rest gently on her arm. "I do not ask this for myself, Christiana, but for the sake of my daughter. Anne will need him to be strong – England will need him to be strong. He will want to hear an account of this from your own lips. He will trust your telling of it. Go to him and speak of what you know and... give him hope."

Christiana nodded slowly and laying aside her basket she rose from the bench. With heavy steps and a heart full of leaden sorrow she walked towards the keep. She felt no warmth from the May sunshine casting its rays above her head.

The guards on duty wore rigid masks of sadness. The great hall was festooned with black drapes that stirred in the draught. At this hour the place should have bustled with life but not a soul could be seen or heard. A tiny door in the furthermost right-hand corner stood ajar; it led to the small private chapel. Where else but in the presence of God would the king be?

Pausing outside the door she took a deep breath. What if he did blame her, or hate her even? Could she live with that? She pushed the door gently and walked inside.

The interior was cold and musty. Two small casements ahead let in the light and to the right of her a glass window glowed in iridescent colour. Tapestries of saints and biblical scenes hung from the walls and in the still air two altar candles burned in solemn reverence. A solitary wooden table bearing a Book of Hours and an open Bible stood between two carved cushioned chairs.

Christiana tiptoed across the tiled floor hardly daring to look at the little body of the prince, cold and pale as alabaster, draped in white robes on a stone slab, strewn with pungent herbs and spices, before the altar. The king was on his knees in prayer; after a while he sensed her presence and stood to his feet, turning to face her.

Never before in her life had she seen a face so ravished and tortured by grief. His cheeks were hollow and white like the rose in stark contrast to the shadow of beard growth across his jaw. His hair, usually so carefully groomed, fell in unkempt strands about his shoulders. Dark and deep like bottomless wells his eyes stared at her.

It took only three small steps and she was beside him, biting her lip to check the flow of tears. With trembling hand she reached out and very gently touched his shoulder. He stood like a statue, unyielding and hard. She gently pressed her fingers into his flesh. He did not move, neither responding to nor repelling her touch. She moved closer and enfolded him in her arms. For several moments she was aware only of her great love for him bubbling up like a spring within her, until she sensed the force of his grief rising as silent sobs that shook his whole frame and then his arms enclosed her tightly.

She held on to him and wept with him – she could do no less. His tears wet her gown, her neck, her hair. With arms around him she waited until his heaving sobs had abated and then she led him to a chair. Sitting beside him she kept hold of his cold trembling hand.

"Why, Christiana?" he said, drawing breath. "Why am I cursed among men?"

"Oh, Richard," she sighed. "You are not cursed. God takes children from peasants and kings alike. Who can say why? In that at least we are all equal."

The king's head was full of the musings that had once plagued his younger days. Throughout his early years when he knew his back to be twisted and with each passing season a little more, he had wrestled with many anguished thoughts. He had many discussions with William Beverley. What sin, whose sin, had caused this deformity? His journey had led him to a deeper understanding of God and a greater dependence upon His mercy; until now when his peace was threatened by his loss.

As she sat there in the tranquillity of God's holy chapel she grew afraid. She was afraid to be alone with him because with her whole being she longed for him. She feared also her own helplessness for she had no remedy, no herb that could ease his pain.

Richard's hand was cold; he shivered. In the shadows of the quiet chapel the king bowed his head. "None can fathom the ways of Almighty God," he whispered at last. "We must trust in His Goodness and know also that there are darker powers at work in this world."

Presently Richard withdrew his hand from hers and walked over to the stone slab where the body of his ten-year-old son awaited internment. Very gently he stroked the fair hair and bending over he kissed the cold white cheek. He turned to Christiana, who stood beside him. "After Eddy's internment I must leave for New Castle; my arrival there is long overdue. But first you must tell me how my child died."

It was not a command but rather a plea, one that she could not refuse, however painful it would be for them both.

"My lord, let us withdraw to the warmth of the hall, for see how cold you are." She took his arm and gently guided him out of the cold air of the chapel. He was shivering for his shirt was thin and he wore no tunic. She drew two chairs up to the spitting fire burning in the middle of the floor and took a fur-lined cloak from its peg and wrapped it about his shoulders. There was wine and goblets on a table against the wall and after pouring the king a goodly measure she bade him drink. Settling herself in the other chair and fortifying herself with the king's wine she began to recall the event, which had shaken to the core every member of the king's household at Middleham.

The day had ended for her like many others. She had gathered herbs under the warm sun and helped to prepare them for Tilly. She had gone over the ledger and all seemed in order. In answer to the king's question, no one had asked for anything out of the ordinary or unusual either on that day or before. Nothing was missing; the poison chest was secured and all in order.

At dusk she had returned to the castle where she had read a little to the countess before retiring to her bed. It took her several moments to relive the following painful hours as the king sat and listened.

At last Christiana's story had come to an end. The fire had

diminished to glowing embers and torches had been lit all around them for dusk was falling. She looked across at Richard, his blue eyes gleaming in the light. "All the hopes and future of this realm were in that boy, snuffed out like a candle," he said painfully. "I doubt my wife will produce another child now."

She leaned forward and touched his sleeve. "Richard, you are the hope and future of this realm. Take the courage of the boar for there are many who love you. And do not give up the hope of more sons; Anne is still young."

She could sense by the way he tensed his shoulders that his back pained him.

"Shall I prepare your physic, Richard?" she whispered. "I will have it sent to your chamber."

There were servants entering the hall to prepare for the evening meal, for life went on. And so she must leave him. Rising to her feet she dared to kiss the crown of his head, caring not who saw her.

As she turned away the king caught her sleeve. "Bring it yourself," he whispered and then let her go.

Palace of Westminster
London
Late January 1485

The palace had an air of bleakness and sobriety this wintertime that had little to do with the weather. There was none of the splendour and pageantry that she had witnessed on her last visit a little under two years ago for the king's coronation. The certainty that the queen only nine and twenty years of age lay dying seemed to permeate even the lavish decoration of this, the most splendid of royal residences.

It seemed very strange to be back here once again, and that at the request of the queen herself. Escorted by a troop of the king's men-at-arms through a cold, barren wilderness of snow and ice Christiana had felt little regret at leaving her home at Middleham.

The months since the death of the Prince of Wales had seemed never ending. The steward finally got his monk and last summertime a most austere, bitter-faced young cleric and two boy apprentices moved in to the cottage. Tilly moved back to the dairy and Christiana spent all her time at the castle. With her beloved Martha buried in the churchyard of Saint Mary and Saint Alkelda everyone Christiana held most dear to her was here in London. For better or for worse this was where her heart compelled her to be.

She barely had time to unpack her gowns into a wooden chest in her chamber when she was summoned to appear before the queen. An usher, who uttered no word as they walked the length of the brightly lit and beautifully painted passageways, escorted her to the queen's great chamber. Christiana hoped her gown of deep blue satin would be presentable enough to meet the queen. It had not travelled well, stuffed into a leather trunk and piled onto a baggage cart.

"My Lady Queen." Her voice was soft and low as she made her reverence at the door of the chamber.

"Who is this, Margaret?" A thin childlike voice came from a small figure lying atop a pile of well-stuffed pillows on the high bed.

"'Tis your herbalist from Middleham. She is here at your request, my queen," replied the familiar voice of Lady Huddleston.

"Christiana?" Anne smiled feebly and attempted to lift herself up onto her elbow. "Forgive me, I am ill and my wit abandons me at times. Come closer." She patted the bed covers with a grey bony hand.

Christiana was troubled by the great change that had come about in the queen since she had last set eyes on her. She lay on the coverlet like a thin winter twig, devoid of colour and life.

"How is the weather?" the queen asked breathlessly.

"The snow still falls, madam, and 'tis bitter cold," Christiana replied.

"Glad I am then for this fire and to be indoors." Anne fell silent and Christiana sat patiently, exchanging a glance with Lady Huddleston.

"Have they told you I am dying?" Anne asked presently.

"Yes," Christiana whispered, "and sorry I am to hear it."

"Have you herbs to cure the consumption? This is what I am told is robbing me of life." Such a question, asked with hopeless resignation, brought deep sorrow to Christiana's heart.

"Dearest Anne," she said. "I can offer your herbalists and physicians such knowledge as I have but I fear there is no cure."

"Then I shall give up all hope except the hope that one day soon I shall see once again my Edward."

Christiana took the fragile hand that lay light as a feather on the coverlet and smiled.

"I am tired, Margaret," the queen said, her breathing slow and laboured as she attempted to suppress a cough.

Christiana took her leave and hurried back to her chamber in the privy palace, feeling a coldness in the air that seemed to seep into her very soul.

Sometime later Lady Margaret Huddleston found Christiana sitting in the queen's chambers in a solemn, pensive mood. The women embraced warmly and sat together on the cushioned window seat away from listening ears.

"I am most distressed to see the queen so ill," Christiana whispered sadly. "Was it sudden? Are her physicians certain it is the consumption?"

Margaret patted the younger woman's hand. "My sister has not been well since the death of her son. She is not strong and has no will to ride the storm that threatens."

Christiana felt the blood drain from her cheeks. "Margaret, do not keep anything from me, tell me all that has happened since last we met," she pleaded.

Lady Huddleston turned her face to the casement and watched the snow as it fell gently past the glass to the yard below. "I doubt I can tell all, dear friend, for much is plotted in secret and whispered behind closed doors," she answered gently.

Christiana gave her friend's hand a gentle squeeze of encouragement.

"The Christmastide celebrations were going well. The queen appeared relaxed, roses bloomed in her cheeks; the king also was at ease. A feast was given for Twelfth Night to which Elizabeth Woodville and her daughters were invited."

Christiana nodded her head; she had heard the news that the king had persuaded Elizabeth Woodville to leave sanctuary last spring and had promised his provision for her and her daughters.

"It was at that feast when it all started," Margaret continued. "Edward's eldest child, Elizabeth, in the fullness of youth and a great beauty like her mother, appeared in a gown of white and gold, the almost match in style and colour to that of Queen Anne, my sister." Margaret paused and took in a deep breath.

"I swear it was no coincidence," Lady Huddleston declared bitterly. "It was her mother, the Woodville woman, behind it. I swear she uses witchcraft for her own ends; rumour has it so and I would say 'tis true."

"To what purpose would she have her daughter dress thus?" Christiana asked, puzzled.

"To taunt and beguile the king and make a mockery of the queen. Do you not see, Christiana, Anne has ten years on Elizabeth of York and has lost her only son, Richard's heir, and if Elizabeth is like her mother she stands to produce a brood of healthy children, boys included."

Christiana sat in stunned silence, staring into the earnest face of her friend.

"And now, Anne is gravely ill and worse." Margaret took hold of the other woman's hand sharply. "Rumour in court has it that Richard has poisoned his wife in order to marry his niece."

Christiana felt the hot sting of angry tears in her eyes. All they had against him was rumour but rumour forged with witchcraft was a powerful weapon.

"It is known that Henry Tudor continues to plot for the English throne and his reward is to wed Elizabeth of York," Margaret continued.

"I see no evidence of poison," Christiana whispered. "Anne herself knows it is the consumption that weakens her. I cannot..." Her lips trembled on unfinished words and her tears fell.

Margaret gently raised Christiana's hand and kissed it softly. "The dark clouds gather and we must be prepared, but for now we must carry on with our duties."

Margaret stood and offered a hand to her companion and together they left the chamber.

Christiana was not to see the queen again until the month of February was in its second week. Neither did she set eyes upon the king; even a glimpse of him from afar would have sufficed to set her heart at rest.

Sir Robert Percy, overseer of the royal household, assigned her to work at the palace herbarium. Brother Luke, the herbalist, was the same aged monk from the Abbey of Saint Peter who she had met on her last visit to the palace. They were aided by Cedric, a young novice, willing to please, if not always able. Much of the herbs used at the palace were supplied by the extensive convent gardens tended by the monks of the abbey, complimented by a steady stream of exotic spices, some of which Christiana had never before seen, from merchant vessels that sailed up the Thames. Trade was slow during the winter months when ships dared not sail and folk even now talked of the time the river froze some fifty years since.

On arrival at the queen's bedchamber Christiana was greeted by one of her ladies with a gentle warning: "Our Lady Queen is in good humour this day and has slept well but take care that she does not become overtired."

After her low reverence Christiana sat on the bed beside the queen, her ladies moving a discreet distance away.

"The weather is a little better this day, is it not?" Anne asked cheerfully.

"It is indeed, madam," Christiana agreed, noticing how the soft rays of sunlight from the window shone onto Anne's waxy complexion, lending it a drop of colour.

"What it is to be in love!" the queen sighed with almost childlike glee. Christiana was not sure whether she should be amused or alarmed for she was never quite sure where conversation with Anne would lead. She sat regarding the queen's pale face with interest.

"When I was a young girl I was so in love with Edward, the Lancastrian Prince of Wales. He was very handsome with a fiery disposition that excited me. I was thinking about him today and how my father brought me to the palace to meet him before he was exiled. We were married in France." Anne breathed a deep and contented sigh and turned shining eyes towards Christiana. "I had no intention of ever marrying my cousin Richard after I was widowed," she went on. "He was too quiet and reserved and in truth I found him boring. But when Father and my Edward were killed in battle I was distraught and Richard was very kind to me. He had a mind to marry me but his brother George forbade it at once." She giggled girlishly and Christiana glimpsed in her face the beauty that had once been hers.

"George and Isabel had me dress as a kitchen maid and hidden away but Richard was..." She stopped abruptly and her face creased tearfully. "Oh he will be so alone when..."

A lady hastily appeared at the bedside. "The queen is tired, Christiana, mayhap you should take your leave," she whispered.

Anne raised a small white hand and shook her head. "Nay," she commanded breathlessly. "Stay a little longer. Some wine, Lady Manleverer."

After she had taken a few sips from a silver goblet Anne turned to Christiana.

"During all the years I have been married to Richard I have come not only to respect and honour him but to love him deeply. There is no better man in all of England."

Christiana felt a hot flush rise to her cheeks. What was Anne trying to say? To what purpose did she make such a confession to her servant?

After a while the queen spoke again. "Do you remember the nettle blossom Martha used to wash our hair?" Christiana nodded, much relieved that talk of Richard was finished. "Can you prepare some for me, Christiana, and wash my hair?" Anne's voice had an almost childlike plea to it.

"It will be my pleasure, madam," Christiana replied and rose to leave.

Lady Manleverer took her by the arm as she crossed the chamber. "Do not be too hasty to bring the nettle blossom," she said softly. "The king's physician has forbidden she bathe. Her body is too weak."

Just as she was about to cross the threshold in sombre mood, the king himself appeared on his way to his wife's bedchamber, a black-garbed man with an ascetic visage bobbing at his side. Christiana caught the words he was divulging to the king: "I must advise most strongly against er... visiting the queen's bed, Your Grace. The consumption is mighty infectious."

It was an awkward moment as both men came to an abrupt halt as Christiana, making a low reverence, sidled past. Her eyes met those of the king and for the briefest of moments their gaze locked. Lempster's eyes, for she recognised him as the one who had given her instruction on the preparation of a poultice, full of contempt, continued to follow the herbalist as she hurried away down the passageway.

Back in the herbarium Christiana sat on a stool and stared at the array of herbal remedies. Perhaps if she could not brew a tisane to wash the queen's hair a preparation of tansy milk to rub onto her complexion would be as welcome. She would send Cedric to the abbey for a jar of dried yellow tansy flowers at the first opportune moment.

She rubbed a hand across her forehead. Was it herbal remedies the queen wanted or perhaps an acknowledgement that the king's heart truly belonged to her, his wife? Christiana still had not fathomed why it was the queen had sent for her and suddenly she felt a deep sadness for the lovely lady.

Palace of Westminster
London
Early March 1485

Christiana sat at a table beneath a small lattice window that opened out onto a cobbled courtyard below. A light breeze wafted in bringing with it unfamiliar smells. Everything about the palace was unlike her home in Yorkshire. Its grandeur and splendour outranked any other royal residence; its wooden carvings more elaborate, tapestries more luxurious and gold and silverware the likes of which could only have been imagined. For all its opulence it seemed to lack a certain intimacy and warmth.

The grave-faced clerk poised over his ledger beside her had scarcely uttered a word in the past half hour except to confirm her accounts, all neatly recorded on wax tablets ready to transcribe to parchment. Brother Luke had developed a palsy in his hand that made the keeping of accounts a laborious task and as Cedric could not be trusted to be accurate she found herself thus employed in the White Hall this afternoon.

At the far end of the hall a peculiar figure raised her curiosity. The afternoon sunlight tipped through a glazed window and within its golden circle a small thin man wearing dark hose and tunic fussed with the folds of an embossed crimson curtain. With his strangely shaped plum-coloured felt hat complete with quivering scarlet plume he had the air of a foreigner about him. Intrigued, Christiana watched as he positioned a large wooden easel, a canvas showing the beginnings of a portrait and a tray of oil paints in a just so manner. His young wiry-haired assistant placed jars and brushes, palettes and rags likewise. Satisfied with their achievements the young man was sent from the room. In the silence that followed the little man twitched around his apparatus, birdlike, nudging a jar here, straightening a brush there.

Presently a panelled wooden door opened in the far corner

and the king entered the hall. The little artist removed his hat and bending double in an exaggerated bow he swept the mosaic tiles at the king's feet with his huge feather. Richard motioned for him to rise and gestured for those present to remain seated.

All thoughts of her accounts driven from her head Christiana stared at the king as he graciously allowed himself to be positioned before the crimson curtain where the incoming rays of light could illuminate his features. He wore a magnificent robe of rich brown sable turned back to reveal the dark stripes and golden bogeyshanks of his doublet beneath. Sunlight glinted on the stones of ruby, sapphire and diamond set in the heavy gold chain draped from shoulder to shoulder. His hair, neatly combed and hanging in waves about his neck, shimmered a deep chestnut. A black velvet beret, with a large pendant fashioned to match the gold chain, fitted snugly upon his head.

He stood, as requested, perfectly still, but she knew that his heart was not at peace by the way he repeatedly toyed with the ring on the little finger of his right hand. His cheeks were pale but caught a blush from the curtain behind his head. His eyes staring from beneath dark brows gave away none of the thoughts shielded within. All these details Christiana took in as though he were a saintly apparition seen for the very first time by mere mortals. But for all his splendid robes and riches he was but a man with strengths and weaknesses like any other.

A small group of twittering court ladies entering the hall behind her dispersed her thoughts and saved her the shame of tears spilling down her cheeks. She quickly turned her attention to the clerk's ledger. Despite her resolve to assist the man she found her mind concentrating less on the blotted figures on the parchment and more on the stilted voices coming from her left.

"How well our king looks in his robes and jewels," remarked one, spreading her ample satin gown across a padded chair.

"Why indeed, my lady, he is most handsome – despite his size," a pink-cheeked young lady giggled impishly.

"Who is the artist?" asked another.

"He is Master Hans Memling from Bruges. He has a reputation for producing a good likeness," came the reply.

The clerk nudged Christiana. "I ask again, is this powdered hawthorn you are requesting?"

Irritated by his question Christiana turned to him. "Yes, sir, the lettering is quite clear," she snapped, although in truth it was not as wax tablets were not the best for accuracy. With a shrug of his shoulders the clerk dipped his quill into the inkpot and continued his laborious scratching in the ledger. Christiana turned her ear once more to the ladies' conversation.

"Such a beauty and so like her mother. I think you are correct, Lady Katherine, in thinking that he painted her likeness too." All eyes were turned to the wall and the painting of Elizabeth of York looking down solemnly upon them in the tight-lipped manner of all royal portraits.

One of the ladies sighed and taking up her embroidery hoop she pushed a silver needle into the taut fabric. "How I do miss our good King Edward. The palace was such a merry place when his court was here with the feasts and the dancing," she remarked.

"Indeed, Lady Toft. I recall well the king's passion for life."

"'Twas a pity the Queen Elizabeth did not always share her husband's passion for life."

"You refer to the queen's dislike of Mistress Shore, I think," one lady observed, to which a stifled cackle of amusement could be heard, sending many a veiled head quivering.

"'Tis not quite the same since his brother took the throne," remarked another tartly.

"Lady Jane, we must not forget that our dear Queen Anne is close to death. We cannot expect there to be much gaiety."

"Even so things are not the same." The speaker lowered her voice. "Many speak ill of the king's preference for northerners. The court is flooded with them these days."

"And have you heard the way those soldiers of his speak, Jane? Not one word can be understood. 'Tis not proper English for sure."

"The Yorkshire man is uncouth and much given to violence, so I have heard." At this remark Christiana shifted uncomfortably in her chair.

"Have you need of leather costrels?" the clerk asked for the second time without answer. "No costrels then," the man stated impatiently.

"Costrels? Yes, two more would be useful," Christiana requested, and the clerk deleted his last entry with such force that he almost broke off the nib of his quill. "And larger ones if you please, for the small ones are near useless," she continued impatiently.

"Do you not recall the Christmastide feast last?" The speaker stifled a giggle with her chubby jewel-bedecked hand.

"Why indeed I do. That was hardly a staid affair," agreed another.

"Do you suppose the girl to be in love with the king and sought to attract his attention? You know how young girls can be. My own daughter..."

"Now you do jest, Jane." This remark was issued with the raising of a plucked eyebrow. "The king surpasses her by years."

"What of it?" whispered another, blushing deeply. "'Tis not that, Jane, but, well, the very thought is incestuous."

"'Tis more likely the king who has designs upon his niece. With the queen dying he will need to look elsewhere for a wife."

"I do not think it possible, Lady Toft. His reputation is quite unsullied."

"Do not imagine the king to be a saint." The speaker shot a furtive glance down the hall. The little artist was still sketching the king – all was well. Heads drew closer. "My chamberer swears that he has a common wench as bedfellow, reputed to be the mother of John of Gloucester."

"The same is known to me," put in another. "But I have heard that she covers her tracks by masking as a herbalist."

A babble of assent and tongue clicking accompanied many nodding heads and a quick glance by one at least in the direction of the clerk's table.

"Well, our King Richard is not so unlike his brother after all." Lady Toft had the last word on the matter.

"There, the ledger is complete." The clerk put down his quill with a sigh of relief.

515

"Then I shall take my leave of you, clerk. I have much need of some air." Christiana stood, gathered the skirts of her gown, turned to face the ladies and walked slowly from the hall through a brood of red cheeks and silently poised needles.

And so it was; a palace rampant with gossip and rumour such as Lady Margaret had foretold and Christiana herself was not to be spared.

The paste would need to cool awhile before Christiana could transfer it to a pot. She stirred it with a wooden spatula as she sat at the bench. It had taken Cedric longer than expected to acquire the necessary herb and it was now the eleventh day of March, three weeks since her last visit to the queen.

Crossing an open courtyard on her way to the queen's chambers a cool wind caught her cloak and she clutched tightly the precious pot. She was grateful for the warmth of the queen's bedchamber.

"Madam," she whispered as she approached the bed and made a low reverence. She had not been prepared for the sight that met her eyes and her heart was sorely stirred. The queen raised a thin white hand.

"Come, Christiana, sit beside me," she murmured. Her attendants had parted the heavy drapes, which had almost concealed the frail figure on the bed, and Christiana walked forward.

Anne's once golden hair was spread across the pillows like tangled sun-scorched thread. There was not a drop of pigment in the face that rested there and the colourless eyes were sunk deep into their sockets. Her unbleached linen bed gown was spotted red with blood. The odour of death seemed to emanate from every pore of her skin, clinging even to the bedcovers.

A wave of nausea and grief swept over Christiana as she sat on the embroidered covers. "I have brought you tansy milk for your skin. 'Tis one of Martha's recipes," she said slowly, feeling very foolish indeed at the notion that a mere herb could help in any way. One of the queen's ladies stepped forward and took the pot from her.

"I thank you. How is the weather?" Anne's voice was so faint that Christiana had to lean forward to catch her words.

"'Tis cold, madam. A wind blows but there is no more snow," she replied.

"Where is the king?" Anne asked suddenly. Christiana glanced enquiringly at the figure of Lady Tempest standing at the other side of the bed.

"I believe he is walking in the garden, madam. Shall I send for him?" Lady Tempest replied.

Anne shook her head. "Christiana?" she said, a little agitated.

"I am here," Christiana answered and took up the tiny hand, more bone than flesh.

"You love him?" Anne asked simply. Christiana looked down at the small hand and caressed it slowly.

"Come, you can be honest with me. It is of little consequence to me now." Anne's words quivered with laboured breathing but her eyes begged for an answer. Christiana would not deceive her dying queen and, ignoring the expectant stares of the ladies around the bed, she nodded her head gently.

Anne caught the sign and smiled. "Somehow I always knew you did. How long?"

"In truth I have loved him since the first day I ever set eyes upon him when, like me, he was but a child."

Anne closed her eyes and one single tear trickled down her cheek.

"Do not reproach the king," Christiana continued. "All men must be forgiven their hot-blooded passions of youth but I swear by all that is holy that I have had no carnal knowledge of him since he took you as his wife." She swallowed the hard lump that was forming painfully in her throat. "I have kept the promise I made to you."

"It is not the sins of the flesh that trouble me," Anne gasped, wriggling her hand free of Christiana's grasp to wipe at her tears.

"It is you he loves," Christiana urged. "Any can see that for he grieves for you." She sat in silence as more tears welled up in the queen's eyes and tumbled down her face.

She took the hem of her capacious sleeve and very gently dabbed at Anne's wet face. "Forgive me, Anne, if ever I have caused you distress. I should perhaps now take my leave of you."

The attendants around the bed parted to allow the herbalist room to depart but the queen shook her head once again. Reaching for Christiana's hand, Anne turned her pale eyes on her face. "You must always be a friend to him. Promise me," she pleaded, "even when he takes another wife as queen, as he must. He has a need for you, for you understand him like no other."

The queen's breathing had become spasmodic, painful, and Christiana waited while Lady Tempest brought wine. The red liquid dribbled down Anne's neck and stained her bodice in her effort to drink.

Christiana's own eyes were awash with tears and she felt a trembling in her limbs.

"Promise me," Anne urged once more.

"With all my heart I promise that I shall always be a friend to him until the king himself sends me away." Christiana dried her tears and bending over the shrunken face she kissed Anne's forehead.

Anne closed her eyes but in the next instant she was overcome by a spasm of violent coughing. At once her attendants were upon her, pushing the herbalist out of the way and lifting the queen as the crimson blood foamed and bubbled at her mouth. Lady Tempest, amidst the mayhem, shouted for Lempster to be called.

Christiana walked over to the window and sat wearily down on the large cushion, her head swimming painfully. Her presence there went unheeded as the women around the bed sought to comfort the queen.

The window overlooked the palace gardens, green and fresh with new life. A neatly scythed lawn ran down to a fountain surrounded by clusters of yellow Lenten lilies. A lone figure on a nearby bench sat perfectly still with legs outstretched and hands clasped before him. Save for the wind stirring his hair he could almost have been made of stone. His slight frame seemed too weak to bear the mantle of grief that hung about him.

From her place at the window Christiana sat silently watching. Stricken with love and sorrow she could not help herself and within moments a cascade of tears had fallen and she covered her face with her hands and wept. She did not stop until she felt a gentle touch on her arm; it was Lady Margaret, her blue eyes compassionate.

"Come, my dear," she said softly. "The queen must rest now and so must you for grief has made you weary."

Taking Christiana's hand she led her from the chamber. "It will not be long now. Death draws ever nearer. We must all be strong for the king's sake."

For four days Christiana bore the sorrow and pain of the queen's illness that kindled afresh the memory of her father's death and Martha's wasting away. For four days she could not apply herself to her work, testing greatly the patience of Brother Luke. On the fifth day she went to the palace stables in search of her brother.

William was making his way back to the stable yard from the armoury and stopped abruptly when he saw his sister leaning forlornly against the post of a stall.

Eyeing William she walked slowly over to him. "Oh, Will, I am taken by such misery, such melancholy," she lamented. "Everywhere is great sadness and pain. I have such a need to be away from here for a while. It must be that you have much work to be done or else..."

William's face brightened and he chuckled. "Your timing is perfect, Anna. I am almost done here. I have to take a turn on watch at the Jewel Tower at nightfall but until then my time is my own."

Christiana returned to the herbarium for a cloak and sought out Brother Luke who was more than happy to give his approval for his assistant to take a little respite. She met William at the belfry in the palace yard just as the large bell was ringing the first hour past noon.

The sky was an uplifting spring blue and the sun shone down upon them as they left the confines of the palace walls. Walking up past the Abbey of Saint Peter and through the narrow mud-swilled streets to the Strand, she gripped William's arm to steady her steps.

"Anna, I have news concerning John," William announced suddenly. "It almost slipped my mind but I heard this morning that he is to be given the Captaincy of Calais."

"Calais!" Christiana exclaimed. "That is hundreds of miles away, Will. I should never see him again."

William chuckled. "'Tis a great honour to be made Captain of Calais, especially as John is still a minor. The king thinks very highly of him," William said jovially. "Your son is fifteen years of age – almost a man. You must let go of him."

"Aye, but France is so far away."

"He will not be going for a good while for he will be sent with Sir Robert Brackenbury who cannot yet be released from his duties at the Tower," William replied encouragingly. "And if you are so worried maybe I can talk to the king and arrange to go with them," he added.

"And then I should be without both of you at the palace. It would be unbearable then."

"Come now, Christiana, no more of this melancholia. We shall see the sights of this great city and then I know where we can buy the best eel pies in all of London."

They passed Holborn Hill where Christiana declined William's invitation to walk up to Tyburn and the gallows on the hill. They passed many splendid and impressive buildings owned by London dignitaries. They walked along many streets that ran straight and narrow and crossed over one another with their ramshackle timber-framed dwellings and dark damp alleyways.

Finally they stopped to rest at the fish market on the quayside under the great stone bridge that spanned the Thames. William glared suspiciously at an old man at the water's edge who offered him a wooden tray containing an array of strong fish-smelling shells. He brought instead two steaming hot eel pies from a vendor standing outside his own shop.

They stood eating them on the slippery bank of the river

looking up at the buildings huddled together above the stone arches of the bridge. Christiana watched the little boats that rowed upriver against the current. She began to relax a little and to enjoy the hustle and bustle of life amongst the common folk of London city.

A sudden unexpected wind from the river blew her gown and she shivered. Glancing upwards she noticed that an army of grey cloud was marching across the sky devouring the blue. Instinctively she took a step closer to William who also, like many others, had his face turned skywards. The uncanny change in the weather and the way the day had suddenly changed from warm to cold began to unnerve those around them.

As they continued to watch an almost unbelievable thing happened before their eyes; the moon, which had been visible though it were day, passed right in front of the face of the sun, plunging London, and for all any knew the whole world, into near darkness. People began to scream and fall to the ground making the sign of the cross, uttering words of an eschatological nature and begging for the forgiveness of Almighty God. The single mournful toll of many church bells was hardly heeded for the discord of wailing, fearful voices.

"William, let us return," Christiana whispered, clutching at his arm.

William's eyes were still watching the sky. After a while he spoke. "See, Anna, the moon is moving away from the sun. It no longer eclipses it – we are safe." He laughed and pulled her close to him. Feeling the warmth of his body and breathing in the familiar smell of horses and leather that clung to his tunic she did indeed feel safe.

By the time they had reached the palace the strange phenomenon had gone and once again the sun shone a golden yellow in an azure sky. Christiana's mood was lighter as she parted company with William in the stable yard. She entered the palace through the White Hall, her boots echoing on the patterned tiles for there was no one about and all was strangely quiet.

She was about to go across to the herbarium when a door at

the far end of the hall opened and the neatly dressed figure of Lady Margaret Huddleston entered.

"My lady," Christiana began. "Did you not see the great darkness? There was much panic on the streets of the city..."

Then Christiana saw the depth of sadness etched into the woman's face and an unshed tear glisten in the corner of her eye. "Christiana," she said, "our beloved queen is dead."

The days immediately following the internment of Queen Anne in the Abbey of Saint Peter were bleak and sombre, the king hardly leaving his chambers and seeing no one. His grief at the loss of his wife had been evident to all. And then, drawn back to his senses by the need to rule his kingdom, Richard once again took his place in a realm seeped in treason and plot.

The queen's ladies were given leave to return to their husbands and children and Christiana wondered greatly what was to become of her since she had no family other than William and her position as companion to Anne Beauchamp seemed all but lost.

The ladies departed over several days; Lady Margaret Huddleston the last to leave for her home in the north.

"I am not certain of what is to become of me," Christiana said with a sigh, watching on as Margaret's attendant packed the last of her possessions into the large chest ready for the journey. "I have had no word from Sir Robert Percy; am I to stay or to return to Middleham?"

"I would gladly have you in my household," Margaret said with a smile. "But I know you will not want to leave the king, and neither can you do so now for you have sworn an oath to the queen to stand by him."

Christiana moved aside as Margaret's chests were carried from the chamber by two burly male servants. Crossing the room to her friend she whispered softly, "You speak true, Lady Margaret, for as long as I am able I shall be close to Richard but I shall sorely miss you, dear friend." Christiana ended her words tearfully.

Margaret took her hands and held them tightly. "And I you, Christiana." She smiled warmly. "It may not be easy to do as you wish but I wager that courtly prattle masters will overlook you in favour of rumour concerning the king and his niece. But have a care nonetheless and remember you have a fine brother to look out for you."

"I do indeed," Christiana smiled despite the tears that began to glisten on her cheeks.

Their final embrace was long and painful and Christiana was grateful for William's presence in the palace yard as Lady Huddleston and her small retinue rode away into the cold misty morning.

Although it was still Lent the king could rely upon the royal kitchens to provide a befitting offering and so would give a modest feast, the first since the demise of his wife, to mark the return to his kingly duties.

Elizabeth Woodville and her daughters would be invited and there would be a welcome return to court for John de la Pole. The king had named his sister Elizabeth's son heir upon the death of his own son. This was a shrewd move according to William, as the Earl of Lincoln was a grown man; his brother George's son, Edward, was still a minor.

Christiana had returned to work in the palace herbarium with Brother Luke and under his guidance had furthered her knowledge of herbal physic. However, her presence at the feast was requested, much to her surprise.

Brother Luke, also a guest, took his place with the court physicians while Christiana was seated amongst the Woodville attendants. Her place was to be midway down the long table beside her Burgundian acquaintance, Lady Francine.

The king, having centre position on the high-backed polished oak chair on the raised platform, looked small and almost hidden from view by the voluminous silk canopy overhead. He was flanked on his right by his nephew and heir, John de la Pole, Earl of Lincoln, and to his left his son, John of Gloucester.

Elizabeth Woodville, looking matronly in her gown the colour of deepest plum, was, as honoured guest, also seated at the upper table. As she moved her capacious sleeves in animated conversation Christiana noticed the overloaded tones of purple dye that caught the candlelight. Elizabeth's two eldest daughters sat on either side of her; Cecily to her left hand and Elizabeth to her right, nearest the king. Christiana marvelled at the beauty of this nineteen-year-old woman, now full blossomed and no longer the sweet child she had last seen at Middleham many years ago.

Grace was said by the royal steward and the food was presented with little pomp or ceremony, observing an air of sobriety in respect for the recently demised queen and the religious dictates of Lent.

"The pear is not to your liking?" The polite voice at her side brought Christiana's attention back to her food for she had been watching the young Elizabeth engaging the king in earnest conversation, leaning provocatively across the Earl of Lincoln as she did so.

Christiana looked down at her trencher where her spoon lay beside a pear dressed in a sprinkling of spices.

"No, no, Lady Francine, please forgive me. The fruit is very good; it is just that I was thinking about the queen."

"Ah *oui*, the queen," Francine replied, noting well where the herbalist's eyes were cast.

The fruit had been taken away and before them a steaming pottage of vegetables and herbs was presented on silver platters. The smell was delicious and Christiana found her appetite returning. Further along the table towards the dais raucous laughter broke out amongst some of the Woodville attendants. A daunting glare from John Russell, the royal chancellor, from across the linen cloth silenced them.

They continued to watch the Woodville ladies as they ate. Christiana had a desire to know the mood of the court and who better to question than a lady of the bedchamber?

"The Lady Elizabeth Woodville does not appear to hold the king responsible for the death of her youngest sons," Christiana said, opening the conversation in a casual manner. The lady in question was all smiles and laughter in the presence of her sovereign. Her daughters likewise were enjoying the king's company.

"What makes you so certain that the little princes are dead?" Francine asked before taking a mouthful of bread soaked in vegetable juices.

Christiana turned her head towards her companion in surprise. "But the talk is that the king has had them murdered to pave his way to the throne," she whispered.

"And do you believe that?" Francine asked without meeting the other woman's gaze.

"I do not doubt the king's innocence," Christiana replied earnestly.

"There is nothing but rumour, no proof." Francine drank from their shared goblet before continuing. "There is no benefit to the king to have the boys murdered; they are bastards, no threat to him."

"They were the focus of a rebellion."

"Indeed, there was a rebellion just after the king was crowned." Francine leaned towards her companion and whispered, "The question is, would a rebellion be to restore Prince Edward to the throne... or someone else? If the princes live then they will be a greater obstacle to the throne for *someone else* than they ever are for King Richard."

The conversation ended then for a minstrel had halted before them to pipe a sweet melody before moving along the tables.

"Ah carp, there is a surprise!" Francine giggled, causing a smile to alight the lips of her companion as more platters were placed in front of them. She passed the silver goblet of wine to Christiana as she piled the fish onto their trenchers.

"It never ceases to amaze me what they can do with a fish," continued the Burgundian woman with a titter. "Regard!" She pointed with her spoon to the king's table where a lavish platter of fish cleverly disguised as venison was presented to his grace.

"That is fish?" Christiana asked incredulously.

"I am certain it is for I do not see our king passing bribes to the church to allow him to eat meat during Lent as some others do."

Sometime later, feeling comfortably full, the guests and courtiers reposed upon chairs and cushions at the side of the hall to partake of their sugared ginger and hypocras and to enjoy some music.

The king sat sprawled in his chair, legs outstretched and eyes closed. John of Gloucester and Lord Lovell were talking in subdued whispers at the king's right hand and nearby the Woodville ladies sat demurely within a circlet of attendants, their veils quivering delicately.

"It is good to see the king more at ease after the pain and sorrow of these past days," Francine remarked softly to Christiana at her side.

"It is indeed, my lady," the herbalist replied, although she knew the extent of his grief and that his manner shrouded the fullness of his feelings.

The lyre player put down his instrument and took up a hurdy-gurdy and tucking it firmly under his arm he dared to strike up a livelier tune, mindful that it was the season of Lent and such merriment was likely to be frowned upon. However, the pipe player followed suit and soon had the point of his red felt hat dancing to and fro. With the increase in the volume of the music voices rose and conversations became more spirited.

"Now where does she go I wonder?" Lady Francine remarked as the two women watched Elizabeth of York leave her mother's side and approach the king's chair. She waited demurely as a groom pulled up a chair for her close to the king. The young lady moved just a little closer to him as she spoke, her blue eyes flashing prettily beneath her lashes, her tiny rosebud mouth curving into a smile. Richard sat straight in his chair and returning his niece's smiles gave her his full attention.

"He is flattered by her interest – what man of his age would not be?" Francine cooed.

"'Tis more likely the king has drunk too much wine and his good sense is dulled," Christiana said irritably.

"Our king takes little wine, although I would concede more than he is used to of late," Francine remarked wryly. "Nay, the king means nothing by his smiles. He is enjoying a little company to ease his grief, nothing more," Francine continued sagely. "But the lady – her behaviour intrigues me; first the letter and now this. And yet many have it that her mother seeks a match for her with Henry Tudor."

"I also have heard this," Christiana replied. "Henry Tudor has made a vow, I understand, to marry the Lady Elizabeth. But tell me, what of a letter?"

"The letter that Elizabeth of York sent to the Duke of Norfolk, a close friend of her father and loyal supporter of the king, in which she openly declares her love for Richard."

Christiana's face reddened. "That is outrageous," she whispered. "When was this?"

"Before Queen Anne's death for her letter expresses a desire that they should marry once the queen is dead."

Christiana sat speechless for several moments as the music throbbed in her head. "Does the king know of this letter?" she asked at last.

"Indeed he does and it has caused him no small amount of embarrassment. 'Tis my belief that the girl's mother was behind it, for she seeks to discredit the king with his loyal supporters. You see, Christiana, like the venison, in a royal court things are not always as they seem.

"If my opinion was sought," Lady Francine went on, "I should say that the girl would make a more fitting wife for the king's son John."

Christiana looked across to where Elizabeth Woodville sat, the folds of her gown spread around her in a regal circle, and noticed the quick violet eyes avidly watching the movements of her eldest daughter.

"And if my opinion was sought," Christiana stated vehemently, "I should say that the king's son deserves better than to have anything to do with a Woodville – and the king knows it!"

The cold stone passageway beneath her bare feet sent a dull aching through her legs as she hurried along. A nightly draught ruffled her gown as she fumbled with the stays of her kirtle. What manner of urgency had caused her to be summoned from her bed at this witching hour? Her mind flew back to a similar dark night at Middleham when she was called to attend the young Prince of Wales. She shuddered in fearful remembrance as she followed the bobbing circle of candlelight thrown by the page's lantern as he led the way ahead.

At the door to the king's chamber she was met by Lord Lovell, his dark eyes tired and anxious. Taking her hand he led her inside. It was warm within; a fire still burned in the hearth. Placed on a large table near the fire was a selection of bottles, phials, tubing and a pig's bladder. Amongst this paraphernalia two jars of black leeches held the corners of a worn parchment displaying astronomical charts and symbols. The heady aroma of medicinal concoctions pervaded the air. Christiana walked past the table eying its contents with suspicion and looked questioningly at Francis.

"The king has felt unwell since he supped this eve," he stated. "I fear that he is now much worse."

Just as he finished speaking the heavy tapestry drapes enclosing the large oaken bed parted and out stepped a tall black-garbed figure with the hunched stance of a crow and a hooked nose to match. Christiana recognised the man at once: Lempster, Richard's physician. He looked down his nose disdainfully at the herbalist and then turned to Francis Lovell.

"Who is this woman, my lord, that you should have permitted her to enter the royal bedchamber?" he asked rudely.

Francis stared at the physician and said, "My Lord Lempster, a word if you please," and drew the man aside. Christiana, leaving the royal chamberlain to deal with the disgruntled physician, approached the bed and cautiously parted the curtains. Richard, wearing only a short paltock, sat on the edge of the great bed; with his arms folded over his stomach he was doubled up across them, seemingly in much pain.

"Richard," she whispered, gently touching his arm. He looked up at her, his eyes large and clear in his pale face. "You must be under the covers where it is warm," she ordered gently. She piled the swan-feather pillows high against the carved headboard before assisting the king onto them and covering his legs with the soft coverlet. She then sat down beside him on the bed.

"Have you pain anywhere else, my lord king?" Christiana asked softly.

"I have a pain and dizziness in my head. I feel a great weakness and there is a prickling in my mouth."

These were words that filled Christiana with dread. She took a deep breath and was turning from the bed to seek counsel with the physician and Lord Lovell when Richard, without warning, leant forward and vomited over the silk bed cover.

"That will be the emetic working its magic," Lempster declared with triumph as he returned to the bedside, Francis with him. "Now at least the woman has a purpose; she can clean up this foul puke."

Christiana ignored the man's impertinence and asked, "My lord what have you given the king?"

For a moment it looked as though the physician was about to reply with yet more words of derision but a sharp look from the chamberlain cut them short. "Hellebore," he spat. "And His Grace will need more of the same if all of the poison is to be voided."

"You suspect poison?" Francis asked, horrified.

"Indeed I do," Lempster replied curtly. Francis shot a questioning look at Christiana who nodded her head in concurrence with the physician's diagnosis.

Francis said nothing for a second or two, seemingly making up his mind on the best course of action to take. Finally he made an announcement. "I thank you for your good advice, Lempster. You may leave us now and be certain that the king is in good hands. I will send for you again if your services are required."

With a dark scowl upon his face the physician left the royal bedchamber, indicating the bottle and spoon reposing upon the table as he did so.

Within minutes these two of the king's most loyal servants had replaced the soiled bed sheets and his sodden shirt. Christiana had given Richard a second dose of the emetic and made him comfortable against a pile of feather down pillows. Francis sat on the bed beside his friend holding a large pewter bowl in readiness.

"How do you suppose this came about, Francis?" Christiana asked. "Who would have opportunity to do such a thing?"

"Any of the courtiers could slip a poison into his wine. Any of the servants, cooks with malice against the king – who knows."

"But surely the king's food is tasted before...?" Christiana reasoned.

"Aye, but 'tis little more than a sniff and a pinch from what I have seen," Francis said bitterly.

There followed a brief moment of silence before Lord Lovell spoke again. "I see here more than a servant's devotion to her master. Your feelings for the king run deeper." The royal chamberlain's eyes met those of the woman who sat beside him. Christiana could make no reply, in confirmation or denial, for at that moment the king began to stir, attempting to raise himself on his elbows. Francis put an arm around Richard's shoulder and eased him forward as Christiana took the bowl and held it before him as a second wave of plentiful vomiting began, leaving the king breathless and weakened several moments later.

Christiana glanced at Francis's tired, anxious face; it was going to be a long night for the three of them.

"Do you suppose any other persons of the king's household are taken ill?" Christiana asked of the chamberlain as he returned from the curtained latrine with the emptied bowl in his hands.

"I am not aware of any," he replied wearily, sitting on the bed once more and placing the bowl beside him.

"Do you recall the food presented at supper?"

Francis rubbed his forehead in concentration. "There was no meat, this being the season of Lent. I cannot remember all... There was fish aplenty and almond custards and syllabubs."

"Was there a dish for the king alone?"

"Yes, of course, the oysters, reserved only for the king."

"Then I will wager that the poison was put into the oysters," Christiana remarked firmly.

At once Francis was on his feet. "I will make enquiries at the kitchens and pantries; I will find out what I can."

"Francis," Christiana called before he had reached the door.

"Procure any peppermint cordials, ale, elderflower, rosehip, any ginger or garlic and return in all haste. The king's health depends upon it."

Christiana decided against giving a third spoonful of hellebore; she had heard of its virtue as a powerful purgative, reserved only for suspected poisoning. She would wait and hope that enough had been given to ensure the complete voidance of the king's stomach.

Alone in the vigil Christiana glanced around at the vast chamber, the farthest end of which was hidden in shadow. Vividly coloured wall murals, painted above the dado and depicting Old Testament characters, came to life in the flickering firelight. Her own eyes were heavy and her back began to ache from sitting for so long on the bed when suddenly Richard opened his eyes and groaned. Christiana fumbled for the bowl and only just had it in place in time before he was sick again. It was almost over; after a moment or two the painful heaving produced nothing but a trickle of bile.

With fearful trembling she set aside the bowl and lay down on the bed beside the king's person. She drew as close to him as she dared and shortly thereafter she felt her eyelids droop and soon fell into an exhausted sleep.

It seemed like moments later when she felt gentle nudging upon her shoulder and woke to find the face of Francis, Lord Lovell, staring into her bleary eyes.

"Christiana you must be away from here at once," Francis declared urgently. "The king's household is stirring." He helped her to her feet and wrapped a cloak about her shoulders to cover her stained and odorous gown. In the bed beside her the king continued to sleep.

"Do you have the cordial and other remedies?" she asked anxiously, remembering her duty to the king.

Francis indicated several bottles and flagons on the table. "Peppermint, rosehip cordials, ginger and garlic."

"You must wake the king and see that he has plenty to drink and if possible have him take a little ginger and garlic in the cordial."

She had done all she could and so, with her head covered

beneath the hood of the cloak and a silent prayer for Richard's recovery she scurried along the corridors back to her own chamber, unseen amidst the waking household.

A pattering of raindrops could be heard against the glazed windows of the White Hall. Candles burned in the circular wrought-iron holders suspended from the beamed ceiling but a sombre greyness persisted. A few people were moving about in small groups or pairs, talking softly amongst themselves, but there was no sign of the king.

Christiana clutched the small wooden chest containing the peppermint infusion that she had made up earlier that afternoon. Close beside her a man in a sodden velvet cape sneezed. Although approaching the end of March and the palace gardens spotted with spring colour and smells there were still days such as this when winter refused to relinquish its hold. She weaved her way amongst the nobles and visitors looking for Richard.

His great chamber had been empty that afternoon when she had returned to enquire after his health. A servant strewing handfuls of dried herbs across the bed covers knew nothing of the king's whereabouts. The two pages polishing the bronze taps on the king's bathing tub paid her no heed save for their quizzical stares.

The king was clearly not in the hall so Christiana made her way to the far end towards the chapel of Saint Stephen. Crossing the passageway she paused to look out onto the open courtyard where the rain blew in a squall. The king would surely not venture out of doors in such weather after his recent bout of sickness, she reasoned. As she came to a side archway leading to the upper chapel she caught the sound of voices from within.

"Now is not the time, Will. Can you not see how ill he is? He was overcome by such sickness last night." The voice she heard belonged to Francis Lovell. She tiptoed nearer to the stone arch around which she could see little more than the stained glass of a window and a section of the elaborate panelling beneath.

"Aye, well, sorry I am for his infirmity, Francis," replied Sir William Catesby, another voice she recognised. "But the word is even now circulating that he was poisoned to avenge the death of the queen."

"In God's name, William, what are you talking about?" the king was heard to demand abruptly.

"In the courtyard just now as I stabled my horse; servants' prattle mayhap but even so..."

"Your Grace, there is a general opinion abroad that it is your intention to marry your niece, Elizabeth of York, now that Queen Anne is dead."

Christiana dared to move even closer at the sound of this, a fourth voice. She caught the king's outburst of sceptical laughter.

"Sir Richard jests not, my lord king," Catesby proclaimed. "He and I are of like mind in this and that you must make a stand against this vile rumour to prevent a public outcry."

"Public outcry!" Richard cried. "What public outcry? Who dares accuse me of having a hand in Anne's death? As to marrying my own niece!" he spat in rage. "By God, what do men take me for? You know full well, Catesby, that I am in negotiation with the Portuguese Duke of Beja as suitor for Elizabeth and myself with Joana of Portugal. What use is an illegitimate wife to me?" The king spluttered and stumbled forward, clutching his stomach.

Christiana was hard pressed to remain hidden and not rush to Richard's aid. She sensed rather than saw that Francis had the king by the arm and was giving him support.

"My king, it is the northerners we have most to fear in this." Ratcliffe's voice was calm. "We can expect an invasion from Henry Tudor any day now. Your throne could be in peril and you cannot risk losing the support of your loyal followers to rumour."

There was a long pause. Christiana held her breath as she waited for the king's reply. It was Francis Lovell who spoke first. "Well, Sir Ratcliffe, what do you propose the king should do?" he asked.

"Call a meeting of the council in the presence of the mayor and alders of the city. Make a formal public denial of his intention to marry his niece, the Lady Elizabeth."

"And let it be done before Eastertide," Sir William added solemnly.

It was not clear whether or not the king had given his consent for the next moment footsteps could be heard approaching the exit and Christiana only just managed to withdraw further into the recess before the figures of Catesby and Sir Richard Ratcliffe emerged.

The king and his chamberlain were standing just beyond the archway; she could see their shadows across the stone floor.

"Send John Russell to attend to my affairs, Francis. I am returning to my bedchamber, I feel unwell," the king said wearily.

Christiana waited until Francis had moved towards the White Hall to seek out the chancellor before emerging from her hiding place. As she did so she almost collided with the person of the king as he sought his way back to his chamber. His face was ashen, his dark eyes troubled and fatigued.

"I have some peppermint... to calm your stomach." Her voice faltered as she saw that Richard was staring long at her. She swallowed hard and held out the small wooden chest containing the costrel. His fingers lingered over hers as he took the peppermint from her.

"Why does no one leave me be?" he pleaded, a desperation in his voice that pulled at her heart. She lowered her gaze, made a low reverence and waited for him to move away.

Palace of Westminster
London
Early April 1485

Christiana walked around the tables and shelves in the herbarium not seeing the bottles, jars and flagons of medicines made up and neatly arranged in rows. Even her nostrils were oblivious to the smells, usually a source of comfort to her. She could not rid her mind of the image of Richard standing outside Saint Stephen's chapel and the pained look upon his face that had little to do with his bodily ailment.

She had a sudden longing to be home in the Yorkshire dales, to see again the wide-open spaces of moorland and to hear the sound of the curlew at twilight. She felt she had a good understanding of why it was that, as Duke of Gloucester, Richard had spent so little of his time here at Westminster.

She touched a jar of oil of St John's wort, pushed it from its place and promptly returned it. She did likewise to a pot of comfrey salve. Her humour was rapidly turning sour. She felt certain that the timely appearance just at that moment of her assistant prevented her from taking up the jars and smashing them against the flagstones.

"Mistress Christiana, is there any work to be done?" the boy asked, standing in the open doorway.

"Yes, Cedric," she replied tartly. "There is always work to be done. Boil up some more valerian – the supply is low, and then you can crush those garlic cloves over there with a pestle. I am going out."

She brushed past the startled youth and out into the grizzled courtyard, leaving the boy quite taken aback by the taciturn mood of the usually amicable herbalist.

There was a sombre air in the stable yard as a steady trickle of rain fell on the cobblestones. She walked across to the low wooden door where a grey head hung forlornly in the rain. She patted the warm cheekbone and buried her face in the rough mane. "White Surrey," she whispered sadly. "This is a miserable place." The horse rattled the door with a hoof and shook its sodden head as if in agreement.

She turned in the direction of a familiar voice calling to her from the far side of the yard.

"Anna!" William emerged from the forge, tawny hair tousled and face blackened from the smoke of the fire. He splashed water from a trough onto his face and rubbed it dry with his coarse tunic before striding over to her.

"'Tis a right wet day for spring," he remarked jovially, looking up at the wisps of grey cloud blowing across the sky. "It will not last long though," he mumbled.

"Why is it you are always with the horses, Will?" Christiana enquired of her brother, her tone not altogether pleasant.

"Unless the king ventures beyond the confines of the city he does not need such a large retinue to guard him so I have other duties which suit me well until I am called upon. Tell me, how fairs the king? I have heard that he was taken ill last night, poison some say."

"The king is well enough in body now that the poison is purged," she replied on a sigh.

"Glad I am to hear it. And what of you, are you ill?" William's brown eyes looked seriously at his sister's downcast countenance.

"I am homesick, Will. I do not care for it here at the palace and would give much to go home to Yorkshire."

"And leave Richard?"

"There is nothing I can do for the king," she returned sharply.

"Well there must be one thing you are able to do for him," William said with a chuckle.

"And what do you mean by that?" Christiana demanded, her cheeks glowing in anger.

"Come on, Christiana. You are no untouched maiden. You know well enough my meaning; you are the mother of the king's son."

"And that makes me a harlot, a court strumpet, does it? Now that the queen is dead I can just jump into the king's bed in her stead can I?" Christiana's face was red with fury now.

"I have spoken to you of this before, William, and it is none of your concern," she continued angrily. She turned from him and with hot-tempered tears running down her cheeks she fled across the yard.

The rain of the past few days had ceased and now the garden was filled with birdsong and a welcome display of buds. Christiana sat on a wooden bench staring at the grimy hem of her russet gown. She was unaware that someone had sat beside her until she heard the melodious tone of Francine's voice.

"Here you are! Someone from the abbey was looking for you earlier to check a supply of herbs. Why, *chérie*, you have been crying. We cannot have this for it will spoil your pretty face, *non*?"

Christiana wiped her cheeks with her sleeve and attempted a smile. "I must go home, Francine. I can bear it no longer here at the palace."

"I see," replied the older woman. "And who are you that you can decide whether you go or whether you stay? Are you not of the royal household under the command and in the employ of Sir Robert Percy?" she asked gently.

Christiana turned to the noble lady and looked into her keen azure eyes. "I do not wish to stay. I will go to the king and ask his leave to return home. He will grant it," she said firmly.

"I have little doubt that he would if that was your true desire but I do not think that he would want it so." Lady Francine smiled and as she moved her head the sun caught the last remaining shimmer of jet in her hair. She had long ago discarded her fashionable hennin, a thing she considered pure vanity, and wore her silver sprinkled hair coiled in a plaited rope at the back of her head and covered only by a modest coif.

"I know how difficult it is to live at court; the gossip, the slander, the fighting like cockerels to win favour. At least you will be near to the ones you love," she added with a touch of nostalgia.

"There is work for me to do at Middleham," Christiana stated untruthfully, imagining with sadness the sour-faced monk whose domain the cottage had become. "I am not needed here. There must be a hundred herbalists at the abbey."

"None with your skill and healing touch. Do not be so sure that you can just return to the castle and claim your right to work."

"The king will make it so," Christiana interrupted.

"The king would sooner you were here," Francine said gently.

"I do not know what you mean, Lady Francine." Christiana could feel her tears threatening her composure and she made to rise from the bench.

Lady Francine put out a jewelled hand to stop her. "Pray be seated. I do not wish to cause you distress."

Christiana acquiesced and taking a few deep breaths she remained seated. Francine took her hand and stroked it gently. At once Christiana was reminded of Martha and the memory brought her comfort.

"I know that you love Richard," Francine began gently. "How you express that love is no concern of mine but I do know that the king is a very lonely man even though he is surrounded by courtiers. He has need of your love and friendship, especially if the talk of invasion by this Henry Tudor is true – and I believe it will happen.

"I too would be sorry to see you leave. I have grown quite fond of you, *chérie*," Francine continued. "Stay here with me and be strong in the face of gossip. You are discreet, not like some of the strumpets Edward used to keep at court." She stifled a giggle with a hand across her mouth like a youthful maiden. "My, my, they were jolly days. See, you are laughing now and that becomes your pretty face much more than a frown.

"Now look, here comes someone else who would rather you stayed, *non*?" She leaned forward and planted a small kiss on Christiana's cheek before standing and walking away, making a low reverence to John as he approached the bench.

Christiana could see that her son was not in the best of humours; his dark eyes were grave as he sat down beside her and thrust his legs out before him.

"Does something vex you, my son?" she asked gently, her own troubles soon forgotten. John fingered the hilt of the handsome sword hanging at his belt. Without looking at his mother he answered her in a voice loaded with anger.

"I have just returned from the hospital of Saint John in Clerkenwell where I heard the king make a most extraordinary speech in which he declared his grief at the death of the queen and, would you believe it, a strong denial of any intention to marry his niece, Elizabeth of York. Why ever should he do such a thing? It was utter humiliation for my father." The boy's words tumbled out on a torrent of passion. "I will not stay in the city with the king to bear witness to such things," he finished breathlessly.

Christiana sighed as she recalled to mind the heated exchange of words she had witnessed in Saint Stephen's chapel several days ago.

"John, the king does not find himself in a favourable position right now. He has suffered the loss of both his wife and son and heir to the throne less than twelve months apart, not to mention the constant threat of invasion by this Henry Tudor. It would be perfectly natural for the king to take another wife as queen; indeed necessary, and granted there have been many rumours that he has designs on his niece. I believe that silly letter she wrote while Anne was yet alive has been the cause of all this trouble. She is but a young girl and may have fallen prey to an infatuation for her uncle – who knows?"

"However that may be, Mother, the king should never have made a public denial of anything of so base a nature. How could anyone believe that my father would even consider such an unholy alliance," he stated hotly.

"Because they do not know him as we do," Christiana replied.

They sat in silence for a while as John kicked the gravel on the path with the toe of his boot.

"It should have been I who died and not Prince Edward," he burst out abruptly. "What use is a bastard to the king?"

John's words held a note of shame and bitterness that caused his mother to recoil inwardly and to sit speechless. Her silence gave John further room to pour forth his frustration.

"Indeed, a king needs a son and heir to his throne and Richard has neither son nor wife. He is no more likely to make me his heir than he is to marry you, a blacksmith's daughter." He turned his dark eyes towards her then; so like his father's and showing the full depth of his pain and anger.

"My dearest son, I wish with all my heart that it could be so but how could Richard legitimise you when the crown was pressed upon him because his own nephews were declared bastards? Your father will not make himself a hypocrite. But know this, John, I gave myself willingly to Richard the day you were conceived and for that I have no regret. The king has raised you as a royal prince. He loves you as much as any father could. It must pain him greatly to see your worth and not reward it. You are young, there is yet time."

She put out her hand to steady his fingers still toying with the hilt of his sword.

"Never again speak of such things, John, for it grieves me sorely. Only God Almighty knows why Prince Edward was taken from us and there is an end to it."

John smiled and on a sudden impulse he wrapped his arms around his mother in a tight embrace. As he drew away, she too smiled, thinking: a man in so many ways and yet still a child.

"A bastard son I may be but you can be sure that I shall be at my father's side when Henry Tudor dares put a foot on English soil," he said passionately before rising from the bench and striding away towards the palace.

May 1485

The king had learned through his network of spies, both at home and across the Channel, that the threat of invasion by Henry Tudor was not only very real but also imminent. Taking this threat most seriously Richard took the necessary precautions to provide for the defence of his realm.

Not knowing where in England the expected invasion force would land the king had to make sure that the coastline was adequately patrolled and alerted. To this end Francis, Lord Lovell, was dispatched to Southampton. The king already possessed a veritable fleet of ships at his disposal and was reputed to be a skilful naval commander himself. Richard had also built up an impressive arsenal of field and handguns and other artillery preparatory to invasion. Commissions of Array had been issued to ensure that at the appropriate time all able-bodied men could be summoned ready for battle.

With much of his strategic preparations met, Richard and members of his household made ready to leave the Palace of Westminster on the eleventh day of May; their destination Nottingham. The castle there was a military fortress favoured by the king and one from which he could act at speed when the need arose, its position being well placed to reach many areas where an invasion could be expected. Here too he would muster his main army.

Much of the country throbbed with the expectancy of war; nowhere more so than within the palace walls at Westminster. There was no way Christiana was not going to join the king on what would probably be the most important military campaign of his life, and so once again she found herself packing up a chest of herbal remedies for the long journey. This time the chest was considerably larger for much of what she had would be part of the consignment of baggage taken to the battlefield – wherever and whenever that might be. There would also be among the king's travelling household barber surgeons and others skilled in herbal medicine.

Christiana was sorry to be leaving her friend and confidante, Lady Francine, who expressed a fervent hope that they would meet again. Brother Luke of the herbarium likewise said that he would miss her skill and wished her well. She could not say, in all truth, that she would miss many others with whom she had been acquainted.

The weather remained favourable as the large entourage of retainers, soldiers and servants of the royal household ambled along with their horses, carts and wagons loaded with provisions and weapons.

Their journey took them close by Berkhamsted. The purpose of the king's visit was to spend a little time with his mother, Cecily Neville, dowager Duchess of York, who had been received into the religious life of the Benedictines at the convent there.

Christiana would have dearly liked to have met the king's mother, not having made her acquaintance at Baynard's two years ago, as the woman was regarded as a great beauty and deeply pious, but Richard's visit to the convent was strictly private.

Almost one month after leaving Westminster the king arrived at his castle at Nottingham mid-morning on the ninth day of June. The great royal fortress built upon a rock rising way above the meadows of the River Trent was an imposing sight to behold.

It took several moments for all the horses, carts and wagons to clatter over the bridge and through the gatehouse of the outer bailey. Riding towards yet another bridge Christiana glanced across at the cluster of buildings to her left and the wide expanse of cultivated land beneath the southern wall. She had stayed here for a few days only during August of the year of the coronation and the grand tour of the realm but she could recall little of that visit, shrouded as it had been in pomp and ceremony.

Riding through the arched gatehouse into the middle bailey the king was greeted by the constable and his lieutenants and servants, who swiftly organised the unpacking of the wagons. Christiana, along with other close members of the royal household, was shown into the great hall where food and drink had been prepared.

It would appear that here also she was not to be treated as a mere servant. Indeed throughout this journey her chambers had been amongst the best and she ate at the king's table with her son; there had never been any private meetings, however, between her and the king.

Two huge grey hounds bounded about the hall excitedly as Richard seated himself at a great oaken chair and allowed his boots to be removed and took the goblet of wine offered. He greeted the dogs enthusiastically and Christiana remembered that the king had spent much of his time here and this castle must have been almost as familiar to him as Middleham. It would surely have held painful memories for him also for it was here that he and the queen received news of the death of their only son.

Against the northern wall of the middle bailey was a row of newly built chambers, splendidly constructed with timber frames and glazed windows overlooking a green courtyard. Looming behind was the magnificent six-sided tower affectionately known as Richard's Tower. It was in one of these chambers that Christiana was to lodge. She could still smell the recently limewashed plaster on the walls and the tapestries were alive with new colour and texture.

Christiana spent much of her time at Nottingham in idle relaxation. John, determined to be at his father's side on the battlefield, spent much of his time training with the king's men-at-arms. Under the circumstances his voyage to Calais had been postponed. They still found time to spend together when John would show his mother around the vast castle or they would walk in the gardens and beyond.

So much of Nottingham Castle reminded Christiana of her home at Middleham and yet in many ways it was so very different. Built upon natural rock there was a labyrinth of underground passageways and caves, dungeons and undercrofts, all with a wealth of history.

"'Twas here, they say, that the constable under orders from the young King Edward, who was then incidentally, only my age, Mother, entered and seized Mortimer, who was the queen's favourite." Light from the lantern that he held aloft danced in his eyes as John stood against the hewn-out rock wall of the cave. He rattled the iron gate guarding the passageway to the outside. "These were put up afterwards as a precaution against intruders."

"Was the queen the wife of the young king?" Christiana asked, intrigued by the story her son was telling as they walked the underground lair of the castle.

"Nay, the queen, Isabella, was the young king's mother. She and her lover, Roger de Mortimer, had overthrown her husband, King Edward the Second, and had him murdered most foully in Berkeley castle."

"Yes, I recall now a story I once heard about that. It was a most gruesome death; poor Edward," she shuddered.

"Well, Mortimer got his comeuppance; he was executed and the castle returned to the king. That brave young king was Edward the Third, from whom our own Richard is descended," John stated proudly as he led his mother up the steps to the upper bailey and into the brilliant sunshine.

"You are well informed of royal ancestry, my son," Christiana remarked, lifting her gown as she trod carefully on the worn steps.

"Indeed, Mother. The king takes a special interest in heraldic arms and their meaning. His royal lineage is of great importance to him. He has commissioned a college of arms in London to keep record of these things."

Christiana smiled and began to walk across the grass towards the keep.

"By the way, Mother, I forgot to mention it before but the king is going to Beskwood on the morrow and requests your company."

"Beskwood?" asked Christiana.

"The lodge in Beskwood Park; the king is going hunting. Do not look so worried. It will be only a small party and I am to be the lord of the hunt. It is my first time so I am honoured. That is why you are invited along – I suppose."

Christiana nodded and smiled faintly. She was not at all sure that she wanted to go deer hunting, strictly a privilege of royalty. At least it would break the monotony and uncertainty of waiting. Tomorrow would be the eleventh day of August and still the king tarried at Nottingham.

The stone and half-timbered lodge with its thatched roof and shuttered windows lay hidden deep in Beskwood Park. Tall oaks and ash of the woodland formed a natural canopy, plunging the building into semi-darkness, and in its shadows creepers grew, covering the stones with a tracery of verdant lace.

A musky earth smell was in the air and in the dampened sunlit shade the sound of almost total silence. Only the jingling of harnesses and the braying of the horses could be heard as the riders dismounted. It seemed to Christiana that the peace and tranquillity were an almost tangible part of an ethereal world.

A huge wooden table bearing an iron candle holder with stubs of half-burned tallow ran the length of the main hall into which the visitors entered. Deer hides, cured, stretched and balding here and there with age, decorated the plastered walls, while from their lofty position stag heads stared down at them, their unseeing orbs ever watchful.

Within moments of their arrival a far door opened and Thomas Danby the gamekeeper entered with three boisterous hounds barking a welcome. Tom bowed to the king and gave a brief nod of the head to his companions. To Christiana he offered a perfunctory smile and nothing more. A serving girl brought in a flagon of ale with bread and cold meat on a pewter platter. The men removed their boots, sat at table and began to eat.

The king, visibly relaxed in his surroundings, struck up a conversation with Tom about repairs to the stakes at the edge of the park. The atmosphere was very informal, so much so that one would hardly be aware that a king sat in their midst.

Christiana began to feel at ease and accepting a cup of ale from John she allowed him to escort her round the room, showing off trophies of past hunts. She smiled into his deep sapphire eyes and was suddenly struck by how easily this boy of hers seemed to blend in with this noble life; a life she still found difficult to embrace even now.

After the brief meal the hunting party gathered in the courtyard at the back of the lodge. Fresh horses were led from the stables and allocated to the hunters. She was acquainted with Charles Pilkington and Robert Harrington who had received a recent knighthood for services to the king. Others were unfamiliar; young men bearing hunting horns and bows with quivers full of arrows slung across their backs.

The Master of the Horse approached Christiana with a slight bow. "I think Misty will do just fine for you, my lady," he said, offering her the reins of a sleek grey mare, not unlike her own palfrey. Christiana blushed, wondering if the man had any notion of whom he was addressing. At that moment Richard appeared beside her to assist her into the saddle, astride like the others.

"I will stay close," he whispered, "this is John's day."

Once underway the hounds barked furiously, the berners on foot keeping them under control. Way ahead the lymer hounds already had their noses to the ground. It was a glorious day, warm and sunny, and Christiana enjoyed the ride through the dappled forest and across open land. Richard rode close by and took great delight in describing the boldness and courage of the stag; so much so that she began to believe it was a sin to hunt him down. She would look across at Richard, looking like any other man in his leather riding attire, his hair blowing in the wind, and her heart would beat with love for him.

After several hours in the chase the quarry was finally run to ground and it was an arrow shot from John's bow that brought the animal down amidst a cacophony of horn blowing and shouting. It was John too, who, given the honour of lord of the hunt, tested his skill in breaking up the deer on the field.

Christiana had no desire to share in the excitement of what to her was a purely male domain, although she had heard that women of noble birth often went hawking. Climbing down from

547

her horse she led it a little distance away into the shade of a few broad oaks. Leaning against the bole of a tree she listened to the hounds moving in for their reward – the intestines of the deer – and the laughs and shouts of the men. She noticed for the first time how warm and damp she had become. The afternoon sun was still hot above the treetops and here and there shafts of light had broken through and warmed the ground. Beside her Misty kicked up the mulch of fallen leaves searching the forest floor for grass. Christiana sighed contentedly, savouring the peace. Two figures, arms about each other, withdrew from the gathering of hunters and ambled through the undergrowth towards her. John's face was flushed with excitement and pride and a smear of red could be seen across his cheek. His father patted John on the back. "The boy has done well," he grinned broadly. He caught her hand and pulled her towards the others. "Come, we must drink to the lord of the hunt and then away to the lodge."

A leather pouch filled with rich red wine was unhooked from a saddle together with a long horn. The bubbling crimson liquid was passed from one to the other with a salutation to Sir John of Gloucester, bastard son to His Grace, King Richard.

The carcass of the deer complete with antlered head was hung reverently over John's horse and the procession moved off towards the lodge with John taking his place beside his father at the front. They had not gone far when someone struck up the note of a hunting ditty and soon the park rang with its merry tune. Tired but joyful they arrived as the late afternoon shadows grew longer and the lodge slowly melted into the twilight.

Mistress Danby, Tom's wife, a tall, strong-looking woman with an abundance of chestnut hair tucked into a wimple, was awaiting them in the hall. She approached Christiana and without any ado spoke softly in her ear.

"Come, my dear. Your chamber is prepared. I will have my servant girl fill your bathtub."

Intrigued and not a little surprised Christiana followed the older woman up a flight of stairs to a small chamber with an open window. A large wooden bed with an array of animal skin coverings filled one corner. Frayed woven tapestries covered the walls. A young girl was already filling a lead-lined tub with hot water, disappearing and reappearing moments later, until it was full. She then threw in a handful of herbs and on a nearby table there was even a tablet of scented soap and a large piece of soft linen. Christiana stood in the middle of the room gaping at it all. Surely all this was not meant for her? When the girl returned with a fresh gown of finely woven camlet dyed a pale blue, the look of utter bewilderment upon her face brought out an amused chuckle from Mistress Danby.

"'Tis the king's orders, my lady. We ask no questions, just do the bidding of our sovereign lord. Now come along or else your tub will be cold."

Alone in the chamber Christiana removed her soiled gown and stepped into the welcoming warmth of the tub water. She washed away the dirt of the hunt and emerged clean and refreshed. She slipped into the gown and sitting on the bed she began to comb her long black curls. She marvelled at the meaning of it all; for the first and probably the only time in her life she was being treated as though she were a noblewoman. The gamekeeper and his wife were obviously loyal and discreet subjects. It felt very good to be away from the royal court with its prying eyes and wagging tongues and maybe Richard felt the same also.

When she went back down to the hall the men were already gathered there. Candles had been lit to replace the dying daylight and a young lad sat cross-legged near the fireplace strumming a soothing melody on a lyre. Richard, his hair still damp from bathing, came forward to greet her, kissing her gently on the forehead. He was wearing a green linen tunic and leggings; only the gems on his fingers set him apart from his fellows.

The delicious smell of roast venison wafted into the room and Christiana suddenly realised how hungry she was. John was given the seat at the head of the table and everyone else sat along the sides, paying no heed to rank. Christiana sat next to Richard and shared his goblet. There was plenty of rich red wine to accompany the huge steaks of venison, loaves of bread and a pottage of vegetables and herbs. The meal was informal and relaxed. Even Tom and his wife and young daughter sat with them at table joining in with the light-hearted banter and quips that flowed freely with the wine.

All evening Christiana was aware of the closeness of the king, the scent of his body, the warmth of his fingers as they touched hers around the drinking goblet and a deep longing for him fired up within her. It had been a day of unexpected events and was it too much to hope that it could possibly end in intimate liaison with Richard? She would not allow herself to think of anything beyond the moment.

It was getting late. The light beyond the casements was no more and all the diners had discreetly departed. Christiana marvelled at such a thing; to leave the table before the king was not proper. Taking up a candle from the side table Richard led her to the chamber wherein she had bathed earlier. The bathtub had disappeared and candles placed around the room lent a soft golden glow to the limewashed walls.

"Why, my lord, you have come to my chamber," Christiana giggled, feeling a little light-headed with wine.

"Nay, my lady, 'tis you who have made the mistake," Richard said with mock sternness. "This is the king's chamber." Christiana looked with surprise into his dark eyes and smiled. He put his arms around her and drew her close. She could not express her love for him; it was beyond the scope of words. She rested her head against his chest feeling the rhythmic movement of his breathing. Drawing apart her eyes sought his and then with a breathless hunger their lips met in kisses hard and passionate. She yearned deeply to tell him how much she loved him but she dared not. Such words would break the spell and all would be lost. Besides, he made no such confession to her.

Tenderly her fingers traced the outline of his face, his dark brows, his pale cheeks and well-defined jaw, as though experiencing a great wonder for the very first time. He returned her caress and let his fingers sweep across her breasts to unlace the ties of her bodice. Within moments they were lying together atop the soft warm deerskins on the bed. There, as the sounds of the night forest drifted through the open casement on a gentle breeze they became one, forceful yet gentle with a tender thunder that lifted them to the pinnacle of ecstasy.

Breathless and fulfilled she clung to him, ever mindful of a closeness that would soon be lost to the confines of memory. Bittersweet tears tumbled down her cheeks as she felt his hot breath on her breast. It was thus entwined that sleep engulfed them, holding them in its timeless embrace until the pearly dawn stole soft foot into the chamber.

Christiana was the first to wake and lying still she watched him sleeping like a babe, his cares and troubles hidden in slumber. She reached down and dared to kiss his lips. He stirred and smiling he pulled her closer to return her kiss. Familiar sounds of the new day could be heard from the courtyard below. Swinging his legs onto the floor Richard reached for his discarded clothes and began to dress.

"Do we leave for the castle today?" she asked, watching him tie the stays of his shirt.

"Nay, I have a mind to remain here a while; hunt a little, ride a little and take ease. I might as well do something while I wait for Henry Tudor's invasion," he said light-heartedly as he bent down to kiss her lips before leaving the chamber.

So it was that Christiana spent the following few days in the company of the king and their son, joining in their princely pursuits during the days and spending her nights in Richard's arms.

On the late morning of the fifth day Christiana entered the hall to join the others as they prepared for the day. Their mood was merry as they ate bread and drank ale. She smiled across the table at her son, seated beside his father, his face radiant; she had rarely seen him so happy.

Thomas Danby had entered the room to check all was well with his noble guests when the great door to the hall was flung open and in strode the steward of the king's castle at Nottingham. The man was red-faced and breathing hard. Their mood changed at once and Richard was up on his feet, his face grave with concern.

That the man was the bearer of momentous news was plain to see. He bowed low before the king, taking a moment to gain his breath.

"Your Grace," he began. "Sir Walter Herbert's men have just ridden into the castle with the news that Henry Tudor and his forces have made a safe landing at Milford Haven and are even now moving across the Welsh Marches towards Shrewsbury."

The north of England
19ᵗʰ August 1485

The following days spent at Nottingham were filled with urgency and anxiety – for the king at least. Christiana saw very little of him.

Commissioners of Array were alerted and armies summoned under their banners. It caused the king much concern that one of his chief allies, the Duke of Northumberland, took his time mustering his troops and did not join the king until the nineteenth day of August. All was then set for Richard's army to move out of Nottingham and journey south to intercept the enemy as he moved east from Wales, heading no doubt for London.

The march was swift and hard and for the most part weary and joyless for Christiana. She travelled with the king's domestic household – those responsible for his personal needs – having little contact with the main body of the army. She was pleased, therefore, to see her brother come alongside her as they halted to rest the horses in green lowland alive with summer insects and flowers.

"Are you well?" William asked, sitting down on the warm grass and offering her a chunk of rye bread. She smiled at him and peered up into the clear azure sky.

"'Tis hard to believe that we are going to battle when all is so peaceful," she murmured, plucking at the buttercups and daisies growing all around her. "Is there any news of Henry Tudor?" she asked warily. William chewed on his bread before answering.

"Reports indicate that he is near to Stone, just north of Stafford and..." he hesitated.

"Well, what of it?" she asked urgently.

"Only that, well it is rumoured that Sir William, Lord Thomas Stanley's brother has met with Tudor," he whispered.

"Then there is treachery?" she breathed. "God help the king."

"We do not know for certain but Richard is most wise to suspect the Stanleys. That is the reason we have Lord Stanley's eldest son, Lord Strange, in our midst."

"We do?" Christiana asked, surprised.

"The king insisted that he was left behind when his father asked to return to his family and own affairs earlier this year."

Christiana picked another handful of grass and let the flowers escape through her fingers.

"Do not fret, Christiana," William advised, seeing her worried frown. "There is time enough for Stanley to commit for the king. He would be a fool to back Tudor with his band of French mercenaries and Welsh barbarians."

The sun was sinking low, painting the sky a glorious orange and purple and spilling gold into the waters of the Soar as they crossed over the north bridge towards the north gate and into the city of Leicester on the twentieth day of August.

Most of the king's northern supporters made camp to the north of the city while he and his lieutenants marched down the main street to the White Boar Inn, situated at the corner of Guild Hall Lane. It was here that the king was to join his most loyal commander, John Howard, Duke of Norfolk, who had arrived a day earlier.

The White Boar Inn was a large and impressive timber-framed building, though most of it was under darkness by the time the king's men-at-arms and servants dismounted in the courtyard. William was amongst those attending to the needs of the horses, checking their shoes and brushing the dust from their coats.

Christiana entered the guest hall through a small door leading from the courtyard and sat down at a wooden table. Before her was a platter of bread, wedges of cheese and a steaming cauldron of pottage. She stared at the meal but could not eat. It was getting late. The rush lights had been lit and men were downing their jugs of ale and settling down for the night on straw pallets against the walls. She took a chunk of bread, broke off a small piece and putting it into her mouth began to chew. It felt like a great rock on her tongue. The palms of her hands were damp with sweat. She began to tap the flagstones with the toe of her boot.

Overhead in an upper room the king was still in council with John Howard, Sir Robert Brackenbury, William Catesby and others. Would he be thus incarcerated all night? She had not seen her son for hours and surmised that he was with his father.

She had a desperate need to see Richard; this would be the

only night the king's army would spend in the town. Scouts had reported that Tudor and his army were now close by at Atherstone. She had not come all this way from Nottingham to let Richard go off to battle on the morrow and not see him one last time.

A door creaked open and William Catesby entered looking troubled and weary. He approached the table and began piling bread and cheese onto a plate and ladling pottage into a bowl. Christiana could contain herself no longer and jumping up from her seat she clutched at the man's sleeve.

"Forgive me, my lord, but I must see the king," she cried with urgency.

Placing the ladle back in the cauldron Catesby turned and stared at the woman.

"The king will see no one tonight. Tomorrow he rides out to defend his kingdom. Whatever business you may have with him will have to wait," he replied abruptly.

"You mistake me, my lord," she urged. "I am Christiana, the mother of John of Gloucester, the king's bastard son. I have travelled with the king's household from Nottingham. Do you not know me?"

Catesby took up the platter of food and turned towards the door. "I well know who you are, mistress, but the king may not wish to see you or anyone tonight." Seeing the plea in her eyes he added: "Wait awhile and I will see."

She watched him as he walked across the hall and disappeared through the door leading to the staircase. Sitting down heavily on the bench she buried her face in her hands and waited. Servants came and removed the remains of the food; most of the lights had been extinguished and the hall was filling up with sleeping soldiers.

A gentle tap on her shoulder startled her. "The king has asked to see you," said Catesby, standing beside her. "Come, I will take you up."

She followed him up the staircase and down a long narrow passageway. The air was musty and heavy with the smell of tallow as she passed lighted candles, their smoking flames tickling the shadows. At the end of the passage Catesby knocked on a door and left her.

The wooden door squeaked noisily on its hinges as she pushed it slowly open and entered the king's bedchamber. Candles in their iron sconces warmed the room with a heady perfume and cast a mellow light around the dark beams. The king was alone standing beside a small table, the empty platter and a jug of ale on its surface.

He glanced up as she entered. His face was pale and heavily lined with fatigue. He had discarded the gambeson and leather hose he had worn for the journey and wore only a shabby paltock.

Christiana did not speak or offer any reverence to her king; she merely walked over to him and held him in a tight embrace. Her tears began to fall in a tide of emotion that threatened to engulf her, wetting his hair, long and loose about his shoulders.

"Richard, I could not bear it if you were to be killed," she sobbed. "Must you go to battle? You are the king. You can send any of your finest men..."

Richard withdrew his arms from her and stared in disbelief.

"Aye, I am God's anointed King of England and bound by an oath of loyalty to my kingdom. Am I some weak-kneed sop that I should send others to battle for my crown and not fight myself?" he cried.

"Oh no, Your Grace, forgive me. It is just that..." She shook her head in shame and felt his fingers, cool and gentle, wiping away her tears.

"I know, I know," he said softly.

"You do not know, Richard. How could you?" she shouted with sudden, angry frustration. "You are a nobleman, a king. What do you know of me, a blacksmith's daughter? All these years I have stood by and watched you with Anne, my heart breaking because I could never have you. Knowing that you cared nothing for me beyond..."

Her heart beat wildly as the words, tumbling out of her mouth, broke on an anguished sob and she beat her fist against his chest. "If only you knew how much I have loved you," she moaned.

He caught her hand and held it still. "If you think that I care nothing for you then it is you who knows nothing," he spluttered, pressing her fingers until they hurt, the blue of his eyes burning like jet in the candlelight. "How could you have not known how deeply I have loved you, still love you?" He turned from her to catch his breath and sighed bitterly.

"Did I not tell you how it must be the day I left Middleham to go to my brother the king? You should have married, Christiana, and not wasted your life yearning for me," he continued with trembling lips.

She stood before him, her throat constricting any words that would form, tears coursing down her cheeks. He moved his face closer to hers and their lips touched in one long tender kiss that left her breathless and longing for more.

"My sweet Christiana," he sighed. "I could never love another woman as I love you, not even my own dear wife." He swept her up in his arms and carried her to the large oaken bed. There he unlaced the bodice of her gown and as it fell from her shoulders she shivered. He held her in a close embrace and pulled her down into the rich depths of the furs that covered the bed. Their coming together was deep and urgent, fused with a tension that confirmed the spoken confession of their love and left their bodies utterly spent.

The room was in darkness, the air stuffy. Her shift had stuck to her body in the heat beneath the furs. For a moment she had no clear notion of where she was and then sensing the presence of the man beside her she remembered. Asleep, Richard was tossing and moaning as though he sought to shake off some hellish fiend that haunts the sanctuary of sleep.

Christiana threw aside the heavy fur and crossing the floor she opened the shutters, letting in a stream of cold air and a silver beam of moonlight. The rattling of the wood had disturbed the king who woke suddenly, floundering in the twilight state betwixt sleep and wakefulness, calling out in incoherent babble. She went to him and held him close, feeling his heart beating furiously and his paltock damp with sweat.

"My love, 'tis but a dream, be still," she soothed, smoothing his hair.

From somewhere beyond the casement an owl hooted followed by the distant call of its mate piercing the silence of the night. After a while all the tension left Richard's body and he sank back down on the pillows. He lay there a long while before he spoke.

"A peasant imagines that his life would be worth living if he had a crown upon his head," he whispered, staring up into the pitch darkness of the high-beamed ceiling. "What does he know?" he sniggered bitterly.

"You wear the crown by the divine will of God, my love," she said, lying down beside him and resting her head upon his chest.

"I was neither ruthless nor ambitious, Christiana," Richard confessed in a whisper.

"I never thought to wear my brother's crown; content only to serve him in the north of England. I could not dishonour the Plantagenet line by allowing the Woodvilles to rule the country I love..." He hesitated and caught his breath.

Christiana held him close and waited, afraid to hear the confession of a desperate man. He turned his body towards her and looked straight into her eyes. She could see the silver glint from the moonlight in the deep blue of his eyes.

"I took the crown offered to me when my brother was declared illegitimate and his marriage void. I did what had to be done..."

Christiana's eyes did not leave the king's face. Was he telling her that he was guilty of shedding the blood of two innocent children? She could not accept that he was; not him. Not the man she knew so well and loved so much. And yet to question him now would be to doubt him. Did she doubt him? Would she love him any less for knowing he was guilty? She stared deep into his eyes and brushed the hair gently from his brow where it had fallen. No, in truth she would not.

"You are the king of England, Richard, and you will go out and meet the threat that has come upon you because you are noble and loyal and courageous. I know that your right to rule England is just and true and not got by foul or evil means. If you die, and God willing you will not, my heart will break but I shall know that you will have died defending your kingdom and there is no death more noble." Christiana's words were drenched in tears but her courage did not fail her.

She saw the tears pool in her king's eyes. "Bless you, Christiana, for knowing my very heart, for loving me and for never doubting me," he whispered.

In the grey light from the moon she snuggled up against him, holding him close until sleep claimed him once more. With all her heart she prayed that Henry Tudor would be forever driven from their land and their lives.

The White Boar Inn
Leicester
Sunday 21ˢᵗ August 1485

A cold breeze curled through the open casement and Christiana shivered. Beside her on the bed the king still slept, the outline of his face just visible in the grey light of dawn. A loud banging on the door, sudden and intrusive, startled her. The voice of a man called from outside in the passage: "My lord king, food is prepared below. Your men are stirring!"

Richard woke with a start and stared at her without uttering a word and in that brief moment of time an icy chill seemed to grip her heart. Then the king leapt from the bed and began to dress. Christiana fumbled with her gown and hastily tidied her hair. Within moments she was slipping away down a back stairway, feeling as much the harlot as some undoubtedly thought her to be.

The cobblestones were still moist with dew and an early mist cloaked the figures scurrying back and forth as Christiana stepped out into the courtyard. Horses whinnied and stamped their hooves, stable hands shouted and bleary-eyed soldiers yawned while holding their jugs of ale.

It was not long before order began to emerge from the chaos; knights mounted their steeds and foot soldiers gathered their weapons. White Surrey was led out of his stall caparisoned in the king's livery and the royal standard bearing the red cross of Saint George appeared dimly in the mist. Outside the courtyard gates still more soldiers were congregating as they emerged from their various billets around the town, their voices sounding loud and harsh. The morning sunshine broke through the mist, striking the metal of sword and battle axe, harness and armour.

Christiana stood in the courtyard watching the scene unfold before her feeling dreamy and light-headed. A sudden hand on her shoulder startled her. It was William.

"We are almost ready. We wait now only for the king." His brown eyes regarded her steadily as she swallowed her painful tears.

William pushed something into her hand – it was a well-stuffed purse. "Here, Anna, take this," he urged. "Hide it well. 'Tis all I have. Should I not return – well you might have need of it." Christiana looked down at the purse and quickly pushed it under the bodice of her gown.

"Will, where is John?" she asked suddenly, looking anxiously around her.

"The king has forbidden him to fight. He is not yet a man and would face almost certain death. Richard will not put another man at risk protecting his son so the boy is not to go with us." Christiana nodded slowly, inwardly glad that there at least was one she would not have to be anxious for.

"John did not take the command too well. He is like as not nursing his wounded pride at the back of a stable somewhere," William chuckled.

A sudden hush descended upon the courtyard as the king appeared at the doorway, resplendent in his newly polished cuirass; the rest of his plate armour was packed into a closely guarded wagon. A squire followed behind bearing the king's sallet with a gold coronet circling the top.

All were now ready for departure, waiting for the king to lead them out. A groom rushed forward and assisted Richard into the saddle. Gathering up the reins in his gloved hand he held White Surrey steady. Christiana looked up into his face; grave, courageous and to her most beautiful. She held the gaze of his deep blue eyes for what seemed an eternity. His lips parted as though he would speak but he did not. He dug his spurs into the horse's belly and trotted out of the wide open gates to a roaring cheer from the waiting crowd.

As mounted soldiers and men on foot turned to follow their king William edged his way to Christiana's side, holding the reins of his horse in his hand.

"Farewell, sister," he said and threw his arms around her. She returned his embrace and held him fast.

"Come back to me, Will," she implored tearfully and watched as he mounted his steed and rode away through the gate.

She stood in the deserted courtyard until the last muffled sounds had faded into the distance and sinking to her knees she wept.

A great multitude of men, horses and cartloads of weapons and armour clattered their way through the narrow streets of Leicester. Trumpeters and drummers blew and banged their instruments as they marched along towards the Bow Bridge and the fields beyond. Soldiers sang their battle songs to encourage the younger men; their spirits were high on this warm and sunny morning.

William rode with the king's horsemen at the front of the army, the great beasts of war jostling and vying for position. Ahead of them all, after the king's standard bearer, White Surrey stepped boldly onto the bridge, his hooves clanging on the stone.

Several horses had followed and William's mount was just crossing the bridge when his eye caught a figure, bedraggled and bony, garbed in grey rags and standing to one side of the bridge. It was not so much her appearance, looking even as she did like a witch from ancient legend, but her voice that drew attention. She was shouting what sounded like curses or oaths in an unknown tongue as she brandished a stick of weathered elder in her skeletal hand.

Her words were drowned just then as a cart, following on behind the horses, lost its balance on the step up to the bridge and overturned its cargo of pole arms, clattering noisily onto the stone. Further up the bridge horses already tightly packed became skittish and kicked out nervously at one another. At the fore the king's horse, jostled from behind, sidestepped into the wall of the bridge and in so doing Richard's gilt spur caught the last pillar and chiselled a mark into the stonework before the king brought him swiftly under control and rode on over the bridge to the far side.

The old hag cackled as a sea of wooden poles rolled towards her feet. Soldiers hastened to right the upturned cart and others came forward to retrieve the weapons. Making no attempt to move out of the way of the soldiers the old woman continued with her spate of oaths and soothsaying. One of the soldiers picked up a stave and thrust the pointed end towards her.

"Move on there, old crone," he shouted. "Unless you have something of value to say be gone!"

At once the cackling ceased and the old woman turned a wrinkled, grimy face towards the man. She stretched her lips into a toothless grin. "Maybe I does 'ave summat t' say," she croaked.

A second soldier heaving a hefty bundle of weapons over the side of the cart shouted, "You mind old Black Annis, Tom. She might just make you a prophecy and then you'll have to part with your silver."

"For sooth I can and you'd be wise to take heed and not mock," the old woman answered.

"Go on then," called the man by the cart. "Do your soothsaying and we might just spare you a dip in the river, but there'll be no silver mind."

Tom lowered the tip of the stave he was holding and nodded to the old woman who raised her staff and closed her eyes. The soldiers standing around exchanged glances with sceptical humour.

"Now I am scared," whispered one with a chuckle.

Suddenly the old woman opened her eyes and announced, "I say this of King Richard; where his spur do strike there too will his head be broken!"

There was a moment of absolute silence from the men around the cart until a shout went up from behind.

"You up there on the bridge! Keep moving!"

With the cart reloaded they proceeded across the bridge to the fields beyond, the hag's words soon forgotten in the song and beat of the marching army.

They camped on Ambion Hill near to the village of Sutton Cheney, clusters of tents and small fires covering the green. Smoke curled and spiralled upwards in the warm summer evening carrying with it the smell of roasting pig flesh. An unnatural calm had settled on the regiments as hushed voices mingled with the last call of birdsong.

William sat cross-legged on the grass sharpening the blade of his axe with a whetstone. A little way over to his left a group of horses stamped the ground and jostled each other as though something unnerved them. Every few moments William would glance in their direction, sure that he had seen the merest flick of a shadow amongst the horses' legs.

He tried not to think of the impending battle but try as he might he could not ignore the familiar churning in his stomach. Nearly two years had passed since he had seen active service and even then his part in quelling Buckingham's rebellion had been slight. He reached over for the costrel at his side and took a long deep drink of the warm ale.

The sound of a bucket overturning alerted him and sure enough there was a figure, a youth, skittish and nervous as a colt, prancing around the feet of the horses.

"Hey, lad," William called. "Come over here. I have a couple of dice; we can play, if you've a penny!"

The youth wore a chaperon upon his head and he had drawn the liripipe around his face concealing all but his eyes. He started nervously.

"You'll unnerve the horses, lad, if you don't move away. The sound of field guns they can stand but not furtive movements round their legs. Come hither I say!"

The boy looked straight at William and then glanced around him. Seeming to make his mind up he crept slowly towards the man.

"Sit you down, lad," said the soldier, offering the boy his costrel and fumbling in his belt pouch for dice. "You look a mite young to be fighting in any battle and not a scrap of armour."

William's eyes narrowed as he looked closely at the boy who had no sooner sat down than he started to rise again like a doe taken fright of the bowman. But William was quicker; in an instant he caught the boy's arm and with his other hand he pulled the liripipe from his face.

"I thought as much," he hissed at the sight of John's startled face. "You were told, nay ordered, to keep away from the battle field."

"Battle has not yet begun," John said petulantly. "Come on, Uncle Will. How can I keep away when my father fights for his crown?"

"You do the king no favours if he has to watch your every move."

"He does not need to know I am here. Do not betray me, Will, please. I can fight as well as any man."

William stared into the boy's pale face, his deep blue eyes twinkling like sapphires in the fading light.

"Your sentiments are noble, John," he said gruffly. "But until you have killed a man and felt the warmth of his blood on your hands you know nothing of fighting." John sat on the grass beside William and took a few mouthfuls of ale from his costrel.

"How is it you have avoided being seen by the king?" William asked after a while.

"My father has gone to the church of Saint James in the village to take Mass," John answered.

"Indeed," remarked William. "It is as well for us then that you are not a spy for the Tudor or we should all be murdered 'ere battle begins." He punched the boy's shoulder playfully and grinned.

"My father will win this battle, will he not?" John asked with childlike innocence. William drew a deep breath and exhaled.

"The king's army outnumbers and outranks that of the Tudor. He has naught but a bunch of Welsh cut-throats and French mercenaries and a handful of traitors to the crown," he said disparagingly. "But we must not forget Stanley, who it is believed could have as many as eight thousand men. Notorious for biding their time are the Stanleys."

"But the king holds Thomas Stanley's son, Lord Strange. I have seen him this day held captive under armed guard in a tent not yards from the king's," John returned.

William smiled. "There is time enough for Stanley to do the honourable thing and fight alongside his king." He ruffled the boy's dark hair. "And you, young knave. Be sure to lie low on the morrow and no chivalrous antics."

The night air was still and warm as grey clouds filled the deep blue sky where a mere handful of stars peeped through. All around the gentle snores and grunts of sleeping soldiers could be heard; some slumped outside the tents where it was cooler.

William rose from his mattress and left his tent. He had a need to relieve himself. Walking between the military shelters to the edge of the camp he could see the pennants, black against the sky, flapping like sails in the sea of tents. The effects of the ale he had consumed earlier had all but worn off, leaving his head clearer.

Once again images of blood spilled and men and horses screaming filled his thoughts. What would become of England and all of them if the king should fall tomorrow?

He relieved himself in some scanty wind-blown bushes and turned to walk back. He was just approaching Norfolk's cluster of tents when he caught sight of a figure running away from the duke's tent, bending low to avoid detection. William thought at first that it might be John again, but no, this figure had the girth of a full-grown man and within seconds he had disappeared out of sight.

Perplexed, William approached Norfolk's tent to see that all was well. The duke's standard fluttered gently on its pole, the tiny crosses on its quarters just visible in the moonlight. The sound of snoring from within indicated that nothing was amiss; there had been no noise of a scuffle. He was about to lift the flap of the tent for a closer look when something shining white in the pale light caught his eye. It was a crumpled piece of thin parchment with a few words scrawled upon it and pinned to the entrance of the duke's tent.

Glancing quickly about him William carefully lifted the parchment and turned to walk away. It was too dark to make out any of the words, written in an untidy hand. Nearing the king's regiment and his own tent he noticed a light coming from within the royal pavilion. He directed his footsteps there. The entrance was guarded by two burly soldiers each holding a polished halberd and with a broad sword at his hip.

"If the king is not yet abed tell him that William Smith of Middleham would speak urgently with him," he whispered to the guard.

One man opened the flap of the tent after a brief glance at his comrade and went inside. William could hear a brief exchange of words and moments later he was admitted into the king's presence.

There would appear to be another who had begged audience with the king or maybe his presence had been summoned for William, although not acquainted with the man, certainly knew of his reputation. He bowed his head politely to Juan de Salazar and caught the gleam of candlelight in his dark eyes and the olive skin of the Spaniard as he swept past him.

Richard sat at a small desk, quill pen poised in his hand, candles burning low at his elbow. William bowed to the king and took a couple of steps nearer. Richard was wearing a heavy padded jack and leather hose. His sword in its scabbard was slung across the table. In the pallid glow of candlelight William could make out the iridescent hues of the noble lettering on a Book of Hours. The king's face was grave, tired, and William noted the dark circles beneath his eyes. Richard rubbed a hand wearily over his face and laid aside his quill.

"It is fortuitous that you are here, Will, for I have penned a letter which I am entrusting to your safe keeping. It must be given to your sister should I not survive the battle."

William stepped closer. "Your Grace," he said. "You will survive the battle..."

The king waved his hand dismissively. "Come, William, you are not some two-faced courtier bred to say and do the right thing in order to win the favour of your king. Loyalty is all that matters to me. We are both soldiers and there should be honesty between us. No one but Almighty God knows the outcome of this battle."

"Aye, my lord king, you are right, but I pray to God that his grace will be upon you on the morrow."

Richard turned to secure a letter, from amongst an array of military plans on his desk, with a blob of wax and his seal. "Now, what is it that you have to tell me so urgently that it will not wait?"

William handed over the parchment without even glancing at the words, doubtful that he could read much of them anyway. As the king read his face drained of colour. "Where did you get this?" he asked, rising to his feet.

"Pinned to Norfolk's tent, my lord king. I happened past just now and noticed it."

"'Jack of Norfolk, be not too bold, for Dickon thy master is bought and sold'," Richard read aloud. "By God," he exclaimed. "Is there no one in this land I can trust? Do all men betray me? Am I not king by right of birth and with the blessing of God and the people?" He sank back heavily into his chair.

William went down on his knees before the king and clasped his jewelled hand.

"My lord, you are rightful king and be certain that you are loyally supported by many. Many who will give their lives for you on the morrow. What more proof would you have than that? Your army is made up of the very best of English nobility, good fighting men. What does the Tudor have? A small band of Welsh barbarians and French mercenaries," William continued vehemently.

Richard nodded gravely and put his hand on William's shoulder. "Aye you are right," he declared softly. "Nothing less than treason is going to prevent me from winning this battle."

The eyes of the king met the eyes of his soldier and for a long, long moment neither spoke. In truth, what could be said? Both knew the implication of the king's words; Thomas, Lord Stanley was and always had been a man who put his own welfare before any other.

Finally the king dismissed him and William bowed his head to kiss the royal ring before rising and leaving the king's presence.

She lifted herself slowly from her bed of straw. Her body ached and a dull throbbing in her head reminded her of her restless, sleepless night in the stable of the White Boar Inn. Outside in the courtyard a blazing sun riding high in the sky told her that it was almost midday. She shuffled slowly back into the hall where the innkeeper's wife offered her bread and ale. She felt too tired and sick to eat and managed only a little.

She had spent all day yesterday after the king's departure looking for John. She had searched the stable yard and enquired of him within the inn. She had wandered the unfamiliar and oddly deserted streets and found not a sign of him.

After a while she left the table and went back outside; she could sense the servants staring at her as they went about their work. How strange she must appear to them, her fine blue silk gown crumpled and bits of straw woven into her untidy hair. She splashed her face with a little cold water from the horse trough and left the inn.

She stepped out to her right into the High Street walking south and passing the great High Cross where the road met with Hot Gate and Swine's Market. A sweltering heat from the rays of the sun burned her head for she had mislaid her hat and sweat poured from her brow. She took the left fork down Hot Gate, along Apple Gate and on towards the West Gate. It would be here, across the Bow Bridge, spanning the River Soar, that news of the battle would come.

Others, eager for news, had also begun to gather, scattering the dust from the parched road into her dry throat. The crowd pushed her across the West Bridge, along the road to the Bow Bridge. Here the masses surged across and spread out into the west fields like an unstoppable tide. Christiana came to rest at the stone pillar of the Bow Bridge at the far side where it began to arch across the river.

She had not been there long when two thinly clad boys, bare-legged and grimy-faced, were seen to be racing across the fields towards the bridge, shouting excitedly, "He comes! The king comes!"

The sound of drum and pipe and singing voices coming from way across the fields was growing ever nearer.

A cry went up. "The king! The king!"

Christiana's heart leapt wildly. Could it be? Was it indeed possible? Did Richard yet live? Such joy was hard to contain. She stood on tiptoe, for she was not so tall, and peered expectantly over the surrounding heads.

She pushed her way to the front just as a great black steed approached and clattered over the bridge in a fury of waving banners and pennants. The rider did indeed bear a crown upon his head, but the hand that held aloft the gleaming sword was not Richard's. He looked around him in bewilderment, scarce able to comprehend the cheering crowd. One of the knights in the livery of the Welsh dragon shouted, "Long live King Henry! Long live the king!"

Men on horseback, foot soldiers, wagons and field guns, women and children all stamped and rattled across the bridge. The people of Leicester joined the triumphant party and turned from the bridge to wave and cheer their new sovereign.

One woman, alone and trembling, remained at the side of the bridge, staring in bewilderment at the remnant of this unbelievable procession. In the wake of the victorious train came their captives; stripped of all but under tunics, feet bare and bloodied, with hands tied by a coarse rope that chaffed their wrists, they were dragged along the dusty road.

As they passed near to where she stood she reached out a hand to touch a sleeve. The eyes that turned towards her were filled with a great sorrow. She bowed her head as he went by; she thought she knew him.

At the very end of this cortège from hell plodded a scrawny, bone-shaking nag. Across its back, swinging limply like merchant's baggage, with a felon's rope around his wrists, was the naked corpse of her beloved Richard.

Christiana watched in horror as one of Tudor's men, walking alongside, forced the blade of his dagger upwards into the bare buttock of the Plantagenet king, withdrawing it with a savage smirk upon his face.

Just as the old horse struggled to step up onto the bridge with its burden, a youth stepped from the crowd and with a birch switch struck the nag hard upon its flank. The horse whinnied and stepped nervously to the side of the bridge. The soldier leading the beast, taken unawares, struggled to bring the animal under control but not before the head of the dead king had been struck against the stone pillar of the bridge.

As one witless and dulled with opium or strong wine Christiana stood on the bridge hardly heeding the shouts of the receding crowds as they followed the newly proclaimed king into the heart of the town. Once through the West Gate the procession was joined by still more bare-footed children and beggars all hoping to benefit from the generosity of a rejoicing army well soaked in ale.

In a moment of utter exhaustion Christiana sank to her knees on the baked earth at the side of the road. A shrill voice, sounding familiar and coming from it seemed a great distance, hailed her.

"Mistress Christiana! Mistress Christiana!"

She looked up to see John's squire, Robert, red-cheeked and panting hard, running towards her.

"Have you seen John?" she demanded, staring into his youthful, tense face. He shook his head sadly but said nothing.

"I fear I have no strength and am feeling ill," she said quietly. "Will you take me back to the White Boar Inn?"

She leaned heavily upon the poor boy for support all the way back to the inn. Her legs shook so violently she could hardly walk at all and her heart was overwhelmed with grief and sorrow but not one tear could she yet shed.

At the White Boar Inn Robert found the innkeeper, who noting the rich attire of the woman and narrowing his eyes at a hint of recognition, allowed them in. The young squire escorted her up the narrow staircase to a small empty room, where she lay gratefully on the bed. The hot afternoon sun shone fiercely through the open casement onto her face but she cared not for she was already asleep.

It was well into the morning when Christiana woke. It was already warm in the small room and her gown clung damply to her skin. She stirred slowly; sleep had failed to rid her of the pounding pain across her forehead.

Once at the table in the hall she forced herself to eat a few mouthfuls of bread and pottage provided by the innkeeper's wife. As she sat eating, the boy, Robert, appeared beside her at the table looking most anxious.

"I must confess something to you," he said, close to tears. Christiana put down her cup of ale on the board and turned to face the boy. He was clearly beside himself with the burden of his sin, so much so that Christiana felt her own heart begin to tremble.

"'Tis my lord John," he whispered. Fearing the worst from his confession Christiana closed her eyes. She felt his hand touch her sleeve. "He followed the king to battle; they say it was fought on Dadlington Field. He begged me not to say anything. He wanted to fight for his father." The boy hung his head in shame. "He did not even tell his Uncle Will."

"Oh blessed Jesus!" she cried and buried her face in her hands. Had all three been lost to that vile Tudor?

"Let us go into the town," Robert offered, "there may be some news."

As they passed through the courtyard gate and round into the street Christiana glanced up to where the sign bearing the name of the inn hung on its pole. With disbelief she saw that the innkeeper, perched on a ladder, had a metal pot and brush in his hand. No longer white, the boar that looked down upon the good folk of Leicester was a freshly painted blue and over his face were the words Blue Boar Inn.

"'Tis the device of the Earl of Oxford, Tudor's commander,"

Robert whispered at her side. "A wise man will always give his allegiance to the victor."

They walked silently down the street, stopping at the high stone cross.

Christiana stood at a loss as to where to go – all around were Tudor's men, drunk with triumph and the copious amounts of ale consumed in the inns of the town, waving the red dragon of Cadwallader.

The world it seemed had turned upside down overnight. Who now would dare carry the symbol of the wild boar? Maybe Robert was right – the wise would swear allegiance to the victor. Had all loyalty perished with the king?

They moved slowly down to the furthermost end of the street and passed under the South Gate arch. The noise and commotion of an excitable crowd met them on the other side, for here stood the imposing gateway entrance into the Newarke. All manner of folk were surging like cattle beneath the great arch for something of much significance that commanded attention lay beyond.

Carried forth on this wave of humanity, Christiana and Robert, clinging on to each other for fear of separation, entered the Newarke. Soldiers brandishing bills were keeping the crowds back from the wide entrance to the Church of the Annunciation of the Blessed Virgin Mary. A body, naked and defiled, was just visible within, raised high on a stone plinth, robbed of dignity and exposed to the leers and taunts of the morbidly curious.

None could now deny the just demise of the usurper, Richard, third to bear that name, calling himself King of all England. And so none could now dispute the victorious and rightful king, Henry, seventh to bear that name, of all England, by the grace of God; so proclaimed the herald stood upon a platform nearby.

Sickened and faint-hearted Christiana would go no closer and pushed her way back towards the gated entrance, but found herself pressed upon and pushed against the enclosing wall and apart from Robert. Here she stood awhile, her face turned away from the hellish scene across the Newarke; an act in a mummer's play from which she felt strangely detached.

Breathing deeply to calm herself she took in the stench of animal carcasses, heaped and awaiting preparation for hide and leather, drifting on the warm wind from the settlement to the south of the town. For what seemed like an indefinable passage of time Christiana sat on the mossy grass in the shadow of the great wall. She caught the sound of passing voices and soon learned that the church in which the body of her beloved Richard was publically displayed was a mausoleum for Lancastrian nobility.

"This *king*, this Henry Tudor should fear for his immortal soul for the way he has defiled and displayed the body of an anointed king." The figure of a man close by, cloaked and hooded despite the heat of the day, spoke his words softly into the crowd. Not all, it seemed, shared in Henry's victory.

Christiana could bear it no longer and standing shakily to her feet she walked slowly back under the arch and found Robert sitting cross-legged by the side of the road. Everywhere she looked men lived and breathed. A boy was chasing a pig across open grassland just across the way, an old man struggled to pull a cart along the road and there against the wooden wall of a shack another was relieving himself.

They walked once again along the High Street. Surely if either John or William still lived they would seek her out in Leicester? As they passed the cross once again the descending rays of the sun were just kissing the stones with gold.

"There is a hospital further along this road, I think... I remember from a visit I once made to the town..." Robert's voice beside her came through the foggy musings of her mind. "The hospital of Saint John the Baptist," the boy continued. "'Tis near to the Royal Prison. There is a hospital in the Newarke... but I do not think any of Richard's men would be taken there..."

With hurried steps, now purposeful, Christiana pushed her way through the throng. They continued silently along the High Street, with its dark wooden dwellings slowly melting into the shadows. On the corner of Saint John's Lane stood the long wooden building, bleak and sombre, the only sign of its benevolence a crooked wooden plaque bearing the words Hospital of Saint John.

The great door of oaken wood stood closed but a bell on a rope hung nearby. With a hope in her heart like the flutter of bird wings Christiana tugged on the rope and the bell clanged loudly.

Several moments passed before a small hole in the door opened and a sharp-featured face with dark thick brows thrust itself through. Immediately Christiana was put in mind of Lempster, the king's physician and momentarily was taken aback.

"Pray excuse me, my lord," she stammered. "I am looking for my brother and son. They were fighting in the battle near a place called Dadlington and may be injured."

"There are no soldiers here," the man replied curtly. "Our benefactor provides for the needs of the good folk of Leicester. There is not money enough for soldiers." With that the door was slammed shut.

With tears stinging the corners of her eyes Christiana turned away and was about to retrace her steps when Robert halted her with a tug at the sleeve of her gown.

"Mistress, wait... Prisona Regis."

A building of cold stone and austere in its regard stood a little back from the road flanked on either side by the hospital and the shire hall.

The two armed guards at the gated entrance to the prison stood rigid as rock and seemingly oblivious to the presence of the woman and boy.

Christiana turned a pale face to her companion. "Could they be held inside?" she whispered.

Robert glanced fearfully at the soldiers. "'Tis a place of incarceration for ones of noble birth methinks."

Christiana remembered the men brought in as captives only the day before; there was one whose face she thought she knew but could not place.

"What will become of these noble prisoners?" Christiana asked, her mind recoiling from any notion that John and William might be within those cold walls of stone.

"They will be held until their captives are able to extract a weighty ransom from their families. They will most certainly be attainted and their lands forfeited," Robert replied. "This is why there is little to gain in holding one such as your brother."

"But what if they have John?" Christiana's voice quivered in the cooling air. "There is none to pay his ransom."

The boy took the woman's arm and gently moved her away from the prison and back down the road.

"If John is in their keeping then 'tis because they have guessed his paternity," Robert replied softly. "They would not want him for ransom, mistress."

Still gripping the woman's arm the boy quickened his pace. "We will journey to Dadlington Field if nothing of them can be found here," he announced encouragingly.

Christiana stopped walking and turned abruptly to the boy. "I am no fool, Robert; I know that if he lives then Richard's son will be in grave danger and we cannot be too forthright in our enquiries."

"If they are at liberty then they will find us," Robert replied on a sigh.

The sun was rolling towards its cradle in the west as they arrived back at the inn.

Christiana was feeling weary and despondent after a day of searching and still no news of John or William and was grateful for a meal of bacon pottage and bread on their return. The hall was beginning to fill up with people; soldiers mainly and most wearing the sign of the red dragon. Many townsfolk would profit from this battle, she thought wryly, as the innkeeper hurried past with several jugs of ale hooked to his fingers.

She looked across at the boy, a mere child of twelve years. His sandy hair fell across his face as he gnawed his bread hungrily.

"Do you not wish to return to your father in Westminster?" she asked. "He is cofferer to the king is he not?"

"Was, mistress," Robert replied, his mouth stuffed with bacon. "Who knows what is to become of him, or any of us now. Nothing will be the same as once it was."

How true that was, she realised sadly. For common folk life would go on as much the same as before like as not, their concern for how many taxes they would have to pay to the crown. But what of those whose livelihoods had depended upon King Richard?

"Go steady on the food, Rob," she advised with a smile. "There is money enough for more yet."

All at once the smile froze on her face. Robert looked at her curiously as her ashen face stared past him to the far wall of the room.

"Is all well, mistress?" he asked, turning around to follow her gaze. The room was packed with folk drinking, playing dice; soldiers laughing and relaxing now that battle was won. He saw nothing untoward.

Christiana put her chunk of bread back down on the table and leaning across to the boy she whispered, "We need to leave, Rob – now."

"Leave now, why?" he asked incredulously.

"Just do as I say," she snapped. "Meet me in the yard; I will find the innkeeper."

Completely baffled by the woman's behaviour Robert went out to the yard. Perhaps he could saddle the horses ready to leave – if she really did mean them to leave.

Christiana made her way up the stairs and quickly along the passageway to the small room she had slept in the previous night. She gathered her few belongings: a cloak, a second gown and a bone comb. William's bag of gold and silver coins she still had beneath her bodice. All the while she was terrified that he might have seen her and would at any moment appear at the door. Her last memory of that vile face dragged up all the pain and suffering associated with it. And yet he wore Stanley's livery; Thomas, Lord Stanley had entered Leicester victorious with Henry Tudor.

She had one leather pouch into which she stuffed everything and hurried back down the passage. There was no sign of the innkeeper so she pushed her way towards the kitchen where she found his wife scolding the kitchen boy for allowing the loaves to burn in the clay ovens as he slept beside the fire.

"Leaving us then are you?" the woman asked, wiping her hands on a hessian apron. Christiana nodded her head silently and followed the woman out to the back of the inn. Here she handed over the required amount for her food and board and those of Robert and the horses, with the distinct impression that she was paying more than a fair price but with little enough knowledge of such matters to argue. It was the last of her own meagre coin, earned as a servant of the royal household.

"'Tis almost dark out there; will you not consider staying until daybreak?" the woman asked, but Christiana shook her head. This inn was far too central to the town and would attract many soldiers; she could not risk that this would be Ralph Hodkin's only night. Besides which, the inn held memories that she needed to lock away in a dark recess of her mind – for now.

The courtyard was deserted save for Robert saddling the horses. The revellers were all indoors and the sounds of merrymaking could be heard beyond the casements. Christiana tied her bag to the saddle of her grey mare; a handsome animal and a gift from Richard for his Royal Progress. As she led the horse from the stall a rough hand held fast the bridle and a sharp voice demanded, "Where do you think you are going with that horse?"

Terrified, Christiana looked up into the face of the innkeeper. "We have paid our due to your good wife and are leaving the inn," she replied, relieved that he was not Ralph Hodkin.

"Not with my horse, you don't," the man replied, tightening his grip on the mare's bridle.

"You are mistaken," Christiana replied with a slight quiver in her voice. "This horse belongs to me; it was a gift from the king."

The innkeeper threw back his head and guffawed loudly. "Why should the king, any king, give a wench like you such a fine piece of horse flesh?"

Christiana looked down at her once beautiful gown, now hanging in tatters and heavy with dust and dirt from the road. Her second gown, bundled up in her saddle pouch fared no better. She pushed back the loose hair that had fallen across her cheeks and felt hot tears of indignation prick her eyes, but before she could answer the man Robert did so for her.

"You have no claim to this horse; it belongs to Mistress Christiana, mother of the king's son."

Christiana's look of horror shot keenly at the boy arrested any further words and he hung his head in red-faced shame. She stood in frightful silence waiting to see if the man had wit enough to make use of the information imparted to him.

"I have no fear of a dead king's whore," he spat the words into the woman's face.

"What goes on here?" The harsh voice of the innkeeper's wife reached them from across the cobbled yard as she marched towards them. Christiana noticed how the man flinched, almost imperceptibly, before his domineering wife.

"Wife, I caught these two about to make off with our best horses. Maybe you should alert the king's soldiers inside at sup," he announced.

The woman stared at Christiana through narrowed eyes. "Let the woman keep the horse; likely 'tis all she has left now that good King Richard is dead," she said firmly.

"But, wife," protested the innkeeper, "that horse is..."

"You, husband, are a fool," she retorted. "King Richard paid you well for your trouble when he arrived here and don't think that I didn't know it. Now, keep the boy's horse and let that be payment enough for your foolishness."

She turned then to Christiana. "Now, woman," she said, "take your horse and be gone. King Henry's men are still within the town and like as not will be supping here for a good few nights yet and we want no trouble. Now, I bid a good night to you both."

"Where are we to go?" Robert asked anxiously as they left the inn and turned back down the High Street towards the stone cross. Stars were already beginning to awaken in a lavender sky. Christiana hardly cared where it was as long as it was as far away from Ralph Hodkin as she could be.

"We need to find another inn and a bed for the night," she replied wearily, "somewhere less grand than the White Boar and more out of the way. On the morrow we will go find Dadlington."

"I heard talk of an inn where the ale is good," Robert offered helpfully, passing the High Cross and continuing down the road.

"I care not for the ale, Robert," Christiana replied. "Do they have comfortable beds or at least a straw pallet near a warm fire?" They were passing along the western wall of the Grey Friars liberty.

"So, Squire Robert, where is this veritable inn for I am tired and in much need of rest," she asked.

"It is not far but we should hurry for soon it will be dark," Robert replied, leading the way east at the end of the High Street, along Friar Lane and towards the marketplace. The only sound to be heard was the clopping of the mare's hooves on the hard baked road and the odd raised voice from within the rickety dwellings along the way.

They reached the end of the lane and over to the right on the market green stood the silhouette of a gigantic elm tree, its black leaves rustling in the night breeze. Beyond, nestled against the southern town wall, was a dwelling, its windows shining bright with candlelight against the darkness; a welcoming sight.

"The Green Dragon Inn," Robert announced cheerfully.

They requested a stable for the horse and, as there were no empty rooms to spare, they had to share with the other guests. It seemed a decent establishment and clean enough although it lacked the splendour and size of the White Boar Inn.

Christiana's bedfellow was already sleeping soundly and, fortunately for her, the woman was slim and took up only half of the narrow mattress. She sat down wearily on her side of the bed and unlaced the stays of her gown. It was warm in the small room and she had worn this gown for several days now and wanted to remove it. A fat bunch of dried lavender sat in a clay jug on the small table beside the bed and Christiana folded her gown neatly with the fragrant flower heads trapped inside the folds and placed it over a chest.

She took up the coin purse and first checking that her companion still slept she opened the drawstring. She had not looked at the contents of the purse since William had given it to her. Carefully she emptied out the coins: gold angels, silver pennies and groats. It was a small fortune; everything William had, given to her.

There was also something else, right at the bottom of the bag, concealed beneath the coins. She slid her hand into the bag and pulled out a curious object; something she had not set eyes upon for many a year and indeed had slipped her memory until now. The edges and surface had worn smooth with the passing of time and the wood had darkened with age but she still recognised it as the little carved wooden horse she had given to William in Jervaulx monastery. How strange that William had kept it all these years – a good luck charm perhaps? Stranger still then that he had not taken it into battle with him. Maybe he had left it to her as a keepsake.

Dear William, would she ever know what had become of him or her beloved son? She sighed and replaced the toy and the coins inside the bag and loosening her garter she pushed it under her hose. The bed was warm and fairly soft though nowhere near as comfortable as the ones she had become accustomed to but she slept little.

Leicester

24th August 1485

The following morning Christiana woke to such a commotion outside the window of her room. She opened her eyes to see the figure of a strange young woman standing beside the bed. Sitting up with a start she recalled that she was in the Green Dragon Inn and this must be her bedfellow.

The woman smiled at her as she tied the stays of her parsley-green gown.

"Susan is my name," she said, lifting her skirts and putting a tiny foot into undyed hose that was most certainly homespun.

"Christiana," the other woman replied, removing the linen sheet and going to the window. It was not glazed but had pieces of horn held together with bits of broken lead. She could see nothing beyond.

"What is going on out there?" she asked, pushing open the window and peering out.

"Folk are gathering for the executions, coming early to get a good view. Men of some note I would say, the common folk they swing from a rope."

The huge elm tree looked even bigger in the early light with its leaves shimmering silver-green. Under its boughs men were finishing erecting a platform that had hitherto sat unnoticed in the darkness; it was the sound of their hammering that had awoken her. There was already a sizable crowd gathering below, the noise of their chatter rising up through the open window.

A cold terror gripped Christiana's heart. Surely they would not kill her son? He was but a child. They could not execute a child, could they?

She tried to hold on to her sanity. They may not even have John. He was probably killed on the battlefield. Better that than this.

"Do you know who it is?" Christiana asked, turning her head.

"William Catesby is one," Susan announced, "and two others. "Do you know him?" she asked after witnessing the look of shock on the other woman's pale face. Christiana swallowed hard but gave no answer.

"Is it true that he is, or was, King Richard's speaker – you know, someone important in the king's parliament? My Jack says..."

So it had been the face of William Catesby that she had seen, dragged sullied from the battlefield without the dignity befitting his rank. She turned away and walked over to where her gown still lay across the coffer. She did not want the other woman to see her falling tears and so she fumbled in her bag, removed her lambswool gown and with trembling hands began to dress. She used the gusset pot beside the bed to further bide her time.

"We can watch from up here. 'Tis the best view, I think, although the innkeeper will charge us for the privilege," Susan was saying. "Jack, my husband, will be sorry if he misses this. Had his head over a pig trough the last I saw and heard of him last night," she chuckled.

Christiana took her comb from her leather pouch and began to tug at her matted hair but these common everyday tasks were little distraction for her fearful mind.

"Here, let me do that for you," Susan offered, taking the comb from Christiana's hand. "By the way, your son I think it was, came looking for you at first light; an early riser is he not?"

Christiana turned her head so quickly that her hair tugged viciously at the comb in Susan's hand.

"John, he is here?" she cried.

"John?" Susan asked, confused. "Nay, Robert. How many sons do you have? I told him you were still abed and to return later."

Christiana sat still as Susan continued to rake through her hair.

"How is it you know this Catesby then?" Susan persisted. "You speak with a strange tongue, where is it you hail from?" she went on, undeterred at having received no reply. "You look as though you've spent the night in a barn by all this straw in your hair and yet that gown over there looks to be a very expensive garment to me."

Christiana sat in silence, her heart trembling and wishing fervently that the woman would go away and leave her be. If she continued to offer the woman no explanation then she would be under suspicion and that she did not want.

"I am come from Yorkshire with my brother. He fought alongside King Richard and alas fell on the battlefield. I am a widow and the boy Robert is my son and soon we shall be returning home," Christiana said quickly and hoped that her untruths would suffice to satisfy the woman's prying. "I knew of Catesby, a fine loyal man and friend to King Richard, so I am told," she added quietly.

"Did you ever meet King Richard? He was said to be a most handsome man, and my Jack says his laws were all set to benefit the common man," Susan continued; nothing, it seemed, was going to quell the flow of her words.

"No, I never knew the king," Christiana whispered after a while and snatching up a cloth on the table began to wipe at her falling tears.

"What is wrong with you, woman?" Susan chided. "'Tis not you who faces the axe," she chuckled mockingly.

Christiana was relieved to see Robert at the door not many minutes later and whispered for him to have a care with regard to his words.

"Have you anything to tell?" she asked urgently. The boy shook his head.

Jack came up shortly afterwards looking much the worse for his night hung over a pig trough. Christiana listened with patient trembling as his wife explained to her new friend that they were merchants; purveyors of cups, spoons, combs, leather costrels and the like. They were in Leicester for the Saturday market when they heard that King Richard had arrived to do battle for his crown with Henry Tudor. Seeing how the town heaved with soldiers they had decided to stay on and sell a few more goods. They had not done too badly so far but it was not always easy avoiding the town sheriff and his men.

"I grow so weary of this woman's constant chatter," Christiana whispered to Robert as they stood by the open casement waiting for something to happen down below. Susan and Jack were watching from the window at the other side of the bed.

It was a good view from up here; right over the heads of the waiting crowd. The executioner, a large man garbed in black, was walking up the steps of the guarded platform, the blade of his axe glinting silver in the dappled light.

"Please God, let it be sharp and swift," Christiana prayed and stared down at the heavy, solid block of wood with its carefully carved and smoothed collar.

There was a sudden hush from the crowd as a group of men climbed onto a platform. From behind the crowd, a horse pulling a cart could be seen approaching from the direction of Friar Lane. The crowd parted to let it through.

Christiana could bear it no longer and bolted from the room without a word of explanation, the boy at her heels. She fled down the stairs and out into the glowing warmth of the morning sun. There was nothing to be seen but the heads of the onlookers. She needed to get closer. Grabbing the boy's hand she pushed and jostled the crowd until they had broken through to the front, ignoring the jibes and insults that came their way.

The cart had reached them; she saw Catesby's bewildered face staring out into the crowd. There were two others beside him in the cart, both grown men, both unknown to her. John was not there; they did not have her son, he was not there. Relief trickled through her body with a fierce trembling.

Catesby was the first to be dragged from the cart and led up to the platform. She watched, senseless, as a gentle breeze slapped his shirt around his bare legs as he stood waiting, hands tied behind his back. She could see the fear in his eyes and the sweat on his brow for she was close, closer than she wanted to be.

"Blessed Jesus, have mercy," she moaned. The priest stepped forward to hear Catesby's final confession and she too prayed silently for his immortal soul. She remembered his loyalty to Richard and paid little heed to the Proclamation of Treason indicted against him as they untied his hands and pushed him forward. He struggled as they put the blindfold on him as the priest, his robes blowing in the breeze, muttered more prayers and made the sign of the cross.

Catesby's head was laid on the block and for a moment she thought that he would have to be held down but suddenly his body sagged as though he had yielded to God's will. When the axe fell it was swift and clean and the severed head dropped neatly into the basket below to a tumultuous cheer from the crowd; the first good red blood to be spilled under the Tudor king that would nowise be the last.

Christiana stood, her eyes fixed on the platform, as the head was retrieved from the basket and the body shrouded and laid to one side. She felt a tug on her hand and realised that Robert was still with her. They had lost their place at the front now and the crowd had them penned like cattle. With a heart heavy with sorrow and a pale and trembling boy at her side the woman heard the thud of the axe and the roar of the crowd for a second time and then a third time.

The throng began to disperse and in its wake the sweet sickly smell of fresh blood sailed silently on the summer air. The bodies were removed, driven off on the cart on which they had arrived. All that remained was the wooden block where the blood was congealing, sticky and black in the heat of the sun.

Her bruised spirit tried to make sense of it all; any wealth Catesby had could be forfeited, a ransom for his safe return was possible, but why his life? In their early days as children at Middleham she remembered Richard talking avidly of the Code of Chivalry; she understood little of such matters.

"How could Catesby be executed for treason when he was fighting *for* the king of England?" She spoke aloud her thoughts to the boy at her side whose only response was to turn a shade of green and sink to his knees on the grass.

"That is no hard question to answer."

Christiana, startled, turned abruptly, recognising the voice at once; seeing the quartered antlers of Stanley's arms embroidered on his tunic and the dark, glazed-over eyes beneath their veil of oily hair struck terror into her soul.

"Our good King Henry has dated his reign to the twenty-first day of August, being the day before the battle," Ralph Hodkin guffawed loudly. "So you see, my little whore, Catesby *was* guilty of treason."

Christiana would have moved away then but for the boy hopelessly retching at her feet. A heavy hand placed on her shoulder further prevented any attempt to escape and she could do nothing but endure the ale fumes, hot and pungent, searing her face.

"'Tis a pity Catesby was our biggest prize. King Henry would have liked the head of a prince no less to put on the block. How fares that son of yours by the way?"

She tried to wriggle free of his grasp but he caught her arm and moved closer.

"I have not forgotten you, wench, and how you lost me my position at Middleham," he hissed and reaching for his belt purse removed an object from within. Christiana gasped as he dangled it before her eyes. It was her garnet and jet necklace that Richard had given her; all these years Hodkin had it in his possession. "Be sure to tell that whelp of yours to watch his back. King Henry wants no pretenders to his throne."

Through tear-filled eyes Christiana stared down at Robert who was wiping his mouth with his sleeve. Ralph gave the boy a sharp nudge with his boot in the small of his back.

"Are you another one of the harlot's brats?" Ralph laughed before stinging her lips with his foul mouth and walking away.

"I am sorry, Robert," she said, lifting him gently to his feet. "Let us go indoors."

There was to be no more searching for John and William that day. Susan and Jack had outstayed their welcome in the town and were moving off with their goods westwards to Tamworth to try their luck there. Christiana paid double the rent for the room she had shared with Susan to ensure that she was its only occupant and took Robert in as her son.

They were both in much need of sleep and rest and this they did for the remainder of the day. At dusk they woke feeling hungry and feigning a headache Christiana asked for food and drink to be brought up to them in their room. She had no desire for any further chance meetings with Ralph Hodkin or capricious guests.

Leicester
25ᵗʰ August 1485

Christiana woke at first light feeling much refreshed. She was determined to make one last attempt to find John and William in the town and then take the horse to Dadlington if their searching yielded no results. Even this proposal seemed a long shot for by now the dead would be long buried and if either one or the other had been injured then they could be anywhere between here and the battlefield. One thing was certain: if John was still alive she must find him before he met with Ralph Hodkin or Henry Tudor, although rumour had it that the king had already left the town bound for Coventry.

At the elm tree she parted company with the boy. Robert was to make a thorough search of the alehouses and inns and enquire of the shopkeepers and tradesmen. Christiana was to visit the churches of which there were a great many. They agreed to meet back at the inn at noon.

Christiana left the marketplace skirting Grey Friars along the High Street until she entered Saint Francis Lane. It was still early and the dew on the grass wet her feet. It was all quiet at the Grey Friars Gateway opposite Saint Martin's Church, save for a grey-cloaked figure keeping a strange vigil, moving furtively along the wall, watchful, alert.

"Good morrow to you, Brother," she said gently. The monk raised his head and concerned eyes met hers. He nodded his head and continued in his resolve.

The woman did not move on. She felt inexplicably drawn to this place and with sudden trembling felt all of her strength dissolve like snow under the heat of the sun. Through a veil of teardrops she took a few steps towards the man. It was not proper for a woman to approach a man under Holy Orders but somehow she was compelled to do so.

"I am looking for my son," she whispered. "He fought for the king... he is the king's bastard..." Her voice broke in sorrow.

With a quick glance around him the monk came forward and guided her through the gateway.

"I have no knowledge of your son," he spoke in hushed tones. "But inside the church the choir is being prepared. Come, you do not have long and by the rules of our Order you should not even be here..."

She stepped out of the church and into the afternoon sunshine, her eyes momentarily pained by its radiance after the gloom inside the chapel. She smiled gratefully through her tears at the monk who had permitted her entrance into their sanctuary, the great wooden door clanging shut behind her.

With the outpouring of her grief and the great flood of tears spent inside the chapel her head had begun to clear. She had said her final farewell to her beloved Richard but her loss sat like a cold, cold weight of emptiness on her heart. Even so she must do all she could to find his son – if he still lived – and her brother.

At the church of Saint Martin the priests were still at prayer and she had to wait before she could ask her questions. No soldiers had come with wounds to tend or to seek refuge within. Neither had they seen any youth of John's description.

Leaving Saint Martin's she hurried along Kirk Gate, up the High Street and turned into Hot Gate at the High Cross. She rushed along Holy Bones but the priests at the church of Saint Nicholas could tell her nothing except suggest she tried at the hospital. She shook her head sadly at this remark, remembering the sour-faced man at the door to Saint John's Hospital.

As she walked down Apple Gate towards the castle she began to feel warm under the strengthening rays of the sun. She crossed into Saint Mary's Lane towards the South Gate when she realised that her way was barred. She halted along the roadside where folk had gathered and now waited expectantly; aware of a muted conversation going on around her she stood listening.

"What excites the crowd?"

"'Tis the king."

"The king? He left for Coventry so I heard, only yesterday. Now he is back?"

"I cannot see the reason he would return to Leicester; if indeed he left at all," a third person interjected.

"Unless it was by the pricking of his conscience that he returned. He had left the corpse of an anointed king to rot like a common felon; how will that sit with his eternal soul?"

"He challenged an anointed king and killed him; that will not sit well with his soul either, especially as he has no right to the crown. He will be paying for Masses to safeguard his soul from now till Kingdom come, like as not."

"Well the corpse is no longer in Saint Mary's so maybe you are right, my friend."

"Henry has a right to the crown now, by virtue of the fact that he won the battle, whatever folk might think. Let us hope that he is well received in London."

Christiana was becoming irritated by the opinions of these Leicester folk but pinned as she was in their midst she had little choice when suddenly from outside the castle enclave the crowd raised a cheer that spread like a ripple along the road.

It was not long before foot soldiers appeared, one carrying the banner of the red dragon high before him, all brandishing halberds and wearing sallets on their heads. Their boots thumped the hard earth beneath their feet as they marched.

Three riders followed the men on foot. On either side of a black steed rode John de Vere, Earl of Oxford, and Thomas, Lord Stanley. Their faces were grave and austere. Riding between them was the man they had declared king. Henry Tudor, wearing a noble robe of richly embroidered gold and scarlet lined with fur, sat tall on his horse and smiled benignly at his subjects as he rode past.

Christiana stared up at him; so unlike he was to the triumphant warrior who had crossed the Bow Bridge three days ago, hot and filthy from battle. He looked to be a few years younger than Richard, no more, and like the Plantagenet king, Henry's most striking feature was his eyes. While Richard's had been warm and gentle, these orbs, pale, grey and close-set, flitted fox-like across the sea of upturned faces. His straw-coloured hair, dull and wispy, having little substance, hung limply about his shoulders and was capped with a black velvet beret.

Christiana remained where she was until Henry and his escort had passed on towards the South Gate and so out of the town. Beside her a man spat onto the ground in the wake of the last soldier to pass by and another muttered a curse under his breath.

So that was Henry Tudor, who, on the outcome of one battle, had made himself king of all England and robbed her of everyone she loved and changed her life forever. It was as though a great cloud had stormed in overhead and blotted out the sunshine. She had not the heart to continue her search and peering skywards she could see that the sun was approaching its zenith.

She turned to walk down Saint Mary's Lane, her steps slow and weary, pushed along by the scattering crowd, and turned into Friar Lane towards the marketplace. The Green Dragon lay peaceful in the noonday sun and quite devoid of life as she crossed the empty hall, the smell of soured ale strong on the air. Climbing the rickety staircase to her room she wondered vaguely whether Robert had returned. She lifted the latch and pushed open the door.

Inside, the room was as they had left it that morning, save for one thing: the figure lying on the bed. His dark hair fell about his shoulders and his tunic was torn and dirty, as were his hose, hanging in threads here and there. There was a smidgen of a downy beard covering his well-defined jaw and a pair of dark sapphire eyes stared up at her from a filthy face. She drew a sharp breath for she had thought at first that she was seeing Richard for so like his father was her son.

She had taken only two steps towards him when she broke down and sobbed; the relief at finding John alive was almost unbearable. Robert, who had been sitting on the bed beside his young master, took a costrel from his belt and thrust it at Christiana. "Have some wine," he commanded.

"Are you not pleased to see me, Mother?" John asked with a weak smile on his pale lips.

Christiana put down the costrel after taking several large mouthfuls and dried her eyes. "Pleased is not the word I would use, my son, I am overwhelmed. Where have you been?"

John turned his face away and closed his eyes. "You know where I have been, Mother," he muttered. She looked enquiringly at Robert.

"I had just been to the Angel Inn across the marketplace," he answered, "and was heading for The Maiden Head on the Kirk Gate when I saw this figure huddled under the Grey Friars Gate."

"I have been inside the church of the Grey Friars, Mother," John continued his story with trembling voice.

"The friar at the gate said that my mother had already been there, not moments since. I did not take his meaning until he said that I had the likeness of my father who lay within the church. I took great care to hide myself beneath my hood... but he knew."

"Oh, my love," Christiana whispered, taking her son's hand in hers.

"He is the king, Mother. He should have a fitting burial in the abbey at Westminster. The friars were digging in the choir floor in such haste that I would wager the hole is not big enough even to take his body." John turned a tear-stained face to his mother.

"I know," she lamented, stroking his hand, "but what has happened to you, John?"

"I did not fight for the king; I ran away," the boy sobbed. "I should have been there with him and maybe..." He sniffed and wiped at the tears trickling down his cheeks.

"You could not have saved him, John," Christiana reasoned gently.

"I was on the top of the hill, standing with Northumberland's men," he continued after a while. "I was keeping out of Father's way, like he said. Suddenly from the front we knew that the king had seized opportunity and gone over the hill. He led a cavalry charge at full gallop down the slope and into Tudor's men, taking out several as he went."

He paused as he tried to recall the events. "It was a purposeful, noble cavalry charge to do away with Tudor once and for all.

"There was much confusion amongst the men on the hill," he remembered after a while. "We thought he had achieved it, Mother, when the king took out William Brandon the standard bearer. A cry went up that William Stanley had committed; at first we thought to the king."

The boy's eyes, bright with tears, searched his mother's face and the pain of betrayal and treason shone out from them. "They fought against him, Mother. They caused his death; he should have won that battle – they killed him and that vile Tudor did not so much as sully his battle axe." His voice was choked with grief and for a while he could say no more.

"Then afterwards," he continued, "everyone ran to save themselves. I ran with Northumberland's men towards Stoke Golding. There I heard that Norfolk fell and so did Ratcliffe and Brackenbury, alongside many others. I do not know what became of Northumberland; reports had him still on the battlefield, though not killed."

"And William – do you know what became of him?" Christiana dared to ask.

John shook his head sadly. "I spoke with him on the eve of the battle. He warned against my fighting." He fell silent for a moment. "I think he was amongst those who went down the hill with the king; if so I do not think he would have survived." Christiana closed her eyes and let her tears fall.

Robert, who had remained silent throughout the telling of John's tale, now nudged Christiana's arm and whispered, "Mistress, I think you should look at his feet. He has not removed his boots since leaving the White Boar last Saturday. When I found him he could hardly stand."

"You have walked all the way from Stoke Golding?" Christiana asked incredulously. "Had you no horse?"

"Any horses not killed on the field were stolen or else bolted," John replied, bracing himself as his mother began to ease his boots over his sore and swollen feet. She gasped when she saw the weeping blisters and sores bled and dried onto his woollen hose. She took her knife and cut away what she could of the dark fabric and then sent Robert for a bowl of water and cloths to soak away the rest.

"I will need a soothing balm for these feet," she announced. "I will go find an apothecary. When did you last eat?" she added, looking at his thin arms and legs. John shrugged his shoulders. "That long ago eh?" she smiled and turned to Robert who had returned with the bowl. "Do what you can for his feet and fetch him a little pottage and some bread. I will return as soon as I can." Reaching down to the bed she took John in her arms and kissed him before leaving the room.

Down in the hall she found Maggie, the innkeeper's wife, a comely woman with a kindly face. Christiana explained that there was a third guest in her room – another son, whose lodgings she would pay for and well. She ordered bread and pottage and enquired as to the whereabouts of the apothecary.

It was as though a small chink of cloud had parted and let a single ray of sunshine into her world. She had her boy back and as soon as his feet were better they would leave this place and return home to Yorkshire. The king and his commanders were gone, bound for the capital, and they would now be left in peace.

Her mind dwelt upon these hopeful thoughts as she walked up the High Street. The town was busy with folk going about their business. There were still a few soldiers to be seen, hanging around idly on street corners or bartering for wares at the many shops along the High Street. Some stood and leered at her as she passed.

She had reached the High Cross when she had the distinct feeling that someone was watching her, following her and had been for some time. She stopped and turned about, peering into the faces around her; women loaded with loaves and yards of cloth, dirty children playing dice under the shade of the stone cross, a dog sniffing and cocking his leg nearby. There was someone in the shadows; a dark spectre, hooded and cloaked, hidden. She grew uneasy and hurried on.

She crossed Dead Lane and saw the school on the corner where the priests from Saint Peter's Church stood and waited for a line of boys to enter. Maggie had said that she would find the apothecary's shop nearby. She came across it a little further on at the corner to Saint Peter's Lane.

Unlike many shops this one had a walled front of wattle and daub and a wooden door; the apothecary must be a man of wealth in this town. The sign over the door showed a painting of a pair of weighing scales and a pestle and mortar amidst detailed sketches of various herbs.

It was dark and musty inside and the familiar smells of medicinal concoctions filled the air. Behind a wooden board that separated the narrow floor space from an impressive herbarium beyond stood an elderly man with his back to her. At the sound of her boots on the stone floor he turned abruptly.

"I beg your pardon," Christiana said, "I did not mean to disturb you." She could see that the apothecary had been measuring white crystals from a jar into the silver pan of his scales. "Perhaps you had better finish your task; you would not want to make any errors with that," she continued, nodding at the jar still in the old man's hand. His eyes narrowed as he looked into her face, the smile he saved for his customers frozen on his lips.

"And you would know what this is I suppose?" he mocked.

Christiana felt her colour rise at once. She did not wish to explain how she had acquired her knowledge of herbal remedies or that she suspected the substance he was holding in unsteady hands to be powder of arsenic, not least because of the way he treated it with such reverence.

"Oh forgive me," she stammered, "I merely meant you should finish your task before serving me."

His face still wearing a puzzled frown the old man turned back to his work. The powder was carefully weighed and sealed in a small phial and the jar was returned to a large chest hanging on the wall where it was secured therein with a heavy key.

"I should like to purchase ointment of calendula and a tincture of valerian if you please," she asked politely. "And maybe bilberry or hawthorn," she added, thinking about their long journey home and the risk of stomach upset on the way.

The old man's eyes shrunk to slits again as he regarded her suspiciously. He was not used to his customers knowing exactly what they needed. He bustled about the jars and pots lining the shelves over his bench.

"You are not from these parts are you?" he asked.

"No," she replied simply. "Maybe also a strengthening tonic if you please, to your own receipt," she added quickly to distract the man's curiosity away from her.

Just then the door opened and in rushed a youth, red-cheeked and panting.

"A good day to you, young Nicholas," the apothecary said smiling. "And how can I be of help this day?"

"I have need of more valerian for my mistress," he replied, still catching his breath.

The apothecary sighed deeply and addressed the woman before him. "The boy's mistress is the wife of an important dignitary in this town and as you can see I am alone in this business and my time must be spent on the needs of the good folk of Leicester," he announced curtly, placing a large pot of calendula ointment on the bench. "You may take this, if you have coin enough to pay, and return this eve to collect valerian, hawthorn and a tonic... to my own receipt," he announced, addressing the stranger.

Christiana knew better than to challenge this man, knowing full well that to do so would evoke further questioning.

She handed over payment for the salve and thanked the apothecary with a slight bow of her head and departed.

She hurried back down the High Street clutching her pot. She had passed the cross and was approaching Kirk Gate when fear gripped her once again; the flickering shadow lost in the crowd. She turned up Friar Lane and quickened her pace. As she passed the church of the Grey Friars she could hear voices singing loud and clear; a sweet harmony on the afternoon air. She almost ran across the marketplace where there were fewer people and passed the shambles and under the shade of the elm.

She was quite out of breath when Maggie stopped her at the foot of the stairs at the Green Dragon.

"Your son is in a poor way," she remarked sympathetically. "I've taken him up some bread and a bacon pottage. There are also some clothes he can have – left behind last week by a guest."

Christiana thanked her and ran up the stairs. The window had been opened a little, letting in a cool breeze. The remains of John's meal stood on the table beside the bed; he had eaten little. She was about to enquire after his well-being when an object, glinting in the light and almost hidden from view beneath a wooden plate, caught her eye. With mounting dread she went over to it and lifted it from the table.

"Where did this come from?" she asked John, dangling the garnet and jet necklace in the sunlight.

It was Robert who answered. "A man called while you were gone. You have missed him by moments. He would not leave his name but said he was an old friend. He said you would know who he was by the keepsake he left behind. He said he would hope to find you in another time." Christiana paled and sat heavily on the bed.

"Who was he, Mother?" John asked, frowning. "I have seen him once before at a hostelry in London. I liked not the look of him then either. He told me how saddened he was at my father's death but how pleased he was that I still lived. He said that he looked forward to renewing his friendship with my mother."

Christiana took the linen stopper from the salve and began to apply it to John's sore feet without replying. She massaged and rubbed the ointment into his skin as gently as she could for her fingers trembled.

"You must know that man," John asked suspiciously after a while. "That is a very fine jewel he gave you."

"His name is Ralph Hodkin and be certain that he is no friend of mine or anyone's," Christiana replied venomously.

"He wore Stanley's livery," commented Robert helpfully.

"He used to wear the boar emblem of the Duke of Gloucester," Christiana informed her son. "Until your Uncle Will beat him to within an inch of his life and he ran away from Middleham with a sack full of the duke's silver."

Robert's eyes widened in wonder.

"This necklace was a present from your father which Ralph Hodkin stole from me when..." She looked down sadly at the jewel beside her on the bed; dulled gold of the chain and the empty claw where one of the garnets had fallen away.

"This man is very dangerous, John. You are not to have anything to do with him nor are you to let him in here again. Do you understand?" She turned to Robert who nodded his head silently.

"Have you a weapon?" she asked abruptly.

"Only a dagger," John answered, bewildered. "I discarded my sword on the battlefield."

"Keep it close," was all she said.

Several hours passed and few words were exchanged between them. Christiana ate some food and checked her son's red swollen feet.

Although greatly fearful of Ralph Hodkin, now that her son was found there was a desperate need to leave the town and return to Yorkshire. She did not allow herself to think of what might have befallen William.

"I have to leave you again," she said, peering through the open window to the deserted marketplace below.

"Where are you going?" John asked, worried now for his mother after her words concerning this Hodkin who might well be still close by.

"I must go to collect more physic for our journey north," Christiana replied. "We leave on the morrow."

"But, Mother, Rob tells me you have but one horse and I am not yet fit to walk and you cannot..."

"I will not be long, I will return by nightfall." Christiana was at the door. "Look after him," she called to Robert before leaving the room and shutting the door firmly behind her, but not before she had caught John's parting words: "Do you no longer care to know what has become of Uncle Will?"

The sun was arcing gracefully down towards the west as she hurried along the High Street. Had Hodkin followed her earlier, hiding in the shadows? How then did he know that John would be in the Green Dragon? He must have seen her enter after Catesby's execution. They must be the reason Hodkin did not leave the town with Lord Stanley. Her thoughts were racing like her heartbeat as she reached the apothecary's door.

There was a small leather vessel awaiting her on the bench inside the shop. There too was the apothecary with a pained and troubled frown upon his wrinkled face.

"There is your hawthorn." He indicated the costrel. "You must return on the morrow for the tonic for I have not had time enough to make it."

"And I have not time enough to return, for I leave this place on the morrow." Christiana fumbled with the string of her purse and thumped more than enough coin to cover the cost of the hawthorn down on the bench, shoved the vessel into her bag and left with angry tears in her eyes.

She took in a few deep breaths of the cooling air before walking back down the main thoroughfare. Of a sudden John's words came back to her mind and she had a deep longing for William; a need to feel his presence and the comfort it always brought. Her tears tumbled in an uncontrolled stream down her cheeks as she realised the foolishness of her desire, for had not John said Will had been in the cavalry charge towards Tudor that had ended in the death of the king?

As she hurried along the now almost deserted street a figure standing huddled in the shadows of a closed-up shop turned a cloaked face towards her. She turned and fled up Friar Lane, all deserted under the black sky. The silhouette of the elm, black as mourning cloth, came into sight as she turned into the marketplace. She could see the outline of the shambles and the empty stalls of the drapery in the distance and the yellow candlelight of the Green Dragon beckoning to her.

It came from the shadows, swift and silent as a hawk: a rough hand fastened over her mouth, hot breath burning her face. She was dragged violently across the wet grass and held against the bole of the elm.

"I am leaving town on the morrow and I feel you owe me a

debt, wench," he hissed. With one hand still across her mouth he began to tear savagely at the bodice of her gown with the other, groping and squeezing her breasts.

"I need to buy some favours from King Henry," he spat, "and I reckon that boy of yours would make a handsome payment." He lowered his hand to feel for the hem of her skirt as she desperately tried to fend him off.

"You see, the Tudor has one big fear," Hodkin continued, "that there are still Yorkists to threaten his hold on the crown, and we all know how weak a hold that is don't we?" he said, forcing her skirt up over her belly to expose her nakedness.

His hand was tight across her mouth and she struggled to breathe and a fierce panic that he might once again overpower her gripped her. In her flailing her hand closed over the hilt of the bollock dagger hanging at the man's belt.

"Who would be a greater threat to our Henry than King Richard's own flesh and blood?"

She just had to make enough room between them to get the dagger out. She could feel his fingers exploring her secret places and knew him to be roused but she stopped struggling. Those few moments when she forced herself to relax were enough to draw the blade from his belt and before Hodkin, in the heat of lust, had any notion of her intent she acted.

All the pain and sorrow, all the fear and anguish of the past four days drew together her strength and determination and she plunged the blade upwards and deep into his stomach. In the moment before death she saw the terror and shock in his eyes and heard the deep-throated gurgle as a rush of warm blood spewed from his mouth and drenched her bodice and bare breasts.

As his dead weight crumpled on her knees she sagged to the ground, his body slumping on top of her. Witless with horror at the enormity of her deed she began to scream wildly and uncontrollably.

She was unaware that Hodkin's body was no longer crushing her and that a strong arm was pulling her to her feet until she felt a sharp slap across her cheek and a voice urging her.

"For pity's sake, woman, hush your screaming or we are all done for!" A cloaked and hooded figure had her by the arm steadying her. He flung off his hood and revealed his face.

"Dear God," she breathed, "Francis!"

The man bent down and dislodged the dagger from Ralph's body and picked up the coin purse that had fallen when her bodice had been torn. Wiping the blade on his cloak he plunged the dagger into a loop on his belt and handed the purse to Christiana.

"Where is John?" he whispered urgently. She could do no more than point a trembling finger towards the Green Dragon.

"Go and fetch him at once and meet me in the stable yard of the inn."

She stared at him dumbstruck. "Go," he commanded, "and make sure you are not seen; there is much blood on your gown."

Sick and trembling she made for the safety of the inn, weeping and stumbling like a drunken whore with her torn bodice. She crept around the back across the courtyard where she was less likely to be seen. Here the only light came from a solitary lantern hanging on its pole in the middle of the cobbled yard. Moving stealthily along a back staircase she reached her room undetected.

At the sight of his mother, her naked breasts smeared with blood and eyes wild with terror, John was grief-stricken.

"'Tis not my blood, son," she assured him. "Robert, pack everything, we are leaving at once."

"What happened?" Robert asked as he shoved their meagre belongings into leather pouches.

"Explanations can wait," she answered sternly.

She changed hastily into her second gown and rolled the blood-stained garment up in the bottom of her bag. She took a handful of silver coins, more than their two nights lodging and the stabling of the horse was worth, and put them down on the bed.

She sent Robert on ahead with the bags to saddle her mare and half carried, half dragged John along the passage and down the back stairs. She felt like a thief in the night as they stole furtively across the yard to where Robert waited with the horse.

John stared in disbelief at Francis Lovell as he lifted him up onto the back of his mother's horse and led it quietly across the cobbles and out of the yard. Christiana looked anxiously around her; she did not want to be accused a second time of stealing a valuable beast. Thankfully all seemed quiet at the inn that night.

Lovell offered no explanation as he led the horse down Friar Lane towards the South Gate, Christiana and Robert following on foot. He bribed the gatekeeper with a well-stuffed purse to let them out and ask no questions. The man saw no harm in that for any trouble a man, his wife and two sons had was leaving the town with him and not coming in.

Francis led them along Millstone Lane towards the Horse Fair lees. The town wall rose steeply on their left side, the ditch dropping sharply at its foot. It was a moonless night and they had to tread carefully amongst the rough stones and grassy tufts along the little used road. A foul smell came up from the ditch where the stagnant water held all manner of filth and human waste.

At the end of the lane and shrouded in darkness was a barn. Drawing closer, Christiana could see that it was constructed of stone and timber with a roof of balding thatch. A faint glow of light showed through the cracks in the wooden door.

As they approached a dark figure stepped from the shadows and pulling open the heavy door he beckoned them inside. Christiana was surprised to see at least a half-dozen men and as many horses standing in the gloom of the barn. Francis reached up and lifted John from the saddle and placed him down onto a pile of straw in a corner.

"Are his feet very bad?" he asked Christiana.

She shook her head. "They are blistered and painful and he will not be able to walk for a few days but they will heal," she replied.

One of Lovell's retainers offered them bread, cheese and ale. As they ate and drank Francis spoke.

"I did not reach the king in time for the battle, much to my regret," he began. "I was keeping watch in Southampton, as you know." He looked at John who nodded his head.

"I arrived in town on the afternoon of the twenty-third and was soon acquainted with the outcome of the battle and that Tudor was calling himself king. I could not move in the streets for soldiers and I had to lie low. Any doubt was put to rest when I witnessed the body of my king displayed for all to see in Saint Mary's Church.

"I was set to leave today; I saw no good reason to stay any longer. I watched Tudor leave through the South Gate and I went back into town to buy food and supplies for the journey home, and George here," he nodded to the soldier beside him, "took a couple of horses to the farrier."

Francis paused, his eyes shining in the light of the lantern. "I had not seen anything of you until I caught sight of you going up the High Street as I stood near to Wygston's House," he continued. "I followed you to the apothecary shop and lost your track on the way back, your pace was too quick. You gave me the slip," he smiled ruefully.

"Why was it that you were following me, Francis?" Christiana asked curiously.

"Once I had no doubt that Richard had fallen in battle my only thought was to make away and seek sanctuary. Until I saw you I had given little thought to John and the pledge I made to his father." Francis stared across at John who sat listening earnestly to every word he spoke.

"I thought that you might lead me to John; I did not know whether he was alive or dead or even in Leicester then. I could not risk giving you a fright in the streets for there were still soldiers about, so I followed you."

"We did not know whether John lived or not until Rob found him this morning outside the Grey Friars gate," Christiana declared, patting the shoulder of the boy whose loyalty had been a tower of strength to her.

"Once I had lost you I threw caution to the wind and took a jug of ale in The Maiden Head Inn, staying longer than I had a mind to and drinking more than I ought to have done," Francis admitted. "It was late when I left and as I hurried down the High Street towards the South Gate I had to stop and piss outside a shuttered-up shop. I could hardly believe my good fortune when down a dark and deserted street who should come hurrying along but you."

"It was just as well for me that you did," Christiana said, shuddering at the memory of her dreadful plight. "What did you do with the body?" she asked quietly.

"I have walked this Millstone Lane enough times to know the postern gates in the town wall," he replied. "There is one near to the Green Dragon and judging by the amount of dung around it I should say it is where the hostler throws out the used straw from the stables. The corpse is in the ditch just below that postern. I removed all the clothes so none can trace him. The body went down with a mighty splash; let us hope it stays hidden and that Stanley does not miss a soldier."

"Was it Hodkin, Mother?" John interrupted for the first time the telling of this sorry tale. She nodded in confirmation. He had no need to ask what it was he was doing, or attempting to do when Francis apprehended him; the picture of his mother's torn gown and terrified face told him well enough.

"Was he known to you? He looked familiar," Francis asked.

"Ralph Hodkin, one-time Captain of the Guard at Middleham," Christiana confirmed. "He was known to Richard also and wanted for theft of his silver and..." She hesitated, looking at her son. "Other things," she continued.

"Not to mention treason against the rightful king of England," John added.

"Then justice has been done and you have nothing to fear," Francis said, taking Christiana's hand and squeezing it tightly.

John stared in wonder at his mother. "It was you who killed him and not Francis?" he asked in surprise.

"He was attempting to rape her, John," Francis returned. "You saw her sorry circumstance. If not by her hand then I should have done the same."

"He would have turned you over to Henry Tudor. You would have been in fear of your life, my son, and I could never have let that happen," Christiana sobbed.

John turned to his mother and took her in his arms and held her tightly as she wept. "I love you, Mother," he said softly.

"We can only stay here one more night," Francis was saying.

"We must all be away at daybreak. There are horses enough for us all and food to last the first day's journey at least."

"Where will you go?" Christiana asked. "Minster Lovell?"

Francis shook his head. "Not yet. We cannot go anywhere they would know to look for us."

A multitude of stars twinkled in the vast expanse of black above her head. A cool night breeze rustled the summer grasses and brought upon it a faint whiff of the town ditch across the way. Beyond the door in the darkness of the barn men slept; but not so the woman whose heart was burdened with sorrow and resolution.

Christiana looked up at the stars and perceiving their mystery and wonder felt a sense of her own mortality wash over her. She allowed the memory of Richard once again to stir the depths of her being. In the quiet of the night her grief and longing for him were kindled afresh but she could cry no more; tears enough to fill an ocean would never drown her pain.

"You should get some sleep, Christiana, for there is a long journey ahead of us on the morrow." She turned her head as Francis Lovell came and sat beside her on the darkened grass.

"You understood me well, Francis," she whispered, looking into the depths of the man's starlit eyes. "I loved Richard with all of my heart. Anything of myself I would have given him, I shall never forget him."

Francis laid a hand upon hers, cold and white in her lap. "Nor I, for he was the truest friend a man could hope to have." He peered into the heavens. "I believe that as long as there are stars in the sky then the memory of our beloved king will live on," he whispered with a sigh. For a while neither spoke and the only sound to be heard was the wind in the grasses.

"It pains me much to say this, Francis, but I will not be going with you tomorrow." Christiana's voice was as gentle as the breeze. The man looked at her in surprise but allowed her to continue. "My brother has not been found, dead or alive. He fought for Richard and nothing has been seen or heard of him since. You will think me foolish but I cannot leave this place until I am certain of what has become of him." She looked skywards at the enormity of the heavens, each light seeming to wink back at her, and she felt so very small.

"I should like it very much if you would take care of my son," Christiana whispered, half to the stars and half to the man beside her.

Francis shifted a little closer to face her. "You have nothing to fear for John. While there is breath in me I swear that I will take care of the boy as though he were my own. That is the least I can do in honour of my friend," he said, looking earnestly into the woman's black eyes. "Besides, I made a pledge to Richard that I would."

"Francis," she breathed as the tears began to trickle down her cheeks. "What can I say?"

"Say nothing, dear lady," he replied and allowed the herbalist to embrace him fondly. Over his shoulder Christiana saw a faint glow of saffron light up the sky to the east; soon it would be time for painful farewells.

"Uncle Will is not here, Mother," John exclaimed. "You must face the certainty that he is dead. You will come with us." The boy was earnest but his mother more so.

"I cannot leave here until I am certain, my son," Christiana returned.

"Then I too shall stay and if we find Will alive we shall all go home together," John declared defiantly.

"John..." Christiana's heart was breaking but she found strength in her resolve. "Where is home? What are we without King Richard? You must go with Francis and make a new life, a new home. I have money enough for now and this is a prosperous town."

"But, Mother..."

"Do not make this harder for your mother, John." It was Lord Lovell who spoke now, his hand firmly on the boy's shoulder. "She is right; you must come with me and she must do what she feels she has to."

The boy said no more and Christiana regarded his face, dark and earnest with its deep sapphire eyes, and felt such an overwhelming sense of love for this child that for one moment she was afraid that her resolve would fail her.

"Francis Lovell has pledged his life to look after you, my son, and as your father's dearest friend there is no better man. Go with him and be sure that if there is any way I can find you again then find you I shall."

The horses were led out into a cold misty dawn and loaded up with what few belongings they had for the journey. Robert Belle walked up to Christiana leading her grey mare. She turned to the boy and embraced him warmly.

"You have been a good and faithful friend to us, Robert, and for that I thank you deeply." She handed him her bag of medicinal herbs. "Be sure to rub his feet with calendula twice daily," she added with a smile.

Turning, she saw that Francis had appeared at her side supporting John, who stood stoically on his blistered feet. She took her son in her arms and held him as tightly as she dared without squeezing the very life from him. "Farewell, my love," she whispered. "And God go with you."

She watched as Francis lifted him into the mare's saddle. She turned to Lovell and held out her hand. He took it in his and kissed it solemnly. There was no exchange of words between them; all that needed to be said had been. Francis inclined his head towards her and walked away to join his men. With the bag of herbs in his hand Robert jumped deftly up onto the back of the horse behind John, giving his master a playful punch in the ribs.

"You boys take care of that horse," Christiana called as they made off down the lane. "Do not ride her too hard for she is fit to carry a prince." She laughed through her tears.

The sky was still a cold blue away in the west but to her right hand in the east a blushing yellow sunrise was blossoming. The hem of her gown was dark with dew as she walked beneath the South Gate archway into the town.

She had nothing but the gown she stood in and a bag containing a few meagre possessions and a blood-stained garment. She still had the purse with William's money; a source of some comfort. Where should she go?

There was still an early morning chill but the sun was growing stronger and warmer to the east. At the corner of Saint Francis Lane she paused. Somewhere to her right, beyond the stone wall of the priory enclave, under the tiled floor of the church choir rested her beloved; melancholia, like rust, was beginning to spread through her veins. She walked on.

She had just reached the corner of Kirk Gate when the sound of horse hooves and harness could be heard approaching from the road ahead. She turned quickly into Kirk Gate to avoid collision with the rider, passing the Guildhall and the church of Saint Martin. At the end of the road glowing softly in the sunshine stood an inn, The Maiden Head. It was not a grand building to compare with the White Boar; the limewashed walls had turned green with moss where rain had dripped from the thatched eaves. She was tired, weary and hungry. She had not eaten any of the food that morning, saving it for the men.

The faded wooden door was ajar so she entered. The tables were empty; she sat down at the nearest one. Fatigue overcame her and resting her arms on the hard wooden table to cradle her head she slept.

The warmth and brilliance of the sun beaming its light through an open window roused her from slumber sometime later. On the table beside her a jug of ale and a platter of bread and cheese teased her hunger pains. Lifting her head she looked bleary-eyed around her. The place was still empty but for a woman scattering threshings and strewing herbs across the flagstone floor. When she saw her lone guest was awake she approached with a smile on her pretty face. She looked to be of a similar age to Christiana, hair coiled neatly beneath a coif and a clean linen apron tied round her waist.

"You look in need of food – please eat," the woman offered. Christiana stared into the woman's kindly eyes for a moment before breaking off a chunk of bread and dipping it into the ale. There were no questions, no explanations; the woman turned from the table and went about her chores.

Christiana ate in silence, grateful for the solitude. When the woman returned later to remove the platter and jug she introduced herself as Martha, the hosteller's daughter, and asked if she needed a room for the night for now that Henry had left town there were plenty on offer.

"I knew a Martha once," Christiana remarked sadly. "She was like a mother to me."

"What happened to you?" the other woman asked gently. "Are you alone? Have you no husband, no father?" Christiana shook her head and the woman went away.

The room at the inn was for the exclusive use of one guest; no bedfellows. It was small but comfortable and the door even had a key so Christiana could sleep in peace. She had spent two nights at The Maiden Head but in truth had slept little but thought much. In a moment of wry reflection she had recalled how Godwin had once told her that she would not survive without a man to take care of her. How right he had been, she smiled sadly to herself.

Christiana spent her time in her room, not caring for the company of the men who frequented the inn, taking all her food alone. On the afternoon of the third day at the inn Christiana was lying on the bed unable to shake free of her melancholia when there came a knock at the door. It was Martha; she held a bundle of green cloth in her arms.

"I have a spare kirtle," she explained shyly. "It no longer fits me; I have become a little fatter I fear," she smiled. "I would like you to have it, Christiana. I have no mother or sisters to benefit from it." The woman unfolded the cloth then and it fell into the shape of a kirtle that did indeed look to be of a size that would fit Christiana.

Christiana stood and put out her hand to touch the offered kirtle and said, "I cannot take this, Martha, without payment for you cannot surely afford to be so generous."

"And can you pay me for it?" Martha laughed. "I can see that gown you wear is cut of good cloth so you must once have been wealthy."

"There was a time when... but no more," Christiana replied gently. "And yes, I can and will pay for this garment."

She took a purse from her belt containing just a few of the coins, the other purse with the greater part of her fortune concealed beneath her gown, and turned it upside down onto the bed. The money clinked into a heap on the blanket followed by the worn carving of a wooden horse. Christiana picked it up and ran her fingers over the smooth edges. Martha stood beside her for the silent tears she shed had not gone unnoticed by the hosteller's daughter.

"Does it hold some sentiment from your childhood?" Martha asked gently.

"It once belonged to my brother," Christiana replied, wiping at her sodden cheeks. "I am here to look for him but I am foolish for he is surely dead."

"How so?" asked the other woman.

Christiana calmed herself and sat down on the bed. "I came here with my brother from Yorkshire. He was one of King Richard's retainers. He fought on Dadlington Field and I know he must be amongst the dead for I have heard nothing of him."

Martha sat beside her companion on the bed. "It has been a week since the battle and the bodies of the fallen will have been buried by now," she reasoned. "If your brother was of noble birth then surely there will be a record of such, if he was killed?"

Christiana shook her head with renewed despair. "Nay, we were but servants. William was a blacksmith turned soldier. No one would note the demise of one such as he."

"On the morrow you can bathe in the tub before the kitchen fire, put on your new kirtle and together we shall find this brother of yours."

Christiana put her hand over Martha's and gently pressed the warm fingers. "You are indeed as kind and generous as your namesake."

Christiana had less than any hope of finding William but she was grateful for Martha; the first to befriend her in this town. True to her word, the hosteller's daughter boiled the water in the cauldron over the great kitchen fire and filled the bathtub for her guest. She even procured the remnants of a soap ball and helped Christiana wash her hair.

A quest to find William was not forthcoming that morning, however, as the inn received an influx of guests just before noon and Martha was kept busy. Sometime later Christiana went downstairs in search of her friend as the inn appeared to be quieter now that the day was progressing into late afternoon. The hosteller, barrel-bellied and surly, was waddling round the tables filling cups with ale from a large pewter jug. In answer to her enquiry Christiana was told that his daughter had received a visitation from her demon and was locked in her room at the back of the inn.

Although fearful of what she might find, having a suspicion of witchcraft common to all folk, Christiana was concerned for Martha so she entered the rear passageway of the inn with caution.

There was an iron bolt across the door to a room at the far end of the passageway. Christiana slid it across, recoiling somewhat at the metallic shriek it emitted. The room was in near darkness for a piece of hessian sackcloth had been placed across the casement to repel the light. Martha was lying on her bed, a damp piece of linen covering her forehead and eyes. She did not appear to have noticed that someone had entered her lair for as Christiana approached the bed, the startled woman let out a painful groan.

Christiana took a step back, unsure of the creature that lay in the bed, but after a while and no further sign of witchcraft she sat gently beside the woman.

"Martha, it is Christiana. Do you know me?" she asked cautiously.

In response a trembling hand reached up and removed the linen strip and Martha turned a pale face, etched with pain and concealed in shadow towards Christiana.

"I am sorry I have broken my promise to look for your brother," she whispered.

"That matters not, do not concern yourself. But tell me what is this that ails you?"

"It is my head, such pain that stabs at my eyes. I have visions and a sickness in my stomach."

Christiana rubbed her brow to recall a memory from a time not that long ago; Prince Edward of Middleham on the night that he died complained of pains in his head and an aversion to light. There had been only one such attack and no one had even so much as thought it might be as a result of witchcraft. Something Martha's father had said prompted her to ask, "Martha, are you inflicted often by this?"

"It is a visitation, a dark spirit that comes upon me whenever my courses are due." Martha turned in her bed and indicated the bowl on the table beside the bed.

"It causes me to vomit and robs me of my sanity," she concluded before bending her head over the bowl Christiana held before her.

As she sat and waited for the woman to cease vomiting Christiana began to think that this was no witchcraft or demonic presence. Many women were taken ill when their courses were due, some badly. The very least she could do would be to procure some white willow bark for the pain and ginger to relieve the sickness.

At once Christiana was on her feet and leaving the room. As she walked through the hall where the hosteller was still serving his customers, though by now not that many, she did not go unnoticed.

"Have you seen my poor girl?" he called to Christiana as she made her way towards the door. "You would do well to keep away from her when she is possessed if you know what is good for you!"

It was but a short walk past the High Cross to the apothecary but her mind was thinking as fast as she was walking. There had been a servant at Middleham Castle in the early days, not long after she arrived. A woman who worked in the wash rooms, wrestling with the linen sheets as she wrung out the water into the great wash tubs. She suffered with persistent headaches and complained of how her sight was affected. Her fellow servants chided her as they were convinced that her blurred vision was due to her being partial to the strong ale she brewed at her cottage in the village. What was it that Martha gave her?

She had entered the domain of the apothecary and was about to engage him in business before the answer came to her. The old man looked up from his work and smiled in surprise as he recognised his caller.

"Ah, so you have not left us yet then? You have come for your tonic I suppose. Well, it is gone, sold. My remedies will not keep forever—"

Christiana interrupted the man; in truth she had forgotten about the tonic. "Nay, I require some white willow bark as speedily as you can manage it."

The old man eyed her once again with suspicion. He said nothing.

"Well, do you have it? A decoction is required to be taken internally." Christiana was becoming impatient.

"Who requires such a remedy?" he asked at last.

"A friend," Christiana mumbled in reply.

The apothecary turned from her then in dismissal. "I cannot be of service to you for I cannot give out my preparations to anyone. I will lose my licence from the Guild of Pepperes. I am sorry, but there it is."

Christiana sighed resignedly. "I am myself an apothecary, although not a member of any guild. I once served in a noble household," she began. "I require willow bark for Martha, the hosteller's daughter at The Maiden Head and also ginger and—"

Her words were cut short by a guffaw from the old man. "Martha, you say? From The Maiden Head? Well apothecary or no you are wasting your time with that one. The poor woman has a visitation by an evil spirit nigh on every month, the moon cycle. Why do you suppose her father cannot find her a suitor? Why do you suppose he calls his inn The Maiden Head?" He finished his rhetoric on a note of laughter.

The old man's wit was lost on Christiana. "I do not believe Martha has an evil spirit," she said with authority. "I am convinced that her condition is brought about by the onset of her courses and furthermore I would like the opportunity to try a remedy which I believe may very well cure her or at the least bring her some relief."

The old man stood before her speechless so the woman took courage and continued further. "You are the only apothecary in this town and with its growing populous you are struggling to meet its needs. Now, if you would allow me to do so, I am able to make up the physic myself, under your authority of course, and for which you will receive due payment."

Christiana felt herself trembling within for such boldness of spirit was quite unfamiliar to her. For his part the old man was inwardly rejoicing. Could this woman be an answer to his prayer? He would say nothing as yet and test her skill and knowledge.

"Maybe, for once I will concede to having a little help," he replied with caution. "But you do nothing without my authority. Is that understood?"

Within the hour Christiana was walking back towards the inn with three remedies in her possession and, she surmised, a great deal more respect from the old apothecary than she previously had.

As foretold Martha's condition improved greatly over the next day or so; the willow bark eased the severe pain in her head and the ginger dispelled the sickness. It would take a while, however, to prove the worth of the feverfew leaves as that remedy was more beneficial when taken over time.

While Martha rested in her room, no longer bolted from the outside, and a stream of sunlight washed the bed covers in a golden hue, Christiana offered to help the hosteller with his work. She had little knowledge in the art of brewing ale so she left that task to Martha's father. She could, however, wipe tables and replenish cups and flagons with ale to pay for her keep at the inn.

Milla, a stout and sturdy kinswoman whose abode was south of the Newarke near the tanneries came in daily to bake bread and cook the food and generally keep order; only the most courageous of men would stand against her disposition.

Christiana was grateful for her presence and took care to

always have her close by; bitter experience had taught her that a man deep in his cups was always to be avoided.

It was not many weeks into her new employment when news reached her ears; news that turned her blood to ice. The day was not so old as yet and Christiana was wiping the wooden tables of the bitter-smelling ale spillages from the previous night.

The door to the street was ajar to allow the fresher air of the town to waft into the inn. Milla's great bulk was obscuring the doorway as she peered out onto the Kirk Gate. It appeared that something of some import had happened in the town and as a group of people were making their way from sheepmarket and down Loseby Lane Milla stepped out to glean what further news she could. Moments later she returned, eager to divulge that news.

"A body has been found," she enthused. "In the ditch water; naked as the day he was born, they say. It must have been that heavy rainfall we had couple of days back, caused the body to float and come aground under the East Gate."

The rag in Christiana's hand ceased its vigorous wiping and she sat down heavily on a chair, her heart galloping in her throat and lips parched and trembling. Naked as the day he was born; Milla's words echoed around her head. The blood-stained gown still in her bag!

"There's nothing to identify him, apart from a big slit in his belly. The coroner wants to speak to any strangers, foreigners, in town to see if they know who he might be."

The words spun round the room in a swirl of mist and she felt sick. Surely she must be found out? She was a murderer and no witness to stand in her defence. She swayed on feeble legs out of the room, down the passageway and into Martha's chamber teetering like a drunkard.

"Christiana, whatever is wrong?" Martha ceased her task of gathering the sheets ready to launder, fearful for her friend. It took a while for the other woman to muster some degree of calm but she waited patiently.

"Martha, are you a true friend? Can I trust you with my life?" Christiana's voice was cracked and broken.

"With all certainty. Please, Christiana, if you are in any trouble then let me help."

With haste enough to cause her words to stumble over one another Christiana relayed Milla's news and then proceeded to construct her part in this scenario: her violation by the man whose rotting corpse was on its way to the town coroner for his judgement; the man's death by her own hand in an attempt to defend herself; the friend, whom she declined to name, who stripped the body of its vestments and hurled it to its grave in the stinking ditch.

"His blood, his blood is on my gown, my gown that lies in the bottom of a bag upstairs in my chamber, forgotten until now," she gasped breathlessly.

Martha's face had drained of all rosiness and she stared wide-eyed at the distraught woman, the woman who relied entirely on her ability and willingness to help. Her mind took only the briefest of moments to resolve the matter.

"Christiana, calm yourself," she commanded softly. "There is nothing to link you to this man other than your own hysteria. None would think to look for or find your gown."

"Nay, I must have rid of it," Christiana spluttered. "'Tis evidence of my guilt."

"All we need do is burn your gown and that is easily done. Milla will leave for home this afternoon and 'tis a Saturday and Father will be at the market to buy the herbs and spices for his gruit."

"How can you burn a lambswool gown? The smell will be putrid!" Christiana asked despairingly.

Martha smiled briefly. "You have not been here when Father tries out a new ale. Folk will think it is just another of his brews gone rancid."

Later that afternoon when the inn was devoid of all folk Martha and Christiana took the blood-stained gown and burned it in a large iron cauldron, throwing in several sprigs of rosemary to disguise the smell. It took some time to reduce the garment to ash enough to bury beneath the soil outside the rear of the inn. Once the last piece of sod had been returned to its place and raked over

Christiana felt much relief, although she sensed that this would not be the end.

And so it was that two days hence an official sent from the town coroner arrived at the door of the inn. He had been given to understand that a foreigner, a stranger from the north, resided under their roof. The coroner would be obliged if the stranger could go just along the Kirk Gate to the Guildhall where a recently discovered corpse lay as yet unburied for want of identification.

Standing amongst the tables and chairs at the inn Christiana was unaware of just how heavily she leaned against the woman beside her. Martha still had her arm as they walked the few steps to the Guildhall and there in the dim light beneath the dark oak beams she saw him. Face to face once again with the fiend who had raped her once and tried a second time; whose loyalties were as fickle as the wind. The familiar leer had sculptured itself onto his green, bloated face and the bulging eyes stared accusingly up at her. Jars of pungent incense surrounded the corpse as it lay on a wooden table but the aroma did little to dispel the smell of rotting flesh.

"Well, do you know him?" A voice beside her jolted her back to the present. "Is he one of yours from the north?" The voice continued to drum into her head. "There were many folk from Yorkshire here in our town, come to fight for that hunchback king. Take a good look – have you seen him before?"

Christiana felt sick. She would be sick or else swoon right here before this despicable coroner if she did not leave soon. She tightened her grip on Martha's arm, closed her eyes and shook her head.

"What was that?" the man persisted relentlessly.

"I have never seen this man before, I know him not." Christiana forced the words out as Martha dragged her from the hall on legs that hardly seemed capable of supporting her weight.

Outside on the street stood the official who had escorted them to the Guildhall.

"He is not known to us so what happens now?" Martha asked, still holding tightly to the trembling woman beside her.

"Well, if he cannot be identified then there is no gain to be had from his body. He will be thrown into a pauper's grave and there will be an end to it." His voice was unsympathetic, noncommittal as he turned to re-enter the hall and his duties.

Christiana remained at The Maiden Head for want of a better place and to be alongside the woman she now considered a valued friend. The time soon came for Martha's courses to flow once more and what once had been a great dread now came and passed with little more than a slight headache that persisted for no longer than one day.

It had been some time since word had reached the inn that the corpse in the ditch had been buried but even this news did little to release Christiana from a state of unbridled wretchedness.

The last of summer was slowly giving way to the glory of autumn, but the splendour of that season hardly seemed to touch the crowded filth of Leicester town. The bronze and gold of the turning leaves seemed to her a mere shadow of the beauty of her homeland and she longed daily for the peace and tranquillity of the dales and wild untamed moors of Yorkshire. More than this her heart ached for William, to know whether he lived or not was a constant desire that left her with nothing but the emptiness of uncertainty.

Although Christiana rarely left the inn the day soon came when she had need to obtain more feverfew leaves from the apothecary. She trudged up the High Street towards Saint Peter's Lane under a shower of cold and wind-blown rain that dripped miserably from her hood and soaked into her worn boots from the squelch underfoot.

She was grateful to reach the shelter of the apothecary shop. The old man seemed to have anticipated her arrival for on his bench stood a glass jar containing dried feverfew leaves.

"I expected you sooner," he announced by way of greeting. "Or maybe your remedy has not worked?"

"Indeed it has, Master Hopton, thus the reason for my visit, to procure more of the same."

Master Hopton inclined his head towards the jar. "It was not easy obtaining more of this," he declared. "It took much persuading for the Black Friars to give it up for their own modest herb garden does not contain much," he finished with a warm smile; the first she had seen him give away.

"Well I am certain that if you knew where to look you would find it growing aplenty beyond the town walls," Christiana responded.

As she was reaching into her purse to take out coin to pay for the leaves the old man put a bony hand upon her arm.

"What say you to helping me here in my apothecary? I am old and my skills are dropping away, like my hair." He sniggered at his own mirth. "You can see how difficult it is for me to manage on my own and although you are a mere woman I can see that you have much knowledge of herbs and their physic."

For a moment or two Christiana did not know how to respond to his request.

"Surely you can be replaced by another monk from the Black Friars and you can retire to their enclave after serving the town well?" she enquired.

The old man smirked. "It has been many a year since I recanted my vows. This is my business; I no longer have connection with the friary."

Christiana pondered her predicament for melancholia had pulled a veil over any vision of her own future. She would not allow herself to believe she had a future without Richard or John or William. She lived with Martha at the inn and wiped tables – was that her future? But she could do this, indeed she could. To rekindle her skill would give a purpose to her life once more.

"I will pay you well for your work, but you do nothing without my authority, you understand?" Guy Hopton was speaking again; she had hesitated too long.

Her mind was set. "I should be pleased to accept your offer of work, Master Hopton. But I shall not move in to the apothecary, for that would not be proper. I shall continue to reside at The Maiden Head Inn but be assured that I shall spend all the daylight hours here at my work."

For a passing moment the old man's face betrayed a look of disappointment but a broad smile soon took its place.

"Not all daylight hours – I am not a slave master. You will observe the Holy Days and Feast Days as befitting any Christian."

It proved to be hard work at the apothecary for Master Hopton was indeed losing his skill and a palsied hand was not conducive to obtaining the correct weight and measure of the remedies. She was also surprised to learn how much more a part superstition played in the art of healing down here than in her native Yorkshire. Many a time did she have to suppress a giggle when she heard the old man prescribe dancing around this or that tree or reciting some hocus pocus incantation to cure some ailment or another. When she questioned him on such matters his reply astounded her: "'Tis what some folk expect and 'tis what Black Annis would prescribe should they go to her and I would sooner have their custom than give it to that old witch."

The weeks moved on and the late autumn winds enticed the trees to divest of their coppery garments. By mid-October the darker days brought a spate of rain, although not the bitterly cold sort that frequented Yorkshire, and the need for cough remedies and infusions to dispel congested chests and trickling noses increased.

Martha's father, the hosteller, had taken to his bed for several days with a winter fever and Martha bore the strain of the extra work. Fortunately for her whenever the need arose their kinswoman Milla always stepped in to lend a hand. It was barely light on one such wet and miserable day when Christiana arrived at the apothecary. Master Hopton was already filling costrels with hot infusions and wrapping them in linen.

"Ah, Christiana, before you remove your cloak, can you take this to Thomas Herrick? His servant has just left; Thomas has taken badly with a winter chill."

Christiana frowned. "Thomas Herrick?"

"Aye, he has a building down on Cheapside by the Saturday market. Be sure you wait for payment. He can afford it; his ironmongery business is doing well, well enough to have repairs done to his shop."

Christiana took the costrel and held it beneath her cloak to keep it warm as she hurried through the streets to Cheapside. The ironmonger's dwelling was easy to find; clad in wooden scaffolding, sodden and dripping with rain. As she stood at the door awaiting a response to her knocking Christiana looked down at her boots. She could feel the cold on her feet where water had soaked through the battered leather and lifted the stitching around the soles. She shivered in the rain. Behind her she could hear the booths and tables being erected in readiness for the market. She doubted there would be much trade in this weather.

The door opened and there stood a servant, his arm outstretched, ready to take the remedy. Christiana held onto it until money exchanged hands and then she relinquished the costrel.

"Be sure to tell your master to take it while still hot," she called but the man had already turned and closed the door.

As she turned to make her way back to the apothecary she became aware that the rain was easing a little; a slither of sunlight was even attempting to poke through the grey clouds. She walked through the marketplace peering into the booths. She had a mind to look for a trinket for her friend Martha; a gift to acknowledge their friendship. Although still wet, the sun was getting stronger and traders were stoically shouting the virtues of their wares and pedlars meandered around with baskets hanging from their necks.

She found what she wanted hanging securely to the side of a basket. On a length of red silk ribbon, the fine workmanship of the pewter engraving encasing a nosegay of aromatic herbs; this pomander would not be cheap, although nowhere as expensive as the true pomme d'amber, or ambergris, of the French pomanders. Martha would certainly have nothing like it amongst her possessions. Indeed, the pedlar himself showed surprise when the plainly dressed woman produced enough silver to pay for a trinket he had carried around with him for several weeks now and never thought to sell.

A wooden booth leaning against the Corn Wall caught her eye as she moved away from the pedlar. Beneath its canopy, spread on hessian sacks, was an array of leather shoes and boots. A brown-robed figure sat astride a stool contemplating the overhead sky. When he saw the woman approach he stood to his feet.

"You have a great need for new boots, methinks," he observed as he pulled and twisted the swollen leather shells encasing Christiana's cold, wet feet as she sat patiently upon his stool.

"I did not think I would have any business this morning as I set off from the friary," the monk commented cheerfully as he measured and tried his boots until he had a near fit to Christiana's feet. He looked up at the woman as he knelt at her side and thought he might try his luck since she was probably the only customer he would have that day.

"Of course, mistress, if you have money enough boots can be made to fit you exactly. It will take time but the waiting will be worth it; no rubbing and chaffing of your feet."

"And where is your workshop?" Christiana asked, looking about her but seeing nothing but piles of shoes and boots.

"At the Austin Friary out of town through the West Gate."

"Do you make the shoes yourself?"

"Oh yes indeed," the monk answered proudly. "Of course I do have help at the friary. There is one man who I swear thinks he's tapping nails into a horseshoe when he hammers the soles on," he chuckled. "He holds the shoe between his legs like it were a hoof."

Christiana's mouth went dry as bone. "This man, is he a monk?"

"Nay, mistress, he is a soldier, or was – there is no more fighting left in that one. He was brought to us from the battlefield at Dadlington."

Christiana began to tremble. "Does this man give a name?" Her voice quivered, her heart stammered.

"He calls himself William."

It was too much to bear. The tears flowed like a torrent down her cheeks and she wept unashamedly before the bewildered monk.

"Oh, mistress, you are ill." The monk stood to his feet looking around him in despair. "Shall I fetch the draper's wife?" He was about to run off in the direction of the drapery across the way when the woman stayed him with a forceful hand upon his arm.

"Nay, I am not ill, please, I need no assistance." Although her chest was heaving painfully Christiana managed to convey her message to the poor man. "I shall purchase these boots if you please; they fit well enough for now. I must get to the friary; this man is my kin, I swear he is my brother, William."

The monk looked at her sorrowfully. "This man you are seeking may not be ready for the world. Are you certain you want to disturb the life he has made for himself?"

"With all my heart I am certain. I must see him; he is my brother. I have longed for the day when I might learn that he lives."

The man sighed. "Very well if you are in earnest. Leave the town through the West Gate and cross the Bow Bridge. You will not be able to approach the friary across the meadow; it will be a marsh at this time of year. Follow the Soar upstream until you reach Saint Austin's well and cross the river over the Little Bow Bridge and there you will see the friary."

The monk tied the laces of the boots and took her coin before watching the woman flee across the marketplace heading west.

Rain had started to fall again by the time she had reached the Bow Bridge. Her legs were aching and her feet, although dry, were feeling the beginnings of a blister or two from the new boots.

She crossed the west fields, heavy with rainfall and traversed the Soar at the Little Bow Bridge, the swollen waters of the river rushing beneath her feet.

The friary, when she reached it, appeared to be very old and not so big for the workings of a Holy Order. She could see the friary building through the crumbling stone of the enclave wall. It was surrounded by a few lesser constructions, one of which seemed to be the workshop where shoes were made; Christiana noticed the pieces of leather and tools lying on the ground outside as she waited for a response to her pull on the bell rope over the arch. All within seemed cloaked in peace and tranquillity.

The bell call was answered by an elderly monk who peered at her with great curiosity. The woman pushed back her cloak to reveal her face, wet with rain.

"You have my brother here," she cried without introduction. "Please, I must see him."

"And who might your brother be?" the monk asked patiently. It was not unknown for the families of their ordained brethren to show their disapproval of the fact that their kinsman had vowed all his wealth to the Augustinian Order.

"It is William, he was a soldier. He makes your shoes."

A light of recognition crossed the wrinkled face of the monk. "Ah yes, William," he muttered.

Christiana had edged her way closer to the wooden door set in the wall and the toe of her boot was almost within the monastery enclave.

"I want to see my brother," she pleaded for a second time.

"You are not allowed inside without permission," the monk replied. "But you can wait in here and I will fetch the Prior."

Rain was pouring down and the cold was clenching at her bones. The man at least had the kindness of heart to allow the woman to enter the building but only as far as a small dark cell near to the main door. There was one bench only and dismal light from a round window high in the wall exposed the green dankness of the stone.

An interminable age seemed to pass before the arrival of the Prior.

"Forgive this lack of hospitality," the Prior explained. "Women are rarely admitted into the enclave of our friary. We are a small order here and lack the space for public areas." He indicated the bench and Christiana sat.

"You enquire of a William, you say?"

Christiana nodded her head in confirmation.

"We have a William amongst us and he was indeed a soldier. He was not in a good way when he was brought to us; he was near to death but by God's grace he lives. Now please listen to what I have to say." Christiana was back on her feet and about to make a third plea to see her brother when the Prior's command silenced her. She sat back on the bench and waited.

"William has suffered terrible injuries on the battlefield but worse than that is the sickness of his mind," the man continued. "He does not accept that King Richard is dead and he blames himself for the death of the king's son. He has a past that I cannot fathom and a confusion of his mind. He seems to think the king's son to be called John. It has taken many weeks for a calm and peace to settle upon him and he is content to work here helping Brother Andrew make shoes which we sell in the town to support our community. I cannot sanction a visit from one who calls herself his sister if it means that the poor man were to lose the little peace God has given him."

Fear and despair gripped her fragile heart. She could not withstand the cruelty of fate that had brought her knowledge that William lived and yet denied her access to him. She turned from the man and fumbled with the stays of her bodice, reaching under her kirtle to where her second purse was sewn. This was where she kept the gold angels; coins of great worth. It was the only thing she could think to do; bribe the man to allow her just one glimpse of her brother. She knew the Church was not without its corruption. As her fingers fumbled inside the pouch they stumbled upon the wooden horse put there for safekeeping. She pulled it from its hiding place and held it up before the Prior.

"Here," she exclaimed. "Give this to William and let him decide whether he will see me or no. You have my word that if he declines me I shall walk from this place and never return." Bold words indeed, but she truly believed that William would never reject her.

The man took the frippery from her grasp, still warm from her touch, and went from the room, leaving her alone. She sank to her knees and prayed that William would give her one moment with him, just one moment to tell him what she needed him to know.

Time passed and finally one of the brothers came and stood outside the cell door and beckoned her to follow him. They walked along a narrow passageway, the worn and faded mosaic tiles paving the way. After several turns in the passageway they came upon a small cell to the right. It did not appear to be part of the row of cells, austere and penitent, that were reserved for use by the monks, but one designed for comfort. The door was ajar and

Christiana stood to one side to allow the monk to push it open. This room had a bed, not merely a raised pallet of straw, clean linen covers, a small table and one cushioned chair. A few meagre candles spluttering in their holders illuminated the solitary figure sitting on the chair.

He was no monk for he wore faded wool hose that had once been dyed murrey and a grey torn linen shirt hung from his shoulders.

The man did not move or even look her way but stared at the little wooden horse that lay in his roughened hands.

The woman felt that her legs had taken root and she was unable to move. Her voice too seemed trapped like a rabbit in a snare. She could not see clearly without getting closer but the man did have William's colouring; hair like the curlew that called across the dales.

A sudden doubt gripped her. Maybe this was not William. She hesitated, unsure. The monk was still standing nearby and his voice recalled her senses.

"Well, here is your brother."

Still the man did not look at her. She entered the dim room and moved closer. She stood before him, waiting, and when he turned his head to look at her a cry of anguish almost fell from her lips.

Surely this was not her William for this face was distorted, misshapen, and her William did not look like that. Her William had been handsome; he did not have a knife wound that sliced his face in two from his temple to his jawbone, still oozing here and there where the skin had not yet closed. But the nut-brown tear-washed eyes that stared up at her surely belonged to her William?

When the dry, cracked lips parted and a single word tumbled out, "Anna," she knew that this was her William. She longed to hold him, embrace him, to kiss him as he deserved, as he had always wanted her to.

She took one more step and knelt at his feet. She touched his arm, warm, living flesh, and her tears tumbled onto his sleeve.

"William, William," was all she could say over and over. "William!"

The man seemed to be bereft of his senses for when he spoke she could discern that his spirit wandered in the past.

"I have not seen the king – where is King Richard? His son is dead, John is dead and it is all of my making. I allowed him to stay on the battlefield. I am to blame. I cannot face his mother, I cannot tell his mother."

Christiana shuffled closer still and whispered urgently to his ear. "William, it is I, Anna. Your Anna, John's mother and John is not dead, he lives."

His eyes burned into her soul but he could not accept her words.

"Nay, John fell, I saw him. They bludgeoned him and stripped him naked and dangled his corpse across a horse."

Christiana's heart was breaking. How could this be? William's mind had become confused; the heat of the battle, the horrific wound he had suffered, all had robbed him of his sanity.

"My dearest love, you must believe me when I say that John is not dead. Our beloved Richard is dead and lies beneath the choir in the church of the Grey Friars but his son lives."

She dared not say more for she was still in earshot of the monk. She stood and left the cell just as the Prior reappeared.

"So you can see how it is with your brother," he exclaimed. "How do you expect him to survive in the world? He has work here and shelter. Have you a husband who will provide for him?"

"I want to take him home. I will provide for him," Christiana said boldly.

"Leave him here where he can be taken care of. Your disturbance will push his mind further into a ravine."

"I have means enough and I *will* take him home."

The rain was coming down in torrents now and by the time she reached the apothecary Christiana was drenched through.

"Where have you been? It was but one errand I sent you on and that this morning. It is past the hour of noon and..." The old apothecary, with spots of crimson glowing on his pale cheeks, chastised her the moment she crossed the threshold.

"And I will stay late the rest of this day to complete your receipts. I am sorry I took so long but there was a matter of great importance for me to attend to."

Christiana removed her heavy cloak and set to work immediately. It was well into the evening before she finished, labouring under the light of several candles.

Guy Hopton seemed appeased now that there were no further receipts outstanding and returned a warm smile as she bade him goodnight before returning to the inn.

The night was cold but she felt hot and light-headed as she entered the crowded inn. She had barely reached the stairwell leading to her chamber when the floor was whipped from beneath her feet and she collapsed in a tepid heap at the hosteller's feet. His strong arms carried her to her chamber where his daughter stripped her of the still damp clothes and put her beneath the bed covers. She lay there for three days, sailing on a fever boat in and out of wakefulness and at such times she was aware only of cool hands soothing her brow and a spoon parting her lips with foul-tasting concoctions that dribbled down her shift.

"God be praised, you are returned to us." Christiana heard the words before the blurred outline of Martha's face filled her vision.

"Returned, where have I been?" Christiana mumbled.

She heard a woman's laughter. "I know not where you have been, only that it was a land of knights and horses, fine silk gowns and Richard and John and William," Martha cried. "Oh and I was also there for you called my name several times. Apparently my knowledge of herbal remedies is second to none." There was more laughter and Martha announced that she was going to the kitchen to fetch the pottage and bread.

Christiana lay there, tired and weary, her head throbbing like the repetitive clonk-clonk of a spinning wheel. She had been dreaming that she was back home at Middleham with her father and William and Martha and Richard and John. For some reason William seemed more real than the rest, as though he still lived and had not died like all the others.

The pottage tasted good but she could only manage a few

spoonfuls. The coarse bread stuck in her mouth like great boulders but it went down with the help of a cup of the hosteller's best ale.

"You are a woman of great mystery," Martha remarked, sitting beside her friend on the bed and gently caressing her cold fingers. "I know so very little about you," she continued. "Was Richard the king?"

Christiana nodded.

"And you knew him, and loved him?" Another question followed by another inclination of the head.

"And who was John?"

"Our son."

Martha sighed; she knew this woman had to be no ordinary guest.

"And does he live?"

Again, another nod of the raven head on the pillow.

"And this other, this William; the one you call brother, the one you were looking for. Now you spoke of him in your fevered state like no brother I would recognise as such. Was he truly your brother?"

The words were gentle but they evoked a spate of tears from the other woman.

"Nay, he never was my brother, but I loved him as such."

"I am truly sorry that he did not survive the battle." Martha squeezed the hand she still held in hers very gently.

It was as though the fever took back its hold upon the woman for she opened her eyes wide and with her hand she gripped her friend's fingers so hard they hurt.

"Martha!" she cried. "He lives, he lives. William lives, I have found him."

Martha shook her head in disbelief. "Oh, Christiana, you have been dreaming. You have laid here in a fever for three days. How could you have found him?"

"Before this fever took hold of me. I walked in the rain to the Austin Friary, Martha; he is there I swear. I must fetch him home." Christiana sunk down onto the pillow, exhausted from her outburst and closed her eyes.

Slowly over the next few days Christiana gained back her strength but said no more about William. It may be that she had indeed dreamt it all.

It was on the morning of the day she was to return to her work at the apothecary that she found it. She was emptying her scrip of the odd bits and pieces that ended up there, all still a little moist from their drenching in the recent downpour – a wooden comb, a braid for her hair, a few pouches of dried herbs – when it fell out amongst them. Round and shiny, the red ribbon a little crumpled, but none the worse for it and still exuding a heady perfume, she held the pomander in her hand.

Hurrying down the stairs she found Martha in the kitchen preparing the fire. She was piling the wood logs into the fender and looked up as her friend approached, seemingly most pleased.

"Martha, this is for you." Christiana held out the pomander towards Martha. "It is a gift I purchased for you from a pedlar at the market but it has lain forgotten till now in my bag."

Martha took the trinket from her friend and wafted it under her nose. "This is a most generous and beautiful gift, Christiana. Many thanks."

Christiana received her friend's embrace with a bubble of laughter.

"I am returning to my work at the apothecary this day," Christiana announced. "Have you seen my boots? I cannot venture forth like this." She looked down at her stockinged feet standing on the cold flagstone floor.

"Aye, they are here, drying by the fire." Martha reached out to retrieve the boots from the corner of the hearth where they had reposed since the day Christiana took ill.

Martha held them aloft. "They are new are they not? When did you purchase new boots?"

Christiana stood rigid, her face draining of colour and a cold prickling spreading across her skin.

"Martha, I did not dream it. I know it now for certain. He is alive. I bought these boots from a monk at the Saturday market, the same day I purchased your pomander. The monk was from the Austin Friary and he told me of William, taken there after the battle. I have seen him, Martha. He does truly live."

A wide grin spread across Martha's face and she laughed. "So has your *brother* taken Holy Orders or is he allowed to leave the friary?"

Christiana did not return her friend's mirth. "It is not so easy for William is very ill. He has lost his mind but I will bring him home. I must."

"Where will you go? Where will you live?" Martha asked the question that Christiana was reluctant to confront.

"I should like to go home, back to Yorkshire, but there is nothing there for me now. I have work here at the apothecary but that not for much longer if I am not about it."

All that day and the following Christiana worked with great diligence at the apothecary. She cleaned shelves, polished the weighing scales, made up any preparations she could in readiness and even took a besom to the floor.

The next day was Sunday so after hearing Mass at the church of Saint Martin just across the green from the apothecary, she lost no time in making her way back to the Austin Friary. It was a gusty wind that slowed her progress this day and not rain but that was preferable.

The same elderly monk answered her bell call as on her previous visit. "So, you have returned," he observed somewhat caustically. "I cannot say the Prior will let you in this time for your brother did not take your last visit too well."

"How so?" Christiana asked anxiously.

"His ravings increased. He was in a state of worry all that day and the next."

"He will fare better when he returns home," Christiana persisted.

Once again the door closed on her and she was left standing in the biting wind. After waiting several moments she was allowed to enter. She was taken to William's small chamber but it was empty and she was asked to wait.

It did not take many minutes before the sound of footsteps, slow and heavy, could be heard approaching. Christiana did not wait for him to reach the chamber before she was beyond the door walking rapidly towards him. He was thinner and his hair had been cut shorter though still brushing his shoulders. There remained a vacant look about him but surely his eyes had smiled when he saw her?

She held wide her arms to pull him into her embrace. At first he did not respond but when she placed her lips over his, misshapen and unyielding as they seemed, she felt his whole body crumble into her arms. He held her so tightly she feared she would lose her breath but she kept him close.

"Anna," he whispered after a while, still gripping her kirtle. "Is it truly you?"

"It is truly me, your Anna." Tears cascaded down her cheeks, wetting his shirt.

"Can you ever forgive me, Anna?"

"Dearest William, there is nothing to forgive you for. John lives and one day you will come to know the truth of my words."

She did not want to let him go for even though his mind was confused and broken, he still gave her the comfort she so badly craved. She had always felt safe and protected when he held her and she still did even now.

"I love you, William. How I love you." Her words spilled forth, cracked and splintered. "I cannot bear to lose you again. Please come back to me. The battle is over, William. The battle is over." She broke down then and wept bitterly on his shoulder.

She felt him pushing her gently away until she could see straight into his face, disfigured, unsightly.

"And would you want this?" he murmured. "A brother whose face should be hidden from the world, a brother who will never work again?"

Christiana traced a finger gently down the scar that ran across his face. She locked her gaze onto his and replied:

"No, William, not a brother, never a brother. But always a man, a man to wed, a man to love, a man I desire with all of my being."

Several moments passed and they were still locked in each other's arms when a voice coming from behind awoke their dream.

"You ill-informed me when you declared this man to be your brother." It was the Prior, standing with hands clasped around a small wooden chest. He handed it to Christiana without explanation.

"And I erred in judgement when I declared this man unfit to enter the world. Take him from this place with my blessing."

Epilogue
Leicester

Christiana brought William back to the Maidenhead Inn where they lived for a while. William had his own bedchamber at the end of the passageway and every night over the course of the following weeks Christiana would come running down the passageway in the dead of night to the man whose midnight terrors would awaken her slumber. There she would lie with him and hold him and calm him until a peaceful sleep took him once again.

It was a few days after William's arrival at the inn that Christiana remembered the wooden chest given into her safekeeping by the Austin Prior. Sitting alone in her chamber where the grey scudding rainclouds obscured the light she opened the loosely clasped lid. Inside were a few scanty belongings; the carved wooden horse, a piece of cracked parchment, a bent metal boar badge, a piece of purple ribbon and a broken belt buckle. Not much, she thought, for a life lived nigh on thirty-three years. She pushed the objects around in the box and then took up the parchment. It appeared to be a letter and most remarkably one intended for her. She unfurled it slowly and let her finger caress the royal seal, still intact.

My Beloved Christiana,

I write to you on the eve of battle. I am confident that victory shall be ours and an end put to this Tudor usurper, or an end to mine own life for I am determined it shall be one or the other.

Know that I have secured a quantity of gold coin within the mattress of the bed in my chamber at The White Boar Inn. It is provision for you, my love, and our dear son, John. Tell him that I loved him well and true and that my noble friend Francis Lovell shall stand as guardian should I fall on the field.

I send this letter by the hand of William Smith, whose loyalty

I have cherished over these years past. I know him to be a good and honest man and John has told me that he is not your true brother.

The said William has promised to place this parchment into your hands should I not return.

My final words to you, my love, convey the hope that you will find the contentment and happiness that you seek and truly deserve. The source of this happiness may be closer than you have hitherto believed.

Farewell, my beloved, and know that I have always loved you –

Richard

She had heard Richard's voice from beyond the grave and it brought her much comfort. He had truly loved her and now it seemed he was giving his blessing for her to marry William. Francis Lovell had faithfully honoured the promise made to his friend and she cared little for the fortune that had been all but snatched from her grasp.

The following day Christiana stood at the Grey Friars Gateway with William. Overhead, a weak insipid sun had broken through the rain-sodden clouds and glistened on the wet cobblestones underfoot.

"Our king and dearest friend lies buried within the Grey Friar's Church," she said softly. William turned towards her, a frown upon his face.

"Truly, William, he fell at Dadlington. Listen to his words." She took the parchment from her bag and read to him, for he had no such skill.

"You would have given this to me yourself had you been able." She took his hand and led him away.

It came to pass that God's grace fell upon these two for not long after this Master Guy Hopton, accepting that his days as apothecary were over, offered Christiana his business, which included the substantial house and herb garden in the prosperous town of Leicester. The only condition he stipulated was that he be allowed to remain at the apothecary until the end of his mortal life, thus ensuring his needs would be met and that she would do nothing without his authority.

As time went on William's nightmares were less frequent and the haze and confusion that beset his mind began to clear. In early spring the following year William and Christiana married under the porch of Saint Martin's Church. It was no grand affair but all those who had become dear to her bore witness: the old apothecary, the hosteller and his daughter Martha – her faithful friend. Even Milla came bearing an armful of fragrant flowers for the bride.

One year later Christiana gave birth to a daughter who they named Anna. William held his child in his arms and wept. That year also brought with it more fortune. The town farrier moved to the south where the town was growing and took work there. His apprentice was not yet ready to take his place and William, who had more than proved his worth on market days when trade increased, took over his business.

It was early April 1487, Anna was a few months old. Christiana had left her baby in the care of Master Hopton. The old man had a reason to leave his bed now that a child needed watching. They were out in the herb garden, the babe in her cradle and the apothecary sitting on the bench admiring the early shoots and buds that sprang at his feet. They were in hailing distance and so Christiana set about her work in the shop.

There had not been many as yet that day requiring a remedy or having a physician's receipt to fulfil. She was washing some of her phials and bottles in a large bowl of water and looked up as the door opened.

A traveller had entered; or so he seemed judging by the dust and filth upon his clothing. He looked nervously about the shop before approaching the bench and the woman.

"I look for Christiana," he whispered. "Christiana Smith of Middleham, Yorkshire."

Satisfied that he had found the woman he sought the stranger reached into his cloak and produced a sealed parchment and handed it to her.

"I am passing through Leicester," he explained. "I require no reply." He inclined his head, turned about and left the apothecary.

Intrigued as to who should care to write to her, she broke the poorly made seal and rolled out the letter. With trembling fingers she began to read.

My Dearest Mother,

I have longed to find opportunity to send word to you. This letter must of necessity be brief but know that I am safe and well. My guardian has proved loyal and true to our king and also to myself.

John de la Pole, Earl of Lincoln, who I think you are acquainted with, sends his greetings, Mother. He recalls with fondness the days gone by.

With all my heart I shall find you when this present trouble is passed.

With all affection –

Your son, John

Christiana was overjoyed to have word that her son was alive and well. She could not fathom why it was he had mentioned the Earl of Lincoln and knew nothing of any present trouble; his words were curious indeed. It mattered not for she had proof that Francis Lovell had honoured his promise. The loyalty that Richard inspired in those who loved him still lived on.

When her husband returned from his labour that evening Christiana showed him the letter. She read it over several times to him as he requested.

"I see in this a warning, Christiana," he offered gently. "These words are encrypted for John must have a care for what he passes on."

Christiana touched his sleeve and smiled. "My heart is at peace, Will, for I know that my son is safe."

From that day forward the night terrors left William for good and his mind was fully restored. Over the months and years to follow the scar that disfigured his face faded and whenever she looked at her husband Christiana saw only the tall handsome blacksmith she had always known. In due course she gave William a son, the likeness of his father, but she never forgot her first born, a child in every way his father's son.

She thought many times of how her life had turned full circle; a life that had begun as a blacksmith's daughter in the dales of Yorkshire and now a life here in Leicester as a blacksmith's wife. Maybe, she smiled, that was how it had meant to be all along.

Glossary

Arret – the lance rest on a breast plate

Besom – a birch twig broom

Black Annis – a legendary figure said to inhabit the Dane Hills around Leicester, reputed to be a witch

Bogy shanks – leg pieces of lamb skins

Bohun Lands – this refers to Henry Stafford, 2nd Duke of Buckingham's claim to his great-great-grandmother, Eleanor de Bohun's estate, which was appropriated to the Crown by Edward IV after the deposition of Henry VI.

Braies – medieval men's underpants

Coffer – chest

Coif – a hood-like cap

Collegiate Status – a church where the daily office of worship is maintained by a college of canons comprising of a secular community of clergy

Colly bird – a song bird, possibly a blackbird

Cruppers – a strap looped under a horse's tail and buckled to the back of a saddle to prevent it slipping

Curlew –a large wading bird with a down-curving bill and brown-streaked plumage

Destier – a medieval war horse

Drahm – a measure of weight

Ewer – a water pitcher made with grotesque animal forms, sometimes called an aquamanile or one who washes the hands of guests at a feast

Flux – an abnormal discharge of matter from the body

Gambeson – a quilted or padded garment worn originally for protection but later worn as a doublet

Kirtle – a dress or gown

Liripipe – a long pipe-like piece of material hanging from the back of a hat or chaperon

Lucet – a tool for making cord

Marshal – castle servant responsible for horses, carts and wagons

Melrosette – a type of jam made with roses

Merrills – a board game played with nine counters

Palfrey – a highly valued type of horse suitable for riding over long distances – not a specific breed

Paltock – a short undergarment to which sleeves and hose could be attached. Later became known as a pourpoint

Pantler – the servant in charge of the bread and the pantry

Papal Dispensation – the right of the pope to exempt an individual from a specific canon law. Matrimonial Dispensation can allow a marriage to take place or dissolve an existing one. Medieval Roman Catholic canon law prohibited marriage between blood relatives up to and including sixth cousins

Pauldron – armoured shoulder protection

Pomme d'ambre – shortened to pomander or apple of amber. Refers to ambergris or whale excrement used for perfume and encased in a pewter/silver container worn around the neck or on a belt

Removes – courses of food with up to five dishes in each course

Rouncy – a common all-purpose horse used for riding or as a pack horse

Sallet – a type of helmet

Scruple – a measure of weight

Shift – woman's undergarment

Steward – the castle servant responsible for managing the domestic household

Truckle bed – a small bed that is stored under a larger one

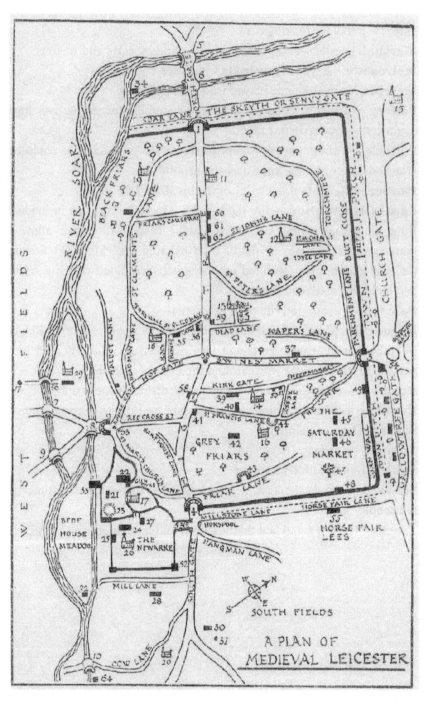

Map based on the map of Medieval Leicester by Charles Bilson, 1920
Reproduced under licence by permission of Leicester University, March 2015

Key to Map of Medieval City of Leicester

1	North Gate	23	Castle Mound	45	Shambles and Draperie
2	West Gate	24	Newarke Hospital	46	The Gainsborough
3	East Gate	25	Dean of Newarke's House	47	Elm Tree
4	South Gate	26	St Mary of the Annunciation	48	Green Dragon Inn
5	North Bridge	27	Wigston's Chantry House	49	Angel Inn
6	Frogmire Bridge	28	Newarke Grange	50	Maiden Head Inn
7	Bow Bridge	29	The Austin Friars	51	St George's Guild Hall
8	West Bridge	30	Hermitage	52	Rupert's Tower
9	Braunston Bridge	31	St Sepulchre's Well	53	Newarke Main Gateway
10	Cow Bridge	32	Newarke Mill	54	Bere Hill
11	All Saints' Church	33	Castle Mill	55	Old Barn
12	St Michael's Church	34	North Mill	56	Little Bow Bridge
13	St Peter's Church	35	Old Mayor's Hall	57	St Austin's Well
14	St Martin's Church	36	Blue Boar Inn	58	Roger Wigston's House
15	St Margaret's Church	37	Lord's Place	59	Free Grammar School
16	Grey Friars Church	38	High Cross	60	Shirehall
17	St Mary de Castro Church	39	Guild Hall	61	Prisona Regis
18	St Nicholas' Church	40	Wigston's Hospital	62	St John's Hospital
19	St Clement's Church	41	Henry Costeyn's House	63	Red Cross
20	St Sepulchre's Church	42	The Grey Friars Priory	64	Mary Mill
21	Castle Hall	43	Grey Friars Gateway		
22	Castle House	44	Grey Friars Gateway		

Acknowledgements

There are of course many people whose support and knowledge have been invaluable and who have contributed to the creation of this book, but first of all I would like to express my gratitude to my long-suffering family. They have been patient and tolerant of my passion for Richard III over many, many years.

My expression of thanks goes to the countless writers of historical fact, however that may be interpreted, whose books and articles have provided the background for my research into the life and times of Richard III. Material provided by the Richard the Third Society was particularly helpful.

I am grateful to English Heritage for kindly allowing me to use the information in their guidebook to Middleham Castle.

I would like to thank my dear friend Carole for providing the images used to create the front cover and inserts.

Last but not least my thanks and gratitude go to all my friends and colleagues who have encouraged me along the way and especially my special friends Sue and Vic for opening their home to me when I needed a writer's retreat.